THE TOWN AND THE CITY

BOOKS BY JACK KEROUAC

The Town and the City
1950

On the Road
1957

The Dharma Bums
1958

The Subterraneans
1958

Doctor Sax
1959

Maggie Cassidy
1959

Mexico City Blues
1959

Excerpts from Visions of Cody
1960

Lonesome Traveler
1960

The Scripture of the Golden Eternity
1960

Book of Dreams
1961

Big Sur
1962

Visions of Gerard
1963

Desolation Angels
1965

Satori in Paris
1966

Vanity of Duluoz: The Adventurous Education of a Young Man
1968

JACK KEROUAC

A Harvest Book

HARCOURT BRACE JOVANOVICH, INC.
NEW YORK

ISBN 0-15-690790-9

PRINTED IN THE UNITED STATES OF AMERICA

To R.G.

Friend and Editor

1

THE TOWN is Galloway. The Merrimac River, broad and placid, flows down to it from the New Hampshire hills, broken at the falls to make frothy havoc on the rocks, foaming on over ancient stone towards a place where the river suddenly swings about in a wide and peaceful basin, moving on now around the flank of the town, on to places known as Lawrence and Haverhill, through a wooded valley, and on to the sea at Plum Island, where the river enters an infinity of waters and is gone. Somewhere far north of Galloway, in headwaters close to Canada, the river is continually fed and made to brim out of endless sources and unfathomable springs.

The little children of Galloway sit on the banks of the Merrimac and consider these facts and mysteries. In the wild echoing misty March night, little Mickey Martin kneels at his bedroom window and listens to the river's rush, the distant barking of dogs, the soughing thunder of the falls, and he ponders the wellsprings and sources of his own mysterious life.

The grownups of Galloway are less concerned with riverside broodings. They work—in factories, in shops and stores and offices, and on the farms all around. The textile factories built in brick, primly towered, solid, are ranged along the river and the canals, and all night the industries hum and shuttle. This is Galloway, milltown in the middle of fields and forests.

If at night a man goes out to the woods surrounding Galloway, and stands on a hill, he can see it all there before him in broad panorama: the river coursing slowly in an arc, the mills with their long rows of windows all a-glow, the factory stacks rising higher than the church steeples. But he knows that this is not the true Galloway. Something in the invisible brooding landscape surrounding the town, something in the bright stars nodding close to a hillside where the old cemetery sleeps, something in the soft swishing treeleaves over the fields and stone walls tells him a different story.

He looks at the names in the old cemetery: "Williams . . . Thompson . . . LaPlanche . . . Smith . . . McCarthy . . . Tsotakos." He feels the slow deep pulsing of the river of life. A dog barks on the farm a mile away, the wind whispers over the old stones and in the trees. Here is the recorded inscription of long slow living and long-remembered death. John L. McCarthy, remembered as a man with white hair who walked down the road in meditation at dusk; old Tsotakos, who lived and worked and died, whose sons continue to work the land not far from the cemetery; Robert Thompson—bend near and read the dates, "Born 1901, died 1905"—the child who drowned three decades ago in the river; Harry W. Williams, the storekeeper's son who died in the Great War in 1918 whose old sweetheart, now the mother of eight children, is still haunted by his long lost face; Tony LaPlanche, who molders by the old wall. There are old people, living and still remembering, who could tell you so much about the dead of Galloway.

As for the living, walk down the hillside towards the quiet streets and houses of Galloway's suburbs—you will hear the river's ever-soughing rush—and pass beneath the leafy trees, the street-lamps, along the grass yards and dark porches, the wooden fences. Somewhere at the end of the street there's a light, and intersections leading to the three bridges of Galloway that bring you into the heart of the town itself and to the shadow of the mill walls. Follow along to the center of the town, the Square, where at noon everybody knows everybody else. Look around now and see the business of the town deserted in haunted midnight: the five-and-ten, the two or three department stores, the groceries and soda fountains and drugstores, the bars, the movie theaters, the auditorium, the dance hall, the poolrooms, the Chamber of Commerce building, the City Hall and the Public Library.

Wait around for the morning, for the time when the Real Estate offices come to life, when lawyers raise the windowshades and the sun floods into dusty offices. See these men standing at windows, on which their names are written in gold letters, nodding down at the street when other townsmen walk by. Wait for the busses to come around laden with working people who cough and scowl and hurry to the cafeteria for another cup of coffee. The traffic cop stations himself in the middle of the Square, nodding to a car which toots at him jovially; a wellknown politician crosses the street with the bright sun on his white hair; the local newspaper columnist comes sleepily to the cigar store and greets the clerk. Here are a few farmers in trucks buying up supplies and groceries and transacting a little business. At ten o'clock the women come in armies, with shopping bags, their children trailing alongside. The bars open, men gulp a morning beer, the bartender mops the mahogany, there's a smell of clean soap, beer, old wood, and cigar smoke. At the railroad station the express going down to Boston puffs shooting clouds of steam around the old brown turrets of the depot building, the streetguards descend majestically to stop traffic as the bell rings and jangles, people rush for the Boston train. It's morning and Galloway comes to life.

Out on the hillside, by the cemetery, the rosy sun slants in through the elm leaves, a fresh breeze blows through the soft grass, the stones gleam in the morning light, there's the odor of loam and grass—and it's a joy to know that life is life and death is death.

These are the things that closely surround the mills and the business of Galloway, that make it a town rooted in earth in the ancient pulse of life and work and death, that make its people townspeople and not city people.

Start from the center of town in the sunny afternoon, from Daley Square, and walk up River Street where all the traffic is converged, pass the bank, the Galloway High School and the Y.M.C.A., and move on up till private residences begin to appear. Leaving the business district behind, the great factory walls are barely within reach to the left and to the right of the business district. Along the river is a quiet street with a few sedate funeral homes, an orphanage, brick mansions of a sort, and the bridges that leap across to the suburbs, where most of the people of Galloway live. Cross the bridge known as the White Bridge, swooping right over the Merrimac Falls, and pause for a moment to view the prospect. Citywards there is one more bridge, the wide smooth basin where the river turns, and beyond that a faroff flank of land thickly populated. Look away from the city, over the frothing falls, and see into misty reaches that include New Hampshire, an expanse of green placid land and calm water. There are the railroad tracks running along the river, a few water tanks and sidings, but the rest is all wooded. The far side of the river presents a highway dotted with roadhouses and roadside stands, and a return gaze from upriver reveals the suburbs thick with rooftops and trees. Cross the bridge to these suburbs, and turn upriver, along the flank of populations, along the highway, and there is a narrow black tar road leading off inland.

This is old Galloway Road. Just where it rises, before dipping once more into pine forests and farmlands, lies a concentration of houses sedately spaced off from one another—a residence of ivied stone, the house of a judge; a whitewashed old house with round wooden pillars on the porch—this is a dairy farm, there are cows in the field beyond; and one rambling Victorian house with a battered gray look, a high hedgerow all around, trees huge and leafy that almost obscure the front of the house, a hammock on the old porch, and a disheveled backyard with a garage and a barn and an old wooden swing.

This last house is the home of the Martin family.

From the top of the highest elm in the front yard, as some of the vigorous Martin kids can testify, on a good day it is possible to see clear to New Hampshire over farmlands and thick pinewoods, and on exceptionally clear days even the misty intimations of the White Mountains are visible sixty miles north.

This house had especially appealed to George Martin when he considered leasing it in 1915. He was then a young insurance salesman, living in a flat in town with his wife and one daughter.

"By God," he had said to his wife, Marguerite, "if this isn't just what the doctor ordered!"

Whereupon, during the next twenty years in the big rambling house, in collaboration with Mrs. Martin, he set about to produce eight more children, three daughters and six sons all told.

George Martin had gone into the printing business and made a great success of himself in the town, first as a job-printer and later as a printer-publisher of small political newspapers that were read mainly in City Hall swivel chairs or at the cigar stores. He was a scowling, preoccupied, virile-looking man, big, genial, eagerly sympathetic, who could suddenly break out into a booming raspy laugh or just as easily grow very sentimental and misty-eyed. He knitted his brow in a kind of fierce concentration over a pair of heavy black eyebrows, his eyes were level and blue, and when someone spoke to him he had a habit of looking up with a startled air of wonder.

He had come down from Lacoshua, New Hampshire, a country town in the hills, as a youth, abandoning work in the sawmills for a crack at the town.

Over the years his family gave character to the old gray house and to its grounds, rendering its shambling air of simplicity, haphazardness, and glass. It was a house that rang with noises and conversations, music, hammer-slammings, shouts down the stairs. At night almost all of its windows glowed as the innumerable activities of the family were carried on. In the garage were a new car and an old car, in the old barn was all the accumulated bric-a-brac that only an American family with many boys can assemble over the years, and in the attic the confusion and the variety of objects were nothing less than admirable.

When all the family was stilled in sleep, when the streetlamp a few paces from the house shone at night and made grotesque shadows of the trees upon the house, when the river sighed off in the darkness, when the trains hooted on their way to Montreal far upriver, when the wind swished in the soft treeleaves and something knocked and rattled on the old barn—you could stand in old Galloway Road and look at this home and know that there is nothing more haunting than a house at night when the family is asleep, something strangely tragic, something beautiful forever.

[2]

EACH MEMBER of the family living in this house is wrapped in his own vision of life, and is brooding within the enveloping intelligence of his own particular soul. With the family stamp somehow imprinted upon each of their lives, they come infolded and furious into the world as Martins, a clan of energetic, vigorous, grave and absorbed people, suddenly terrified and melancholy, suddenly guffawing and gleeful, naive and cunning, meditative often and just as often ravenously excited, a strong and clannish and shrewd people.

Consider them one by one, the youngsters who are taking in impressions of the world around as though they expected to live forever, on up to the elder members of the family who find assurance everywhere and every day that life is exactly what they always supposed it to be. See how they all go through their succession of days, the robust exuberant days, the days of celebration, and the days of sickness of heart.

The Martin father is a man of a hundred absorptions: he conducts his printing business, runs a linotype and a press, and keeps the books. In the midst of this he plays the horses and places his bets with a bookie in a downtown back-street, Rooney Street. At noon he carries on a shouting conversation with insurance men, newspapermen, salesmen and cigar store proprietors in a little bar off Daley Square. On his way home to supper he stops off at the Chinese restaurant to see his old friend Wong Lee. After supper he listens to his favorite programs, sitting in his den with the radio on full-blast. After dark he drives over to the bowling-alley and poolroom which he supervises, in order to bring in a little extra money. There he sits in the little office talking with a congregation of his old friends while the billiard balls click, the alleys roll and thunder, and everywhere there's smoke and talk. At midnight he finds himself in a big poker or pinochle game that lasts long into the night. He comes home exhausted, but in the morning he's off again to his place of business trailing cigar smoke behind him, shouting good mornings to his associates in the shop, eating a hearty breakfast in the diner by the railroad tracks.

On Sundays he absolutely must go driving in his Plymouth, bringing with him a good portion of his family that wants to come along. He drives all over New England, exploring the White Mountains, the old towns on the coast and inland, he wants to stop off everywhere where the food or ice cream looks good, he wants to buy bushels of Mackintosh apples and jars of cider at the roadside stands, and whole baskets of strawberries and blueberries and as much corn as he can carry on the floor of the car. He wants to smoke all the cigars, get in on all the poker games, know all the roads and shores and towns in New England, eat in all the good restaurants, make friends with all the good men and women, follow all the racetracks and bet in all the bookie-backrooms, make as much money as he spends, kid around and laugh and make jokes all the time—he wants to do everything, he does everything.

The Martin mother is a superb housekeeper who according to her husband is "the best darned cook in town." She bakes cakes, roasts great cuts of beef and lamb and pork, keeps her icebox bulging with food, sweeps the floors and washes clothes and does everything that the mother of a big family does. When she sits down to relax, there she is with her deck of cards, shuffling, peering over the rim of her spectacles and foreseeing tidings of good fortune, forebodings of doom, omens of all sorts and sizes. She sits at the kitchen table with her eldest daughter and discerns the news in the bottom of her teacup. She reads signs everywhere, follows the weather closely, reads the obituaries and notices of marriage and birth, keeps track of all illness and ill-fortune, of all bustling health and good luck, she traces the growth of children and the decline of old men all over the town, the omen-tidings of other women and the approach of new seasons. Nothing escapes the vast motherly wisdom of this woman: she has foreseen it all, sensed everything.

"You don't have to believe it, if you don't want to," she says to her eldest daughter Rose, "but I had a dream the other night that my little Julian came to me at night, right into bed like he used to do when he was too sick to sleep or when he was scared of the dark, like he used to do that year he died, and he said to me 'Mama,' he said, 'are you worried about Ruthey?' and I said 'Yes, darling, but why do you ask me?' and he said 'Don't be afraid for Ruthey any more, it's all right now, it's all right now.' He kept saying that: 'It's all right now.' And he looked just like he was the weeks before he died, with his little brow all pale and covered with perspiration, his little sad eyes wide as though he wanted to know why it was that he had to be so sick. It was such a *vivid* dream! He was right there in front of me, Rose! And I told your father about it and he moved his head, you know like he does, from side to side, and he said 'Let's hope so, Marge, let's hope so.' And now you see!" she concludes triumphantly. "Here's Ruthey home from the hospital and all well again, and we thought she was in such great danger!"

"Okay!" cries Rose, holding up her hand in an affectionately taunting manner. "That's the way it was."

The mother looks up slowly and grins. "All right," she says now, "you can say what you like, but I understand it better than all of you. I dream, I get nervous when something wrong is going to happen, and when there's going to be happiness in the house I feel that too—and that's just what I've been feeling all week, ever since I had that dream about Julian. I saw it in the cards too—"

"There she goes!" cries Rose, shaking her head in a gesture of stupefacted defeat. "Now we're going to hear all about it."

"It always happens like that," says the mother firmly, as though the girl had never spoken. "My little Julian tells me all these things. He hasn't forgotten us and he's still taking care of us, even though we don't see him—he's still here."

"Aw, Ma knows what she's talking about, don't you worry," says Joe, the eldest son, with a sudden quiet tenderness, as he smiles bashfully at the floor, and paces around the kitchen. "She knows what she knows."

And the mother, smiling a faint ruminant smile of consolation and joy because her Ruthey is home from the hospital, because she has foreseen it in a dream and in her cards, sits brooding at the kitchen table over her teacup.

The eldest daughter, Rose, is a big husky girl of twenty-one, the "big sister" of the family, the mother's constant companion and helper, a robust creature full of hilarity and vigor and warmth, possessed of a large and generous nature. She stands by her mother's side peering anxiously into the icebox, she walks around the kitchen with the heavy steps of a pachyderm that make the dishes in the pantry rattle and jingle, she hauls in the wash in huge baskets from the yard. When her favorite brother, Joe, comes home from his constant wanderings she whoops raucously and chases him around the house. When news comes to the house of catastrophe or great triumph, she exchanges with her mother that swift glance of stunned prophecy.

The few boy friends that she goes out with are all big husky creatures like herself who work on farms or drive trucks or handle the heavy work in factories. When one of them cuts his finger or burns his hand, she sits him down and administers the necessary aid, and scolds him furiously. She is the first member of the family to get up in the morning, and the last in bed. As far back as she can remember she has been a "big sister." There she is at dusk, standing in the yard taking down the wash, packing it in baskets and starting back to the porch, pausing for only a moment to scowl at the children playing in the field nearby, and then shaking her head and disappearing inside the house.

The eldest son is Joe, at this time around seventeen years old. This is the kind of thing he does: he borrows a buddy's old car—a '31 Auburn—and in company with a wild young wrangler like himself drives up to Vermont to see his girl. That night, after the stamping furors of roadside polkas with their girl friends, Joe runs the car off a curve and into a tree and they are all scattered around the wreck with minor injuries. Joe lies flat on his back in the middle of the highway, thinking: "Wow! Maybe it'll be better if I make out I'm almost dead—otherwise I'll get in trouble with the cops and catch holy hell from the old man."

They take Joe and the others to the hospital, where he lies in a "coma" for two days, saying nothing, peeking furtively around, listening. The doctors believe he has suffered serious internal injuries. Once in a while the local police come around to make inquiries. Joe's buddy from Galloway, who has only suffered a minor laceration, is soon up out of bed, flirting with the nurses, helping with the dishes in the hospital kitchen, wondering what next to do. He comes to Joe's bedside twenty times a day.

"Hey, Joe, when are you gonna get better, pal?" he moans. "What's the *matter* with you? Oh, why did this have to happen!"

Finally Joe whispers, "Shut up, for krissakes," and closes his eyes again gravely, almost piously, with mad propriety and purpose, as the other boy gapes in amazement.

That night Joe's father comes driving over the mountains in the night to fetch his wild and crazy son. In the middle of the night Joe leaps out of bed and dresses and runs out of the hospital gleefully, and a moment later he is driving them all back to Galloway at seventy miles per hour.

"This is the last time you're going on any of these damn trips of yours!" vows Mr. Martin, puffing furiously on his cigar. "Do you hear me?"

His mother fears that he will come home on crutches, maimed for life, but in the morning she looks out the window and there's her son Joe stretched out in the backyard underneath the old '29 Ford, launched on an overhauling job, with a smudge of oil on his lip like a little mustache so that he looks "just like Errol Flynn" somehow. And the next day, Joe is to be seen high-diving from the window of a tenement overlooking a Galloway canal, in the mill district, where he has himself a sweetheart. Joe always has a job, always earns money, and never seems to find time to mope and sulk. His next goal is a motorcycle wild with rabbit-tails and blazing buttons.

His brother, Francis Martin, is always moping and sulking. Francis is tall and skinny, and the first day he goes to High School he walks along the corridors staring at everyone in a sullen and sour manner, as though to ask: "Who are all these fools?" Only fifteen years old at the time, Francis has a habit of keeping to himself, reading or just staring out the window of his bedroom. His family "can't figure him out." Francis is the twin brother of the late and beloved little Julian, and like Julian his health is not up to par with the rest of the Martins. But his mother loves him and understands him.

"You can't expect too much from Francis," she always says, "he's not well and probably never will be. He's a strange boy, you've just got to understand him."

Francis surprises them all by exhibiting a facile brilliance in his schoolwork, amassing one of the highest records in the history of the school—but his mother understands that too. He is a dour, gloomy, thinlipped youngster, with a slight stoop in his posture, cold blue eyes, and an air of inviolable dignity and tact. In a large family like the Martins, when one member keeps aloof from the others, he is always regarded with suspicion but at the same time curiously respected. Francis Martin, a recipient of this respect, is thus made early aware of the power of secretiveness.

"You can't rush Francis," says the mother. "He's his own boss and he'll do what he likes when the time comes. If he keeps so much to himself it's because he has a lot on his mind."

"If you ask me," says Rosey, "he's just got something wrong up here." And she twirls her big finger around her ear. "You mark my word."

"No," says Mrs. Martin, "you just don't understand him."

Ruth Martin at this time is eighteen years old, a senior in High School. She goes to the dances, the skating parties, the football games of high school life, a diminutive, quiet, well-mannered little girl with a cheerful and generous temperament. She is a well beloved member of the family of whom it is expected that she will marry in time, raise her children and meet responsibilities in her patient, reliable and merry way, as she has always done. Now she wants to attend a business college in order to learn secretarial work and be self-sufficient for a few years. Ruth is that kind of a girl who makes no smash in the world, the girl you never hear of, but see everywhere, a woman before all things who keeps her soul to herself and for one heart.

✦

Thirteen-year-old Peter Martin is shocked when he sees his sister Ruth dancing so closely to another boy at the high school dance—after the annual minstrel show in the school auditorium. Looking over the entire dance floor, rose-hued and misty and lovely, he decides that life is more exciting than he supposed it was allowed. It is 1935, the orchestra is playing Larry Clinton's "Study in Red" and everyone begins to sense the thrilling new music that is about to develop without limit. There are rumors of Benny Goodman in the air, of Fletcher Henderson and of new great orchestras rising. In the crowded ballroom, the lights, the music, the dancing figures, the echoes all fill the boy with strange new feelings and mysterious sorrow.

By the window Peter gazes out on the brooding Spring darkness, burning with the vision of the close-embracing dancers, stirred by the tidings of the music and filled with an infinite longing to grow up and go to high school himself, where he too can dance embraced with shapely girls, sing in the minstrel show, and perhaps be a football hero too.

"See that fellow with the crew-cut?" Ruth points out for him. "The chunky one over there, dancing with that pretty blonde? That's Bobby Stedman."

To Peter, Bobby Stedman is a name emblazoned on hallowed sports pages, a weaving misty figure in the newsreel shots of the Galloway-Lawton game on Thanksgiving Day, a hero of heroes. Something dark and proud and remote surrounds his name, his figure, his atmosphere. As he dances there, Peter cannot believe his eyes—can this be Bobby Stedman *himself?* Isn't he the greatest, speediest, hardest-running, weavingest halfback in the state? Haven't they printed his name in big black letters, isn't there a slow pompous music to his name and to the proud dark world surrounding him?

Then Peter realizes that Ruth is dancing with Lou White, himself. Lou White, another remote and heroic name, a figure on rainswept or snowlashed fields, a face in the newspapers glowering in exertion over the taut center position. . . .

When Lou White comes to the Martin house to take Ruth skating, Peter stands in a dark corner and looks long at him in sheepish awe. When Lou White stays awhile to listen to the Jack Benny program, and laughs at the jokes, Peter is completely amazed. And when again he sees him on the day of the big Thanksgiving game, far down on the field hunched over the ball,

Peter can't believe that this remote god has come to his house to see his sister and laugh at jokes. The crowds roar, the Autumn wind whips among the flags around the stadium, Lou White far away snaps back the ball on the striped field, makes sensational tackles that evoke roars, trots about and is cheered thunderously off the field as he leaves his last game for the school. The bands play the alma mater song, broken in the wind.

"I'm going to be playing in this game in two years," says Peter to his father.

"Oh, you will, hey?"

"Yes."

"Don't you think you're a little too small for that? Those boys out there are built like trucks."

"I'll get bigger," says Peter, "and strong too."

His father laughs, and from that moment Peter Martin is finally goaded on by all the fantastic and fabulous triumphs that he sees possible in the world.

If on some soft odorous April night the twelve-year-old Elizabeth Martin is seen strolling mournfully beneath the dripping wet trees, pouting and fierce and lonely, with her hands plunged deep in the pockets of her little tan raincoat as she considers the horrid legend of life, and broods as she returns slowly to her family's house—be sure that the darkness and terror of twelve-years-old will come to womanly days of ripe warm sunshine.

Or if that boy there, the one with the resolute little face, who wets his lips briefly before replying to a question, who strides along with determination and absorption towards his objective, who tinkers solemnly in the cellar or garage with a gadget or old motor, says very little and looks at everyone with a level blue-eyed stare of absolute reasonableness, if that boy, nine-year-old Charley Martin, is examined carefully as he goes about the undertakings of his self-assured and earnest young existence, dark wings appear above him as if to shade a strange light in his thoughtful eyes.

And finally, if on some snowy dusk, with the sun's sloping light on the flank of a hill, with the sun flaming back from factory windows, you see a little child of six, a boy called Mickey Martin, standing motionless in the middle of the road with his sled behind him, stunned by the sudden discovery that he does not know who he is, where he came from, what he is doing here, remember that all children are first shocked out of the womb of a mother's world before they can know that loneliness is their heritage and their only means of rediscovering men and women.

This is the Martin family, the elders and the young ones, even the little ones, the flitting ghost-ends of a brood who will grow and come to attain size and seasons and huge presence like the others, and burn savagely across days and nights of living, and give brooding rare articulation to the poor things of life, and the rich, dark things too.

[3]

OVER GALLOWAY and over this house the weathers proceed, flanking across the skies in seasonal majesty. The great Winter rumbles at its very foundations and melts, there is water trickling underneath the snow, the ice-floes throng at the Falls, and the air is suddenly noisy with a lyrical thaw.

Young Peter Martin hears the long echoing hoot of the Montreal train broken and interrupted by some vast shifting in the March air, he hears voices coming suddenly on the breeze from across the river, barkings, calls, hammerings, which cease almost as soon as they come. He sits at the window awake with expectation, the eaves drip, something echoes like far thunder. He looks up at broken clouds fleeing across the ragged heavens, whipping over his roof, over the swaying trees, disappearing in hordes, advancing in armies. There's a smell of gummy birch, rank and teeming smells like mud that's dark and moist, of dark unlimbering branches of last Autumn's matted floor dissolving in a fragrant mash, of whole advancing waves of air, misty March air.

There's something dizzy and wild in his heart, he hurries out on the street and paces the sidewalks, all around him there's a grand melting, blown adrift, something soft and musical, a thaw, a hint of warmth, a breath. On the street the sagging snowbank, the running gutter, the noisy thaw, the lyrical newness everywhere. He hurries along filled with unspeakable premonitions of Spring, he must hurry over to Danny's house and play with him in the melting snow, make snowballs, throw them across the misty air against black oozing tree-trunks, shout amid all the sudden sounds that carry in the air from everywhere.

"When the snow melts we'll play pepper just to unloose the ole throwin' arm, get that homerun swing back, huh, Dan?"

"Yow!"

The boy's "Yow!" echoes across the field like the sound of a horn. They build a snowman and riddle it with snowballs, and now dusk is coming and March sky is mad and lowering with angry, purple clouds. In a moment the sun is going to break through and flame in all the windows of Galloway, the mill windows will be a thousand red flambeaux, something will slant across the skies and over the river.

"Yow!"

Then the rains come, April washes the snow with water and carries it down to the mad roaring river, tree-trunks come floating down from New Hampshire, the falls are in a turmoil, gray, dirty yellow waters boil and explode on the rocks heaving up sticks and logs. The kids race along the riverbank throwing things in the water. They build fires and yell jubilantly.

One day, suddenly, dusk settles in a hush of quiet, the sun goes down huge and red, and an odorous silent darkness takes over, as treeleaves swish softly in a breeze all smelling of foliage and loam. There's a big brown moon rising on the horizon. The old people of Galloway go out and stand on the porch awhile, remembering the old songs. Big George Martin lights a cigar and looks at the moon. The fragrance of the cigar smoke lingers on the porch, there's no wind, no more noise and fury. "Will you love me in December as you do in May . . ."

In the morning, as the sun comes up warm, as a vast chorale of birds is taken up in the branches everywhere, as the suggestion of sweet blossoms spreads in the air, it is May.

Little Mickey wakes up and goes to his window: it's Saturday morning, no school today. And for him there's a still music in the air like the faint sound of heraldry over the woods, like men, horses and dogs gathering under the trees far across the field for some joyous and adventurous foray. Everything is soft and musical, and sweet, and full of longings, misty hints and unspeakable revelations that float in the gentlest blue air. There, in the blue shadows beneath the morning trees, in the cool speckled shade, in the new green misty color of the woods far off, in the dark ground still moist and all covered with little blossoms, there is his hint of glorious spreading Summer, and the future. Mickey dashes out, slamming the kitchen door behind him, goes rolling his old rubber tire with a stick. He journeys down old Galloway Road over the cool dewy tar, on each side of him the birds are singing, he wonders when there'll be apples in old man Breton's orchard there. He figures this year he will explore the river in a boat. This year he will do everything, boy!

In the middle of the morning Mickey watches all the big guys at the ballfield slamming their fists into their gloves, throwing a brand new white baseball around. Someone has a bat, hitting light bunts, the boys stoop to pick up the grounders and yell, "Uff! I got them old kinks this year!"

Someone hoots under a high fly, punches his glove, pulls it down, trots around awhile, lobs the ball back easily. It's Spring training time, they've got to watch "the old arm." Mickey smells the fragrant cigarette smoke in the morning air where the older boys stand around talking. Big brother Joe Martin is winding up leisurely, throwing to another boy who squats with a catcher's mitt. Joe is a star pitcher, he knows how to take his time and get the old kinks out in the Spring. Everybody watches as he lobs the ball in easily, with a sure motion and a deadpan face. A minute later he's whooping with laughter when someone gets a knock on the shins from a hard grounder.

In his mother's cool shady kitchen, Mickey devours a bowl of cereal and stares at the picture of Jimmy Foxx on the box cover. His chums are coming up the road, he can hear them, they're going off to play cowboys on the hill. He's Buck Jones all the time. They're out in the yard now, calling:

"Mick-ee!"

Mickey comes storming out of the kitchen with both guns blazing, "Kow! kow! kow!" and dodges behind a barrel; the others take cover and return fire. Someone leaps up, twists, contorts, and falls slain to the grass.

In the Spring night, Joe tunes up the old Ford and roars off to drink beer with his buddies. And on the first warm June night, Mrs. Martin and Ruth dust off the old swing in the backyard, put cushions on it, make a big bowl of popcorn, and go sit under the moon, in the waving black shade of the high hedges.

A cousin sits with them in the breezy night, exclaiming: "Ooh! ain't the moon grand!"

Old man Martin, banging around the kitchen making an egg sandwich, mimics savagely: "Ain't the moon gry-and!"

The three women out in the yard, swinging rhythmically in the creaking old swing, are telling each other about the best fortune-tellers they have ever known.

"I tell you, Marge, she is *uncanny!*"

Mrs. Martin rocks in the swing, waiting patiently, with slitted eyes, skeptical.

"She foretold almost everything that happened that year, detail by detail, mind you!" And with this Cousin Leona looks up at the moon and sighs, "The irony of this life, Marge, the irony of life."

The father of the house stomps out of the kitchen with his sandwich, mimicking again, savagely: "Oh, the irony of liaf!"

The women rock back and forth in the old creaking swing, reaching mechanically into the popcorn bowl, musing, contented, belonging to the wonderful darkness and the ripe June world, owning it, as no barging man of the house could ever hope to belong to any part of the earth or own an inch of it.

By the New England lake on a July night, the young people dance in a lanterned breeze-ruffled ballroom, the lights are soft blue and rose, the moon is bright on the dark waters out beyond the balcony. The songs are sweetly felt, to be sweetly remembered. The young lovers cling, whisper, dance. On a diving raft off the lake beach, young people sit with their feet dangling in the soft waters of the night, they hear the music from the ballroom floating over the lake. In a honkytonk saloon where Joe is drinking beer by the gallons and dancing the polka with big Polish and French-Canadian blondes, the smoke is thick, there's tumult of fiddles and stamping feet, and the sight of the lake and the moon out the screen windows is darkly beautiful, a lone pine soughs in the breeze just outside the windows. A lonely youth sick from beer and dizzy with the night's fragrance walks along the shore of the lake in a confused reverie. He hears music coming from over there, where they dance, the dark breeze brings it to him in a remote fusion of melancholy sounds. The cool potent heavy-scented magnificent night, the smell of pine, the reeds swaying in shallow water, the thronging sounds of toads and crickets, and the great round brown moon with its sideways brooding, somehow compassionate, sad big face.

In the hot August fields of afternoon, farmers bend in the shimmering haze to sweating sun-tormented chores. The little children flap in the brook like fish, they dive from the bank and from trees like little white minnows. In the shade of the pines, beneath their breezy symphonic soughing, way down to the fields, the brooks, across aisles of golden sun and pale green space, see the farmers, the children, and beyond, the rising smoke-stacks of the Galloway mills shimmering afar.

There's weary heat in Daley Square, the streets are airless, the houses hot, at noon the white-shirted, straw-hatted, sun-flushed people move in a sullen throng. The insurance man pauses on a blazing streetcorner to wipe the perspiration from his hatband, the rednecked traffic cop stands stiffly at his position, and Mr. O'Hara, a city comptroller, moves slowly about the dark stuffy corridors of the city hall, greeting a clerk:

"Couldn't be any hotter, could it!"

"Paper says there'll be showers tonight."

"Hope so, hope so."

George Martin comes home from the shop at evening, entering the house in a weary shamble, sweating and red-faced, wheezing with discomfort and disgust. Little Mickey watches his father remove the coat, the necktie, the wet limp shirt, watches him fall in the old leather chair in the den and light another cigar. The hot red sun slants in through the drawn shades, the house is breathless and lazy. Peter is sprawled on the cool linoleum floor of the sunporch with a glass of lemonade, the radio gives out the drowsy, humming, catcalling, hooting sounds of a Red Sox game being played in hot blazing Boston.

"What's the score?" calls the father.

"Tigers three to nothing. Bridges is shutting them out."

Mr. Martin waves his meaty hand in disgust, puffs on his cigar, sighs. The crowd suddenly rouses itself as someone is rounding first with a double to left field.

"Cronin!" calls out Peter. "McNair is scoring, Foxx is up next!"

The sounds of the game quiet down again, there's the murmur of crowd-conversations, someone suddenly whistling, the drone of an airplane in the lazy Summer sky, someone catcalling the pitcher from a coaching box. The announcer waits listlessly. He repeats: "Two and one, two balls and one strike."

Suddenly there's coolness, the sun is a deep red, a wind comes over the meadows from the river. The Martin mother is frying hamburger in butter, Ruth is banging around the kitchen setting the table, the icebox door slams, the quart of milk is placed on the table.

"Supper'll be ready soon!"

"I want to see what happens in this inning," calls Peter. He rolls over to a cooler spot on the linoleum, leans his cheek against the smooth floor, waits sprawling for the events on a hot dusty infield in Fenway Park in Boston.

Mr. Martin rattles the newspaper and glares at the editorial, puffing angrily. "Now the crazy bastards want to raise the city taxes!"

Mickey wanders out in the yard, where Charley is repairing the bicycle in the sun-heated garage, sweating, absorbed, industrious Charley. Mickey looks up and he can see his brother Francis sitting by one of the bedroom windows, musing.

The breeze is cooler, the sun is almost dark red, and here comes Joe in the old Ford from his day's work at the filling station. Now it's suppertime and, in a moment, it will be summernight.

And so one night as little Mickey is ready to go to bed, he sits awhile on the front porch of the house—the whole gang has gone home to bed—and as he sits there, he notes the subtle coolness in the air, the premonition of something different, the approach of schooldays again. Above him is a starwealthy sky, Augustcool and calm, full of misty light and a sting of coolness. Everything smells old and dusty and weary from the long Summer; and he realizes that the games he has been playing all Summer with the gang have also grown old and dusty. He goes to bed with a vague feeling of melancholy and loss—and suddenly, in the middle of the night, he awakes with a start, with joyous terror.

His window is rattling, there is a wind outside bending the branches back and forth, he hears apples thudding to the ground! From the North, from his window, he sees night clouds—he smells a prophecy—he closes his window tight—it rattles! It begins to rain!

He gets another blanket for his bed. He lies there in bed thinking, beneath the quilt, full of wild new thoughts. Autumn! Autumn! Why is he filled with such a huge excitement, with such glee and jubilance? What is this that comes now?

He falls asleep and dreams of wild winds, ragged racing clouds, cities in the North along seacoasts where the mad spray flies. And when he wakes up in the morning, there it is, in the smokey-red dawn, a kind of tender blue char through the morning sky, the sky singed brown in its borders,—and there, clean new rain on dark tree-trunks, and something wild and fresh in the clouds.

All through that day the clouds assemble and form in great knots and frames on the horizon, something whistles across the land, a leaf flies.

The days tumble one upon the other, and one night, finally, Mickey is washing his hands and his ears carefully, going to bed early, full of piety and reflection, getting up in the chill morning to go to the first day of school. The oatmeal and toast await him in the kitchen, there's something fragrant and warm by the kitchen stove, outside it is chilly and raw. He starts off with his brand new pencil-case smelling of new leather and rubber. And lo! there at the school are all the other kids of Galloway, and not one the worse for it!

So when the sun of October slopes in late afternoon, the children scurry home from school, make footballs out of stuffed socks, they leap and dash in the powerful winds and scream with delight. Fires are burning everywhere, the air is sharp and lyrical with the smell of smoke. There are great steaming suppers to be eaten in the kitchens of home as the raw October gloom gathers outside, and something flares far off. The children are off again at dusk, they form excited groups in front of fires, the iron-gray clouds mass together and move across the skies. There on the street corners are the men and boys gathered, discussing some rumorous tidings, some news, some furor that can be sensed in the very air—football, maybe, or the big heavyweight championship fight, or the elections. The leaves are piled in the gutters, the supper lights are glowing warmly in all the houses, smoke whips from the chimneys, the whole evening echoes with the calls and cries of children, the barking of dogs. Someone is smoking a pipe and striding the street. The streetlamp at the corner-store sways shadows in a big black dance, the store sign swings and creaks in the wind, leaves fly, apples thud to the ground in the orchards, the stars are blazing in the somber sky—everything is raw, smoky, and terrific.

Peter Martin strides downtown to the library, returns with books and brisk scholarly intentions. Francis winds his scarf around his neck and scowls. The father comes in the house calling: "What's there to eat? I'm hungry!"

Now above the tawny fields converge the snow clouds, there are gray skies sullen with omens of snow, it's November. The first icy winds come blasting across heaths that were summery landscapes—and snow follows, flying and blown forward in a vast sweeping shroud. The brooks freeze up, at night the skaters build great bonfires, there are shouts in the frosty air, the scraping ring of shovels, a soft, locked silence in the air. Here are the fields of snow along which solitary walkers make their mark on Sunday afternoons, and pause to watch the rose light creeping over the milky hillsides, or to shake a snowpile from a sapling's lap. And bitter December follows, savage with sleet and raw storms and news of catastrophic blizzards yet to come tomorrow.

The old house weathers another winter upon its hill, with its windows flashing the sun by daytime as the winds whip snowdust about the eaves where the long icicles hang, the tree-branches scraping and knocking against its side in the long howling nights. The wash in the backyard flaps and ripples stiffly, and here comes big Rosey wrapped in a bearish coat, with the tip of her nose so red and snuffling, her big raw hands gripped around a basket again. Joe is in the garage racing the motor of the car, his father is barging around a corner of the barn looking for some old cans of anti-freeze, the eternal cigar trailing smoke behind him, and he swears now because it is so cold and the roads are so bad.

George Martin goes into the town in the February morning and eats breakfast in the diner. He slides open the diner door and ducks out of the wintry blasts. There's the steaming racket of lunchcart cookery, men eating and laughing and yelling at him to close that door, and there's the frost on the windows rosy from the winter dawn. George Martin the printer consumes two batches of pancakes with Vermont maple syrup and butter, ham and eggs, toast, and three cups of coffee before he goes off to his work.

"Think you'll last out the morning, Martin?" yells the counterman.

"Hell, I'll be back in an hour for some more pancakes!"

Laughter rattles the frosty windows as Martin slides the door and strides off across the railroad tracks in the blasting wind. He comes slamming into his plant, kicks off his galoshes, rubs his hands zestfully, lights a cigar, and plunges into workaday matters at hand among old ledgers and galleries of inky type.

"Cold enough for you, George?" yells Edmund the pressman jubilantly.

Living continues in Galloway like the seasons themselves, nearer to God's earth by these weathers, through which life pulses processionally in moods and leaps and bounds, while the moods of the universe flank across the skies endlessly.

[4]

ON A MOONLIT NIGHT in a grove of pines, among the tables and benches of some forgotten picnic ground, a place where there were lights festooned and the music of oldtime waltzes beneath the trees, somewhere in 1910 in the marvelous New England Spring night—George Martin had first seen the girl who was going to be his wife. Her name was Marguerite and she was French and pretty. George Martin the workaday young man had considered his life and the commands of his soul and decided to court this affectionate, simple, and sensible young lady. And he married her. His thought was: "Marguerite is a *real* girl."

Marguerite Courbet was the daughter of a French Canadian lumber worker in Lacoshua who had saved his money and gone into a profitable little tavern business, only to die swiftly and tragically at thirty-eight from heart attack. This left her an orphan, her mother being dead since her infancy, and subsequently Marguerite was taken in by her father's sisters and went to work in the Lacoshua shoe-shops on her own initiative, as a girl of fifteen making herself self-dependent from that time on. She had always been a cheerful, rosy-cheeked, affectionate kind of woman in whom scarcely a trace of the effects of a tragic lonely girlhood were evident, save for an occasional air of grim quiet that orphans have in moments of reflection.

In the early years of their marriage, in those days when people hung strings of beads in the livingroom door and placed huge kewpie dolls on top of the piano, when the young husbands and wives went forth on Sunday afternoons perambulating the swaddled child in a basketwork carriage, when the young husbands wore high stiff collars and Homburg hats and trousers that pegged in and made them look spindly, when the young wives wore great hats and long gowns and flopping fur neckpieces, the young Martin couple got along together through the early nervousness of marriage as well as they could manage.

She sometimes waited up late for him while he played poker with the boys backstage at B. F. Keith's, and when he got home she cried and he tried to soothe her tears, and then he would refrain from playing poker for two whole weeks and the honeymoon would resume. Each time he went back to poker her tears were less bitter and dumbfounded and, after each sad reconciliation, sweetly, meditatively, their marriage was that much sounder. The children began to come, Martin rented the big house on Galloway Road and left the insurance business to go on his own as a printer, and in time the real tone and substance of their marriage began to take form.

Marguerite was a devoted mother whose marital love for her husband had decreased in proportion as her family grew and as she expended more and more time to the children, but in her relations with him there was a simple and dignified tenderness, an occasional argument that flared up funnily and was forgotten, and a mutual wondering love for the children and the home that bound them together more than anything else could. They were partners, they were people who still retained an old racial simplicity and earnestness with regard to the home and the family, and after several years of marriage and those few early misunderstandings young lovers have, there never again entered in their minds any thought of acute self-interest in the ways of nuptial advantage. Everything was directed towards the family which was well-knit thereby. In this manner did they succeed in finding happiness and a grave truth through nature's own old ways. They were an oldfashioned couple.

There was no official religion in the family, but the mother had always taught the legend of the Catholic religion to those of her children who seemed most interested. As a result, on church holidays such as Easter or Christmas, some of the kids went to church with her, or else did not, all according to whimsical family trends. In this manner some of the young Martins grew up under the influence of formal religion, while the less susceptible ones had practically nothing to do with it. It was a unique situation —especially since the death of little Julian Martin when the grieved and remorse-stricken mother had felt it her mourning duty to acquaint her more devout children closer to the church and its meanings. No family tension was created by this, since the children saw religion as a kind of activity, like school, instead of as a divine ordaining, and they never made comparisons.

Martin himself was not a church-going man. His contact with the Catholic religion had been through his own mother, a devout Irish Catholic woman whose name had been Clementine Kernochan. Both he and Mrs. Martin believed that there was a God, and that there was a right and wrong, and that the virtuous life of love and humility was God's own life. "And who has never really believed in Jesus?" he would ask.

"I'll never be sorry I raised those children that way," his wife would say. "It was an education they couldn't have got anywhere else, it's something that'll always be right and good for them now and later in life. And as for all my children, I brought them all up to know right and wrong and what God wants of them."

"Marge," Martin would say slowly shaking his head, "Marge, I've never had any complaint with the way you raised the kids. Whatever you thought was the right thing for them was all right with me, God knows."

And now when most of her children were grown up, reaching the age when they were ready to start their own lives, this mother's serene love for them had not abated. She was a lonely woman, an orphan through and through, surrounded by the fruits of a rich life spent with Martin in his house and in his town, yet forever haunted by the memory of her lean and terrifying girlhood. And so she would often sit sewing by the window in the front parlor and spend whole afternoons looking out on the road, waiting for her children to come home from school or from whatever they were doing, without knowing why she sat there or what it was that she was waiting and looking for. She was the mother of eight children, the wife of a good and respected man in the town, and yet there was something strange in her soul that she could not understand. She was a woman with a deep everlasting conviction in the pith and rightness of her life, and still there was something that brooded in her.

One memory haunted her more than any other, reminding her of this lonely unknowable feeling in her life. It was when she had been a young mother at twenty-four, she was calling her children to supper from the back porch of the house, shielding her eyes with one cupped hand as the sun was breaking through great frames and knots of gray March clouds at dusk, suddenly sending its magnificent red light down upon everything. She was calling out the names of her children, and her children were abroad in the strange otherworldly red light of late afternoon, abroad in the sighing organ sounds of dusk, calling back to her. And she had paused, uneasy, standing there on the porch in that strange red light, and she had wondered who she really was, and who these children were who called back to her, and what this earth of the strange sad light could be.

It had all passed swiftly, but in that one moment that she could never forget for the rest of her life, had been made implicit to her the essential chronicle of her somehow irrevocably orphaned life, her orphan loneliness.

"I don't care what anybody says," she would say, "I worry for my children and I want to help them always. Yes, you're all growing up and you'll all be going off to live your own lives soon, but that doesn't mean that I'm not your mother—and that I still don't love you as much as when you were all my babies."

"We're not talking about that!" someone would shout, laughing. "We're just kidding you about the way you worried when Joe was gone on his trip!"

"And why shouldn't I? I prayed for him every night. I asked God and I asked my little Julian to watch over him. It was the least I could do while he was away from his home," and saying this she would nod her head in a firm and satisfied manner.

"Well, that's the way you are, Ma," some son would speak up softly. "What the heck—mothers are like that."

And here she would wink both her eyes in a humorous awkward little gesture of delight, a characteristic of hers that made the others grin fondly, and they knew she was right and wonderful.

Then they saw her when she peered over glasses at the cards spread out before her teacup, consulting the fates, contemplating destiny, tracing the pathways of things in time and season. They saw her cook food and mend clothes and do the house-work, then they saw her sitting by the window and window-gazing, they saw her there in the house, sometimes grim and quiet and ruminant, at most times busy and serene, full of motherlike purpose, a most strong and reassuring woman setting the very world on its course for them, by day, by night, by the years—for she was their mother.

[5]

WHEN JOE WAS thirteen years old, and Peter nine, and Charley five, they carried out an expedition that the family never forgot. The expedition was really Peter's idea but it would never have panned out without Joe's determination and striding generalship.

Peter's best pal was Tommy Campbell, also nine years old at the time, who lived up the road on his father's farm. Like almost every other kid in Galloway, Tommy could not make up his mind whether Friday night was more exciting than Saturday morning, or even whether Saturday night itself could contest the issue. On Friday night school was all over and in that throbbing darkness all one had to do was sit back and think of the whole weekend of freedom ahead. But the weekend could not properly begin till Saturday morning at eight sharp when, after a hurried breakfast of cereal with bananas and sugar and milk, the whole broad world of daylight and skies and trees and woods and fields and The River were just waiting to be had. However, just because the weekend *began* at eight o'clock sharp on Saturday morning did not mean that it could be quite so mysteriously enjoyable as the Friday night anticipation of that beginning. There was something about Friday night that none of them could deny. It was richer, more leisurely, they made plans, mapped routes and campaigns, sat back and stretched their legs, pondered, meditated on affairs to come, consulted with fellow chieftains, laughed *tolerantly*, moved about casually. There was no rush, no losing of one's head, no sinking feeling of desperation that it was all slipping away in the hour-glass of day. Friday night was a time for lounging, far-seeing, statesmanlike convocations.

And then there was Saturday night which had a peculiar taste and tone of its own, compounded of funny-papers piled in inky-colored bundles in front of the candy store, the empty thrilling house after the folks go out for the night, and the midnight secrecies of staying up to read *The Shadow* undisturbed, or *Star Western*, or *Argosy*, or *Operator 5*, or *Thrilling Adventures*, or a glue-smelling, thick-bound, page-worn library book like *The Last of the Mohicans*. Saturday night was a great time in its own right.

While Tommy Campbell might have spent some time trying to sift one great time from another, it was incontestable that Sunday morning was bad. Sunday morning was a suffocating kind of time, when you ate bacon and eggs for breakfast, and then put on a necktie, and waited around while your mother and your sister took hours to get ready, and finally took you off to church. All the daylight and open skies and trees and woods and fields and The River were postponed for the day. You hated those woods and fields and that River on Sunday morning, not so much because you couldn't have them but mostly because *they* didn't care whether you had them or not. You went to church choking at the collar and suffocating and dying, and your mother's perfume on her church clothes was enough to put an end to you for good—it went in your nose and down your throat and you choked on it. The smell of incense in the church, and the smell of three hundred other perfumed mothers and sisters, and the smell of the pews, and the smell of burning tallow—that was enough to smother the life out of you. Everything smelled like Sunday. It was all so far away from the soft, almost velvety overalls well-used and well-worn through so many adventurous, interesting, serious darknesses.

So Tommy Campbell decided to run away from home and make every day a Saturday. His little brother Harry, who, like Charley Martin, was five years old, approved mutely of the idea when Tom put it to him one Friday afternoon. So they started out from the house at once and had not gone two hundred yards when Harry sat down to rest, to think awhile and look back apprehensively at his father's farmhouse where the road turned. He had never been so far away from home. His big brother knew what was "going through that head of his," so he took him by an ear and led him along another two hundred yards. But by that time Harry's ear was getting used to it and he kept balking back like a mule. Brother Tom grabbed a fistful of hair, which gave him a better grip, and plodded him along another two hundred yards.

When they came to a boathouse on the river at the city limits of Galloway, and Tom showed him the boat they were going to steal after dark, little Harry decided he wanted to come along after all, no need to drag him any more. They sat there and waited for the sun to go down; meanwhile Brother Tom foraged around the woods until he found a suitable number of clubs and rocks that he could use to break the padlock on the rowboat. They sat there looking at the rowboat bobbing up and down slowly in the water, and waited excitedly for the sun to go down.

When Peter Martin came drifting along the river's edge with a stick, Tom told him where they were going. Peter sat a while with them and scaled flat rocks over the water till they bounced. Then he went home to supper. When the sun went down, Tom broke the padlock and he and his little brother went rowing up the river towards New Hampshire. When Peter finished his supper that night, he wished he had gone with the Campbell boys.

The next day Mr. Campbell and some policemen came to the

Martin house and consulted with Peter's father, and finally they called Peter into the front room.

"Listen, son," said Mr. Campbell sadly, "my Tommy and my little Harry ain't been in sight for twenty-four hours. You know they ran away from home, don't you?"

"Yes, Mr. Campbell."

"And you know which way they went, don't you?"

Peter looked at his shoes. Then one of the policemen kneeled in front of Peter, and tweaked his jaw, and laughed, and said: "You tell us which way they went, because you see if you don't, they might get lost and starve to death in the woods. *They* wouldn't like you to let them starve in the woods. We've got a car outside and if you tell us which way they went we'll let you ride with us . . . if you want."

"That's right, Petey," said his father. "Tell your father where they went."

Peter went out on the porch and pointed the wrong way, towards the hills. "They went that way, to the hills, they said they was going to the ocean and get a ship to China." Peter had often thought of doing this himself and it seemed like a good lie.

The whole police force went searching through the hills all afternoon. Peter stayed in the barn with little Charley. At dusk, Joe came in with a rubber tube and began patching it up at the tool table. Peter told his big brother all about it, and Joe rubbed his jaw and sat down to think.

Finally he said, "Tell you what. We'll go up the river first thing in the morning and warn them. We'll start at five-thirty. Tonight we'll sleep in the barn."

Little Charley said he wanted to come along. Joe and Peter looked at him, wearily, and decided they might as well take him along or he might tell somebody.

"That's the trouble with the whole bunch of you!" cried Joe, telling them off. "I dunno *why* I'm doing all this for you. I got other things to worry about, I got my own troubles. I can't be spending all my time getting you kids out of jams!"

They had two bunks on the second floor of the barn, where they slept sometimes in the summertime. There was a ladder that led up a big hole in the floor big enough for lowering bales of hay, as had been the case in the old days when the Martin house was a farmhouse and the littered field in back was for growing crops. Now the barn was just an old sagging shack of boards good enough to keep the car in, mixing up smells of gasoline with the old smell of cows dead and gone and manure all dried like tinder between cracks in the floor. But it was a good big barn with a tower on it that could be reached by climbing another ladder, where Joe and his buddies often went to play cards on rainy days. Joe himself had made the two bunks on the second floor with boards and put in old mattresses and horse blankets to sleep in. Joe's bunk was the top bunk; Peter slept in the lower bunk with Charley that night.

It was May and they had to argue with their mother before she let them sleep up there so early in the year. She stayed in the barn five minutes talking up to them in the flickering darkness before she went across the yard back to the house. She knew something was *up*. They talked and told stories until the candle burned down, and then Joe said: "All right, guys, let's get some shuteye now, we gotta hit the trail at five-thirty sharp." And they all turned over on the crinkly mattresses, and closed their eyes, but it took them all an hour before they could sleep.

At dawn Joe heard the Campbell rooster crowing up the road and jumped out of the bunk to the floor. It was cold and foggy and still dark outside. He put on his boots and his heavy shirt and his leather vest, and fixed his pants inside the boots and laced them up, and woke up the boys who were sleeping together like two kittens in a basket. "Okay, you waddies, hit the deck! We got a lotta ground to cover today!" Then he busied himself around the barn getting his things together—his knife, his big work-gloves, his flashlight, his hand-ax—all the while singing his favorite song:

"O the hinges are of leather, and the windows have no glass,
And the board-roof lets the howling blizzard een—
And you kin hear the hongry coyote
As he sneaks up through the grass,
On my little old sod shanty on my claim—"

Peter and Charley were not so keen on the idea any more; it was so cold and damp and dark. They turned over like a team in the blankets, but Joe said: "Don't you boys be gettin' yourselves comfortable or I'll haul you right out of that bunk!" Then Joe lit a candle and hunched down to hone his knife, and the two kids watched him with wonderful fascination and wished that they could do things the way Joe did them. This made them want to get up and be just like Joe, so they finally got up.

Peter went to the big hole in the side of the barn and looked out at the misty darkness over the river two hundred yards away. But then, on the other side of the barn, the east side, he looked through the window and saw the pink sky over the hills far away, and it certainly was beautiful, and it made him want to get going and find the Campbell boys somehow.

They sneaked into the kitchen and made bread-and-butter sandwiches with bananas and apples, and Joe told them how to wedge the lunch bags underneath their belts at the side. The whole house was silent and sleeping upstairs, they could hear their father snoring and the clocks ticking, they could smell the sleep coming from upstairs, the silence and the innocence, and the strange kind of funny ignorance of it. And when they sneaked around the kitchen on the creaky floor they had a feeling of secret excitement and gladness that clutched at their throats and made them want to yell and sing and wrestle, except that it would wake up everybody upstairs.

Joe led the way striding across the yard and across the field in back of the barn. Beauty, the old collie, came out of his doghouse yawning and followed them silently across the field. They went across the highway, over the ditch, across the high grass by the river, and then up along the riverbank in single file in the wet grass, Beauty following them silently, just as silently as he had joined them in the Martin yard . . . and still yawning.

They headed up the river as the sun came up brightly. They rested two miles up the river and ate some of the apples, and threw the cores in the water, and sat there chewing grassblades and thinking.

"From what I figure," said Joe, poking a stick in the ground and drawing a line, "in that boat they can't go fast, upstream, and they musta fooled around a lot, so we oughta ketch up to them this afternoon. And you know what? I'll bet you a thousand dollars they won't go no further than the Shrewsboro bridge"—he made a mark across the line—"because after that they're in New Hampshire deep and they'll be coming to some rapids up near that town up there. And they'll get scared, because they're just a coupla crazy brats like you!" He rubbed up the lines and threw the stick away.

They went on up the river another two miles, the dog leading the way now that he knew they were following the bank. At eleven o'clock he came trotting back with a dead crow hanging from his mouth and Joe took it and flung it in the river and pushed Beauty in the water so he would swim around and get clean again. Beauty came scrambling up the bank, dripping wet, and shook himself furiously, showering everybody. That was when little Charley made the first sound he had made all day long: he cackled and rolled in the grass, happily, for incomprehensible reasons of his own.

They moved on till noon when it got hot and dusty, even on the river trail, and little Charley said he was thirsty; so they went into a pine wood across a dirt road to look for a brook, and found one gurgling over some rocks under the pines. They drank the cold water and soaked their hair in it, and stayed there awhile resting in the shade, Charley falling asleep for a few minutes. Joe took his hand-ax and cut himself a big staff from the birch on the hill the other side of the brook.

They went back to the river trail and trudged along till three o'clock in the afternoon. Far up ahead the forested bends kept turning and losing themselves in the white hazy shimmer of the river so that it never seemed they were getting anyplace. But around three o'clock they came in sight of the Shrewsboro bridge. And sure enough, there up ahead, on the bank, sat Tommy Campbell and Harry Campbell, motionless, propped up in the high grass, communing sorrowful thoughts of their own and thinking how hungry they were.

Tommy Campbell was glad to see them. He jumped up and came running over, hurdling the ditches with a yell ("showing off as usual," as Peter said) and laughing and trying out Joe's hand-ax on some bushes. They broke open the lunches and all five of them ate everything up in two minutes and threw the banana peels in the water. Everybody was chattering except Joe, who was hunched at the rowboat pulled up on the sand.

They spent the rest of the sunny afternoon sitting in the high grass by the water. It was a beautiful, lazy afternoon, breezy and soft. Tommy Campbell just lay back and kept spitting silently through his teeth in the breeze that made the grass wave. The way he spat out over the grass was the calmest, laziest sight Peter had ever seen. Little Harry Campbell lay on his elbows looking fixedly at the ants on an anthill beneath his nose, and Charley just hunched up with his hands around his knees and watched his big brother Joe. Joe was inspecting the rowboat from stem to stern and not talking to anybody. Peter began to realize that Joe had come only on account of that boat. He kept inspecting it and looking underneath it and going out every now and then to row around on the water.

Suddenly it started to grow cloudy, and in several minutes, before they could talk about it, some rain began to fall in hard scattered drops. Joe rowed back quickly and pulled the boat up on the sand and yelled: "Okay, you guys, make for the bridge and pick up all the sticks and paper you see on the way. Come on, come on!"

They all ran for the bridge picking up sticks, and by the time they got underneath it the rain was coming down thunderously, and it was getting gray all around, and a powerful wind came sweeping down the river and turned the water dirty and dark. Joe was struggling along the shore dragging the rowboat over the shallow water. He was alone, and he was cursing, and as usual he was deep in lonely thought.

And then, suddenly, it was almost as dark as night and it was getting windy, cold, and damp. Little Harry Campbell began to cry, but he was "a crybaby anyway," and Brother Tom told him so, though he felt sorry a moment later and sat him down roughly beside him. But Joe got a big fire going with the sticks and the lunchbags, a crackling big inferno of a fire that made everybody feel good again, they all stood around it rubbing their hands and laughing, jabbering away. Everybody was waiting for Joe to say something, too, but he was just staring into the flames and thinking. When they looked up from the flames all they could see was blackness and black water and rain falling, and a few lights far away across the river.

The wind began to blow howling hard, and suddenly it shifted and all the rain slanted in underneath the bridge and spat smoking in the fire. The boys ran to the other side under the bridge and huddled up on the sand and watched their fire die down. Joe was cursing, trying to start a new fire with some old damp paper. Little Harry saw a rat scampering across the sand and started crying again, and even Peter and Tommy Campbell were ready to cry, but little Charley Martin just sat there watching his brother Joe, not saying a word. They looked around with frightened eyes at the great desolated woods and the dark river and the whole wilderness of rain around them. It seemed to all the boys that there was something they had betrayed, something that had to do with home, their parents, their brothers and sisters, even their things in drawers and boxes in closets and chests —and that this now was their dark punishment. They looked at each other and wondered what was going to be done now.

That was when the police cars found them. The men were driving over the bridge and had noticed the fire down on the sand and the shadowy boys hovering around it. Old man Campbell came hopping down the bank through the brush on his farmer's legs and hugged his boys to him and cried. The cops were just behind him shaking their heads and glaring at the older Joe. Finally George Martin came, huffing and puffing through the bushes and yelling: "Great God a-Mighty! Here they are!"

"Thank the Lord we found you," cried old man Campbell, hugging his boys, "or this would have been your last night on earth for sure! Your mothers are worried and waiting for you, boys! Let's all go home and have some nice hot chocolate and cake!"

Hot chocolate and cake was nothing to sneeze at, Tommy Campbell told Peter a few days later, and that was why he went home that night, that was the only reason why. Peter asked him why, then, was he crying and kissing his father when they found him? Tommy Campbell did not seem to recall any such sissy act on his part. "We were eight miles up that river," he said, "and I was aiming to go eight *thousand* miles up that river if you hadn't come and messed up our plans."

So they walked away from each other and did not speak for six weeks, until it came time to swap all the magazines they had, which they had read over and over again, since it was difficult to go out and buy some new ones just like that, and they had to make a swap *some*time, even if it meant speaking to a particularly unreasonable individual and making a truce with him and swapping magazines without noticing *him* so much—which they both did.

In time, all was infolded in the earth again, in the glee of home again.

All that was two months before the death of Julian Martin. When little Julian died the afternoon the priest came to the house, Peter ran out in the yard when his father drove home and clutched him by the arm and cried: "Hey, Pa! Francis is dead, Francis is dead!"

"You mean little Julian, Petey-child, your poor brother Julian." And the old man shuffled into the house and closed the door sadly.

Through all the dark terror of coffins and the crape on the door and weeping relatives, Peter could not erase the horror and mystery of telling his father that Francis was dead. Francis was Julian's twin and looked just like him; he was sick all the time like Julian, and yet it was not Francis who had died, it was Julian. Even when they lowered Julian's little coffin into the grave, as his mother and sisters cried and sobbed and all the relatives stood with heads bowed, Peter kept thinking that it was Francis' coffin—because Francis was not at the burial, he was home, sick in bed. Even as they covered that coffin with earth in the grave Peter kept thinking about Francis.

In bed that night he suddenly remembered a year ago when Francis was sick in bed. He had come running into his room with a *Star Western* magazine to show him the pictures, laughing and sitting on the edge of the bed, and Francis had slapped him in the face hard and told him to go away. Peter could never understand why he had done that.

Then Peter had gone to the desk-drawer in the den where his sister Ruthey kept her holy pictures: Ruthey made these holy pictures herself, and they were very beautiful; she sold them at Easter-time and Christmas from door to door to make pennies. Peter took a pile of them and went back quietly to Francis's room and, while Francis slept, he laid them all around his head on the pillow, at his side, even at his feet, all over the bed till he was surrounded with holy pictures. Then Peter got down on one knee and whispered to the holy pictures and tiptoed out of the room. He prayed again in his room to God that the holy pictures would work and make Francis better.

When Francis got better a week later, Peter figured that the holy pictures had worked well, and everything was all right again.

His parents laughed and chuckled over this and thought it was cute. Peter could not understand what they were laughing about and went about his business as before.

[6]

WHEN GEORGE MARTIN went to work in the mornings he got up bleary-eyed out of bed, and coughed so thunderously that he could be heard way out on the road. He yawned, and grunted, and coughed tremendously out of his massive chest again, gasped and wheezed, pulling on his trousers and socks and shoes, and went limping downstairs in a gouty sleep-drunken waddle that shook the very walls of his house. In the bathroom he barged about swooshing water everywhere, he shaved and combed, his huge explosive cough rang out once more, and finally he emerged trailing cigar smoke behind him, wearing an expression of scowling morning absorption, picked up his hat and a handful of cigars and the *Racing Form* in the den, and left. And once more they could hear the great racked and blasting cough outside as he slammed open the garage doors and drove off to work.

"When your father coughs, it comes like a bolt of thunder," the mother would say. "I don't know how a man can cough like that and not fall dead right on the spot."

"Well," Rosey would say, "I guess he's got enough beef on him to stand the shock."

Then Martin would drive downtown to the Square, park the car in a lot behind his printing plant and walk across the railroad tracks to a diner where, in the company of other businessmen, he would eat his usual big breakfast.

In these surroundings Martin was always regarded with a curious respect which his townsmen seemed to reserve for him alone. He was unique in the fact that, while being a businessman of some consequence in Galloway, he at all times maintained an air of humility among other men, or joked and kidded with them with the verve and excitement of a big child who has yet to learn the advantages of secretiveness, sly restraint and silence. He was a man whom you addressed as George; his demeanor did not require that you address him as Mister Martin, nor at the same time could you properly call him "Georgie." The particular dignity of the man seemed to be best shown in the way that other men referred to him as George, plainly, simply, and with deep respect.

"That's the way George is, yes."

"Nice fellow, George."

"He's got his faults but he's a pretty fine man."

"Straight as they come."
"Man from Lacoshua, isn't he?"
"Yes, I believe George came from Lacoshua. Oh, he's been around here for some years, but he was born up there."
"A good man to do business with. That's what I'm told, anyhow."
"Oh, yes, George is all right."
"Except when he loses at cards."
"Well, I guess it's pretty hard to be a good loser, and George is no exception. But I'll tell you one thing about George Martin—he'll give you the shirt off his back."
"Is that a fact!"
"Yessir. Couple years back he loaned some money to a man and when everything fell through and this man went bankrupt, why, George never said a word, and today they're as good friends as ever. I happen to know this man, he's almost back on his feet today, and George never once put the matter up to him."
"Well, some men can afford to do business that way, of course."
"George is fairly well off, but he does work for his living. I can tell you one more thing about George: he's gambling too much: I'm told he neglects his business pretty much nowadays. Of course I only hear all this, I can't say for sure for myself. But that's what I'm told."
"Is that a fact!"
"Of course he's always been a big one with the cards but now he's playing the ponies too, you know, and sometimes they say he's in that club on Rooney Street eight hours a day. As you can see, that's going a little too far. 'Course I'm not certain about all this, as I say, this is what I'm told."
"Well, George was always a pretty heavy gambler. Friend of mine tells me about those big poker games they used to have backstage at the Keith's theater years ago, back in the twenties, when George was in the insurance business."
"Yeah, I remember, only George was out of the insurance business then, I believe he was just starting out with his old theater paper—what was the name of it?"
"That was the old *Spotlight*."
"That's right, the old *Spotlight*. Yes, they used to have some big games in those days. I believe George Arliss himself was in one of them, a game that lasted a whole weekend!"
"George Arliss, the actor?"

"Sure thing. George Arliss used to come to Galloway with a troupe. Didn't you know that, Henry? Hell, vaudeville in those days! The Marx brothers when they first started out with that high ladder act, and a hundred others I can't even remember—Van Arnam's old minstrels, Ruby Norton, Lydell and Mack, Harry Conley, Olsen and Johnson—"

"I remember them."

"Hell, I remember all of them. In those days they had the poker games, right here in B. F. Keith's, and George never missed a one. They say he used to be the last man to go home and the first one to come back."

Meanwhile George Martin himself would arrive at his printing plant and go in to work. He would light his second cigar of the morning, sit down in the swivel chair before the old rolltop desk and scowl at the papers and affairs at hand before him. By this time his pressman Edmund would be busy getting the two presses ready, maintaining his usual absorbed silence in which there was just the hint of an alcoholic taciturnity, and old John Johnson, who had been Martin's linotype operator for seventeen years, would come in all wrapped up in a great winter coat, a hunting cap with earmuffs, a huge woolen muffler and the kind of overshoes that New Hampshire farmers wear.

At around ten o'clock the tradesmen would start coming in. At this time the plant would be thrumming busily in all its parts, and Martin, wearing antique gold-rimmed spectacles on the bridge of his nose, and an old gray woolen sweater with buttons down the front that gave him an odd, shambling, patriarchal appearance at his work, would be standing before huge galleries of inky type scowling over an infinite meticulous labor that was like the weft of time itself. With his abrupt, stunned look of wonder he would look up at the tradesmen who approached him and stare at them as though he had never seen them before, and then say finally: "Why, good morning, Arthur. How's the boy this morning?"

"Just fine, George."

"Is that shipment of paper coming?"

"Sure thing, George. I just dropped in to see about next Saturday night."

Around eleven o'clock Jimmy Bannon would come tottering and weaving into the shop, gape jerkily around him, and moan hello to Martin over the roar of the presses. Whipping out a sheaf of papers from his shapeless coat with a motion jerking him violently aside, he would go staggering onward to the typewriter; and with his eyes rolling, beseeching, his neck working, he would fall in the chair and hurl himself back and forth ecstatically placing the paper in the roller, till suddenly out of all this tormented riot of the flesh, moaning and crying out his thoughts and his head flopping in heat of gruesome intelligence, he would begin pummeling the keys and these neat, sober and conventional words would emerge on the page:

> "Galloway, Nov. 3—Rep. Frank Grady, Fusion candidate for Mayor, announced today he will appeal the decision of District Court Justice James T. Quinn, who yesterday dismissed a suit by Grady over the engineering cost records of the Spool Street project, on the grounds that it was improperly filed . . ."

Jimmy Bannon, a spastic paralytic, was editor of the small political weekly which Martin printed. Though he had to weave and totter through all his days and nights, though he had to eat alone, and live alone with an old sister, though he had to withstand the curious and pained stares of the people of Galloway as he stumbled drunkenly along the streets, and though his life was one explosive jerking and craning of the neck, it was said that Jimmy Bannon was one of the shrewdest men in the town, that he knew more about city hall than anyone else, and that he made his living by merely withholding a tenth of the information which he had on every politician who had ever held office in the past twenty-five years in Galloway.

Jimmy Bannon had a license and drove a car, and people would stare unbelievingly as they saw the car come weaving slowly up the street, with its driver rolling his head ecstatically and bowing to the wheel. Often he would sound the horn to greet some pretty girl on the sidewalk, moaning his libidinous halloas with a rapture of the angels.

On those mornings when he sat before the poor typewriter and pounded it mercilessly with his flung and flailing fists, and drooled upon its keys, Martin and Edmund and old John Johnson would look at each other with rare sorrow and regret. Here were these four men at work in the morning, each on his own job, all old friends of some years' standing, and there passed between them an unnamable feeling of kinship that found its profoundest focus in the person and incredible situation of Jimmy Bannon. Men suffer because they are built for suffering, and Jimmy Bannon, a ferocious caricature and sum of their lives, was there in the morning with them.

One of Martin's oldest friends was Ernest Berlot, a barber who had made a fortune in the theater business once, strewn it everywhere in an orgy of spending and gambling and high life, and finally lost it altogether, returning gray-haired to his old trade as barber. But, strange to say, he had continued in his wild and boisterous ways even then, since he was a man of strong natural vigor. When Martin had met him they had gone out together on a long series of memorable toots through the years that to this day were still remembered by all the fishing-boat skippers, hotel managers, bartenders, and gambling-house owners throughout the length and breadth of New England. But Berlot had aged swiftly and was now a melancholy old man. When Martin dropped in occasionally at his barbershop in the early afternoons for a haircut or a chat, they looked at each other with that special sorrow that a couple of old pals have after all the years of beautiful association.

"Here comes George," old Berlot would say, looking at Martin with tired eyes, without cracking a smile, staring at him solemnly and with grave affection written on his gaunt, seamed face.

"There you are, you old reprobate. I've been looking all over for you!" Martin would cry.

"Looking all over for me? You know your way here."

"Here?" Martin would say incredulously, looking around the barbershop with all its array of bottles, shining mirrors, ornate old cuspidors, potted plants in the window, and antique barber chairs. "I didn't expect to find you here. I only came here as a last resort. Why, I've been looking all over for you, I was over to Jimmy Sullivan's, I looked in to the Golden Moon, Picard's, I asked everybody if they'd seen you and, by God, nobody had!"

"Ah, you're fulla bull, George. You know I don't drink no more."

"Why, what do you mean, Ernest? Finally I went over to the Frontier Club thinking you were dead drunk in the back room maybe, but you weren't there either. I said to myself, now where the hell could Ernest be? Maybe over to Charley's in Lawrence?"

"Ah, you're crazy, George."

"Why, what do you mean, Ernest?" And with his clumsy jest

wrung dry of every further possibility, Martin would roar with laughter and clap old Berlot upon his stooped, melancholy back and shove a cigar in his hand.

"Give me a haircut, you old bastard!" he would cry out. "You can't say I'm not your pal. I've been coming for my haircuts all these years and I've never complained once."

"What do you mean, you never complained once!"

And while Martin would chuckle uncontrollably in the barber chair, old Berlot would smear shaving cream over his old friend's face and knead it devotedly with his huge hands in a brooding and affectionate revery, all the while scowling and shaking his head as Martin continued his clumsy jestings, as other men in the barbershop smiled at these two oldtimers.

When Martin left the barbershop, he was always overcome with a strange sorrow, and thought to himself:

"Ernest is so old now; he's getting so old. God! To think that so much comes to so little, to think that life is really that short. I'm getting old too. My God, who can say the things people have known and the things that have been forgotten, in all the thousands of years. God, how short everything is, just a snap of the finger, everything's all over."

In the early afternoons Martin would finish odds and ends in his shop before going off to his favorite bookie joint to spend an afternoon of blissful horseplaying. Sometimes, at around two o'clock, an old priest by the name of Father Mulholland would come into his shop to see about the regular printing of collection envelopes and letterheads and other matters pertaining to his parish. He was a tall venerable old man who at one time had been connected with a parish in Lacoshua, and had known Martin's mother and father long ago.

"Someday you'll see my point, George," he would say on occasions when they argued about religion. "Your mother was one of the most devout women I've ever known, and her father, John Kernochan, was a man of God if there ever was one, a truly religious man in his time."

"Wait a minute, Father! Aren't you getting a little ahead of yourself? You couldn't possibly have known John Kernochan. Let's see, old John died in 1880 or thereabouts, isn't that so?"

"George, you forget that I'm a very old man," Father Mulholland would say with a humorous pursing of the lips. "You don't seem to realize that I have been walking this earth for eighty-three years, and that I have been doing it in the official service of God for sixty-one years."

"You don't say!" Martin would cry with astonishment, removing the cigar from his mouth a moment. "And I thought you were only in your seventies."

"Now when your mother married your father, Jack Martin, she married a good man, but he wasn't a religious man. But yet I always knew that afterwards, as a result of their union, something profoundly devout would result. You see," the old priest would chuckle, poking Martin in the arm, "you see now how true that is! Here *you* are, a man yearning after God and after His light if I ever *saw* one! Yes, sir! And your children, the little ones, little Michael, Peter, Ruth and young Francis, all of them have the makings of splendid Catholics and certainly that of splendid Christians."

"True, Father, but I ask you again, would a little water and a few words in Latin make them any better? You say that I'm a man yearning after God—and isn't that more than you can say of a lot of yearners we both know? Do I need an official writ to prove that I'm a Christian? When I want to do good and be good . . . if at all possible?"

"We've talked about that so many times before, George, and we never do reach an accord, do we?" The old priest would look up with a soft prayerful chuckle and shake his head with a slow, senile, wondrous trembling. "Yes, yes. You're a stubborn fellow, George."

"Here," Martin would say, holding out his hands, "let me put it this way. If I were a farmer, I'd plow my ground and look to God as my only witness. Now, as a printer, living in this town among these people, I plow the ground that I have, I'm in business, and God is still my only witness. I don't see how the church can come between a man and his God without somewheres breaking the direct contact. Look at these collection envelopes—of course you understand, Father, that I'm only doing this for the sake of argument—"

"Of course, George!"

"Then look at these collection envelopes. Of course I realize that the church is not self-supporting, it's not in business, it needs the contributions of its parishioners and supporters, and all that. But haven't you seen this sort of thing exploited, corrupted?

Father Mulholland, in your sixty years as a priest you certainly must have seen it!"

"I have seen it."

"Well, what about it?"

"Are there not priests who are the representatives of God, and are there not priests without whose business acumen, without whose tireless efforts, there would be no church? Of course you know that the higher the priest, the more he is a politician. You know that."

"I didn't know that exactly."

"Someday, George, I'll tell you the story of modern Christianity. It's a long and complex story, involving much high politics." Father Mulholland would purse his lips in pedagogic musing. "But now I want to ask you: if it is necessary that there be two worldly priests for the sake and the support of one genuine, devout, God-like priest, do you think the game is worth the candle? You remember the great Father Connors back in Lacoshua. Is it worth it?"

Martin would shake his head with wonderment. "Yes, by God, it's worth it. Father Connors. Yes, yes. He was a priest. There's only one priest I know who topped him. And that's you, Father, and I mean it sincerely, believe me."

"Come, come! Only a minute ago you were ranting and raving about my corrupt little collection envelopes."

"No, that's not fair. I was only saying for the sake of argument! I want to ask you something: here you have your parishioners going to church on Sunday morning, receiving Holy Communion, walking back to their seats with a mighty holy look. But while you're sitting in your rectory on Saturday night, Father, I've seen them out on the streets and in the saloons, and there's nothing holy about them then! Oh, it's that *look* in church that beats me! I don't know where they learned it! What about that, then, Father Mulholland. Don't you admit that there's just a little teeny bit of hypocrisy there!" And Martin would roar with laughter, poking the gangling old ecclesiast in the arm, and looking up eagerly in his face to see any signs of discomfiture there.

"George," Father Mulholland would say, "George, I believe you fancy yourself a philosopher. I'm not going to answer your question. Indeed, I'm going to let you think about that question yourself."

"I'll think about it, Father, and what will be my conclusion?"

"Well, now," the old father would say, carefully adjusting a battered old hat on the top of his head, looking down at Martin with a gleam of joy in his eyes, "supposing that come Sunday morning our friends whom you describe were still, as you say, bamboozling around, heh?"

"By that time, Father, they're dead to the world. I know!"

"But not dead to God, evidently, because they all seem to turn up in church in the morning."

"They do! But that's only because their conscience bothers them!"

"My dear George," the old priest would chuckle, gripping Martin's arm and shaking him gently, almost deliriously, "you're arguing with yourself, not with me. Now I'm going to leave you to *your* conscience and go away." And he would gently clap Martin on the shoulder and gaze down upon him with his huge expressive visage of benevolence and old friendliness. He would leave with a cheerful backward wave of his hand and glide out of the shop, stooping in the doorway to pass. Martin would watch his departure with sorrow and wonder, because he was such an old man, because he was such a rare and marvelous person, and a priest.

There was something in Martin's heart that never ceased its wondering and sorrow. There were days when everything he saw seemed etched in fading light, when he felt like an old man standing motionless in the middle of this light and looking around him with regret and joy at all the people and things in his world. Men saw him laugh and chew on cigars and talk excitedly and grow angry, but they never saw him in his lugubrious rueful solitudes when he choked with inexpressible sadness. He saw men cheat each other, he heard scorn every day, he saw bewilderment in the eyes of other men, he wandered through a harassed cycle of anger, guffaw, malice, hate, disgust, weariness. Then in a moment he embraced life and ran benevolently, joyfully, through it, only to resume suddenly a morbid, sometimes wicked, melancholy in which he was black with hatred and scoffing. But once by himself, in the antique light of his profoundest comprehension, he saw all these things, he stood apart from them, with infinite old regret, he wondered and lamented and cried out to himself, and repined in loneliness.

"This is it," he would think. "This is the way life is. It's such a strange thing—oh, it's so funny, so short, God knows what it is."

In moments like this, he gazed brooding at his children, and wondered what it was that weaved and weaved and always begat mysteries, and would never end.

He was also a lively man. In the Jockey Club he spread his form sheets out on the table before him, sipped from a cold foaming glass of beer, smacking his lips, lit a fresh cigar and plunged into his figures with absorbed gusto. At evening he came home and ate like three men. And later at night, as he was deeply involved in whether or not he should call the other man's bluff or raise him a stake, he sat there puffing thoughtfully on a cigar, fidgeting his chips and grinning at the other man slyly.

All this was the likes of Martin's days and nights.

[7]

ONE SPRING gloomy young Francis Martin discovered that he was in love. He was seventeen years old, just finishing his last year of high school, and thinking mistily of going to college in the future.

Her name was Mary and she was an Irish beauty with black tumbling hair. One look from her and Francis was frozen in his soul. He knew that she would always hold him with those eyes of hers and laugh, somehow, because of it.

He had met her in school where, in an English class, she sat diagonally in front of him and cast her locks about on drowsy afternoons. He was the most brilliant student in the class and before long she was casting her locks about for him on those lovesick, heartsick afternoons which are nowhere sweeter than in high-school classrooms.

"Francis, read sonnet twenty-nine for us," the proud old woman teacher would suggest dreamily. It was close to the end of the hour, time for poetry and lingering moods of "beauty and truth." In the back of the class the boys drowsed sullenly. In the front part of the class stood tall spindly Francis, surrounded by the girls.

Francis reading in a precise, mature manner:

> *"When, in disgrace with Fortune and men's eyes,*
> *I all alone beweep my outcast state,*
> *And trouble deaf heaven with my bootless cries,*
> *And look upon myself, and curse my fate—"*

"Francis! *Deef* heaven?"

"Yes, Miss Shaughnessy. I believe 'deef' is the Elizabethan pronunciation. And it makes for better poetry than *def* heaven."

"Well, we'll look that up," the old woman smiled dreamily. "And, class, I want you to notice how Francis does his own thinking about poetry. You mustn't only read, you must also read yourselves *into* it."

The boys in the back of the room looked at each other with a bland indifference.

Francis continued:

> *"Yet in these thoughts myself almost despising—*
> *Haply I think on thee—"*

And here, turned up to him from around curling locks, were the dark bewitching eyes of his beloved Mary. . . .

In the lyrical Spring evening, then, he would start out for her house, borrowing his brother's bicycle, and pedal slowly across the town in his stern and invincible manner. She lived in the southern part of Galloway, in an old ramshackle farmhouse on the banks of the Concord River there. And whenever he rounded the corner of the highway and came gliding on soft rubber tires towards her house, with its vines over the porch and its drooping trees, with the dark river beyond, and the aura of pastoral simplicity all around, it never failed to cast a spell of fearful enchantment over him. At times he was hardly capable of controlling his wretched excitement, and more than once came wobbling to a stop at her fence post.

Her brothers, rawboned youthful farmers who called him Frank, were always sitting around in the soft evening darkness whittling and telling stories that were of no consequence to him.

"Hey, Frank!" they called.

"Here comes old Frank!"

"Frank" would thereupon go up on the porch, where Mary sat with her mother and a few kid sisters in creaking hammocks, and he would stand tensely against a post in the dark silhouette of the vines.

"My, Francis, you look to me like you're getting thinner all the time," the complaisant mother would say. This would please Francis considerably, it suggested that he ought to be fed and taken care of by someone like Mary.

In the same complaisant manner, Mary would survey him in smiling silence.

Later, when they were alone on the porch and the others were getting ready to go to bed, Francis would say: "Look at that moon. It never looks more beautiful than right here in South Galloway."

"Oh, you and your poetry."

"Well, what shall we talk about?"

"I don't know, don't ask me."

Then Mary would brood so voluptuously, so sullenly, with a heavy-hanging rueful lip and dark impenetrable eyes.

"God, your eyes!"

"What about my eyes?"

"They're so beautiful, honest."

"You're always saying that, Fran-cis. Look at them, look at them," and with this Mary would open her eyes wide and comically stare at Francis, a little cruelly too. He loved her more than ever when she treated him like a fool.

He never wanted to kiss her because she was altogether too voluptuous—her lips were too yielding and rich when he pressed his own against them, his hand around her waist inadvertently probed too much soft shapely flesh. These were things about her that he never dared to dwell upon because he loved her as if she were an angel. Darkly, with a bitter melancholy, he wanted to spend the rest of his life watching her sulk and brood. This annoyed Mary.

"Kiss me, Francis. You're an awful *tease*."

And afterwards, as the night grew chilly, he would put his coat around her, and she'd sit wrapped in his arms staring off into the darkness. Her voice would get husky, a faint smile playing at the corners of her mouth, and while speaking she would look at him occasionally with those eyes. He continued to stare at her intently, in such a way as to insure her being bored with him and yet made curious by turns.

"Francis, you're very smart, ain't you? Someday you're going to be a big success. What are you going to do?"

"I don't know, but I know I'll make a lot of money."

"You're a funny fellow. I wonder what it would be like to be married to you. What would you do?"

"What would I do?"

"Yeh. Do you know anything about women, about love?"

"Oh, I'm not interested in that, not now, I mean."

"I know you're not. You're funny. That's what *I* mean."

"Mary," he would say, "look at me."

"Why?"

"I want to see your eyes."

"Other fellows always want to neck. All you want to do is look at my eyes."

"What other fellows?" Francis would inquire a little hotly.

"I had other fellows before I met you, what do you think?"

"Yes. Mary, if we were married, we'd—" But he could never go on and explain to her that he wanted to spend the rest of his life watching her, scrutinizing her moods, devouring the dark pouting sight of her.

"We'd what?"

"We'd be together, wouldn't we?"

"Well, *naturally*."

"What I mean is—"

"Oh, go home, Francis; you're crazy. I'm not going to school tomorrow, I'm going to pretend I'm sick. Come and see me Thursday night."

"Thursday! That's almost a week!"

"I'll write you a note tonight and have Jimmy give it to you in school. Go home now, I'm sleepy, I want to go to bed."

"All right, Mary. What will you write in the note?"

"How should *I* know?—I haven't written it yet!"

And Francis would leave sheepishly, turning to watch her enter the house in her lazy sorrowful way. All yawning and abstracted and tired of him and of everything. That was when he loved her the most.

He would pedal the bicycle homewards across the dark fields, always stopping near a cemetery to lean on the handlebar and consider the vision of his beloved Mary. From the top of a hill he could see her house down by the river, down by the silent slow-flowing Concord that Thoreau had known a hundred years ago, that Francis knew now with all the special enthrallment of morbid concentrated love. She was in the house now, she was moving about in her morose dissatisfied way, that light that was being dimmed was the light in her bedroom, she was in bed now and staring in the darkness with her fulsome pout. He pedaled homewards in dreamy meditation, pursuing Maryish thoughts to all their dark recesses.

In the morning he stalked the halls of the high school looking for the boy, Jimmy, who would bring him Mary's note. It was thirty minutes too early; there was no Jimmy, there were hardly any other students, just an old janitor sweeping the halls. Now when the students began to arrive in laughing groups, there stood Francis by the main door searching every face. Jimmy lived next door to Mary, he had access to her miraculous presence when she wanted him to deliver notes, he saw her day after day moving about in her windows or out in the yard—he seemed to be more fortunate and favored than any other Jimmy in the world.

The boy finally arrived, holding out a note.

"Mary Gilhooley told me to give you this note, Francis."

"A note?" Francis would inquire with raised eyebrow. "Oh, really? Let me see it."

The moment the little freshman was out of sight, Francis would stalk away clutching the note in his pocket, and hurry down to his locker in great hungering strides; there, amid the shouts and clatter of the other boys, read the note in trembling secrecy, staring around him with a speechless astonishment as though a certain power in it were raising him, mad and seaweed-trailing, up above the surface of the common sea to unspeakable heavens.

Dear Francis,

Gee, I am so tired this morning I can hardly open my eyes. I can see Jimmy next door eating his breakfast so I guess he is almost ready to go to school so I better make this one short. Bessie is going to spend the day with me and we are going to listen to the radio. I'll think of you every time they play something nice.

All my love, Mary.

During his morning's classes Francis repeatedly took the note out of his pocket and examined the writing. He searched for hints in the very flick and shape of the letters, in the pressure of the pen on key words such as "dear" and in "you" and "love." He seemed to find a special pressure upon the word "all" in "all my love." None of the musical utterances of Shelley and Shakespeare could be so surrounded with lingering, rare, shadowy darknesses like this. He placed the open note atop a page of poetry—and he compared for hours between the lines.

Sick and drooping with love, he purchased a birthday gift for Mary in a Galloway jewelry store—a single string of fine smooth pearls—and placed them delicately in a red velvet box. On a soft May evening, he started out once again on the bicycle in all his severe and melancholy demeanor, and crossed the town thoughtfully, a moody inscrutable swain maddened by the witchery of his goal.

That night of her birthday, a night that he was never going to forget, he arrived at the old farmhouse and was greeted by her brothers.

"Hey, Frank! Old Frank! You looking for Mary?"

"She just went for a ride with Chuck Carruthers. You know old Chuck, the football player!"

"He came here in a Ford convertible."

"And where did they go?" Francis asked feebly.

"They went that way."

"She'll be back, Frank. Sit down and make yourself comfortable."

"No," said Francis quietly. He looked down at her two brothers from his bicycle with an air of cold indifference. "By the way, when she gets back, give her this, will you?" And he handed them the box of pearls.

They called after him and yelled "old Frank" but he was speeding away down the road, away from her house, away from the town, towards the woods that stretched before him in flowery darkness.

He came to the railroad bridge and stared down at the waters. There were some children yelling on the river bank and splashing around in the water. He heard someone calling. "Fran-cis! Hey, Fran-cis!"—a distant, mysterious call.

And it was Mary. Down by the water's edge he saw a Ford convertible coupe, and Mary herself waving at him and smiling. A tall well-built boy in a bathing suit stood beside her grinning as he wiped his hair with a towel.

Francis got off the bicycle and directed it down to the water's edge over a path that ran through the bushes. He came slowly, sadly, while Mary was sauntering up to him with a casual and lazy petulance.

"I didn't know you were coming tonight!" she was saying in her sullen way. "Why didn't you call me?"

He stood motionless, staring at her out of the depths of a raging and futile loneliness. He could see her pouting lips, her dark smoldering eyes, her hair tumbled over one side of her face in the evening breeze.

"It's your birthday," he said listlessly. "I thought I'd surprise you."

"But you should always call anyhow. I have other plans sometimes."

"It doesn't matter, it doesn't matter!" he hissed savagely through clenched teeth, and turned away to close his eyes and think. He suddenly knew that he had frightened her by this sudden show of pent-up anger, and whirled about to smile and say: "I'm sorry, I guess I should have called."

She stared at him curiously.

A moment later he wandered after her towards the beach and the car. It was growing darker and the other boy had turned on the headlamps of the car while he dressed behind the open door.

"Come out of the water now," called Mary to the children. "Cissy! Maggie!" She stamped her foot. "I'm gonna tell Ma on you if you don't come out this minute."

"Aw, you're a scaredy-cat!" yelled the boy who was dressing. "Someday I'm gonna throw you right in the water and then you'll learn how to swim!"

"No no no!" she squealed. "I'm afraid to drown, I'm afraid, *honest!*" and she bent over quickly to stifle a little delighted laugh.

Francis stared at her with amazement.

"Honest, Francis," she went on, turning vivaciously with a toss of her head to him, "I'm afraid to death of drowning, ever since the Crouse boy drowned last summer. Oooh! you should have seen him when they dragged him out. I was there. My father found him. Oooh! I'm scared to death."

"Then you mustn't go swimming," said Francis decisively, almost as though talking to himself.

For the next few minutes he was silent as he gazed at Mary, and listened to her talking to the children, watched her dry them off with a towel in a brisk and motherly way that sent pangs of unspeakable loneliness through his heart. "Mary, Mary," he kept saying under his breath, framing the words with his lips in soft prayerful entreaty. He wanted to take her in his arms and walk away, carry her away, as far as he could go, till they came to some place where there were no people at all, and dark silence.

"Mary," he said out loud, with a start.

She turned her dark gaze upon him.

"Come on with me, on the bicycle. We'll go for a long ride." And he put his hand on her shoulder very lightly, with tense fingers.

"Oh, we're going for a ride on the highway for some ice cream, up at Bill's," she cried gleefully. "And potato chips too! They're real good at Bill's. Come on with us if you want."

"If I had a car I'd take you to Bill's every night," he said softly.

"Oh, don't be jealous, Francis; it's not like you."

"I'm not jealous," he replied with a little sniff.

"Well, *say* something!" she cried suddenly.

"Huh? Well—I think I'll go home, I think that's what I'll do now, go home."

"If you want."

"That's what I want," he said to himself out loud, fumbling with the bicycle and starting to turn miserably. At that instant Chuck having finished dressing and combing his hair on the beach, now appeared before them in the bright light of the headlamps. He shambled gracefully up to them with a proud lithe step over the sand, a big healthy good-natured athlete with an ingenuous grin and a handsome, offhand manner.

"Hi there, Martin!" he greeted. "Coming for the ride?"

"No, I've got to go some place."

Chuck flicked the towel at Mary and whooped with laughter, yelling: "Well, come on, we ain't gonna stay here all night! Come on, you kids, get in the car! Everybody get in!"

Mary went running into the car, calling back something to Francis which he never heard, and in a moment Chuck was racing the motor of the car.

Francis hurried away, pushing his bicycle along the path with a feeling of dry rotten horror in his heart.

The car was moving along the old dirt road, its headlights reaching over the bushes where he was walking, and in a moment he knew his wretched fleeing figure would be revealed in shafts of light for all to see. He suddenly threw himself on the ground with his bicycle and lay breathlessly embracing the grass in darkness.

He heard the car move slowly up the road, and Mary's voice crying in the soft night: "Where's Francis? I don't see him anywhere! He just disappeared! Where is he?"

"Maybe he's a six-day bike champ!" the football player shouted, and a moment later there were no sounds but that of the retreating car and the soft trilling of crickets all around.

Francis lay there on the grass for a long time, until he finally came to his senses, realizing that he was lying in the middle of the woods in the cricket-stirring night, under a vault of terrifying darkness. He looked around him on one knee with a wondering and crazy lonesomeness.

In the same half-demented state he stood up, got on the bicycle and started up along the path, turning into the road and cycling along with that feeling of crazed wonder. He couldn't believe what had just happened; he tried to ignore it. "I'll think about it later," he said absentmindedly, and mused upon the countryside and the branches under which he glided swiftly.

Thus he picked up speed and came rolling along past the ramshackle old farmhouse where Mary lived, almost in high spirits now as he thought about what he would do tomorrow after school at home. But Mary's two brothers were there smoking in the darkness of the porch steps.

"Hey, Frank!" they called. "Mary's gone swimming by the railroad bridge. We just heard."

"Did you find her, Frank?"

"Yes!" called Francis as he pedaled past them. "She's swimming— And I hope she drowns!" he added in a choked cry they could not possibly have heard over that distance. And instantly the tears burned in his eyes, and he sped home weeping on his bicycle.

By the time he had arrived home, put up the bicycle and gone into his room, stamping around with the proud manly determination never to see her again and turning his thoughts to new matters, he suddenly couldn't get over the thought that Mary had been searching for him while he lay hiding in the dark bushes.

He heard her say over and over again: "Where's Francis? I don't see him anywhere! Where's Francis? where's Francis? where's Francis?"

So now young Francis was learning to weave himself into his own cocoon of tormented adolescence. All was harshness around him. He was biding his time and waiting with sad patience until life would open up for him as he desired it should. He was a musing, discontented, lonely young reader of books, of which there are so many in America scattered thinly and almost pathetically throughout the towns and cities: easy to hurt, open to abuse and scorn, much too sensitive in a thoughtful formal loneliness to withstand the harsh buffooneries, the horse-play, the animal brutality, the wild carelessness of a savage rhapsodic America in its shouting youthfulness. He was alone and fearful, and sometimes also scornful. He was different from the other kids his age who generally spent their time in ice cream parlors, on drugstore corners, on athletic fields, on dates at the movies and dancing. He was different from them and he was proud of it.

At seventeen, now, he may be walking home from the library at evening with a few books under his arm, or taking solitary walks at midnight, or sitting in his window reading after school, or drinking a coke at the corner drugstore in absorbed melancholy, but all the time he is balancing life and death, stumbling through a thousand moods of horror and hate, watching himself step discreetly through all the philosophies, sects, factions and cults of a hundred books, living the despondencies of many heroes—Jean Valjean, Prince Andrey Bolkonsky, Anna Karenina, Greta Garbo, Byron, Tristan, Hedda Gabler.

He goes to the library, and spends the morning poring reflectively through several biographies. Every now and then he looks up with an amused but rather sheepish smile. At noon, he lingers around Daley Square examining the townspeople of Galloway with secret pleasure and a feeling of aged understanding. Even when his father goes by among all the others, walking slowly to lunch in conversation with other businessmen in the rippling sunlight, he watches him secretly from the doorway. Even then Francis is filled with a strange pleasure and the belief that he is the only mortal soul in the town who has frighteningly understood the meaning of life and death.

[8]

YOUNG PETER MARTIN was busy trying to make the Galloway High School football team. It meant glory and triumph, and fame in Galloway, and little else was on his mind as he hurried home after dark each evening, late for supper, weary and absent-minded with all the hundred details of his goal. His mother would feed him great boiled dinners and he would eat them with a voracious abstracted intensity, mulling over his chances and ripping at the bread and meat at the same time, as though everything were part of one great hungry plan to succeed.

"How you making out on the team?" his father would ask him kiddingly, but in a goodnatured tone.

"We'll see, we'll see," young Peter would reply grimly. "I might even get my uniform next week!"

He was fourteen when he first reported to the football practice sessions. He was growing but he had not grown enough. The coach and his assistants never gave one look at this boy who still seemed like a child, who was indeed a child, who was hardly grown enough to push a watercart around the field for any length of time. At the first day of practice, after going through routine calisthenics with everyone else, Peter collapsed on the grass and lay there sick for an hour trying to recover while all the others dashed around, jumped in the bus and went home all flushed with the excitement of the first day's workout. Peter had then trudged home three miles, depressed by the very thought that he couldn't even make it to the bus.

But he kept coming to practice, and later that season he was always seen standing around the edges of the squad on the field, attired in a pathetic nondescript football outfit that someone, probably the team manager, had happened to consign to him just because he had proved so obstinate coming to practice. Once in a while one of the assistant coaches would beckon him out to the middle of the field to stand there as a kind of defense dummy, around which the luminaries of the squad dashed and capered in all their recognized glory.

Still young Peter would stride back home at dusk, his mind teeming with the possibilities of his future as a football hero, hurrying into the house where his mother waited anxiously with his huge supper kept warm, and he would again tear into the meat and bread and consider the glorious triumphs that awaited him.

The following year, although he was only fifteen years old and still growing, he was already a junior in school and the better part of his high school days were spent.

"Don't be discouraged, Petey," his father would say to him, chuckling. "After all, you skipped grades in grammar school because you were such a smart little cuss and now you find yourself almost finished at high school. I don't want you to feel bad, understand? It's not your fault, you're just a baby."

"I'm *not* a baby—I'll make the team this year!"

And that year he stood around on the edges of the practice field and watched, and waited for a chance to be beckoned out on the field to stand as a defense dummy, or to just be seen doing some impossible feat under circumstances which would suddenly, miraculously arise. He dreamed all day long in classrooms of some such circumstance: he saw himself being called out to play defense during an actual scrimmage by some stroke of luck that would take him only a minute to conjure up. He would spend hours brooding over what he would do: someone would throw a pass, destined for the great Bobby Stedman or for Mike Bernardi, the coaches would be standing around with impassive faces waiting for the play to materialize, the newspapermen would smile at one another saying, "There goes the old razzle-dazzle pass play!" Suddenly, out of nowhere, a swift stocky figure would blaze across their vision, leap up and intercept the pass, and come roaring down the field, at top speed, eluding all flailing arms, dodging and weaving and opening bursts of phenomenal speed that would simply astonish and amaze everyone present.

In his classes, at home while eating, in bed at night, and at the practice field during long sun-slanting October afternoons young Peter would lose himself in such reveries, and tremble at the very sight of Coach Reed whenever that venerable old mastermind would glance his way. Yet when practice came around he just stood there in back of the squad, lonesome, insignificant, shy, all decked out in another miserable hand-me-down of a football uniform, and tremble in his knees whenever a coach so much as looked his way, or one of the team's stars brushed shoulders with him.

His father came to watch practice one day, and as the old man sat in the empty grandstands and saw his little son standing drooped and sad at the back of the squad, never so much as taking a step forward or doing any of the little capers that the other boys performed regularly as a means of catching the coach's eye, he realized that Peter was not only too young and undersized for the brutal game of football but also too gentle and modest in his ways. No one would ever notice him on this or any other field.

He waved at his son and the boy smiled back shyly. George Martin went home shaking his head ruefully.

One day the coach was running the varsity team through a defense scrimmage and suddenly he was looking directly at Peter and several other young outcasts who spent every day faithfully standing around just as he did. Someone had just been injured and a replacement was needed in the fourth-string backfield that was scrimmaging on offense. It was a drowsy Monday afternoon, there were many absentees.

"Get one of those kids there to fill in!" the great coach barked. The assistant came over and scrutinized the kids with a sullen air. Several of the boys stepped forward eagerly, though with a little hesitation, while Peter stood back watching, almost blushing. It so happened, however, that Peter looked the least delicate of the lot—at fifteen he had begun to grow muscular bulges on his legs—and the assistant, staring with a dull expression of boredom, finally looked around the others and beckoned him over.

"You there! Step into the backfield. Get a helmet over there."

Peter dashed to the sidelines and picked up a helmet with trembling fingers. The next moment he dropped the helmet to the ground, gulped, swallowed, and picked it up again. Someone had to help him put it on properly, as he stumbled wretchedly to the scene of the play.

"Hurry that kid up!" roared the great Coach Reed as he waited for the distraught scene to end, but Peter had suddenly discovered that one of his shoelaces was untied and there he was fumbling on one knee and looking up with a kind of despair.

Finally everything was set, and Peter found himself huddled among ten sweating grimy scrimmagers listening to the orders for the next brutal smashing play.

"You, kid," barked the assistant coach in the huddle, "take out the end. That one there. Do you understand?"

"Yessir!" mumbled Peter. He was scared to death.

Explosively the play developed and Peter found himself rushing towards a tall rangy youth who came flailing straight at him. Peter lowered his helmeted head and pushed head-on, and just as he made contact he felt the explosive crash of bone and muscle encased in hard canvas, and fell to the ground momentarily stunned, feeling that all this had happened long ago in that precise dizzy way. He felt sickened and mortally afraid. The others returned to the huddle, Peter wandered after them in a daze, wondering why everything was so strange, staring around him incredulously.

"The same play!" barked the assistant coach. "Give those first-stringers a real workout!"

And Peter heard these words from far away.

Once more the center snapped the ball back and Peter realized that it was time again for him to rush the tall powerful player who had just smashed him to the ground with his pumping vicious knees. But all at once, in the flash of that moment, a surge of fear and lonely anger ran through him, he had a vision of retribution, he looked at the other boy and saw the gleam of dumb brutality in his eyes, he sensed something powerful and bloody between them and them alone. In the next instant, snarling and weeping and blind, Peter was running as fast as he could and smashed straight into him, shoulders first.

The tall youth was cut down sharply.

"Nice block!" called the assistant coach.

The tall boy, whom Peter now more or less recognized as Al MacReady, the famous Galloway end, slapped Peter briskly on the back and said: "Nice, nice."

Back in the huddle Peter glowed with the first triumph of his work: a sharp pain in his shoulder was dissolving quickly and seemed to be making his blood beat warmer. He danced nervously and champed the turf.

"Wait a minute," said a quiet voice behind. Up stepped the venerable Coach Reed himself, staring over the field with eagle's eye, musing, profound, big, approaching them with hands clasped behind in majestic authority. He leaned into the huddle and spoke to the panting youngsters in a deep gruff voice, his breath smelling of tobacco, wheezing softly with a sad asthmatic labor, a sadness that amazed Peter who had never stood so close to him. "We'll try a switch here," the old man growled. "And let this kid here carry the ball, on the eight end-sweep. What's his name? What's your name there?"

"Martin," gulped Peter.

"You know the eight sweep?"

"Yessir."

"All right! Go ahead." And with this the old man backed up, hands clasped behind him, and waited for play to resume. "Be alert out there!" he called out to his regular players on defense. "Don't let these kids pull one on you!"

At this the varsity players steeled themselves, champed, leaned forward eagerly, and waited for the play. One of these regular players was creating a sensation that year as a phenomenally savage tackler on plays breaking through beyond the line. He was a wiry powerful little Irishman named Red Magee who could come slicing into a play and send it scattering to four corners through sheer zest and wiry guts. Now, at the coach's words, he danced and champed in vicious eagerness and waited for the play.

When Peter found the ball twirling back to him he was already running slightly forward, nervously, but once he had the ball in his hands he was off to the right in a wild sprint, literally running around his own blockers and finally sweeping wide around the end, around the tall Al MacReady who tottered reaching for him and fell, while all the others seemed to sway in Peter's direction without actually getting underway. In a moment Peter was all alone running down the sidelines and looking back foolishly, as though he were just as embarrassed as the players. The coach blew his whistle to call the play back, but at that instant Red Magee came with the speed of a bullet upon Peter, who had stopped running, and smashed full force into him, cutting him down with a sudden sharp thud as the ball wobbled up into the air and the two boys scattered over the buckets on the sidelines. Peter saw stars.

"Dammit, I blew the whistle on that, Magee!" roared the coach across the field. "The play was over!" He turned and muttered something in the assistant's ear, and they both smiled faintly.

Magee jumped up and trotted back to his position jubilantly. He was known as the devil of the squad who could never control his own wild viciousness, and on Saturday afternoons at the big games the crowds roared with appreciation at his fiery, colorful, violent antics.

Peter wasn't hurt, but he returned to his position slowly, thoughtfully, as though he were dazed again, and incredulous as before.

"That was nice running, sonny," said Coach Reed directly to Peter. As they huddled for the next play the boy was suddenly conscious of the old man's hand resting on his shoulder, and he gulped with fear and amazement. What would his father say if he could see this moment now?

"See what you can do on the off-tackle seven. You know it?"

"Yessir," swallowed the boy.

"All right!" roared the coach over the field. "This kid'll give you another chase. Move in there, Bernardi, you're too far back. On the ball, on the ball! You won't be able to loaf Saturday! If a kid can run around you what do you think Lynn Classical will do? Stedman, wake up!"

And thus, in the drowsy hum of the October afternoon, Peter waited panting for the ball to come back to him, his knees trembling, his blood pounding from all the running. And again the play developed explosively. There were violent biffings and scuffings in the line as he waited for the ball to hit his hands. When it did, he was off like a deer once more, running up the backs of his blockers, teasing around them like a dancer, slicing through to the open spaces beyond the line, and opening up more speed. He was fifteen yards beyond the line and still running, arching his back as he flanked around someone's reaching hand, stopping, jumping over a leg, darting aside to continue along in a forward sprint, and moving towards the open—when suddenly he was confronted by Bobby Stedman the backer-up defense man and someone else, and he veered charging to the left only to see a glimpse of Red Magee come sluicing at him in a flying tackle, which he dodged coyly by stepping back and moving forward again. The whistle blew again as Peter and Red Magee glanced at each other furtively.

"What's the matter with you guys!" the coach was roaring. "I want you to wake up!" And in a wheezy confidential whisper in the huddle he said: "All right, try it again, sonny, on the two hole; shift on the left, you kids." And the old man stepped back thoughtfully.

And again Peter found himself waiting in the drowsy sun, sweating, panting, grinning with fatigue and joy, pounding his hands impatiently for the ball as the lines met, and biffed, scuffled, opened up for him. He ran sharply to the left, according to the play he knew so well from long lonely memorizing, and then cut back inside straight for the "two hole": it was wide open, he ran directly through it at top speed, like a scared rabbit into the open. But just as he was emerging, the wiry little figure of Red Magee hurtled through the air straight at him, Peter saw everything, and there was a terrific collision of bone, muscle, and canvas that could be heard in a loud "whap!" clear across the field.

Peter stood rooted to the ground from the shock of the head-on collision, one leg placed deliberately in front of the other in the frozen act of running, and Red Magee, similarly frozen in the act of tackling, lay sprawled on his knees with both arms around Peter's hips, moaning: "My neck, my neck, ooh, my neck!"

And like a limp rag, in a dead silence that followed, the boy rolled over clutching his neck, while Peter stood horrified and dazed, looking down, the ball still hugged to his side.

Everybody ran up to the injured player. There was a confused minute during which the coach's car was brought up and Magee was carefully placed in the back seat. He kept moaning and clutching at his neck, and staring about with a white look of fear.

Peter stood petrified at the back of the crowd with the ball still in his hands.

"Did he break his neck?" someone whispered.

"It sounded like *something* broke!"

"They're taking him to the hospital. Holy cow!"

Peter was standing back there understanding that in some way, somehow, he had cheated the older boy into thinking that he could easily be knocked down, by submitting motionlessly to the first furious tackle on the sidelines and by dodging the second attempt with a meek agility. But just now, seeing Magee coming at him ravenously in one of his famous slashing tackles, he had nevertheless rushed straight at him with driving knees and with all his headlong might, deliberately to deal him the full force of the weight and power he knew he had and that he had so far concealed.

"What did I do?" he asked himself in terror and wonder.

They drove Magee to the hospital, but in ten minutes word was received that he had not broken his neck, that he had only suffered from shock and would recover overnight.

"That was like a couple of locomotives meeting on the same track!" said Coach Reed gruffly and the whole squad laughed.

Thereafter for the rest of the afternoon Peter was the center of interest. He was taken aside by one of the assistant coaches and the long onerous task of learning all the refinements of play was begun for him. He spinned, reversed, faked, shifted, learned all the rudimentary motions of the subtle powerful backfield action. He was awkward, bashful, foolishly nervous—but something exulted in him, and the coaches were watching him carefully, with a kind of scowling pride. Old Coach Reed himself sauntered over and watched impassively, turning occasionally to a curious newspaperman at his elbow and talking in a low voice. Then he would turn again towards Peter and roar:

"Relax! relax! When you spin don't think of anything else but the spin, and *then* start running. Just think of the ball and your three steps, understand?"

After practice, when the raw October gloom gathered around the field and all the players had run in for their showers, Peter was still running and spinning and handing the ball on reverses while Coach Reed and his assistant stood by, barking at him in the sharp frosty air.

"No! no! no! Make your pause, and *then* turn!"

"And when you turn, pivot on the right foot, the *right* foot!"

Thus, sweating and panting and joyful, young Peter was sent in to the showers: and there, in the steaming clatter of the shower rooms and the lockers, everybody was coming over to talk to him, the varsity men themselves—Mike Bernardi, even Bobby Stedman—on down to the lowest subs. Where yesterday he had sat dressing in a dark corner of the noisy rooms, today he was the center of the whole raucous exciting scene that he had been watching so long in lonesomeness. He danced under the steaming showers, dried himself vigorously, dressed, combed his hair, and waddled about with the limp of a bonafide athlete at last, proud and battered and fatigued.

And then in a whirling confusion of events he was given a regulation football uniform with a huge numeral on it, his picture was taken by a local news photographer, Coach Reed came over and asked him about his school grades, the team manager hurried over with two pairs of brand-new shining backfield shoes, and Peter thought he would go out of his senses from all the excitement and tumult that suddenly surrounded him and filled his heart with dizzy unbelief.

He hurried home, striding along joyfully in the dusk, gloating over what his father would say and what the whole family would say, thinking all the feverish thoughts of youthful glory and triumph, he gazed into the faces of everyone passing him on the dark streets and wondered if they knew about this, or what they would think when they heard, and the whole raw October darkness of the evening with its flying leaves and powerful winds and flares of fire from somewhere was all his. In his deepest soul, deeper than the regret of his heart, he gloated and boasted because he had almost broken Red Magee's neck: for Red Magee had tried to smash Peter Martin to a pulp and everybody had seen the result, everybody knew Peter Martin was the vanquisher.

In the strong autumnal winds he rushed along ignoring the new dark knowledge he now half-understood—that to triumph was also to wreak havoc.

The smoke was whipping from the chimney of his house, he leaped up the steps with glee, smote the side of the house with delight, walked around the porch taking deep breaths of air and looking up jubilantly at the stars, and then he plunged into the house to tell them all the news, to sit down at his mother's table and tear at another great meal of meat and bread and potatoes in hungering rout.

During the remainder of that season Peter was sent through the paces of grueling interminable backfield drills, spinning, faking, reversing, ducking and weaving through all the hundred intricate movements of the play, growing so painfully, brutally fatigued sometimes that he wished he could just fall on the ground and give it all up. But the moment he was off the field, once more he would start weaving and spinning with a mad urgency, even while walking home; or in his room he would stand in the middle of the floor and start all over again, holding the football to his stomach, handing it out, spinning, stepping. If he could have carried his football into the classroom, he would have done it. He slept with the football on a chair beside his bed, and in the morning he would pick it up and turn it over and over in his hands before breakfast.

The awkward, shy, shambling movements of the novice on the football field gradually became the movements of a swift and knowing halfback, he began to step about with graceful assurance, impassively, and smoothly, darting off with a thrum of powerful trained speed, his eye considering all obstacles with a crafty deliberation, his whole body swaying one side or the other in quick judgment.

Before long he appeared in his first big game—considerably awed by the vast excitement of the stadium all around, but successful in making a favorable impression on everyone in the last few plays of the game. His father came to watch him at practice almost three times a week now, standing on the sidelines puffing a cigar in blissful absorption.

The local sportswriters knew Coach Reed was grooming several young members of the team for future stardom, but it was not until the last practice session of the year, when they were all standing around watching practice for the big Thanksgiving game, that the old coach directed their attention to the other side of the field, to Peter who was making practice runs with the second team on the snowy turf:

"And there's your next year's Bobby Stedman," announced the old man in his famous impassive way.

"Pete Martin?" the reporters chorused in surprise.

"If that's what they call him," replied the old coach with his famous twinkle of the eye, "if that's what they call him, I guess that's who it is!"

[9]

AND YOUNG JOE MARTIN at this time was driving great trailer-trucks on the route up to Portland, Maine, over nighttime highways that roared unto dawn from powerful motors and huge revolving hissing tires, along blazing macadams that stretched miles ahead all bright from lights and neon roadhouses, highway lamps, gas stations and diners, rolling on through the coastal night in thundering breakneck speed. He had found a job that suited him wonderfully.

In the high cab he sat grimly through the night hurling the immense machine along with an exultant feeling of joy and accomplishment. Sometimes, when he had to slow down before country intersections that criss-crossed the great broad speedbelt of the highway, he could feel the massive push of the trailer behind him with its tons of cargo, like a Gargantuan nudge in his back, and then when it was time to pick up speed once more, from first to second to third to fourth speed in a series of straining bucks and bolts, he could feel the powerful motor grinding and pulling with irresistible force until it raced along again in headlong catapultion on the straightaway. He would unleash wild whooping cries of delight. On downgrades the truck would gain a giant momentum, he would jam in the clutch and let the whole mighty bulk roll in silence, and then at the foot of the upgrade he would again step on the gas and send himself roaring uphill in unbelievable glory.

In the first weeks of his new job he unleashed whoops of joy a hundred times the night. He was twenty years old now and "crazier" than ever.

Near Portland, in a truckman's diner, he met a whole covey of waitresses who took to him as fish take to water. He sampled them one after the other: and often, in the gray dawns when it was time for him to drive the truck back to Galloway, he would leave his lady fair and leap up to the high cab of the mighty truck like a gallant mounting his warhorse, and roar off throwing back kisses. It was around this time that he found it expedient to sport a dashing little flick of a mustache, just above the lip in a thin brown line which, together with his laced boots and riding pants and visored cap, contrived to give him the appearance of a first-class ladykiller and handsome libertine. He was trying to save his money; in a few months he was going to be seen on a flashy new motorcycle—and then, as he put it himself: "Here I come!"

Women loved him because he was boyish, and men slapped him on the back and bought him drinks because he was manly. And all the time he whooped with laughter, told interminable stories, strode about insouciantly, and passed everything off as great fun and good times.

But in all this whirl of long blazing white highways with their roadhouses and diners, the men and women eating and drinking, the laughter, the love-making, the raucous jokes, the beer, the jukebox music, the miles of smooth macadam through pine woods and the roar and rush of the driving, the huge presence of the truck, the weary ecstatic nights—in all this, the swashbuckling young Joe was also a kind of grim, workaday, lonely Joe. Sometimes he would park his truck along the highway and pause to smoke a cigarette thoughtfully—or at other times, taking leave of his friends in some reeling Portland saloon, he would take solitary walks around the town and stride along in boyish reverie.

One time he stopped the truck at a diner outside a small Maine village and there met a strange and lovely girl who didn't seem to pay much attention to him. She was a waitress, and when he got to know her she pointed out her family's house to him, just a half a mile away on a hill above the highway. It was a charming colonial house surrounded by the stark trees of New England winter. Her name was Patricia. She was going to school days, and earning her spending money by working as a waitress.

Something in this little out-of-the-way diner outside a small village attracted Joe, and before long he began to stop there all the time for his meals and relaxation and his weekly flirtation with the handsome Patricia, who received his thrusts with a wise and ladylike charm. She was a tall angular girl, with something gaunt and beautiful in her face, dark serious eyes, long lashes, strong white teeth, and a full-breasted feminine figure. In due time she learned to accept and anticipate Joe's frequent visits and flirtations, they shoved nickels in the jukebox and danced, she made him great batches of pancakes, strong coffee, special home-made donuts just for him, she waited on him exclusively when he was there, and before long she was taking rides in his truck with him to Portland and back. She was the kind of girl who would wear overalls to go truck-riding and who drank beer prodigiously, danced well, walked in a long loping stride like him, laughed a lot, and was always ready to follow anybody she loved "to hell and back," as she had learned to say from Joe.

"When I get my motorcycle," Joe told her jubilantly, "we'll ride *all* over and go *every*where! Hey! Can't you see us whippin' along at eighty per under the moonlight? Wahoo!"

"Yes, but you don't get drunk till the ride is over, Joey boy."

"For that you gotta kiss me!"

And she kissed him, suddenly, with a powerful surprising passion.

Joe became a familiar figure in her home, parking the truck in front on the highway and striding up the lawn to play with the dogs and her little brothers and sisters. Patricia's mother baked cakes for him to take along on the grueling journeys. Her father slapped him on the back and told him jokes. And sometimes, when Joe left for a week's time and saw Patricia waving sadly at him as he drove off, he could realize all too well that this was "getting serious" and that he liked her "too much."

"Ah, but she's a great kid!" he would laugh, and think with delight about her as he hurled his great truck along the speedways of the night.

"Where you been hangin' out, Joe?" his Portland cronies shouted at him when he began coming around again in the wild saloons there.

"Aw, I found the sweetest kid in the world, no kidding!"

"What's her name, Joe? What you holdin' out for?"

But Joe was too wild and too young to brood over a woman for any length of time, and gradually he began to neglect the diner where she worked. He returned to his old ways, to the blind routs and drunks and poker games with his truckdriving, happy-go-lucky comrades—half of whom sported the same kind of little mustache, and all of whom were young wildcats and wranglers like himself.

Those days Joe would sometimes arrive back in Galloway drowsy with fatigue, wheeling the great truck into the garage. He would step down wearily from the cab, smoking a weary cigarette, pausing in the little office-shed to engage in banter with the garage-men and drivers who looked upon him as a great fellow and a good worker, and then trudge on home to go to sleep for twelve hours at a time.

Joe was indefatigable in his pleasures, wonderfully liked by everyone, coveted by women of all kinds, strong and responsible at his work, spendthrift with his time and money and laughter. Yet in his inmost soul, like every other man, he brooded and was restless and dissatisfied and always looked to the future as a challenge and a sad enigma. He wanted a motorcycle so that he could hurl himself plummeting and roaring along to anywhere, he wanted the camaraderie of his pals, he wanted women and more women, plenty of beer and food and money, he wanted everything that a carefree youngster wants—but at the same time he knew that there was something else he wanted, that he did not know what it was, and that he would never get it. To all his friends and to his family he was just Joe—robust, happy-go-lucky, always up to something. But to himself he was just someone abandoned, lost, really forgotten by something, something majestic and beautiful that he saw in the world. Someday on his motorcycle he wanted to go far out across the U.S.A.—just for the "hell of it" and just for something else, too—to see sublime mountains, massive canyons, great mountain forests drumming in high winds, lakes where he could pitch camp, the deserts and the mesas and the great rivers that somehow had forgotten him, the vast "man's country" of his boyish dreams. Joe sometimes really believed that he should have been born elsewhere and in another time. He could work with all his energy for fifteen hours a day on some old motor in a garage, and then suddenly gaze off and recall somehow that he was lost and forgotten by that sublime meaningful world that gleamed in his vision: and where he got that vision he did not know.

He sometimes spoke about it with Francis who "knew everything."

"Dammit, France, I wish I could have lived in those days when you rode on horseback and all you had ahead of you was this big unexplored space, the wide open spaces, and everybody had to pitch in together to put up a cabin or build a saloon or haul a wagon across a river."

"You mean the frontier days."

"When men were men," whooped Joe, "and guys just practically owned everything they saw. *You* know . . ."

"No, I don't know."

He would tell his father about it and the old man would instantly fly into a political rage: "You've got something there, Joe! That was when America was America, when people pulled together and made no bones about it."

"I know, but what I mean—"

"In those days," thundered the father, "there was honesty and there was good living. Things were hard, the poor devils sometimes got snowed right under by tough breaks and big blizzards and Indians, anything at all, but by God it made better men! Those pioneers were the men who made this country *great*, before it started to fall apart in the last thirty years, they were the fellows who took it upon themselves to leave comfortable communities and strike out with their wives and kids to build a new country. And now! Now you can see what all their suffering and sweat is coming to—"

Which was not what Joe wanted to talk about. It had no name, he did not know what it was. It was just a boyish dream, his own secret sad dream. And so like any other man—and he was already a fine and true one at twenty—like any other man he brooded in his heart's restless unknowable depths. While he worked and drank and laughed and knocked around.

[10]

THE MOTHER completes a chore in the kitchen, listens to the late evening news on the radio, has her cup of tea with crackers, and yawns, and tells Rosey to close the windows upstairs. To eat and to sleep, to have a house and to live in it, to have a family and to live with them—these are the things she knows. To bask in the days that keep coming and going, to keep the house warm and clean and enjoyable, to prepare food and eat it and store it, to conquer sickness, keep things together, preside over the sweet needs and plain satisfactions of life, and to order the furies of existence around all these things—this is what she knows, and she understands that there is nothing else to know.

The depth of a woman's heart is as unknowable as that of man's, but nothing like restlessness and feverish rue ever abides there. In the very deeps of this heart are contained all the secrets, and the one plain secret of life, which is something that is homely, coarse, sensual, and deep, something that is everlasting because it is serene and waits patiently. A man may spend the night tracing the course of the stars above the earth, but the woman never has to worry her head about the course of the stars above the earth, because she lives in the earth and the earth is her home. A man may yearn after a thousand shades and shapes that surround his fevered life, but to the woman there is only one shade and one shape to things, which she forever contemplates in the fullness of her profundity, and she never loses sight of it.

Some men dig into the earth to excavate whole lost cities and civilizations, they want to find otherworldly mysteries and strange things never known before. But if you dig into a woman's heart, deeply beneath whatever surface it presents, the deeper you go, the more woman there is; and if you're looking for mysteries there, you'll find that they don't matter.

The Martin mother was this kind of deep woman, who could look upon the lives and activities of the world around her with the judicious and patient eye of an eternity, knowing that all fuss and furor would end, all joy and all tremendous spiritual fret would end, and things would grow back into their proper ways. Thus, sometimes when her three eldest sons chanced to be eating at the same table on some occasional noon, she would feed their plates and hover about and watch them from her corner of the table with a blissful, ruminative, shrewd smile.

As they talked and ate and smoked, receiving coffee and dessert in that contented absentminded manner that men have at table, she would notice how each one of them burned and raged with a particular loneliness, a special desolate anger and longing that was written in each pair of eyes, and she knew that all men were the same.

What did it matter if Francis suffered from the rue of abandoned love, embarrassed and haughty and dark with hate, and pale with loneliness, all wrapped in his books and thoughts and in his solitary habits? His mother knew that he ought to eat more, and sleep more, and take care of himself for a long life that was ahead of him in spite of everything, including himself. Somehow she knew that whatever Francis did it would all amount to the same misuse and folly and waste that all men practiced—he would continue on his melancholy path, loving the sorrow and abandonment of his own heavy heart, staring into abysses, trickling himself away in black ennui, sitting by the ticking of a clock, with a book, a thought, a thinlipped morose idea. But to her it all seemed dignified and beautiful nonetheless, because he was a man, and the sorrowful misguided man is a beautiful and forsaken creature.

And Joe. What did it matter if Joe had a thousand raging enthusiasms, was always working and running around and spending his money, or if he was lonely in the company of many women and scores of men, or if he sometimes filled himself up with whiskey so that he could reel blindly across the night? What matter if he whooped with laughter and wet his lips in his brief boyish way and strided around town in his rough workboots and visored cap and yet at the same time felt lost, forgotten, deserted by something that he wanted and could never even imagine—it would all amount to the same thing. Joe would get married, have children, work, rage about in all his manliness, grow old and die, leaving more life behind him and die in dumb wonder with work-gnarled fingers and far-gazing wasted eyes. He could never know the immeasurable pricelessness of the present, the very moment of being his coarse, sensual, and beautiful self, and the women watched him and loved him because he was so blinded.

Young Peter, with his brooding ambition, a trifle slyer than the other brothers, but blinder by far, a pouting, disgruntled, lunging youngster with a thousand confused desires, who could look about him with profound wonder and glee and gravity, and at the same time never see himself there or anywhere, who chased the future with maniacal desperation and ran smackdab through all his days and nights with wild eager amazement, who would one day hurl himself against all stone walls available and get up sorrowfully to find some more, and be loved by women because he was so saddened—the mother knew him well also. He would catapult himself in loneliness towards more meaningless goals, like all men, and he was all so rueful, rough, noble and sensual in the eyes of this silent mother.

She knew that, though women are sometimes lonesome, men are always lonely. She knew all these things and yet there was no wonder in her heart, but peace, blissful contemplative womanly peace, knowing plainly the purpose of knowledge.

It is amazing how women *are* women, even in childhood. Little Elizabeth stands in the middle of the field watching her little brother Mickey make a fool of himself rushing around madly for more fuel for the fire, which rages at the mouth of a discarded sewage pipe, making the smoke spout from the other end of the pipe and dancing in the smoke like an Indian. Little Liz knows that this will add nothing to the natural peace of life. It's supper-time, time to go home and eat and grow stronger, but Mickey wants to dance in the smoke, and make more smoke to dance longer, and he won't go home to eat until he's exhausted and bored with the smoking sewer-pipe.

"Come home! It's time to come home!" she cries.

Mickey dances in the smoke. "Wheeeooo!"

He burns a finger in the course of the fire-dance, and when they get home Lizzy rubs butter on it to relieve the pain, and pushes him away saying: "You're cra-zy! Go away!"

She watches him broodingly as he rummages around for cookies, she is silent as she watches him with his dirty face and hands, his burned finger, his snuffling nose, and the way he scratches his head violently and walks off with the cookies to munch on them idiotically. "Cra-zy!" she says. But she follows him into the other room to watch some more.

The old man comes home from work and lights up a cigar and sits down with the evening paper, and when Ruthey asks him what he will have to drink with his supper he looks up with a dumb and startled look, stares at her with disbelief, rattles the paper, puffs on the cigar, and says: "Why, I don't know, anything, I guess, anything at all."

"But you got mad yesterday because there wasn't any coffee."

"Coffee?" he grunts, as though he had never heard of the stuff. "Well, that's fine, coffee'll be fine," and he goes on reading the paper. And she stands for just a moment watching him, with a faint, helpless, skeptical shake of her head, a sudden faint grin that always says, "Isn't that just like a man!" Then she goes back to the kitchen to make the coffee just the same.

And big Rosey knows them. She stands arms akimbo, a great warder of the keys to peace and comfort. She makes no bones about them: they are no more coarse, sensual, and beautiful than she is. (But yet she knows they really are.)

When by some chance the Martin house is empty of its men for a short while, the women in it—woman and child—are smitten with their own kind of lonesome understanding, and look at each other with feminine knowledge, in that smart and swift understanding glance that communicates all the depthless womanish comprehension there is in the world, and sometimes too they look at each other with feminine glee.

And the men rage on in loneliness.

[11]

IN HIS SENIOR YEAR of high school Peter was sixteen. His shyness, his shrewd and dogged ways, his blue eyes gazing from underneath a shock of dark hair, his boyish pensive determination, were not in the least offset by his having grown a brawny, powerful physique. He was built like a rock: broad of shoulder and chest and girth and thigh, weighing close to a hundred and seventy pounds while standing only five feet eight. But still he was like a child. And no one noticed him in his school until the day of the first football game, when he scored three long-running touchdowns, and went back to the bench to rest until next week's game while managers threw hooded jackets over him and patted him on the back, and the crowds roared.

He was publicized as a great "climax runner" in the newspapers. Instantly he had hundreds of friends, students and teachers alike, and he scarcely knew what to do about it all. In the company of his fellow teammates he soon learned the knack of limping and swaggering through the halls of the school in all the glory of a famous school hero. Yet when he was alone he continued to pursue a bashful and unobtrusive path through his world, always wrapped in deep thoughts of the future, and of future glory and triumph. Now he had begun to think of college, of being a great scholar and college football star, of being a great man eventually.

At the high school dances he suddenly found himself pursued by the young ladies, though he did not know how to dance, and on top of that could not have carried on a conversation with a girl for a minute without blushing and stammering like a rapturous idiot. Instead he hurried home and studied, and when his schoolwork had begun to seem trivial and too limited, he began to read Dr. Eliot's "Harvard Classics" from shelf to shelf, thinking that in this way he would soon become conversant with all the knowledge in the world. He half understood what he tried to read and plunged on, trying to master everything in sight.

Towards the end of the season the Galloway team began to meet stiffer competition from teams all over New England and in time Peter found himself working like an ox on the gridiron. In some games when there were many injuries, he carried the ball all afternoon and plunged and dove and smashed his way on play after play, with fatigue, a bloody snarling mouth, a bruised and knotted body, and something that was like powerful disgust in his soul.

In the shower rooms after the big games, he and the other gladiators were watched broodingly by coaches and newspapermen and rabid followers as they undressed wearily, showered, dressed again and then sat in melancholy fatigue. There were banquets and testimonials and a thousand slaps on the back, and they were always weary and full of premonition of another week's smashing brutality. But when they limped and swaggered around the streets of Galloway, or in the halls of the school, it was always glory, and they knew that was all they wanted.

In one game it rained in torrents upon a muddy field, the stands were filled with people who huddled under umbrellas and raincoats and newspapers, and Peter crashed and splashed his way through the misty, mud-splattered chaos, and exulted. And in the morning he saw his picture in the newspaper, a dark misty print covered with blotches and grotesque muddy figures, he saw himself driving forward in a fabulous world of darkness and rain and heroism: just as he had once seen the pictures of Bobby Stedman and Lou White long ago. This then was the completion of his first ambitions—but it wasn't enough, there had to be more, there had to be much more.

The final game of the season, the big Thanksgiving Day contest in a concrete stadium that always drew enormous crowds, was the game of games, towards which all the enthusiasm and energy of the team, the school, and the followers were directed each year. The newspapers gave the game a front page spread in special editions, the two local radio stations carried a play-by-play account of the game over the air. Terrific rivalry was thus generated between the two opposing teams and between the two towns themselves, Galloway and Lawton.

Thanksgiving morning was the occasion for great migrations by auto and bus up the river to the great stadium, people bet on the outcome of the game on streetcorners, little children leaped about and screamed with delight hurling stuffed socks and stayed close to their radios when the game was on. The game could be heard over radios in poolrooms, fire stations, and police stations all over town. The streets of the towns on that morning were practically deserted; passers-by were in the habit of shouting to one another: "What's the score now?"

That year both teams had rolled up powerful records in New England and were meeting for what promised to be a championship clash of "herculean proportions," as the papers put it. Among the record crowd assembled in the big stadium that year were a good many of the Martin family who came to see their own kin represented in a great event, the Martin father himself at the vanguard of their grand entry into the stands. Men called to him and he waved back his cigar. He was tickled pink and he didn't care who knew it.

With him were his wife, Joe, Mickey, Ruth and Elizabeth, all bundled up in warm clothing and flushed from the cold wind and the excitement. Flags whipped atop the rim of the stadium, brass bands blared and paraded on the white-striped field, great raw November clouds marched across the skies, everything was gray and windy and thrilling, and their own Peter was donning the attire of battle underneath the very stands where crowds roared.

It was the first football game in the Martin mother's experience, and when she saw the parading bands down on the field, she cried: "I don't see Petey? Is that him there?"

The old man laughed, and just then the Galloway football team appeared trotting out on the dark field, the crowds thundered in ovation, the drums sounded, and the old man cried. "There he is now! Marge, there's your boy down there now!" And there were tears streaming down his cheeks. He didn't care who knew it—he was proud enough to cry.

"Where? Where is he?" the mother cried.

"That's him, Ma!" shrieked Mickey. "Number five. See him? In the back there! Hey! Hooray, Pete Martin!"

"Wheee! that's my brother!" cried Ruthey.

"Does he see us?" asked the mother anxiously.

"Of course not!"

"My, but everyone's cheering for him!" said the mother proudly. "Has he scored a touchball yet?"

Joe grinned. "Ma, the game ain't even started, and it's not touchball, it's touch*down*."

"It's so cold today, I hope he doesn't fall down on that hard ground!" the mother said. "My, everyone's yelling their heads off!"

"Come on, Petey! Earn your turkey today, my boy!" howled the old man. "Score a touchdown and by God you can have both drumsticks!"

"Hey, Martin!" yelled a man several rows away. "After this game maybe he'll be so hungry he'll want to eat the whole turkey!"

"That's all right with me!" howled Martin. "By God, that's all right with me! He's my kid and he can do what he likes!"

People all around them laughed, and one man reached down a bottle of whiskey, crying: "Your kid's playing in this game? Pete Martin? Here, have a drink on me. Can't say I'm not doing my bit for the Galloway team!" And a small cheer was raised all around them.

The teams returned to the locker rooms for final instructions, the bands paraded on the dark field, there was noise and furor and autumnal excitement everywhere.

In the chilly locker room Peter sat on a bench tightening his shoes and thinking. The old coach prowled in front of the players barking instructions and warnings at them. They could hear the faint music of the bands outside, the clonking of cowbells, crowds roaring—and all of them were swooning with fear, swallowing and gulping, terrified and lost.

"Don't think you're gonna have an easy time out there!" barked the old coach. "Oh, no! Don't think you're going out there and pick daisies with these Lawton boys. You haven't noticed how small and dainty they are, have you? You won't go out there and waltz around a few times, and say thank you, will you now!"

The boys laughed, and gulped.

"You noticed how big they were, didn't you? You saw that DeGrossa boy who plays center for them, hey? He weighs about two hundred and twenty pounds, stands six feet three inches in his stockings?"

They had also seen the expression of fierceness on his face.

"You saw that line, didn't you? Solid all the way through and twice as wide, like trucks, hey? And those backs—what did they look like to you?—like demure young girls, perhaps?"

They had looked like leopards, somehow, and the players gulped and swallowed.

The door of the locker rooms burst open and a man in white knickers shouted: "Two minutes, Coach Reed!" With the sound of his urgent cry came the roar of crowds, the music, the bells clanking, the drone of an airplane overhead, and the school cheers raised in vast whistlings and zis-boom-bahs and sudden rousing songs. Above them they heard the stamp of many feet, and the beat of many drums.

The door closed again and a hush of silence prevailed in the gloomy locker rooms. The old coach looked at his young players and said nothing. Everyone held his breath and looked at the old man who had hounded them and fatigued them and driven them all year long through a hundred days of bone-rending football, and suddenly, somehow, they felt a strange affection for him: he had been like a harsh father to them.

"There's nothing to say," said old Reed with a shrug of his shoulders. "There's positively nothing to say," he said helplessly, and looked at them with bland open eyes.

Everyone waited breathlessly. The old man stalked around once more in woebegone silence. They realized that they loved this gruff old man.

He stopped and stared at them once more with a bland open expression, while his assistants stood behind him, grim, almost panic-stricken, pale and drawn like the players themselves.

"A whole year's work," said the old coach. "A whole year pointed to this game. This is the only game that really matters. You were all kids once and you remember other Galloway-Lawton games, you heard them on your radios, you wanted to grow up and play in this game. Well," he said, staring at them, "here you are.

"I'm gonna slap my hands together in a moment now," went on the old man, "and what are you gonna do about it?"

There was a pause: and then all the boys cheered the old man and leaped up, he clapped his hands, the assistant threw open the door, and out they swarmed into the cold winds, out to the dark white-striped field, racing furiously in the wind and exulting, and all around them the crowds roared and the bands drummed and blared, something in the air was like thunder and battle and glee.

They saw the Lawton team across the field in a huddle of great captains, standing in the wind in their dark uniforms, helmeted fantastically, all grotesque, wild, and ominous; they saw the officials in white placing the new yellow football on the kickoff line; they saw the whole mob-swarmed terrific stadium in a gray windswept blaze of vision. Whistles were piping in the air, silence was falling over the multitudes, the game was ready to begin.

And then when Peter saw the ball up in the air, wobbling and windswept, and saw it bouncing down before him, he was mortified with fear. Then he lunged for it, picked it up, snarled, and ran straight downfield with all his headlong might, crashing and stamping through a confusion of hard bodies and falling finally on the icy midfield beneath ten others, and the game was on.

"Woohee!" his father was howling way up in the stands. "Did you see that? Thirty yards back he took it! What a runner!"

"Hooray! hooray!" Mickey was screaming.

"What happened?" cried the mother. "Was Peter down there? Everybody fell down!"

"I'll say he was!" shouted Joe. "He was down on the bottom!"

"Have another drink, Mister Martin!" called the man with the bottle. "That runback was worth a nip. Have another drink, Mister Martin!"

Down on the field the teams lined up, the linemen digging in low and glaring at each other, the backs crouching, the quarterback calling out numbers with his whole body jerking behind each shout, the officials waiting expectantly nearby, and all of it windswept on the dark field to which all eyes were fastened excitedly. The lines collided, biffed, scattered, long rangy youths sprawled, someone ran and ducked into a pileup of bodies, and it was no gain. The cowbells clanked, someone shouted: "Come awnnn, Gallo-wayyy!"

"What's happening? What's happening?" demanded the Martin mother with furious innocence.

The crowd suddenly roared as someone ran wide around end, around reaching hands, arching his back and waving one arm, cutting back suddenly on dancing feet, wavering, darting aside, plunging on a few yards and pulling along to a stop under a pile of bodies. The crowd's roar surged away into droning chattering sounds, cowbells and drums rang in the sharp air, someone whistled.

"What was that?" cried the mother, tugging at Joe's sleeve.

"Petey! Gained five yards!"

"Come on, sonny!" howled the father. "Keep it up, boy!"

Suddenly the crowd was on its feet again with a sharp roar as someone darted through hugging a ball and ran straight ahead and then to one side sprinting, wide, arcing towards the sidelines, and running out of bounds.

"Petey ran up a first down!" shouted Joe to his mother. "Did you see him?"

"No, no, I don't see anything."

"Hooray, hooray!" yelled Liz, waving her school flag.

And thus the game carried on in the grayness, both teams digging in deep and plunging and scrambling, and to the Martin mother nothing seemed to happen whatever. Indeed, as the first half wore on, Peter was brought to a standstill in his running, as well as his running teammates, and the Lawton team just fought and plunged and gained nothing either, and the half ended without a score in a game that depended on the defensive ability of the team lines.

"Well," said the old coach back in the dank locker rooms, "I told you it would be like that. I told you, and now you know."

The players lay sprawled on the floor panting, looking up at the old man with helpless weary eyes.

"I want you to try more passes. I want you to try the forty-seven in their end zone and try the trick pass over the end's head. And you linemen: you're getting fooled on their mousetrap every damn time! Every damn time! I never saw the beat of it! Magee here is playing the best defensive game in the backfield; you other backs are loafing. MacReady's doing fine covering their offtackle plays. The rest of you are just a bunch of dummies!" And he went on like that for fifteen minutes, stalking around the gray damp room, looking at them fiercely, and then wearily, and staring at his assistants dumbfoundedly as though he had never seen them before.

"It's like I told you fellows. This is the game. Go out there and bring yourself some pillows, why don't you, so the ground won't be so hard! Or why don't you bring out some poetry books and read them some poetry? See how they'll take to that! Huh?" he barked, and glared at them. And yet they knew they loved this old man.

They went back for the second half.

"Come on, boy!" howled old man Martin in the stands.

Again the teams dug in deep, glaring at each other, smashing at each other, scattering and scrambling in tremendous bone-bruising collisions that were not heard high in the stands. And on the field itself the roars descended to the thudding field like one vast whispering sigh, like vague distant commotions of sad excited humanity.

"Come on, you guys!" the little quarterback piped in the huddles. "Let's go, let's go! Time's running out! The offtackle six! Martin!"

And up in the stands the crowds roared and saw Peter swing wide with the ball in one hand gripped like a big egg, and turn in swiftly towards the scuffing lines and break through at headlong speed, and go breakneck up the field with his legs twinkling in the gloom, pursued by dark figures, smashed down by dark figures on the white chalk-stripes.

"Was that Peter?" the mother cried. "I saw him fall down, number five! Oh, my goodness!"

Again there were milling plays in the November gloom, scatterings, dodgings, pileups of bodies, and the pipe of a whistle in the keen air.

"It's such a funny game," said the Martin mother, turning to Ruth. "Nothing happens, everybody falls down. My goodness!"

"Come on, my boy!" shouted Martin in a powerful voice. "Come on, son!"

"Ten minutes left to play!" someone shouted. A cowbell clanked wearily, the cheering section whistled vastly, sighed, said zis-boom-bah; and there was a roll of drums. Again the teams collided on the field below and the players reassembled slowly, meditatively.

"Mickey," said the mother, tugging at the little boy's coat, "tell your mommy what the score is."

"Zero to zero!"

"Tell your mommy what that means!" she demanded.

And now suddenly the crowd rose to its feet with one roaring cry of surprise, explosive and vast, as a Galloway player swept wide around the end, leaped into the air, twisted, and shot the ball several yards over dark helmeted heads, as another Galloway player paused, twisted, reached out for the ball, barely grasped it in his fingers, turned and went plummeting downfield along the sidelines. The roaring of the crowd surged and grew thunderous, the Martin mother jumped up on her seat to see, and she saw a figure racing down the sidelines, shaking off tacklers with a squirming motion, plunging through others with a striding determination, tripping, stumbling, staggering on half fallen and half running, straightening out once more, plodding, faking, yet suddenly approaching the goal line in a drunken weary run, staggered aside by another lunging figure, momentarily stopping, then carrying on again, striding to the line falling, with a dark figure smashing into it, now wavering on bent knees, now finally diving over and rolling in the end zone triumphantly.

It was a touchdown at last.

"Petey! Petey! Petey!" screamed Ruth and Elizabeth in unison as they jumped up and down on the seats, as the great crowd roared everywhere around in tremendous jubilation.

"What happened?" cried the Martin mother in despair.

"He did it!" howled the Martin father with indescribable amazement and excitement. *"By God he went and did it!"*

"He did what?" the mother cried.

"He scored, mommy, he scored!" little Mickey screamed.

And there was a tremendous bedlam of sounds and noises and cries everywhere, confusion and drumming, and the Martin mother suddenly sat down plunk on the seat and stared straight ahead at people's backs.

"Don't you understand, Ma?" cried Ruth, bending down to her mother. "Petey scored a touchdown, we're winning the game!"

"On account of Petey?"

"Yes! yes!"

"Hooray!" cried the mother, leaping up on the seat, and she grabbed Ruth's flag and began waving it with wild excitement, and hugged her husband and kissed him furiously on the cheek, while he hugged her and lifted her up and down shouting. And the man with the bottle stumbled drunkenly down to him and thrust the bottle in his hand.

"Finish it!" he shouted. "It's all yours, by gum, it's all yours, the whole damned quart!"

After the game was over, the cheers of the crowd subsided into one vast excited murmuring and laughing, everyone began to mill towards the exits, music sighed in the wind behind them, desultory drums beat sadly over the battered field. . . .

Martin stood alone looking over the stadium while his family called to him from the exit ramps. He stood motionlessly, with tears in his eyes, and he spoke to Joe who waited silently beside him:

"By God, Joe, I'll never forget this day as long as I live. That boy— Well, I just don't know how to say it."

"He pulled one right out of the hat, all right!" chuckled Joe.

"He did more than that! I just don't know how to put it— I mean I knew he was going to do *some*thing. You know? It's the kind of kid he is, he's capable of doing almost anything."

"Well, let's go home, Pa, and we'll see him at the house."

"That kid! I remember when he was just so high, just like little Mickey, just a shy awkward little tyke. By gosh!"

And then amid innumerable honkings of horns, shouts, sudden small cheers, wild singing, and the sharp whistles of traffic cops, the crowds began to leave the stadium on the jammed highways, their cars fluttering back bright banners and confetti, some cars racing by others with a sudden rout of singing and cheering, a long honk of horns and shouts out the windows. The big game was over and everybody was going home to the turkey dinner, everybody was hungry.

And the November noon sun broke through, great gaps of blue sky appeared, and on the highway the automobiles flashed brilliantly in the sun as they migrated back to Galloway. The silent deserted Square of the town was suddenly flooded with honking victorious cars, flutters of colored paper were thrown out the windows, the young people were shouting: "We won! We won!"

And in the dank locker rooms back at the stadium the victorious Galloway team hooted and hollered in the hot soapy steaming showers, they danced on pink feet, hurled towels about, jumped over benches, slammed locker doors, sang in chorus—while not far away, in another damp room, the Lawton boys sat dejectedly and mumbled to each other and smiled sadly. Thus, not long after, both teams emerged from the dressing rooms limping and battered, combed and sleek and proud, and shook hands before the busses, under the curious stare of rabid football fans who stayed to watch.

"Next year," the young players told each other, smiling.

"Better luck next time!"

"You played a great game."

"We were lucky!"

Then the Galloway bus roared home triumphantly with the

boys singing loud and lustily—mainly the substitute players who were never too weary and proud, like the regulars, to sing and exult out loud. The bus wheeled into The Square where crowds waved at them, and at the high school mobs of youngsters waited, cheering.

To Peter all this was like a dream, he stared at it wearily, almost indifferently; and although his name was on everyone's lips, he wanted to duck off by himself and wonder about it. He hurried off the bus, spoke for a while with a few excited admirers, strode through the basement of the school, slipped unnoticed out the back way, and soon found himself walking along a canal near the mills. He could hear the scattered shouts of the young people back at the school. He smiled to think that much of it was due to him, to him alone, to think that so much of that noise was mysteriously his own weary indifferent doing.

He was amazed.

People passed him on the street and Peter stared at them with wonder. Now they knew his name, they knew of him; if they hadn't been at the game itself they had heard about it on the radio, they would read it in the newspapers or hear about it from others. They did not know who he was, as he passed them on the street. He was only one of them, and he would be forgotten in a week.

He hurried on home, and gloated because no one noticed him. He wished suddenly that no one would ever notice him again and that he would walk through the rest of his life like this, wrapped in his own secret mysteries and glories, a prince disguised as a pauper, Orestes returned from distant heroisms and hiding within the land, stalking unknown within the land under powerful autumnal skies. But why was it they did not notice him any more than before?

When he had crossed the White Bridge and struck for home in a hurried stride, people began to notice him on the street, the boys in front of the candy store stared at him in awed and curious silence, some of them yelled out from across the street:

"Great game, Pete!"

"You gave 'em hell, boy!"

And Peter smiled and hurried on beneath great black branches of November. Yet somehow now, he felt that he had almost betrayed everyone he knew by having performed great feats that required their silence and praise, their awe and embarrassment.

When old Judge Clough stopped him on the sidewalk in front of his sedate old home of ivied stone at the foot of Galloway Road, shifting his rake from one hand to the other in order to shake hands with him, saying, "Congratulations, my boy!" and smiling a quick twinkling smile, Peter felt a twinge of fearful remorse, that he had brought this venerable white-haired old man of the law to shaking his hand and praising him, that he should stand there and receive his distant magisterial praise.

But running down the street towards him, hooraying and yelping with delight, came his two kid brothers, Mickey and Charley, hurling a football high up in the air and dashing about in emulation of their big brother's now-famous touchdown, and for the first time Peter was glad that he was a hero. The eyes of all the neighborhood were upon him, he came walking up the street wearily, and here now his own family was coming to him cheering and proud and glad. Mickey climbed up on his back and sat on his shoulders, Charley walked proudly alongside throwing the football back and forth, saying: "What a game! I heard it all on the radio. You shoulda heard the announcer go wild when you made the touchdown! Yow!"

"Tara-tara!" trumpeted Mickey magnificently from his swaying perch. "Here comes Pete Martin! Tara-tara!"

And up at the house the front door was open and his father was standing there waiting for him.

"Swifty Martin!" he called from his house in a thundering voice, grinning slyly, puffing on his cigar. "Welcome home, Swifty Martin!"

Peter ducked into the house still holding Mickey high on his shoulders, his mother rushed up laughing and crying, "My he-ro! My hero!" as everyone laughed. There stood Francis in a corner with a bemused smile, Joe was pouring out a glassful of wine, the sisters were kissing him, and on the table the great roast turkey lay upturned on a platter surrounded by all the steaming dishes, glassware, silverware, and white linen of a huge holiday dinner.

"Now you're going to sit down right there, and begin to eat, and eat until you can't eat another mouthful!" the father was shouting excitedly. "Come on, take off that big sweater, make yourself at home! Joe, bring over that glass of wine!"

"Give him a chance to wash up first!"

"Wash up! Go right now and wash up! Here's your wine! Anything you want is yours." The father was out of his wits with joy and celebration. "Here's a cigar, by God! Take this cigar and smoke it—"

"My goodness!" the women cried.

"He's a man, ain't he? He can smoke a cigar, dammit! Besides he doesn't have to train any more till he gets to college now. Come on there, All-America, show 'em what you can do."

Peter stood in the middle of the room, holding the cigar and the glass of wine, laughing and bending over with laughter with all the others.

"Let's eat! It's time to eat!" yelled the father. "Rosey, bring out the gravy, bring out that other bottle of wine, bring out my whiskey. Oh, but you shoulda heard the twelve o'clock news on the radio! If I ever meet the dirty rat who wrote the news!—"

"What's the matter?"

"He said that when you caught the pass you romped—mind you, you *romped*. Listen, you smashed for that touchdown! They're trying to give all the glory to the guy who threw you that measly little pass in mid-field, they're trying to say that you just caught the pass and danced over safe and sound, and by God—if I ever—I'll wring his scrawny neck! I never saw such a hard-won touchdown in all my life! I never saw anybody get hit so many times and stay on his feet so long! I never did see anybody run so beautifully and so strongly, and now they're going to spread this bull around that you just danced around and romped over the goal after catching a *pass!* This is the *crummiest* town anyway!"

"Take it easy, Pa!"

"Well, dammit, I'm *mad!* I'm mad enough to break somebody's neck, and I'm gonna break that radio announcer's neck this week!"

"Dinner's ready!" called the women from the dining room.

"Everything is yours, Petey, my boy," cried the father with sudden tears in his eyes. "Everything in this house and in my possession is yours. Sit down here with your family and eat, my son, eat your fill. It's a day for celebration and happiness, it's a rare day, my boy, a *rare* day in this kind of world. Believe me, boy, you'll realize what I mean someday—"

"Now you're not going to start making speeches!" cried Rosey, incredulously.

"I can't help it, dammit, I feel—well, I don't know how to say it, I just feel—happy and sad! This is my own boy, today he showed the world what he could do, I'm proud of him and I don't care who knows it! I don't care if I do make a fool of myself! He's *my* boy, that's all there is to it!"

"Well, don't start crying about it!" said the mother. "Everybody's hungry and it's time to eat. Ruthey," she said in a low voice aside, "what kind of a highball did you mix your father?"

"If I feel like crying, dammit, I'm gonna *cry!*" shouted the old man. "But I'm not going to cry! Here, here, everybody sit down and eat! Sit the hero over there by his mother, let her cry over him, I'm all through. All I'm gonna do now is eat! Then I'll go out and wring that announcer's neck!"

"Oh, boy, what a turkey!" spoke up Peter, holding his knife and fork in his fists. "Let me at it! I was thinking about it all morning."

"If you're a hero, Petey boy, it's because your mother feeds you like a horse," said the old man sadly. "Here, what the hell, it's Thanksgiving today, isn't it? Let's have a little toast. We're not Pilgrims and we're not religious in the way they used to be, but at least we can have a little toast. Give the kids some wine, Marge; let's all drink a toast—"

And the kids were giggling under the table.

"This is a good, *good* day—this is a rare day. You'll all understand what I mean someday. You forgot Francis there, give him a glass of wine, give my boy a glass of wine. They did this a couple of hundred years ago right here in New England, they rejoiced, we'll rejoice. Here! a toast to our boy, Pete, and to the whole family. Everybody drink up!

"Now!" he concluded. "Everybody eat! I'm ranting on like an old fool. Don't pay no attention to me, eat!"

2

At twenty young Joe was the victim of the early fatalism that says: "What's the use anyway? Who cares what happens!" That frame of mind proceeds on towards even greater excesses in the name of despair, while all the time it is only the sap of youth running over, running wild.

With his brother Peter riding high on the wave of marvelous success, and his brother Francis having completed high school and making ready to go to college—while Joe himself had quit school impatiently to get jobs—and with things moving on, Joe now found himself alone and insignificant in his own eyes. He was the eldest son and it began to occur to him that maybe he was the shiftless son, too.

A kind of lyrical ecstasy possesses certain young Americans in the springtime, a feeling of not belonging in any one place or in any one moment, a wild restless longing to be elsewhere, everywhere, right now! The air is balmy and springlike, redolent with so many musics from everywhere, everything seems to describe dizzy circles, there are illimitable thoughts of long spaces and long voyages, it is a strange, maddening but still as yet ecstatic feeling of irresponsible wanderlust of the soul, responding to everything at the moment—"I don't *give* a damn!"

Joe was in just the mood to come across Paul Hathaway. In his new job driving for a big company that ran trucks on the four-hundred-mile run between Boston and Baltimore, he was assigned as a junior driver and his senior partner turned out to be this man.

Paul Hathaway had been driving trucks for fifteen years during the course of a hectic whiskey-drinking life and three wives. On their first trip south in the huge aluminum-bright truck-trailer, down U. S. highway No. 1, Joe got to know Paul well. He was a fierce and lonely man, about thirty-five years old, with a swarthy pockmarked countenance, dark blazing eyes, and an angry brooding manner. He always held a cigar butt clamped in his teeth as he sat high in the cab driving. He spoke very little, for the most part listening to Joe's interminable talk and laughter with a sullen discontented scowl. But when they stopped at a diner for food, he would never let Joe pay the bill, got very angry about it if Joe insisted and covered him with a contemptuous look.

"Ah, what a lousy rotten life!" Paul Hathaway would always say, his dark eyes burning with hate and loneliness. Young Joe began to like him very much, to look upon him as a man with a real heart and a torn aching sense of despair, which appealed to him deeply.

They had made several trips together down to Baltimore and spent time in the Pratt Street saloons there, drinking, and talking, dancing with the women, reeling drunkenly down dark streets at dawn and waking up next day in some flophouse near the waterfront. Back in Boston the same thing began all over again: they staggered around South Boston or Charlestown, slept anywhere they could, returning home to Galloway next day dirty and bleary and disgusted.

Paul Hathaway was married to a shrewish worthless woman who, the moment he walked in the door, was on his neck with a thousand curses and maledictions, complaints, whining tears, and shriekings of disgust. She always ended up throwing things at him. They lived in a shabby old rooming-house over a canal in the Galloway mill district.

Through some drunken miscalculation Joe happened to sleep in Paul's rooms one night after a big binge that began in South Boston and ended on Rooney Street in Galloway. He woke up in terror. There was such a noise and furor coming from Paul's bedroom, such shriekings and cries and the smash of glass, that he thought the man was beating his wife to death. Hurrying over to look in, he was amazed to see Paul lying on the bed calmly smoking a cigarette and contemplating the ceiling, while his wife raved in a tantrum, throwing objects on the floor and pointing her finger at him in trembling rages.

"Everybody's talking about me, you no good basted, and you know damn well why! They see you come home drunk, they say here comes Minnie Hathaway's drunk husband again. *When* you come home, which ain't often, you no good rat! And here I sit waiting for you, I haven't got enough money to buy a dress, I have to wait here while you go drinkin' and whorin' all over the country. It's bad enough in your own hometown, you have to go out with out-of-town whores! Someday I'm gonna buy a gun and shoot you dead! Someday I'll just leave and never come back! Don't laugh, I can take care of myself, I can get a job and be happy again, be young like I used to be! I don't need you, you lousy bum!"

Paul only turned his dark, tortured face to the boy in the doorway and said in his gruff voice: "Good morning, Joe."

And outside the dirty snow was melting in the streets, the canal whirled by floating refuse of March, the mill whistles blew, all was defeat and squalor and empty beer bottles in the hallway.

"On top of that you have to bring home all your damn drinkin' bum friends and dirty up my home. You have no consideration for *me*. You go drinkin' and whorin' right here on Rooney Street while I sit here with nothing to do, thinkin' you're out working and making money for our home, and all the time there you are three-four doors away having the gad-damnedest time of your life while I *sit* here, *sit* here, *sit* here!" And she screeched in a seizure of ungovernable fury.

Paul Hathaway withdrew a handful of bills from his wallet and threw them at her feet, and reached over to the table by the bed and helped himself to another drink of whiskey, all in profoundest silence and calm.

Joe hurried out of the house feeling ashamed and terrible, but after a while choking with glee at the thought of old Paul lying there taking it all so calmly and drinking his whiskey. He never went back to Paul's home but thereafter they were closer friends than ever. Several weeks later, when Joe was driving back through Maryland, he stopped the truck along the highway and turned to Paul.

"Man, I'd like to know what I'm doing driving this truck. Just look out there: a highway, lights, a big moon above, a breeze blowing over the fields. Hear the music from that diner? See these cars going by full of beautiful women? Back and forth, back and forth, from Boston to here, and what do we get for it? All we do is drive and drive, get more tired all the time, every drink we take makes us worse. No kidding, that's the way I feel right now!"

"Aff," said Paul, waving a contemptuous hand, "I been feeling like that all my life."

"It's a crazy world," said Joe.

"It's a lousy rotten life!" corrected Paul. "You saw my wife Minnie, didn't you? You saw what kind of a loudmouthed fleabag she is! Well, that was my third wife and every single damn one of them was just like her! All three!"

Joe scratched his head, grinning.

"That's women for you!" shouted Paul. "They're all alike, I never did meet one who had any sense, I never will! The only one who was any good, maybe, was my first wife. Jeanie. She's in Pittsburgh now. But even she was a loudmouthed nagging goat. I always tell them to go do their gad-dam washing, that's all they're good for!"

"So here we are, sitting in this truck," went on Joe dreamily, "tied to it like a couple of slaves, and look at those snazzy cars go by full of beautiful women. Wham!"

Paul waved a contemptuous hand and looked away.

"I could take this big baby and drive it right out to California," cried Joe triumphantly, punching the wheel of the truck. "Just think of it, man! We'd go in swimming at one of those big beaches, Malibu or whatever they call it, just for a swim, that's all, drive three thousand miles just for a swim."

"You're crazy," said the dark Paul, looking away.

"Yeah! Drive through the desert, through Texas, Arizona, stop off for a drink now and then, pick up the broads, go swimming, drive on out to the coast! Can you see it?"

Then they were silent in the truck, the windows open to the soft Spring night with all its odors of loamy fields and flowers and the sharp pungent smell of exhaust fumes on the highway, and the heat of the highway itself cooling under the stars, and the fried-food smells floating in the air from all the places. And Joe was full of crazy music and desire and suppressed wild shouting, he was smoking on his cigarette with a desperate restless anguish; while Paul sat there glowering straight ahead, mumbling to himself, cursing and brooding.

"I'll tell you something," Paul now said finally, angrily. "My wife left me this week. I didn't tell you but she left me last Thursday."

"Where'd she go?"

"How the hell should I know!" he shouted bitterly. "She just left, that's all!" And he looked at Joe with a confused abject wildness.

"What're you gonna do?"

"I dunno what I'm gonna do," muttered Paul quietly.

"You mean you miss her?" shouted Joe incredulously. "Brother, I don't want to say anything, but she was a wild woman."

"She was a wild woman," echoed Paul quietly, "but she was a woman, she was my wife. My third wife. I dunno, maybe I'm crazy. I did tell you about Jeanie in Pittsburgh?"

"Your first wife, or was it your second?"

"Don't be a sarcastic young punk, it don't fit you! Yeah, my first wife."

"What about her?" demanded Joe with mounting glee.

Paul, for an answer, reached into the cab compartment and pulled out a quart of whiskey and drank in grave silence.

Joe once more was full of wild mute desires.

"Paul, let's do something! Dammit, I want to do something, I don't know what!"

"Ah, you're crazy."

More silence—and Paul continued to drain the bottle in fierce lonely reveries. Joe got out of the truck and began throwing rocks over the fields, as far as he could throw, way across the moonlit fields.

"We dumped the load in Baltimore, didn't we?" said Paul suddenly from the cab. "We dumped the junk on Pratt Street. We're going back to Boston empty, ain't we?"

"Yeah, what about it?" cried Joe, grinning.

"I mean we ain't hijackers, are we?"

"What're you talking about!" shouted Joe with laughter.

"Ah!" said Paul, and he turned away and drank some more. But suddenly he got out of the cab and took Joe by the arm. "Listen!" he said angrily. "You think I'm drunk?"

"Damn near it!"

"That's beside the point. Look, let's take off!"

"Take off?"

"Take off, gad-damn you, take off!" he yelled. "Can't you speak English? Let's take off in the truck and go to Pittsburgh!! I want to see my wife Jeanie—"

"Jeanie? You said she was your first wife!"

"She's still my wife, damn you!"

"What do you mean?"

"Aff!" cried Paul bitterly. "I got three wives and I never divorced! You understand?"

"Ain't that bigamy or something?" cried Joe gleefully.

"Who gives a damn what it is! All I know is I got three wives and I never divorced. I want to go see the one in Pittsburgh, right now, this minute. Let's take off! Joe, I'm a fool for my wives! I'd do anything for them. I want to give Jeanie some money, I just want to see her, damn you! You don't understand, you're just a young punk."

Without a word Joe jumped up in the truck and started the motor with a roaring blast. "Come on!" he yelled jubilantly. "Let's go!"

"Turn the sonofabitch around!" shouted Paul, beside himself with excitement now. "We gotta go back to Route 74 and up to Harrisburg and hit the Turnpike west! We'll be in Pittsburgh long before morning! Turn him around!"

Joe flung the huge truck-trailer around in an arc and sent it roaring back down the highway in breakneck speed. And they were off.

And thus, in this manner, without a second's forethought, Joe and his melancholy wild friend began a mad voyage that was to take them a thousand miles up and down the seaboard and into the middle west, in a truck which was now technically a stolen truck. All of it was done without a moment's reflection and when they would remember it later on they would only recall the wild rushing speed of the truck, the moon meadows along the highway, the shouting and laughter in the high cab, the lunch diners along the road, the music and the madness of the Spring night and the American spaces. They never did find Jeanie in Pittsburgh.

Four days later they arrived back in Boston. They drove into the big garages on Atlantic Avenue at nine o'clock in the morning and got down wearily from the high cab, while men rushed up wanting to know what had happened, where they'd been, what was the idea, what was going on here!

And Paul only said: "You guys give me a pain in the neck."

That is what he said, despite the fact that they were in trouble up to their necks. At this casual and matter-of-fact remark, Joe burst out into an uncontrollable whoop of laughter right in the face of the irate company official himself. He and Paul looked at each other with that furtive solemn look of two men who have gone through things together with the same idea, the same madness, known each other perfectly through a rout of days and nights, and therefore don't really care what other men think or say about them.

Luckily, Joe and Paul merely lost their jobs. The police were not notified, and the company claimed their back pay for the wear and tear on the truck.

A few days later Paul Hathaway disappeared from Galloway, wandering off somewhere without a word to Joe, going off to continue being his selfsame raging self in some other surroundings which would always be identical somehow with his dark and anguished atmospheres. Joe wasn't to see him for several years.

Joe spent a few days after the incident lounging around home with a kind of white look of sickly penance about him. His father was far from pleased with him, his mother shook her head sadly and said: "Ooh, Joey!" and looked at him with faint sorrow and regret. His brothers and sisters grinned at the strange pale sight of him.

After the initial anger and shock, the father gradually lapsed into a chuckling reminiscent mood and was heard to say at the shop: "Dammit! but that kid is a genius for getting into jams! I used to be the same way back in Lacoshua, always getting into some holy mess or other, and how the old man used to blow his top!" And he laughed his hoarse savage laugh.

And presently Joe made up by getting a new job in town. He started out the first morning with a lunch packed hopefully by his mother, he spent the cool morning working absorbedly over an old motor in the downtown garage. In the hot afternoon he sweated underneath some battered old heap of a car. At dusk, sweating and work-wearied, he was washing cars and changing tires and mopping up the lubrication pit and swearing under his breath because it was just his luck to find the worst job he ever had. The man expected him to do all the work around the place for a very small salary, long hours and six days a week. Suddenly Joe wanted to go off again on a wild wonderful trip out West, anywhere, everywhere.

At supper that night he told his father he was going off again, and the old man objected, at first with bewilderment, and then sorrowfully: "Joey, let's forget about the mess you got in, like it never happened. This is *your* home, fella, you stay right here and don't go getting all kinds of ideas in your head about what we think. We don't think anything. Now ask your mother if I'm not speaking the truth."

"I know that, Pa, but I just feel like I'm hanging around doing nothing. You know it's terrific country out Pennsylvania, Ohio, out that way!" Joe cried eagerly. "Out West, Pa!—I'd like to tear right out to California and see what kind of work they got there!"

"I'm going too!" yelled little Mickey suddenly. "I wanta go run a saloon in the West like the Silver Saddle in Tombstone, like the one Buck Jones goes to!"

"Ah, you're crazy, it's only a picture!" said young Charley contemptuously.

"But what are you going to do, Joey?" the mother spoke up anxiously. "You just can't go like that, you have no money. Where will you stay?"

"I'm gonna hit the road, Ma! I don't need any money!"

"That's right!" cried Peter with an excited laugh. "All you do is hit the road, you're on your own! I'd do it if I wasn't going to college—I'd go with you tonight, Joe, no kidding!"

"Who's asking you?"

"Ah!" said Peter, turning away.

"I don't want to hear any more about it, eat your desserts," said the mother, and she piled some dishes together in a loud impatient manner.

"Ah, Ma, he's old enough to know what he wants to do, the bum!" said big Rose scornfully. "Don't you worry, he'll come crawling back soon enough, I'm not so sure about all this hit-the-road stuff."

"Ah, you're full of beans!" cried Joe, slapping his big sister with a napkin. "How do you like that! She thinks she's the big stuff all right! I know she's not the *little* stuff, she's too *big* for that!" And with simultaneous raucous whoops of laughter that reverberated throughout the house, Rose and Joe chased each other out of the dining room, Rose unleashed wild hoots of laughter and chased him into the kitchen, around the kitchen, out in the hall, through the front rooms and back down the hall, with the kids yelling and laughing. Finally Rose was sitting in a chair trying to catch her breath while Joe sat on her lap and called her his "best girl."

"By God, you ain't much to look at, but you're my best girl."

"Ah, get away, you bum!" gasped Rose breathlessly. "I wasn't born yesterday, you know! I'm not one of your little dolls!"

"My best girl, Rosey. Listen, Rosey, make some of that walnut fudge tonight, make me some fudge before I leave you and go to California—"

"Yes, yes!" chorused the kids. "Make some fudge, Rosey!"

And then, out in the yard just before sunset, in the soft Spring dusk all flower-scented, cool, and echoing with the muted far-off sounds of the town, by the tall hedges just sprouting green buds, under the big trees, Joe and Peter stood playing catch with a brand new white ball. Mickey and Charley conducted a game of their own alongside with an old taped ball, and Francis leaned out of a window upstairs watching them below in impassive silence. No one said a word, there was just the meditative gum-chewing windup, the leisurely throw, the plunk of the ball in the glove, the dreamy gazing away. Little Mickey and Charley stood alongside imitating their big brothers to perfection, winding up leisurely, with a blank, impassive, gum-chewing expression, throwing nonchalantly, gazing away in musing reflection, standing there with all the calm and control of big-leaguers warming up before a game, just as their brothers were doing.

"Whattaya say, Francis," Joe called up. "How about coming to California with me! See the world!"

"No, thank you," said Francis with quiet amusement from his perch.

"Don't tell me you want to stay in Galloway all your life!"

"Not exactly."

"You can't go through life reading books!"

"Don't worry, I don't intend to."

"It's all right having a lot of brains, but where's the fun?"

With this Francis pulled his head in, and disappeared inside the house.

Then, in the darkness, Joe sat on the porch long after the others wandered off in the house or went to bed. He sat in the white moonlight remembering the night in Maryland when he and Paul had started off on their wild trip . . . just a few nights ago . . . and all because the night had been so fragrant and vast, so mysterious and exciting, so vastly suggestive of the million things and places awaiting them there in the dark whispering heart, just like the night that spread before him now.

There were dim lights burning far off on the highway, on the river. There were lights even beyond those, stretching miles off in the night; he wanted to go there, to see what was there. There were lights like that stretching across the country, across all states and cities and places, and things happening everywhere even now. "Even now, even now," he kept thinking. There were bridges swooping across rivers and Mississippis, cities at night casting halo-glows in the sky seen from far-off, there were giant water tanks waiting by the railroad tracks in Oklahoma, there were saloons with checkercloth and sawdust and fans overhead, there were girls waiting in Colorado and Utah and Iowa towns, there were crap games in the alley and a game in the back of the lunch-cart, there was soft odorous air in New Orleans and Key West and Los Angeles, there was music at night by the sea and people laughing, and cars going by on a highway, and soft neon lights glowing, and an old shack in Nevada seen across the wastes. There were men drawling in Louisiana, Negroes whooping with laughter and flashing knives in backstreet Savannah, construction jobs blazing in the Missouri sun, there were the morning hills of Pennsylvania, a small cemetery on the slope-side, towns in the valleys, the gaunt hill-boys, and Ohio once more. Joe had to go see it all, even now, even now.

The next day he told his mother he was going to a movie—so she would not feel bad—and he started out for California hitch-hiking, just like that.

[2]

EARLY ONE morning in May, Mickey Martin sat at his little desk by the window of his bedroom with his chin resting in his hand. He gazed outside at the misty green fields across the old road, brooding out the springtime dawn. It was the morning of a big day in his life. He was going to the races at Rockingham with his father, and then in the evening to dinner in a big restaurant and a show in the big Boston places. He was all ready to go, he was up and washed and even combed, while his father still slept and snored in the other room.

It was not quite yet six o'clock in the morning. He had been up since five; he was getting mighty impatient.

To this boy of New England the May morning was like faint music in the woods again, some unspeakably exciting foregathering of events far in the deep shade of morning pines, all of it stirring there. He could hear it all faintly in the woods from far away, from across the fields and pastures, in the cool misty morning air, and he wanted to go there too.

The first miraculous May morning had come, very suddenly,

very softly, and everything was green in the trees and fields, the sky was blue, the air was golden pure, and everywhere there rang the tiny peepings of a thousand foregathered birds hidden in the branches.

When this season comes in New England, a boy is suddenly aware of the whole world awakening with him to all the new things there are, and will be. The time of wintry storms and staying indoors has passed, one more year is achieved towards manhood, and all the plans hatched at the school desk or in the room are almost ready at last to be performed, in the green and sun-glorious summer.

Mickey was going to be captain, manager, coach, pitcher, scout, president, owner, and star of that year's baseball team. And "him and his chums" were going to build a secret mysterious clubhouse somewhere along the dump shacks by the river, with secret doors and hideouts, and passwords too, with each member of the gang (he being X-1, the Chief) equipped with all the necessary tools and garb of dark and disguised espionage. And he would "make" a story of his own just like the *Little Shepherd of Kingdom Come.* And he would take Beauty Junior his new dog and teach it to race faster than any other dog in Galloway, and "him and Mike" were going to get a rowboat and sail up the Merrimac River, way up in the reaches of New Hampshire there, and maybe up there was a real Injun Joe and real river bargemen cussing and working away, and fires on the bank at night. . . .

There were so many things to do, he realized now as he sat before the window and watched the springtime morning unfold mistily before his eyes, so many things to do and there wasn't a minute at all to waste. It was time to go and wake up his father.

Mickey tiptoed down the hall and peeked into his parents' bedroom. There he saw his mother fast asleep but his father stirring slowly and turning over; the birds were peeping and quivering in the leafy branches just outside the screen windows.

Mickey waited until he saw his father yawning and yumming, staring up at the ceiling, scratching his head, whereupon the little boy cupped his hands over his mouth and whispered:

"Pa!"

And the old man turned his head around and stared at him.

"It's seven o'clock, Pa!"

And still the old man gazed at him with something like disbelief for a moment, and then it seemed presently to dawn on him what day it was and what they were going to do, and he grunted.

"What time we leaving, Pa?" pursued Mickey in the same furtive whisper, with his hands still cupped over his mouth and fidgeting and squirming around the doorjamb as though he didn't want anyone else to see him there.

"Right now," grunted the old man, staring calmly and gravely at him. "I'm getting up now and then we're off," he said in a hoarse gruff morning voice.

And with this, big Martin heaved himself up and over into a sitting position on the side of the bed, and as he did this there was a sharp crack of floorboards, janglings of bedsprings, one mighty groan of the bed posts and his own explosive grunt which he emitted inadvertently in his exertions, and his wife who had been sound asleep up to this terrifying moment shot up her head and stared wildly around, crying: "My God!"

"Sorry to wake you, Marge," the old man growled sheepishly, "but we've got to leave early."

"Where? What?" cried Mrs. Martin sleepily. "What time is it? What?" She rubbed her eyes for a moment, and then she noticed Mickey standing behind the corner of the door, and cried: "Well, for goodness' sakes, look at Mickey! What are you doing up so early!"

"We're going to the races!" he cried proudly.

"Now, at this time of the morning?" she said sleepily. "What are you two up to? I'll have to get breakfast," she added as an afterthought and at once started to get up.

"Now don't get up, Marge," protested the old man anxiously. "We're having a bite of breakfast downtown. Don't bother, don't bother, we'll manage all right."

"We're gonna eat breakfast in the Astoria Cafeteria!" announced Mickey proudly. "I'm gonna have a baked apple with ice cream and some pancakes and syrup and everything."

"My goodness' sakes," said the mother, and she got up straightaway, pausing now for just a moment to peer outside the screen window, in front of which she stood in her long cotton nightrobe in an attitude of sleepy delight, crying out: "Oh, the pretty little birds! Listen to them there! Oh, my!"

"Marge, we'll manage. Don't bother getting up, will you?" And Martin stuffed his shirt in his trousers and hurried out the door, but she followed them downstairs just the same.

And then for the next few minutes the father was in the bathroom coughing thunderously and barging around and swooshing water in the sink, while Mickey sat by the screen door gazing out at the yard and his mother took milk out of the icebox and fussed around the kitchen, and finally the old man emerged from the bathroom all shaved and combed and sleek, with a big cigar trailing smoke behind him and an absorbed morning frown on his face, and he marched into the den, picked up his racing form sheets from the desk, stuck them in his vest pocket along with a handful of cigars, he sharpened a few pencils, stuck his straw hat on the top of his head, and he was ready to go.

The mother stood in the middle of the kitchen floor staring at both of them with her arms folded helplessly and she kept saying: "My goodness gracious. Why didn't you tell me? I would have got breakfast for you. You can't leave on an empty stomach. Drink this milk—and Mickey," she said, plucking at his coat, "why did you have to wear that awful old coat. Why didn't you wear your nice new one! Drink your milk. What time will you be coming home?" she demanded anxiously.

"We'll be back late tonight. Don't worry about a thing."

"We're gonna eat steak in Boston and see a movie tonight!" Mickey added excitedly, and he rushed on the porch and vaulted over the railing.

"Well," said the mother ruefully, "you should have eaten something just the same."

And coughing thunderously, grunting, chewing his cigar, Martin backed the car out of the garage and turned down the driveway along the house, where he waited gunning the motor impatiently while the mother plucked at the boy's clothes on the porch and combed his hair. And when Mickey jumped in the car she was standing in the kitchen doorway with her arms pressed to her shiveringly, calling out every last-minute instruction and suggestion she could bring to mind, looking up at the sky to see if it was going to rain, warning them not to eat too many hotdogs, and so on, and finally they drove out on the road and started off with Mickey waving back delightedly to his mother and shouting: "Bye, Ma! bye, Ma! We're gonna win a hundred dollars today! You wait and see, Ma!"

And all around the Martin house in the trees and hedges, and in the branches that canopied over the old road, the birds were singing, they were darting and fluttering in the small green leaves.

It was morning, and the boy was with his father.

"Now," said the old man, "we'll spend the morning at the shop and see what kind of figures we can get. I think I can spot a couple of good long shots today."

"And me," said Mickey solemnly, "I'm gonna handicap them and write it on the typewriter."

So they talked about these things, and ate breakfast down at the Square in the cafeteria where the sun streamed in upon the clean tiled floor that had just been mopped, and everything was brown and gold—strong coffee brewing in the big urns, the fat half-grapefruits in the chipped ice all golden in the sunlight, the brown mahogany panels, the gleaming food counter, and all the men that were there in the morning eating and talking.

Mickey ate his breakfast quickly, waiting impatiently while his father talked to some men at the other table, and then they strode off to the shop to get busy. Mickey made a list of the day's entries, and carefully, judiciously picked them according to his own calculations. The old man spread out the *Morning Telegraph* before him.

Old John Johnson came in at ten o'clock, looked at them a moment, removing the pipe from his mouth, and said: "You know, if you two boys can't figure out how to beat the races, I don't believe anybody will."

"What have you got there in the eighth race, Mickey?"

"Green Swords!"

"Green Swords? I never heard of that plug."

"He'll win the eighth race! He's a chestnut gelding out of Sickle!" blurted Mickey eagerly.

"He's a what? You see that, John? This kid even knows the sires and the whole stud line. He don't care about the figures, he's got his eye on class! Ha, ha, ha!"—and the old man tousled Mickey's hair gleefully—"that's my crazy little kid!"

Martin fell to chuckling hoarsely and shaking his head, and went back to his figures with fresh absentminded zeal.

At noon the two gamblers were all set to go. They stuffed their papers and figures in their pockets, bought a scratch sheet on the Square, the old man went in the bank for an extra wad of money, they had a quick lunch in the Chinese restaurant where Martin kidded with his old friend Wong Lee and gave him a tip on the first race, and they drove off in the warm sunny afternoon, down the green wooded Merrimac Valley and then north to New Hampshire to Rockingham Park in the hills.

Rockingham was like any other race track on a warm drowsy afternoon, but to Mickey it was all gold and magic. In front of the gates there were the cries of hawkers and tipsters selling their tips—"The Kentucky Clocker" or "Lucky Morgan's Green Card" —and there was the flutter and furl of flags atop the grandstand and in the pavilions, the smell of hotdogs and beer in the warm air, hot sunlight on the gravel, and that feeling of lazy excitement which a racetrack evokes when people are entering at the gates and the vast unseen presence of the great track itself awaits them beyond the grandstand with its sudden far-spreading acreage of green infield, its sweeping turns, toteboards, distant barns, and bright striped furlong poles along the rail a mile around.

It was the immense, stirring, drowsy scene of a day's fate and fortune for all the prancing beautiful horses, and the jockeys, owners, trainers, and bettors gathered in the warm sun there, an epic of men and horses and money that thrilled the little boy's imagination, filling him with wonder that all of it at sundown would be irrevocably recorded in the closely packed files of "the Turf"—and in the gray past-performance charts of the *Morning Telegraph*, to be examined years later with recollection and wonder: "8 Rkp May 4 '41—Choctaw 106, Mandy Lou 109, Fading Sun 111." And the remembrance of forgotten horses, old jockeys, the dust at the far turn, and the sun waning behind the hills.

It was always glory before the first race, before the day's events would begin to pass into turf records and the old legend of the files, and Mickey missed none of it. While his father pored over his papers and went betting at the windows, Mickey leaned on the paddock rail and examined the horses with fascination and joy, he consulted his program to check on the lineage of the noble horses, he loafed around listening to the talk, and for all the world he was an aristocrat and sportsman of the turf, never betting, never growing bitter because some horse or some rider seemed to lag on him, always idling there with an eye for a beautiful bay's sheen and flank, for the nimble legset of a famous jockey, for the brilliant silks of the stables, and all the harness, the shiny boots, the saddles and gear of the sport which he gloatingly accepted as the sport of kings. When the bugle blew and the horses paraded from the paddock to the post, Mickey followed them along the rail and never took his eyes off them, it was all gold and magic for him.

His father had bet fifteen dollars across the board on a two-year-old filly in the first race. She was frisky, arrogant, bright chestnut in the sun, her jockey leaned over and cooed in her ear, she champed and minced: her name was Flight. And Mickey watched her every movement as she paraded along the track with the other horses towards the far chute, he noted her dances and her quick canters out of line, he watched her jockey's silks until he had them burning in his mind's eye, so that when the horses were standing solemnly in the starting gate a half mile across the field he could still see Flight and still notice the peculiar seat of her jockey as he leaned to pat her on the neck.

"What's she doing now?" the old man demanded.

"She's stubborn, she keeps backing out of the gate."

"What are they doing?"

"The men are pushing her in from behind. Now she's jumping up!" cried Mickey excitedly.

And the crowd breathed "Ooooh!" as they saw a commotion far across the track.

"She's gonna ball up the whole works," muttered Martin gloomily. "I shouldn't bet on these two-year-olds. They're all nervous wrecks!"

"She's on edge, Pa!" said Mickey eagerly.

"What's she doing now?" the father demanded anxiously.

"She's shaking her head from side to side. Yow, is she stubborn! She's holding up the whole start!" Mickey cried with delight. "Wait now. It's gonna come now."

And suddenly across the drowsy afternoon fields they saw the horses lunge in a body, they heard the faint d-r-ring of the gate bell, the clocker's flag fell, and the horses were rushing forward along the chute with surprising speed in a cloud of dust.

"Come on, Flight baby!" howled the old man, jumping up.

And the crowd yelled as one of the horses suddenly shot out front and twinkled swiftly along the rail with its tail streaming back and the jockey hunched over motionlessly.

"Who's that?" shouted the father.

"Flight! Flight! Look at her go!" yelled Mickey.

With gloating disbelief they watched the russet-colored horse streak down the backstretch a full seven lengths in front of the pack and going away all the time, going away to ten lengths, running alone far ahead of the pack as though it were running for fear and faster all the time.

"Yaa-hooo!" howled the old man. "*Look* at her go!"

Flight was at the far turn almost instantly, turning in and seeming to run slower now as she came running around towards the grandstand, seeming almost to crawl now as she negotiated the turn, and suddenly wheeling into view at the head of the stretch all spindly-legged and flailing and wild in a frantic knock-kneed sprint, turning down the stretch crazily, racing down along the rail wide-eyed and straining—and behind her the pack came turning into the stretch in a cloud of afternoon dust.

"She's all alone!" shouted someone with angry amazement.

"Whoooeee!" howled Martin.

And Flight came galloping past the grandstand with her jockey turning in the saddle and looking back in a stiff posture, and almost standing in the stirrups as he cantered her across the wire, grinning.

On that first race Martin won thirty-six dollars clear. He was beside himself with jubilation, plunging back into his figures and papers with renewed anticipation, looking up for only a moment to stare delightedly at Flight as she was being unsaddled in front of the judges' stand.

"Good girl, good girl!" he called out. "See, sonny, did you ever see such a beautiful creature as a thoroughbred racehorse!! Isn't she a beautiful sight! And such noble animals, so patient, so loyal. They will do anything their masters ask them to do—the poor noble beasts!" he cried.

Mickey stood along the rail watching Flight in the winner's circle, watching her old trainer come loping up and caressing her on the brow with a tender stroke of his hand, watching the jockey jump down, croon something in the horse's ear, and go stepping nimbly into the weighing room with his saddle over his arm, a dusty tired little man with a brown, seamed, goodly face and great powerful hands and wrists. Then the stable boy threw a blanket over Flight, gently took her halter, and walked her off back towards the barns—and both of them trudged silently along the rail, Mickey following—and he listened to the stable boy cooing and sing-songing to the solemn silent horse, then he watched the horse toss her nose over the boy's head neighing faintly, and then nuzzle her nose in his neck and show her teeth in a playful grinning gesture, and snort softly and wearily. He watched them loping off to the barns until they were out of sight, and he wondered what it would be like in the evening when the races were over and the boy would sit on a bale of hay in front of Flight's stall and talk to her while he whittled on a stick, in the soft springtime night of the hills. He wished he could be a stable boy too, and a jockey, to have the mighty friendship and silence of a horse, the faint neighing, the clopping on the stable floor, the soft snort and grin, and all of it in some warm summer-night under the stars and trees of the American racetracks.

He went back to the paddock to look at the horses for the second race, and it was all wonder and beauty.

After the third race the sun had disappeared behind gray clouds, a few minutes later it started to drizzle, and then it was raining softly—and the odors of hay and damp manure from the barns and the paddock was strong and fragrant in the air, the earth of the track smelled rich and loamy, the lights of the toteboards blinked in the dimness, and far beyond were the low gray hills of New Hampshire almost invisible in the gray mist. The whole tone and tenor of the day's racing, and the track itself, had changed into something less festive and bright and flag-rippling: now it was raining, it was gray, the horses were wet and melancholy looking, the jockeys were grim at their work, and everything seemed more businesslike and thrilling somehow: the trainers and owners huddled in the paddock wearing raincoats and talking in low tones, the bettors converged under the grandstand and smoked and talked and consulted their selections, and every now and then Mickey saw some stablehand or groom hurrying through the crowd to make a bet at the windows as though some exciting, important developments were transpiring in the misty rain.

He stood beside his father under the grandstand among all the men, and they ate hotdogs and drank root beer, and watched the toteboards blinking in the grayness.

"Now the track's muddy," said the old man gloomily. He had won no money since the first race and he was now some twenty dollars in the hole, looking very discouraged and glum. "I dunno how to figure this next race. If this keeps up we won't have any money left for a feed and a show in Boston." He looked down at Mickey sheepishly.

"No!" cried Mickey.

"Well, what can I do? I haven't hit anything since Flight. I got too cocky—I bet too much on the last two races."

And they watched the rain gloomily and stood there side by side with their hands in their pockets, and then finally the old man laughed hoarsely. "Cheer up, sonny! We'll see what happens."

But after the seventh race the old man had only ten dollars left and he was disgusted. He had thrown away his papers and figures, he was growing angrier by the minute, and finally he wanted to go home.

"Let's get out of here, for God's sake!" he growled angrily. "Everything's gone wrong today, I never saw them run so crazy. Something must be fishy somewhere—these birds around here are always up to something!"

"Let's watch the last race!" Mickey begged him anxiously. "I wanta see Green Swords. I don't want to go home, Pa," he cried.

"Pretty sad, hey?" the old man snorted. "Here we were going to have a big feed in Boston and then go see a good show and enjoy ourselves, now look what your silly old man has done—lost all his money like a damn fool." He tore up and threw away the tickets for the seventh race, and kicked the bits away with a vicious, rueful swipe of his foot. "Who's this Green Swords you're always talking about?" he asked curiously.

"He's been running in Louisiana all winter, Pa!"

"Louisiana? How do you know that?"

"I follow them at Fair Grounds. See? Green Swords runs in handicaps down there"—Mickey picked up an old discarded *Morning Telegraph* from the ground—"now they've got him up here."

"You figure they sneaked him up for a killing? Let me see that damn paper!" And they pored excitedly over the horse's record as the bugle blew for the last race and a flurry of excitement ran through the crowds.

"Well, by God, I never heard of the plug, but like you say he's running way below his class."

"Sure!" cried Mickey excitedly. "You never heard of him because he's all the time running down in Louisiana. Look at his odds, thirty-to-one! Nobody around here ever heard of him either. Huh?"

The old man peered at the toteboards and rubbed his chin musingly.

"By gosh, he's got a beautiful price on him all right. Might almost be worth a try."

"They sneaked him up!" stated Mickey triumphantly. "You wait! Now he's gonna win and the owners are figuring to win a lot of money. You watch!"

"You may be right," said the old man dreamily. He took his last ten dollars out of his pocket and looked at it. "I got this last ten bucks left—I guess we're all washed up as far as going to Boston is concerned—so we might as well bet, and get it over with, and go home, huh? If we're going to lose we might as well do a job of it. Huh?"

And they looked at each other judiciously, and then at the ten dollar bill.

"He went down to eighteen-to-one!" observed Mickey, peering at the toteboards.

"What? Somebody must be wise to something at that! Come on!!"

So they hurried to the betting windows, and the father bought the tickets win and show. "Now," he said, pulling out his empty pocket, "look at us bums! And you told your mother this morning we were going to win a hundred dollars. What a laugh!"

The race was at a mile and a sixteenth. Just as the horses were being led in the stalls, the sun suddenly reappeared through a gap in the clouds and everything was hushed and ruddy with fading light, a coolness and freshness spread in the air, the rain-water dripped from the grandstand roof and twinkled in the puddles. To Mickey it was like the last day of the world, the late afternoon of time and destiny, the sad glowing reddish light that he always remembered from his childhood as the companion of hushed and muted wonder. And now he was afraid.

"Is that your plug there, Green Swords?" the old man asked dubiously. "In stall eight? By golly, he looks like he's half asleep. Look at him standing there with his head hanging between his legs."

And suddenly there was the sharp d-r-ring of the starter's bell, the crowd rose, the horses lunged forward chopping and galloping in the mud.

"Well," said the father, throwing a little kiss with the tip of his fingers, "good-bye ten bucks!"

Green Swords was running in the rear of the pack, heaving and straining and plodding in pursuit. But in the backstretch they watched him nose slowly into the pack at the rear of the close file, and hang there with his tail streaming.

"See!" cried Mickey proudly. "He's a slow starter. Wait ti they come in the stretch."

"Yep, just wait," said the old man gloomily with his face averted from the track, yet occasionally looking again with a rueful curiosity.

The horses bobbed along the backstretch in a dense pack for a while, then they reached the far turn and seemed to come to a standstill as they milled around towards the grandstand again, and in the red light there they seemed to merge into one moving dragging mass. Mickey had lost sight of Green Swords in the melee, but the announcer had him running in eighth position.

"Hear that?" cried the old man angrily. "Eighth, next to last! And that's the way they've been running for me all day, all day long!"

Mickey looked at his father with terror in his heart, he saw the light of the red fading sun glowing in his face and in his eyes, etching every sign of disappointment and rue in his expression, and suddenly he felt like crying.

But the roar of the crowd as the horses neared drew them to their feet. They watched avidly as the horses came wheeling into the stretch all spindly-legged and swerving and splashing. The puddles in the track were red in the sun, the faces of the jockeys seemed dark and intent as they whipped and leaned in and booted, the horses bobbed in a body. They all came down plunging by the seventh pole in the thrilling approach to the finish that drummed dully below the roar of the crowd.

Mickey was searching frantically for Green Swords in the midst of all the horses, and suddenly he found him all mud-besplattered running in the middle and swerving to the outside behind six front horses in a grim lonely struggle to get out of the pocket and run free.

"There he is! He's trying to get on the outside!"

"I don't see him! Where's he running?"

"Seventh!"

"Oh, my God!" cried Martin and he stood up and smote his brow with disgust. "Let's get out of here!"

"He's still running!" cried Mickey. He watched the horses toiling down the last eighth of a mile, they all seemed weary and plodding in the mud and Green Swords seemed to be running with his head down, running low and steady, and slowly creeping up along the pack from the outside. Mickey jumped up on the seat, leaned back squinting to judge the distance remaining and the slow momentum of Green Swords' advance, and suddenly he was horrified to realize that Green Swords would certainly make it in another eighth of a mile but there wasn't time, they were almost at the wire. Green Swords seemed to sink lower in the mud and drive harder, he crept up, they all swept to the sixteenth pole, and passed it, and just before the wire the leading horse faltered bobbing his head, slipping a hoof in the mud, the other horses surged up in a phalanx of straining necks, and Green Swords suddenly flashed low past all of them and was forerunning across the wire a half a length ahead of the dense moiling pack and the jockey sat up jubilantly.

His father was already on his way out of the aisle, looking towards Mickey perplexedly.

"He won! He won!" screeched Mickey.

"Who won?" the old man grumbled. He saw Mickey running towards him with a delirious look of joy.

"He won! Green Swords won!"

"He did not."

"He did! There! They're putting up the numbers. Number eight! Green Swords!"

The old man looked at the toteboard, frowning; he could not see that far. "I don't think—" said the old man doubtfully, and just then above the hubbub of the crowd he heard the announcer say casually:

"The winner, number eight, Green Swords, by a half a length."

He took his boy and embraced him wildly, yelling "Waa-hooo!" and shaking him deliriously. He was out of his senses with joy. He cried: "Poor little kid, poor little Mick, I didn't believe you! To think that I didn't believe you!—"

And Mickey laughed with savage delight, and in the next moment they were scuffling down the stairs three at a time, the big man leaping clumsily and whooping, the little boy darting and weaving among the crowds towards the five-dollar window, where they rushed up breathlessly and waited in line punching each other playfully and beaming at everybody around and laughing.

Martin had bet five dollars to win and five to show, and he collected one hundred and seventeen dollars in all.

"Now we'll go to Boston and have a big feed, hey, sonny-boy Mickey!" yelled the old man jubilantly as they counted the money and pawed at it in his hand and scuffled back and forth looking at it and grinning at everybody and sort of dreamily, absent-mindedly looking for the exit gate. "Whattayou say we both eat a couple of steaks apiece, hey?"

"And then we'll go to Thompson's and eat some ice cream!"

"All the ice cream you want!" shouted the old man triumphantly. "All the steaks and chops and lobster you want, sonny, all the ice cream and pie and cake in the world! Everything! Fried clams! hot dogs! hamburgers! sauerkraut and franks! What'll we eat? Where'll we start?" he cried happily. "Boy! I'm as hungry as a horse! What about the Old Union Oyster House for some lobster meat and melted butter? Or maybe we can go to Jacob Wirth's for beans and brownbread, or knockwurst, or steak, and some of that nice Bock beer for me? By golly, I'm starved! Huh, Mickey?—or Pieroti's for some nice thick chops? Huh, sonny? Where'll we eat? Where'll we start?"

They swaggered arm in arm out of the track and drove off towards Boston, triumphantly hungry and gleeful.

And the sun went down on the legend of Green Swords in the last race, the solemn chronicle forever recorded in gray files. The sun sank and the highway lights blinked on along the road in the fogs of dusk in New Hampshire.

[3]

FRANCIS MET a strange man that summer. He was in the Galloway Public Library one day scanning a shelf of paper-backed French novels—he had begun reading French prior to his enrollment in a college that Fall—when he heard someone step up softly behind him, pause, laugh dryly, and say: "*Comment!—on lit le français dans les petites provinces des Etats Unis?*"

Francis turned and stared at the man.

"I was only expressing my astonishment—" Wilfred Engels bowed slightly, his coat over his arm, his sweaty collar undone, smiling, mopping his brow—"my astonishment in finding a young man interested in the French originals in this little provincial American town." And with this he laughed again and toddled away.

But a moment later Engels turned around and came back, and introduced himself suddenly in an ingratiating manner—

"You may wonder about me, I can even see it in your eyes now, you're asking yourself: what can this seedy *outré*-looking man be wanting with me, I was only minding my business! Tell me immediately though, do I bore you, does it pain you to have to stand here talking to me!—"

Francis began to stammer something.

"Good! good! You have that sensitive regard for strangers that so few Americans have. But I will be brief: I'm here in this gloomy little town on a business trip, I walk the streets in solitude, alien, you see, alien and alone and far from home, I come into the library to get out of the rain, and lo! I find this intelligent-looking young man reading casually through the pages of Julian Green, Balzac, Stendhal . . . But that look in your eyes is still bewildered! Believe me, I've been in America long enough to know what that look means. . . . What's your name?" he asked suddenly, bending forward stiffly.

"Martin—"

"Believe me, Martin, in France, in Europe, people who are perfect strangers speak to each other like this every day!"

"I didn't say anything," grinned Francis.

"Ho, ho, ho!" the man roared with laughter, as the librarians looked up with annoyance. "Now I feel better, I have a witty acquaintance. I was feeling *very* disconsolate; outside in those rainy streets it's like a scene from Flaubert. What would you say to some tea?—I'm curious to know what a young man like yourself *thinks* about, really! You look so different from all the others—"

"Well—" began Francis.

"Don't feel called upon to humor me, whatever you do!" he cried, holding up his finger with a strange cackle.

"Well," said Francis, "it struck me funny—I mean the tea, the tea!"

"I want to know what you *think* about in this out-of-the-way part of the universe," said Engels with sudden gravity, staring at Francis intently, with a squint from behind thick lenses. "Believe it, it will be like an education for me. Do you feel particularly *accosted?*"

"Oh, no, no."

So Francis got his raincoat, amazed, snickering under his breath at the thought of the whole thing which was assuming such funny proportions. "What a character!" he thought. "Who would have thought it possible!" They hurried across the street to the lunch-cart near the railroad tracks. As they sat in a booth by the steamy kitchen door, the counterman stared at them, finally leaned over, and said—

"What'll it be, fellers?"

—and they ordered tea.

"Tea!" he cried, staring at them. "Tea?" He looked around wearily. "Well," he sighed, "I don't know. I'll see if I got some tea-bags left."

And the tea was brought to them in great cracked coffee-mugs. It was all too rich for Francis to believe.

"I'm Viennese-born, you know," resumed Engels, lolling back in the booth now with a delighted air of conviviality, "but you see I was raised in Paris. I suppose you know all about Paris?"

"I've read about it."

"Ha-ha! Wary and cautious!" Engels produced a long cigarette from a case and tapped it dreamily now. "Perhaps you're wondering what my business is. You don't think, 'Ah, a businessman, a Babbitt!' That *is* the furthest thing from your mind, isn't it? Well, you see, I'm connected with an export company in Boston, and here in your charming little town they manufacture textiles. You see before you a businessman, a mercenary man, completely Americanized and mechanized in his three years in the States."

"You've been here three years?"

"Yes! I've taken out my citizenship papers, the call of the dollar is too strong, I can't resist it!"

He removed his thick-rimmed glasses and began to polish them in a slow, deliberate, musing way. Francis saw that he was well in middle age, with drooping lidded eyes and a round face like an owl's, with something weary and bland in the expression not at all in keeping with the way he gushed joyously, with a faint suggestion of irony about the brow that you could not say was not somewhat heightened by a deliberately raised eyebrow. Francis marveled at the whole odd, dark, sharply intellectual, strangely distinguished look of him, amazed that he should be in Galloway on a rainy Friday afternoon.

"Perhaps we can swap ideas! That's what I like! And who knows, perhaps I can teach you a few things—I was a teacher for a while, you know. Ah! I've done many things in my long and obscure career. Perhaps I can tell you about it sometime, a lesson in stubborn resistance to the wretchedness and futility of our times—" He gazed away angrily. "However, you've saved my life, you're going to turn business into pleasure. I shall have to come around here every now and then. What's more, you've resurrected my faith in America. Yes!"

And he went on like that for a bit, as Francis grew somewhat embarrassed. Suddenly Engels stopped and laughed nervously:

"Look here. Martin! Is that your first name? Francis? Well, believe it, I've been putting on an act for you, a sort of Continental act in the worst taste. But you knew, didn't you?" And he looked away gravely. "But understand, I was only trying to impress you, to interest you first off. The fact is, I'm just a lonesome old fool and I wanted to make friends. I rather imagined you felt yourself a young romantic in an unromantic town when I saw you poring over the French novels."

"I don't fancy myself a romantic," said Francis soberly.

"Everyone is so serious in this country! It's really refreshing, believe me. But shake hands, Francis Martin, we will be friends. I'm very glad to know you now."

He laughed with a kind of gloating rapture, and they spent the rest of the afternoon in the lunchcart talking, Engels mostly, with great verve and excitement, Francis listening, curiously, trying to make him out, trying to decide what it was that he wanted to learn from this mysteriously eloquent, somewhat ridiculous, nervous, somehow grossly important odd sort of "European" man.

They promised to meet in Boston in a few days, where Engels said he knew a lot of interesting people who were, like himself, "radically involved in art and politics and change." "You see, you're not really alone in your opinions of modern life! You ought to get around more!"

After that Francis mused alone in front of the library. It was about six, it had stopped raining, everything was clean and fresh, with a washed glitter around the library and city hall, a luminous gap in the clouds, a clear afterglow; all of it, suddenly, in his reverie seeming somehow like a French town in the Provinces to which he was magically transplanted after his long talk with the interesting gentleman from France. But he saw how far from a French town Galloway really was—he laughed thinking of it—he saw the redbrick mills, the dirty alleys behind the saloons on

Rooney Street, and then the Victorian houses with potted plants on the screen porch.

And when he got home, he saw the ugly old gray house, the yard littered with boards, buckets, old car seats, empty oil cans, a hose and a lawn mower. From the house the two radios blared swing music and baseball scores. Inside Elizabeth lay sprawled on the floor reading *Thrilling Love Magazine* and *Movie Screen*; Charley was reading *Popular Mechanics*; the father was reading the Galloway *Evening Courier*; Peter was oiling up a football; Ruth was talking inanely on the phone with one of her boy-friends. Everybody was doing something—but nobody was *thinking*, nobody was interested in anything finer, more beautiful, more exalted.

"My God," thought Francis, "there's no culture at *all* in this place!"

Francis and Engels met and talked and strolled the Galloway streets all that summer. Francis even went to Boston and visited some of Engels' "political" friends, who had parties and discussed "issues" and went to concerts and rallies. Some of them were Americans who were politically and artistically fiercer and angrier than Engels could ever be; art students, young writers, law students, actors, college instructors, all kinds of people, young and old.

What was most important to Francis was that for the first time in his life he heard spoken—and spoken in the articulate fluent language of "contemporary thought"—all the misty indistinct feelings that he had been carrying around with him for the last few years in Galloway. At last he realized that he had not been alone in these feelings. Elsewhere in the world other men and women lived and felt and reasoned as he did, other men and women were dissatisfied with the way things were, with society and its conventions and traditions and grievous blotches, other men and women wandered lonely in the world carrying in their hand the bitter proud fruit of "modern consciousness." They, like him, had been frightened and alone at first, before discovering there were others.

And he was amazed to think that a whole coherent language had sprung into being around this restless, intelligent, determined trend, this gentle, invisible revolt in America. They had words to name the key complaints and frame the major solutions, vast studies had been undergone in many fields in an effort to widen the disclosures of this new knowledge, thousands of people scattered everywhere in the country were reading the same rare unheard-of books.

They had the words, they had their habits and demeanors, their kind of living, their common characteristics and the places and shows and restaurants and hangouts. Above all, they had this universe and the strange names and stars that constellated it: Freud, Krafft-Ebing, Kafka, Jung, Rilke, Kierkegaard, Eliot, Gide, Auden, Huxley, Joyce: names which, when first heard, brought so much mystery and joy and curiosity into his soul. He had one whole vision of this new kind of life and all the people with their books and ideas who were shaping it.

"I'm glad to see you have chosen to go to Harvard, Francis," said Engels. "It *really* is one of the very few decent universities in the whole wasteland. There's Berkeley and Chicago, and, of course, Columbia and several of the eastern universities. But outside of that—my God! The others exist primarily as processing plants for football players and dizzy coeds, *really!* And some of the Jesuit colleges are just bastions of reactionary Catholicism."

So Francis could think of "Berkeley" and see great numbers of "real intellectuals" gathered there, walking the campus at evening in groups and cliques, speaking fluently all the magic words and all the magic names with a bland, almost disinterested assurance, but with a kind of soft earnestness too, a whole new exotic world suddenly discovered in the vast midst of a drawing, stammering, brute-like America. He could hear the words, the terms—"frustration," "compulsive neurosis," "oedipus complex," "anxiety," "economic exploitation," "progressive liberalism," "the facts"—he could hear the casually uttered names: Picasso, Braque, Cocteau, Heidegger, Tchelitchev, Henry Miller, Isherwood—and he could see the places and be amazed because they suddenly existed and awaited him quietly.

"There's hope," Engels said. "There are a lot of good people coming up, and things are changing. The depression did it in a way. In many ways the depression was the best thing that could have happened here: Americans were frightened and sick—and like sick men they slowed down a pace—and new ideas moved right in and quite admirably promoted this change in all directions."

And Francis gladdened in these discoveries of an America that was not at all like the futility he had always known in Galloway.

A strange thing happened one night when Wilfred Engels left for New York. He had visited Francis in Galloway and they were just running into the old turret-topped depot for his train, when they bumped into Peter and his chum Danny.

"Oh, this is my brother Peter," introduced Francis.

"Well, well!" cried Engels, gripping the boy's hand. "This is an unexpected pleasure!"

"Francis has been telling me a lot about you, Mr. Engels."

"You're the one who's going to college to play football!" Engels cried. "The athlete who will never open a book!"

"I don't know about that," said Peter, grinning. "Who says I'll never open a book?"

"I know you football players," laughed the man, clapping Peter on the shoulder. "You always end up selling life insurance, that's what you learn in college! You'll join a fraternity, have a lot of admiring friends, and then sell policies at alumni reunions the rest of your life!"

Outside in the lashing rain the train was chugging in with a great furor of steam and bells and rolling gigantic wheels. The depot floor trembled. In the sudden excitement of the moment, Engels staggered to the door with his suitcase. He kept shouting to Peter, as they all straggled: "Oh, I know you, I know you!"

"I know you, too!" Peter was shouting, turning every now and then to look at Danny with a frown of amazement.

"And what about your friend there, what's *his* name? Danny? What does he do? What's he got up *his* sleeve?"

Danny glowered and said, "I work for a living, I work in the mills."

"Ah, he's the dour one!" cried Engels. "Why didn't I meet you before! This is terrible. Just as I'm leaving! And now you're all going to college—except the gloomy millworker there—you're all starting out on your lives! I'm getting on a train and going off to the ends of the night with my suitcase—just a lonesome old fool. Uprooted and drying up malignantly, in my own ancient and malignant juices—you understand that?"

The boys stood around on the platform a little abashed. Engels seemed ready to burst into tears, but again he clapped Peter on the shoulder and cried: "I know you, admit it! You're the type who deliberately conceals his true self from the world! Isn't that true?"

"Well—"

"Be a good brother to Francis there, remember that! As for me, I'm just lonesome and silly and right now I'm going off to the ends of the night. I'll write to you, Francis, first thing in New York! Good-bye, good-bye!"

The train chugged and rumbled off in the lashing rain. They saw him waving and smiling and disappearing, and then the sorrow of a departing train in any night rain anywhere fell over the platform. They ambled back inside the depot with their hands in their pockets, and finally sat down on the old benches.

"That guy's *nuts!*" said Danny with amazement.

"I thought you said he was a smart man, Francis. Who *is* that guy?"

"He had a couple of martinis before we came here and he's a little drunk, that's all," said Francis wearily.

"What a character!"

They heard the train howling far off in South Galloway, the rain drummed on the high roof of the old depot, and the silence of a departed train and an excited departed voice was all around and haunted with sorrow.

And Francis, strangely, was suddenly thinking of Mary Gilhooley whom he had loved in high school and by whose house in South Galloway Engels was now speeding in a train, in the night rain, over the bridge and over the selfsame beach where she had rejected him that night, long ago. It was all so sad.

"He's a very intelligent man, Pete. You didn't catch him at the right time, that's all."

They stared outside at the glistening cobblestone street, the streetlamps dripping in the rain, the cars passing solitary in the rainy darkness, the dull glow of the factory windows ranked bluish beyond the brickheap alleys. There were puddles in the street, and rain drumming and splattering everywhere.

They got up and ambled to the doors.

"Look, there goes Nutsy De Pew," remarked Peter. "What a crazy maniac. Look at him—drunk as usual—going home to sleep it off."

And Nutsy went stumbling by outside, and then there was

nothing but rain and puddles and the glow of a red neon upon the cobblestones, and the drumming hush all around.

"Someday I'm gonna get out of this lousy town," said Danny. "You know?"

No one said anything and they stood there with their hands in their pockets and looked at the rain. Somewhere far off they heard a faint howling sound, drowned immediately by a wind-blown gust of rain on the roof.

"Well. Let's go to Nick's across the street—have a cup of coffee."

The door of the depot opened and a gaunt old ticketmaster came in, shook the rain off his coat, turned, stooped to a spittoon with a finger against his nose, and snorted. Now he strolled slowly across the worn planking of the depot floor, and looked up at the clock on the wall, and stopped to check on his own old pocket watch, and ambled on slowly to his office cage, and yawned. And the rain drummed and drummed above on the old roof.

"Well—what about that coffee."

"Huh?"

They stood in the doorway staring at the rain, waiting. Francis was lonely, and bored, bored. Everything was like it had always been, like he had always known it, like he knew it would always be. God, but he was lonely and bored.

[4]

IN THE MARTIN HOUSE on the second floor facing north was Peter's bedroom, a room that looked out on the old road, the pine forests, and the hills that were blue on gray days. Peter had shared this room with Joe as far back as he could remember but now, while Joe was away, it was all his with all the potent secrecy that a room can have when it is inherited and becomes a solitude. During that summer he therefore rearranged a few things, pushing his cubbyhole desk up by the window, converting Joe's bed into a kind of couch against the wall—his "thinking" couch—hanging a few college banners on the wall along with some track medals and a framed newspaper picture of himself scoring the Lawton game touchdown, installing a battered book-case that he had made with some old boards and stuffing it with old books,—and then he observed the whole effect with pleased admiration.

Now he was "really collegiate" and all set to go to town. And he spent many days that summer just sitting at his desk over a book and staring dreamily out the window. On rainy days he saw his future in the distant hazy swell of the hills on the horizon, in the dim blue reaches there, and dreamed and dreamed of greatness. There was never anything else that could hold his dreamy attention: all was the fulfillment of himself, the future, greatness, a heroic struggle and overcoming of all obstacles.

And in the next room, in the bedroom shared by little Mickey and young Charley, a room facing north also, Mickey was wrapped in the same kind of burning vision of life as triumph. Mickey had Erector sets, he built toy cranes and trucks and conducted great engineering experiments that seemed impossible at first but eventually succumbed to his grave cunning: and after reading *Huckleberry Finn* he deliberately wrote out a river adventure of his own in a nickel notebook, a carefully wrought-out epic called *Mike Martin Explores the Merrimac.*

Moreover, Mickey conducted a whole, perfectly ordered, imaginary "world" of his own which was exhaustively set into motion and recorded each day in his own "newspaper," printed by hand and illustrated in pencil. Sports predominated in this world: it was all horseracing, prizefighting, baseball, bowling, basketball, hockey, football and the financial successes thereto, and throughout its blazing legend and all its dusty files the name of "Mike" Martin predominated: Mike hit the most homeruns, batted .395, was the greatest money-winning jockey of the turf, the world's unchallenged heavyweight champ, the best fullback a college ever had, the fleetest of all sprinters (he also ran the mile regularly in 4:04 flat), the most phenomenal of all duckpin bowlers and one of the richest adventurers in the United States with holdings and ranches and wives all over the world.

Not that he had no competitors—he had many. The newspapers which he himself printed and published attested to all this in great eight-column headlines—and who could deny it when the greatest publisher and editor in the United States was also the selfsame, one-and-only, genial, robust "Mike" Martin? There was no sadness, and no madness, only stoutness of heart and vigor and strength. There were "soreheads," the ungenial but still-as-yet fierce and mighty competitors in a world of lances and shields

American style, but these "soreheads" always succumbed after terrific listings on the windswept field of the earth, and the cheerful, canny, beloved and powerful heroes prevailed.

On the rainy summer days when the blue haze shrouded the hills and the landscape outside, Peter sat at his desk over elementary books on algebra, geometry, and French—credits he needed in prep school that year—and, smoking his very collegiate pipe, he considered exactly how he would set his destiny underway, where it would need a heroic push, where it would call for cheerful humble patience, and where it would approach its fruits and the time for ecstatic immortal immolation. He had visions of great achievement in the preliminary, almost unimportant stages, that is, impressing the women, amazing the men, scoring all the touchdowns, displaying brilliant scholarship, winning the awe of all: the humble beginnings exploding suddenly into triumph, all by virtue of his natural unalterable heroism, the great achievements piling up in pyramidical hugeness, approaching now the point of immolation in the vastness of all—he saw himself founding families and lines, organizing world events, pointing to necessities and hoisting them into place, arranging, disarranging, revising pitiable errors of others, getting everything fixed to his own satisfaction, standing there a grave, powerful, humble leader of men and things—and then suddenly disappearing in a mist of immolation, to the utter astonishment of the world around him, disappearing into the immense haze of the universe, in the Valhalla of himself and of everything.

He had gone to church on the raindark Good Friday afternoons, and so had Mickey, all silent and solemn, and he had seen Jesus suffering and heroic, dark, dark Jesus and his cross, dear great sacrificial Jesus the hero and the lamb, and he had wept at the spectacle of that heroic sorrow—and then he had gone to church, and Mickey too, on the bell-golden Easter mornings of sun and flowers and seen Jesus arisen triumphant, immortal, radiant and true—and all the occasional yawning mortals sitting beside him in the pews, the ones who coughed and fidgeted irritably and dozed and yum-yummed while the mighty drama of life's meaning was marching all around them, these were the "soreheads" of the earth indifferently turning away from immortality and heroism, abysmal, empty, and unamazed. That was not for Peter, not for Mickey. They had to be heroes or nothing.

✦

The night before Peter left for prep school he lay in bed and felt that strange mingling feeling American boys have when they are about to leave home for the first time: that drowsy fear of leaving the bed, the room, the house that has always been the first comfortable basis of life before anything else, the house that is as familiar and plain as an old sweater, to which one always returns after excitements and fatigues to sweetly sleep: and yet at the same time he felt that similarly drowsy excitement of going off from the house—to railroad depots, coffee counters, new cities, smoke and furor and windsmells strange and new, to sudden unimagined vistas of river, highway, bridge and horizon all sensationally strange under unknown skies, and the smoke, the smoke!

He stayed awake until four in the morning—after dark hours of writhing tormented excitement and lonely reveries where he babbled to himself whimsically ("Well, here goes Martin in the morning, here I go!")—and at eight he got up all tense and feverish, snapped shut the suitcase all neatly packed with shirts and socks and coats and trousers, put on his new sports jacket, stared at himself in the mirror, and went downstairs.

His mother was in the kitchen making his breakfast. And while she picked and plucked at him, told him what to wear on cold days and what to eat and how much to sleep, what to do about his laundry and what to say to the nice man who was going to be his Dean, he just sat brooding and nodding his head. Because it was a raw gray September day and the air was fraught with gloom and with a faint wild excitement too, and it was almost as though he could grab his mood right out of the air if he could only determine whether he felt sad or joyful leaving home for the first time. It was something appalling and heavy, like his suitcase, something that choked at his throat, like the starched shirt and the new tie, to be "going away"—although he would be back in six weeks for Thanksgiving—and yet too there was a tremendous furor waiting for him outside, somewhere, beckoning him to come on, come on.

"And don't forget to write me the moment you get there," his mother kept saying. "Tell me if you need anything. Your money should last you the first week. And send home for anything you need."

"Yep."

"Be sure to be nice and polite and make a good impression on your teachers there—"

"Yep, yep."

"I'm so proud of you, you look so nice and clean this morning!" she said gladly.

"And stay that way!" cried Rose, picking a thread off the hero's sleeve. "Don't go getting all dirty on the way up and look like a bum when you get there!"

"Yes, ladies, I will."

"And don't forget to be the star of the team," said his sister Ruth eagerly. "That's the important thing!"

"And don't get hurt!" added the mother with a frown, and she plucked at his collar.

And as Peter ate his breakfast and looked out the window broodingly and saw the hills and the mist far off, something stirred and thrilled in him, he gloated, he was on the verge of diving off a high place into the open air—yet when it actually came time to pick up his suitcase, move to the door, and kiss his mother and sisters, he felt sick at heart and almost wanted to cry. He couldn't tell them that he felt this way, he "had to be a man." But they saw the thin film of mist in his eyes and kissed him affectionately.

"I'll be back in two months, it'll only be two months," he kept saying.

"That's right, the time'll fly like anything! Before you know it, you'll be back home!"

"Sure!" cried Peter, reassuring them desperately.

"Poor baby!" said Rose. "He's just a baby! Be sure and write to your big dumb sister now! And when you come back a big sleek college man don't be holding up your nose at me!"

"What are you talking about!" cried Peter angrily.

"Don't miss your train, Petey!"

"Holy cow! Is it already half-past?" And suddenly there was another wild flurry of kissing and good-byes, Peter hurried to the door almost stumbling, his mother plucked at his coat collar, someone opened the door for him, he rushed out saying, "Here I go now! Here I go!"

He hurried down the road swinging his suitcase, he turned and waved to his mother and sisters once more, he strode determinedly now down to the bottom of the hill, and they saw him bustling off into the "world" with a jaunty, scowling, absorbed air.

There was only sadness for him now in the gray morning mists, and a dull pang of regret in his heart, and dread. On the highway the cars and trucks went by in all their busy, self-absorbed unconcern, it was a morning world of bustle and business, everything seemed to be mocking his solitary little sorrows, there was no room here for him and for the hesitations of a boy walking down the road with his suitcase. He felt very glum and the day was gray.

His chum Danny met him at the bus stop by the bridge, as prearranged. They looked at each other with a hearty, congenial, yet bewildered cheerfulness. This had all been talked over before: Peter was going off to make good, Danny was staying behind to work in the mills, but somehow, someday, both of them would be rich and successful, and they would always be friends.

"Well, Zagg"—Danny had always called Peter by this name, ever since they were kids—"so you're off at last—and it's like I always said, you're on your way."

"Aw, I hate like hell to leave Galloway, honest, that's the way I feel!" confessed Peter.

"A little lonesomeness for your hometown won't do you any harm, Zagg, it'll make a better man of you." And Danny pronounced these words in his dour and gloomy way.

"I know, Dan, but— Gee, if you only knew how I felt when I left the house. I dunno—but there's something so damn sad about leaving home, you know?"

"It's *gotta* be that way!"

"I know—but it makes a lump in my throat, you know? I guess I'm crazy but that's the way I felt. And now— I feel a lot better now, I guess I feel like hitting that old road! Ha, ha!"

"That's the spirit, Zagg. That's the only way to be!"

"You've always been my best friend, Danny!" said Peter, suddenly mortified. "And someday you're gonna be a great man, I know it! You're too much of a good guy!" He squeezed Danny's shoulder impulsively. "Someday I'll be saying the same thing to you, wishing you luck on your way, and we'll always be friends!"

"You bet, Zagg, we'll always be friends!"

And sorrowfully Peter watched his unhappy buddy go off to work, he felt worse than ever—but suddenly it came in the gray air: a truck roared blasting by, someone shouted, there was a thronging of sounds everywhere as though his eardrums had just popped, everything was noisy and lyrical, the Falls thundered at his feet, smoke passed in the sky overhead, he was blinded and deafened for joy.

He was leaving home but now he was striding off into the

smoky center of things, for the first time "on his own." He was a man with a suitcase and a walletful of money and each of his gloating hungry wits, and there stretched the future dizzily before him in dimness! and roads and bridges and cities! and smoke, smoke, smoke!

When he got on the train and sat in the coach among the men with their morning newspapers and cigars, and the conductor made a gruff joke when he collected his ticket, and the man sitting next to him politely opened a conversation about the weather and the international situation, Peter realized with glee that he had a new status as a man of the world. He even smoked a cigarette and expressed the opinion that the international situation was pretty bad at that, and the man vehemently agreed with him all the way to Boston, as smoke flashed past the windows and swooped upwards into the gray air of morning.

The prep school was up in Maine, not far from Augusta, in the heart of the rolling woods and fields of some of the finest country in New England, and it was called Pine Hall. It was relatively unknown but it was just the place to get his credits and prepare for college—and, of course, also, it was a hideaway breeding-ground for college football stars. He had his choice of almost any college after that year. And among other things it was also an exclusive sort of school for rowdy young socialites expelled from the Andovers and Exeters for their prematurely dissolute ways.

Pine Hall had a charming little campus of old redbrick Georgian buildings covered with ivy, with peaceful walks running around the halls, all of it in the shade of noble pines and spruce. There was a village a mile away, soft farmlands to the south, forested hills sweeping north with their wild hint of moose and mountain brooks, and a fresh, greendark, northern atmosphere to the whole surrounding country that immediately delighted Peter's fancy for rustic solitudes. Now he pictured himself studying diligently in the school library and then going off on long meditative walks in the woods and fields with a copy of Horace in his back pocket.

But before he could really look around and enjoy things he found himself on the football field with some twenty husky youngsters from all over the East. He was faced with another grueling effort to make the varsity and hold his own—and here he discovered to his dismay that the players in this school were all high school stars like himself, much bigger and better than the average high school regular, and each convinced of making the team. Yet, of all the high school "phenoms" gathered there, at least half of them would have to succumb to the competition and play a secondary part in the team's destiny. Peter was crushed with the thought that he might wind up among the unlucky ten, the others looked too big and too good for him, and they looked fierce.

That first night he suffered dreads and a feeling of defeat, he brooded in his room and wrote a despairing letter to Danny back in Galloway, and then he went out for a melancholy walk to the sleepy little village, and noted gloomily that everything closed up at ten o'clock.

And he was going to spend eight months in this place—eight months of gloom and defeat and shame! For the first time in his life he felt completely abandoned and helpless and thoroughly frightened: what was he to do? He remembered all the loving care of his mother when she packed him off, the proud excitement in the house the night before he left, his sister reminding him to be the "star" of the team—and God! now it was questionable if he could even *make* the team! He remembered his father telling the men that his kid was going to "knock 'em out" this year, he remembered his kid brothers and their chums cheering him when he walked up the street, and above all he remembered the Lawton game and the Thanksgiving dinner afterwards at home and all the innocent joy and delight and glory of that day. What a fool!—to plan his life around glorious deeds, to thrive on that and nothing else, and finally to bring himself foolishly to things that were beyond his power and then stop there in full humiliation for all the world to see! And all the horror crept up in him, he wanted to go away from everything and never come back, he wanted to bury himself, drown himself, die—do anything but live and admit this final humiliating impotence and defeat.

And what was most horrible to him that first night was the final terrible realization that he was only Peter Martin, only Peter Martin—and who was that in the world? Who was he, if not some sort of impostor and stranger and scoundrel, who somehow managed to fool people and even his own family into believing that he was Peter Martin. Who *was* he?

He was no one—he felt his arms and legs, looked at himself in the mirror, looked out the window in the dark Maine night, and he was no one. He was a ghostly stranger, he was a dreaming forgotten thing, and he was an anguish-stricken humility, and nothing else. He felt like rushing into the next room, where he heard the voices of his new teammates. He wanted to go in there and confess to them that he was a fake, an impostor, a stranger to them, he felt like going in there and shouting for their forgiveness. . . .

But he fell asleep exhausted; and the next day out on the field he put on his helmet, gritted his teeth, and suddenly found himself breaking through the line of scrimmage and running off on a giddy succession of touchdowns that had the coaches looking at each other in grim wonder. And the other boys to whom he would have confessed the night before were now looking at him with grins and blinks of respect, in silent manly admiration—and Peter was shocked and angered at himself. Somehow more than ever now he wanted to take them all by the shoulder, look at them, tell them that they did not understand, they did not *understand*—

But in the succeeding days he found himself consorting with scores of cheerful friendly boys, he had excited talks with his coaches and teachers, the studies began, the little campus grew wonderful as the leaves on the occasional maples began to turn red, and the air sharpened. There were bull-sessions at night in the lamplit rooms and the light streamed out on the walks and the pines, there was music in the village hall on Saturday night and many pretty girls to dance with. Something strided jubilantly across the land. And Peter almost with tears in his eyes late one night realized that other people were also strangers to themselves, and were lonely and troubled like him, and sought each other out cheerfully and with friendship, and perhaps even sometimes felt like he had felt the first night, like confessing everything, confessing all that was so dark and lonely and crazy and fearful in the heart. And he shook his head wincing at the thought of it. He had never felt anything like that before—yet somehow he knew that from now on he would always feel like that, always, and something caught at his throat as he realized what a strange sad adventure life might get to be, strange and sad and still much more beautiful than he could ever have imagined, so much more beautiful and amazing because it was so really, strangely sad.

✦

That year at Pine Hall Peter had a "great year." Everything he did was excellent and wonderful. He was a devastating fullback on the team both on offense and defense and as a triple-threat. He led the track team in scoring, and played on the baseball team in the Spring. He was on the honor roll in his studies and liked by his instructors. He was one of the most popular boys in the school and had scores of friends, and he shone with the young ladies of the village both in the dance and out in the lovers' lane. He ran a typewriting agency for extra spending money, and also composed English term papers for the others at a fee. He contributed stories and articles to the various school publications and rather fancied himself a Hemingway that Winter after creating a minor sensation on the campus with a story entitled "The Counterman, the Drunkard, and the Collegian." He learned to go around in dirty black-and-white saddle shoes, and sloppy lounge jackets, he played tennis with the girls from town and was to be seen going in Marty's for a coke after a fast set in the hot sun all dazzling in white ducks and sneakers. He became conversant with the profounder "procrastinations" of "Prince Hamlet the Melancholy Dane." And when he wrote home he sometimes pulled out a beauty like "inordinate" to mean "too much," or "*raffiné*" to mean "refined"—all for the edification and amaze of his family.

He was seventeen years old, of medium height now, and weighed a hundred and eighty-five pounds. He was a real bozo, yet very sharp—if he wanted to show you how well his coat hung and draped he stood with one foot turned aside as in the *Esquire* ads. He knew all about jazz: his chum Dick had a "terrific" collection of Eddie Condons and Kid Orys and Muggsy Spaniers; and another chum, Jay, had a "great" collection of Roy Eldridges, Choo Berrys and Coleman Hawkins. Someone else had Gershwin, and Debussy, and Stravinski. Everybody had music. In every room there was a little radio blaring on the dresser, and the occupant was always combing his hair and getting ready to go out on a date. Peter himself had a tom-tom drum which he pounded with the "Sing Sing Sing" beat—"just like Krupa" too.

They were madcaps too, and the maddest of them all, the "crazy" Mac, had a job in town walking a ninety-year-old man up and down Main Street in the evenings, for which he was paid a wage of fifteen cents a night—and he never, never cracked a smile. Then there was Tony the halfback from Somerville, Mass., who got drunk one night on a half a barrel of beer and tore up a small tree by the roots out on the green and took it to bed with him.

On the bottom of Peter's scorecard the Dean wrote: "A good scholar and a fine citizen," and Peter sent that on home, along with a copy of the school paper with his own stories ringed in pencil. He also sent home photographs of himself to his Galloway girl friends, and he even had one of them up for the Spring prom, and sent her back home properly impressed. His relationship with this poor girl was completely blank.

There was the whole round of liniment-smelling lockers, the musty classrooms, the boiling odors of the dining-hall, the chilly assembly hall, the library smell of bound volumes and varnish, the crisp evergreen and ivy smells of the campus—all the odors and sensations of a prep school for boys, and with it all, the incessant chatter and activity and eager excitement of the busy regimens, and the constant glee and snickering that goes on at all times. It was funny and wonderful to sit around and talk about how really "crazy" a certain instructor was in his private life, how he had once registered in a hotel as "Apollo Goldfarb" and another time as "Arapahoe Rappaport" and how he really was a "very funny guy." It was amazing to discover how so many things were really funny. It was fun to shout and joke in the dining hall, and to choke with laughter in French class when Mac deliberately mispronounced "Monsieur le Coq"—and never, never cracking a smile, the triumphant wit and hero of three hundred gleeful souls.

It was funny to see Rocco the big Italian guard from Bridgeport, Conn., conversing seriously with little Rodney Mason the president of the Philolexian Club (probably about exams)—and in the school paper they would write it this way: "Buddies Moose Rocco and Rod Mason seen talking over old times on quad—" which would convulse the entire school. "Flash Mason and The Moose." It was the funniest thing anyone had ever heard, it was dark and daemonic with furious glee, and in the old dorms at night in the creaking halls there was wicked, ravenous, brooding joy.

During Easter vacation Peter received a letter from one of the great school madcaps and wits, which ran convulsively as follows:

Dear Hashoodfludnistnizaaflem,

I thought I would write you a letturd as I just found your undress among my *things. Short* of that I was going to ask Rod the Flash for *it*. I hear the Moose is seriously thinking of *grabbing off* the ingenue part in the Pine Hall production of "Ah Wilderness!" That sounds good but I'd rather see him in Oscar Wilde's "Lady Windemere's Fan." As I write you the stomping, rollicking, scintillating, solid, hot, strains of Guy Iturbi Ignacz Lombardo are filling the air. To say his occarino and glackenspiel sections have improved is an understatement. Look out Blue Barron and Leo Reisman! Give my regards to Kensington Kaplan. I hope this reaches yours, Rodney Martin.

(signed) Cunny Keane Tracer of Lost Loads.

There was all this gleeful demonism, and a thousand absorbing and wonderful things to be done, and parties and dances every week, and the fascinating vistas of new study, new languages, new knowledge—vistas that were just like the blue pine hills and the gray dimness to the north that they saw outside the classroom windows.

And Peter went on long solitary walks through the woods with his copy of Thoreau in his back pocket, he tramped contemplatively across birch fields and groves of pine, paused at the frosty brooks and saw the sloping red light of Sunday dusk move across the blue snow, and came tramping back to the roast beef and the noisy dining-hall raging with hunger and joy.

Even though he was homesick at times, it was a "great year"—and he only realized it insofar as it promised other "great years" of joy and success in college, he only enjoyed it insofar as it pointed to the future. He was bulging with youthful confidence and vigor and health, his cheeks were smooth and pleased, his eyes sparkled, and the whole world was singing.

In the Spring when graduation time came round, the raw Maine Winter gave way to a sweet and lovely May, incredibly tender, fresh and green, full of morning musics and cool gold-flecked shade in the campus yards. Peter opened his window on the morning of graduation and looked out, and felt like singing. Everything he had done that year seemed excellent and wonderful, and all was warm sunshine, peace, birdsong, and loafing young joy. The bells rang in golden light, the boys walked the greens in dazzling white attire among the proud visiting families and girl friends, there were rippling soft sounds of voices in the May morning air, laughter—and something gleeful and wicked that promised the night again, the dark wonderful night that had been their partner in crazy snickering joy all the year long, and that also promised a whole golden and richly dark summertime of home again, home again.

When Peter got home he found himself swamped with scholarship offers from several of the bigger universities in the East and from two in the deep South. He was definitely "hot," he was the "flashy Massachusetts back" they spoke of in athletic offices and coaches' locker rooms, he was scouted and discovered and tabbed and grimly sought after. He was going to become famous, he was going to be the dark swift figure with twinkling feet that is seen in the Pathé Newsreels galloping across chalk-stripes in the terrific, mob-swarmed, Autumn-dark stadiums of America as jubilance strides across the land.

At home that Summer he put on his old blue denims, went swimming in the brook in the pine woods with his chums, loafed around reading Jack London and Walt Whitman, went fishing, played baseball and drank beer with the boys.

And it was that Summer that he met Alexander Panos, who was to become a great friend of his youth, a comrade, a confidante in the first glories of poetry and truth. Panos was the first boy Peter knew who was interested in books and things for the sake of themselves, who spoke of "ideals," "beauty," and "truth." One of the first things young Alex did was to read him Keats' "Ode to a Grecian Urn" while Peter was swimming in Pine Brook, and their friendship opened up into a springtime of wonder and knowledge.

This boy was a Greek who lived across the river in an old ramshackle house with a huge family of wild emotional high-strung sisters, brothers, parents, aunts—and one old grandmother who still longed darkly for the Isle of Crete again. It was a noisy turbulent household ringing with the sounds of loud argument and emotional voices all day long and night, there were tears, tantrums, furies of recrimination, sulks, tender reconciliations, laughter, music (Greek records on the victrola, and the radio, and the piano, and a mandolin)—there were great celebrations on all holidays, and an awful tearful grief whenever some relative died in Galloway, where most of the Greek families were related to one another so that there was always a funeral someplace. The mother was half Russian, and the whole family was tumultuously religious in the Greek Orthodox faith. The children and the grownups all looked alike, with curly black hair, broad expressive Slavic mouths, flashing dark eyes, and olive-skinned complexions. Alex himself represented in his appearance the very sun and zenith of their fiery romantic look. The Panos house was visible from Peter's house across the river; he had seen it many times in the past, a rickety mournful-looking thing, but he could not have known that one of the great friends of his life lived there.

The strange thing was that young Alex had known Peter when they were little boys, although Peter couldn't remember, until Alex told him the story:

"Oh, I remember you well, I'll never forget it!" he cried excitedly. "It was during the time of that Greek-Irish fight in the sandbank, remember?"

"The Greek-Irish fight! Sure I remember! That was a war that lasted almost three years—slingshots, fist-fights, rocks! Sure I remember."

"Well," resumed Alexander Panos with a sad smile, "that was when I met you, and your brother, your big brother I guess it was."

"That would be Joe."

"Joe—yes, his name would be something like that. Joe! You see, one day I was coming home from school, when a bunch of Irish kids surrounded me on the sandbank and began pushing me around and hitting me and everything. And your brother Joe was going by with you, you had fishing poles, I guess you'd been fishing—"

"Oh, now I remember *you!* You were that little curly-headed Greek kid they were shoving around that day—yeah!"

"Precisely, Peter. You forgot, probably your brother Joe doesn't remember either—but I remember, oh, how I remember!"

"And Joe broke up the fight!" Peter recalled triumphantly.

"Yes, he broke it up. Do you remember I was crying?"

"Yeah."

"And your brother Joe just stood there and looked at the kids running away and he was swearing at them, and you—you walked up to me and asked me if I was all right."

"Did I? I don't remember that."

"Do we ever remember our true selves? . . . I remember, I remember," said young Alex with a sad smile. "Oh, God! after that I couldn't forget you and your brother. But it's strange that I never saw you again after that—until this Summer. We had moved away. God, that was years, years ago."

"It sure was!" laughed Peter. "We must have been eleven years old, and Joe was about fourteen then."

"I was the curly-headed little Greek kid on the sandbank," said Panos, smiling mournfully. "I didn't have a chance to tell you the other day, and I wasn't sure until I'd seen you again that you were the same kid. But you are. Your eyes are still the same—that was what I remembered: your eyes, when you walked up and asked me if I was all right. Forgive me for saying such silly things," he grinned sheepishly, "but that's how I remembered you. It was I—the curly-headed little boy on the sandbank."

"Well, I'll be damned! Wait till I tell Joe!"

"And where is Joe now?"

"He's been gone more than a year, he's working all over the country. We got a letter from him from South Dakota last month."

"You know," said young Alex sorrowfully, "that's exactly how I imagined your brother—the one who chased the kids away—that's how I imagined he would be when he grew up: roaming around the country. I used to think about both of you in strange reveries. . . ."

"Oh, he's a great guy!" cried Peter, grinning.

"I knew that then," said Alex sadly. "I knew he was great even then, and I know now he will be a great man. And you too."

"All because we chased the kids away!" laughed Peter.

"It was the way you did it," Panos said gravely. "Your brother cursing because he was angry at injustice, and you, by the way you looked at me. I shall never forget the sympathetic eyes of that little boy."

"And to think—" said Peter, embarrassed, "to think that I couldn't even remember that time. It was so long ago!"

"So long ago," echoed Alexander sorrowfully.

This was young Panos. He remembered the incident of the sandbank with all his heart and with all the soulful intensity of his nature, more than Peter and Joe could ever dream. In his room in the ramshackle Panos house he wrote poetry on reams of paper and actually splashed them with his tears, and barged around the littered room brooding, and wept again when he heard a violin concerto or songs like "April in Paris" or "The Boulevard of Broken Dreams," or a melancholy, anguished Greek song on the victrola, he went into ecstasies reading Byron and Rupert Brooke and William Saroyan, sometimes he opened his window and howled down his hosannahs of joy on startled passers-by.

Whenever he went downtown to Daley Square, he walked about in his erect mien, sometimes with tears in his eyes because "nobody understood." People stared at him in smiling amazement, because he was the strangest and most foreign sight to behold in all the town—excepting one Mohammedan woman who lived in the Greek coffee-shop district on Commerce Street and was seen wailing on the streets to Allah each sunset, a woman with whom young Alexander was on the most amiable terms.

He was eighteen years old—and in high school he had actually risen to a high rank in the school brigade, sporting polished boots, riding crop, visored cap and all, he had been a very dashing Cossack of a youthful officer, and an exceptional scholar as well. He had fallen in love with a girl in school and haunted the poor girl's house in striding midnight anguishes; he had contemplated the waters of a Galloway canal at three o'clock in the morning because her family didn't want her to go out with a Greek; finally he had confronted her on the street and professed his love in a broken, voluptuous voice, as people stared, and as the poor girl stood fidgeting and grinning.

His clothes were always shabby, unkempt, darkish and antiquated—yet always worn with great dignity, as though he were proud and noble in his poverty—his "poverty" being a romantic fancy with no real basis in fact. He haunted the Galloway library, went to all the movies and applauded excitedly by himself whenever something amused him or impressed him, he wrote irate letters to the editor of the Galloway *Star* protesting various injustices that had come to his ravenous attention. He prowled the riverbank on rainy nights and terrified himself with thoughts of suicide and death, at Greek weddings he went around kissing all the bridesmaids and being boisterously gay, and at Greek funerals he sobbed with grief at the side of his wailing aunts. He was an amazing gleeful figure different from anyone else in the businesslike town, and he flaunted his strangeness and impulsiveness with a nervous joy, sometimes going to great extremes to astound people on the streets, like wearing a garland in his hair or going about with fifteen or seventeen books under his arms and staggering from their weight. He was not of this world.

And Peter was amazed and delighted with him because he was such a "Marius" of a poet—Peter had read *Les Misérables* and Marius was his hero, Marius was the soulful and sensitive dreamer American boys are always discovering in European literature—and so that Summer, in the raucous beery atmospheres of Rooney Street saloons and at the moonlit lake dances with the gang, in cool soda fountains and the hamburg-sizzling lunchcarts, at the drowsy pine brook and on bustling Daley Square at noon, in cafeterias and movies and in the sleepy old depot on rainy nights, in all these plain homely places of the Galloway and American world, it was marvelous and gleeful to be with a Marius, a real romantic fiery poet sprung out of the pages of some fantastic story, it was better than a show and crazy with fun.

Peter and his old chums Danny and Scotcho and Berlot spoke of Alexander:

"That crazy bastart Alex!"

"What a guy! Did you see him last Saturday night when he jumped up on the table and began to recite poetry!"

"Yeah. He don't give a damn."

"What a happy-go-lucky maniac!"

"And then he starts singing that Paris song, 'The Boulevard of Bwoken Dweams'—"

"And crying all over the place!"

"Everybody's looking at him but he don't care, he goes right on reciting poetry and yelling his head off."

"I gave him a cigar Sunday night and he almost choked on it. You shoulda seen him smoking that cigar! He he he!"

"What a good kid he is, though, you know?"

"Yeah—Alex is a damn good kid. A little crazy but the best damn kid in the world."

"He's got a heart, you know?"

"Yeah."

"Where is he now?"

"Oh, he's probably home writing poetry. Don't worry, you'll hear every line of it Saturday night!"

"That crazy bastart Alex!"

One day that Summer Alex took Peter to his house and introduced him to his mother, telling her in Greek that he was a dear friend of his and a good boy to his own mother, whereupon the sorrowful old woman clasped young Martin by the hand and stood gazing at him with tears in her eyes—as though she was receiving him into the family—while some of Alex's sisters stood behind with a joyous yet mournful air, and the whole ramshackle house seemed to brood all around with a dark ecstasy, something was dreaming wildly in the corners, something melancholy and griefstricken lurked in the very odors of cooking and in the old furniture in the dank front room and in the lopsided porch out front where the children were chattering and screaming at each other.

One day Alex stopped on the sidewalk when they were walking past a little crippled boy in a wheelchair, and he began crying. Peter asked him what was the matter.

"But don't you see the brotherhood of man in that little boy's eyes? Oh, don't you see?" he choked convulsively.

And Peter the grave, plain-mannered, unobtrusive, football-playing young American boy could only stand there and be struck by the wonder of such a heart in a human being, and at the same time feel a burning embarrassment because it was all so demonstrative and tortured, somehow all so unreal.

"You don't understand!" Alex kept saying.

"But I do understand—it's only that . . . that you don't have to show your feelings that way, people will just think you're crazy."

"Let them think whatever they wish!" Alex cried proudly. "I'll always do what my heart tells me to do, and to the devil with what people will say."

"But other people feel like crying when they see things like that," said Peter angrily, "but they don't go around showing off."

"Showing off!—you have the cruelty to stand there and tell me that I'm showing off! No! you don't understand!"

"But I do!"

"I have feelings that other people don't have. Can I help it? Can I help it?" shouted Alex.

"But other people *do* have those feelings! I have them too!"

"No, no, no. Not like I have, Pete. Not like I have—"

"Pig's ass!" muttered young Martin.

"No, no, no! And I don't mean it as insulting, but no one in the world can feel the way I do when I see a crippled little boy, or a sick old woman, or someone dead in a coffin! Don't you see? The brotherhood of man appears to me in all its heartbreaking glory, and then everyday life suddenly doesn't mean anything any more! I just see the soul of the whole whole world, nothing else! What do I care about what people do! Oh, Pete! Pete! If only you knew what goes on in my soul!"

They often argued because there was a powerful division in their personalities and backgrounds and upbringing that could have separated them before their friendship could grow. But Peter was always wonderingly aware of the essential fury of Alex's really sensitive heart. He knew he was a good-hearted and generous boy, and Alex was always aware of the underlying tenderness and understanding in Peter himself, and they stuck together. For there was also great exuberance, affection, and sheer gladsomeness in their friendship, they were young and hopeful of everything. They got boisterously drunk with the gang and everything was all right.

That Summer Peter saw very little of his brother Francis, who had begun to spend more time around Boston with his new acquaintances after his first year at Harvard. Joe, of course, was away, and Peter's only contact with him was through writing. One of Joe's postcards that Summer said:

> Howdy Pard, I'm sure glad to hear from you and know that you're well. Don't be so damn tight with your letters—use more paper and more than one paragraph. Give me the lowdown on the boys and the goings on. Adios, Joe.

It was postmarked "Sundance, Wyoming," where Joe was working on a ranch now.

In September Peter packed up again, said good-bye to his family—this time with more cheer and self-confidence than when he left for prep school the year before—and he started off for his first year of college feeling that everything was opening up for him, feeling himself grow stronger by the hour and more "experienced" in the ways of the world. He was now embarking on a greater adventure—a big college in a big city: he was going to the University of Pennsylvania.

[5]

AND WHAT DOES the rain say at night in a small town, what does the rain have to say? Who walks beneath dripping melancholy branches listening to the rain? Who is there in the rain's million-needled blurring splash, listening to the grave music of the rain at night, September rain, September rain, so dark and soft? Who is there listening to steady level roaring rain all around, brooding and listening and waiting, in the rain-washed, rain-twinkled dark of night?

What do little children think when it rains on the roof all night, on gable-top and turret? What do little boys write in their diaries? What does little Mickey say tonight?

"Rain today. No school. Played in my room all day. Ole Charley and me played games in my room tonight. Gee, it's raining."

How does the rain needle softly on the waters, and roll with the old river in darkness? Who walks along the river listening to the rain? Alexander Panos—he walks the town at night in sheets of shrouded rain.

"And I know that I shall die young, I know that I shall die . . ."

In his room, in the feverish white light of the bulb, in the littered room of papers and books, he writes at his desk, he writes to Peter at Penn, and the rain patters on the windowpane, the rain beads his windowpane and rolls softly like tears. . . .

"Pete, old friend, don't think me insane, but I know, I *know* that I shall die young, I know I shall die— And yet I am not sad, no, I am not sad— Here tonight it is raining in Galloway—and the nostalgic reverie of old songs returns—'April in Paris,' Peter, and 'April Showers' and 'These Foolish Things' and 'In My Solitude'— And why do these songs return to me always, and so many others— 'Jalousie' and 'Dark Eyes' and that 'Boulevard of Broken Dreams'— The oldies stealing back to haunt me in the faint melody above the pitter-pattering rain—"

The pattering drone, the lull, the drowse of water falling, and all the thousand little rain feet in vast and twinkled dark, and all the old gaunt houses waiting beneath the trees, with dripping weeping eaves, and huge rotted sea-smells of rain all around—and the river bulging slowly—

—Don't forget to close your window before you go to bed, Ruth!
—Pretty wet outside, hey, Ma!
—Gee, it's raining.

Foggy rain falling on Galloway, Galloway dark at night, the streetlamps dripping—rain spearing down the darkness, splashing in the street—the vast million-twinkled rainsplash all around, all around—and the old wagon in the rain, the soggy rag in mud, the tin can tinkling in the alley—and the town sleeping in the rain, and the old dark river there—what did it say? What did it say?

Old Ernest Berlot the barber lies abed listening to the rain, it splatters and shatters on the courtyard, it drums and roars, vast, vast, and God, but it's strange, he remembers so much, and God, but he feels sad and old.

Splashing rain, splattering, dark and wet, in all the puddles and cobblestones and gutters, and this immense old silence in the town, all thoughts rain-drowned, mute, and dark . . .

—So like I say, I always thought Bob was a pretty nice fella, you know? After all is said and done, you know?

—Give me another cup of coffee while you're there, will you, Jimmy?

—Yup. Hey, gee! It's really coming down now, ain't it? Look at it coming down out there!

—It's really raining all right.

—Gee!

All of life is soft and dark now, and the huge and shrouded rain falls everywhere, in warm and rain-blue dark:

It falls in the muddy loam beneath the pines, in the marshy bottoms of rainwashed earth, in the secret thicket of the wet woods at night, in the brooding hidden ditches, the culverts trickling, in the mystery and darkness of rain-haunted woods and heavy-hanging trees at night, in puddled earth, in rain-darkened bracken at the end of the road.

And the rain falls sleeping on swarded meadows all greendark and damp, it falls washing on old stonewalls, and weeping on marble stone, and flowers there, and wreaths, it seeps and washes into every secret deep.

It falls on highways too. George Martin comes driving home in the rain-hushed midnight hour, his lights go reaching across the slanted rainfall, across the asphalt glistening wet, and the rain spears in his window, the windshield wiper blurs and clicks, blurs and clicks, blurs and clicks. . . . What wonder and strangeness is in his heart? What does the sudden sight of the town all desolate and rain-blurred there, its lonely lights haloing in darkness, its empty streets, its houses brooding under trees, what does the sight of the town rain-drowned and silent do to him? What awaits him there?

All thoughts, all hearts are melted softly, and asking rainy questions, and waiting and listening all night long.

The river swells and elbows darkly through folded shores, all bulging, all softened by rain.

Still the shrouds of rain come down.

[6]

FRANCIS WAS BEGINNING his second year at Harvard that Autumn—a brilliant student handling all his courses with ease, occasionally lagging in his duties but easily catching up in a few nights' work, moving along towards his degree with an indifferent and rather lonesome air. He had no goal in mind. Like most commuter students at the college he never mingled with the others as much as he would have liked to, and often when walking around the Yard he had the nagging uncomfortable feeling that he didn't "belong" at all. He went home every night by painful circuitous routes, taking the subway to North Station in Boston, then the old smoky rattling trunkline train to Galloway, and finally the bus from the depot to his family's house. He carried his books with him on these daily journeys, and sulked miserably, and arrived home tired and discontented.

He considered it emblematical of his uninteresting fate that of all the people he could have known at Harvard, it was a commuting student who attached himself to him. The student made it a regular habit of sitting next to Francis on the train and conversing eagerly till getting off at a little country town. He was a strange, shapeless kind of person, named Walter Wickham. He staggered under the weight of scholarly tomes, always attired in the same tight-fitting suit, the same black shoes, the same battered hat, always wearing an expression of absorbed eagerness and zeal.

Francis wanted to know the "least objectionable" Harvard men —this is the way he actually mused on it—the ones who *looked* like Harvard men, who spoke and acted and lived like Harvard men. He saw them everywhere on the campus, in the lecture rooms, on the Cambridge streets, elegant, casual, well-dressed, a little facetious and exclusive, always suave-looking and composed and luxuriously belonging to the place the way he never could.

He wanted to find some way of earning money so he could afford to live on the campus itself; sometimes he almost wished he was a football player like Peter and receive the various benefits accruing from that status. His father paid his tuition but the rest was a little too much for the Martin budget now. Meanwhile he scrimped and saved money for trips to visit Wilfred Engels in New York.

"Ah, well," he thought, "there's a saying about wearing old shoes gracefully." He thought of young Samuel Johnson who had hurled out of the window at Oxford a pair of new shoes left at his door by some charitable nobleman. "Some philanthropist from a middlewest brewery clan may leave a can of beer at my door—or a barrel, perhaps, which I could go about in."

It amused him to consider that he was no better than a pauper in what was universally regarded a rich man's college. And when Wickham habitually rushed up to him on the train and dropped his load of books on the seat in an inelegant, slapdash, high-school way, Francis was always rather amused—embarrassed also, perhaps—but amused. Wilfred Engels was his one contact with "interesting" people, but Engels' stay in New York was still indefinite and Francis was not brash enough to look up the people he had met at Engels' parties.

Meanwhile, Peter had broken his leg in a freshman football game against Columbia that Fall. For several weeks he went hobbling around the Penn campus with a crutch and a plaster cast on his lower leg. Though he looked a little drawn and disheveled from the discomfort of his injury, he nevertheless began enjoying college life and his new-found leisure tremendously.

Alexander Panos came joyously from Galloway to visit him, and they took a train to New York for the weekend, spending avid days and nights exploring the great city together. They drank beer in longshoremen's bars, stood vigil on Brooklyn Bridge in the dead of night, visited museums and theaters, sailed on the ferry to Staten Island, and quoted poetry at dawn in scraggly streets. The ardent young Greek from Galloway, happier than he had ever been in his life, stood on the parapets of parks bawling great cries to the rising sun, while Peter grinned beside him.

One Saturday night they were crossing the cobblestones underneath dark girders of the Third Avenue el, Peter limping with the aid of crutches. An illkempt man came staggering out of the shadows of a doorway holding out a cigarette butt in a gesture demanding that someone light him up. And at the same moment they saw two men strolling nearby who were, inexplicably, Wilfred Engels and Francis Martin. Francis looked dark and severe in the New York night.

"This is crazy!" yelled Peter. "What are you doing here?"

"You've already made a new friend, I see!" laughed Engels, rushing over, delighted.

Peter was leaning on the crutches holding out his cigarette, to which the shabby stranger bent solicitously, nervously, trembling, muttering incoherent speeches: "Fine-looking boy! Too bad, too bad, you hurt yourself. Hurt your leg, huh?" He held Peter's arm with a long, bony, shivering hand.

"Well, how are you, football player!" greeted Engels, joyfully extending his hand to Peter. "I see you've become a martyr in the great American cause for bigger and better concrete stadiums!" He pumped Peter's hand vigorously, and then shook hands with Alex Panos, who was flushed and pleased to be meeting a "real sophisticated New Yorker" for the first time. Francis, displeased somewhat, stood back watching in silence.

The hobo continued to stare intently at Peter during the flurry of greetings and conversations, and went right on talking incoherently. "Even if you hurt yourself—I wish I was you! No kidding! Fine-looking boy—young—got your life ahead of you. You got your health just the same—"

"Hey now," cried Peter, pressing the man's shoulder and laughing, "you don't look *un*healthy to me! What've you got to be so gloomy about? You got a couple of drinks in you, you feel good, don't you? You've got just about as much money as I have, which is none, isn't that so?"

The man flinched back, as though he had received some profound insult yet wanted to avoid embarrassing Peter.

"I'm not bumming money off you!" he yelled anxiously. "I only wanted a light! I'm no bum, I'm no bum!" He looked around at everyone and nodded his own eager confirmation, keeping his grip on Peter's arm.

"I don't mean that," said Peter. "I mean you talk as if I were a happy-go-lucky millionaire or something. I'll be down on the Bowery with you before long, don't worry!"

The man was ravenously excited. He was getting more attention than he had had for years. He stood there by a sooty girder weaving and grinning and showing broken yellow teeth, looking up and down the street with an expression of idiotic joyousness, gazing at them benignly, cocking his head one side sentimentally, examining them all with the fervent enthusiasm of an old friend. Suddenly he heaved himself up to full height and cried: "I've got my health, huh? Is that what you say?"

"You look all right to me."

"Okay," he cried, poking Peter in the ribs, laughing savagely. "You have it your way!" And suddenly he pulled up his pant leg and held up his foot for all to see. There was a dirty bandage flopping over his ankle, and above it a ghastly sore surrounded by shining swollen coal-black flesh all the way up to the knee. He held it there, swaying drunkenly and grinning with inquisitive slyness.

Wilfred Engels gasped in horror: "Good heavens! Could that be gangrene?"

"That looks terrible!" cried Peter. "How did you get that?"

"I stepped through a manhole on Second Avenue last week. It's getting worse, huh?"

"It's all infected! You've got to go down to Bellevue and have it cut!"

"Cut? Whattayoumean *cut?*" the man demanded, with a look of fear.

"I mean cauterized!" yelled Peter with a kind of nervous relief. "Go right down now! Here's a nickel for the subway!"

"I've *got* a nickel!" yelled the poor man indignantly. "You think they'll fix it?" he asked anxiously now.

"Sure! You gotta go down right now!"

Engels and Francis had moved off to the other side of the sidewalk. "Come along, come along!" Engels called out now to Peter and Alex. "There's no sense standing around there, let's go have a drink."

"Don't mind me! Go ahead with your friends," cried the man, gripping Peter's arm again and pushing him back and forth slightly. "Don't mind me, I'm nothing, I'll be dead in a couple of days."

"No!" cried Peter. "Take this nickel and go down to the ward, they'll clean it. Take this quarter too. Eat! You need some food, some energy, or that thing'll get you! You can't go around like this!"

"Peter, are we going?" called Francis. "Please! Let's go now."

"Now go and do as we say," said Peter, shoving a coin in the man's side pocket. "Isn't that right, Al?" he demanded. "Shouldn't he do that?"

"By all means," said Panos in a deep, sad, grave voice. He had been watching everything in silence.

"You think I ought to?"

"Right now, man, right now!" And Peter started off on his crutches. And presently the old hobo weaved off down the street, under a streetlamp and around the corner, and he was gone.

"There he goes," said Peter, "back to a *bar*. He'll just drink up my thirty cents. I shouldn't have given it to him. Geezus, do you realize that man's going to be dead in a couple of days, just like he said?" The two boys stared at each other gravely. "Did you take a last look at him? He looks like death already, it's in the rings around his eyes. The poor old bastard."

"I understand perfectly what you mean," said young Panos slowly and sadly.

"It's horrible!" cried Engels, coming over. "You shouldn't have touched him, God knows what he has."

"That man will be found dead by the cops in a few days," mused Peter. "They'll find him on the sidewalk all black up to his eyes."

"Ugh!" said Francis. "I don't see how a man can let himself go like that."

"The streets are full of such men," said Engels. "But at least," he went on, "you've done your good Boy Scout deed for today, Peter. Oh, you football-playing Samaritan!" he chuckled richly, pressing Peter's shoulder.

"It takes money to be a Samaritan," said Peter.

"How can a man let himself go like that," said Francis again, "staggering around the streets, drinking, with a leg like that? He doesn't seem to mind anything."

They took a cab to a bar uptown, and sat at the clean mahogany bar, in the dim lights that glowed from behind glittering bottle displays. There was a low fulsome murmur of engrossed voices all around, soft music, the smell of clean leather and Scotch and soda.

"Well now," said Engels jovially, "that was a little touch of the lower depths, wasn't it? I can see, Peter, that this is the sort of thing you and your young friend here are fond of exploring in New York." He paid for the drinks, as he had for the cab, and waved their contributions away. "What do you think, Francis? Does all this appeal to you? Should we join the boys in these forays into the highly cultural parts of the city?

"Tell me," he demanded, tapping Peter's knee, staring at him gravely, "where are you going tonight, for instance? What are you going to do?"

"We weren't thinking of anything special—"

"What? No waterfront saloons with sawdust on the floor? No all-night movies on Times Square?" He laughed, hugely amused. "What do you say, Francis? Doesn't it sound like the *real* thing?"

"Well—" said Francis, pursing his lips. He was not really sure whether Engels was being ironic. The other two boys were grinning foolishly, completely abashed by this banter of Engels, which seemed so urbane, disturbing and richly droll.

It was not strange that these boys from Galloway were somewhat impressed by Engels that night—all three of them, the moody discontented Francis, the brash, amazed, and delighted young Peter, and the ravenously excitable young Alex Panos. They were sitting in a cocktail lounge with him in the great rare city of their youthful hopes—New York, the unbelievable and miraculous place of places that had been the lore of their hearts since childhood, the road's end of young aspirations and secret boyish plans. Engels, somehow, was a man who belonged to it and seemed to understand and own it all.

After that weekend Francis decided to come and live in New York as soon as he finished school. Someday, like Engels, he too would have an apartment, with friends and associates in for cocktails and dinner each Saturday night. They would talk about the newest books and plays and art exhibits, exchange gossip, meet new people, encounter new ideas, and partake in all the thousand excitements that made up the brilliant surge and rush and style of life in New York. It was a hint of his heart's desires.

[7]

PETER WENT HOME that December for Christmas week.

He sat in the train wide awake at dawn, and leaned his head wearily against the back of the seat with his face turned to the frosted window in grave attention. The Boston-bound express sped eastward in the frozen Rhode Island dawn, and he suddenly sensed a new joy swelling up in him, something strange, something exultant, something that came to him from the scene outside the window where the sun had just appeared on the gray horizon and was spreading a cold rose light over the snowy fields and lonely farmhouses and over the forests of ragged birch that were everywhere slowly turning away from the sweep of the train's progress, all of it remote and beautiful through blurs and streaks of blown snow and flying steam that whipped past his window from the locomotive. He realized, almost with a shock, that nothing could be more beautiful to him than these stretches of snow and these woods all tainted pink from the dawn. It all belonged to his own New England; he was rediscovering his earth, which he had been away from too long, it seemed.

Warm little kitchen lights were coming on in the isolated farmhouses out there below the high immense skies, shining through pale mist across the snow, twinkling like messages, filling him with the wonder and delight of coming home, reminding him of cozy warmth and snugness in blankets of dawn with windows rattling in the wind and the house full of smells of oatmeal, toast, and coffee in New England winter mornings.

What was it to which he was returning? What had he left behind only a few months ago as inconsequential? Now it came back to him with the full impact of discovery, brooding out there in the stark frosty air. He wanted it back for himself again and for always. It was his land, his own land.

The locomotive whistle howled across the snowy woods, again and again, and each time it blew he was overwhelmed with an indescribable joy and longing for home. It was all there, the wild, crude birch forests and the orderly fields surrounded by stonewalls, with the lonely-looking farmhouses standing desolate alongside their woodsheds and wells and barns, casting long shadows on the snow, and he knew that the farmers were getting up and putting on their shoes by the kitchen stove, their wives pouring water in the coffee pot, the chickens waking and preening in warm fusty coops while the rooster crowed in the snow.

It was the morning of a December day in 1940, he was eighteen years old, a football star at Penn, and he was coming home for Christmas.

After the first months of his freshman year with its dark campus at night when soft golden light shone in library and lecture-room windows, after his wanderings in New York and Philadelphia, he was now returning to something wild and crude, to deep snow and raw gray skies, a flight of dark birds over the pines, to ice-locked brooks and kids skating and shouting in the frosty air, to old woodstoves in saloons and men in boots and jackets, to the New England of towns and woods and snowstorms and deep star-sparkling nights. He realized now with strong conviction that nothing which could be taught him in the university could ever touch the wild joy in his heart, the plain powerful knowledge of things, the boyish glee and wonder he felt now as the train bore him back to the weather and veritable landscape of his soul. He wished that he would never have to leave Galloway again. Nothing that the university taught him could match for him the power and wisdom of his own kind of people, who lived and drew their breath in this rugged land joyous with tidings of towns, plain, homely, genuine and familiar, that he saw rolling by him again.

Restless, feverishly happy, Peter walked through the train as it sped clackety-clacking on the last lap from Providence to Boston. The coaches were filled with sunlight, men were awake and reading morning newspapers, the sparkling snowy countryside swept by outside—and it was then, with the shock of strangeness and half-remembrance, half-prescience, all half-dream and half-reality, that he saw his brother Joe sitting casually alone at the other end of a coach.

Joe—sunbrowned, fierce, meditative and watchful at the window, with a little half grin of anticipation on his lips, ragged like a hobo with long hair and dirty workclothes and a tattered canvas bag at his feet, coming home at last from his tremendous roamings, coming home incredibly on the same train as Peter in the same snowy world of morning.

Joe looked up casually—spurting smoke from his nostrils, full of thoughts—and they looked at each other dumbly. Joe frowned with surprise and disbelief, Peter's heart pounded and he hurried over.

Joe suddenly let out a wild whoop of amazement.

"Don't tell me it's YOU!"

They swung each other around on gripped hands and pounded each other and blushed with tears of embarrassment and joy, and passengers in the coach turned and smiled.

"You didn't tell me you were coming home for Christmas! Geezus, Joe, where you been?"

"Sit down! Sit down!" yelled Joe. He whacked Peter one on the back that sent him staggering down on the seat, he joyfully punched him, and shoved him back and forth. "Fancy meeting you on a *train!* I just got on this thing in New London a couple of hours ago! I've been hitch-hiking up from New Orleans till I won money in a crap game in New London last night!" With an agile and anxious movement he held out a light to Peter's cigarette and his own, inhaled smoke prodigiously, blew it out his nose in sharp spurts, impatient and absorbed and feverish with excitement.

"What happened?" asked Peter with shining eyes.

"You mean the whole trip? The whole year and a half? Man, I've been everywhere!"

"Wow—"

"I'm *tired,* Pete, I want to rest, I'm sick of roaming around. Wait'll the family hears about this! What about *you?* What's this I heard about your leg? Ma wrote me a letter and told me you hurt your leg!"

"Against Columbia frosh," laughed Peter. "It was nothing, just a small bone cracked, it's all right now, good as new."

"What about next year? Will you be able to play next year?"

"I tell you it's good as new!"

"You sure?" cried Joe anxiously.

"Sure I'm sure."

"It better be!" cried Joe, intent and troubled.

"I'll bet you've been *all* over!"

"Ah, I'll tell you all about it later! Right now we'll hit Boston and have a few beers, hah? Like I told you, I won a few shekels in New London. This calls for a *celebration!*" He wetted his lips, then caught Peter's eye again. "We ought to hit Galloway around eleven o'clock and surprise the old lady, hey, Petey? Wait till she sees both of us waltz in, huh? And the old man!" He whacked

Peter jubilantly again as the train rushed on to Boston, and the day was almost insane with joy.

In a few minutes the train was slowing down to the great South Station. They jubilantly gathered their things and hurried out across the huge, dark, smoke-smelling shed, out among the crowds that filled the vast marble floor of the station, and then out on Atlantic Avenue with taxicabs bleating and maneuvering about for fares that poured out of the station, and heavy trucks rumbling by on the cobblestones, policemen's whistles shrilling, cars and busses swoshing by over the dirty snow with tire-chains beating and ringing. The sharp frosty air of Boston with its smoke and sea-smells sent shivers up and down Peter's spine.

They hurried along the narrow crowded streets towards North Station, hitting a half-dozen bars on the way and gulping down beers. They were swaying and almost staggering up to North Station, buying tickets, exultantly boarding the dusty rattling trunk-line train to Galloway. They rolled over the white countryside beside long stretches of forest and field and icy pond, and finally, almost suddenly—to Peter who was half-drunk and chattering eagerly—they were clacking on a bridge over the Concord River and the conductor was calling:

"Gallo-way, Gallo-way."

All of Peter's emotions rose marveling in his soul, and a film of tears came to his eyes. He was home and his brother Joe was miraculously at his side. The locomotive whistle was howling at the gates of Galloway where years ago as a boy he had lain in his room listening for it in the night dreaming of voyages and great personal events, and he knew that now the sound of the whistle was carrying across the rooftops of his hometown, clear across the river to his family's house on the old road, and he knew that he would never grow old and weary of his life.

High and hilarious they started off on foot from the depot, and soon they were striding up the hill over icy ruts on Galloway Road engaged in gleeful conversations in the wind. There it was, the big wind-belabored weather-sheltered house, their home. In a moment Joe broke into a run and went sprinting over the snow-deep lawn, hurdling over bushes and running around to the side of the house to the windows of the living room where he crouched furtively and peeked in. Peter followed.

"Duck!" whispered Joe. "I see them—Ma and Rosey. I knew they'd be in there. Look at 'em, knitting away like fiends!"

Peter peeked in, and he saw his mother and Rosey sitting in old brown wicker chairs rocking back and forth, their hands fluttering swiftly over needle and yarn. He heard the mumble of their voices; and a bright patch of sunlight fell on them, illuminating their meditative, placid, blue-eyed faces in a cheerful winter morning brilliance that sent pangs of joy through him. The bright chintz curtains, the shiny top of the mahogany table, the clean smooth linoleum on the floor, the gayly colored cushions on the wicker settee, all of it was just as he had expected. Kewpie the cat lay dozing warmly in an old sweater in the corner.

When Joe began to tap on the window-pane the women looked up sharply with the inquiring, incisive air women have when they're home and there is a knock from outside. When they saw who it was, they turned to each other that swift glance of stunned prophecy. They rose from their chairs with a cry and came scurrying to the door. Joe bounded up the steps. In a moment he was being smothered with kisses, the women were crying: "It's Joey, it's Joey! He's come back! Oh, my God!"

Peter came after him into the warmth and the smells of boiling meat and vegetables that filled the house. It made him furiously hungry, wildly glad.

"And Petey!" Rose whooped with delight. "The two of them together!" She grabbed Peter in her powerful arms and kissed him violently on the cheek.

"My Petey's home too!" called out the mother. "Oh, this is too much, my two boys together, my boys are home," and when Peter kissed her she threw her arms around both her sons and hugged for dear life.

"I'm hungry, Ma!" yelled Joe with a shout of laughter. "What's that chow I smell! What've we got for dinner?"

"Oh," cried Mrs. Martin beside herself with uncontrollable joy, "I can't believe it. I was expecting my Petey home from college, he wrote me he was coming, but you, Joey, you never told me you were coming home. Now he's come home for Christmas! Rosey!"

"Joe, you old son of a gun, where the hell have you been!" cried Rose in her high raucous yell of greeting. "And don't give us any of your lies!"

"Never mind that, I'm hungry!"

"He's hungry again. He's always hungry. Get away from me, you old bum. I'm all out of breath!"

And they both laughed their high whooping laughter.

Then they all went into the kitchen, and the mother, with a flushed and anxious expression on her face, wiping tears from her eyes, was at the refrigerator pulling out great quantities of food from her larder. "I've got some nice Maine sardines here," she said, "and here's some bacon, eggs, ham—and here's some hamburger steak nice and lean I got yesterday, and milk, and here's some lettuce and tomatoes. Do you want a nice salad? And some beer if you want it, some fruit salad, pineapples, peaches. And here, do you want some beans? I baked them Saturday, they're still very good. Here's some peanut butter, jam—"

"Whoa! wait a minute, Ma!" cried Joe, running up and putting his arms around her. "We don't want all that. How about a cup of hot cocoa, huh?"

And Rose was standing at her mother's side peering anxiously into the refrigerator.

"And here's some nice cheese I just got at Wietelmann's," the mother went on, oblivious of everything in the world except that her sons had been starving to death away from home. "Oh, and if you want a snack before dinner, if you want a little lunch before dinner I can fry you some of this nice tenderloin steak—and I've got a few lamb chops left if you'd like that. Just say what you want. And here's some nice canned asparagus tips and ripe olives. Oh, and I've got plenty of Vermont maple syrup here. Do you want me to make you some pancakes?" And as she said this, all the food was coming out of the refrigerator and being piled on the kitchen table.

"No, no," cried Joe, "just make us a cup of hot cocoa! We're not hungry, I was just kidding, we ate in Boston!"

"Unless you want a nice bowl of peasoup?" the mother inquired anxiously. "I made it last Friday, it's very good. Or maybe you'd like to try some of the boiled dinner that's on the stove?"

"No, no, Ma! Cup of hot chocolate! Hey, Rose, tell her we ain't hungry!"

But Rose herself was not easily to be dissuaded. She crossed the kitchen floor with the heavy step of a pachyderm, the whole room trembled and a rack of dishes in the pantry rattled and jingled, she said: "You're going to eat something with that cocoa! How about a couple roast-beef sandwiches?"

"Yes," said the mother, "there's that, from Sunday's roast. Or you could have—" She paused awhile as she hauled out a big roast of beef from the ice box and stacked it beside everything else on the table, then she began to rub her lips meditatively. "Rose!" she finally said. "What else is there?"

"Ain't that enough?" called Joe. "Hey, Ma!"—and he rushed up and kissed her again. "That's enough, hear?"

She wiped a tear from her eye and shook her head sorrowfully. "Oh, Joey, I've been worrying about you, so long. Where have you been?"

"I worked on ranches, ships, all that kind of thing, and I worked hard and ate like a hog and I saw the most wonderful places. Look at me! Look how tan I got!"

"And you, Petey?" she wailed softly, turning to Peter with one hand still clinging to Joe's arm. "Your leg, your poor little leg!"

"It ain't so *little!*" called Joe with a wry grin. "He's all right now! He was a big star on the freshman team at Penn, Ma, a future all-American is what he is! Hey, Pete?"

And Peter began dancing around the room to show his mother that his leg was healed up and well. "See, Ma?" he cried. "It's nothing, it's good as new. I told you in my letters a million times . . . didn't I, Rose!"

"Ah! he's all right," said Rose, coming up to Peter and throwing her arms around him. "He's all right, the little bum."

"Oh, my goodness, I'm so happy I don't know what to do," sighed the mother finally. She took down an apron from a hook and wound it on. "I've never been so happy in all my life. I knew something was going to happen, Rose, I told you I felt something, you remember when I told you that I had a dream, I—" And she fell silent, shaking her head, reflective and inscrutable in her own grave joyous thoughts, and vigorously began cutting bread and getting the lunch together.

"You see?" said Rose, nudging Joe in the ribs. "Watch her . . ."

"Aw, Ma knows, Ma knows," said Joe, chuckling, and then he brought his hand down on his knee with a resounding slap: "We're going to have a big celebration!" he cried. "Hey, Rosey, ain't we? We'll get drunk New Year's Eve on a nice big quart of good Scotch, huh? We'll get the old man piffed again! Hyah! hyah! hyah!"

Then he threw himself back in the chair and emitted a loud happy sigh. "Home again, what a deal! Bring on that food! From now on I'm just gonna sit back and take it easy just like it was when I was a kid. No more flophouses and bunkhouses and going broke and scrounging around for me. . . . Nosir! Home again!" In a few moments his mother had prepared a stack of thick roast-beef sandwiches, and Rose followed bearing a kettle of steaming hot chocolate. All four of them fell to eating and drinking elatedly, in an atmosphere that made the two brothers realize more than ever that they were home again.

[8]

LATER IN THE DAY Peter went upstairs to the attic to find some old books packed in a trunk. Up there, for purposes of study and solitude, Francis had arranged himself a little room in a partition of the attic at the back of the house where the east gable protruded from the sloping roof. Rose had said Francis was not in, but Peter peeked in and was surprised to find him seated at his desk turning over the pages of a paper-backed book. The slant-ceilinged little room was stuffy and close from the heat of a radiator hissing steadily at the valve, warmish with a faint odor of wine.

"How are you, Mr. Bones!" yelled Peter.

Francis looked up blandly. "Hello there. What are *you* doing around here?"

"Didn't you know I was coming home for Christmas?"

"Yes," said Francis vaguely, "but I didn't know it would be so soon."

Peter sat down, and lit a cigarette, and instantly jumped up nervously. "What's that book you've got there? Oh! It's in French!" He took the paper-backed volume and scanned the title—"*Les faux monnayeurs*. What is that?"

"It's a novel by André Gide."

"What's it all about?"

"What's it about? Well, I suppose it's about the falsity of people in particular, and everything in general."

"Where did you get the book?"

"Ah . . . why, I got it right here in Galloway, in the public library."

"You did!" cried Peter. "Oh, yes, now I remember—they have a shelf of French literature in the back over by the shelf for cook-books!"

Francis had produced a bottle of wine from a desk drawer and was wiping off some glasses.

"What's that . . . *wine!*" said Peter. "I'll be damned."

Francis glanced at Peter curiously. He cleared his throat and said, "It was rather a surprise to find Gide stuck in there by your cookbook shelf amongst the Zolas and Dumas and Hugos of French morality."

"It was?" burst out Peter with a sheepish and confused grin.

"Well, yes. Not, of course, that it's to be held against the city fathers of Galloway. . . ."

"Why's that?"

"Well," said Francis wryly, "I don't know exactly why's that, but maybe you could say that to insinuate the notorious Monsieur Gide among the most respectable and honored French writers would constitute . . . well, you know—"

"Oh, I see!" cried Peter. "And what was this guy Gide notorious for? What did he do?"

Francis cleared his throat again. "Well . . . he was noted for his monstrous perversity of character, his monstrous opinion of bourgeois Europe, for one thing. Ah, why, he's even been considered by some of the most valorous pedagogues of French letters as a . . . as a seditious churl—"

"Yes?"

"And, ah, in some quarters he's regarded as an unnatural corrupter of French youth." And with a kind of lonely disconsolate glee Francis began to chuckle as though somewhat overcome by the sound of the words.

He uncorked the wine bottle with a gallant flourish and poured Peter a glass. "Here, try some of this, it isn't exactly the very best—but it's not too bad."

Peter took a long gulp and nodded eagerly. "And this Gide . . . why do you read him? I mean all the business about the churl and all that. I mean—*you* know!"

Francis smiled. "What *do* you mean?"

"How should I know? What does he *write* about?"

"People."

"And they're *all* false? Do you think that everybody in the world is false? Do *you* think the world is false?"

"Do I?"

"Yeah! What's your philosophy? Do you have one?" blurted Peter, blushing.

Francis cleared his throat, with a somewhat askance look out the window, and a little frown of amazement, although he was somewhat pleased also.

"For instance!" cried Peter, holding up a finger rigidly. "Just tell me one 'for-instance'! We have a guy at Penn who does nothing but sit around drinking coffee and talking philosophy and he's always saying 'for-instance' and showing what he means. He's pretty smart too."

"Well, you just don't pull for-instances out of the hat. *You* give me a for-instance, for instance . . ."

Peter doubled up with a crazy laugh and threw himself down on the chair. "No, wait!" he cried. "I always wanted to know what you think. We're taking philosophy this year. I have a lot of ideas myself but I never can put them together nice and logical. My philosophy is that you can't explain the world. It's too big and it's too crazy and sometimes it's funny and most of the time it's . . . strange."

"In the first place," said Francis, pursing his lips, "I don't believe in mysteries. Obviously there's mystery in your *strangeness* idea. As for the world being funny, I don't know. If nightmares are funny . . ."

"Is that what Gide says?" said Peter almost sullenly, with sudden curiosity.

"I don't suppose so—perhaps it's taken for granted. He's just a typical European intellectual. His concern is with truth and the stupidity of the world . . . and his enemy is society, I suppose."

"High society?"

"No, people . . . everybody."

"So *everybody* is false?"

"I didn't say that. He just understands that men have organized themselves in an insane way that's almost impossible to untangle and almost too much for the man of sensibility to bear. . . ."

"Yeah?"

"And finally, on top of that, there's the nightmare in all its clear full contours"—Francis mused with a smile—"at all times too, unexpected and vast." Francis got up to close the window, which was open an inch at the bottom, and came back and gently lowered himself back in the chair, where for a moment he sat in absolute lassitude, with his thin hands drooping over the edge of the chair as though they were broken at the wrist. He stared emptily out on the sunny snow-flashing day.

"Here's a for-instance!" cried Peter. "Take today. See all the snow out there and the icicles on the houses and the sun shining, and the kids sliding down the hill having a big time. Look down the road there, here comes Charley and Mickey home from school. See them? Charley on the bike, Mickey walking beside him. They come all the way from school and now they're hungry, they're ready for a big meal. Look at the pretty girl down there sliding with her kid brother on the sled. Take all that. What do you think about it?"

"What do I *think?*" laughed Francis. "Gad!"

"Yes! I mean, do you enjoy it?"

"But that's utterly beside the point."

"No, it's only a for-instance," cried Peter, almost pained. "See? It's another philosophy! If you didn't have eyes and if you didn't have feelings and senses all that would be still out there, but you wouldn't know about it, you'd be sitting here, it would be out there and you wouldn't know a thing about it. You wouldn't be able to *enjoy* anything—"

"That would be sort of nice," murmured Francis faintly.

"No!" laughed Peter savagely.

"Well, now, here's *another* philosophy. Take that day of yours outside, and turn it into a night, a cold night—it isn't day all the time, is it? That's only the half of it . . . the other half is night, you know. And so, we have our consciousness of that night and therefore we have our consciousness of the necessary and natural brutishness of things, don't we? And wouldn't it be better, then, if we had no consciousness at all."

"What do you mean?" asked Peter. "The night would be nice, you'd go out and take a nice walk, get some fresh air—"

"I mean the night that's icy blackness. The one you can't live in. The one we have. The *true* one."

"What?" asked Peter, a little embarrassed and stricken by Francis' tone.

"Your winter night . . . all merciless and hopeless, the one that kills you in the end, the one that has no consideration of any human pith or earthly significance except to destroy all of us completely. Tell me about that one. Tell me about your precious *senses* that inform us on the subject—"

"Well, I don't know," mumbled Peter, a little confused.

"They tell you about our crime—"

"What crime?"

"Well, *ours*. They tell you about it in various ways—original sin, Darwinian drive, Freudian unconscious, whatnot . . . But our only crime is that we were *given* that consciousness of yours, isn't it? Without it, I suppose we'd be a large group of innocent louts. It might be better."

"What about the churl man of sensibility?" cried Peter, shrewd, flushed and watchful.

Francis nodded, smiling, almost eagerly. "We strike out at each other automatically, snarling and clawing. That's what they call crime, or sin, that's what we are—sinners. But our only crime is our innocence. Our only responsibility is there, and it is *not* a responsibility. A perfect set-up for the gods, a perfect set-up for the night, and in another sense a perfect set-up for entrenched reaction."

"What a lot of stuff!" yelled Peter, amazed. "How can you believe all that?"

"Isn't it true that all they told you when you were a kid turned out to be a lot of crap? They told you about God as soon as you had Santa Claus in doubt or before, *someone* did. Yet you ought to know by now there's no Godliness anywhere, and there certainly is no God to comfort and watch over us. Maybe you might even, in the sophistication of modern times," he went on, "be forced to admit there *must* be a devil even in spite of the fact there is no God. Certainly the brutality on all sides is evident, all the Godliness must be hiding out somewhere. It's a force, a *weight* of persuasion. And then they told you about love, didn't they? Yet you ought to know by now, really, that it's impossible to love in the middle of so much icy night and unhappiness."

"I don't know . . ." muttered Peter, a little frightened.

"Surely at some time it'll occur to you that love's just a word describing the fiddling around with flattery and deceit that makes you feel a little better for a moment. And then justice. They imprint that word in stone all over the world, on friezes around court-house buildings. Yet you ought to see, or perhaps you sense it now, that justice isn't the concern of men in this world. Men are too unhappy for *that*. You can't blame them, there's no so-called faith, life's too *short* for that, there's no time. The icy blackness doesn't last long, just long enough to choke you and freeze you to death."

"But I don't *believe* it!"

"Why not, if it's the truth."

"I don't know," said Peter. "Why should you believe what those guys say?" he suddenly asked slyly.

"What guys?" cried Francis with an amazed laugh.

"What do you care what *he's* got to say—Gide . . . or guys like Engels."

"Who's talking about *them?*"

Peter stood staring doggedly out the window as though he would lose his persuasion, if Francis were to catch his eye and begin laughing in his strange mirthless way.

But Francis had wearied of the conversation, he was wiping his hands with a towel at the sink in a brisk and absorbed manner, and Rosey downstairs was calling them down to eat.

It was a strange conversation that Peter never forgot.

[9]

IT WAS CHRISTMAS week, and for young Charley it was nothing but troubles.

At fourteen now, he was in the ninth grade in school where his marks were somewhat below average, though not for lack of intelligence. A strange, quiet boy, interested much less in book-learning than in what was to be learned from old rusty automobiles on the junkheap or from the thousand machineries all around him. At home he was the self-reliant, unobtrusive, almost solitary little son who more often than not was to be found in some obscure corner of the house or cellar or garage tinkering meditatively with some gadget that had come to his grave attention. Among his neighborhood pals he was always, by silent and inscrutable consent, the "leader of the gang." This was due, no doubt, to his awesome air of concentration and the way he had of assuming all kinds of responsibilities in the innumerable circumstances that offered themselves in their play. Like his older brother Joe he had the same peculiar mannerisms that hinted of an absorbed self-assurance: he replied to a question only after a brief solemn wetting of the lips, he walked with a long determined stride towards his object, and he gazed at people with the same calm, level, blue-eyed mien of absolute reasonableness, as though nothing could ever faze or mystify him. But unlike Joe, whom he greatly venerated in his quiet way, young Charley was much less gregarious and less lively.

He was in trouble and, to make it worse, he was alone and unwatched in his tribulations. This, however, was just the way he uncompromisingly wanted it. A week earlier, in the company of several other boys with slingshots, he had broken a window in the home of a certain crochety old man well known in the district for his hermit-like and testy disposition. This old man had submitted a formally written report to the police insisting that the culprit, the "young thug," be apprehended and punished at once. Charley heard about this and was scared. All his chums laid low and kept mum and went about for days with secretive, pale airs.

But an efficient motorcycle policeman, known throughout Galloway as Tooey Warner, was assigned to investigate the source of the vandalism, and that was the end. This terrifying policeman spent several days browbeating schoolboys in the neighborhood and eventually found out that Charley had done it, or at least had been the leader of the barrage. That same afternoon, when Charley was coming home from school, the same day his big brothers came home, Tooey Warner roared up on his motorcycle, pulled up to the curb with a screeching skid, took off his glove, yelled, "Come here, you!" and, when Charley came over, the cop slashed the glove across his face with a vicious swipe.

"All right, let's go down to the station, wise guy. Get in!" He gunned the motor with an awful roar and adjusted his goggles.

"But, wait a minute, Mr. Warner!" cried Charley terrified. "I didn't mean to do it, I just shot over some trees and it hit the window. Honest! I'm willing to pay for the window!"

But Tooey Warner never felt that his job was done until he drew repentant tears from his miscreants. Again he slashed Charley across the face with his glove, drawing blood this time with the small steel button on the wrist. He was the most scrupulous and brutal cop on the force. Though it could never be said that he did not display equal intrepidity with regard to adult transgressors of the law, it was household knowledge that the schoolboys were his choice specialty.

"Honest, Mr. Warner!" cried Charley now, a little tearful, realizing somehow that he was expected to cry, "I didn't mean to do it. I can pay for the damages if you let me—!"

"Why you little punk, where would you get the money? Do you know what you did? The damages are nine bucks!" And the cop punctuated this with another sharp slash across Charley's face,

"I can pay for it," said Charley, grimly, in a quiet voice.

Tooey Warner glanced at him with a severe stare of repressed rage, a-tremble with elemental vitality. He had a lot to do that day, he was harried on all sides by his work and his wife and the hatred of almost everybody in town, and suddenly, sighing, his chest almost collapsing, his eyes losing their fire and growing stony, he became a bored policeman and took out a notebook. He wedged his glove temporarily under his arm and began to execute a slow scribble. It took a long time. Then he snapped the book shut and looked squarely into Charley's eyes.

"Listen, you little bastard—Friday afternoon! You show up at old man Bennett's house with that nine bucks, I'll be there to check, and if you don't show up I'll beat the living hell out of you, myself, personally. It don't make no difference to me. All you young punks are alike. Another trick like this and I'll send you up to reform school, remember that! All right!" He adjusted his goggles again. "By Christ, I'll fix your little ticket, do you hear!"

Charley braced himself for another stinging blow but without further ado, Tooey Warner re-adjusted his glove, patted his visor briskly, jammed the starter with a violent kick, and with his legs magnificently atilt like a jockey on a renowned horse, he roared off in a blast of appalling glory that had long been the living image of bane and woe to every Galloway boy old enough to walk.

Charley knew he was going to have a hard time raising the money and meeting his awful deadline. It was the furthest thing from his mind to ask for help from his parents. On the first day of his labors on the city dump, after school, he found that, at the rate he was going, he wouldn't have enough time to salvage a sufficient amount of scrap—metal fixtures, bits of lead and brass, old aluminum pots and pans and such—to sell to the notoriously tight-fisted junkmen and at the same time make the deadline. He had to start playing "hookey" from school to spend the whole day at his task. This raised the problem of absentee notes for his school principal. He was full of troubles.

Silently forbearing and self-reliant, Charley decided to worry about all that later and concentrated on the first thing at hand—gathering scrap on the dump. He had only four days to make it. It was a bitter and grueling task, in the dead of winter, on steep snowy banks swept by insistent winds all day long. He foraged and grubbed and labored among rusty fenders and old chassis, oil drums, tin cans, empty tomato crates and whiskey bottles that covered the sloping floor of the dump—which was really a floor and not a ground, with its sagging spongy layers of old coalesced swill and ashes, underneath which furtive dump rats scampered in their burrows.

He worked there in a fury of energy, tearing off shapeless masses of junk to clear away whole areas of snow so that he could see what was to be found, until his hands were raw and cut and his face burned from the perpetually smoking fires. He was alone in the deserted slopes. Even the dogged grubby junkmen had been discouraged by the winter cold, and the air about him was foul from the smell of burnt-rubber smoke, from rancid exhalations that steamed up out of whole sections of ancient sour rot and from the general teeming putrescence of winter dampness on a dump along a river that received sewage and dye-mill disposals the year round. It was a stretch of the Merrimac River some distance below the White Bridge falls and about a mile below where it flowed so placidly, broadly, and undefiled off the Martin home on Galloway Road. Such was Charley's fate. . . .

Down by the water's edge near a cluster of big rocks he erected an ingenious shelter where he stored his day's scrap, before carting it at nightfall to a young friend's backyard not far from the dump, and which he also used as a dressing-room. He could not come home for dinner at noontime all dirty from the junkheap, when he was supposed to be in school all morning, so he hit on the idea of preparing a bundle of old clothes, old shoes, towel and soap, which he took with him every morning from home along with his schoolbooks, and every noon after his morning's work he changed in the shelter, washing with snow melted in the sun in a bucket, and then went home for dinner looking clean and scholarly. Then, at one o'clock, he returned to the dump for his afternoon's work, changed back to his working clothes, hid the bicycle in the shelter and started in again in pitiable laborious measures.

On the third day he was getting desperate. He had only collected a few dollars' worth of junk, at most, and his last day of grace was approaching swiftly and hopelessly. At one o'clock he was hurrying across the Rooney Street bridge on his bicycle for another desperate afternoon's work. The clear sharp pristine air was all sparkling with snow and icicles, the kind of day he used to enjoy. Suddenly he heard someone calling him from the board-walk of the bridge. It was his sister Liz. She stood there with her hands lodged casually in her coat pockets and with an expression of unmistakable severity on her rosy young face.

"Charley Martin, tell me what you are doing out of school!"

"Hah?"

"And don't give me that stuff either!" She stood there, tall and calm, surveying him with an air of sisterly sternness. It was a little difficult to make convincing, however, due to the fact that she was wearing a boyish half-length raincoat over a pair of bright blue slacks, and looked a blithe winsome high-school girl from top to toe, scarcely authoritative.

"What about you?" yelled Charley, snickering.

"Never *mind* about me! I want to know what *you* are doing out of school!"

"Ah, Liz, it's a big story. You don't want to hear it, do you?" He suddenly laughed savagely. "What you doing in slacks? You didn't have those on this morning at breakfast!"

"I told you never mind about me!" she said slowly through clenched teeth, slitting her greenish eyes, pointing at him. "I want you to tell me that long story of yours. Where were you headed? Tell me!" She took the bicycle and shook it angrily.

"The dump over there."

"And what for?"

"I'm collecting junk so I can sell it. I need some money bad."

"And what for?"

"Because."

"What for?"

So Charley had to tell her all about it. Anyway he trusted and loved Liz. But while he told her about his predicament with the police he couldn't keep a straight face, somehow. She was standing so gravely, so solemnly before him, a fellow hookey-player.

Her own eyes gleamed a little, with infectious gravity, but she said, "Listen, sonny boy, this is nothing to laugh about, those cops are *tough*. We've got to get you out. How much money did you make so far?"

"Gee, only about two bucks, Liz." He turned away to snicker.

"Cut that out! And we're not gonna stand here in the cold talking about it," she cried sharply, and lowered her head a moment to think, with a quick brooding movement of decisive reflection, while Charley leaned his chin in his hand with a bored expression. "And don't be such a wise guy!" snapped Liz, noticing his little gesture of manly patience. "You think you know everything, don't you! Well, listen to *me*—I'll get the money for you in the bank this afternoon and you'll go and give it to that old fool right away, tonight! That's what you're going to do, Mister Martin!"

"Oh, no!" cried Charley, surprised. "I'm getting that money myself with the junk I sell—"

"Shut up! You've only got two dollars' worth, you nitwit, and you haven't even sold it yet! You'll never make it!"

"I'll make it, I reckon. . . ."

"Don't give me that cowboy talk! I'll break your head!" she yelled, shaking the bicycle furiously. "You're not going to get all dirty on that filthy dump and maybe catch a disease."

"I figured it out," returned Charley quietly, reverting to the tone of voice he used whenever he carried on judicious discourses with himself, "and I reckon I can make it easy. . . ."

"What did I tell you about that cowboy-reckon talk!" shouted Elizabeth, stamping her foot on the boardwalk. "You're going to go right back to school this very minute. I'll write your absent notes for you, and that's *all* there is to it!"

"No."

"Are you going to do what I say?" she said finally.

"I *can't!*"

"All right then," she said with the crisp finality of a woman making up her mind, "if that's the way you want it, okay. Get off the bike and let me get on—"

"Why?"

Liz shook the bicycle again peremptorily. "*Because*. I'm going back to Dotty Beebe's house and get into some old clothes. And I'll meet you on the dump in ten minutes."

"What?" howled Charley.

"Listen!" Elizabeth hissed through her teeth, and she took Charley's jacket lapel firmly in her strong hands. "I've made up my mind and you're gonna keep your big mouth shut this time."

"But you're not gonna dig for junk?" he cried incredulously.

"That's it," she recited in a kind of monotone. "Now *shut up* and get off that bike."

And Charley got off, and stood there scratching his head. She mounted the bicycle with an air of busy authority, and said, "Now!

I'll meet you over there across the bridge in ten minutes. Be there!" She pedaled off. Charley walked across the bridge, and waited for his sister in complete bafflement. Liz was his strange, wild, unpredictable sister all right.

She was back in fifteen minutes roguishly attired in dungarees and a brown leather jacket, wearing shoes and a pair of work gloves she had borrowed from her girl friend's brother while he himself was in school. They promptly started off across the field.

In a matter of minutes they were both rooting and digging about on the junkheaps, calling excitedly whenever they found some odd scrap that seemed valuable, tossing it on the pile in Charley's shelter down by the rocks with a feeling of mounting efficiency. The girl found an old rusty aluminum frying pan, one magnificent iron kettle with the handle partially broken off, and an old black fireplace grate. The boy, with an eye for larger details, found a huge sheet of metal that rumbled like thunder when he struggled down to the shelter with it.

Liz, the strange impulsive Liz, was enjoying herself very much. To her, the fact that she was grubbing on the city dump with her kid brother, wearing a man's crude workclothes, playing hookey from high school on a cold December afternoon, was a fantastic and wonderful adventure she was convinced no other girl could appreciate. She hated "most girls" anyway and the strict conventions by which they generally behaved. The original, the different, even the shocking thing, in her proud and exultant belief, was the only thing to do. She had long been a confirmed tomboy. She believed fiercely in everything that this kind of American female child believes in—the besting of snotty little boys in fights and races and tree-climbing. She had nothing but contempt for the fluttering little girls who gave up easily and resorted to feminine wiles. She wanted to go slapdash through the world anyway she liked.

Yet, with all that, everything about her already suggested depths of charming tenderness, infinite and womanly. At sixteen she was comparatively tall, erect in bearing, with a luxurious head of brunette hair, and eyes that really were lustrously green. In the way that she jumped down the slope of the hill with a graceful dainty bend of the knees, her hands waving in the air timorously for balance, in the way that she paused sometimes to stand and gaze with that patient, silent, and voluptuous brooding that women have, in all those things was the eloquence of a truly beautiful mien and manner. She was Charley's sister and his best friend.

At that moment, however, neither Elizabeth or Charley was going unnoticed. As they dug and ripped and dragged the junk down to the shelter, and shouted jubilantly to one another in the wind, a young man, who had just driven up in an old 1928 Chevvy sedan with the back seat and windows removed to make room for loads of all sorts, was standing on top of the hill watching them with a puzzled and curious air.

It was their brother Joe. Having spent the day working on the old Ford in the Martin barn, he had decided that certain parts in the old car needed replacement, so he had borrowed the rickety Chevvy from a friend to drive down to the dump to see what he could find among the wrecks regularly dumped there. Joe stood now, peering down intently at the two youngsters trying to decide what they were up to.

Some schoolboys, their shadows cast far along the brow of the slope in the slanting afternoon light, had paused on their way home from school. They also stood on the hill watching Charley and Liz, with motionless, brooding curiosity.

Suddenly one young schoolboy, with a casual and incredible show of perfectly composed cheerlessness, picked up some rocks and began to throw them down at Charley and his sister. The whole thing happened so swiftly that at first the two kids below couldn't understand what was going on. When the steady beat of rocks all around them apprised them of the little scoundrel's purpose, they began yelling up angrily at him. But the schoolboy stood calmly surveying them from his advantageous hilltop and kept throwing more and more rocks. His schoolmates hurried away in embarrassment and dread.

Charley picked up some rocks of his own and furiously began to loft them as far as he could towards the schoolboy. This only urged the little knave on to greater efforts, perhaps out of a kind of coldblooded desperation. He proceeded to intensify his assault with vicious enterprise and actually stoned Charley on the leg. Charley let out a yowl of rage and charged right up the hill over heaps of junk that gave way and slipped under his feet in his scrambling haste, but he was bound to get him. And just as he reached a fairly stable stretch of ground and was running straight up to the tormentor in a hail of rocks, one of them struck him squarely on the forehead and he fell on his knees.

When Liz saw Charley fall she let out a howl of her own that struck doom in the heart of the little fiend. She came charging uphill with appalling speed in great antelope strides, terrific with girlish wrath and he, sensing the imminent end of his advantage, decided to run away. But just then Joe swooped down at him and took him by the arm and shook him off his feet.

"You crazy little bastard, what are you doing?" Joe yelled.

Charley had risen to his feet again, with that unpredictable obstinacy of his nature, and he came charging the rest of the way up the hill with blood streaking down his face, grimly silent, his teeth bared. With a frantic lunge the schoolboy disengaged himself from Joe's grip and began to run for dear life across the field.

Liz had come up, and she and Joe stood rooted to the spot in fascination as Charley raced off in pursuit of the schoolboy. In the hushed silence of the terrible moment that followed they could hear the sound of small feet running over the rubble, frantic and absolutely urgent, until Charley dove in a long flying tackle and sent the other boy crashing to the ground.

"I think I'd better go over," said Joe.

Charley merely pulled the schoolboy to his feet by the collar. For a moment it seemed as though some unspeakable violence would erupt, but nothing of the sort seemed to happen. Charley just held his adversary by the back of the collar and stared at him without a word. The other boy, meanwhile, had craned his neck around to avert his eyes from the sight of Charley's bloody face, yet every time he tried to jump away, or just look away, Charley tightened his grip and pulled him even closer, until finally with a slow, hesitant, almost hypnotized movement the little rascal had to turn his face to Charley and look with fearful blindness at him.

"Look what you did to me," said Charley in a low voice. The cut on his forehead looked bad, but it was nothing more than a minor laceration.

"Do you see what you did to me?" said Charley quietly.

The schoolboy lunged convulsively aside, but to no avail. Once more he was brought face to face with his fearsome victim.

Liz and Joe walked up and waited nervously to see what would happen. Suddenly Charley flung the other boy around with amazing swiftness and delivered him a tremendous kick in the behind.

The schoolboy went sprawling on his knees from the force of the kick, but almost as instantly he was up on his feet racing off, with such frantic exertion that he plunged headlong on his knees again where he groveled for just a moment with great clutching fury, got up, slipped, all in an ecstasy of savage futility, and finally made off in a crazy sprint across the field. Charley for his part didn't choose to pursue the matter any further. He stood at ease, with almost sad composure, and gazed after the schoolboy's retreat with a calm, baneful eye.

Joe got some band-aids out of the car and wiped up the cut and bandaged Charley's head.

"Well!" he said. "I don't know what you two are doing here, but I never seen a better boot in the you-know-where! Hyah! hyah! hyah!" He examined Charley's cut again with careful gravity, and Elizabeth watched anxiously.

"Now! I guess that'll be all right for now. We will wrap a handkerchief tight around your head, so, and damn if you don't look like Captain Kidd. Now!" he said, folding his arms. "Lizzy, what's this all about? Why aren't you in school?"

They explained everything to him.

"What! Nine bucks for a window!" Joe commented. "Why, that old crackpot's off his nut! Somebody ought to shoot that cop Warner, he's too damn rough on kids. He's had it coming to him for years." Joe walked to the edge of the hill and scanned the whole length of the dump in silence. He strode back reflectively.

"Look, jerks, now that you started this crazy business we might as well finish it. In the first place, you morons, you're not working the right side of the dump, it's over *that way* that you find where the city trucks dump their loads every day, the new wrecks with good bumpers on them, and sometimes good motor parts too. I'm looking for an oil filter myself," he added speculatively. They were leaning on his every word eagerly, because if anybody knew, Joe knew.

He walked around the Chevvy, lit a cigarette, suddenly jumped in and yelled, "Come on then, what are you waiting for?" They went rattling over the rubble down to the other side of the dump, bouncing and swerving crazily. Each of them was grinning with sly delight, as though something wildly funny had suddenly come into the air.

Joe parked the car by the water's edge. "Now!" he said, and

marched off towards the nearest old wreck where he immediately appraised the general situation and sprang into action. First he lunged at a kind of old rusty bar protruding from a tangle of junk and immediately wrenched it spectacularly from its moorings, in a furious display of industry. With it he began to belabor a single headlamp on the front of the wreck until it was lopped off. "Fifty cents!" he called out. "You see how it's done?" He threw his cigarette away and looked around authoritatively.

"Charley, you take that piece of iron and pry out the tire on the front wheel," he commanded. "There's another tire on that old Nash there. And you, Liz, you carry all of it back to the car and the stuff you already picked up this afternoon." Having dispatched these orders, Joe fell back to his work with sensational vigor, on an ancient ruined Graham this time.

In that manner, under Joe's supervision, as the dusk slowly deepened, the three of them managed at last to pile up more than a sufficient amount of scrap and junk to meet Charley's poor needs. The boy was all amazed and joyful. It was as though the world had come back to him again, back to reclaim him after disasters and isolations to keep him infolded in sweet and safest brotherly darkness.

"Look all the stuff we got!" he yelled. "When we going to sell it, Joe?" he cried with shining eyes.

"Right now, pardner," said Joe very severely. Charley leaped away in ravenous excitement, and Elizabeth watched with brooding satisfaction.

It was getting dark, and as the wind rose driving ghostly snow across the murky fields, as a thousand ranked windows glowed in the Galloway factories across the waters, the two brothers and their sister loaded the back of the Chevvy, and rattled off along an old dirt road that wound away from the river into the woods.

The junkman was a rather moronic person by the name of Zouzou, who lived in a dilapidated old farmhouse at a fork in the roads leading out of Galloway into Norcott, New Hampshire. This Zouzou could not have been much more than thirty years old but owing to the idiocy of his nature, and perhaps also as a consequence of the incredibly lonely life he lived as a hermit junkman, he already presented an appearance of the most extraordinary decay. His skin was like wrinkled brown parchment, he had a toothless mouth and a senile pointed chin that was always drooling and unshaven and trembling from moronic excitement, and in the way that he walked and moved around there was a strange and disorderly energy like the last shaky vigors of an old man.

When they arrived at Zouzou's farmhouse, it was completely dark except for one dim light burning in the back kitchen window. Charley led them around to the back and knocked. In a moment Zouzou himself opened the door and emitted a meaningless giggle. Behind him they could see a littered kitchen table upon which was his supper. An empty can of beans lay beside a frying pan in which the beans had been heated and out of which he had evidently been eating with an enormous ladle of some kind. On the wall beside the table there was a ring screwed into the woodwork to which Zouzou had apparently attached a towel irrevocably. It was the dirtiest towel the Martins had ever seen.

Charley indicated to Zouzou the purpose of their visit, and the simpleton straightaway picked up his oil lamp and went out in the yard to see what they had. After a cursory examination of the load he turned to Charley—while Elizabeth and Joe stood back in the dark outside the range of the weaving lamplight—and he uttered a sentence of jargon which young Charley apparently understood.

"He says to drive the car in the barn. We're in!"

Joe gravely drove the car into the ruined old barn, and there, by the light of his oil lamp, Zouzou unloaded the junk onto the ground and grunted something that sounded like "Oui!" each time he found some object particularly suited to his liking. Finally, having examined everything, Zouzou sat down on the ground in front of the enormous pile and began to thumb a corncob pipe reflectively.

"What do we do now?" Joe wanted to know.

"He's thinking," said Charley with a touch of impatience. "Give him time to think."

Finally after minutes of pipe-smoking and smacking his lips to say, "Pah! Pah! Pah!" he rose and left them waiting in the barn.

"What'd he say, for krissakes?" cried Joe in stupefied amazement.

"He'll be right back," said Charley, deep in thought. In a moment Zouzou was back with some money in his hand which he now held out to Charley at arm's length, with a suspicious glare. Charley took the money and counted it. It ran up to ten dollars and eleven cents. When he at last looked at Zouzou and nodded in mute agreement, Zouzou exploded into a wild maniacal laugh of happiness.

"Hokay! Hokay!" yelled Zouzou, and picking up his lamp he beckoned them out of the barn. "Ginjale! Ginjale!" he was shouting.

"He wants us to have some ginger ale in his house," explained Charley eagerly.

But suddenly Zouzou had jerked his head around in a birdy movement of demented attention and was holding up his hand stiffly for silence. All that could be heard was the whistle of the wind through the niches of the barn, and the scraping of branches overhead, and the soft sift of snow under the door. At last, without turning his head or relaxing his tense mad stare, he said something happily to Charley.

"What's this?" cried Joe. "What's goin' on?"

"He says that was his sister just then," said Charley around his hand. "He says she's been in the parlor for ten years."

"You mean he's got a sister living here?" cried Elizabeth anxiously.

"Naw, his sister's dead! He's always telling us his sister's still in the parlor."

"Well," said Joe, turning to Elizabeth, "I reckon it's just about time for us to be moseying along."

Charley seized Zouzou's hand and shook it firmly, and Zouzou went, "Hee hee hee!" bidding him good-bye. They jumped in the car, waved to Zouzou, and lurched off, while Zouzou stood out in the middle of the road waving his lamp gleefully at them.

For Charley, who sat looking out the window bubbling over with pleasure, with his eyes turned away from Elizabeth and Joe for fear they would catch him with their laughing eyes, the day seemed now full of strange crazy glee—and all his fears and bruising terrors, his troubles and lonely unconsolations, were gone.

And when they would get home now, in a few minutes, his father would be standing there in the kitchen with his gape of wondering curiosity. He would stare openmouthed at them for a moment and then ask what it was all about, and scratch his head, and frown, and peer at them, and wonder about it, and go back to the den. His mother would be full of anxiety and solicitude, peering at them shrewdly, knowing everything. Peter and Ruth would be there, grinning, and Mickey would be watching in wistful silence. Rose would be there saying, "Well, well, well, it's about time!" Francis would be somewhere brooding about the house.

In the smoky air of evening now, there was something mad with glee, something that laughed in a soundless choking in the dark.

It seemed to Charley that he knew what this something was. He had been with the children at dusk when they suddenly leap up and tumble over and yell in diabolical delight, for no earthly reason, as something passes by in the dark smoky air, and the children have understood it so well.

[10]

WHEN CHRISTMAS EVE came that year, the winds died down as if pious. A hush of nipping cold descended and caked the snow and filled the air with a silent locked frostiness. After nightfall huge and lustrous winter stars appeared to reign over the miraculous stillness of the night.

To little Mickey it was all miraculous, a simple verity, the truth of Christmas which was the doing of little Child Jesus, and of God, to which he, Michael Martin, was tremblingly and joyously prepared and given over.

The very sheen of starlight on the glossy snows, the little red and blue and green lights in the windows of homes, the icicles hanging from eaves—all these things, in the silence of mystery and prophecy fulfilled, were the altar flickers and divine meanings that had to come every year at Christmas. Reared in the Catholic myths and understanding, he walked in the frosty night and was a saint. Little Mickey, moody, dreamy, full of childlike revery, was wrapped in a silence of pieties, while all the others laughed and yelled and talked and enjoyed themselves. "Like it was New Year's already!" he thought darkly, almost scornfully.

They had all been skating at the pond a mile or so down Galloway Road in the evening, everybody—all the kids, Peter, Charley, Liz, her girl friends, Peter's chums, Joe, some of his buddies, and boys and girls from all around—dancing like shadows by the roaring bonfire, and scooping around in great swishing zigzags. Some of them were singing and yelling; some, like Peter and his friends Danny and Scotcho and Ernest Berlot Jr., were nipping out of bottles of brandy; some, like Liz and her boy friend Buddy Fredericks, were skating in beautiful arm-locked waltzes. The night's numb frosted air was sharp with cries and murmurs and shrieks.

But Mickey skated around the fringes of the pond, alone, thinking, looking up at the North Star, running a stick in front of him like Dit Clapper the hockey star, pushing along doggedly deep in his own amazing thoughts about Christmas and everything, and once in a while—when no one was near—singing "Silent Night, Holy Night" in a small, high voice like the choir boys at midnight Mass. Once Charley came wobbling over on skates to show him the big studded Western cowboy belt Joe had bought him for Christmas.

"But you ain't supposed to look at your presents till midnight!" cried Mickey, astounded.

"It's all right; Joe said it was all right to wear it skating tonight!"

"But you can't do that," scoffed Mickey. "Don't you know nothin' about Christmas? You didn't open *my* present did you!"

"I don't even know where it is. Say!" Charley laughed savagely. "Rosey was lookin' for *you!* She's lookin' for your presents to wrap 'em up in paper. She's been wrappin' presents all day, up in the bedroom with *big* piles all over the bed and she's wrapping 'em with *ribbons*. Did you know there's a big party going on at the house now? Mr. Cartier and Mr. Mulligan and Mrs. Cartier and Mrs. Mulligan and everybody. Pa's in the kitchen making drinks and they're playin' the piano and singing. It's crazy over to the house—"

"I wrapped 'em myself," muttered Mickey, "and they're hid and nobody can see them till midnight. They're hid in the cellar."

"What?"

"My *presents!*"

"What'd you get me, Mick, what'd you get me? I bet you can't never guess what I got you!"

They had bought scout knives for each other, and they both thought it was going to be a big surprise, too. On the other hand they both *wanted* scout knives.

At eleven o'clock Peter—their big brother Peter, a hero of heroes, a captain of captains among the little high-school football players who were skating all over the pond with their Galloway "G's" on heavy woolen sweaters and nodding and blushing whenever Peter chanced to look their way, an unfathomable football player at Olympian Penn—their big brother Peter was standing on the bank, with his skates around his neck, by the roaring bonfire, calling out to them, through cupped hands: "Heyyy, Mick! Hey, Char-lee! Come on home. . . . We're all getting a ride home!" Everybody piled into a rattling car that belonged to Ernest Berlot and Peter's wild chums, who were a little drunk now. They wanted Peter to join them in further celebrations in the Rooney Street saloons, and they all went speeding back down Galloway Road, Joe and Liz singing crazy songs, Mickey sitting on Peter's lap in front, some other kids from down the road riding on the runningboard and yelling in the wind, Berlot the driver tooting the horn wild and insistent.

When they came in sight of the Martin house, Mickey's heart filled with pleasure when he saw the soft lights in the windows and the curl of smoke winding from the chimney. He knew that Christmas was always beautiful. Every room in the Martin house that night was lighted up to serve one purpose or another. When they parked in front they could hear a chorus of voices singing in the front room, and great adult roars of laughter, the celebrating elders having a big time. "Just like it was Saturday night!" Mickey thought darkly again.

The kids giggled and peeked in from the front porch, at Martin, and Mrs. Martin, and the Cartiers and the Mulligans and other guests who were gathered around the piano with drinks in their hands. George Martin, almost as drunk as a lord, was singing loudest of them all, while the mother sat at the piano playing with a radiant and happy flush on her face. It made Mickey happy, yet also somehow sad to see his mother laughing and playing the piano like that. At Christmas, he always liked to just sit beside her on the couch. She let him have red port wine to drink with the walnuts, and watch the warm soft lights of the tree, red and blue and green, and listen to Scrooge on the radio. He liked to listen to Scrooge every year. He liked to have the house all quiet and Scrooge and Christmas songs on the radio, and everybody opening the Christmas presents after midnight Mass.

He liked it when his father sat in his chair with a clean white shirt and a necktie and a vest, and a fresh cigar, eating candy and nuts and fruit out of bowls, laughing, talking to everybody, sitting there all neat and combed and rosy-faced from the holiday. He liked to have his mother putting tinsel and cotton snow and bulbs and decorations on the Christmas tree, and Rosey helping her, and a big turkey roasting in the oven and filling the house with its delicious smells, and Liz on the floor reading the funnies, and Joe and Charley, and Ruthey and Petey all there, the whole family in the quiet house at Christmas.

They all went in the house. The singing went on around the piano; big Mr. Cartier was doing a crazy dance with his wife's hat on backwards. It was too much for Mickey who had to sit down in a corner and giggle. For a moment he was worried when the Christmas tree shook a little from side to side, but it had been well secured to the floor—Joe had done the job himself—and he guessed it wouldn't fall over. He went over and threw more tinsel on the branches.

Ruthey was whispering to Mrs. Mulligan: "That's Mickey's blue star up there on top of the tree. Every year we've got to get up on a chair and put it up, or *else!* You know, or *else!*"

Mickey heard, but he paid no attention, he just stood before the tree with his hands clasped behind him. Then his mother came running over and threw her arms around him saying: "Oh, my little Mickey! He loves his tree so much!"

"Where's your present to me?" cried Ruthey. "Where did you put all your presents?"

"In the cellar."

"Well, it's time to bring them up now! Bring them up and we'll lay them under the tree with all the others."

So Mickey went downstairs and came up a moment later with a pile of packages all crudely wrapped his own secret way.

"Oh, you wrapped them up nice!" cried Ruthey. "But I'll fix them up with ribbons and everything. Is this mine? Oh, I can tell what's in mine!"

"No, you can't!" Mickey affirmed sternly. "How can you, if you ain't seen it?"

"I can guess, can't I? It's about big enough for a bottle of perfume."

"Ha, ha, ha!" he laughed savagely. She had guessed it right on the nose. He smote his brow incredulously: "Boyoboy, are you *off!* You're a million miles off!"

"I am?" murmured Ruth with hesitation, realizing somehow that he was taking the whole thing altogether seriously, and in a rush of tenderness she kissed him impulsively on the cheek. She knew what it all meant to passionate Mickey, Christmas, and the realization of his feelings filled her suddenly with a longing to guard over his little devotions.

"At midnight," she said to him softly, "in about a half an hour you and I and Ma are going to midnight Mass and when we come back everybody'll open their presents. And I'll bet you'll be a million miles off guessing what *I* got *you!*"

"Oh, *your* guess was a billion miles off!" yelled Mickey with a broad smile.

"Well, then I'll get a big surprise. And I bet you can't *ever* guess what I got for you. There it is there under the tree."

"Let me see!"

She handed him a large package. He judiciously weighed it in his hands, turned it upside down to see if it would rattle, or make any revealing noises, he shook it, held it up to the light, put his ear against it with a crafty mysterious look. He wanted Ruth to think that he had secret methods of his own for determining such things.

But finally he admitted, "Naw, I can't guess."

"You're no better at guessing than *I* am!" Ruth laughed and kissed him once again.

Then there were more uproars in the house as Mr. Cartier yelled, "Beans! It's time to eat them beans! Where's the bean-pot? George, I'm genuinely sorry, I know you had them baked beans done for Christmas morning tomorrow, but I gotta eat them beans!" They trooped into the kitchen where Mr. Cartier began to eat the beans.

"Well, I'll tell you," said Martin, "if you want to make up for this, ask Santa Claus if he's got a woman who can bake a pot of beans like Marge and *that's* what I'll take!"

The noisy merriment swirled and rolled, it was as though the very windows were rattling.

Joe and Rose were opening up another bottle of whiskey, and Peter came hurrying into the kitchen with some ice cream and ginger ale. He gave Mickey a glass and showed him how to make an ice-cream soda. Out in the parlor Liz was dancing around with Charley trying to show him the jitterbug, and suddenly Liz swept Mickey up and danced him around the room, and he jumped about to show her he could do a better job than Charley.

It was almost time for midnight Mass now, but everybody was having so much fun and everything was so crazy and funny that Mickey almost didn't want to go to church after all.

Finally his mother got their coats, and they started out on foot with Ruth, and walked off in the frosty quiet night.

Mickey was sublimely happy now. All along the streets people began to appear from their houses, afoot or in cars, all moving in the same direction. It amazed Mickey that the whole night was full of voices and the crunch of steps over the hard snow, even though it was almost midnight. And again and again he looked up to gaze at the stars, which seemed to touch the rooftops of the houses, icy bright and trembling and hovering over the snowy chimneys and over the sleep of little children smaller than he who believed that Santa Claus would soon be climbing down those chimneys.

From the open door of the church warm golden light swarmed out on the snow. The sound of the organ and singing could be heard.

Inside the church there was the delightful smell of overcoats fresh from the cold night mingled with the incense and flowers. Everyone was settling down for Mass, the men fingering their hats devoutly, blowing their noses, looking around and nodding, the women adjusting their hats and prayer-beads with sharp prim movements.

Mickey gazed with fearful awe at the beautiful crib on one side of the gleaming white altar, representing the Christ child in the manger, the mother Mary bending over him silent and immobile, Joseph standing mournfully by, all of it bathed in the soft blue light that came from the enormous star. The three Wise Kings stood apart, with concentrated devotion, frozen in sorrowful intensity, as though they knew that the whole world was looking at them and the moment must never be disturbed, nor the little Child Jesus who lay in the crib in a halo of silent miraculous light.

The choir boys, who had been quietly assembling on each side of the altar, began to sing in small high voices.

"Oh, they sing like little angels," whispered the mother ecstatically to Ruth, and she dabbed at her eyes with her handkerchief. "I can't help it, I have to cry when I hear those sweet little voices."

Three little girls, wearing the uniform of the church's sodality, came out and stood in front of the communion rail and raised trumpets to their lips, while titterings went softly around the pews, and in clear though occasionally flat tones they began to play "Hark, the Herald Angels Sing." The voices of the choir boys and the sudden soft inclusion of the organ accompaniment turned the rendition of the little girls into a huge success, and when they hurried back to their front pews everybody was smiling benevolently in their direction.

Finally the priest came out followed by his train, and everybody rose for the beginning of Mass.

Standing next to Mickey throughout the Mass was a wiry little man who gave off a very strong odor of alcohol. He stood stiffly and motionlessly with his hands clasped to the pew in front of him or sat in an erect and rigid posture without moving a muscle, as though he might have been afraid that the slightest move would betray the fact that he had been drinking. When he kneeled, he lowered himself with slow and painful dignity to the knee-rest and hooked his elbows over the pew, taking firm hold with his hands, in a movement that was furtive and at the same time singularly devout. Mickey could not take his eyes off the man's great powerful brown hands as he draped them over the pew and clutched at the wood, at the great knots of muscle and vein on them and at the large black rosary beads that were wound delicately about the hands and hung rattling gently against the back of the pew. It seemed strange to Mickey that this man had come to midnight Mass. In spite of his small stature he looked fiercely powerful and strong, almost savage, his eyes were dark and authoritative and the cords in his windburnt neck stood out like pillars, and he seemed to Mickey like a wild hermit from a mountain cave with all his silent ferocious mien.

When communion time came, the man turned to the big woman next to him, and nodded to her, and instantly a file of children started from the pew followed by the big woman and the little man, who walked and hobbled like the bow-legged French-Canadian farmer that he was. They all marched slowly down to the altar where the little man ordered the procession of his family along the altar rail by a series of imperceptible signs. Mickey watched broodingly as the man and his family kneeled at the altar.

The little altar bell jingled as the priest raised the ciborium. Everybody in the church lowered their heads, but Mickey raised his head slightly and thrilled at the sight of the vast plane of bowed heads everywhere, until he caught the eye of another little boy who was looking around, and they both dipped back quickly.

Mickey was now growing a little tired of the Mass. He wanted to go back home and open the presents and see what he had for Christmas. But he began to do another rosary on his beads for fear he had not prayed enough. It was then that his pensive gaze fell once more on the manger scene beside the altar, and a shiver of surprise ran through him. For a moment he imagined that he himself lay in the crib, that he himself was the Christ Child and that the Virgin Mary was his own mother. This strange feeling grew in him until he held his gaze fixed on the beautiful scene hypnotized with wonder. The scene almost seemed to come to life for him and he fancied that he had seen a blush of pleasure growing on Mary's cheeks. And at that precise moment, a low mournful note from the organ filled the church, and with unaccountable swiftness Mickey's eyes burned with imminent tears.

He was carried away by a fearsome emotion of great sadness, the kind he felt when he was alone in his room in the middle of the night.

Then the boy looked up again at the altar manger and saw that he too must suffer and be crucified like the Child Jesus there, who was crucified for his sake, who pointed out his guiltiness that way, but who also pointed out what was going to happen to him, for he too, Michael Martin, was a child with a holy mother, therefore he too would be drawn to Calvary and the wind would begin to screech and everything would get dark. This would be sometime after he was a cowboy in Arizona on the Tonto Rim.

And then he thought about his brother Charley. Did he hurt him that time when he threw a piece of slate, and it hit Charley in back of the head, and Charley ran in the kitchen crying?

"Charley! Charley!" the boy thought to himself with anguish. "I didn't mean to do it, honest! I didn't know! Forgive me, God!—Jesus!—Joseph! Charley, forgive me! Like Pa forgave you for breaking those windows! Oh, Charley, will my Christmas present make you glad? Will it make you like me? It's a good scout knife, I bought it on money I saved since way back in October." These were little Mickey's rushing inward-tortured thoughts—and he sighed now, suddenly.

The altar boys were singing again, with a vigorous tone of completion, the Mass was almost over. The altar boys were sinners and hypocrites, he knew some of them, especially Mulrooney there in the back, so innocent-looking, who killed snakes along the river by frying them in tin cans, and blew up frogs with straws, and the blond boy Bailey who sold newspapers and hit Raymond one day in the schoolyard and made his nose bleed. But they too were being saved. Although they could do what they liked: he was headin' West himself, soon, mebbe.

Suddenly Mickey wondered if everybody else believed in God like he did. They had told him Santa Claus first—he was God's friend, they said—but now he knew that was just a lot of stuff for kids. Was God really everywhere around and not just sitting in heaven not looking down? Everybody in church went about under God's look like they were only lining up after recess, and yawning, and coughing, and fidgeting. The little noises of noon and the smell of lunches and orange peels and the crunching of shoes in the gravel in the schoolyard: that wasn't God! And the priest talking about how the people did not give enough for the parish, and the way the people threw their money in the baskets, angrily almost, that wasn't God! All this shuffling and coughing and *nose-blowing* in the church wasn't God!

Yet all the beautiful singing and the organ in the church, yes, it was God's music for God. But he also liked "Home on the Range" and "Bury Me Not on the Lone Prairie" just as much. These songs made him see the cowboys loping across the sage on their mustangs in the big sad sunset and made him cry for the death of waddies in the Montana roundup.

Now, in a minute, it would be time to go home, to walk in the late night among all the people smoking and laughing and heading home to open presents and eat and celebrate, and across the field, under the stars, in the shadows of the houses where the little kids were sleeping, maybe this year he would see the Angel walking in the snow at last.

[11]

ON NEW YEAR'S EVE the snow was flying in large soft flakes over Galloway. In Daley Square the snow fell upon the festive crowds hurrying to a thousand and one destinations and celebrations in theaters, nightclubs, bars and private parties all around town. The whole town seemed steeped in joyous, far-crying silence in the breathless snowfall, all of it giving the night a mysterious and thrilling excitement that was everywhere in the air.

Peter and Alexander Panos were seated in the Square cafeteria by the big plate glass windows facing the street, both of them full of wild anticipation, waiting for the others to meet them there, meantime discoursing excitedly. They were to meet Peter's gang in front of the cafeteria, after which they were all to go to a Rooney Street saloon to meet up with some of Alexander's friends. There was a dance at the Admiral Ballroom that Peter wanted to attend, there was a party somewhere else, and the whole night was throbbing and unfolding nervously, happily. In the short time left to themselves alone in the cafeteria Alexander was busily engaged in making his usual report to Peter about what he had been doing all week, and inquiring eagerly after Peter's activities, as though he hadn't seen him for years, as though they had but a few hours left on earth together.

"Time! Time!" cried Alexander. "There's my greatest enemy. There are so many things to learn, to do, and time rushes past! I *should* be finished with my research on Byron within a week. How I have been *working* on that thing! After that, Pierre, I'm going to embark on a thorough study of philosophy. You should *see* my room! Yesterday I read and wrote for eighteen hours straight and in that time I drank *sixteen* cups of coffee and smoked *three* packs of cigarettes. The place is literally a battlefield of paper strewn all over the bed, the chairs, the floors!" And Alexander cast a melancholy look at Peter and held out both his hands helplessly. "But Byron . . . that ultramagnificent Byron! *'Tis time this heart should be unmoved since others it has ceased to move* . . . Oh, God!"

"I wonder when those guys will get here!" said Peter absent-mindedly.

"Don't you see the sweep of that remark?" cried Alexander. He ruminated darkly awhile, resumed suddenly on another tack: "At any rate my study of philosophy will be as thorough as time will permit. That's the whole trouble with these dramatic schools —the emphasis is on art and the drama, there's so little to be learned there in the way of philosophy and history—don't you see?" At this time he was attending a dramatic school in Boston, and rushing around with exotic little girls in slacks who wanted to be like Luise Rainer. These were his happy days.

"We've got to get to a liquor store soon," put in Peter anxiously.

"Yes, oh, yes, Pierre. Oh, I forgot to tell you! I met a *real Norwegian* in Boston this week who attended one of our rehearsals. He told me about his brother in Oslo who died leaving behind *huge great* unpublished piles of writing! Imagine—and you should have seen this Norwegian fellow; he's a simple man, married, with three children in Kristiansund." Alexander smiled his great twisted smile and shook his head sadly and looked at his friend. "Just an ordinary man, Pete, but in his commonness there was a touch of greatness. Do you understand?" He looked anxiously for Peter's reaction.

Peter nodded. Then he cried: "Where *are* those damn guys! Here we are with a thousand things to do, it's New Year's Eve, it's eleven o'clock, and they fool around and keep us waiting. I'll bet I know what happened: Danny's singing a song in the middle of the street, they can't get him in the car, he's plastered to the gills. What a bunch of guys!"

"Yes, Peter," echoed Alexander slowly, raising an eyebrow, "what a bunch of guys. . . ."

"There you go again!" laughed Peter, jabbing Alexander in the shoulder. "A Norwegian guy you like very much, you said he was an ordinary man. But just because my gang aren't intellectuals you don't like them."

"But I *do* like them!" corrected Alexander gravely, slowly. "Ernest Berlot I particularly like and I'm trying to help him out intellectually as much as I possibly can. I'm having him read the plays of August Strindberg now, you know. Ernest will learn—"

"Berlot's reading *who?*" cried Peter with an amazed crazy laugh. "Do you mean to sit there and tell me you're making him read . . . *plays?*" It was too much to believe.

"Why," replied Alexander, "he likes Strindberg *very much*. He thinks his plays are *very good*. He told me so himself. He said, 'Alexander, these are very good plays.' He said it just as simply as that."

"But he's only pulling your leg, you crazy maniac!" cried Peter. "He wouldn't read a book for *fifty dollars!*"

"Oh, no! I saw him myself when I went to his house the other night. He was sitting in the parlor reading Strindberg when I rang the doorbell, I saw through the front window. He was wearing glasses and reading *very* intently. When he came to the door he said, 'Al, these plays are very weird but I'm catching on as I go along.' Don't tell *me* about Ernest Berlot. I know him as well as you do now, you know. The others—I'm not particularly antagonistic towards them. Scotcho is a good kid at heart. As for Danny, you know I hold nothing against him, it's just that he's smug because he has to work so hard, and makes an *awful* issue of it. Incidentally, I wrote some more poetry this week." He rummaged unsuccessfully for several moments through all his pockets.

"Christ-on-a-bicycle! Where *are* those guys!"

Francis Martin, having diverted his time in one of the Galloway theaters earlier in the evening, came walking slowly into the cafeteria for a cup of coffee. He had just seen a very poor movie which he had expected to be a great deal better; he was engaged in a series of sulky thoughts. When Peter hailed him from the other side of the cafeteria, he seemed reluctant to acknowledge the greeting, and came over slowly.

"Come on with us, Francis, we're going to have a big night!"

Alexander extended his big paw to Francis, smiling broadly. "I haven't seen you since New York!" he cried. "How've you been? Did you like the movie?"

"You mean the one across the street? Rotten," said Francis, and with this he sat down at their table, almost tentatively, on the edge of a chair.

"What about it?"

"The gall of that plot. As if it had never occurred to anyone before that a rich idler, by God, can be just as much a *gentleman* as a self-made man! Isn't that astoundingly revealing? That Hollywood!" He looked out the window at the rushing crowds.

"What's on your mind these days?" demanded Alexander with eagerness.

"Flight. I'm getting the hell out of Galloway. I am sick . . . and . . . tired . . . of . . . Galloway."

"Wonderful!" yelled Alexander in a bawling voice that drew the attention of everyone in the cafeteria, even the people coming in and out the revolving doors.

"I didn't tell you, Pete," said Francis. "A friend of mine is helping me get a job in a music store in Boston. I may be able to live in Cambridge from now on—"

"And then, later, *Paris!*" bawled Alexander, spreading his arms. "And someday we will all be remembering Galloway and the nostalgia of our youth here. We'll even remember this night in the cafeteria, on the eve of a New Year, 1941, and lost moments once unwanted. Oh, if I could only find that poem I wrote last night!" He fumbled again furiously among his pockets.

"If I ever went to Paris," said Francis, unexpectedly pensive, "I think I would be very happy. . . ."

Berlot's car finally pulled up in front of the cafeteria, and Berlot jumped out grinning broadly, waving at them in a commanding beck. The two boys, dragging the reluctant Francis along with them, got in the car, which started off instantly.

"You're late!" Peter yelled happily to the general company, which consisted of Berlot, Danny Mulverhill and Scotcho Rouleau, the three youngsters who had driven the skating party home on Christmas Eve. Alexander and Francis sat back bored.

"You know why we're late, Zagg?" yelled Berlot, flushed with liquor, eager for the big night. "This crazy bastart Danny here got in a big argument with Richman at the theater . . . huck huck huck! Tell 'em what you were saying, D.J."

"D.J. ain't talking," replied Danny solemnly. Berlot and Danny and Scotcho were ushers at the Monarch Theater not far from the Square.

"Two big burpers discussing Wall Street, that's what they were! Huck huck huck! Imagine talking to his boss like that! Richman actually thinks D.J. knows what he's talking about!"

"I told him Consolidated Niblick was going up several points before the snow stops flying," growled Danny solemnly. He was a great character, Berlot was mad about him, and so was Scotcho, and so was Peter. But Alexander hated him somehow.

"There! there! before the snow stops flying, Consolidated goin' up! That's what he told Richman!" yelled Berlot, in such excitement that he swerved the car out of its course for a moment and skidded in the snow and started a big commotion in the main street traffic. "Huck huck huck! Tell 'em what else you said, D.J.!"

"Who is Richman?" inquired Francis quietly at this point.

"He's the owner of the Monarch Theater," explained Peter eagerly.

"Richman's main trade is all the old washerwomen on Back Middle Street," interposed Danny wide-eyed and solemn, staring at Francis whom he knew only slightly. "Every Monday he has Buck Jones and Roy Rogers and big western pictures, and all the old washwomen from Back Middle Street come shuffling into the show with their pots and pans and brooms to see the westerns—"

"They do?"

"Sure! Do you know what they do? They just sit there and watch the picture, they don't even know what's going on, and everytime Buck Jones shoots the villain their jaws drop out."

Francis turned a curious stare to Peter.

"Sure!" yelled Berlot. "Ten cents' admission. He fills the house with old ladies. And that's how he made his million! Sure!"

By this time the car was parked not far from the center of the Square, Berlot having driven around the Square three times during the conversation. Now he had turned off the ignition and was leaning back with his hat slumped over his eyes.

"Whattaya want to stop *here* for!" yelled Scotcho, who sat between his two cronies in the front seat. "I thought we was going to the Rooney Street joint to meet Alexander's intellectuals!"

Alexander's intellectuals were several youngsters from Galloway who attended Boston College, three rather dour young Irishmen who read Aquinas and were proficient in mathematics. They were to meet in a bar on Rooney Street.

"Why did you park here!" Scotcho suddenly yelled again at Berlot, who turned and looked straight at him under the slump of his hat with grave surprise.

"Why," said Berlot, "just for a little nip."

"But we're late! Not that it makes any difference to me!"

"We're *awfully* late, Ernest!" put in Alexander emphatically from the back seat. "They're *very* good kids and you really ought to meet them."

"We'll just have a little nip," said Berlot, and he produced the bottle, uncorked it and drank several leisurely gulps. "I gotta catch up on that drunken D.J.! I'm about ten nips behind."

So the three wags in the front seat silently gazed out the window at the people who went by on the street.

"Hey, there goes Beansy," said Berlot quietly.

"Don't let him see us, we'll never get rid of him!"

"Good old Beansy," chuckled Berlot. "Do you know what Blowjoe Gartside did to him once, Pete? You were at college then, last month. He took Beansy and hung him up on the fence outside Mulvaney's bar, he was so drunk. No bull! Beansy was so stewed he couldn't talk, he couldn't walk, he couldn't see. He had a bottle of some stuff that he gave me a drink of. You know what it was? Shellac! Shellac mixed with alcohol! I swear on the Bible on my mother's name!"

"That's Beansy."

"Do you know his mother throws him down the stairs when he comes home drunk? You ought to see her—a big woman two hundred pounds, she works in the silk mills. When he comes home drunk, she goes out and when he gets to the head of the stairs, she just lets him have it, wham! Beansy has to go and sleep it off in the depot. And listen! Another time, last winter, I think, he was so drunk he let it snow all over him right outside the car. He fell right outa the car, out on the highway. That was the night I was dead drunk in the back seat. I woke up at six o'clock, and no Beansy! I got outa the car, all I could see was a big hump of snow on the ground. It was Beansy, dead to the world!" And Berlot leaned out to stare up the street. "There he goes . . . ! To Rooney Street and Middle Street to hit the saloons and see what he can get. He never gets it. At midnight everybody'll be smooching with his girl and Beansy'll be alone."

"Eleven-fifteen," put in Scotcho wistfully. "Another forty-five minutes and it'll be 1941. Imagine that!"

"Do you know that Beansy thinks he's a matinee idol?" said Danny, turning to everybody. "I caught him once in the men's room at the theater, admiring his profile with another mirror that he carries with him, getting a *side view*. New Year's Eve and he won't even come near a girl. He's afraid of them. He told me once women carry hatpins in their stockings to stab a guy with—"

"*Who* is Beansy?" inquired Francis suavely. Alexander was sitting beside him, dark with weariness.

"That was him went by just now!"

"Hey, Francis," cried Peter, "did you know that Berlot's old man and Pa used to be big buddies in the old days?"

"They used to hell around together," explained young Berlot eagerly, "they used to go to New Bedford on big fishing trips and get blotto right in the middle of the ocean. Huck huck huck!"

"Really!" cried Alexander, his patience having long been exhausted, "you're keeping those three fellows waiting an awful long time. Why don't we follow through with our plans for the night as we're *supposed* to do."

"Okay, we'll go see the intellectuals," said Berlot, and he started up the car and drove it slowly along the street.

"Look! The Greeks in front of the Y. You know what those guys think? Every woman that passes by falls in love forever with them." Saying this, Danny leaned forward to stare with grotesque stupefaction at the clusters of young men lounging in front of the Y.M.C.A. building. "That's why they stand there with that dreamy look in their eyes and smoke big pipes. Sure! That's what they think! See them showing their profiles to the women? Look at 'em swinging their chains. Hey, Zoot!!"

"There's that crazy Remo!" said Berlot, pulling the car to a sudden halt in the middle of the street. Another car swerved around crazily.

"He's a good basketball player, that crazy Remo."

"He's drinking and tailing around so much in about a year he'll be in *Shrewsboro* with the nuts!" Berlot suddenly stuck his head out the window and yelled: "Hey, Remo the madman!!—"

The boys in front of the Y.M.C.A. looked around and waved derisively as the car went by. But a moment later Berlot stopped the car again at the curb and fumbled in the locker for the bottle.

"Whattaya stopping for again!" cried Scotcho.

"Do you want me to get out and *push?*" cried Alexander now.

"Ah, take it easy, Alexander," said Danny in a soothing voice. "Man, don't you realize it's New Year's Eve? Don't you realize that this is a tough life, that there's a whole lifetime of worry ahead of you? Why should we always be in a hurry in this world?"

"The Prince of Crete must never hustle!" put in Scotcho with emphasis.

"The Prince of Crete?" echoed Francis softly.

"Sure! Alexander is the Prince of Crete," explained Danny, turning to stare at Panos, rolling his large yellowish eyes in mocking amazement. "What a good kid you are!" he suddenly cried with a shout of laughter, and under the sway of some powerful secret mirth he began to pitch over and choke with irrepressible laughter.

"Oh, what's the use!" sighed Alexander. He howled, in all good humor, with a helpless wave of his arms, and at this the bottle was instantly thrust upon him by the boys in the front seat—it was the big chance they had been waiting for—and he was loudly adjured to drink and drink more, which he at once proceeded to do in prodigious wild gulps as everyone cheered.

"There you *go!* There you *go!*" yelled Danny, beside himself and leaning solicitously over Alexander from the front seat, even kneading his hair enthusiastically. "Drink! drink! For tomorrow you may kick the bucket! Do you know something, Al? It's a tough life, I don't have to tell you that. The world is full of sorrow, old ladies trudging to the mill for the dead man's shift, or going to the Monarch to try to enjoy a movie, old men mopping floors. Oh, Al, if I were as smart as you I could express myself better. You know," he went on, suddenly turning to Francis Martin with a sincere air, "you don't know us very well and we don't know you very well, all we know is that you're Zagg's brother and that's good enough for us. What I'm trying to say is, we're not a bunch of fools like we seem to be—you know? I work in a mill, Francis, from three in the afternoon to midnight, in the daytime I go to high school trying to acquire myself a little education. I work hard, so do these guys. So let's all be friends, it's New Year's Eve, dammit. If I was only intelligent enough, like you or Alexander, I'd express my thoughts better, you know? But accept my fondest—gentlemen, all of you!—hand me that bottle, quick—to all ye merry goddam gentlemen, I bequeath the happiest of all new years on this crazy screwball earth! Hup!" And he drank a tremendous gulp of whiskey, and sputtered and coughed and choked, and tears came into his eyes, and Scotcho doubled up in hysterical laughter.

"Let's go!" yelled Berlot, throwing the empty bottle out of the window and jamming in the clutch. The car hurled forward with a great jump, and they were off at last to the Rooney Street barrooms.

As they charged into an upstairs saloon, Scotcho and Berlot immediately broke up two girls who were dancing together and whirled them off in crazy jigs. Francis and Alexander took up the rear in a more or less decorous fashion. But the moment Francis saw what it was going to be like—the dancing rooms roaring and shaking with the stomp of feet, the French-Canadian millhands cavorting with their women in that stiff-necked, white-collared way workingmen have on holidays, and the midnight hour approaching and things getting progressively noisier—he decided to go home and go to bed. Without a word to anyone, he went down the stairs, winding his scarf around his neck, and started up the narrow snowy street.

And as he walked home at a steady pace, everywhere around him, along Rooney Street, along the canals, the town was beginning to raise broad sounds of revelry that mounted as the midnight hour drew near. Meanwhile it had stopped snowing suddenly, a wind had come up and was blowing the fresh clean snow about the streets, and an occasional break in the clouds revealed sudden sparkling stars. It was colder now.

"What an unbelievable gallery of imbeciles that brother of mine parades around with!" he thought with a grimace. "Friends! Does he think the whole world will be *friends* with him? What chaos! Everywhere, nothing but chaos!"

He walked along absorbed in his own thoughts, jostling through occasional crowds, passing saloons and restaurants and diners in which people had begun to blow on paper horns and shake rattlers in a frenzy of merrymaking.

He turned smartly into a narrow side street and strode along past huddled tenements. Lights were burning in some of the windows and Francis could hear all kinds of merry noises inside. "Happy New Year!" he smirked. "Ring out the old, you idiots. Ring in the new—ring in more stupidity, more brute misery, more nonsense, more chaos. But, in God's name, don't fall out of line or the next in rank'll flog the living daylights out of you. Look out for that budget. Responsibilities to meet, you know. Love your wife and kiddies, forward the sub-human race. Learn to accept the whip of your next in rank. Don't revolt, whatever you do! The whip and not death! As for me, ladies and gentlemen, I'm going to desert the sinking ship."

He stopped on the bridge above the Merrimac Falls which were crashing about in a frothy steam beneath the high windblown stars of midnight. Shivers went up his spine.

"God!" he shuddered. "How horrible it would be in that water now. Will you look at the way those damned ice floes get tossed around on the rocks!"

He lingered there at the railing and watched moodily below.

Suddenly a car raced wildly across the bridge and zoomed past Francis, and someone leaned out the window and waved and yelled: "Don't jump, Bud, don't jump!! Hap-py New Year-r-r-r!" And almost before Francis could look around the car was veering crazily around the corner intersection and racing off downtown.

He hurried along thinking and burning, and finally he was walking up Galloway Road towards the house, and the sounds of the celebrating town faded far behind.

"These ridiculously cold climates," he sniffed. "The South is what I want—Mann's South, or Gide's, or Goethe's, the Mediterranean South, the Venetian. Remember that poem you wrote about that? What a timid little fool I was! I wonder how many fellows like me have wasted away, fretted, written poetry in a thousand chaotic American towns like this one until they decided to get out! And how many girls too? I wonder where all the girls are who read Willa Cather and Edna Millay and Gertrude Stein. They're the people I'm interested in, saved by their sensibility. What do the rest of them amount to, for God's sake? Great hordes of them, like ants. They struggle to find the meaningless ant-hill."

Francis stopped in the middle of the road and looked at the big shambling Martin house. He remembered his boyhood now as he stared at the house. This was the house he had been born and raised in, and yet what proof was there, in this wintry desolation of midnight, that anything had ever happened to him? "Looking at that house makes me feel absolutely certain that I never belonged there anyhow. Where's my Venetian sun, my own future, my Riviera, my marble plaza? Where will I be when I've managed to extricate myself from all this forever?"

In the Martin house now, in the creaking secrecy and isolation of midnight, in the gleeful choking excitement of midnight when Mom and Pop are not home, in the dark spooky hallways of house, in the screaming glee of attics, dark corners, under-the-bed, behind-the-door, back-of-the-sofa, as winds moan and windowpanes knock, and something stalks creeping in the darkness, in all this the Martin kids were converged now, hiding, running down halls, screaming horrendously, crawling on hands and knees, giggling, snickering, choking, saying, "I see you! . . . peekaboo!"—for it was midnight, and the house was dark, isolate, thrilling, and it was theirs for the night.

"Where's Joe? Where's Joe?" the Martin kids were screaming now in the dark wind-demented house of midnight.

"He's hiding up in the attic, I bet!"

"Let's go catch him! He's hiding up in the attic! Let's go catch him!"

And they all scurried up to the attic looking for their crazy big brother Joe, the gleeful kids Mickey, Charley, even Lizzy tagging along—but when they got there, he wasn't hiding, he was just sitting before an old chest pulling out a lot of old clothes.

"Look at all this stuff! D'jever see so much junk! Who's gonna put on this old dress? Who wants this old straw hat?"

"Oooh, let me!"

"Let's play some more hide-and-seek, Joey, please, Joey! hey, Joey! huh, Joey?"

"Wait a sec, I wanta see what else is in this big old trunk."

"Hey, looka me! I'm Zouzou! I'm Zouzou the junkman! Giddap, giddap, horse!—"

And the wind beat around the attic gables, something creaked in a dark corner, and the house was spooky and rich with darkness and all fabulous.

"Ooh! look at this!" cried Lizzy, pulling out an old 1910 dress, and she began putting it on, the floppy hat, the floppy shoes too, and strutted around clomping, so solemn, and the kids rolled on the floor and choked, and Joe scratched his chin, and the wind beat against the attic, the timbers creaked.

A child, a child, hiding in a corner, peeking, infolded in veils, in swirling shrouds and mystery, all tee-hee, all earnest, all innocent with shiny love, sweeter than a bird, pure with pretty gleaming eyes and rosy lips and the crazy little grin shining out, all writhing and quivering with phantasy and understanding, and the possibility of tears, unaware of duskish birds with disillusioned eyes flying nearer, but not now, oh, not now—the child, unknowing, yet best knowing, Godly all-knowing, the child crieth—"I see you. . . ."

Francis came in the house and went upstairs to his attic room, and lay down on his bed, in his dark nook, to meditate. And all around the house, upstairs, downstairs, everywhere—strange noises, unexplained titterings and tappings, creakings and scamperings, whoops and gasps and something hiding and playing in the dark, and commotions and conniptions all over.

What was it all about? Good God, what was it all about and what were they doing? He had not been that kind of child. Were they peeking at him now?

No, he had not been the same kind of child, he had been sickly and inactive (Francis reflected this now, darkly)—a child given to long profound solitudes and lone reveries during which he had imagined himself a hero, a prince, a great prizefighter, a warrior and a god. Owing to his delicate health, of course, he had not been able to take part vigorously in the ordinary activities around him: but even afterwards when in normal health, none of the things that children did had particularly interested him.

"The mother seems to think that it was a tough break for me to be sickly," he mused now as he stared at the dark ceiling, "but, heavens, the more I think about it I realize it was actually a boon to me someway. How else could I have been vouchsafed boyhood moments of contemplation while all the other kids were out in the fields and streets competing in their silly games? It was good for me. I learned what was rare, beautiful, fine, higher. It's the same story with a lot of great men. If I want to be great, I know the secrets—"

And nothing was further away from his mind than the naive and absurd hopes, the sentimental belief in the eventual wonderful fruition of his life, that his family placed in him—in moments when they considered him the "queer one" of the family who had "something on his mind" and who would one day pop up and surprise them all by some fantastic feat of brilliance that would make them all proud of little Francis—nothing was further away from his mind than these things.

"I feel like someone lost in a strange, hostile foreign country," he mused. "Like the other night when the old man raised his glass to me—what was it, Christmas night?—'Here's to you, Francis,' he said, 'here's hoping for the best.' That sentimental sad look in his eyes: he hates me and he's ashamed of himself for hating me, and he knows that I know it, too. Because I didn't get a job the moment I got out of high school, like all the other poor simple jerks around here, because I don't listen to his stupid stories, because I keep to myself. Oh, that gets him mad! What was it Gide said about the bourgeois father? But it really gets him mad. Anyway how I would have loved to return his toast that night, by executing a low formal bow. . . . Ah, well, it just isn't done in this neck of the woods." He smiled in the dark.

(Someone said "Wooo!" far below and a little foot tapped slowly, and there were laments as if solemnly meant to spoof all sorrow.)

Francis turned over on the bed and stared at the wall. "Oh, that stupid bunch tonight! That gang of Pete's! That awful Greek of his and that awful Danny with his sentimental little speech to me. My silence disturbed him also. That's what the old man principally hates about me—that silence. . . . And all those people with paper hats. New Year's Eve indeed—what a horrible thought that there's going to be another full year of it! And what makes a man keep on going?" he thought with a frown. "I wonder when the next depression'll hit me. Baudelaire was depressed all his life. There are so many things to make one sick nowadays, enough to make Baudelaire pale in comparison. . . ."

(A door creaked open slowly below, little feet ran bumbling, there was a pause, a hush, a smothered peep, a watchful waiting, another pause, another hush, and rattle-bang-slam the chair turned over, and whoops, and gallopings, and crazy laughter . . . all in the house, all in the house.)

And whether his family knew it or not, he was now about to set himself free.

"There's what was so exciting tonight walking home," he agreed happily, "just the idea of freedom, of finally making a decisive step. A simple little job in Boston, maybe something much better later, and just leaving this town and this house and going off as *myself*—as old F. Martin himself—that's a thought of freedom. It upset me wonderfully." He sat up on the edge of the bed. "No more my father presiding at the supper table, with that provincial wedding picture of him and my mother hanging on the wall like a Damascus sword, like something out of Julian Green's novels, a grim reminder for all the kiddies of their respective fates."

(Sudden silence as the wind ceased, and a shush, a hush, the squeak of a mouse . . .)

Suddenly he felt terribly lonely. He lay on the bed and turned over on his side again. He heard the sound of car wheels crunching over the snow in the driveway below, and voices. It was his parents and Ruth and Rosey coming back from the party at the Cartier's. He went to the window to look down solemnly at them from his dark perch.

"A brilliant evening was had by all," he whispered sardonically.

(Downstairs the scattering of little feet in the bedrooms, and snickering shushes, as little forms burrowed under blankets and smothered with glee and waited all breathless and mad.)

Francis sprawled back on the couch, and suddenly, a moment later, he was fast asleep with all his clothes on. He dreamed in the darkness of corridors alive with human forms, and suddenly again there were sounds outside. Francis raised his head and blinked at the gray light in the window. It struck him strange that he had been asleep for hours. He listened intently to the shouts and singing out on the road. He recognized Peter's loud voice in the midst of all the others. He got up and went stealthily across the attic to the front gable of the house and looked down on the road. He saw Berlot's car parked in front of the house, and Scotcho sitting disconsolately on the runningboard as though sick, and Berlot and Danny supporting Peter between them and walking him around and around in the snow, meanwhile keeping up their loud chorus of shouting and singing. The dawn wind swirled snow sweeping around them.

Francis hated scenes and dreaded one even now in his sleepiness. He hurried back to his room and put on his coat and tiptoed downstairs. He closed the front door quietly behind him and walked across the snow to the car.

"What's the matter with my brother?" he asked sleepily.

"Is he plastered!" yelled Berlot in the frosty stillness. "Huck huck huck! You know what he did a minute ago? He said, 'Gentlemen, if you will be so kind as to allow me to beg your indulgence, I should like at this moment to give myself over to the lower . . . no, the baser instincts.' How did he say it? 'Allow me, gentlemen!' Something like that! And he stuck his head out the window and . . . urp! Huck huck huck! That's Zagg, that's Zagg for you—!"

"Geezus, boys," Peter was moaning pitcously, "geezus, boys, geezus, boys—I don't want my mother to see me, I'm shot, I'm shot . . ."

"That's all right, Zaggo!" sang out Danny, dragging Peter around once more and tousling his hair violently. "A little fresh air will revive you. Pull yourself together!" he shouted, slapping him several times on the face lightly, turning away to laugh savagely at the absurd comic drama of the situation. "Bring yourself to your senses, man!" he cried with a stupefied stare of bulging eyes.

"Your brother Francis'll get you safe in bed," Berlot reassured Peter as he led him to the porch. "Damn old Zaggo, are you tanked!"

Peter slipped and fell and sprawled over in the snow.

"Awake the dawn!" yelled Danny now as he picked up a handful of snow and fluttered it down upon the sleepy disconsolate Scotcho, who did not even look up. "Ye gods, gentlemen, am I the only clear-headed man in this crisis? Must I bear the brunt of the catastrophic times? Hah? Our ship of state is foundering! The helm is spinning on its widget! Hey, Francis, what do you call the thing the helm spins on in all them big stories? Oh," he howled, suddenly running down the road with his arms outspread, "the dawn cometh and spreadeth rosy-fingered Alexanders everywhere . . . everywhere!"

"The Mouse is a big poet this morning," said Berlot admiringly. "We been to every joint between here and Boston. . . ."

Francis took Peter under the arm and helped him up the porch steps, whereupon, amid effusive farewells and singing and declamations, the gang got back in the car and roared off down the road.

Francis led Peter stumblingly into the house—just as the grayness was spreading over the sky and the first winter birds were chirping in the high snowy hedges. He led him up the stairs slipping and falling to his knees and growling and creating sudden loud commotions against furniture. After interminable fumblings, he had him safely in the bedroom that Peter shared with Joe. Beneath a dumpy patchwork quilt that the mother had made with her own hands Joe lay snoring peacefully. Peter threw off his clothes helter-skelter all over the room and miserably crawled into bed. Joe turned over snorting on his side, and in a moment they were both deep in sleep.

Francis stepped out in the hall and paused for a moment in the gray darkness. All around him, in all the bedrooms, there was the slow rhythmic deep breathing of the entire family asleep, like one single and mysterious slumber, the strange hush of silence that prevails in a sleeping house in the dawn hours, the moody human presence of silence and soft repose incomprehensible between the waking furiousness. He rubbed his eyes sleepily and leaned back against the wall, as though suddenly he had forgotten where he was and what he was doing. He was wrapped in a mood of uncomprehending lethargy, scarcely awake, and yet aware of a certain breathless suspenseful gloating in him as he lingered there in the dark hall, listening and looking around with a kind of wondering and crazy lonesomeness. The old worn carpet of the hall, the chest in the corner, the familiar doors leading to the bedrooms, all dim in the gray light, and the warm odors of drowsy sheets and pillows, the gentle breathing, and the silence—all of it brooded around him in profoundest absorption. He took a step forward and gloated in the loud creaking noise it made.

"What am I doing here?" he suddenly thought. "Who am I?"

Mechanically he opened the attic door and walked slowly up the narrow staircase. In his room he looked vaguely around as though he had never seen the room before, not *this* room, and he stared out the window at the gray snowy dawn, walked around for a moment, stopped before the mirror.

"Francis Martin, Francis Martin, Francis Martin," he kept thinking, and he ran his hand through his hair and gaped at himself in the mirror. A moment later he was back on the couch and fast asleep again.

(And the little ones were sleeping too.)

[12]

GEORGE MARTIN was on the verge of losing his business. When he saw that bankruptcy was a distinct possibility, he suddenly didn't want to do anything about it and stood back, watching with mingled horror and delight.

At fifty he was experiencing that second restlessness of manhood which is just as intense as the first restlessness of youth, just as wild, and open to springtime lurings, and subject to lonely futile whims, as that first urge to burst out of the shell of sameness and loneliness which men always know, but never conquer in peace and patience as women somehow do in time. He suddenly wanted to see what it was like to consider losing his business, to consider ruin and humiliation and the somehow thrilling exile of it all, just to see "what would happen."

When it became evident to some people that he was hopelessly behind in debt and in payments for the mortgage on his expensive printing machinery, which he had slowly been paying up over the years, and that he was losing ground rapidly in volume of business due to neglect and much time spent gambling, he cried: "Ah, I don't care what happens! Anyway don't get all excited, nothing'll come of it, I can build this business up again just like I built it up out of nothing twenty years ago. What kind of a fool do you think I am!"

They told him that if he continued to spend all his time playing the horses and gambling and neglecting his business he certainly would not be able to build it up again.

"And suppose the thing did fall down the hole!" cried Martin heatedly now. "I'm sick and tired of this place and everything in it. Do you realize that I've been working my head off in here for twenty years and I never hit higher than six thousand—and that was a big year! And what have I got to show for it? Sure, sure, I didn't save my money like some people do, but I worked damn hard."

"Well, you've always made a good living," they said.

"A good living!" snorted Martin. "I'm just disgusted with the whole thing, I've had my fill of it! By God, I wish I were free to pack up and leave the whole shebang, go off and follow the ponies or something, that's what I wish!"

"But you've got a wife and kids," they grinned. "That you can't do."

"I know some people who would, but not me, not me!" cried Martin sadly. "I'll just have to stick it out and drum up new business, that's all—just stick it out as usual."

But he wished he could leap right out of his life as George Martin. The wildness and desperation of a moody middle-aged despair was clutching at his brain and making him dizzy with terror and suspense, he felt like a little boy hanging by his arms from a high tree just to see what it would be like to "risk everything." He felt a tremendous desire to become even more sorrowful and lonely than he had ever been, he knew that this was goading him on more than anything else and it was a terrifying unspeakable thing.

Even when a man he knew as a mortgage speculator came sniffing around the shop under some flimsy pretense, he continued to talk about chucking up the whole works with a savage and irrepressible glee.

The loyal young Edmund warned him: "Didn't Jimmy Bannon put you wise to that guy that was snooping around this morning? You shouldn't have talked to him about those things!"

"I know, I know," said Martin sadly, "and I also know who sent him here, you know the bunch." And he suddenly laughed savagely—because it delighted him to think that while toying with the idea of giving up his business and walking off free of its cares and burdens, he could also toy with the bated greedy emotions of a small clique of men who were anxious to snatch the ground from under him, for purposes of personal profit and also of spite. He knew them all and he didn't like any of them. He knew the shady dealings some of them had pulled in the past, but they would not get the satisfaction of spite from his side. All this made him giddy.

But a moment later he couldn't understand the overpowering folly that was coming over him, he looked at Edmund working silently at the press and realized that he was also toying with his hard-working loyalty, he thought of his unsuspecting wife and the family, he thought of what his favorite little Mickey would think of him, he thought of everything that had gone into his business, his youth and the talent and diligence of a whole lifetime. He thought of the big Fridays when he had some of the children like Ruth and Lizzy and Charley and Mickey come up to help fold the weekly papers, and the "picnics" they had in the shop, and he even began to look around the place and think about each object and the scenes of the mysterious past which they occasioned in his memory. He felt strange.

He realized how funny it would seem to get up in the morning and not drive down and park the car by the canal and the railroad tracks, have breakfast in Al's lunchcart, and then come in the shop to his cluttered desk and his galleries of type, and say good morning to Edmund and old John, and then watch Jimmy Bannon come in at eleven all weaving, twitch-drunken and tortured, and then to work there all four of them in grinning joy. He thought of his little shop with a thick weeping feeling of consolation, he nodded his head saying, "Ah, yes, ah, yes, by golly!"—and he was logically and firmly convinced that his whole life's work was right here in the familiar dumpy little warehouse floor by the canal. Yet he was making up his mind to chuck up the whole thing even as he was walking around the plant looking at it. Even as he was smiling at the sight of a new steel filing cabinet which he had bought only three months before, his smile suddenly turned inward, and he thought of "what it would be like" in an immediate dark future of proud bitter sorrow.

Somehow that was what he wanted—that sorrow, that freedom to be haughty with failure and loneliness. Somehow he felt he would find out things that he had never known before this way. At fifty that was what he wanted, his new self engaged in strange new things. He exulted in these crazy thoughts even as he was firmly convinced that it was all mad. He thought favorably about all the joy and confidence and struggle that he had brought to it, through hard times and easier times, he thought of these heartening aspects of his business—and then he simply decided he was sick and tired of joy and confidence somehow, he wished to feel bitterness and rage again, and dark loneliness again, as in his youth.

"You damn fool," he thought scornfully, "you want to be young again and go around enjoying your misery? Is that all?" And he laughed at himself sarcastically.

Ten times a day he thought of a new aspect of his desire to quit, and each time it was crazier than the other, and he knew that he just wanted to quit, that was all.

"By God, I just don't want to be bothered any more!" he suddenly cried out loud in the shop, but neither Edmund nor old John heard him in the noise of the machinery.

"Now I know, now I know," Martin kept thinking in disgust.

"All the dirty business in the world and it's me, too! I'm no better than the others and I never was. The same crazy stubborn streak that makes people do such awful things—and there I was telling myself I couldn't figure out all the killing and the wars and the robbing and the cheap chiseling. What a laugh! I'm just as bad as the rest."

"And why *should* I stick it out?" he thought in swelling anger. "I don't have to! By golly, I've made up my mind, bad streak or no bad streak, that's what I'm going to do and God can hate me all he wants."

Now the moody urge towards unhappiness and the bitterness and rage which it would sanction was begun. What a powerful, stubborn, magnificent stupidness Martin felt as he thought of opening his hands in dramatic stiffness and letting his business go crashing down! What a thrill it gave him to surprise himself and do the unexpected thing, the thing that would brand him a fool and stand him humiliated! To feel that he could experiment with his own life's blood and undergo that dark thrill of promising himself some good and mysterious effort later on in the strange humiliated future!

The moment his wife learned about the situation and they talked about what to do, he deeply realized that he had been indulging himself in whims and fancies like a schoolboy. He saw clearly that there was no other course but to rescue his affairs as best as he could and go on with his business as before. In her presence, life became as simple as bread and drink, as profound as night and day, and all the wild moods and whims that he had a day before now appeared as mere unnecessary morbidities in the sunlight of the earth, her earth.

"No, no, you can't do that, George," she protested firmly, quietly, with grave sorrowful tears, "it just wouldn't do."

"Don't you think I know that, Marge?" he cried, anguished. "But, good God, I'm so tired, so tired of the whole thing, I just can't stand any more of it!"

"It's your nerves," she said quietly, "that's all that's wrong with you. All you need is a rest. Then you'd realize that you mustn't do this. George, you don't want to finish your days working for somebody else and not being certain of anything. You can't be sure of what can happen later on, in case you get sick or something—and after all the work you put into it, George!"

"I know, I know, I think of the children too!" he cried. "You're absolutely right. I agree with you a hundred per cent. But if you only knew, if you only knew!"

"I know, I know," she said slowly, "you're nervous and you're lonesome and maybe you're having your own kind of change of life. Don't laugh, that isn't so crazy as it sounds, George!" she protested sadly.

"Ah, Marge," he chuckled, coming over and kissing her, "you have the damnedest ideas sometimes—but I give you credit for one thing, though you may say some pretty silly things sometimes, I give you credit for having more brains than I have, in the end." He looked at her with delight, and then turned away again brooding and fidgeting and full of chagrin.

"It's your nerves, George, you need a rest!" she stated firmly. "I'm as sure of that as I can be sure of anything. What you need is a good long rest and time to think—and maybe you shouldn't even think at all, just rest."

"Yeah, relax, relax! like old Joe Cartier tells me to do!" he cried bitterly. "Well, I just can't, that's all! I don't know what's the matter with me but I just can't take things as they come. You're all perfectly right, I *am* crazy! Sometimes I wonder how you ever did stand me!"

"Oh, you're no bargain, all right—"

"So I'm not such a bargain, hey?" He grinned foolishly. "Well, by golly, for once I agree with you. I'm not! This time I almost proved it." He hugged his wife and looked at her sadly. "Look, Marge, go put on your best bonnet and let's get the car and go out some place, huh?"

So he remembered her then as the pretty French girl at the picnic grounds long ago, with her yearning, quiet, courageous little look, the great friend and companion of his life. The thought of how he had almost forgotten her and everything she meant to him in a foolish reverie so far from the core of his real life's desire, was enough to shrivel up his heart in shame.

She went and put on her "best bonnet" all flushed with the delight of the occasion, and the kids were amazed to see Ma and Pa starting out of the house together arm in arm, all dressed up and going no place in particular, just for a "few glasses of beer" and to talk and be together, no movies or parties or anything like that, just going out by themselves to be together. And Martin that night was like a man who realizes, in the presence of a woman, that the earth is not mad—it smiles.

The next day everything went up in a man-made smoke. The clique of men who had been watching Martin's every movement like vultures bought up his mortgage, made a few arrangements, and sat back waiting for Martin to have to retire from his business. It was the "well-known squeeze play," as Edmund solemnly judged it, and there was nothing that anybody could do about it.

"Well, that's it," said Martin wearily, "I should have been more careful. That's it and that's all."

And the motives of greed and spite which these men were exhibiting were enough to eat up Martin's soul, it was the grand fruition of his worst fears about what they might do, and of the ultimate corruption of ordinary men. At the same time it was also the mysterious act of reality which completed the intentions he had had all along and closed the door irrevocably upon the whole uncertain affair: they had him where they wanted him, and that was where he really, secretly wanted to be, no matter what he tried to tell himself.

What shocked him frozen, in black realization of how mad men could be, was an unexpected thing: it turned out that two of the machinators in the sordid deal were men who had been former close associates of his, two men he had always habitually trusted as a matter of course, as he would trust the light of the sun, two men he had even respected for their quiet dignified mode of living, their charming little families, their manner of civility and plain sense and agreeableness. He could never possibly have dreamed that they would be involved in any such scheme against him or against anyone else either.

"Wally and Jim!" he cried in amazement. "You're not telling the truth. There must be some mixup!"

"No, no, no!" moaned the paralytic Jimmy Bannon, waving his finger in grotesque rapture at Martin.

"Wally and Jim!" cried the old man, dumbfounded. "Well, what do you know about that, those two fellows!"

It was mad, mad. The windows were darkened, the world was mad and rumbling with doom, all deranged and sickly.

"I don't believe there's anything you can do, George, if those guys choose to run you out," said Edmund gravely.

"Thath what they're gonna do, Joth!" howled Jimmy Bannon, rolling his head mournfully.

He had lost his shop at last. Now that it was all over he wanted to be alone, to think about it, he wanted to get in his car and just drive around on deserted country roads.

When he went driving that day he kept looking at the farmhouses, among their fields and trees and homely stonewalls in the beautiful summer sun and shade of late afternoon, he kept wondering what the farmers were thinking there, if their lives were in any remote way similar to his own, if they had troubles and fears and crazy lonesomeness such as he had, and if they had also known men whom they liked and respected who had suddenly turned against them and turned the world into a place fearsomely lonesome. The winey glory of the sun was making deep green shade at the well, by the far stonewall, at the dusty old door of the red barn, a world of sun making grainy gold in the grass and shimmering across the fields, making speckles of shade in the woods of the afternoon earth. It was strange, strange.

But when he had driven back to Galloway and the town was all a-bustle in the early Saturday night rush of excitement and shopping and going-out, when he drove by the barbershops and saw the men getting their Saturday night shaves, when he saw the men standing at the bars, foot on the brass rail and hat shoved back, and he saw the little children darting in the shadows and yelling with glee, and all the crowds milling in the lights of Daley Square, he suddenly felt cheerful and almost jolly.

It made him laugh now, to think of Wally and Jim and what they had done.

"Those things happen, hey?" he laughed. "Well, they can have it, that's not for me! They can be as crazy as they like; by God, I've still got my own honesty and my own soul! I may be broke, but I've still got my own soul!"

He got his two old friends, Joe Cartier and Ernest Berlot, and they went to their favorite club on Rooney Street for a complete night of drinking. Martin had some money on him and he insisted on spending every last cent of it on his two old cronies who were good enough to drink with him when he needed them and their grave good presence.

"Don't look so gloomy!" he kept shouting at them all night. "Drink up! Have a good time! Be happy! Don't worry about me,

I can get a job anywhere anytime, and make as good a living as I've ever done. Billy! another round of drinks!" he howled.

"Well, kid," said old Joe Cartier ruminatively, "I guess what has to happen, happens, and it shore ain't no good to cry over it."

"That's right," said the old barber Berlot with a wry smile, "you remember what *I* lost in my time. I guess I'd have been crying about it for fifteen years if that's what I'd have done."

"There you are!" exulted Martin. "We may be broke, but we've got our own honesty and our own souls! I don't think any of us need worry about what we've done in our lifetime," and he gripped their shoulders broodingly.

Later on in the night he wept when he heard a young Irishman sing in a sweet tenor voice all the old songs that recalled his youth to him.

"Isn't it funny the way you start out on your life," he cried mournfully, "thinking that the whole world is a beautiful place just waiting for you to make your way in it! It's a beautiful dream you have when you're young, before you learn how some men can be, how things can break. But, by God, boys, if I had to live it all over again, I would! I would! Because it's a sweet life when you come down to it! Listen to that boy sing—there you have all the sweetness and beauty of life put together in one lovely song, and what more could you ask for? At least we've got that, we've got beauty and a few sweet memories and those poor little kids of ours we put in the world, who trust us and love us and believe in us so much! It's a sweet life. Forget everything else, I say, because it's a sweet life and God is good to us in the end."

At four o'clock in the morning the two oldtimers carried him home mumbling and exhausted and drunk, they helped him upstairs in his house, undressed him fumblingly while his wife hurried around preparing sedatives, they dumped him in the bed, looked at each other helplessly, and then tiptoed sheepishly away and went home.

And little Mickey, aroused from sweet grave slumber by all the noise and terrible excitement in the house, stood now in the doorway and looked at his father fearfully as he lay there mumbling and drunk in the bed.

Yet on Monday morning the big man was up bright and early, shaving and dressing and eating breakfast in grave, scowling, meditative silence. Mickey watched his father—his clean white shirt-collar tight and neat against the ruddy flesh of his neck, his eyes sorrowful and thoughtful, his face set in morning absorption and determination, his prim and solemn movements all betokening a new purpose and many anxious considerations. His wife spoke to him about little things and he stared at her with his agonized brooding tenderness. Then he went quietly out of the house, without a word, got in his car, and drove away.

That morning he got himself a good-paying steady job in a downtown printing plant, came right back home and told his wife that everything would be all right again now.

So George Martin, in the space of a week, had lost a business valued at some twenty thousand dollars, had drained his last savings from the bank in order to meet most of his debts and avoid the dishonor of a complete bankruptcy, and was now become a wage-earner in another man's firm after twenty years in business for himself.

Yet the shock of this really stunning change was received calmly, cheerfully, even gleefully by the Martins young and old. They had always been vigorously absorbed in living itself, never quite conscious of those finer points with regard to "position" in a community, thus heedless of that delicate, invisible, yet definite change that had come about in the family's worldly status. It was even possible they would have to move out of the big house and find a cheaper place to live. Yet their only thought was of the humor and pathos of the situation and the chagrin of their father. They rallied around him laughing with him, and all were immediately concerned with the simple matter of earning more money all around.

They sat around the front room in the evenings that summer and talked:

"Now you'll know how it feels to have to get up and hurry so you won't be late for work!" cried Ruth to her father goadingly.

And they all laughed eagerly, the laughter ran through the house, the kids sat on the edge of the sofa watching and listening in rapt fascination, the mother was making lemonade for everybody in the kitchen, the father sat back in his chair grinning.

"Ah, whattayou mean?" he snorted, winking quickly aside at the kids. "Now wait a minute! What makes you think I had such an easy time of it working for myself. I notice you used to get mighty, mighty tired just folding those little old papers for me at the shop, I used to have to carry you home, you little sparkplug you!"

She sat on the arm of his chair teasing him: "Now you'll know what it feels like to punch a time clock at the last minute!" And she pushed him on the arm and made a wry face.

The kids yelled with laughter.

"Okay, so I'll punch a clock, what about it!" cried the old man grinning, and he tried to think of something funny to say. Then the mother came in with the lemonade, and they all sat there late into the night laughing, arguing, shouting, almost *celebrating* this strange new turn in the family's fortunes which was so exciting and wonderful, somehow, because it made them all sit together in the front room and have "regular parties," as Mickey delightedly saw it.

Joe was inflamed with a new idea in the heat of all the enthusiasm.

"See, Pa? I saved a lot of money on my trip and sent it home to Ma. Now it'll come in handy. I know a guy who wants to sell out his gas station. Just a little place on Kimball Street, two pumps and a lubrication stand. I'm gonna take it! Monday, by God, Monday!"

"I'll be your helper, Joey!" cried out Charley, tugging at his big brother's arm. "After school. I'll work real good! You know I'm real good!"

"Sure thing."

"Ma!" cried Charley. "Maybe I can quit school now and just work for Joey, huh? I don't have to go to school any more, huh? I want to start working!"

"You will not," said the mother, peering at him.

"And me," said Mickey, frowning thoughtfully, "I'm gonna start a paper route"—and he looked around at everybody grinning sheepishly.

"Say," said the old man, looking up at Ruth and winking, "maybe that'll solve all our problems. Mickey'll start a paper route."

The family roared with laughter. People passing on the road outside might have thought that a great celebration was going on in the Martin house. In the heart of such a family, whether mere events were happy and good and wonderful, or unfortunate, even calamitous, they could never really be discouraged or disheartened, they could only be excited and gleeful and, in the end, all together. Together there was never really cause for anything but rejoicing, the sheer force and joy of their numerous presence was in itself a surging enthusiasm, they looked at each other and knew each other well in that casual, powerful, silent way that brothers and sisters, parents and children have.

Big Rosey, for instance, the big sister and lusty guardian of their lives, was sitting beside young Peter on the sofa chuckling and then roaring with laughter and throwing in a few digs herself when someone kidded someone else. Peter, sitting beside her meditatively yet watching everything with deep pleasure and consolation, was amazed at this big girl, the very bulk and consequence of whose hearty chuckles and shouts of whooping laughter and huge convulsive movements made him joyful that she was just there and was his sister. He couldn't have known why. It was her presence, the great and good mystery of her being there beside him, and of all the family being there with him, and he being with them. To feel these unknowable yet so overwhelming affections for his brothers and sisters and parents, to see them there in the room with him and laugh with them, this was gravity and glee and wonder.

And the father himself was most thankfully aware of these things that bound them together: he wondered that he should ever have rued and regretted any mistakes in his life, any decision and miscalculation, when it was so that all things were equal, all things were bound together, and all things were the same and just as well with his family and its single beating heart.

No one was really downcast: the mother herself spoke of going back to work in the shoeshops if it ever became necessary. Even young Lizzy wanted to leave high school now and get a job.

"What's so horrible about leaving school!" she muttered in her proud scornful way. "What do I care about history and books. I want to make some money and have a good time. Phooey!" she cried.

"She wants to make some money so she can go to Hollywood and be a big actress!" goaded big Rosey, stroking Lizzy's head teasingly. "Look at her! Ain't she a raving beauty?"

Elizabeth stuck out her tongue at her.

"Look at that!" whooped Rosey. "Ain't she the ladylike one! Just like Greta Garbo! She's gonna go to Hollywood and become a big actress and then she'll come around here in a fancy car all dressed to kill and stick up her nose at us!" She stroked her kid sister's head gleefully.

"Is that what you'll do, Liz?" chuckled Joe fondly. "Ain't you going even to say hello to me when you're famous? And after all the times I used to let you play baseball with the boys! When all the other girls were playing house in left field, Liz used to rap them singles to right field! Hyah, hyah, hyah!"

They all rocked with laughter again, and Elizabeth scowled and smoldered.

"All right," she said, "laugh. I'll make more money than anybody. Just wait."

"Will you buy me a cup of coffee when I meet you outside the Ritz?" the old man asked with heavy innocence. Again they all roared with laughter and slapped their knees, and Liz stalked fiercely out of the room. But she was back again in a minute flouncing around gayly and snorting down her nose at Joe and Rosey.

Thus it was—a convocation of resolves and excitements. However: "There's no point in staying home now that I've got this Boston job," Francis told Peter. He added, with a wry smile, "I see no reason why I should clutter up the house anyway, do you?"

"Clutter up the house? What are you talking about?"

"Oh, that's just the feeling I have. It was a silly thing to say anyway." He smiled a little wistfully. "I just have more fun in Boston." He was starting another year at Harvard that Fall.

In the mornings now George Martin drove down to work with his favorite daughter, Ruth. Trim, businesslike little Ruth, who had always been so cheerful and reliable, so dear to him, and a comfort to his heart, who knew him perhaps better than anyone else in the house, who was ultimately a great loyal friend of his life, she and he went to work together in the same printing shop, working just a few feet from each other at the linotype and at the folding machine, looking up from their tasks every now and then to exchange merry glances of delight because they were working together now.

And it was such a joy and gladness for the troubled old man to see his Ruthey there, working with him in the morning, evidence enough that he was not alone and scorned in the world, as he could so ruefully feel, evidence that the sun shone on the earth even through all the error, misery, and madness of things which he told himself were, when all was said and done, mere caprice and accident.

3

THAT SUMMER Tommy Campbell, Peter's boyhood partner in the prowling riverside adventure, sandy-haired, vigorous, intelligent Tommy, showed up in the uniform of the United States Army.

It was dusk, hushed and summer-still, and in the reddening light of New England June, Peter and Alex Panos were sitting on the porch tilting their chairs against the wall of the house and talking. Peter had just completed his first year of college.

They saw a figure striding up the road a half-mile away, they could see the soft dust he raised in the road as he walked, and they noticed that he was some sad and lonely-looking young soldier. Alexander commented on him, saying: "Look at that soldier coming up the road, lost and sad in thoughts of death!" But they did not actually recognize him.

At the hedge, young Tommy Campbell cried out: "All right, you two civilians! Sound off!"

The two boys just gaped.

"I'm off on the Road to Mandalay, you deadbeats!" cried Tommy, swaggering up the walk. "You better take one good last look at me because you won't be seeing me for a long time!"

And they were amazed because he had "gone and done it"—for Tommy had always boasted that some day he would travel around the world and be an "adventurer." He really looked like one now. He gripped their hands enthusiastically, squeezed their arms with a strong manly grasp, laughed, and told them that he was going to the Philippine Islands in a few weeks.

"No more hoeing the rows for me for a while." And he smoothed his sleeve and put his leg up on the porch banister in a casual, elegant, and soldierly manner. "You guys can stay home and read books and go to school—that's not for me any more. No more 4-H club for me either, that's for girls all right. I want to see the tropics, I want to see *pygmies* and weird birds!"

"So that's where you've been all this time!"

"Yep. Maneuvers in the West Indies. Didn't you read about them in the papers, down in Martinique? That's where I've been. What are you guys up to? I mean these days," he grinned slyly.

And there was nothing, absolutely nothing they could say.

That night the three boys really had a go at it conversing on all subjects and weighing the drift and possibility of their respective fortunes in the world. They solved all the problems of existence and the universe and rubbed their hands in anticipation of new ones. They sat in Peter's bedroom in a litter of books and papers and letters, smoking cigarette after cigarette, drinking coffee by the pot, laughing uproariously, talking about women, politics, books, and the soul of man. It was all exclusively their subject in the smoky little bedroom there with the patchwork quilt, the football pictures on the wall, and the bright lace curtains that puffed in the summernight breeze.

Gleefully they decided to go out and sleep in the woods at Pine Brook that night. Peter stealthily went downstairs to an old chest and smuggled some blankets out on the porch, where he hid them beneath the hammock. Then he went back upstairs and they drank more coffee and talked a lot more until two o'clock in the morning, when they decided to set out with the blankets.

"This is a night I shall never forget," said Alexander, jubilantly slurping up his coffee. "I shall never forget it because, don't you see, it's so *damn* significant, honest! Just think! Tommy is going off to the Orient, we're saying good-bye to him. Don't you see, Peter! After all the years that you've known Tommy and played with him as children, after all the dreams of youth. It's a parting of the ways, for all of us, and really sad! We're on the threshold of a new age, and God knows what it's going to be—in any case, hugely important to mankind! And how is each one of us going to fare in the great convulsion of the times, what are we going to contribute individually? What will we contribute to the great brotherhood of mankind?"

"You know, Alex, that's one thing that's always amazed me about you," spoke up Tommy with an eager smile. "I was going to write a play last year with just that as a theme, with a character like yourself in it speaking up for the brotherhood of men. But as an anti-thesis I was going to have someone else representing the voice of necessity and practical philosophy. You see the conflict there?"

"But, of course, Tommy, it's my whole life—sensing that conflict and being tortured by it," said Alexander, amazed by Tommy's words.

"You know, I believe you," grinned the good-natured farmboy. "But here's the way I see it, the raw truth of it: I never got time to write that play, due to Spring plowing and my father needing a new pasture fence. So you see, the conflict answered itself. I didn't have to write the play, it was all there. Spring plowing and a new fence, contributing to food and livestock for the citizens of the world, in other words, the brotherhood of men in action."

"Yes," said Alexander vaguely—he was worlds apart from this idea—"yes, I see." And he fell silent, typically, only to burst out moments later with raucous exuberant laughter as they swung the subject to something else. It went on like that for hours, with Peter dashing about making more coffee and getting cake from the breadbox. Finally they were ready to go out and sleep in the woods.

Just as they were getting ready to leave Peter's room, a sudden light tap was heard on the door and Mrs. Martin appeared in the doorway with a sly smile on her face. They looked at her, dumbfounded.

"I know what you young devils are up to tonight," she said, pointing a finger at them and shaking her head. "Don't think I don't know about those blankets you hid on the porch. Hey?"

The three boys glanced at each other with a kind of sheepish pleasure.

"Yes, yes," she went on, "I know. You were planning to sleep out in the woods, out in the woods in the middle of night where you can catch cold in the mist and get bit by spiders and snakes. You couldn't fool me!" she smiled cunningly.

"Well, no!" protested Peter with pleased astonishment. "Not exactly! We were just going to go down to Pine Brook—and go in swimmin' this morning, early this morning—and—well—"

"Go in swimming at this time of night?" And she sat on the edge of a chair and clucked her tongue almost mournfully. "Oh, no, no, no," she said sadly. "It's dangerous to sleep out in the woods like that. You never know what kind of bugs and snakes there are, especially by the water like that."

"Hey, Ma," cried Peter gleefully, "look at Tommy here! He's a soldier, he's going to sleep out in the jungles in the Philippines and everything like that. What about that? Huh?"

The boys laughed excitedly.

"I know, I know," replied Mrs. Martin, "but it's not right just the same. You've got a nice warm house, why should you go out and sleep in the cold wet woods like that? You've got a nice bed here and there's an extra bed up in the attic, the boys can sleep here, there's room for both of them. You won't get chilled and you'll be comfortable and before you go swimming you can take sandwiches with you and a bottle of milk if you like. Now isn't that a much better idea?"

"But what about the jungle, Ma?" cried Peter, laughing.

"I don't know about the jungle," she said with a sudden sad absentmindedness. "No, I didn't make the army, I didn't make the wars they have either. Why, if it's going to mean jungles for Tommy there's no sense in this now."

And it seemed so true to them suddenly. They all stared at her rapt with fascination as they thought of her warm quilted beds, her clean house, her food in the icebox, her warm radiators in the winter and all the things of a homestead. They remembered how good these things were to come back to after a night of drinking riot and weariness, how really sweet these things were, and how they never actually thought of them.

"Yes," she went on, "you should all be grateful that you have nice comfortable homes if nothing else in this world, you should be very grateful and make use of them and enjoy them while you can. Now isn't that true?"

And they thought of "wars and armies" and of men who were the opposite of Mrs. Martin with all their flimsy tents and trenches and guns and cauldron-food and bloody battles, and they grinned fondly.

"Now," she said, "maybe you should do as I say and you'll see that the old lady isn't so dumb. Sleep here and then get up early in the morning and go swimming when the sun's up and all the birds are singing and it's nice."

"Okay, Mrs. Martin!" said Tommy Campbell, jovially going up to the mother and putting his arm affectionately around her. "You're absolutely right! We'll do that, we won't sneak out, honest! On one condition, though, and that's if there's any caramel pudding in the icebox—"

"Well, there isn't any right now, but I'm going to make some Sunday and if you want to come and visit Petey again—"

"Ho ho ho!" yelled Tommy happily. "I was only kidding you, Mrs. Martin. I'll do it even without the caramel pudding. Remember when you used to make caramel pudding for me and Pete on rainy days, when we used to draw pictures up in his room? Boy, was that a long time ago!"

"Yes," said Mrs. Martin almost quaveringly, "I do remember, and now look at you, a soldier and everything. Why did you go and join the army! I think there's going to be plenty of time for that later—"

"You know me, Mrs. Martin, always on the go!"

"Well, I'm going over to see your mother soon and have a good long talk with her. Good night, boys, and remember what I said" —she turned and peered at them severely—"no sneaking out of the house!"

But after she had left the room, Tommy leaned towards the others and whispered: "When the sun's up and all the birds are singing. But what about *bats* and night mist!" They laughed splutteringly. "But we'll do as she says, I'm tired anyway. Let's get some shuteye and go swimming first thing at dawn."

So they slept in the house that night. Mrs. Martin had exerted her last benevolent powers over the comfort and well-being of Tommy Campbell and the mysterious likes of him in his generation, the kids who were going off to war and death. She perhaps did not know this; they could not know it. What happened that night Peter was to remember later with a distressed sorrow.

At dawn, bleary-eyed but joyful, the three youngsters took off across the wet dewy fields and went into the woods to the brook among the pines, where they had done the old swimming as little kids. And just as they got there the sun began to come up, the mists stirred over the hillsides and over the placid brook, birds peeped in the pines, the last pale stars trembled, and great light began to overspread the world.

"Rosy-fingered dawn!" howled young Panos with indescribable delight, and they were all awake now, strangely ecstatic, and each began to sing, babble, and wander around in the woods throwing sticks, Alexander himself singing in a loud bawling voice that might have been heard two miles away in the profound stillness. He even ran tripping to the top of a little hill, yelling joyous hosannahs and holding out his arms to the sky, while Peter and Tommy watched him, amazed.

Peter, for his part, kept looking up at the sky and yelling "Space!" or down in the water with a show of moodiness, saying "Lucidness," or stamping his feet on the ground and repeating over and over again, "Solidness, solidness, solidness," though he hadn't the vaguest idea why he enjoyed doing this. And Tommy Campbell, flinging his tunic over his shoulder in the warm morning, began to sing in a high cracked voice, *On the Road to Mandalay*, which echoed and re-echoed in the woods, especially when Panos lent his own thunderous voice to the refrain. They felt wonderfully foolish and happy and they let go with anything that came to their minds.

"Because the sun is coming up!" howled Alexander. "Only because the sun is coming up! We came here just for that!"

"We thronged!" shouted Peter triumphantly.

"Yes! Through the woods!" bawled Alexander. "Oh, listen to me! Beauty is truth, and truth is beauty, and that is all ye need to know!"

"Chambers of beauty!" cried Tommy Campbell, pointing to the rays of light streaming down between the pines.

"God's cathedral-l-l!" called Alexander through cupped hands in a great shout that carried across the fields, and they all laughed savagely.

Then, as the sun came up in full brilliant array far off over the hills, fanning light all over the sky and gilding little dawn-clouds that were regimented beautifully overhead, the boys fell silent, in awe, and stood on the two little hills watching, Panos and Campbell on one hill, and Peter alone on another, all of them brooding and reflective. It was a strange little moment of meditation in the deep stillness of the morning, with only the sound of a farmer's horse neighing faintly far away and clip-clopping on a road, and someone whistling far away, and a barndoor closing.

They trudged back home wearily, after a quick shivering swim in the brook where Alexander splashed about prodigiously, screaming: "Mumbo Jumbo God of the Congo and all of the other Gods of the Congo!" Now, their meditations over as whimsically as they had begun, they jabbered excitedly all the way home; Alexander wound a flower around his ear, Peter chewed the stems of long grass, and Tommy strode along like a prophet, carrying a huge limb from a rotted tree. They happened to see two veiled old ladies trudging along the road, apparently towards the church in Norcott, two darkly-clad old women faithful to some endless novena. Peter pointed at them with the air of a prophet, saying: "Fear." Alexander went into a little dance that was intended to represent fear, and Tommy Campbell raised his huge tree-bough and waved it thrice in solemn blessing.

They strode on home eagerly, hungrily. Alexander cried: "Up there!" and they all stopped. Alexander was pointing at the sky, saying: "Glory!" They all stared up at the sky.

"Here!" cried Tommy Campbell, pointing to the ground at his feet. "Death!"

Alexander knelt on the ground and tenderly took the flower from his ear, and laid it down, and covered it with a little bier of earth, his whole body, meanwhile, seeming to tremble suddenly from some spasmodic feeling.

"What's left of life," he said mournfully, "what's left of life, a little flower. Immortal little flower that venerates us, that venerates us and all that this morning means. Weep for the little flower, weep for the petals in its heart, weep for us, weep for us!" He knelt there, while the boys watched grinning, he knelt there and seemed to be wrapped in a secret, prescient ecstasy of what his life was to him.

And then they went on home.

[2]

IN THE WARM SUMMER NIGHT all cricket-stirring and soft, under tall drooping trees and the sultry stars of night in June, on the side of a dark road, below gaunt telephone poles and the long swooped wires, on the road where cars passed in a lonely spear and reach of lights with a haunted rush of voices and radio music faintly inside, the roadhouse glowed red neon and blue in softest darkness among congregated gleaming cars on the white graveled drive. Music came pulsing in the air, and the noise of laughter and dancing and all the singing, lyrical, somehow hopelessly sad sounds that Americans make at night.

Liz Martin came walking down the road dressed in slacks, carrying a small handbag, looking around somewhat frightened yet with childlike haughty scorn, a lonely and disconsolate figure in the weaving light of passing cars. She had got off at a bus stop half a mile away.

She came to the red neon roadhouse beneath the trees and stopped, with a rueful and attentive air. The music pulsed faintly, the cars gleamed darkly on the white bright gravel, the ventilators roared whirring above the door, summer moths fluttered in the neons.

"Liz, gal," she said to herself, "what are you waiting for?" She wondered if she had "lost her nerve." She stood there on the driveway in front of the entrance awning trying to decide just how to go in the place.

A party of people came out, laughing. Behind them sudden loud jazz pounded into the night. The faint tinklings of a piano came from far back. She saw a smoky flash of dancers huddled under low rafters, dark shadowy figures nodding in the pink-blue light, a gleam of bar and bottles. The door closed, the music became a muffled pulse, the cricket-sounds swelled up all around, the people drove away crunching over the gravel. Again she was alone.

"Liz, gal," she said, primming her hair abstractedly, "there's no sense just standing out here. You've got to go in."

Even as she said these things to herself, grinning because it was so silly to stay there talking to herself, she knew she was scared to death to go in, she knew it was almost too much for her to walk in all alone and do what she was going to do. She had come to see about her man Buddy Fredericks, who had not showed up for their date that night. He was playing piano inside. She was determined to find out what was wrong, why he hadn't come as he always did on Friday nights. And with that saucy, petulant, yet grim little manner that girls have on such occasions, she had started out after him from the house, fuming with indignation and wrath. But now she was scared by all the noise inside, and leaned on a car, and bit her lip, and wished that Buddy could be like he was a year ago when he had his motorcycle and would just come and get her and go riding, before he had to start being a musician, before he had to go and trade his motorcycle for a piano.

The night, all around her, was the way it had always been with her and Buddy before—cool, dark, vast, mysterious: with the river gleaming in starlight when they roared speeding down the highway, and she hugged close to him, and they sang shouting in the wind. It was the way the nights were when they would go to "their spot" on the riverbank and spend the night eating fried clams, talking, singing, telling stories, kissing, making love, thinking about what they would do when they were married. The crickets in the mist, the great shadowy meadows, the far-off hoot of the Montreal train, the little lights gleaming far away in the summer darkness, and always the cool lapping sound of water at night—that was the way it had always been for her and Buddy before. Now he was inside this noisy laughing place with a lot of people, and she was scared—and jealous.

"Liz," she said to herself again, "it's now or never." With this she drew herself erect, ran her tongue speculatively around her cheek, tightened her handbag against her, and marched straight up to the door and opened it.

She blinked at the heat and fury inside. The floorbeams shuddered from the stamping of many feet, the din that rose to the low ceiling was deafening, she could see nothing but people crowded and elbowed in a solid moiling mass. There was a sensual reek of cigarette smoke and liquor in the air, and she was conscious of many eyes looking at her from the dimness.

Almost blindly Liz marched straight ahead towards the bandstand on the other side of the room. She was not going to be diverted from her goal by anything. She pushed her way through the crowded dancers who were whirling, bouncing, swerving, colliding, bowing, laughing and shouting, all in the din of booming, beating, furious, almost insane tempo.

Now with a roll and racket of the drums the music stopped. There was shattering applause, and for a moment only the babble of voices, the tinkling of glasses, the deep thrumming roar of the ventilators. Then the piano started, a saxophone moaned, the band struck up the quiet blues, the dancers shuffled and embraced on the floor. A blonde girl stepped up to the microphone and began to sing.

Liz walked right up to the bandstand, pushed her way with proud scorn through a group of girls standing in front of it, and stood staring at the pianist solemnly.

He was a big shambling youngster with a cigarette stuck in the corner of his lopsided grinning mouth. He sat hunched over broodingly, his long hands reaching, his eyes staring in a dreamy absent-minded reverie, and he played softly, moodily, as though to himself.

"Hey, you!" she said.

He looked up startled.

"Come here, you!"

"Huh? That you, Liz? What the heck you doing here?"

"Never mind that. Come here."

"What do you mean, come here? Can't you see I'm on!"

"I don't care what you're on," said Liz contemptuously. "Come here."

"Ah, don't be crazy, Liz!" laughed Buddy suddenly. "Man, sometimes—hey, listen to this!" he cried enthusiastically, beckoning her with his head. "Listen to this—those chords I was working on. Come here, come here, don't be crazy."

Liz went over and leaned on the piano, and looked at him wrathfully, with a film of embarrassed tears in her eyes, curling her lip angrily.

"Listen, you," she said in a very low voice, "why didn't you come tonight?"

"Because I had to play here!" he laughed. "I had a last-minute call!"

"Why didn't you tell me?" she demanded intently. She knew the girls in front of the bandstand were watching her and laughing, but she didn't care, she didn't care about the whole roaring place.

"I didn't have time, crazy!" laughed Buddy, pushing her lightly with a big meaty hand. "Come here, come here, listen to these chords, dizzy!"

"You're lying," she said half-heartedly, looking at him now with a wary, amused eye, knowing that everything was all right again.

"Okay, so I'm lying," the boy frowned. "Here's the chords I was telling you about—wait a minute," and he paused broodingly while the singer sang slowly to the end of her chorus in the sudden hush of a suspended tempo, then he struck his chords softly, with great spread-eagled fingers, and stared at the keys moodily during the applause.

He got up—tall and big, slouching and shambling dreamily, somewhat consumptive—and took Liz to a corner table and ordered her a coke. He was dark, with pensive brown eyes, slow lazy movements, and a way of staring into space absentmindedly when someone spoke and turning to gaze at them with a serious, stupefacted, scrutinizing earnestness.

Liz was looking up at him gleefully now. "Oh, I know you weren't lying. Don't look so stupid!" she cried happily.

"Who's looking stupid?" he mumbled in his absentminded way.

"You are! You don't even know that I was jealous!"

"Jealous? Why?"

"Oh, never mind!" she cried in his face angrily. "How can you be so big and foolish! You're so foolish—and so *big!*" She stamped her foot and sulked.

And he chuckled, hugely pleased, staring at her with fond amazement. He not only liked her, but actually she was the only girl he had ever noticed particularly. For the most part he went around wrapped in his own thoughts like a great brooding monk, always thinking about something other than what was directly at hand—a dreamy, shambling, overgrown boy with strange notions of his own, thoughts of his own, and music in his mind . . . destined, somehow, to forget his life in a dream. He had spent his boyhood on the farm, and then, in high school, where he had met Liz, a few piano lessons had suggested to him that he become a jazz musician. He was a good one now, with an inborn genius for music, and the restless exploring originality of the American jazz musician. He dressed smoothly, sleekly, with his immense size forty-six drape jacket, long lapels, a bow tie, and a way of wearing his clothes with a catlike slouch and angular ease. He was only eighteen years old. And the sharp, vivacious, abrupt Liz was the girl who could wake him up and make him pay his amazed attention to her.

"That singer," said Liz now, as the jukebox music resumed thrumming and low, "I'll bet she's making eyes at you. And all those girls standing in front of your piano. That's *my* piano!" she cried. "Damn bunch of flirts! Why did you have to get a job in here!" she demanded.

"This is a good place! Do you know what I'm getting for tonight? Fifteen bucks!"

"Well, what about that singer?"

"Her? She's married to the drummer. You're crazy."

"Well, I saw her looking at you, brother."

"Yeah?"

"Yes! Don't look so happy!"

And they sat at the little corner table looking at each other with a kind of grave, absentminded delight. Soon they were holding hands casually and looking around the room in solemn curiosity. They were young and they forgot one moment from the other.

"Buddy!" said Liz finally. "You're not mad at me for being jealous."

He grinned and shook his head.

"It's only because I love you so crazy, Buddy," she whispered savagely. "Buddy, do you love me as much as I love you? Now, *really*, do you?"

"Sure."

"And you're going to be my husband," she stated firmly.

"I guess so."

"You *guess* so! Don't forget, you!" she whispered in a sulk. And suddenly there were tears welling in her eyes and she was looking at him, studying his face intently, and trembling convulsively as though she was going to cry. She felt that furious longing for him to "notice" her, that longing possessiveness that was the one ruling passion of her life, something she remembered from way back as a little girl when she would protect little Mickey in a fight, or even Peter on one occasion, and take them home and make them play with her. It was always that dreamy absentmindedness of them that drove her furious to own them, make them stay beside her dreaming. But when *they* noticed her she was always scared.

"Take it easy, Liz!" pleaded Buddy softly and swiftly in her ear. "Don't cry. You know I mean every word I say."

"Oh, you're so dumb!"

"Okay, I'm dumb," he laughed, squeezing her hand in his sudden, earnest, astonished way.

"We'll be married and we'll have children and we won't ever see nobody else," she pouted darkly. "You're so big and dumb. I want you for myself. I don't want other girls around. I don't want them to look at you because you're mine. You belong to me. You do, you know. Buddy, you've *got* to!"

"How can they help looking at me!" he shouted, laughing. "I'm sitting right up there on the bandstand! Crazy Liz!"

"We'll be married and we'll have lots of children and we won't see anybody else in the world," she said simply, and then she broke out in a gleeful little laugh and kissed him quickly. "I don't like it here in this damn place. I wish you weren't a musician—but that's one reason why I love you. I love you because you're a musician and a big fool."

"Great," he grinned absentmindedly.

"You're going to be a great musician, I'll help you," went on Liz as though reciting things to herself. "And I'll be a great singer myself like Martha Tilton. That's what it's going to be," she said firmly.

When it was time for Buddy to go back on the bandstand, he got up slowly and lazily, tousled Liz's hair in his fond abstracted way, winked at her, and went shambling back to the piano, and she watched him with proud approval, with brooding satisfaction.

The drummer struck a cracking rim-shot and the band was off once more on a fast swing beat. All the dancers began to bounce in unison, tall girls were held off at arm's length, scissoring sexy knees swiftly, pulled back suddenly to whirl and bounce, flung away again scissoring and bowing. The room seemed to rock from dancing and din, the smoke was thick and heavy, the waitresses scrambled through the crowd with their trays yelling orders, everyone was talking or shouting. The saxophone player with a sweating bursting face was playing with his eyes closed, driving the instrument up and down, standing with his legs wide apart. The drummer grinned and bobbed his head steadily as he snapped the snare brushes. Someone was drunk across the way, there was a weave of bodies in the dimness, the manager came rushing up, a glass smashed, someone was being thrown out.

Liz watched all this with a scowl of displeasure. Only her Buddy was calm and beautiful to look at in the whole place, he just sat slouching at the piano with his hands reached out, motionless, executing soft tinkling interplays in the wild music and noise, grinning secretly over his ideas. Only Buddy was like that in the whole place, Buddy and maybe three soldiers who sat at the table in front of Liz. The three soldiers sat motionless, sullen, a little drunk, watching with bleary eyes, paying no attention to two military policemen who stood in the corner twirling their heavy sticks abstractedly. They and Buddy had other things on their minds, dark and meaningful, besides frolic and screaming. Most of all Liz hated the girls who were there "making damn fools of themselves."

She hated the whole fury and clamor of it, she wanted to get away and go with Buddy to their own place on the riverbank where they sang to each other and ate fried clams and talked about things, where everything wasn't crazy and honkytonk and silly like this. She knew what she wanted. Only she and Buddy, together, alone in all the world in dreams, was good, only that was true and wonderful and good.

It was her first furious smothering love.

When the club closed for the night, Liz and Buddy drove out to Bill's on the highway and bought two containers of fried clams, then out along the dark river several miles to "their" spot on the riverbank beneath a grove of pines, where they sat down on a bed of green grass, just by the water.

The river was sown with starlight, bright and misty, flowing hugely in its dark tidal silence, all mud-smelling, all rippling soft. They could see the railroad tracks gleaming across the river in dark thickets there, the Montreal train was howling almost out of earshot upriver, faintly interrupted in night airs. The breeze harped softly in the pines overhead, the water lapped at their feet. It was the great nighttime and summer's joy of their hearts. When they thought of each other, they always thought of each other on the riverbank at night, their faces dark and dreaming and the mysterious shadow of themselves in darkness, speaking softly in the pine-scented darkness, sighing, waiting, and sweetly kissing.

"Hey," said Liz huskily in Buddy's mouth, "I don't want ever to go home." She had said that a thousand times. "We'll always come here," she said simply. "This is our place. Someday when we're rich we'll come back here and build our house right here. A twelve-room house."

"Say, this wouldn't be such a bad spot for a house!" cried Buddy, looking around with dreamy amazement.

"Just leave those things to me," she said, "you just think about music and how to become a great pianist and play with Benny Goodman. I'll figure the rest."

"Yeah? You're supposed to become a singer too! How will you work that in?"

"I'll do that, too," she said firmly, "I'll do a lot of things."

And they ate their fried clams, and munched, and looked around.

"I just remembered a great song today!" cried Buddy. "I'll bet you can't remember it. I'm going to make an arrangement of it. *She's Funny That Way!*"

"Oh, I know *that!*" said Liz scornfully. "Huh! Listen . . . I even know the words. *I'm not much to look at,*" she sang, "*nothing to see—just glad I'm living—and happy to be—I've got a man—crazy for me—he's funny that way.*"

"Bet you don't know the second chorus!" he cried gleefully. "*I can't save a dollar—ain't worth a cent—but she'd never holler—she'd live in a tent—I got a woman—crazy for me—she's funny that way*. Think of the beautiful chord progressions in that, beautiful but simple, just pure!"

"And the words!" cried Liz, kissing him. "I've got a man crazy for me. You *are* crazy for me, aren't you, Buddy?"

"Let me finish my fried clams. For me it would be I got a *woman* crazy for me."

"Am I as good as fried clams?"

"Maybe with a little tartar sauce—"

"Oh, you wheel you!" she sniffed with delight.

And then they lay back with their arms as pillows and looked up at the milky stars and talked.

"You look at those things long enough and you're knocked out," said Buddy, staring astonishedly at the stars. "They're so far off, you know?"

"What do you expect!"

"I mean they're so *far*, so far gone! Deep! You look up there long enough and it's just like looking into a big hole, you're afraid you'll fall in it—like when you drink too much."

"You're crazy," said Liz fondly.

"I used to go to Smitty's house and play records and play piano and then at midnight go out on the porch and drink a can of beer. He lived right by the railroad, you know. I used to watch those passenger trains clipping along to Boston and New York and then Chicago, right under the stars, and I used to think—someday I'll be able to play like Teddy Wilson, I'll have that left hand of his. Boy!"

"You'll play better than him," said Liz. "You'll play in Hollywood and Chicago and Florida and every place. And I'll be with you . . . I'll be the singer, you'll be the leader."

"Nobody can play better than Teddy Wilson, dope! Look at that star there. It's gold!" he cried, amazed. "The others are all silver and that one is gold!"

Then they were almost asleep from the drowsiness of lapping water and the breeze, and the cool enfolding flower-smells all around, and the grass underneath them that was like warm hay in the cool night—the young lovers, on the starry shore at night, in the bower, dreaming of trains and far-off cities of jazz.

"When we're married we'll wake up in the morning and tell each other stories," said Liz. "That's how we'll wake up. We won't need an alarm clock. And then we'll run down the hall on a nice big thick carpet that tickles the toes and go take our showers together. Then we'll go downstairs and have a ranch style breakfast. Hmm! And for lunch what'll we have? Cheeseburgers! pineapple salad! Hmmm!"

"You want some more fried clams, greedy?"

"How *did* you guess!" She tinkled with laughter.

"Finish them. I'm all through. I'm almost ready to sleep. It'll be dawn soon. The sun always comes up," he said sleepily, "all the stars and the sun on a wheel, like a big, slow ferris wheel rolling in the universe. Someday I'll use stuff like that for lyrics—nice love song with different lyrics. Not just love, dove, blue, you, June, moon—but real beautiful words. Did you ever hear that great blues *Black and Blue?* That's a colored song from New Orleans. *Oh, my sin is in my skin, Oh, why do I feel so black and blue?* . . . Guy sitting in his shack on a gray Monday morning, it's drizzling and he's real depressed, he's sitting on his old rickety bed, just feeling rotten."

"Tell me some more!" cried Liz eagerly.

"That's all."

"But there's more to it! The rickety bed—tell me a story about it!"

"Ah, I feel too lazy."

"He's alone on his rickety bed! You've got to tell me stories. You've got to learn *now!*" she cried.

"Tomorrow. I hear music right now. Chords, melodies, chords—if I could hit the chords I hear, I'd be so great. Mad chords full of new sounds and all kinds of . . . colors almost . . ."

And they brooded by the riverbank.

"Boy, is your old man going to be sore this time!" cried Buddy, sitting up. "It's almost four! That old man's going to hate me!"

"I don't care. We'll be married soon and then they won't be able to tell me what time to come home.

"I hate it at home!" cried Liz, sitting up suddenly. "My father's so gloomy because he lost his shop and we have to save money and everything and scrimp. I hate it there now. I want to go away with you. We'll be married soon," she pouted.

"You're always talking like we're getting married next week!" chuckled Buddy, pushing her away playfully.

"Next month."

"Next month? Are you crazy?"

"Yes. You'll get that job in Hartford and we'll go live there."

"I don't know if I can get that job!" he laughed.

"But you will," she said quietly. "Then we'll get married. I love you, I love you, I love you. Then we'll be together always. I want to live in the same house with you, I want it to be my house. Yes."

"I won't be making enough money to get a house!" He laughed again.

"Yes," she said. "Oh, be *honest*, honey!" she cried, wincing.

"How, dope?"

"I'll get a job in a defense plant in Hartford. You play with the band and I'll work in the defense plant. I'll make a hundred dollars a week."

"Say," mused the boy, "maybe I could get a job in a defense plant too, and play with the band at night, huh? Maybe we'd really rake in the dough that way!"

"Of course, you fool!" she said scornfully now. "Let me do the thinking in this family. You just lay there and think about your *mad chords*."

"Poo!" said Buddy, blowing in her face. He rolled away dodging her hand, they laughed and squealed wrestling on the ground, they threw pine cones at each other, they raced in the woods, and they were alone in the middle of their own nighttime earth, in gorgeous darkness, in the bower, alone and hidden in the land—and they were happy now, they were young, they didn't care what would ever happen.

[3]

ONE NIGHT in July Peter was coming out of a movie with some of his usher chums. It was about eleven o'clock of a warm pleasant night with a yellow halfmoon just rising into view over the rim of Daley Square buildings.

Liz Martin had been waiting and watching for her brother Peter from the window of a sandwich shop across the street. Now when she saw him scuffling about on the Square she ran out and called him, and he looked up with an angry preoccupied glare.

"What do you want? Can't you see I'm going some place!"

"Look," she said scornfully, "just forget that silly gang of yours for a while and come with me. It's important. I want you to make a big promise to me."

He looked at her with curiosity; he had never seen her looking so flushed and delighted. But he also noticed she was raggedly nervous.

"What do you want me for?" he demanded.

"I want to talk to you." She tugged on his arm impulsively. When Peter didn't budge, she looked up pleadingly at him. He saw the terror and loneliness in her eyes, realizing at once that she had been waiting for him for hours during the movie.

He went with her, with some embarrassed reluctance arranging to meet his buddies later, and they sauntered around the Square a few times.

"Now we'll walk home," said Liz gravely, "and by the time we get there you'll promise me." She had taken his hand, to his dreamy surprise.

"But you haven't told me what's up!" he cried.

"I'm going to marry Buddy," she said simply.

"You're going to marry Buddy, okay. What am *I* supposed to do?" he said very casually.

"I'm going to Hartford tonight and I want you to help me. I want you to promise—now!" And she stopped in the middle of the sidewalk staring solemnly into her brother's eyes, searching his face eagerly and nervously for signs of his disapproval.

"Now?" murmured Peter absentmindedly. "Say, wait a minute! You mean you're sneaking out, you haven't told Ma or Pa?"

"*There!*" hissed Liz wrathfully. "There it is! Even you! Even you!" She looked at him with tears in her eyes.

"What do you mean?"

"Oh, don't be so damn dumb!" she cried out.

"Wait a minute," said Peter. "You know you don't have to run away at all, if you want to marry Buddy. Who's going to stop you? Nobody can say anything to stop you. You know how Pa is, he'd never really try to stop you if you wanted—"

"I know that!" she snapped.

"Ah—big mysteries," sighed Peter wearily. "You and your mysteries, always."

"It's not that either, Petey. I don't want to go through all that stuff with *you!* I don't want to go through all that with them. I don't want to see anybody or talk about it with anybody, I just want to go. Don't you understand? Just go, go, go!"

They strode along rapidly.

"Do you understand?" she insisted, looking in his face.

"Sure I do. Still you don't have to go like that, running away. What'll Ma say, what'll Pa say? They'll be worried. Holy cow!"

"You're afraid," she said contemptuously, "you're afraid of what they'll say if you help me. And I thought you weren't afraid of anything."

"I'm not afraid!" he cried hotly. "I'm just thinking about you. And money! How much money have you got? And where's Buddy if he's going to marry you?"

"In Hartford. He doesn't know I'm coming."

"Great! He doesn't know you're coming."

"He expects me two weeks from now when he finds an apartment for us, but I'm coming tonight."

"Why doesn't the guy come and get you if he's going to marry you?" demanded Peter with stout indignation.

"You still haven't promised!" she persisted shakily.

"Promised what?"

"I want you to sneak my suitcase out of the house."

They looked at each other with a kind of crazy desperation. They were hurrying along the street in the general direction of the river and home, not even thinking where they were going. Peter was shaking his head, asking himself if anything had ever been so crazy. There was something else on his mind also, it was annoying him, he couldn't figure out what it was.

"I hid my suitcase under the bed, see?" Liz was telling him eagerly. "The big one that weighs a ton. I hope you can handle it without making any noise—without waking up Ruthey! Hear me?"

"I'm listening," he said. Now it came to him, as for the first time, that his sister Liz had packed all her things in a suitcase and was actually running away from home, tonight.

"I'm taking the one-thirty train. I got my ticket yesterday. Hear me?"

"Good God, yes, I hear you!" he cried irritably.

"I'll wait for you on the corner while you get it," she said gleefully now, squeezing his hand, almost laughing with delight. "Then we'll go get my train—and Petey, you'll see me off, you'll kiss me good-bye. I'm scared!" she brooded suddenly. "I want you to be with me when I leave." And she started to bite her fingernails furiously, searching eagerly once more in Peter's face as they hurried along.

But he was scowling and preoccupied.

"I know what you're thinking," she said. "You're mad. You're mad because I'm running away and you'll have to tell them you helped me."

"I'm not mad!"

"You're mad because I'm going to get married and I'm not your little sister any more. Huh?" she asked nervously.

"You're crazy!" he muttered.

"I'm not doing wrong, am I? You know that, too. That's why I came to you to help me, because you're not afraid of anything, you don't care, and sometimes you're just like me!"

"You came to me to help you!" he echoed sarcastically. "One suitcase! You and your big dramas!"

"But I always made big dramas, remember? The time you told me a secret about who started that big fire on the river. It was you, but nobody ever found out—and I made a big drama of it, don't you remember? I sealed the secret in a box, my Chinese box, and I burned it on my altar. Remember? That was me and my big dramas. Petey, I'm not crazy, am I? You don't think I'm crazy!" she demanded anxiously.

"Oh, Liz—no, no,—but why do you have to do this, like this!" he stammered chokingly. "I mean—well, dammit, I dunno."

"Big dramas," she continued in a daze of recollection and fright. "You know why I always liked big dramas when I was young? Because people are such fools, oh, such fools!" she cried. "They let everything go to pot. If they lie, they forget about it the next day. Imagine! I lie too, but it's important when you lie, the reason must be remembered. And, Petey, I always keep secrets. I could kill people who don't keep secrets!" she cried almost in a rage, through her teeth. "That's why I didn't ask Francis to help me tonight—he's home tonight—he was right there on the porch and I didn't even ask him."

"Francis?" said Peter, surprised.

"And I didn't ask Joe either. Joe was in the house at seven before he went out. Do you know why I didn't ask Joe?" she confided in a low voice.

"Huh!" scoffed Peter, pretending that he was not curious.

"Because Joe would laugh and change my mind if he wanted to, and if he didn't want to change my mind he'd just laugh. He'd laugh at my big dramas. But you get *mad!* You're not laughing, Pete—you just make believe you're laughing."

They had crossed the White Bridge and had stopped in the middle of the sidewalk.

"Now what?" Peter was muttering in tortured confusion.

"I've got enough money, don't you worry! Buddy's got a lot of money, he's got two jobs in Hartford. Look at my money!" she insisted, holding it in front of Peter's face. "I'm glad I'm quitting that damn job in the five-and-ten. Now I'll get a good job in a defense plant."

He smote his brow in despair.

"What's the matter with you?" she cried, laughing. "You're more scared than I am! But you'll keep my secret! There's got to be two or three persons in the world who believe in your secret secrets, and always believe, always. Otherwise I don't want to live," she brooded. "Not if there aren't three persons like that. Isn't it silly to live? The things you have to do to live!" she cried, blushing.

Peter chuckled now.

"My brother and my husband and my son," said Elizabeth suddenly, and she stiffened quite dramatically as though struck by an astounding idea. "They will always believe in my secrets!"

"Where do you pick up all that stuff?" asked Peter with amazement. He was used to hearing his sister talk on and on like this, yet it seemed that he never really heard her before.

But she was squeezing his hand desperately. "Go get the suitcase. Quick, Petey, quick!" Her hand in his was trembling and thin, and he was embarrassed.

"Look!" he cried. "Don't be scared—there's nothing to be scared about."

"I won't be, as long as I've got my three persons."

They were at the foot of Galloway Road by the gas station on the highway, the station was closed, the corner was dark under tall close-packed trees with the river breeze blowing through the branches softly. Peter was just standing there abstractedly—but Liz was pushing him to get started. Halfway up the hill he turned and looked at her standing alone and ruminative, waiting and rueful under the trees, so forlorn-looking on the dark street corner in the night, very much alone—and he realized that she was his "little sister" and she was going away at night with her suitcase, going away from the house and the place they had always known together.

When he came to the house and saw how dark and silent it was with the family gone to bed, and when he saw the yard where they had played games together so often, the place by the hedge where Liz had kept her "altar" and burned great secrets so solemnly, and all the little places in the yard that he knew so well—when he saw all these things, and the halfmoon that seemed to touch the east gable on the roof, and the window just below it that was the window of her bedroom, he felt stranger and more confused than ever, and now suddenly very heartsick.

"I don't like it!" he heard himself muttering over and over. "I swear I don't like it."

He went in the house quietly and wandered upstairs, moving slowly in the darkness, meditating as he groped along. He knew what he had to do, but he hated to do it.

Ruth was sleeping soundly in the sisters' bedroom. The other bed belonged to Liz, it was nearer the window and the dim moonlight fell across the clean smooth spread in leafy shadow—and it seemed to Peter that there was something haunted and forsaken in the sight of her bed. Someone had made the bed neatly that morning, probably Rosey or his mother. It was smoothed carefully, with loving skill, Liz was expected to sleep in it tonight as she had done all her life. He felt more helpless and terrified than he ever remembered.

With a feeling of silly lonesomeness the boy pulled the suitcase out from under the bed and listened breathlessly to the slow dragging sound it made in the sleeping house. Ruth did not stir. She was sleeping, he could see the faint pout on her face, he fancied wildly she was really awake and knew all about it and was playing cat-and-mouse with him. He stared at her.

"Damn it all!" he thought fretfully.

He stepped out of the room on tiptoe carrying the heavy bag. Out in the hall the old boards creaked. He could hear his father's lion snore in the other room.

"Petey!" his mother said from the darkness. "Is that you, Petey?"

"Yeah!" he blurted.

"Go to bed, it's late."

"I'll be back—the guys are outside," he lied swiftly.

"Don't stay up too late, Petey."

"Okay."

He whistled casually, faintly, and went downstairs taking care not to bounce the suitcase against the banister. At that moment someone came in the kitchen door downstairs.

"Petey!" his mother called from the darkness. "Is that Liz coming in now?"

Peter knew it was Joe from the barging-around in the dark kitchen. "I guess so," he said, gripping his head with anguish.

"Tell her to come to bed."

"Okay, Ma."

The sound of her voice from out of the darkness and softness of the sleeping house was faint and sorrowful, and he was out of his mind with the thousand little anguishes that he suddenly felt everywhere, the brooding griefs that stalked slowly in the house, that seemed to surround him in the darkness.

He hurried down the stairs and quickly placed the suitcase behind the couch with a desperate one-handed hoist that almost sprained his wrist. Now he was swearing up and down with pain and torment, rubbing his wrist and hitting himself on the side of the head like a madman.

He went in the kitchen just as Joe was putting on the light. They looked at each other and said nothing. Peter drank a glass of water and Joe sat down at the table and began to read the *Popular Mechanics* he had brought home with him from the gas station.

"Are you coming in or going out?" Joe inquired.

"Going out. The guys are down on the corner."

"Hand me that piece of cake on the breadbox before you go. I'm dead on my feet, I pumped an hour straight before closing tonight. What a night!"

Peter gave him the cake and started to go, then suddenly, sheepishly, he turned back and took a bottle of milk out of the icebox and poured a glass, and set it down before his brother with a strange forlorn look.

"Well, thanks, Jeeves!" laughed Joe, looking up surprised.

Without a word Peter went down the hall, hauled the suitcase from behind the sofa and slipped quickly out the front door. He waited a minute in the deep shadows of the hedge until he made sure Joe wasn't looking out the window. He could still see him sitting in the kitchen with bowed head, reading and eating the cake. He, too, looked alone and forsaken. For a moment Peter thought he was going to start to cry, it was all too much for him, he didn't know what to do or think or say, he was depressed and sick.

"Ma's always awake," he thought heartbrokenly. "Poor Ma. I dunno—I wish Liz—I wish somebody'd do something."

He hurried back struggling to his sister with the heavy suitcase. At the corner bar he phoned for a cab and they were driven down to the depot. Elizabeth's train was due in a half an hour; they went across the street to the cafeteria. They sat at a table by the plate-glass windows where they could see the ancient turret-topped depot across the street, the tracks, the signal lights, the old brown boxcars standing in the darkness by grimy redbrick warehouses, the cheap hotel with its red neon, the little depot lunchcart along the tracks—all the things in America that people notice when they go journeying, which they look at with a sense of awful loneliness and dread.

Peter began to eat a plateful of frankfurters and beans, suddenly discovering that he was ravenously hungry. Liz ordered toast and coffee, but seeing how hungry her brother was, she gave him her toast.

"Eat something, eat something!" Peter kept telling her. "You're going on a trip, you've got to eat!"

"I'm not hungry. I wonder what Buddy'll say when he sees me."

"Good God! Don't you even know?" he cried. "What are you going to do when you get to Hartford? It'll be about four o'clock in the morning when you get there. Oh, this is whacky!"

"I'll sit in a cafeteria till morning," she said simply. "Then I'll go to Buddy's place and catch him just when he's going to work. That's what I'll do."

Peter kept looking at the clock as though he were waiting for the train himself but Liz just sat drinking coffee and thinking out loud about all her poor childlike newlywed plans.

Peter grew hungrier and hungrier, for some odd reason. He went back to the counter for an order of bacon and eggs, but he discovered he only had twenty cents left in his pockets and came back to the table morosely.

"Where's your food?" Liz demanded. "What's the matter with you? I know you're hungry—I know you when you're hungry, you never stop eating. Go get some food. Here! Take this dollar and buy all the food you want," and she pulled a bill out of her purse.

"Don't be silly!" he cried.

"If you don't go get it, I'll get it myself!"

"Look, I can't be spending your money, you need it for your trip. What do you think I am!"

"Eat, dammit!" she cried angrily. "If I can't feed my brother when he's hungry, I'm not worth marrying."

"I'm not hungry."

"You are too! I know you. Go ahead, get some bacon and eggs, get some of those lamb chops there. I've got lots of money. Do you hear me?" And she took Peter's hand and thrust the dollar bill firmly in his fist.

"I don't want it."

"By God, I'll bash you over the head!" she yelled furiously, as people looked up astonished.

"You need this," he said, about to fling the dollar back at her, but then he saw that her eyes were misty and she was looking at him sorrowfully, almost mournfully, with a poignant heartsick loneliness that made him choke up with anguish. He wished she would come home again and stay—but there was nothing for him to say.

He took the dollar and went and got another plate of food, knowing now that it would please her hugely if he ate. Moreover he couldn't ignore the fact that he was mad with hunger, too. She watched him eat with brooding satisfaction.

"God, you make me hungry when you eat like that!" she said, fascinated. "You ought to get a job eating in a restaurant window, everybody'd rush in to try it."

"I don't know why I'm so hungry," Peter said sadly.

"Oh, look!" said Liz, excitedly. "I bought a pack of Camels. See them? I'm going to start to learn to smoke tonight. I'll smoke on the train. Buddy smokes Camels. He'll like me more if I smoke too, the same brand as him. I'm going to do everything he does. When we wake up in the morning I'll always light up two Camels for both of us."

Peter stared wonderingly at her over his food.

Suddenly there was the rumbling of the train coming. They took the suitcase and ran across the street, right up to the platform where the giant engine overtopped them passing in a tremendous flare of red smoke and roaring steam. And they saw the weary faces of travelers in the windows of the coaches that glided by and stopped.

It was time, time. Liz and Peter looked at one another. He brushed her soft sister's-cheek with his lips, and swung the big suitcase up on the train platform. They looked at each other once more, she kissed him swiftly and stepped up. Suddenly the train was moving, moving.

Peter was stricken with a lonesome terror: he jogged alongside the train looking up at Liz, and she just stood there looking down at him sadly, waving.

As the train picked up speed, Peter ran with it. When it was really underway, he stopped, and waved at her for the last time—forsaken little Liz going off in the night with her big suitcase. Then the train rumbled off, sudden silence passed, he heard a vast breeze passing through branches everywhere around, the locomotive whistle howled going away, the tracks gleamed nakedly in the moonlight—and he was sick now with a crying lonesomeness, he somehow knew that all moments were farewell, all life was good-bye.

He went home, he walked under the dark swishing trees of home and July and nighttime.

[4]

GEORGE MARTIN sat on the dark porch of his house with his son Peter in the cool, breezy, starwealthy darkness of a late August night. The trees and hedge all around swished softly and swayed, nodding and bowing in the dark advancing wave of the breeze. They sat brooding on the porch.

It was the night before Peter was to go back to Penn for his second year, and it was also the night when the women of the Martin house began packing in preparation for moving away from the old house to a new home in a flat. The Martins could no longer afford the old house, and now that Elizabeth, Francis and Peter were going to live away from home it was not practical to stay there even if they wanted to.

It was a beautiful night, rich with steep sheer darknesses, and the high looming shadows, the moving boughs, the swaying street-lamps of the old road, all of it overvaulted tremendously by the great chunky nodding stars of August bending close to rooftop and treetop, blazing there close-packed—and the old man and his son sat on the porch on their last night together in the Martin house.

"So there it is, Petey, my son," spoke up the father mournfully. "There it is. Your little sister went and got married at eighteen and I guess I'm to blame. And just look at us there"—he pointed inside the house where Mrs. Martin and Ruth and Rosey were rolling up the rug in the front room—"moving out of the house we've been living in for years and years, farther back than you or Charley or Mickey or even little Lizzy can remember. And your little brother Mickey's up in his room wondering what it's all about, the poor little beggar. Ah!" he cried bitterly. "It's too much, too much!" and he shook his bowed head slowly.

"Pa, don't worry about it," spoke up Peter gently. "After all, a lot of families move from one place to another all the time. And as for Lizzy—why, hell, she's not the only girl who gets married at eighteen, a lot of them do. That's what she wanted to do. That Buddy Fredericks is a nice guy." He looked at his father anxiously.

"Young Fredericks is a nice boy," agreed old Martin sadly, "I've nothing against the boy. But Lizzy is too young, much too young to get married, she's only a child, my little girl, just a little kid. You don't understand, you're too young, you'll never understand!"

And after a long brooding silence Peter said: "I guess everything turns out the way it's supposed to, doesn't it?"

"Yes, yes," sighed his father wearily, "it does that. And all on account of my own damn foolishness—"

"What do you mean!" Peter laughed angrily.

"My own foolishness, Petey, I should know better than anyone else why this family is falling apart, and still, still, I'm not entirely to blame, you can only do the best you can—"

"Who says this family is falling apart? Who says that?" cried the boy, laughing, trying to cheer up his father, poking him on the arm. "I never heard you say *that* before! Not you!"

And his father sat shaking his head in the darkness, saying nothing, and all around the million treeleaves were swishing and rustling in the night, trembling together on drunken boughs, all a-hush and vast, whispering and sweet in darkest shadows above.

"And now they talk of war," said the old man, sorrowfully staring up at the trees, "and they talk of sending kids like you across the ocean to fight and get killed. That's what they're talking about now, more and more every week. Kids like you and Joe and maybe Charley in time—and even kids like poor young Buddy Fredericks—all kids, all of you. I wish I could help you all, you just don't know what you're in for in this world now. Do you hear me? You just don't know what you're in for now! Just a lot of poor kids. We're all in for it. I'd like to ask God what it's all for!" he whispered hoarsely, wearily, entreatingly.

They were silent on the dark porch: and then, once more in that first sad year of saddest understanding, young Peter was overwhelmed with a tearful wrenching sadness that made him want to cry, from awful knowledge, to see his father sitting there beside him so full of sorrows and heartstricken love and mortal loneliness. He seemed old now, suddenly so old as they packed up the things of his house inside, as he sat thinking of his youngest daughter who had left his house, as he rued the ragged way he was losing his house.

"Pa," said Peter with a choked sobbing voice, "I think everything'll be all right now, honest!" And he couldn't say any more, he didn't want his father to know that he felt like crying, and yet he wished there would be a way to let him know.

"Yes," echoed the old man, "everything'll be all right now."

"You have a good job!" cried Peter. "And Joe's garage is coming along great, he told me so himself. We're all making money, even Charley, and I'll have a job on the campus this year and send some money home to Ma whenever I can, see?"

"No, no, no, don't talk like that!" cried the old man quickly. "I don't want you to be sending any money home, do you hear me? We'll make out, we'll make out. Petey, my little boy," he said, gripping Peter's arm, shaking him gently, "all I want you to do is to make good in college and in football. That's about all that's left to me in the world. Petey, all the pride I've got left is you, in you, do you understand?" he cried anxiously. "Something may go wrong with the others—and, God knows, it'll kill me over and over again and break my heart a hundred times—but if anything ever goes wrong with you, I just don't know what I'd do. Why, Lord," he suddenly chuckled gleefully, "don't you remember when you were just a little tike and I used to throw you a football and make you catch it? Huh?" He tousled Peter's hair roughly. "And, Lord, you were such a chunky little kid, rosy cheeks, plump, strong as an ox, always smiling, always smiling! I want you to go on smiling," he continued gravely, "that's the way I want your life to be. If anything goes wrong with you, I just don't know what I'd do."

"But I can send Ma a little money, you know."

"No, no, no! You've got all you can handle there with your

studies and your playing. No, no, no!" he cried angrily. "You hold up your end of the battle and we'll hold up our end here. I'm banking on you to make good, if only because I can go and tell some of these punks around here that my son is a great star and a great boy—and if only because I want you to go on smiling all your life the way you used to do when you were just a plump little tike with rosy cheeks. Sonny, sonny!" he cried unhappily. "Listen to me! Do what your old father says, I know best. Study! study! Work hard and make good. There's never anything wrong with a man who always, always tries! I want you to be that way—" He gripped Peter and looked at him for the first time since he was a child with the tender gaze of an anxious, pleading father: "Be my good boy, Petey, be my own good boy."

Peter stammered something, embarrassed and stricken with imminent hot tears.

His father got up. "I'm going in now and see if I can help the ladies with the packing," he said, with sudden wry amusement. He slapped the side of the house with his hand. "This old house, by golly, this old place of mine. I remember the first time I saw it, years ago. I always used to think it was too big and too far from town." He leaned back and looked at it. "Yep, I hate to leave it now. Funny, I didn't think I'd ever feel this way about the old joint. Got some nice trees around here, nice fresh air." He sniffed the air and looked around ruefully. Then he chuckled. "Years ago I always wanted to leave, I always thought it would be great to leave sometime. Well, I'm leaving it now, all right!"

"Well," said Peter sheepishly, "it'll be a change to go somewhere else." He looked up at his father with a quick grin.

"Yup. I guess I'll go in now and go to bed." And Martin waited by the door, slapping the wall of the house again and again nervously. "You go to bed early and get some sleep, Petey. I'll see you in the morning, give you a sendoff on your big year. Your old man'll be praying for you tonight, Petey," he said in a trembling voice finally, and he wandered into the house and closed the screen door behind him, and Peter was alone on the porch.

He was alone on the porch and his father was gone, and something mournful was left behind to brood by him in the darkness, something old and sorrowful, and something unspeakably good and kind and wonderful, his father the strange, great, brooding companion of his life, whom he had never realized before for the dark near figure that he was, immediate, close, loving, anguished, right at his side speaking to him and gripping his arm—his father.

And Peter, realizing these things, knew that he was no longer the joyful eighteen-year-old boy of little more than a year ago in prep school, the boy of powerful sensual vigors, of food and drink and sleep and tremendous pagan indifference, of life as a delicious loafing laziness, sensuous and profligate routs, and stupefacted appetites. He knew that at nineteen now, somehow, something in him was done and finished and departed, strange melancholy forebodings were in him, and a heaviness of heart, a dark sense of loss and dull ruin, as though he had grown old at nineteen. Suddenly it seemed to him that college and football were no longer important, and suddenly he thought of war, and felt a thrill coursing in him. And all the suitcases and college banners and sharp sport jackets and pipe-smoking, quipping, wry mannerisms of college life were ridiculous as he thought of them.

And something dark, warlike, mournful and far was suddenly brooding in the air.

Peter thought of his home now. This was the last time that he would ever sit on his front porch and look out on Galloway Road, yet this too was almost a great strange thrill coursing in his veins. His tall dark singing trees there, swaying in the breeze, swishing leaves in a million hidden places, bending by his bedroom window as they had done for him all his life, rustling softly against his window screen, his tall dark singing trees—he would see them no more, he would have to pull up his stakes and roll, and they were singing him a farewell song, the winds were going softly through the branches and a sound was advancing in the night, and it was a farewell hushing song. . . .

Something mournful, dark, and far off was brooding in the air, across his fields—and he would never come back here again, this was the last time, the last night, and then no more, no more. Where was he going? And his father's voice speaking to him in the darkness was still haunting, still heard. The trees swished and swayed, weaving-drunk with a hundred moving dark boughs,—and it was a farewell song. He remembered how the days of his boyhood here had been rich and golden, tumbling one upon the other, he remembered all the places around the house and the road, the places he knew so well. And Elizabeth was gone far away from these trees, his little sister, Lizzy gone away. It was strange, she had heard these trees, she had been under them and had heard them, in her room she had heard them long in the night swishing by her window—and his father's house was dark now in the middle of the night, and the starwealthy sky vaulted over, bending near and milky-blurred by the highest waving treetop—and there was the hush of silence and night, the song of a million trembling treeleaves, the dogs barking far off, nighthawks in the field mists, crickets, crickets, further vast dull boomings of distant forests in the wind, the whole world brooding and sad and whispering at nighttime, in the starpacked Augustcool night, and somehow, now, omened with war.

It was a farewell song all around and he was never coming back again. It was farewell, sweet from his trees, dark from his high shadowy trees, and he was alone on the porch, for the last time on the porch beneath his bending trees. Now he would pull up his stakes and roll, and go far away, and never come back here—and the trees were waving a vast soft song, a million tender rustlings for him, for him alone—and there had been tears in his father's eyes in the darkness. They had rolled up the rug in the house that night, the women had rolled up the rug—and where was Liz tonight? Where was little Lizzy, his sister? Now everyone was asleep, and he was alone listening to the serenade of his dark old trees, the lullaby of his boyhood trees, and he knew he didn't want to leave now, he knew he would never come back, it was the farewell song of his trees bending near him, farewell, farewell. . . .

[5]

A FAMILY leaves the old house that it has always known, the plot of ground, the place of earth, the only place where it has ever known itself—and moves somewhere else: and this is a real and unnameable tragedy. For the children it is a catastrophe of their hearts.

What dreams children have of walls and doors and ceilings that they always knew, what terror they have on waking up at night in strange new rooms disarrayed and unarranged, all frightful and unknown. More than once little Mickey Martin woke up in the middle of the night in the new flat in Galloway where his family had moved that very day, and went to the window to gaze down on the iron-gray street, and the naked trolley tracks, and the empty sidewalk, with a feeling of panic and forlorn doom.

The next afternoon Mickey started home from school in the wrong direction, towards Galloway Road and the old house, not realizing that he was doing this. Suddenly remembering that he actually did not live there any more, Mickey turned and pulled his steps in the other direction. A moment later he was suddenly plunged in an awful confusion as he positively could not remember which way he was supposed to go to get home. Trembling and almost on the verge of crying, he started to walk towards Galloway Road again, feeling that this was distinctly wrong, virtually a sin, and at the same time again remembering with an awful painful impact that they did not live there any more.

The little boy paused on the bridge in long meditation. He was amazed and confused, and all his thoughts were frightened. Again he pushed himself back towards his real home, thinking, "Gee! Oh, gee!" He was almost panic-stricken at the thought that perhaps nothing was real, that he was wandering in the world alone, that he had no home actually, and that he himself was an intruder and a ghost in the real world of regular ordinary things. He hurried towards home and he was almost fearfully amazed when he saw familiar faces on the streets, and saw that he was noticed, and heard the children calling him. Now he wanted to brood and imagine that after all a great joke was being played on him by God, and that he was arriving to this neighborhood from some long dusty journey around the world, just a fantastic stranger grim and weary and looking for a place to rest. When he opened the door and walked in the house he was overwhelmed with a strange, yearning, wonderful gratitude and joy.

This new home was situated in a neighborhood denser in population than that around the old house on Galloway Road, and made up largely of wooden tenements and small closely-packed bungalows, with stores and shops nearby that made it a small kind of shopping district for the suburban homes and farms thereabouts. It was a flat, on the fourth floor of a wooden tenement house, consisting of four bedrooms, a livingroom, large kitchen, and bath. There were two suspended porches front and back overlooking a busy street on one side and the roofs of small houses on the other. It was a spare, white-washed, square wooden building, a typical example of New England French-Canadian building, roomy, drafty, yet oddly comfortable and homelike. Heavy telephone wires swooped past the windows, the gaunt telephone poles seemed to lean athwart the porches, the hallways were musty and creaky—yet something in the air outside the windows was high and lyrical, swooping and powerful, for there were vistas and views, the house was built on a rise near the river, and you could see the town across the river all redbrick and smoky, the bridges, the falls, and on the other side the fields and lorn birch and small farmhouses, and the hills.

In October—for the family was moved in and unpacked by then—great northern clouds moved above at dusk gilded hugely by the sun, and the street below rang with the cries of children, the roaring of busses, and the laughter of drugstore corner boys. It was lively indeed. And Mrs. Martin often said: "Oh, it's nice and lively here, I like it very much."

And surprisingly enough she seemed to be enjoying herself more than anyone else, she soon established her place by the front windows when it was not too cold to go out and sit on the high porch, and there she could see everything, the street below, the river and the bridges, the lights, the people, the cars going by, and the fields and woods far off that darkened and became vast, impenetrable and pin-pointed with lonely lights at nightfall. And soon everyone was reconciled and even pleased with their new home: it was full of old comfort and a thrilling, close-packed secrecy that the other house did not have.

The rent in this flat turned out to be extremely reasonable, due to some sort of odd oversight on the part of the old, deaf French-Canadian landlord who came regularly by the month, collected the rent, and accepted bread and milk at the kitchen table (a custom Mrs. Martin was well conversant with). He would puff on his pipe a few times, and leave solemnly for another month.

The father had his job in a printing plant downtown paying him good wages; and Ruth helped the family considerably with her earnings and contributions; as well as Joe, who however was not making as much with his little gas station as he might have wished, due to its bad location on an out-of-the-way street. But with the low rent, and the three incomes, the family was at least well on its feet.

Peter, away at Penn, was doing his best to earn his own way. Francis was completely on his own in Boston, where he had his job in a music store, making himself more and more indispensable to the department he worked in, and continuing his studies at

Harvard. And it was not strange that Francis should be showing this kind of ingenuity and self-reliance over and above Peter's sad half-hearted attempts on the campus, because somehow everyone knew that Francis would be able to take care of himself in these matters. They had long ago decided that he necessarily was alone in the world.

They missed Francis at home. He only came back infrequently and briefly, picking up his clothes and things by slow stages, and coming and going about the house in his old, silent, meditative way.

"Well, by God, Francis is showing some brains, all right," said the father, shaking his head. "He can take care of himself, no doubt about that. I sort of always knew he'd be able to do these things, though I don't know why exactly. Just a hunch he gives you with that look of his—he's had that look always, even as a little kid." And the old man was silent at the thought of it, at the thought even of the little Francis who had once come into his office years ago, unannounced and roaming from school, a sickly-looking, shy, moody little boy of eight, to watch his father all afternoon long in a reverie of child-meditation and wonder. The old man remembered that incident now with surprise and regret.

Big Rosey had begun to leave home also, attending a nurse's school in a nearby Massachusetts town and coming home only when she had the time. Thus the mother was in solitary charge of household duties, but since the numbers in the household itself were depleted by one half, the work was not so strenuous as before.

The kids, Charley and Mickey, went to school and lived their self-absorbed children's lives. They came home at dusk out of the shadows of noisy scuffling and shouting and joy, they came home with flushed cheeks, ate prodigiously, slept greedily, and went to school in the mornings swinging strapped books and arguing loudly.

A few times Mickey had picked up his glove and bat and started back to his old neighborhood on Galloway Road, where the gray turreted house still stood—empty and window-gaping on its hill now. He had started back there to go and play with his gang, but they didn't seem to care whether he was around any more, new groups had formed, new conspiracies were in the furious air, and Mickey was the stranger, the lonesome unknown returning. How many times he had started back towards his new home in the tenement, stopping to look back at the old house longingly, with a strange feeling gnawing at him, as the long sun-slanting light glowed in that world all a-murmur with his departure, as the chimneys smoked, the children shouted and leaped, and none of it was his or for him.

And Francis, now, when he came home on a weekend from Harvard the first time, suddenly saw with some misgivings how far down his family had had to go in order to maintain themselves and live. It seemed to him that the tenement flat was a scene of spiritual deprivation, and even horror. He had now grown used to sedate brownstone Cambridge and to a more cosmopolitan scene and existence. To see his own family living in what might well have been called the slums, though not on the order of the Rooney Street slums in Galloway, was a fact that served to remind him how very close he might have come to such a life himself. Fortunately, of course, that year marked the first completely independent circumstances of his young life: he had his scholarship, his job in the music store, and modest savings to tide him over. He saw that he was "lucky."

He looked silently into all the rooms. The bedrooms were all doubled up with two beds, clothes and belongings were hung and piled indiscriminately behind doors or in flimsy cardboard closet stands, in bureaus and boxes, all in confusion, and what furniture his mother had not sold to finance the moving bill was closely distributed everywhere so that there wasn't much room to move about in—a family being always reluctant to part with too many of its belongings. But a lot of things were missing: the sewing machine, some living-room furniture and commodes, desks, the piano, old things that had had some charm.

Then there were the musty hallways smelling of cooking, four flights up from the street-front with its drugstore and barber shop and lunch diner, and the suspended porches leaning into space by telephone wires, and the noises of the street. And there was no attic here where he might have sought out his solitary habits.

"My father's downfall, as you might call it," he wrote in a letter to Wilfred Engels that night, "has certainly wreaked havoc with what little charm there was in my family's surroundings. It's quite sad and sometimes I wish I had money, I could help them. This year I feel for the first time a definite surge in myself towards some real energy. That remark in Goethe's notebooks about the horses, the chariot, and the control over the reins, where he cries: 'That's mastery!'—this I might yet feel and with conscious materialization. It's all connected with my plans for the winter, which are taking shape. There's a man at Harvard—Wilson, you might have heard of him—who wants me to help him on research for an anthology of German Impressionistic poetry in the Twenties, some fine things there. All for pay under the N.Y.A. setup. Also, some of us are thinking of a little review, and I might be in line for an editorship. However, meanwhile I have a few odds and ends to clear up. Picking up the last of my things at home—(including the silver cord?)—and I suppose none of us will be the worse for it. I can't rouse any feelings of a definitely filial type, only the most humane and objective. Nothing gained is nothing lost, though. I feel rather strange as I write this at my brother Joe's desk all cluttered with dime magazines and sparkplugs and tools: I feel that something is over and done with. A little sentiment creeps in. I'm staying over tonight, and tomorrow: the lash, the horses, the mastery?—and off!"

He retired early, sleeping in Mickey's bed, his mother piling an extra blanket on him and his father coming around anxiously to the bedroom to say goodnight. All night long his parents had gone to great pains reminding him that he was more welcome than ever in this house, although they seemed to know, as he knew, that it was somehow all over, almost as though he did not seem like their son any more.

"There's nothing here for you that can compare with the old place, or with the places where you live in Boston, but just the same, if you ever need to come back and live at home, for any reason—well—" and the father trailed his words helplessly.

"Sure, Pa," replied Francis simply.

"We don't want you to go and think that there's no room here, because there is! With Lizzy gone and Rosey and Pete too most of the time, why, we could always manage. And you know under the circumstances this was the best we could do—"

"Well, naturally—"

"—and humble as it is, as they say, well, it's your home and it's yours as well as ours. So if things were ever to take a turn with you, and, God knows, I'm not wishing you anything like that, well, you can always come home."

"There's always room for one more!" cried the mother, laughing. "If you want a corner to do your reading in, we can find it!"

"Like in the old days, Francis," said the old man, grinning—

"always room for one more, so we had the whole bunch of you, one after the other.—Ha, ha, ha! Look at the expression on his face, Marge!—What's the matter, Francie? Think your old man went too far?"

"Oh, no, no, no—"

"Well, anyway, now we're doing the best we can, all of us," Martin added gravely, "and I guess that's about the story right there."

Francis was strangely flushing: he was tucked in bed, his mother was covering his feet with another blanket, and both his parents were hovering solicitously, worriedly over him as he lay there flat on his back in the bed. He suddenly realized that he could not remember anything like this in a long time. And it seemed like an awkward, terribly embarrassing and even horrifying situation from which he had no means whatever of escape, there was nothing for him to do but lay there and look up at them. He felt naked with helplessness.

"Well," he said with an effort towards finality, "I hope—I sure wish I could—well, yes, if anything like that comes up I'll certainly come home. It will be the sensible thing to do—"

"You'll come home for Thanksgiving?" his mother asked.

"Well—no. I have to go someplace then, but Christmas, yes."

"Yes, yes; come home for Christmas," said George Martin with a drawn expression. "Give us a chance to do a little for you, if you understand that. Your father feels pretty low about all this, boy."

Francis nodded and swallowed: he was just then incredibly embarrassed by his father's sudden feeling.

"But it was the work of some power higher than us, so we shouldn't really complain."

"It's comfortable here," said Francis.

"Oh, yes, we'll make out, don't worry. It's just that we don't want you to think this is not your home too— Well, what the hell, you know?"

"Surely."

When his parents had bid him goodnight and left the room, Francis turned over quickly in the bed, quickly and with furtive sudden joy, and stared at the wall. He felt terrible somehow, yet relieved now, remembering what he had said in the letter to Engels about flying away in the morning, and remembering his room at Harvard and the things in it, and what he would do tomorrow when he got there. He stayed awake and stared wide-eyed at the wall for a long time, and suddenly it began to occur to him that his eye was fixed all this time upon a little picture that Mickey had tacked on the wall by his bed, a little paper with a drawing that he had done on it with crayon, depicting a forest with a river and a little boat with someone in it. It was a pathetic little picture and Francis began looking at it, inadvertently snuffing a little, as though amused, although he could not imagine why, and then he tried to go to sleep. . . .

The afternoon of that same night Mickey had gone straight from school to Joe's gas station to watch Joe and Charley at work on the cars. But one thing had led to another and long after suppertime his two big brothers were still tinkering around, grease-smudged and absorbed, and Mickey was getting very hungry and tired and impatient.

"Wait a minute, wait a minute," Joe kept saying to him, "we'll be going home in just a minute. Go play in back of the station—and hand me that wrench there," he added musingly.

And Mickey went behind the station and passed the time away throwing empty oil cans around and lighting small fires to burn the leaves. It got darker and colder and he was hungry and wanted to go home. The great harsh ragged skies of October were everywhere around with their huge tumultuous clouds and their premonitions of awful darkness, and the winds began to blow all demented with blown leaves and dust and dark fury, and Mickey, dressed only in his light school clothes, began to shiver, and feel gnawings of hunger in his stomach, and pangs of vague fear—as though again the world were closing in on him and suffering him to great terror. And more than that, the fact that he still had his schoolbooks with him and his school clothes made him feel foolish with his two brothers in their dirty coveralls, and with nothing to do while they absorbedly fixed cars and paid no attention to him.

"When are we going home, Joe? I'm hungry! I'm cold!"

"Here's a dime, Shorty. Go get a sandwich in the diner across the street and warm your fanny in there. We gotta finish this job tonight."

He waited and waited, and then finally, long after dark, Joe and Charley closed up the station and they all started for home in the rattling old Ford. But they had to stop at a junkyard on the highway to pick up some old parts, and that took another half-hour while Mickey waited in the car cold and hungry and miserable. How the little ones are always kept waiting in a car—suffering and waiting it out in such mute silence while their elders pore absorbedly over some damnable gadget in the ragged wintry night! He sat there shivering and watching them at the other side of the junkyard bending in solemn concert by the glow of a flashlight over a rusty old heap, and he watched them mournfully, waiting and waiting.

But lo and behold! here they came, they were all through, and it was time to go home for supper. "Time for some eats!" cried Joe, rubbing his hands together and starting up the car—and they drove off down old rutted roads, the old Ford rattling and jumping, the cold bitter wind blowing in through the windows, his brothers silent and meditative and gravely smoking their cigarettes.

Now suddenly Mickey saw his family's new house: they had come back from the junkyard by another route and quite taken by surprise he realized that they were in the neighborhood: with a shock he now saw the tall four-story tenement and the familiar windows and porches of it, and he even saw his mother moving briefly in the window of the kitchen. It was incredible.

"Hey!" he cried. "That's our house!"

"That's right, brilliant," muttered Charley.

"It's nice and warm up there!" said Mickey suddenly, looking eagerly at the house and the windows all warm and glowing in the dark. "We got food up there too! Supper, huh!"

The two older brothers looked at each other grinning.

"Boy, I'm tired too!" cried Mickey with satisfied emphasis. "Yessir! And I got a nice bed up there and everything. Gee, I thought we'd never get home. That's our house up there," he said again, sticking his head out the window of the car and looking up as they parked in front of the house. And he ran out of the car and up the stairs with a wild glee. This was his home, his new home, and it was as good as any home he would ever have, and in there he had food, and warmth, and a nice dumpy bed, and his mother and father and family: that was all he could think about. He was ecstatically happy, he was grateful, grateful, more than he had ever been.

In the house he looked at everything with profound satisfaction, even the chairs and tables, and he kept looking at his mother, as he sat waiting for supper at the table, with an expression of laughter and happiness on his face. Then he watched his brothers come back from the washroom all pink and clean and he watched them sit down to eat. And he went to his room just to look at his bed—and though Francis was sleeping in it that night—it still looked like the most wonderful, the warmest, coziest, finest bed in the world, and he went back to the kitchen filled with happy thoughts, noting how the frost was forming on the windows outside, how dark it was out there, and how warm and glowing it was inside his house.

[6]

PETER MARTIN was sitting in his room at college on a cold gray afternoon, bending absorbedly over a physics text, when suddenly he looked up with startled surprise and hurled the book over his shoulder against the wall. A wave of nausea had come over him. He got up and went to the dresser to look at himself in the mirror.

"Cripes, what disgust!" he cried out loud, and then fell to walking up and down the room and rubbing his chin speculatively. He hadn't shaved for several days, he felt the rough raggedness of his chin with pleasure, and he was even pleased with the dirty old corduroy jacket and the baggy pants he wore, but at the same time he had a distinct feeling that he was living like a tramp. Again he looked in the mirror. Just below his image he saw the half-empty whiskey bottle on top of the dresser.

"Jerk!" he muttered, and put the bottle away under his shirts in the drawer, where it could no longer impress the maid who cleaned his room.

He went to the window, which faced a stone archway, and looked down on the students scuffling by in strident talkative groups, and brooded watching them. "What's this? What's this? They're all walking around as though they knew what they were doing, and exactly why."

He went over and picked up the book and arranged its pages and spread it out on his desk again, and sat down. Motionlessly he studied the text for about a half hour, making faces at the pages, sighing, doodling with a pencil as he went along. Finally he closed the volume with a decisive air.

Now he was ready. It was three-thirty and he had to report to the physics laboratory at four for a makeup examination.

He put on a battered coat and went out, trailing his steps casually along the hall, as though he might change his mind. Suddenly he stopped at one of the doors, knocked and went in. Inside it was half dark. Someone was lying on the bed, and there was a strong smell of beer in the room.

"Hey, Jake Fitzpatrick!" yelled Peter. Not getting a reply, he pulled the other boy by the leg until he had him almost out of the bed. Fitzpatrick woke up with a violent start and looked around.

"What are you doing?" demanded Peter, turning on the light curiously.

"I was writing a story. . . . I must have fallen asleep right in the middle of the thing!"

Fitzpatrick, a slender, nervous, curly-headed Irishman with a lopsided, grinning, strangely pathetic face, looked around with wonder and began to scratch his head. "A damn complex thing it was, too. All about a guy who meets a girl in a bar, but the girl—"

"Tell me tonight. I've got to go to an exam."

"Well, yeah, be seeing you tonight."

"What are you going to do now?" demanded Peter enviously.

"Finish the story I guess. I think it was good, damn good!" And Jake got up and lifted a glass of stale beer to the light, examined it gravely, swirled it around a little bit to make foam, and finally drank it. "Ain't you going to football practice?"

"After the exam," sighed Peter, going out, "just in time for scrimmage under the floodlights." He closed the door and went back down the hall to his own room, where he sat down on the bed and put his head in his hands, and considered everything gloomily.

Sitting where he was, and looking towards the window where everything was gray and cold-looking and yet somehow thrilling, he suddenly realized that he did not want to go to the laboratory to boil water and measure the pressure of gases. He wanted to go back to Jake Fitzpatrick, and talk and tell stories with him, drink and get drunk, go out in the gray streets, and walk around and look at all the people and think about them. He grinned happily.

And just then his buzzer rang, the whining sound blasting through his ears sharply, and he threw his hands up in despair, clutching his head, and ran out in the hall crying: "I'm coming! I'm coming!" At the telephone he bellowed irritably: "Yes! yes! hallo!"

"Hi!" cried a girl's voice.

"Judie?" he asked.

"Fine, how are you? Are you thirsty?"

"Yes," answered Peter passionately in a hoarse whisper.

"Okay," sang the girl. "Come to my house—nobody's home—I got wine."

Without another word Peter hung up the receiver, ran down the stairs, out to the street, across the campus, dashing through traffic like a halfback in flight, into an apartment house foyer, up the stairs. In the hallway a girl stood holding the door open for him.

"How's Hamlet today?" she said, hurrying after him down the long dark hall.

"Thirsty."

She poured him a waterglass full of wine and he began to drink it, sprawled out on the couch with his feet against the wall, one hand dangling to the floor languidly.

"Don't call me Hamlet. Hamlet never studied like Faust in his dungeon with the skeleton heads."

It grew darker outside and suddenly it began to snow in thin flurries, and the neon lights began to glow. Peter drained his glass of wine, received another portion, drained that, and suddenly grabbed the girl by the arm and pulled her down on the couch with him. "I've got to go to the laboratory and measure the pressure of gases," he said in her ear. "Where's your aunt?"

"Out."

"Fine. We've got just ten minutes."

Ten minutes later he was running across the campus to the laboratory and up the long stairs, his coat flying behind him, his hair all wild, his lips stained with kisses and wine, all fever and excitement.

Soon he was sitting on a stool at a long table, alone, in front of a little stove upon which he was boiling water, and on his lap he made notes in a notebook, meanwhile gazing out the window down on the narrow streets below, which were whitening with snow. He felt very gloomy. He couldn't understand the experiment and he was doing it all wrong, and in the little office just off the laboratory he could see the physics professor himself seated at his desk correcting papers and puffing on his pipe—a man, there, who understood things and had a sure and earnest interest in the world, science, and the livelihood of man! Peter was appalled.

What could he do in a world like this? Again he gazed moodily out the window, and suddenly a great nervous exaltation swept through his whole being, he was whipped with a feeling of great joy. Down there it was getting dark, it was snowing more heavily, and the narrow gray streets, the stone canyons with people walking to and fro in them with twinkling feet, were suddenly mysterious and amazing and beautiful. It struck him as wonderful that people were walking back and forth along the street. Just a moment ago he had been running down there himself all ravenous with things to do and get done. It was the world itself, to which, as he hovered there, he was descending for the first time in his life, amazingly as from some unknown previous dreaming existence in dark Galloway. He was seeing it all for the first time with eyes of wonder. He was amazed because of life, because of sheer human presence on the earth.

After he had strapped on his shoulder pads in the cold gloomy locker rooms at the practice field, he took out a letter from his mother. In her long, calm, folkwise language, she had written telling him that his father had taken sick and was bedridden at home, and could not work for two weeks. It suddenly occurred to him happily that he could go home to Galloway a few days to see his father. He was only a sophomore, working his way up to the first-string backfield, perhaps in time for the Army game in three weeks.

Then, in the raw attritive dusk of late October, when the skies were like torn and forlorn rags above the floodlights of the scrimmage field, the Penn squads rammed and smashed at each other on the busted turf. Coaches stood around in windbreakers and baseball caps, shouting with small fife-like voices in the wind. It was a long scrimmage session, longer than usual because of the presence of certain visiting coaches and reporters who had come to see the practice for the big Navy game that Saturday.

These luminaries of the sports world were standing by on the sidelines huddled miserably in winter coats, rubbing their chapped hands, holding the brims of their hats in sudden gusts of cold, and stamping their feet with a kind of impatient sadness. They were the writers for the great Philadelphia papers, and writers from New

York and all over the country, "prognosticators" and "experts" and "beloved columnists" from Chicago, from the Coast, from the Big Ten country, writers from the Associated Press and United Press, sad-seeming, shabby-hatted, grim and weatherbeaten men—with the coaches who looked just like them, including two famous coaches of Dartmouth and Brown. Though there was a lot of excitement in the air because of the big impending game, they were all perhaps thinking of their warm cozy offices, after all, of hot coffee in cartons and the mellow briar pipe and talk of the "gridiron," certainly of anything but this desolation and this plain which was not all really like the columns they wrote ("Pressbox Jottings, by Pop Sampson"), or like the neat plays on blackboards with chalklines showing just how everything works.

The players meanwhile—Peter among them—were grimy in their red and blue uniforms that were now as dark as winter clay, all of them perspiring in the cold, some of them with their sleeves rolled up, some without stockings so that their bulging calves were smeared with dirt and blood. They sniffled sadly and spat, and gasped to catch their breath, and sighed.

"Again!" barked the head coach.

One-two-three, rackety-bang, slam, whap! The poor fullback for the fortieth time was flattened like an omelet at the line of scrimmage by a phalanx of 220-pound guards and tackles whose names were Bjowrski and Mierczacowicz and "Big Moose" Marino of Scranton.

"Again!" shouted the coach.

There happened to be a certain flaw in the fullback's spin that evening and this had to be ironed out at all costs. "We're going to get that damn thing right if we have to stay here till midnight!" shouted the coach, pointing up furiously at the floodlights, whereupon all the visiting writers guffawed on the sidelines and the visiting coaches smiled grimly.

Peter was smack in the middle of these great head-on detonations. He and another boy, an end, were going through the same blocking assignment in each of these repetitions of the play, with the absentminded sorrow of two men trying to ram down a heavy door and failing forever because the door was unbendable. The door in this case happened to be a gigantic tackle named Makofskik who was so unbelievable that several weeks before, just for laughs, he had reached out and raised Peter to the ceiling in the locker rooms. Peter's job was to "hit him low" while the other boy "hit him high" so as to make some attempt to take the monster out of the play. However, at each sad repetition of the play, though they managed to rebound again after initially hitting him and thereby somewhat holding him back, he always reached out over their heads and caught the lunging fullback with one meaty hand and brought him to a dead stop. Were it not for the fact that this gave ample time for several other ferocious players to smash the poor fellow underneath and out of sight, he would just simply plunk him down on his back, turn around and walk away.

Once, however, Peter and the boy hit the big Pole so astutely that he fell down and the harried fullback gained five yards. On the next play Makofskik was like a mad bull. Peter was coming in to "hit him low" when the great hamhock hand presented itself to his countenance and he was brushed aside with the distinct consciousness that his neck was snapping somewhere, after which someone ran up his back with the cleats digging in. This, it turned out, was the triumphant fullback who had managed somehow to elude the great hand and gained about a yard—a hardwon yard on Peter's behind.

And then, disentangling themselves from sorrowful heaps, the players rose again with doleful eyes, hands on hips, and waited for orders, and sniffled and spat.

Finally, however, the coach had drawn aside a moment and was talking to the famous men on the sidelines. It seemed to the players that the scrimmage session was over at last. They began talking a little and laughing happily. "Hey, Moose, what happened that time?"

"Whaddayamean?"

"How'd my shoe taste?"

"I'll shoe you—ya Dago."

Someone said something dirty in whispers; they all laughed. (The players were forbidden to swear.) They all kneeled there on the ragged clods of dirt, spitting mud and wiping their mouths of blood, great massive tackles with their hands hanging like beefs, long rangy ends with melancholy eyes looking down, chubby Armenian guards with thighs like posts, and compact halfbacks with gaunt scarred-up faces looking up at the sky absentmindedly. They all swore under their breath, and groaned, and sighed. They were all waiting for the coach to send them into the showers. They thought of this with such sore joy and consolation, of the warm locker rooms, the steamy showers, great good rubdowns with liniment, then a big meal at the training table and some sleep in their comfortable dormitory rooms. They all looked longingly down the field at the warm golden lights in the raw dark, they waited and prayed.

But on the sidelines one of the visiting reporters was rubbing the side of his nose quizzically. "Well now, coach, what's this I hear about all these speedboys you got under wraps for the Navy? Is that just a rumor, a lot of hopeful optimism among alumni or is it the real McCoy?"

"Yeah, coach, what's the story the cognoscenti has been airing abroad?"

"How about a little show, off the record?"

So in answer the coach only grinned faintly and walked back to the field blowing his whistle.

The reporters nudged each other gleefully. "Here we go!" "Now we're going to see some of that backfield speed he's supposed to have!" "This is what the Middies are going to see on Saturday afternoon!"

Weary Peter was on one knee thinking soft and tender thoughts of Judie and of the sophomore dance in rosy lights with plaintive moan of saxophones and of his warm room in lamplight, and books, and all such joyous college-boy thoughts that come in the hungry Fall. Suddenly he realized that the scrimmage on the wintry plain was not over in the least, and that they had called the play where he himself had to come around and take the ball on a reverse. He hardly had time to compose himself before he was off with the ball and snickering. "Holy cow! Holy cow!" he kept thinking, and it was all so absurd. They charged at him and he just circled around further back, laughing and thinking about it, and strangely, suddenly infuriated at the sheer foolish indignity of what he had to do in the world. At one point it was almost as if he might suddenly throw the ball up in the air—and walk away, or go into a sudden sheepish foolish dance and make faces at the coach, thumb his nose at everybody, and run lickity-split down to the furthest glooms beyond the floodlights and disappear into the night over the fence, and just keep going down the streets of Philadelphia, football uniform and all, out to the furthest ends of the Autumn night somewhere.

Instead he heaved and strained with all the tremendous discomfort of his furious calling, he circled back, yelled crazily at everybody that tried to tackle him, zig-zagged his way through, somehow eluded everything (no one particularly wanted to bother catching him), hurdled and hop-skipped and whirled, and in a moment was all alone down by the goalposts pulling up to a stop and suddenly standing there motionless in thought, staring at the warm light in the windows of the locker rooms down at the end of the field, as if meditating something, and holding the football out in the palm of his hand, like one who studies the acorn.

But the coach was piping him back with the whistle. "Come on back here, you won't get away with it twice!" The reporters were slapping their knees for joy on the sidelines, and the weary players were sniffling and spitting and waiting with their hands on their hips, and sighing.

Finally, in the locker room, he remembered his mother's letter and his desire to see his father.

He remembered what he felt in the laboratory and in Jake Fitzpatrick's room, he recalled also the excitement of trains and travel and the going and coming in the world itself. He could leave all this, if only for a few days, and rush off to things again. And a pang of loneliness hit him as he thought of his father sick in bed and the thoughts and anxieties that old man would feel now that he could not keep up with his job in the Galloway printing plant.

After he had dressed, Peter went to the office and talked to the coach.

"You'd better go home, then, for a couple of days at least and see how things are," growled the coach. "Try to be back for Thursday—this is no picnic party here."

So Peter rushed back to the college dormitories with mounting excitement and happiness. In a matter of minutes he was packed and ready to go home. He left, cigarette in mouth, hat pushed back, lugging his bag, hurrying along jubilantly, yet scowling, preoccupied with voyages, prowling about in the world he had just discovered with all his secret and disordered moods.

When he arrived home, he found his father mournful and pale in his sick bed.

"Well, Petey," said the old man with a bitter smile—"it's just another one of those things. We get nothing but bad luck."

The doctor had ordered Martin to stay put in bed for at least two weeks. He had pleurisy and trouble with his liver, he was feverish, irritated, gloomy, and harried with worries.

"I can't work—I guess your mother told you that. I guess God is punishing me for giving up the shop. But I'll be back on the job in two weeks, it's no great tragedy." And with this the father returned his gaze to the window, vacantly, yet in another moment he was looking eagerly at Peter, almost bashfully too.

"I notice," said Martin presently, "you seem *dissatisfied*. Anything wrong at college, hmm?"

Peter made a wry face.

"Something's on your mind. You know when I went to visit you there last month you were in bed in the middle of the day."

"Why not?" said Peter arrogantly. "I stay up all night studying."

"Then how can you go to classes?"

With languid weariness Peter sighed, "Somedays I don't have any."

The father sat up in the bed and fixed Peter with an earnest stare. "I'll bet my bottom dollar there's something in that little blockhead of yours but you don't even know what it is yourself. Well, go ahead, go ahead, I don't care. I haven't got time to worry about all of you, sick as I am and out of luck as I am. Do what you like. But you know how I feel about what you do, Petey, you know how I pray for you."

Peter was seething with indignation. He felt like stomping out of the room and out of the house. He pictured himself doing this, slamming the door, proud with rage, noble with absurdity.

His father was talking in a new tone of voice, he could hear it, but he was thinking about something else in a tense reverie; it wasn't for a full minute before he began listening again to his father's words.

"You remember when you used to run that old linotype in the shop—?"

"The linotype?"

"Yes. By God," laughed Martin hoarsely, "and you were *good* at it too! I was just thinking, if you had a chance you could fill in for me at the shop, for a couple of weeks. Of course, it's just a crazy thought. If it wasn't in the middle of the football season you could do it, you see? I mean take a couple of weeks off from school."

"Oh, sure."

"The way *you* study, I mean!" And with this Martin guffawed with his savage sheepish glee, and then fell to scratching his chin judiciously. "That's absolutely out, of course, just a notion. Ah!" he suddenly sighed disgustedly—"and yet who knows? If that boss feels like it he can give that job to someone else, just because I miss a couple of weeks. That's the way they are in this town." He looked at Peter with his frank blue eyes wide open.

Peter disagreed. "He won't do that. Your boss Green? It's not your fault you're sick, and you're a good worker. He won't want to lose you."

"I'm not so young as some of them."

"He'd have to be a regular bastard to fire you."

"I don't know the man," said the father simply, "he may do anything he pleases. But I'd just better get well as quick as I can."

They looked at each other mutely. And although nothing further was said, Peter was greatly disturbed.

Peter wandered out of the house, took a bus downtown and strolled curiously back and forth in front of the printing shop where his father worked. He went in finally and came face to face with the boss.

"Hello, Mr. Green," said Peter, grinning foolishly, half expecting the man to know that he was George Martin's son. But the printer only stared.

"I'm George Martin's son, Pete—"

"Oh, yes. How's George now? Any better?"

"Yes. He'll be in bed another two weeks though."

"I know," said the printer.

"Well," began Peter, and then he could think of nothing further to say, and the printer, someone having called him from the other side of the plant, hurried off with a gesture telling Peter to wait a minute.

Everybody was working and self-absorbed in the busy plant, and Peter felt foolish standing around, more so because he did not really know why he had come here.

"I don't like that man," he thought, watching Mr. Green. "I don't want to work for him," and in another moment Peter would have left the place, but he changed his mind and waited nervously.

The printer came right back, and Peter declared: "I see you've got someone working in my father's place."

"No," said the printer with his perpetual harassed frown, "no, I'm trying to get someone down at the union though. I might get a man in the morning."

"I used to run the linotype in my father's shop," blurted Peter. "He had a shop, you know. I guess you know that."

Mr. Green made absolutely no comment, either by word or expression, but kept staring at him.

"I was pretty good," Peter went on, affecting now a casual air, and walking over to one of the two linotypes. A man was working at the other one and he too stared at Peter.

"Well, this man here's doing twice the work," said the printer with his worried air. "We're way behind on our orders. Did you run this kind of machine?"

"Yes, this kind here."

"Well—do you want to fill in for your father?" Green was peering closely at Peter.

"But you're getting a man in the morning, aren't you?" returned Peter, peering back insolently at him. "I don't know if I'd be as good as a union man," he added haughtily. "But I'd be pretty good."

Still the boss was not sure what Peter meant, and suddenly, smiling, Peter strolled out.

He went home to supper without telling anyone where he had been, what he had done, or what he had thought of doing. The next night he dropped around again at the printing plant to see if Mr. Green had found a substitute operator, and learned with a strange, grave feeling of relief and reassurance that a new man had been hired for the two weeks. Then he packed up and got ready to go back to Penn and studies and football. He was angry, confused, utterly baffled. Just before he left he kept looking at his father in his sick bed, trying to think of something to say.

"I'll be home after Thanksgiving," he told his father. "It's only a few weeks from now, just a couple of weeks—"

"I know," said the old man. "Don't worry about a thing now, just get back to your schoolwork and your duties and football and everything. We'll be all right here."

And he and his father embraced awkwardly, and Peter hurried out of the flat, feeling sheepish and sorrowful. His brother Joe drove him down to the station.

"Well, *that's that!*" Peter found himself thinking on the train.

As it pulled out, he saw a familiar curly head of hair several seats in front of him. It was Danny on his way to Boston too. He had a quart of whiskey with him in a paper bag.

"I called you and called you in Galloway!" yelled Peter as they stood in the windy roaring partition between the coaches. "Where were you?"

"Zagg," said Danny, with great sincerity, "I been drunk for three weeks. Ask Berlot if that isn't true!"

"Why, you maniac?" asked Peter with indescribable delight, tousling Danny's head from sheer joy.

"I quit my job in the mills, I finished my course in business school, I'm gonna start working as a typist in Boston next week."

"And you get drunk, Mouse? I thought you'd be happy!" Peter was really surprised.

"So did I, Zagg. I've been working so hard and so long to get out of those mills, and that damn town. Now I'm out, now I'm a free man, and I feel miserable, Zagg, I feel miserable. Between the mills and this new job of mine I have three weeks with nothing to do but enjoy life, so I went and got married to a huge beautiful quart of whiskey, Zagg, look at it!" He held it up and looked at it reverently. "Do you understand that remark, Zagg?"

Suddenly Peter was seized with a tremendous mournfulness of heart as he thought of his father sick at home, of his strange visit to the printing plant, of Joe at the station, of his mother working in a shoeshop, of the lonely woe of his life at college, and now the brooding melancholy Danny. And all these things conspired together, and he and Danny arrived in Boston an hour later roaring drunk.

Peter had twenty dollars on him, and in the back of his head he planned to take the first train to New York after the bars closed in Boston. But they went to the Imperial Cafe on Scollay Square, a great multiple saloon with two floors and half a dozen sections, a place of stomping and noises and occasional brawls, full of sailors, seamen, and women. They toasted each other ecstatically, vowing they were the greatest friends on earth, and really sincerely believing it, vowing never to part again.

In the morning, blood-red drunkenness roared in Peter's head. He woke up in an expensive-looking hotel room. Beside him was a scrawny middle-aged woman snoring horribly. The boy leaped out of bed in blind dismay, paced up and down the room smoting his thighs and swearing and muttering. He stopped every now and then to peer with fascinated disgust at the toothy dame in the bed. He looked at his wallet, which had only eight dollars left in it, and he was sick at heart, completely dumbfounded with himself.

"My father's sick, my mother works, gives me a little money. My brother works, my sister works. Everybody believes in me because I'm in college. Danny is my friend. I go out with him and desert him for this *thing* here I don't even know. What am I doing? Oh, Christ, what am I doing to everybody!"

He tiptoed out of the room finally, leaving the woman to her fate, and hurried to a cafeteria where, over a glass of tomato juice that he could not drink, he literally stared into the abyss.

"I have no honor. I haven't got the honor of an animal. If I had any honor, I'd never do things like this." He looked around the cafeteria at other men. They all looked so morning-decent and morning-honorable and morning-purposeful.

Peter miserably made his way to the train and back to Philadelphia to school. His schooldays were almost over. The way he learned, and what he learned, he knew now could not be learned in any school.

[7]

IT WAS SATURDAY afternoon. The huge crowd filled the stadium and the ocean-roar of their jubilation was carried on radios all over America. The batteries of newsreel cameras clicked mysteriously high atop the pressbox. In the pressboxes men trained fieldglasses on the battered plain below as if they were generals of war. In the closing moments of the final period the piteous songs of the losing side were raised by choirs of faithful alumni, and fifes blew on the field, and muffled drums dolorously beat out the doom of certain hopes and certain destiny.

Young Peter sat on the bench, a new sophomore halfback, hooded among the others in the shades of historic day, aching and burning in every bone to run out into the middle of the field which was like the middle of the world's life, and stand there among these great sanctifications which, for his soul, were like the Tribute of the Angels in the great arcades of Judgment Day.

In the last minutes of the fourth quarter, his turn came. He removed his hood and ran out among the echoing hums and roars of the game's sad completion. He did not dare raise his eyes to the multitudes.

There were dazzling final plays in the gloom, mysterious reverses and sudden rips of speedy backs through the Navy line, sprawlings, convergences of tumbled bodies, flash passes, short gains. Suddenly, in the smoky dusk amid roars, there were two penetrations deep into the Navy backfield by some strange ghostly Peter who was almost impossible to see. He seemed so small and so furiously diffuse in his diving and ducking through tormented bodies—all in the shady dimness as drums boomed mournfully.

Hundreds of miles away in New England his father sat wild-eyed at a small pitiable radio. There, too, it was dusky and dim at the windows, raw October night was rattling at the panes, and the announcer was shouting remotely:

"Another long gain by Pete Martin of Penn! Straight through the middle and down the side, and out of bounds on the thirty yard line! First down and ten to go! Peter George Martin from Galloway, Massachusetts, he's a sophomore, five foot nine, a hundred sixty five pounds. How he GOES! Another one of Penn's great new backs . . . O'Connell, Singer, Angelone, Martin . . . auguring badly, wouldn't you think, Bill, for Notre Dame next month? And, oh, that Penn line, it's like a battering ram. Navy have their backs to the wall now! . . . Shift now to the right, single wing, six-three-two defense for the Middies—and there's the gun! The game is over! Penn wins! The game is over!"

And sadly the game is over, there are great movements and departures in the gloom, the last music of brass-bands and drums, the lamentation of alma mater song sung by choristers with whiskey bottles and battered hats, the last echoes of the huge darkened stadium that is slowly emptied of all its eager life. The game is over.

The lights of Philadelphia burn in oncoming night beyond. Everyone is going off to eat, there will be drinking in bars, and parties, and wild hilarities. And the football players, taking showers or combing their hair or being rubbed down by some consoling trainer, are thinking of the soft sweet girl awaiting them for the dance.

This was when Peter saw the joys of his college life—always on the Saturday night when the game was over and night spread its rewarding darkness over all.

The following week Peter got a letter from his father, from a town in Connecticut called Meriden.

> Hello there, Swifty Martin! [it read. The envelope was also addressed to "Swifty Martin," for the father wanted the football coach and anybody else in the school to know that his son

was a great swift halfback.] Six-thirty in de mawnin and de ole weazel is up and around thinkin about home and wishin a lot of empty wishes. Well, to be brief, here I am settled down in a new job. Yup, you guessed it. When I got out of bed and went back to my old job at Green's it wasn't there for me any more. I'm not as young as I used to be, and they had a young man there who seemed to be doing pretty well for himself. No need telling you how I feel about Green pulling this kind of thing. Knew him off and on in years past while in Business in stinktown. Well, I could have guessed that he'd turn out to be a stinktown stinker himself.

My new job here is fine and dandy, got it through the union, good bosses, good boys to work with. It's not a bad little town to work in, not 'tall. No complaints except lack of heat in the rooming-house and bum food in the diners. I send home most of my pay every week. Doesn't leave me much. Once in a while I bet 50¢ on a pony, or go to a movie. But I'm worried about you, Pete, because you are so very dear to me, *so very dear!*

I know that you're lonely at school, that there's something on your mind bothering you. The world's in such a mess, all you poor kids are mixed up. Keep your chin up and just wait for the best, or the worst, whichever Fate chooses to deal you. But be brave, be gay, be a genuine man whatever you do! That's the way to live. Don't worry, don't repent. Work hard and do your best, it's the most any of us can do. Your family's behind you and loves you. Give thanks to the forces of nature that bind us all through life.

Your lonesome old Pop.

P.S. And I thought I'd write you a cheery letter! Well, I'll send this off anyway. Heard you last Saturday on my radio—so proud, so dearly proud of you!

This letter stunned Peter. He had taken it out of the mailbox and read it walking slowly upstairs to his room. Now, in his room, he sat with the letter open on the desk, with the radio playing Beethoven. He stared blankly out the window.

"Well, *that's that!*" he thought immediately.

And gazing out the window at the campus, he suddenly felt a great loathing rise in him. "And now I'm supposed to go to football practice!" he cried out in the room and, jumping up, he pulled the shade down and plunged the room in dreary half darkness. He sat down again at the desk, peering in the gloom at his father's letter.

He sat there a long time without seeming to think anything. Through it all, he began to feel a tremendous thrill in his veins, like a pulsing, and something that was like an aching restlessness in his muscles and nerves and very bones.

"It's human life I want—the thing itself—not this," he said to himself with happy surprise.

He got up, so violently as to knock the chair back, punching his fist into his hand, burning with energy and wild feelings. With a jubilant and determined movement, he tore his coat out of the closet, and went out, closing the door. He hardly knew what he was doing.

He had decided to quit the football team, he was not going to play any more football.

"So simple, so simple!" he kept thinking.

He plunged along in the wind, coming to a bar. There was Jake Fitzpatrick drinking beer and talking to the bartender. He had probably never come to this particular bar before in his life, but there he was inside. Peter snickered gleefully and went in.

"Martin!" called Jake happily. "Say! why you looking so pleased with yourself?" he demanded.

"I decided to quit football, stick to my studies, stick to the human things!" rattled Peter. "Look! my hands are shaking. I'm all excited. That's what I'm going to do."

"When?"

"Starting now. I'm a free man, a human man. I'm going to stay right here all afternoon."

"What's that letter you got in your hand? Ah—I know, it's your draft board. And that surer'n hell explains it all." And Jake chuckled.

Peter jammed his father's letter in his pocket. He had been walking down the street with the letter in his hand. "That letter made me decide to quit football!" he suddenly blurted.

"Who's it from?"

"It's just a letter," said Peter with a distant air. "Well, it didn't make up my mind, actually, but it helped. It's just a letter—"

"Well, drink up! Say—" Fitz cried now, "why don't you go over to Judie's and bring her down here? I get a kick out of that girl. Really interesting—in a crazy way."

"Yeah, that's it!" agreed Peter.

He hurried out into the cold night to fetch Judie, bounding along nervously but with a strange reeling swagger. He was back on the campus in a moment, looking around rather angrily and with a foolish lonesomeness. He had come to a full stop and stood slumped and meditative right by the library entrance. He was taking his time going to Judie's house across the campus. His heart was pounding and pounding harder.

"What I'm going to do," he thought with great difficulty, framing the words in his mind, "is think very slow. God!"

He strolled around the campus looking at it with great curiosity, as though he were a visitor, stopping now and then to peer at some monument or landmark with that curiosity visitors have. Yet he was thinking about something entirely different.

He was wondering how he could possibly bring his radio with him on the train, perhaps carry it under his arm, get a seat to himself, and lay it there beside him and take care that it wouldn't fall off when the train started and stopped. A hundred such details crossed his mind. When he lit a cigarette his hand was trembling violently.

"That's what I want to do. That's what I *know* I want to do!"

A half hour later Peter Martin was walking across the campus with a heavy radio under one arm and a big suitcase gripped in the other hand. He was moving in the shadows, staying close to walls and taking absurd long-cuts where it was darkest. He was actually leaving college altogether.

When he got on the trolley and arranged all his belongings around him on the seat, he sighed vigorously: "Well, that's that!"

A student sitting across, whom he knew vaguely, was glancing at him curiously. Peter, roused out of good-natured lonesomeness, glared back with such angry flashing hatred that the poor fellow buried his nose in a book all the way to the railroad station and never looked up again.

In the phone booth Peter again felt awful twinges of foolishness when he heard Judie's voice over the phone protesting: "But, Petey, don't leave college! Don't give up your football! You don't mean to tell me you're going back to that awful hometown of yours! You're crazy if you do that!"

"What do you mean I'm crazy!" he shouted.

"Oh, never mind. All you think about is yourself—what about *me*? What are you going to do about me?"

"I'll write and I'll save money and come down and see you all the time, that's all."

"Sure," she murmured sadly.

"All right, all right!" he shouted, hitting the wall of the booth. Finally they said good night and Judie was almost crying at the end.

After hiding away from the family for one moody week, wandering in New York till his money ran out, Peter proudly came home like a veritable hero under cover of the sensational worry he had caused everyone.

The moment he arrived, he got a job in Galloway. With the job, in a big gas station in downtown Galloway, and the beginning of his contributions to the family budget, he knew that he was "making up" for his rash decision. These things done, he was absolutely ready and waiting for his father and the objections the old man would raise about his quitting school. He was actually waiting for this with a resentful air, ready with a hundred deliberate scornful replies.

Sure enough, without a moment's hesitation, within the first hour of his arrival in Galloway that Saturday, Martin hunted down his son, and strolled casually up to him at the place where he worked. Peter was bending over a motor in the yard of the station, all dressed up in a new suit of coveralls, his hair slicked back smoothly, his hands just a little dirty from the work.

"Hello there, son!" greeted Martin with a forlorn show of cheerfulness.

Peter did not seem surprised. "Well, well! Pa! How did you know I worked here?" And it was almost as though he knew his father would come that very moment.

"Oh, Joe told me," replied the old man casually. "What are you doing there? I didn't know you were a mechanic . . . I thought Joe and Charley were the only mechanics in the family."

"I'm *not* a mechanic," replied Peter almost petulantly. "I'm just lubricating this car in all these little oil cups here. This chart shows where they are on a Nash. Then we pump some grease in the transmission, all over, from below in the pit there. Good job, huh?"

"Good pay, I'm told," said the old man, looking around curiously at the clean, spacious, well-organized station. "These people seem to know their onions. I used to bring my old Plymouth around here in the old days, but it wasn't the same kind of a place then—"

So then, while Peter bent there to his task, and his father stood watching him, there was a moment of terrible silence. Everything that they had to say to each other was frozen in them.

"I just thought I'd come down to see how you were getting along—"

And once more they were silent. At that moment they heard the radio inside the station and they could hear the announcer's excited voice, and the roar of crowds, and band music, the distant triumphant fanfares of a great Saturday afternoon game somewhere in America. Peter had grown numb with embarrassment and closed his eyes secretly over the motor, shuddering at the thought of his father standing there beside him.

"I wonder what game that is?" the old man spoke up with a kind of abject curiosity.

He looked blandly at his father: "Michigan-Iowa, I think. I'm not sure."

"Well," said the old man in a distant voice, looking away, lingering there, standing with his hands in his coat pockets, "what time do you come off work?"

"About six."

"Be home for supper?"

"*Certainly*," said Peter very deliberately.

"There's a lunchcart across the street," the old man said suddenly, "I think I'll go in for a hamburger or something like that. Feel a little hungry."

Peter looked at him for the first time. "I'll be finished with this in a minute. Go ahead and I'll be there—in a minute. I could stand a cup of coffee myself."

"Okay, Petey," said the father as though they had finally come to a great sorrowful agreement. "I'll be sitting in there." And he went off across the street, Peter standing and staring after him with the most mortified feeling that he had somehow slashed this man across his crestfallen eyes, in some vicious and thoughtless way.

He went to the lunchcart a few minutes later and joined him at the counter where, as things always go in lunchcarts, there was a lot of talk and laughter among the men, a radio playing loudly, and people coming in and out in fresh bursts of enthusiasm. So they just sat at the counter watching and listening.

And the fact that he and his father had yet to mention the thing that was burning in them, the gentle madness of this, the complex delicacy of it, the manly tact and sorrow of it, the unknowable things they were sharing together that afternoon, all this was gripping him and almost breaking down the scornfulness he had planned to use. Peter wished his father would speak of it, say something, argue with him, even get mad at him, shout at him right there in the lunchcart in front of all the men.

Presently, though, as both of them sat there in profoundest silence, and Peter was about to tell him what he had thought up in the way of plans for the future, the door opened again and a group of men who knew Martin came in.

"Well, how are *you* boys?" greeted Martin jovially. "You know my boy Pete here. How're things going at the plant?"

They grouped around for a moment, and Peter realized with a burning anger that his father was an object of curiosity to them now, where once they had rallied around him, as he had seen them do as a boy, with a genuine politeness and admiration.

"Hear you're working out of town now, George," one of them said, rather curiously, yet with no intended slyness, though it showed up somehow in all their faces as they listened altogether too quietly to his answer.

Peter bent over his coffee cup in a tense rage.

He heard someone ask: "What's *he* doing?"

"Pete, here? Oh," laughed Martin, "he speaks of freedom." It was just a little jest, and no one quite understood it. For some reason the youngest man in the group snickered. Peter's heart pounded like a triphammer, the blood rushed to his face sickeningly yet with curious exaltation, and he turned slowly on his stool, with great deliberation, bringing up an utterly mean look full into the young man's face, and said angrily:

"What's the matter?"

"Huh?"

Peter almost instantly blushed, the tears were coming into his eyes from embarrassment, still he continued to stare indignantly into the other's face, while everyone watched, and for a moment he had a wild fearful impulse to throw his fist into the other's face with all his might, to break up everything there in front of him in a chaos of fury.

There was an uncomprehending silence for a moment, and then, as in a dream, the men filed away across the lunchcart to get a booth, and Peter, his eyes blurred, was just stupidly staring into space with his neck muscles bulging and his fist unknotting slowly, his whole being shuddering from within. The oldest of the men was still standing alongside his father, gaping at Peter.

Suddenly Martin chuckled hoarsely. "By gosh! Little Petey used to be *so* shy, *so* shy! Remember him when he was that high, Bill, a shy little kid like my Mickey, never saying anything 'tall. Say, what's the matter with you there?" he laughed.

Peter got up and walked out of the lunchcart with a feeling of numb humiliation. His father joined him outside in a moment.

"That was a funny thing to do," he said curiously. "You never used to be like that—"

"The way that guy laughed! Who *is* that jerk anyway?"

"What's the matter with you?" cried the old man angrily. "They didn't do anything. I know those boys fairly well—"

"Bunch of wise guys. Didn't you see the way they were, didn't you see them—don't you notice anything?"

"Yes!" roared the old man. "I notice you're no longer the same little Petey who was so modest and so cheerful—"

"To hell with little Petey!"

"That's right, that's right, go ahead and say it!"

"Say what?"

They glared at each other with looks of pure hatred.

"Gee!" cried Peter with a flooding sense of terrified dismay. "Didn't you notice how they *looked* at you and talked about you working outside Galloway, in that damn smug way. Pa, that laugh!" he pressed desperately.

"I didn't notice anything of the sort. It's that neurotic way you kids are beginning to have, that's what it is, I guess."

"What do you mean, neurotic!" said Peter through his teeth, with intense loathing suddenly for the mere sound of his father's voice.

"That's what they teach you in college, I guess, that's what they learn in Harvard and Penn. They certainly turn out smart boys these days."

Peter was speechless with rage. "You be careful, Pa, what you say. You can't say—"

"What do you mean by that, sonny?" said the father meekly, with soft pain in his eyes yet his lips curled in disgust.

"You can't say that!" burst Peter with the foolish realization that he didn't know what he meant.

"I don't understand you any more," said the father.

"What!" cried Peter. "How can you be my father if you don't understand!"

"No, I don't understand you," declared the old man emphatically, his voice trembling. "I don't think I'll ever be able to understand you again now. Do you realize that, Petey? That's what a father has to go through in his life? He must lose all his children one by one, because God wants them till they get old, then he's going to throw them away. But when he throws them away I won't be around to help any more. That's the big trouble—"

"Pa," began Peter eagerly, "you know I wanted to come home and help out, don't you? You remember that night last Summer when we were on the porch and I told you how bad I felt leaving home—"

"No, I don't remember that."

"Didn't I say it? I went to school and I couldn't concentrate because of all that. All the trouble at home!" he cried with a great sigh. "Then you got sick. You know, I went down to Green's that day to see about the linotype job!" He looked at his father triumphantly. "You never knew *that*, Pa!"

The old man seemed to be thinking about something else.

"I'm not telling you everything because— At school I was miserable, I didn't want any more of it, that or football or anything. For another reason by itself, not home. I went down to Green's and thought about taking over your job for two weeks. Even then I was thinking of quitting school. Ma was talking about working in the shoe factory. I saw everybody working and just managing to live, how unhappy it was, all of a sudden, for the first time."

"What happened at Green's?"

"He wouldn't hire me," said Peter eagerly, "but I talked to him a *long time*. See, I tried to help even then!"

The father shrugged.

"Ah, there you go," snarled Peter suddenly. "I guess you'll never believe what I say. Okay." And he shot a glance at his father filled with hatred and mistrust and yet also with a furtive crestfallen curiosity, for he suddenly realized that he had simply lied.

"It's all the same to me, Petey," said the old man, brooding. "You know what I wanted you to do. However, it's your life, not mine." He stood there, staring gloomily into space. "In my old age I wanted a son doing big things. You don't know what a kick it gave me telling the boys that you were on a big college football team. You may laugh, but I was damn proud of you."

"Now you're not proud any more!" scoffed Peter.

"I'm just as proud of you as ever, only now I haven't got anything to say to those fellows. They're going to ask me what happened to you, and what will I be able to tell them?"

"Ah-ha!" persisted Peter with the same mocking indulgent air. "So that's what you're so worried about—won't know what to tell the boys. Tell them all to go to hell for me, won't you?"

"Don't think I wouldn't, if I felt like it," said the old man with a bland, preoccupied look. "No, it's not that at all. It's *you* I'm worried about."

"There's nothing wrong with *me!*" the boy fairly shouted. "I'm perfectly all right and I know *exactly* what I'm doing!"

"Exactly what you're doing," sniffed the old man. "Isn't that just fine and dandy. Nineteen years old and he knows exactly what he's doing. Yessir, they make 'em real smart nowadays, mental giants. Here's a Martin who's a mental giant—no, wait a minute, there's two of them, two Martin mental giants. Mister Francis and Mister Peter!"

"I don't give a damn what Francis is, but don't class me—I know what I'm doing, for the first time. Leave me alone!" he suddenly added.

"Leave you alone?" echoed the father wonderingly. "Why, has anyone in the house ever bothered you or told you what to do, or pushed you around, and tried to run your life? You kids have always had perfect freedom and all the encouragement in the world."

"All the encouragement in the world," said Peter now with a dark gaze. "Remember the Lawton game of 1935?"

"Well?" said the father. "What's the Lawton game of 1935 got to do now?"

"Oh, nothing," said Peter, waving his hand, brooding, shrugging finally. "It's no big thing. You just said"—and here Peter began to blush, feeling very foolish. "Well, it's nothing actually."

"What, what?"

"You said I was too small to make the football team," he said almost slyly but with an attempt at being casual and matter-of-fact.

"Did I?"

"Yes! I remembered that, but you don't. I went out for the football team and it took me a long time to make it, but I made it, didn't I? I finally made it in spite of you."

"Petey, I don't remember saying anything like that. I may have said it, okay. Still what difference does it make? You're a grownup boy now."

"Well, I don't want to play football any more," burst out Peter in one breath, grinning.

The father was exasperated. "Good Lord! All this has nothing to do with it at all! *What* kind of boloney have you been picking up? You were just a wonderful little kid, then, I remember you with your little baseball cap and your glove. Lordy, I remember the look of yearning and shyness on your face, and the things that you seemed to want to do, right in your eyes—"

"Yes yes yes yes," sighed Peter irritably.

"Now—look at what you've done. Giving up a scholarship in a fine college, and all the friends and connections you were making there, the career you could have built out of it— Giving all that up for what? In this world of hard times! For a job like this, in this stinktown of stinktowns. I tell you I'm just baffled, that's the only word I can think of!"

Peter was no longer angry and resentful; he was smiling gently while his father spoke.

"If I want to go back to Penn, I'll just go back, that's all. Right now it doesn't interest me."

"*You*'ll never go back there, not after what you've done!" Martin almost shouted.

"If you only knew what you've done, Petey! It's a hard world! All the poor people in the world, the poor struggling masses, fighting and scampering after a bit of bread, and you, just a boy with no knowledge of life, no years of harsh experience, no understanding of what hard times actually are—you do this thing with a song in your heart!"

"A song?" said Peter, pleased.

"Oh, it's hard, Petey, to make a living!"

"Who wants a living? I want life—"

"You're just playing with *words,* sonny, words you learned in books."

"Do you know there's a war coming!" continued Peter, ranting. "Even if I had stayed in college I'd be yanked out, and soon! Nobody's going to college in the very near future. Do you know that Mel Barnes left the team the same time I did, to go and join the Air Force? You didn't know that, did you? That doesn't interest you because it doesn't fit in with what you want to think."

"Do you think you can do what you like all your life?"

"Yes! Why not?"

Martin laughed hoarsely. "Poor kid, poor kid! You don't even know what you're up against." He laughed again and shook his head sadly. "The trouble with us Martins is that we can't get along in the world, some things in it are so ratty, and we have to turn away, we always turn away."

"Oh, forget it, will you, Pa? *I'm* not worried."

"Well, you have your little job here," said the father, indicating the gas station across the street. "I guess there's work for you to do there this afternoon. I won't bother you any more."

"You're not *bothering* me."

"I'll go home and shut up. You'll be home for supper, then?"

"Of *course*," continued Peter. Feeling suddenly ashamed, he added: "I'll be home for supper, Pa, and I'll see you there." But the old man was walking off, and Peter watched him go with a sudden rush of regret.

He went back to work in the lubrication pit with a feeling of gloomy disgust. At six o'clock, when he was through work, he was overcome with depression, and walked home in the tremendous windy November darkness, as great boughs cracked overhead, as the last leaves flew across arc-lamps.

And suddenly that night his father, clapping his hands together and holding them there in sorrowful reverence, cried out of the dark of the parlor: "The things, my son, the things!"

[8]

JOE MARTIN happened to be spending the Sunday afternoon in a bar when news of Pearl Harbor was announced over the radio. He was drinking with Paul Hathaway, who was back in Galloway for the first time since the truck trip. The first thing they did, in company with several others, was to put down their drinks and tear off in a body to the recruiting station at the Post Office to enlist on the spot. Somebody wanted to call up his girl first, but they shouted: "Come on, Romeo, this can't wait!" They soon learned that the enlisting machinery was going to take its own slow time, and they all had to go home for supper.

George Martin, on this day, was alone in his rooming-house in the Connecticut town where he worked, when the news came over his little radio. He was shaving and he stared at himself in the mirror with exasperation.

"Now they've done it, they've done it again! We'll hear all about it before it's through, and after it's through! Now they'll start passing out the buttons, and then when it gets good and bloody they'll start passing out the medals. Now all the idiots in the country are going to rise to the top. It's their time."

He didn't care who heard him in the adjoining rooms.

"This is the time for the fools to swing into action. And this is the time for the good youngsters, the brave ones, to get themselves killed and to kill other brave ones. I've seen it all before, here we go again! And my three boys—*four* boys with little Charley, fifteen years old and who knows? My boys! my boys!" he cried with dawning anger and disgust, and he slammed around the room.

Martin remembered that he had really felt the same way in 1917 even as a young man, and it was all coming to pass again, the same stupid and violently unreality of things gone mad. It seemed more unnecessary and obsolete and insane than ever before. He wrote to his wife that night:

"The poor American people! All the fools in the world take us for millionaires living in mansions. They attack us because we're supposed to have so much money and to be so arrogant because of it. And what is it they're attacking? Some poor devil who works his heart out because his parents and his grandparents had to work so hard and taught him the life of work too. And he is such a peaceable man, the American, the first really peaceable man! All he wants is to live, raise a family, work, and make his life more enjoyable and kind-hearted. Is it any more than that, after all? And I'm not referring to the middle class or whatever they call themselves with their fancy houses and fancy lawns like they have up on Wildwood Drive in Galloway and their fancy jobs in banks and Chambers of Commerce. I'm referring to the *people* of this country, the poor devils who have to work hard for a living and believe in their families and in a Godly good life.

"Well, Marge, here it is again. The Great Boobs are on the warpath, and someone, somewhere, is turning out the garbage that's going to blind everybody to the real facts of the world,

American or otherwise. Kiss my dear children for me. There's a long road ahead and all we can do is wait, we helpless ones."

In Galloway, the little kids ran out in the fields at dusk and yelled and screamed because they thought the Jap planes were going to come over any hour. Mickey was with them and they all went "Ra-ta-ta-ta-ta!" like machine guns, and wrestled each other furiously.

Peter, at this gloomy and obsessed time of his own life, went walking around Galloway late at night when everyone else was asleep and virtually listened to the silence. The river continued its slow thundering hush through the town, the cold white moonlight shone on the frozen canals and made its midnight glow between windswept desolate tenements on Rooney Street.

Peter was a year too young to be eligible for the Selective Service draft, but he had heard about the merchant marine and he pondered this as the first great step of his new life. Curiously, however, he never thought of this in terms of war, but in terms of the great gray sea that was going to become the stage of his soul.

And after his midnight striding meditations he would always come back to the house, haunting his family's sleep in the kitchen with a cup of tea, his cigarettes, and a long moody penetration of great books. In the morning, bleary-eyed and satiated, he went off to work in oily coveralls and brooded in the lubrication pit all day, thinking thoughts of Unknown Seas, and Circles Drawn at Midnight, and the Great Snow White Albatross.

Mighty world events meant virtually nothing to him, they were not real enough, and he was certain that his wonderful joyous visions of super-spiritual existence and great poetry were "realer than all."

He began to adopt his father's habit of looking up with stunned wonder when someone spoke to him, yet with a slight difference, screwing up his face in angry earnestness, flicking face-muscles impatiently and with profound deference to the speaker. This came to such a pass one week that he did nothing but flick his face-muscles in front of everybody. Alone, he even practiced it, gravely, in the mirror, and glared at himself.

He was reading all the great books and moving around in the world wrapped in the gloomy cloak of himself at nineteen. Moreover, he was certain that his life was over, that he was going to die a young death, and that his last days were going to be spent in striding, silent, scowling enigmatical greatness. Still, at that time, he was as handsome and sturdy as any other man in Galloway, and when some girl happened to catch him by surprise with a happy morning greeting, he would suddenly blush and smile with fumbling uncomprehending sweetness. Then, his heart hammering away, he would hurry off to think by himself.

One night the melancholy young Greek, Alexander Panos, met him outside the Galloway library. Outside, because he had specific orders not to interrupt Young Faust's "study of everything." Peter came out at closing time, nine o'clock, lighting a cigarette, scowling and muscle-flicking over the flare of the match, stuffing his books grimly in his pockets and ready to go on up the street. Out of the dark alcove came Alexander, smiling sadly.

"What's that you're carrying?" barked Peter, almost annoyed, as though he had sensed his presence in the darkness nearby and wasn't in the least surprised.

"Some things I want to show you," replied the young poet. "Wait until we sit down some place. How are you tonight, Pete?"

"All right, all right!" barked Peter. "Same as any other night. Let's go!"

They walked across the canal near the Y.M.C.A. and Peter glared at the young Greek athletes lounging against the rail twirling key-chains. They did not however notice Peter, whom they would ordinarily have noticed because of his reputation as an athlete.

He spat casually into the canal, saying, "Where shall we go?"

"We can go to the cafeteria on Daley Square and have coffee, or—"

"Yeah, we'll do that. Say, what was that you were saying about Gothic art on that canal bridge Monday night?"

Alexander collected his memory and pointed towards the library. "You mean the bridge over by the Greek church. I was saying that on each side of the canal you have the Gothic soaring St. Matthews cathedral and then the Greek Byzantine with its inward dome."

Peter nodded absorbedly.

"Gothic immensity, don't you see, placed next to Byzantine sensitivity. But, of course, I'm prejudiced," he smiled. "Did you ever stop to realize what an unusual city Galloway is!" continued Alexander eagerly.

Peter laughed sarcastically.

"I understand, but still, even in this city, only a canal separates two schools of architecture. And the view from the Rooney Street bridge is very beautiful. People park their cars on the bridge on Sunday afternoons, people from New Hampshire and Connecticut and Maine, just to watch the river and the horizon!"

"Hmm," said Peter, preoccupied with something else now.

"I've got so many things to tell you tonight," began Alexander, inhaling eagerly on a fresh cigarette. "I haven't seen you for two days. Where did you go last night?"

Peter spat again into the canal. "I went out with Berlot and the boys. We met Scotcho and Danny and some of the other guys and made the rounds of the joints. Gartside had his car and we picked up Grimy Gertie in the Yellow Moon."

"That horrible gangbang? Pete, not her, really not her!"

"Yeah, sure," said Peter casually.

"Don't enumerate the details, please! I know all about it," said young Alexander with a princely melancholy.

Peter was slapping his knees and laughing with high pleasure. "Oh, Al, you poor miserable maniac, are you horrified?"

"Really, Pete," Alexander stammered earnestly, "I don't object at all—but a sensitive person like you . . . What of your soul?"

"My soul isn't sensitive," cackled Peter, "it's in the gutter where it belongs." But instantly he brooded again.

"I have no objections to Bacchus and Venus, but, Pete, the things you do when you go out with that gang! Don't you see that we must learn to discriminate? There are greater and finer things than dallying around with mad strumpets! The world is opening with new hopes and greater ideals and you want to fulfill minor and cheap sensations! Isn't that silly? Pete, I hate like hell to talk like this—it would be so much easier to praise you than disagree with you—but just think, a full-scale war against Fascism is on! And think of Tommy Campbell, Tommy with whom we saw the sunrise last summer, and now he's in Manila and the Japs have taken Manila! Have I hurt you talking like this?"

"No, go on. But there's no definite news about Tommy yet. He may have escaped in the jungle."

"That's all I have to say. Please don't misunderstand me!"

"I haven't," laughed Peter. "What say, shall we stroll toward Daley Square?"

"All right."

A moment later, after dark consideration, Peter was saying: "Al, about that Grimy Gertie business, don't go thinking for a minute that horseplay like that influences me. You know how much I've been studying since I left school, you'll never know *how* much. All I do is study," he concluded fiercely.

"Yes, of course," said Alexander. "I know it well, I never get to see you any more. But I want you to keep it up. Someday we'll both be great men."

Right on Daley Square among the crowds of the town, Alexander began again: "Oh, Pete, the war has come and it has wrought sad changes. I'm lost now more than I've ever been before, and I know you feel the same way too, I can tell."

Peter was scowling because Alexander talked too loudly among the crowds.

"Don't you remember, Pete, the first time I met you, on the sandbank when we were children, you and your brother Joe?"

"I know, I know."

"And when I introduced you to my mother for the first time, how she knew!"

"She knew what?"

"That you were like a brother, that I looked upon you as my brother. She knew that instantly from me, though I never had to tell her. And then, Peter, recall how it was when we went to New York and met your brother Francis and that man Engels. And then, one of the greatest moments of my life, when I finally met your brother Joe last year. How I almost cried when I saw him! Don't you realize that I can't forget that day on the sandbank years ago? My whole existence and faith is almost based on that one day! Not completely, of course, for I have loved—loved Julia Browning so much, even when she laughed at me on the street that day. Pete, I was only sixteen."

"You always were an amazing maniac," chuckled Peter.

"Of course, a maniac of sensitivity. And now, tonight even, what a strange love I feel for poor Alice—"

"That's the poetess in Boston?"

"Yes, you'll meet her and see what a great woman she is. Most of all, though, I love poor Maria. If you could only see Maria," he said sadly, "if you could only see her eyes."

Maria was a girl from New Hampshire whom Alexander had met somewhere in Boston through his friends, and it was said that she only had another year to live. However, Peter was dubious about this. His total knowledge of the girl had come from Alexander's own lips, and he knew that Alexander was capable of fabricating stupendous romances and literally believing in them.

"A year to live, and the sadness of her eyes, Peter. I want to marry her but she refuses. She refuses angrily and sends me away, and I go and weep by the Charles River—"

"How could you marry? You haven't got any money and you're still going to school."

"In that one year we could concentrate all of existence!" sang Alexander joyfully, as people turned to look and Peter scowled at his shoes. "But more than that, I ask myself now: where are my former joys? Where? Like that morning as a little child when I looked carefully at my first flower, or when I read Homer for the first time in Junior High. And the time my favorite aunt died and I learned the lesson of tears at twelve. Where is that morning you and I and Tommy Campbell went to Pine Brook at dawn to see the sunrise and sing? Remember how I buried the little flower in the earth? Was it for Tommy that I buried that flower?"

"No one knows how Tommy made out," persisted Peter.

"But I knew then, I knew! Don't you see, Pete, life can't hide anything from me!"

"Well—"

"And now, Pete, everything seems gone! I know I will die young, before I'm twenty-three. What blackness is closing in on me! It almost seems to me as though you were the last of the human beings on earth for me."

Peter looked away, not knowing what to say.

"Peter, always remember that I have never been hard or insincere, I have always expressed my feelings in spite of what people might think."

And Peter grinned, rubbing his jaw.

"However, I am more reserved nowadays, much more aloof than I have ever been," continued Alexander, walking erectly and with a stately air. "The glories of youth may have vanished, but always the Prince of Crete maintains his dignity. 'Weep not for the poets, for they carry the tears of six thousand years.' Isn't that a good line? I wrote it last night, in the midst of a paper on George Bernard Shaw."

Walking around the downtown streets, they ran into a football man from one of the Boston colleges that had bid for Peter's enrollment a few years back. He was an assistant coach on the team and lived in Galloway. He nodded to Peter and stopped.

"Whattayasay, Martin, how're you making out?" the burly coach inquired, a former player himself, standing before Peter with the serious frowning demeanor football men have when confronting one another.

"Okay," replied Peter, frowning. Alexander stood apart, waiting disinterestedly. "How are the things at the college?" inquired Peter casually.

"Fine. We ought to have a good team next Fall, though I don't know how many men we'll lose to the service. I heard you left Penn," he added with curiosity.

Peter shrugged, rousing up the old defenses he had been using for months against a question repeatedly asked of him around Galloway. "Oh, yes, I guess I outgrew the urge for football. Anyway, the war's breaking up everything in the colleges," he added lightly, and frowned again.

"Well," the man smiled, "not yet, not quite yet anyway. What's the matter, college football too much for you? You were doing damn well from what they tell me. How was the team down there?" he asked professionally, after a moment of Peter's silence.

"Pretty good," said Peter casually, pleased because the team "down there" was far more famous around the country than the man's own team.

"Well," said the coach, glancing at his watch, "I hope I'll see you around, and—good luck," and he walked off briskly, Peter staring after him with a false smile that changed into a scowl of displeasure.

"That's all, brother," he muttered indistinctly to himself.

"What?" demanded Alexander with curiosity.

"There's the guy who once called me up every night for a whole week trying to get me to go to his school. Now he gives me a brushoff, a nice slick one. Did you notice his smile?"

"Oh, what do you care, Pete?"

"I don't."

But Alexander looked mournfully at Peter. "Dear friend," he said, "there are things more important than athletics in this world, in spite of what your father tries to tell you. I understand how he feels about it, I can read the great disappointment in his eyes. You see, Peter, even though Mr. Martin doesn't like me, I can understand him—"

"Yeah, yeah."

"And it was your own decision to quit football. After all, look what's going on in the world now, a great new struggle for freedom and liberty. It's your own mind that decided what you should do now, your own conscience. I think your decision to go to sea in the merchant marine this spring is a great and noble decision. You don't have to do it, and there's so much danger now, with the submarines and everything."

"I just want to go to sea," mumbled Peter, full of gloom.

"I'll never forget that letter you sent me!" Alexander cried with a sudden piteous, broken smile. He had acquired the smile from Paul Henreid, the movie actor.

"What letter?"

"The one from New York, where you went after you quit college and before you came home. Remember? 'I am driven and weary,' you wrote, 'and I don't know where to go. In one stroke I've changed my life, given up its first crude direction. But I'm still young, and therefore I believe there's still love in my heart.' Don't you remember writing that from New York? I've memorized those lines, they're great! Pete, you will never know how I felt when I received that crumpled little letter, you will never know the pain that I felt!" Alexander had stopped in the middle of the sidewalk and was squeezing his fist with the other hand. "I went upstairs to my room and pounded the walls and wept bitterly!"

Suddenly the tears were trickling down his face as he stood there, and Peter, completely abashed, looked away furiously and glowered darkly upon the whole thing. How strange his life had become! Yet there was an overwhelming warm joy in his heart because his friend had understood so well. He wanted to take Alex's hand in both his hands, and press it warmly, thanking him and blessing him somehow, but he realized he could never do that, and he wondered mournfully why.

He only said, "Well, Al—that was wonderful of you—but, hell, don't cry about it or anything like that. Don't—"

"Don't what, Pete?" smiled the young Greek. "You mean on the street? Look, there's no one around, the street's deserted—this is Commerce Street, there's the police station, and I wept, that's all. I won't embarrass you any more. Remember always that I'm Latin, warm-blooded, I'm half-Russian, I'm Slavic, and I have these emotions, and I express them. You're a Martin and I'm a Panos, that's all. Let's go have a cup of coffee in the cafeteria. I'll show you the letter I got from Alice, another beautiful letter, and a quotation from Barbellion, another from Saroyan. I have a million things to tell you. After a few months, we'll probably never see each other again for the duration of eternity. Many of us here in Galloway, your brothers and my brothers, and the kids we know, will get killed in this war, many of us. Tommy Campbell is only the first to go, don't you see? 'So we'll go no more a-roving,' Pierre."

"Is it as bad as that?" grinned Peter.

"You mark my words: these may be the last months of our friendship in this life."

Thus they were, young Panos and young Peter, both of them nineteen years old.

[9]

EARLY IN THE SPRING Joe Martin enlisted in the Air Force. Just before he was called to active duty he suddenly felt a strange powerful whim to go and see the girl he had known long ago in his first truck-driving days, Patricia Franklin. She was not working in the lunchcart on highway No. 1 any more, but he promptly found her at home, and with her fiance moreover, a grocery clerk named Walter. But Joe only laughed at this and came to Pat's window late that night and threw pebbles and made her come down and talk.

She came down wrapped in a coat, and in the darkness where they argued, she told him emphatically and sadly that she was serious about Walter. She even laughed at the incredulous, red-faced Joe when he stalked with crazy determination straight towards the woods as if he was going to spend the night there.

He had rented a room in a small hotel in town. He came back afresh in the morning with an air of giving Patricia his final ultimatum, and, of course, she laughed again. He stormed out once more, though with the sudden stricken feeling that she was the most beautiful creature he had ever seen, especially now that she laughed at him that way. She was now so beautiful and unapproachable that his heart was bursting with all kinds of strange new griefs and the one grievous joy of humiliation he had never known before.

"All I do is die! Why, she's the most knocked-out broad I've ever seen in all my life! And she was my girl! What was the matter with me two years ago? Why do they do this?"

He strode around the little town thinking of her beautiful dark eyes, her long brown hair, her soft white skin, her sweet and luscious mouth, her very flesh, and the loveliness of her when she put on her little threadbare coat and came tripping down the stairs to talk to him. The whole day was suddenly enchanted with her presence in the earth thereabouts. He stared at trees wonderingly. What was he doing here? It seemed that everyone in the village existed only because she was nearby, dwelling and abiding. Was she with Walter? His heart dropped like a rock in his belly and for a moment he bent in a sudden swoon of horrible disbelief.

He spent the afternoon in his hotel room with the newspapers and a pint of whiskey. Ah! he was going off in the Air Force, and she was just another girl, there were millions of them everywhere, and she was no prettier than the others.

He barged around the room beginning to feel the wild triumphant effects of the liquor he was drinking straight out of the bottle. "I wish Hathaway was here, I'd get him drunk. Or some of those guys—those mavericks from the ranch, like Red, or Boone Waller. What a character that Boone was! I think I'll write him a letter, right now!"

And Joe sat down at the writing table and began to write a letter to the ranch-hand in Wyoming, but a minute later he crumpled up the paper furiously and hurled it against the mirror, and grinned. He paced up and down the room musing feverishly. "Dammit, those women get beautiful when they turn you down. They get that glow in their eyes and suddenly they're built like Mae West. They get soft and beautiful when you can't get them any more, they're like a million dollars—and just like a wife ought to look. Oh, a wife!"

It grew dark when he had finished the bottle, and he got up and flung himself on the bed and soon fell asleep. Around nine o'clock he woke up as he heard his floor crack loudly, and someone gasping almost inaudibly.

"Who's that?" he yelled, flying to his feet, half-asleep and tottering and uncomprehending. He heard a brief muffled cry of fear, a girl's cry.

"Joe?" she said.

"Patricia?" he mumbled unbelievingly.

"Joe, where's the light? I can't see anything."

Patricia herself found the light switch and clicked it on, flooding the room suddenly with a bright glaring light that made Joe wince.

"What's going on?" he croaked hoarsely. "What is this?"

"Do you know that I've been waiting for you since six o'clock at home?" she said gravely. "You said you were going to come back. I told Walter and broke my date with him—well, we usually go dancing tonight at the lake. I told him I was going to see you and he understood—"

"What are you doing standing in the middle of the room?" he cried irritably. "Sit down!"

"Listen. I know *everybody* downstairs, my father's best friend runs this hotel. I told them I was just coming up to see if you were in."

"What are they doing," grinned Joe, "listening at the plumbing pipes?" As Joe said these things he had the strange sensation that it was two years ago and not now any more—as though in his sleep he had forgotten something important.

"Well, listen, Joe," said Patricia gravely, "if you're going to tell me what you wanted to say, or whatever it is, let's go outside someplace, we can't stay here."

He began putting on his shoes, still yawning.

"You're acting strange," said Patricia almost curiously.

"I am?" he said, looking up solemnly at her.

"You're not like you were this morning or last night," she said with pique in her tone. Joe was too sleepy and still a little too drunk to notice, and he spent the next few moments gravely washing his face and combing his hair, and even inspecting his face in the mirror awhile. Patricia just stood rigidly in the middle of the room watching him, her lip curled up in a kind of disgusted and irritated fascination, until he was ready to go, when her expression resumed its judicious blankness.

Joe suddenly turned and stared at her. "Say, wait a minute!" he said, sitting on the edge of the bed and rubbing his jaw and looking vacantly straight ahead.

Patricia stared at him indignantly and with some confusion.

"I mean, this is funny, isn't it?" continued Joe with a mischievous, tricky, lopsided grin on his face. "About us and everything, and the way we've been arguing. And you coming here."

"Joe, I told you I can't stay in this room and I also told you—"

"Hup!" cried Joe, standing up rigidly like a soldier at attention, but the tricky grin was still on his face. "Say, wait a minute! It *is* funny. Because when I woke up just now I almost forgot that you were Mrs. Fancy-pants now and no longer Pat Franklin—practically. I looked at you and everything seemed fine and nice, but now I just remembered—" And with this he wandered out of the room a little absentmindedly, opening the door and leaving it wide open behind him, but suddenly, with an infuriated bitter feeling that he could not conceal from her, he came back in the room just as she was following him out, and picked up his shaving kit from the dresser and stuffed it in his overcoat pocket, and went out again.

"That's that," he muttered. "I'm going down to the Ford now and I'm off. Want me to drive you home? I've got the old rattletrap with me."

She said nothing, and suddenly Joe turned around and went back in the room, where the light was still shining, and sat on the windowsill gloomily. Patricia stood in the doorway in her threadbare coat—pensively. Joe jumped up and opened the window and looked out, where the snow had piled up an almost eerie silence in the streets.

"I'm going home now, Pat, and don't ask me why I came," he said over his shoulder. "It was good while it lasted and I guess you agree with me."

"Agree? About what?"

"About me leaving!" he suddenly almost yelled, and she was startled, even scared of him for a moment, and stood back against the door looking at him.

"Yes," the girl said at length, quietly, "I think that's the best thing for you to do. I'm sorry you had to make the trip."

"Ah, shut up!" he snarled.

"Yes, yes!" she suddenly snickered. "You're right, I should never talk like that. Huh?"

Joe was fumbling earnestly in his pockets for the car keys and at the same time for a cigarette. There were tears in his eyes. He loved her so much.

Pat immediately walked across the room and handed him one from her purse and lit a match for him and held it up. He leaned to it abstractedly.

"It all makes pretty good sense," continued the girl in a firm, motherly tone of voice, "because after all you didn't show up for two years and you didn't even write, and now you're going in the air force, and, well, as you say—that's that."

"Yep," said Joe, "that's the ticket. By the way, say something to your mother for me, and the others. I better be going now before this storm gets bad."

And he suddenly planted a firm swift kiss on her lips, with the flair of a man kissing a woman good-bye impatiently, except that he lingered on her mouth for just the space of a moment more. He suddenly tore himself loose and walked off towards the door. And just as instantly he was lunging back and gripping her by the shoulder, as she herself stood there devouring his eyes with her own welling eyes.

He pulled her to his side and began walking her towards the door, with their sides pressed tightly against each other and undulating closely. Finally, stopping short at the door, they turned to each other without parting, rolling into each other slowly, and embraced in a slow, feverish, tremendous kiss.

"Yes, this," Joe whispered in her neck, "this is the way we are."

And Patricia was lost in the deepest, most loving silence.

Joe and the gloomy brooding Paul Hathaway went off to basic training together at an Army camp in Alabama.

In the train at night while all the recruits howled and sang and told stories, Joe and Paul sat together silently and contemplated the rolling earth of mid-America by starlight, and wondered about their lives past, this inexpressible present, and their future in war and sadness. Paul Hathaway sat motionless with his dark face lowered scornfully to the vast night outside and he thought of his whole meaningless ravaged life. "I've been a bum all my life," he said, "maybe I can do something worthwhile now, something different, maybe. Listen to those kids singing like they didn't know they was going off to get their heads blown off. Christ, it's nothin' to sing about. Crazy bunch of basteds!" His dark eyes burned. "But me, I've been a bum all my life, and it don't make much difference. So that's that."

"Hey, you guys, how about a game of poker?" yelled somebody.

"Shaddap," said Paul Hathaway with indescribable scorn.

And Joe just sat there reading and rereading this letter from Pat:

Dear Joe,

Promise me you'll write and tell me where you're going after basic training. What I said goes: where you go, I go. It doesn't matter where, I'll get a job and a place to live and when you have days off on leave I'll be there to take care of you. I don't want to be away from you any more, and I don't want you to forget me again like you did the last time. If you do, Joe, it will be very easy for me to die. Do you understand that? Maybe I'm crazy, but don't get mad at me for loving you and wanting to follow you. You're mine and I'm yours, and you know I always was yours and always will be. I'm crazy about you, darling, please see that. There's nothing else for me to do but be beside you, just beside you. Oh, how I miss you now.

Pat

Joe was destined not to leave Paul Hathaway's side during the entire next two years in the service, thanks to their amazing luck. The swirl of orders and assignments and missions that were to come never separated them completely and always landed them back together in the same outfit and for the same duties more or less, to their wild yelling joy. This was just as the two cronies wanted it, naturally, and they helped the situation along by means of indefatigable intrigue and teamwork. After six weeks of basic training in Alabama they were sent to Denver for Air Force training.

It was from there that Joe wrote a letter to Patricia. She promptly came out in a bus across the massive land, the Eastern hills, the Mississippi Valley, and the Great Plains altogether—two thousand miles of earth and America that she had never seen and that she was seeing now through the brooding eyes of love and sadness and womanly grandeur. When she got to Denver, weary and lost and frightened in the clanging morning streets of a new strange city, she made up her mind to stick it out. She got a job that very morning as a salesgirl in a department store, got a room downtown on Grant Street, and settled down to be near her Joe, just as she said she would.

She even got a girl friend for Paul Hathaway. After long nights of dancing and drinking in the Larimer Street saloons, she cooked great breakfasts for the two soldiers, pressed their uniforms while they slept, woke them up with cigarettes and cups of coffee, and always sent them back to camp with a wonderful feeling of sweetness and joy. And all this was done in humblest loving silence.

"Say, you joker, that's some girl you've got there, that Pat!" admitted Paul Hathaway reluctantly. "I never did meet a girl like that before. And she followed you all the way out from back East."

One Sunday afternoon they had a picnic in the mountains, Joe Martin all trim and handsome in his uniform, Paul Hathaway grave and good-looking and soldierly with his parade cap tucked a-slant on his head, and Patricia, smiling and darkly beautiful, and little Bessie, whom Pat had brought along for Paul. They had their picture taken. It was a picture that Joe was going to keep in his wallet throughout the war and years later. It was a picture that really contained the lovely image of Patricia's brooding devotion to him, as well as the whole legend of wartime America itself, a picture upon which was written the great story of wandering, sadness, parting, farewell, and war.

One night Patricia and Joe passed the railroad station in downtown Denver, and there were the young wives with babies in their arms, the young soldier-wives who were beginning to wander the nation, tired and lonely and all wrapped in visions of love and remembrance and desperate devotion, traveling the thousands of night-miles across the continent in search of some pitiable little home or situation that would bring them close to their young husbands, if only for a few months. Joe and Patricia gazed at them with compassion and confusion.

"See, Pat, that's why I don't think we should get married now, that's my real reason," Joe told her gently. "Understand that."

"Oh, but I wouldn't mind, Joe!" she said joyfully.

"I know you wouldn't and *they* don't either. But hell, look at those poor kids and just imagine what they're going through just for the sake of— Well, I don't know."

"All for love, Joe," she smiled.

"Yeah."

"You can't tell a woman what isn't right, Joe."

"Look at that little one there with the baby. She must be all of eighteen years old and look how tired she is. Where is she going, what is it all going to lead to? Nobody can tell about these things any more."

"It's happened before. But I'll do whatever you say, darling," Pat whispered.

They sat in the railroad station that night watching the young wives and the young soldiers and sailors sleeping on benches, passing the greater part of the night among the kids of their own generation as though they suddenly felt they didn't belong anywhere else.

Joe bought a fifth of whiskey and passed it around among the soldiers, while Patricia minded babies for the girls who had to make phone calls or get ready to entrain once again. And they all sat around chatting through the long night-hours while the trains arrived, discharging more and more of them, and trains departed, and good-byes were called, and more of them came and went, and they all looked somehow alike, mournful and lonesome, the young wives and the soldier-boys and the young civilians on their way to camp. In the station that night, a Carolina boy plucked on his guitar and sang songs, and the stationmaster, speaking over the public address system in the hollow, echoing, mournful voice of railroad stations, was calling: "One-thirty Rock Island train now loading on track four for Omaha, Des Moines, Davenport, and Chi-caw-go, and points East—Union Pacific train for Cheyenne, Salt Lake City, Sacramento, San Francisco, and points North to Portland, Tacoma, and Seattle, now arriving on track two—"

The great wartime wanderings of Americans were just beginning. Great troop-trains rumbled by in the night everywhere, in Louisiana, in Oregon, in Kansas, in Virginia, and how many soldiers were in each of these trains, and what were their thoughts in sum and total and dark intensity? And the young wives were riding the trains with babies in their arms, and brooding, and waiting, and writing letters, and listening to the long hurled-back mournful howl of the train in the dark outside. Always, somehow, it was night, and the rolling land at night, and weary harassed sleep in coach-cars, and the railroad stations again, and a hollow melancholy voice calling the names of places:

"Santa Fe, Fort Worth, Dallas, Shreveport, and New Awrleans—"

And "Boston, New York, Philadelphia, Baltimore, Washington, Richmond, and all points South—"

It was a railroad landing and the crowds of khaki-clad soldiers searching eagerly, or waiting casually, or singing and shouting, and the sad blur of their faces as the train departed, and the vast infinite rolling land again, the oncoming of nighttime again, the clacking wheels, and thoughts, thoughts, thoughts in the night once more. And it seemed to be raining all the time too; and so many letters were written.

Dearest Joey,

We received your lovely letter and we're all so proud of you for your promotion to Sargent. And aren't you the fancy one going to Florida! Send me an orange, Joey, and send me a picture of the palm trees down there in sunny Florida. We are all well and we all love you and pray for you. Do your best, sonny boy, that's all you can do, and take care of yourself, be extra careful. Your old mom prays for you every night and prays that you'll be safe and sound no matter what. Here's a big kiss from the whole family, including one from the old weazel himself your father.

Mom.

[And in the father's handwriting]

Hi there, Sarge! Remember me to the Southern belles down there!

This is the pitiful way it was: and all the eerie feelings that young men were having in some strange part of the country far away from the places that had always been familiar in their lives, which were become unreal and fantastic now as a dream, and maddening and sorrowful too; and all the night-dreams woven out of three thousand miles of continental traveling and ten thousand miles of earth-traveling that were so gray and strange and pitiably enacted upon some deranged little map of the mind that was supposed to represent the continent of America and the earth itself. Sailors dreaming of the sea as some poignant little lake, or of their movements north and south, east or west on the terrific seas, as on some gray little canal or river, with life teeming on the banks; soldiers dreaming of America as some packed little place with mysterious fields and roads leading directly within walking dream-distance from state to state, or of islands in the Pacific as little puddle-jumps in the sweet small lake of the mind—all the vast and oceanic and terrific distances compressed by human necessity into something no bigger than a field, and a lake, or the palm of a hand.

And then the bugle blowing in some Dakota army camp, and the rawboned, windburnt boys waking up again to the clear cold mornings and great snow-distances and distant hills, to drafty barracks and rough khaki trousers and the heavy G.I. boots clomping, waking up to steaming breakfasts, hot coffee, a cigarette, and then the windswept range and the peppery chatter of rifles firing in the frozen air, the broken cry of a sergeant, a puff of smoke, and someone rubbing his raw chapped hands together and grinning steamily in the morning air.

Or the Coast Guardsmen on some heaving little cutter off Labrador waking up to the violent squeak of the ship, the pitching and flopping on the waves, the wild dawn-light over the seething field of waters, and the cook's slop bucket flying garbage into the sea, the acrid nauseous smell of cigarette smoke in the mess, the big red-faced gunner's mate from Iowa slopping catsup all over his eggs, the little mascot-pups yapping broken cries in the North Atlantic wind, the rigging by the afterdeck squeaking and straining and the flag cracking in the wind, and the wide mournful spread of slow, smoking merchant ships crawling in formation around the horizon all dark and low-slung and cumbrous in the sea.

Or the big B-17 revving on the field and blowing everyone back windswept and grinning, and the pilots striding across the field with their strapped-up gear talking earnestly and gesticulating, and the grimy mechanics scowling in the shed over a cup of coffee and a cigarette, and the noise of mighty engines deafening the morning air in multidiscordant whining roars everywhere, and the sudden flash of sunlight off a passing wing, and men looking up absentmindedly and with pondering afterthought at the sky.

It seemed as though a whole nation of men and women were beginning to wander with the war. They traveled on trains and busses and their familiar unknown faces were suddenly everywhere. In far-away towns where eleven o'clock had once been silence and the swish of treeleaves and the sleepy rush of Pinefork Creek, and the echoing howl of the Eleven-O-Two, now it was the crowds of warworkers hurrying for the busses and the midnight shift at the vast swooping sheds three miles out of town.

Far off across a dusty Virginia field men toiled with their Lilliputian cranes upon the gigantic Gulliver-structure of the War Department, and it all shimmered and wove fantastically in the sun. Great flat dusty gashes were gouged into green fields as airfields came into being. By sleepy coastal villages they put up the shipyards, and inside at night huge hull-shapes were spawned by lights and sparking torches. Out of tremendous sheds that stood on the horizon a mile long they wheeled out the incredible airplanes and bulking tanks. Nothing seemed to get done as men and women went back and forth, talked, ate, slept, made love, "put in their hours," drank, collected paychecks, argued, fought, leaned absorbedly over blueprints, hammered away at steel, walked around in absurd circles. Yet trains whipped across forlorn wildernesses and suddenly flashed past long camouflage-painted walls and fences surrounding whole territories of tanks and airplanes, and returned swiftly to the wilderness. Long flat-cars hauled big boxes across mountain passes, barges appeared in the Hudson River majestically bearing mighty gun-barrels and gun-mounts and Army locomotives and whole fleets of trucks, and out of the Golden Gate sailed the new heavy cruiser low and long and bristling in the waters. And suddenly, in some sleepy Indiana town, a jeep came bouncing in, stopped abruptly, someone got out with a red flag, and the khaki trucks came roaring one by one with the mystery of thousands suddenly passing and going somewhere swiftly.

It was like this, and it was more than that, and no one could fathom it and see it all at the same time. It was carried on night and day around the terrific cycloramas of the land and spread-eagling far overseas incredibly. No one could see it, yet everyone was in it, and it was like the incomprehensible mystery of life in the world itself, grown fantastic and homeless in war, and strangely haunted now.

Elizabeth and Buddy Fredericks got on a train and went voyaging across the lonely darkness and by pin-points of light to Detroit, Michigan, to get jobs there in the vast war plants. And they rode the train together, big dreamy Buddy sprawled in the seat, dozing, then waking up and slowly grinning at Liz, who sat knitting and scowling through the night.

"Long trip, huh?"

"Yes."

"But we'll get there all right, Liz."

"Yes. And my baby'll be born in Detroit."

"I should hope so."

"Go back to sleep, honey. Get some sleep."

They went to Detroit simply because there was more pay there, and because they wanted to travel around and see the country.

In Detroit Buddy got a job in a tank factory, and Liz got a job in a ball-bearing plant as piecework-checker, they rented a little room in a friend's home in Grosse Pointe Park, and they settled down to saving money and dreaming and eating and sleeping and loving. Then when the baby was coming, Elizabeth stayed home knitting small things and brooding joyously and writing letters to her mother at home.

These were the happiest days of her life.

One Saturday morning that winter, big Buddy came home jubilantly from the night-shift, humming in the trolley. He strode home happily, another week's work done and another paycheck collected, his thoughts filled with music. Then he saw a bar, and it looked wonderful, opening up at eight o'clock in the morning, swept fresh and clean for a new day, with the bartender raising the shades, and a truckman rolling in a barrel of beer from the street.

Buddy breezed in, ordered a glass of beer, and went to the jukebox and played Coleman Hawkins' "Body and Soul." He suddenly loved Liz more than he ever had—as a true wife, after all. He rushed out of the bar and literally ran up the street, and went dashing across the yard, and up the stairs.

And there was Liz sleeping in his big blue pajamas. He turned on the radio to Happy Joe's morning show. He shot up the shades to let in the snowy light, and threw himself on the bed beside her. He felt fine.

"Wake up, wake up, Liz, you little thing!" he cried, beaming with happiness, muzzling her hair and seizing her body and shaking it, and finally drawing her to himself.

She was half asleep, crying, "What?" and burying her face in his neck. "What?" she cried sleepily.

"Come on, come on!" Buddy whispered gleefully. "Get out of bed and let's go! Don't you hear the radio program? I put it on for you. I found a place where they have Hawk's 'Body and Soul' and it's terrific. Liz, last night on my way to work I passed under a window over the drugstore on the corner and what do I hear but a guy blowing some fine trumpet accompanying a Tatum record! I was stoned! I backed up and looked in and I saw a bunch of musicians sitting around drinking and playing records, I even saw a clothes closet full of mad suits and ties! I tell you, Detroit *jumps*, Liz! But no kidding, come on, let's go out!"

"You're crazy! It's not even morning yet."

"Of course it's morning, look outside. 'Oh, what a beautiful morning,'" he sang. "There's snow all over Michigan, all over Ontario, it snowed some more last night, it's great!"

"Okay."

"I know what you need, a cigarette—something else too. Feel your face and your lips, all hot and dry, you've been sleeping. I'll kiss your lips till they get cool again and wet again."

"Oh, no!" cried Liz, turning over and flushing furiously with the excruciating embarrassed modesty of a young wife.

Buddy lit a cigarette and leaned over her and placed it against her lips with a pleased grin, and suddenly Liz was wide awake. "Oh!" she cried. She sat up in the bed rigidly. "You wanted to kiss me!"

"Sure!" said Buddy proudly. "Let's go out and drink some beer."

"Hm. Kiss me," said Liz, and he kissed her.

Happy Joe was screaming on the radio in their favorite radio program. It seemed that in the course of an advertisement of "Ontario Furs" a train was thundering into town bearing a load of furs, and Happy Joe and his assistant were enacting a little drama in which they were supposed to be unloading the furs on the freight platform. "Hand me that crowbar!" "Okay, Joe!" yelled the assistant, and there were great noises of grunting and gasping, and groaning boards over the air, and then: "We almost got it now—almost!—keep pushing down! Okay! Here it comes!" —and then there was a great sound of cracking wood and final tumultuous completion and the two men rapturously breathing joyous "Oooohs!" and "Aaaahs!" and swooning deliriously over the contents. "*Will* you *look* at this! this *wonderful* Persian paw coat, and *only* three hundred dollars, mind you!"—"Oh! and will you *look* at *this* one, Joe, isn't it just *divine!* A sable-dyed muskrat with flaring sleeves and all for three hundred and ninety-two dollars, can you imagine, can you just *imagine!*"—"Oh, Joe, I think I'm going to feel faint! Yes, I think so now, I definitely feel it coming!"—"Water! Water! Help! Charley is passing out! He has just seen the new shipment of superb Ontario Furs at new all-time All-American low prices!"—"Water! in the name of mercy, water!"

Liz and Buddy were crazy about this madcap program, they always listened to it and it always represented morning and a new wonderful day to them.

"Okay! I'm going to get up!" cried Liz, and she jumped out of bed in the flopping pajamas that Buddy had worn on their wedding night, and she ran barefooted to the bath.

Liz took a shower and went back in the bedroom to put on lipstick. And there lay Buddy sprawled on the bed snoring, dead to the world. Liz rolled him over, undressed him deftly, pushed him under the covers, and patted everything in place. Then she went to the window, looked out at the beautiful snow awhile, lowered the shade that he had just raised so jubilantly, turned off the radio, hung up his clothes, and got into bed with him.

And she leaned on one elbow, completely awake and beaming now, unable to sleep any more, with Buddy embarked on a whole day's sleep at last. There was nothing else she wanted to do that morning: just look at Buddy asleep, just think and plan, just be there with him in their new sweet strange life together—that was enough for her.

But ten weeks later her baby died stillborn in a Detroit hospital. It would have been a boy.

For this poor girl, only nineteen years old and horror-stricken by the sudden grievous sharkish thrusts of death and agony, lying in the pain and suffering darkness of a hospital—the loss of a little life, her young husband's grief and anxiety, the nights in the dreary hospital, and even the sheer agonized womb of her womanliness—became the sign of everything that was harsh, cold, ugly, dreary, dark and hopeless in life. She never saw the baby and she preferred to think that it had not been a baby after all but some growth that had to be taken out of her, some disease that she had to have before regaining her health. She bit her fingernails and considered all this desperately. She was disgusted.

She vowed darkly that from now on her life would be smooth as silk, luxurious, easeful, warm and bright and gorgeous. She grew sick and tired of the sympathetic young nurses who fussed around her and wondered how they could spend the rest of their lives working in these "smelly horrible hospitals."

She grew irritated with Buddy, snapping at him. "Oh, stop coming around here to look at me like that! Why don't you go out and make some money? Real money, for God's sake!"

"Maybe I can get a car next month. That would be good, Liz, we could take trips and—"

"Well, get it! And when I get out of here I'm going to buy all the clothes I want with that damn money I saved."

Buddy was crumbling within from grief and boyish despair. "Gosh, Liz, take it easy; everything'll be swell from now on. I wrote to your folks and your mother's coming out to see you—"

"I don't want to see her! I don't want to see anybody!" she cried fiercely. "I want no sympathy from my family. They never knew how to live anyway and they think a thing like this is just routine, it happens to everybody, 'It's life!' they say. I can hear the old biddies in Galloway gossiping about it, 'Oh, isn't it just too *sad!*' They're all fools and bores, and from now on you and I are going to live, *live*, understand?" she cried, clenching her fists.

"Sure we will, Liz—"

"We'll leave this lousy town and go to California, do you understand?"

"Certainly, baby," said Buddy, taking her hand and holding it against his cheek mournfully.

And then the sickened demonic Liz cried in his arms, kissed him tearfully, held him close, trembled miserably, asked him to promise never to stop loving her, gazed desperately, sadly into his eyes, and wiped his poor tears broodingly. But when he left Liz was silent and meditative in her bed, dark with vows and torn with horrible fury.

[10]

FOR PETER an incomprehensible, misty, guilt-stricken, haunted kind of time had begun. He was bewildered by some unnamable guilt that weighed on him because Tommy Campbell was gone, and lost on Bataan, the pale memory of him like a face in dreamlike darkness. Others—Mike Bernardi, who had played football with him, and wild Ernest Berlot, and bitter sad Danny, and his brother Joe and Paul Hathaway—were dispersed and gone in the war. There were a lot of the boys still in Galloway waiting to be called, but the thought of the first few who had gone and joined up was like a moan, a whisper, something stricken and done forever, so manly and pitiful.

Of course he and some others sometimes scoffed at the idea of making suckers of themselves and rushing off to get shot up. But at night Peter walked the Galloway streets that seemed empty now, and it was as though he heard the distant solemn voices of these youths adjuring him, phantom-like, calling him because he was not with them. Lost, haunted, almost forgotten, where were they all? They were scattered all over the U.S.A. and in England, and Australia, and India, and Pearl Harbor—but where were they in the actual night of time and things, what was it that was so ghostly and lost across the skies of the night? His very life itself had become haunted. He had grown guilty and old. Boys who had admired him because he was a football hero were now gone away, truer heroes than he could ever be. In some way, he had deceived them all. He was twenty and that was the way he felt.

One July morning in 1942 he left home with a seabag full of workclothes, walking in the cool shade along the little white fences behind the tenement. He hitch-hiked to Boston and wandered around Scollay Square buying a seaman's wallet and a knife and cap. He waited around in the maritime union hall all afternoon for a job on a ship, and finally, late in the day, he was boarding a big cargo-transport ship in Boston harbor, on the Great Northern Avenue docks.

He stepped upon a quivering gangplank for the first time in his life, with a feeling of the most tremendous joy—just as the dusky afternoon was darkening over solemn harbor waters, and strange dark light was bending over wharves and the ships and by dockpiles on the waterfront. No one was in sight, on all the piers, and ships, and railyards, nothing moved, all was haunted, it was like being alone in all the world, amid docks and edifices and warlike projects. He had never felt so ghostly alone in all his life.

The ship was a looming gray mass "just back from Iceland" they had told him in the hall. She sat there amidst her smoke-wreaths and swooping seagulls squarely and flatly in the waters of the slip, so much like an immense gray bathtub somehow, with unfathomable superstructures, her slanting hull streaked with rust, a thin stream of water arching from the scuppers and splashing below, and the mighty bow standing high above the roof of the wharf-shed all huge and prescient with battering storms and strange northern seas. It was the first time that he ever saw a ship with the incredible knowledge that he was going to sail on it.

When he walked across the sagging boards of the gangway in the silence of destiny he felt a strange stirring in the pit of his stomach, a wondrous, lonely, half-frightened joy warning him that he was walking directly into the portals and maws of the awful sea itself. At twenty he was going on a ship, a great proud bark back from homeless seas and Icelands, bound for other and perhaps stranger and darker lands and seas than any ever wandered before. So it seemed to him in the mystifying solitude of deserted afternoon, in that moment of haunted gloom before lights come on in the world.

But suddenly the lights did come on, the galley portholes glowed and made pale mysterious reflections in the oily waters below. A guard suddenly appeared at the head of the gangway, checked Peter's papers, and inexplicably vanished. Peter hurried inside the shambling old vessel, as something unspeakably exciting gripped at his throat.

In there, in deserted dim alleyways, it was even more awesome: the stewish smell of a galley for the first time, and the smells of paint and cable and oil and rust, and all the steel bulkheads and portholes, the strange melancholy insides of a ship. Two men moved past him suddenly and casually in the alleyway, going up a ladder, silent, with the dreamy impassivity and old routine of seamen. Perhaps he had arrived among the lost men of the war, two of them had just brushed past him.

He found himself in the big galley, the kitchens of the ship, and there, standing in the midst of great aluminum cauldrons, huge pots and pans, and a cook-range big enough to boil a hundred ordinary kettles of water, was a mighty Negro cook, six-foot-five, peering into steaming soups. With a corncob pipe clamped in his teeth, he ruminated over whole vatfuls of brothy soup, humming in a deep basso some strange and mournful melody that Peter had never heard, as darkness pressed in at the portholes and the world outside receded.

"Well, boa! so you done laid down a hipe!" moaned out the cook in a deep and massive voice as Peter walked by with his seabag.

"A hipe?"

"Yeah, boa, you done stole the chickens, ain't you? You reckon you can run, and run, and run down that road till the day you dah?" The big man peered down at Peter squinting and twinkling. "Well, thass allright, 'cause old Glory's on yo side, cause HE'S done laid down a hipe a LONG time ago!"

"Glory?"

"Thass ME, son! Ain't nobody else! Thass ME!" He stared sideways down at Peter.

"Where was that?"

"Boa, you mean where Ah stole *my* chickens? Umm!" he moaned tremendously, turning great dolorous brown eyes overhead, puffing on his pipe, going "tsk! tsk! tsk!" "He wants to know *wheah* was dat! BOA!—that was in Savannah, Jawgia!"

"Savannah?"

"Ain't dat what Ah said?"—hoarsely. "You lookin' fo de purser to sign on? Is *dat* what you layin' down right now?"

"Yes! Where can I find him?"

"You find him right now drinkin' up de likkah ashoh! You ain't goin' find *him* right now, son! You jist find you a bunk. Go oan now, you only a chile. Glory ain't got no time to waste wid you." He looked earnestly at Peter. "Go *oan*, boa! Go lay down yo *hipe!* And den you come back heah, in dis galley, and eat yo denner! *Heah* me?"

And big Glory moaned and hummed, and could be heard all over the ship, like the great voice of grieving doom.

In the large messhall, a withered skinny little man without teeth and a little witch jaw sat dolefully at a mess table talking to a sleepy disconsolate listener who wore an apron. They were all alone there in the sea of tables.

"You understand," the little seaman was saying as Peter passed, "I don't like the idea of sailing the *Westminster this* run. You understand my point! They got our number now. [Cough! cough!] They almost got us the last time near the straits. . . . You understand the way it is, they track you just so long, they get their bearings, they lay for you. [Cough! cough!] Then boom! It's to be expected, you understand. They got our number now, I tell you." And the little man wiped his eyes with a blue handkerchief, and stared after Peter with polite curiosity, while the man in the apron just sat looking down at his feet.

It felt stranger and stranger. Peter wandered down the grimy alleyways until he found a room with several empty bunks. He threw his seabag in an empty locker, thinking suddenly of home. He got out a pad and wrote a long letter to Judie Smith in Philadelphia, and sat down again on the bunk with his head in his hands.

He went up on deck after a while. It was dark now—and yonder, over the mystical water Boston blazed her diadem of lights. Standing on deck in the darkness, it occurred to Peter that nothing in the world could be so chaste as a ship moored at a city's dark dockside while all the world brawled and reeled in the lights beyond. All the lonely ship-lights in the bay showed where the patient hulls were berthed and anchored, where they loomed, in enfolding shadows, like the kneeling nuns of the sea—while young sailors on watch wished they were brawling around Boston's bars with the rest of the crew, but were bounden, like adolescent monks, to the monasterial harbor-night of duty and truth.

A launch drifted by, softly puttering, beaded with lights, and someone cursed just a hand's-breadth away, it seemed. "Dammit, when you gonna hand me that line, boy, next week?" Water gurgled, the launch puttered away, and then the same old harbor silence in the summernight.

The *Westminster* was leaving in two days. Longshoremen suddenly swarmed all over her with paint buckets and blowtorches and cables. Booms were brought into play to load on great supplies of lumber, barrels of oil, T.N.T., and all kinds of construction equipment. The waterfront slammed and roared all day with tremendous activity.

Peter knew he had time to go back to Galloway and say goodbye to his family, but suddenly he just wanted to leave. The possibility that he might never come back was a deep, joyful, even pleasant thought at times, full of dark heroism and wonder, a magnificent thought of death itself. He clung to it grimly with a touch of horrified realization that it might be stupidly true.

Yet his dreams aboard ship as they prepared to sail were all eerie and haunted with awful guilts. He dreamed that his mother and father were standing beneath a sky demented and dark, holding out their arms to him, crying: "Oh, Petey, what have you done to us!" And it seemed that he should never have done this to them.

Alex Panos came to Boston to see Peter off. They met at the pierside lunchcart.

"But suppose you never come back!" Alex cried in desperation. "Don't you realize, Peter, that they're torpedoing ships by the scores and that thousands of seamen have drowned! Couldn't I go along with you? All I'd have to do is get papers and scramble through red-tape for a day or two, and we'd be shipmates! Peter," he added solemnly, "I have seen death-flowers in the eyes of your shipmates. Honest I have. . . ."

"But it's nothing like that," scoffed Peter. "A lot of ships are going through—most of them make it, this old tub'll make it. Look at her! She'll have no trouble. I have a feeling . . ." He gazed ruminantly.

"I know that feeling of yours—I know it in reverse, old friend. But if you want to go on alone, it's all right with me." Alexander lit a cigarette with a distant melancholy air.

"And why the hell do you think I joined the merchant marine?"

"I know—we all feel that terrible sadness now, about Tommy and all the others. And I know your mind is made up. You want to get away from my influence, as you call it. All right, all right. In this filthy little lunchcart on the Boston waterfront maybe we're seeing each other for the last time."

"Don't be silly."

"This is the way it will eventually end. . . ."

"When I get back I'll get you drunk on a *hundred dollars'* worth of champagne, how's that sound? I'll be rich, man, full of money!"

"Good-bye, Peter. I really have to catch my train now."

"Can I meet you tomorrow somewheres—before we sail? After that I can't get off the ship. . . ."

"This is the way it will eventually end." And, mysteriously, Alex walked away for the first time in their friendship with absent-minded sorrow. The gods that had whispered in his ear were neither deceiving, nor playful. It was the last time they ever saw each other.

That night Peter went ashore with some of his shipmates. They went to South Boston in a raucous gang, drank enormous quantities of beer and whiskey, got in red-eyed fights for no reason at all, ran yelling through the streets jubilant with doom, howled for some legendary madam beneath a window and were showered with a bucketful of hot water, slept sprawled in doorways, came straggling back to the waterfront just as red dawn was breaking over the masts of fishing smacks along Mystic Avenue, and slept a fitful hour before Glory came into the foc'sle moaning:

"Seven o'clock, an' not a *soul* in de galley. GIT UP! Git up, you drinkin' boys! You done laid down yore hipe las' night an' now you all want to go to heaven and git paid, but you doan want to work, you doan want NAWTHIN' A-TALL! Not a *soul* peelin' them potatoes an' onions an' washin' them pots 'n' pans!"

Peter had innocently signed on as a scullion, this was his first day's work in the galley. In the steaming heat of a July morning amid odors of hot swilled dishwater, rotten slop in the scuppers, grease and lard and bilgey slime in the galley drains, Peter, bleary-eyed and disheveled and sick, was weighed down with the thought of all life as one tale of disgust and dirty toil.

He managed the day's work with fatigued wonder and went to bed early. And during the night a passenger train was shuttled into the great wharf-shed and five hundred construction workers boarded the ship with their tools and gear. Everything was made ready, security was clamped down, men moved around in the engine-room firing the boilers and on deck in the smoky dawn hauling in some of the lines.

In the morning, as a cool, almost autumnal wind blew across the harbor making the waters chop and dance, he woke up to the tremendous vast shuddering "BAWWW!" of the steam whistle. It was the *Westminster's* cry of departure. He hurried to the port-hole to see the dock slipping by slowly and silently, the longshoremen standing idle by the bits, smoking and smiling, yelling "Come back home!" and "Take it easy now!" Great pistons began to rumble in the ship's bowels, the ship trembled, and they were moving. He realized as if for the first time that this great ship could actually move.

Away from the mournful tangle of his young life, and his sorrows and guilts, his parents and friends and Alexander and his sad dreams, out to the cool windswept sea on a bright winey morning. It was incredible and wonderful, like a happy dream. The mighty thrumming pistons backed the ship out into the bay, and the rudder was set around in a churning roar of water that smelled of oil and kelp, and the nose of the ship turned ponderously to face the sea, and slipped on with slow mounting power through the mine nets, past the last two lighthouses at the entrance of Boston harbor.

Far ahead of the *Westminster* and her sister ship, the *Latham*, two destroyers prowled the horizon like lowslung tawny seacats, their guns pointing like bristles up and down and every way, as the slender hulls heeled and pitched in the sea. On the *Westminster* itself soldiers monstrous with earphones and orange lifebelts suddenly appeared at the gun stations. They stood almost motionless, as though listening at once for the sounds of the war.

With an unknown fear Peter began to feel the big ship beneath him rock deeply in sea-swells. A powerful wind blew from the north over the capering waves. On the flying bridge stood the captain of the ship, a stout man, scanning his own ocean-world to which Peter now felt suddenly and irredeemably delivered. He was scared, for the first time, more scared than he would ever be again on the sea. He looked aft for Boston receding in a thin smoky line. There was no turning back now from the unknowable.

Down in the galley, as bright morning sunshine poured in the portholes, there were turmoils of activity Peter had never believed possible. All kinds of cooks and helpers had miraculously appeared for the sailing, wearing fantastic cook's caps and white aprons, slamming pots, waving ladles and great knives, shouting to one another in Spanish and Chinese and whooping Harlemese. Two little cooks with wrinkled necks jabbered away in a secret terrifying Morro tongue. They were frying hundreds of eggs and thousands of bacon-strips at the great ranges, roaring with talk and laughter in the confusion of steam, cooking-smoke, clattering dishes, clanking pans. And in the midst of all this noise, Glory walked calmly about his kitchen with the dignity and vast acumen of Chief Cook.

At sunset, after raucous suppers in the messhall among hundreds of seamen and construction workers, Peter put on a peacoat and went up on deck. There was no land in sight now, just a long sash of bloodred sun laning to the ship. It was keen and cold, with shagginess in the great sky, a cold grandeur in the air, an intimation of October in the sea.

"We're meeting an explorer ship off Cape Farewell, Greenland," Peter had heard someone say in the messhall. "Then it's any place in the North, I guess. . . ."

"What're we doin' up there?"

"We're going to build an airbase somewhere in the Arctic, that's all. . . ."

Beyond the wild red sunset, around the horizon towards the north, the sea stretched a seething field that grew darker as it merged with the lowering unknown sky. Somewhere up there was the Arctic Sea. Peter stood on the bow in the powerful headwinds gazing that way with an inexpressible sense of amazement and expectation, full of confoundment that in that direction, to which they slowly pushed, there could be no warm light and comfort and no friend, only the North, the far White North as ruthless and indifferent as the ocean's own overlowering night.

He made his way below through crowded alleyways to the big messhall. The men, hundreds of them, had cleared all the tables and spread blankets over them and started big crap games and card games. They were drinking coffee and talking excitedly in buzzing groups. Most of them were fantastically attired in boots and jackets and mackinaws, many of them wore beards. Most of them were already drunk and there was much coming and going among the construction workers from the messhall to the rooms above where the drinking took place more or less unofficially. The dice-players snapped their fingers and whooped and yelled, everybody crowded up money-in-hand, the card games puffed up smoke, a heavy sullen curiosity sometimes suddenly brooded throughout the hall. The seamen, sheathed with knives, were in the middle of everything with their rolls of money; a barefooted deckhand held the floor with an amazing run of throws that raised uproars of excitement. Even the Chief Mate and some other officers were watching curiously from the staircase. Old Glory sat in a corner with a few of his cronies, puffing on a corncob pipe, watching everything with his great brown mournful eyes. Someone sitting on the stairs was strumming a guitar. Only half of the men wore their lifebelts, the other half did not seem to care.

Everywhere throughout the great ship there were men—in the barber shop topsides where the supply of shaving lotion would be drunk in a month's time, down in the bowels of the ship in the engine-room, and in the foc'sle, and men gambling in the messhall, men eating in the galley pantry, men talking in the staterooms, officers conferring on the bridge, kid seamen playing cards and reading in bunks, soldiers at the guns or in their quarters playing records, captains and mates convoking over maps, men brooding in their bunks alone, men on deck staring at the darkness. It was a whole world of men, eight hundred of them, talking and gambling and smoking and reading and drinking as the great dark ship pitched through the night, towards the furious North. The *Latham*, the sister ship, likewise a glittering infolded world of eight hundred men moved a mile alongside in the darkening sea.

Day after day the ships went further north, past the coasts of

Maine, Nova Scotia, Labrador, Newfoundland, through the fogs, over the ghostly Grand Banks, out into the ocean-spaces. The air grew colder and the winds stronger, something hoary and gray came into the sea, the water in the scuppers became ice-cold, the sunsets lowered fabulously in icy fierce colors. Finally they were sailing the waters off Greenland, off Cape Farewell. Another escort ship joined them—and they plowed on up beyond Iceland, up into the Arctic Sea and the tremendous storms off the rocky sawtooth coast of Central Greenland.

It was the immense, lovely, cloud-sashed Arctic sunset at midnight, the icebergs as big as hills a mile off, with waters crashing slowly and ponderously upon them, the porpoises with their Mona Lisa smiles disporting and diving in formations, and bitter cold, and north pole grayness ahead. It was the fantastic North of men's souls, the place of unbelievable desolation and final solitude, the place of Thor and the Ice Kings and monarchial coasts, the place of whales and polar birds, of craggy rocks washed by forlorn waters thousands of miles from man, the last place.

They turned in towards the coasts of Greenland finally, in August. One morning Peter got up and looked out the porthole and saw sheer brown cliffs of the summer North rising steeply not thirty feet from where he stood. They were going up a fjord, fifty miles inland among stillnesses, crags, Northern lights, sudden eskimos in kyaks drifting by with grins of tender idiot welcome, fifty miles nearer the three thousand miles of vast inland snow, fifty miles underneath the mighty mountain ranges that brooded unseen by man and bare of life forever.

He gaped. It was all so far from what he had expected of the "adventure of the sea," so far from archipelagoes and Polynesias, the coral pearls and encantadoes of the sea, the wreath and the horn, the lost capes, the impossible lagoons and gardens of the South. It was this instead.

He thought of Galloway with a smile.

The ship stayed in Arctic Greenland almost four months, inland upon the fjord waters, while the workmen unloaded trucks and small cranes and power engines from a freighter and towed them ashore, and blasted rock, and leveled primordial ground, and piled up the lumber and spawned a small raw town in the rocky wastes. They measured off a vast rocky level for an airfield, and started blasting straight off. Meanwhile the *Westminster* and the *Latham* sat at anchor and fed and bedded the workers until they had built and appointed their own kitchens and messhalls and dormitories ashore.

It was an amazing and well-coordinated subjugation of the wilderness of rock at the ends of desolate earth, full of foresight, vigor and determination, typically American in dispatch, although no one seemed to think much of it. The workers were too absorbed to think, and the idle seamen were too bored to care after going ashore once or twice during the first days to explore the empty shore.

For a while there was absurd trading with the eskimos. Fish-spears and harpoons and stinking furs were exchanged for a handful of oranges or an oiler's cap. Peter acquired a harpoon in exchange for the sweater he had worn on the football team at Pine Hall, gleeful that an eskimo would be rushing around wearing the famous Number Two of the Class of 'Forty. Eventually everybody got bored with trading too, with everything, and refused to be interested in anything.

Months went by on the ships, everybody played cards and read, and ate and slept, and talked and argued, and yawned, and stared into space, and did what little work there was, and yawned again.

"Hey, Kenny! I just thought of something. Were you ever up a flagpole?"

"*What?*"

"A flagpole—did you ever climb a flagpole?"

"Listen to him, listen to him. . . ."

"Because if you did you should have stayed there, you'd make a damn nice flag with your big flap. . . ."

The snows came. The men rowed back and forth between the two transports and visited and gambled and gab-fested interminably. On the *Latham* they sat around drinking coffee, bearded and bored, and someone said, "Well, I don't care what you guys say but I'm telling *you* we're not going home, we're going to England to load on, direct from here, and on up to Archangel, Russia, and then *back* to U.K. to load on just in time for the invasion armada to Japan, the big blowoff in the Spring. Around Good Hope and over to Australia then up to Japan, thousands o' ships—"

"Ah, you're crazy."

"No, not Japan, *Turkey!* Go bowlin' right through the Med fleets to Turkey, then the armies will push north, and, my fine lads, it'll be a lucky day when *you* get home again. That's what they're sayin' now, go ahead and worry and figure it up and down but it won't do you no good, it'll be a pretty far day when you get home again—"

"What I figure is, if not Turkey, if not Turkey see—"

"Yeah, if not Turkey, chicken."

Four thousand unknown miles away from home, they were all haunted, lost in premonitions of never returning, delivered to the nothingness of the earth, forsaken among rocks in the rim of the world, forgotten in the homelands of snow, as-if-doomed within the gates of a misnamed impossible continent. And where was home? And their grievous families? and the soft, sweet summerlands they had left behind it seemed forever? They all felt this and none of them could speak of it.

Sometimes Peter dreamed of the entire Arctic Ocean as an estuary; all Greenland a grounds, a park; every mountain a knoll, every jagged fjord a brook; and all the round warring world a sweet fatherland.

They started home, finally, in November, raising the great anchor and chain, pointing ponderously around to the mouths of Greenland and the seas again, gliding between forlorn mountains, passing the washed rocks of eternity, and out upon the black waves.

One night, in pitch darkness, Peter was in his bunk dozing when the alarm bells rang janglingly and the buzzers whined and terror gripped all their hearts.

Filled with dreamy disbelief of the moment, expecting it all to stop somehow, Peter waited, and listened to the sudden booming of depth charges, and the wild scramble of running feet on the deck overhead. "Why are they all running about, the idiots!" he scoffed in the darkness, and turned over.

Suddenly his mirror on the locker door fell on the deck. "What am I doing down here?" he thought, sitting up. A vast sustained roar, far off, and wails and cries directly overhead sent him running topside with his lifebelt. "Please, God! please, God!" he thought. There, in the ocean-night, a mile away, the *Latham* was burning and sinking in the icy sea. They all huddled together, staring at the evil red glow on the waters that seemed to burn so calm there.

"They got the *Latham!* They got the dynamite!"

"She's going down!"
"Hey, Chuck! Where are you, Chuck?"
"Is this boat number five? Hey, is this boat number five?"
"Everybody take it easy! Stand by! Easy! For God's sake . . ."
The red smoke flared up slowly far off.
"Look at her!"
"Somebody cut a raft down, we lost a raft!"
"Oh, Lord, Lord, Lord, Lord . . ."
"She's going down!"

It was all terror, a nightmare, an evil dream, they all huddled together in the pit of night and said "Who is this?" and wandered around stumbling on the deck and folded their arms over their beating hearts and prayed.

"They got the sub!" someone howled somewhere.

"Hey! Hear that?!! They got the sub! Chief says the corvettes got the sub!—"

"They sank all the subs! They sank all the subs!—"

The red glow had faded and the *Latham* had expired out of sight while they milled around talking and shouting. Men were strewn and lost a mile away on the ungodly waters, it was too much to fathom, too much to believe, no one knew what to think at all. Even after the all-clear was sounded they stayed on deck peering anxiously over the waters, and talked and paced up and down and waited. Some of them were silent thinking of the men on the *Latham*, of their familiar faces gazed at and understood for months, months of loneliness, deprivation, meaningless fond conversations, those selfsame faces gone down now to drown in black waters of unbelievable night. It was too much to believe.

And then dawn came and the remaining ships in the convoy, two Canadian corvettes, a destroyer, the freighter, and the *Westminster* appeared to each other in the gales, busily fuming black smoke, driving on relentlessly, a congregation of barks and phantom friends emerging to each other in the grayness. It was all over now, the *Latham* was gone.

In the waste-waters, the homeless waters of the world, they stood on deck gripped with loneliness and terror as never before, and between them and the deep was just the poor ship's hull. Now they knew that the land was their home, as all men realize for the first real time only on the sea.

A light beamed across the bleak waves, a blink-light warm and soft from one of the corvettes sending an all-secure message to the

Westminster, and the warmth and beauty, the benevolent intelligence of that little light—why had it not prevailed for the *Latham?*

Peter could not understand it. He leaned wearily on the rail, on his elbows, gazing down at the ship's side where it rushed through the foaming waters, and he could not understand it at all.

The world was mad with war and history. It made great steel ships that could plow the sea, and then made greater torpedoes to sink the selfsame struggling ship. He suddenly believed in God somehow, in goodness and loneliness.

He thought what he would do if the ship was torpedoed like the *Latham*. At first he could only think of easy survival. His shipmates perished and drowned because it was possible; he survived because it was impossible to perish, he clung to some poor support in the sea and was found and rescued by men. But each day-dream successively grew more difficult, he was less fortunate, and finally he was helpless, eventually he was sucked down in the wake-whirl of the sinking ship and blinded in the world of water. No amount of day-dreaming could dispel the single choking horror of this one irredeemable thought: to look about him within the bowl of a water's cosmic dreary night, to be falling within it forever, to smother and roll beseeching, to open his mouth to yell where there is no sound.

When he thought this final unthinkable thought, Peter resolved to take a razor blade and put it in his watch pocket, wrapped carefully in cloth, and keep it there—for the time, the night, when he should find himself floating alone in these Arctic sea-immensities. Better than to drown, to sink downward with a water-logged life jacket, or to roll over numb and lean his face softly in the waters, or to hang suspended by a kapok on top of the ocean-valleys—better than that would be to slash his wrists and expire dizzily and dreamily in his own pool of blood. He began to examine his wrists, the blue veins that throbbed on them, the tiny capillary tracings, the cords that pulsed, the smooth, delicate, and infinitesimal vitalities that conducted his own poor warmth—which he would spill at one stroke among immensity.

He lay in his bunk thinking thoughts like these and then, towards morning, he would hear the homely slambang and clatter of ovendoors and pots in the galley, he would begin to smell the aroma of bacon frying on the range, and oatmeal steaming, and eggs boiling, all the quaint manly preparation of food on the dawn's salty ocean—and he was restored to his better understanding.

One night in the highest fury of an Icelandic storm Peter was with his chum, Kenny, a young dishwasher of lonely charm who bore himself with a beautiful and aristocratic air among the sordid hipsters at the sink and was, as Peter came to learn, the near-alcoholic son of an old and wealthy family in New York. They stood on the bow of the *Westminster* shouting and yelling and singing, huddled in their coats in the blasts of wind, ducking the wild sheets of spray that palmed over them vastly, full of wild glees and sudden homecoming joy. Kenny was yelling, "Ain't fit night for man nor beast! What think ye, Pegleg?"—and he limped around the deck, and spat, and squinted.

And Peter, "Aye, One-Eye, Aye! Man never spoke truer word than ye speak this night!"

They limped about and staggered afterdecks to the emergency steering wheel (an obsolete piece of equipment on that voyage) and gripped it desperately and pretended to wrestle furiously, at bay with the tempest.

"Full fathom five my father lies!" called Peter in the gale. "Pearls be his eyes, his bones of coral made!"

"Aye, Pegleg, such be the fate of all men of the sea, ye true seadogs!"

About ten minutes later, a terrific pillow fight had begun in the empty dormitories topsides, organized by Kenny in whose melancholy there was a disposition to craziness. Peter and Kenny and a half-dozen others creeped about in the dark, they crawled on hands and knees ravenous with suspense, crazy with joy, laughed savagely, hurled and smashed with pillows until the feathers flew, hid behind bunks and pounced on one another, wrestled and rolled and hurled whole mattresses across the ship's-darkness, chased each other all over the ship—all upon the thunderous waters of stormy night, in the middle of a grievous sea war, not seven days after the disaster of the *Latham* and the death of hundreds of themselves.

The ship neared home waters around Christmas. Everyone had grown a bushy beard and anticipated the long-awaited thousand dollar payoff and made lists of expenditures and argued and felt better than they had in months. Peter stalked the decks, scanning the horizon for signs of land, any land. Now he wanted no one to believe that he would die and never return, he wanted to hurt no one ever again in any way, he was in love with life and never wanted to leave it again. He thought ecstatically of towns and cities, of streets with houses in them, of windows in the houses and the lights in the windows, of people going down the empty streets, of the sweet things of the land. He thought of things he had not seen for six months in the rocky wastelands of Greenland and on the sea—"women's legs," and doorways, and neon lights—the things of the land and of men's life there. He dreaded the day he would have to go to sea again. He wanted to see his family again, his mother's house, his father's face.

One gray morning as Atlantic clouds scudded in the ragged skies, suddenly they were putting in to the coasts of some gray, solemn little country. Peter leaned on a rail gazing avidly at the rocky headlands, the lighthouse, the brown winter meadows beyond, roads, trees, and windswept little cottages facing the sea, and church steeples, and a little man absurdly riding down a road on a bicycle—a little port all true with human presence. It was Sidney, Nova Scotia. To Peter it was the earth again, the land which was their home, the actual sweet sad place of life again. The crew feasted their eyes and felt some deep comfortable joy returning.

A launch came pitching furiously in wild sprays to the *Westminster* with an absurd little man, bowler-hatted and briefcased like a burgher of the world's morning, clinging precariously to a stanchion and hailing the ship with pathetic eagerness. Everyone stared at him. It had been so long since they had seen a man like that, it was good to see him, so solemnly funny. Weary and bearded they watched him gravely as he leaped furiously from the launch to the Jacob's ladder over five feet of tossing water, without a hitch, quite cheerfully risking his neck and his neat black suit for the sake of the morning's affairs. He came clambering up the ladder with all the agility of some one enthused and busily concerned with commerce in the little port-town beyond.

The *Westminster's* captain was at the ladder. The little man suddenly presented him with his card.

"MacDonald Company, sir, Ship's Chandlers, at your service, sir!" he piped briskly.

"Ship's chandlers?" growled the old man. "I don't want no damn ship's chandlers. Where's the pilot around here?"

"Here comes another one," said the Chief Mate, staring with disbelief at another absurd little launch that came pitching and flying to the ship.

"And who is *that?*" demanded the captain. "I suppose that's Angus Mahoney and Company coming to polish the brass? Get off my ship, goddamit, and next time wait until a man's got himself cleared away before *you* come scampering up. Get off!" he roared. "What kind of a place is this anyway? I can't even get my pilot and put in before some pencil-peddler comes. . . . *Who* is that coming alongside now? Get off my ship, *you!*" he yelled, turning again to MacDonald and Company, who promptly bowed, grinned around at everyone with toothy friendliness, seeming to say "Ah, well, all in a day's work," and went scampering down the ladder again, card, briefcase and all, full of cheerful enthusiasm, not at all insulted or hurt, and made another spectacular leap across the bay upon the bobbing little launch, waved briskly, and went pitching and jiggling back to land with one hand gripping the stanchion and the other holding down his bowler hat in the scuddy Atlantic winds.

It was something so funny, so pathetic, so human. Peter was filled with an absurd desire to go scampering over the ladder himself and rush off into "these things"—whatever they were, the land, and ports, the crazy streets of life, men and the pitiful things they did, their furious meaningless strivings, scampering for their bed-and-soup, wearing bowler hats.

They made it home for Christmas. In Boston, in the snowy mysterious streets, they straggled off—bearded, fierce-looking, carrying harpoons and furs, and wallets full of money. They straggled off into the world again, back to the streets of life again without so much as a howdy-do or good-bye, each to his own fierce and secret pleasure, each wrapped in his own dream of hopeful joy.

At home in Galloway things had changed in Peter's family. Ruth was gone in the Women's Army Corps and Rosey had transferred to an Army hospital way out in Seattle. And with Joe in the air force, Liz gone off, and Peter bound to the articles of the merchant marine and regular war voyages—and the father still forced to work away from home—the Martin parents had decided to try to reunite the home in some way. The old man was able to secure a linotype job in New York if he wanted it, and the mother was certain she herself could get a job in the shoe factories there. So they planned to move to New York and bring the children, Mickey and Charley, with them.

"My!" exclaimed the mother when they sat around the sad little table-tree that Christmas. "I was born on a farm in New Hampshire and now I'm going to live in New York! It's going to be easier for all of you to come home on furloughs and visit me—won't it? New York is right near everything, isn't it, Petey? Maybe even Liz can come and visit me now."

"Well," scowled the old man, "it might be worth a try. By God, it might be the thing at that!" he cried, shaking his head. "We'll see, we'll see, we'll have to do *something*. There's no sense the way it is now!"

And Alexander Panos was gone from Galloway. He had joined the Army in October. Peter visited his family and they told him that he had turned down a chance for a commission, saying: "I want to be among the humble ranks."

Peter walked the streets of Galloway at night for the last times, the empty snowy streets, his friends all gone, something gloomy and finished at home, and the war sighing far off. Everything was coming to a close in Galloway and something else was approaching. He was ready for new things and sick of soul with the old haunted vanished ghosts of life.

Judie Smith was living in New York now, in an apartment of her own, waiting for Peter to come and join her there. They had written long letters and something like love throbbed in Peter's mind when he thought of her—his dear, wild, glad-eyed Judie of the college days. He yearned for her after all the watery bleakness of the world.

The *Westminster* was sunk that winter. Peter was sailing on a freighter to England when he heard about it. The *Westminster* was sunk in the dead of night, in February, somewhere in the North Atlantic, with a loss of over seven hundred lives, including scores of crewmen who had sailed with Peter to Greenland. And the great galley, Glory's galley, and Glory himself, and the mess-hall where they had eaten and gambled, the foc'sles where they had talked and played cards, the bunks where they had slept and sweetly dreamed, and the dormitory where they had romped gleefully with crazy joy—the old creaky melancholy ship itself was down in the bottom of the sea now, sea-sunk forever in foundered night. Fish were wandering in the pantry; old Glory was aglow in coral balconies.

Yes, the summer before, on the Boston waterfront, Alexander had seen death-flowers in the eyes of Peter's shipmates.

[11]

FRANCIS, completing his courses at Harvard in the Spring of 1943, was more amused than anything else when he took the mechanical aptitude test for officers' training in the Navy and miserably failed it. At first he didn't understand what this would mean. He had passed everything else with flying colors, the physical examination, the intelligence test, and even the chatty, almost social interviews with a board of polite and witty officers. One of these officers came over to Francis, as he sat awaiting his fate in an anteroom.

"Well, Martin, I'm sorry, and surprised! I thought you'd pass everything without effort, at least it certainly seemed so to me."

"Well," smiled Francis lightly, "what does this mean? Is the Navy rejecting me?"

"Oh, no. It only means that you'll be transferred to V-6—"

"And what's that?"

"You'll be an enlisted man training at one of the centers, probably Newport or Great Lakes. Your chances of getting a commission now depend on how well you make out as an enlisted man. First there'll be boot camp—"

"Boot camp?" Francis now realized what had happened, and he was suddenly infuriated. "I'm a college graduate and I can't get a commission?"

"Not if you can't pass a mechanical aptitude test," said the young Ensign with an air more distant than a moment before. "A lot of fellows are like that . . . they have high intelligence quotients but like you they don't know a bolt from a screw, and that's usually something they can't help either, from long habit. But I was really surprised!" he grinned.

"Yes," said Francis coolly, "I suppose I'm cut out for lesser things."

He was told to wait a couple of weeks before he was to be called for induction.

Everything had happened so swiftly, the abrupt end of his studies in college, this sudden rebuff from the Navy, that Francis was stunned. In a matter of days his whole life had been changed from the leisurely, absorbed life of the campus with his fairly eminent scholarly and social position in those surroundings, to the situation of a Navy "boot" waiting to go to one of the raw windswept camps of the war with hundreds of other raucous sailors-to-be. It was too much for Francis; he was alternately amused and angry and disgusted.

He went to New York and spent his remaining two weeks of freedom living in Greenwich Village with the motherly little intellectual girl he had met at college, Dora Zelnick, in her apartment on Eighth Street. He saw a lot of Wilfred Engels and went to countless parties where everybody got drunk and got mad and argued all night, and then his time was up and he had to go back to Boston to report for active duty. He was never angrier in all his life. Ironically, he was put on a train that went back to New York that very same day, and onwards to Chicago, to the Great Lakes training base.

It was a windswept plain, blue-gray wooden barracks everywhere, and dust swirling between the buildings in wind blowing from the lake. Francis, huddled miserably in a blue peacoat, with tan leggings around his legs and a blue peacap drawn over his brow, wandering around alone at dusk, dejected and lost, not knowing what to do with himself. There was a library in one of the wooden buildings at the end of the camp: he often wandered there.

It was the cold floor of the barracks at night and the raucous boys putting up their hammocks and writing letters home on top of seabags, and the Chief bawling them out in a booming raspy voice, and finally the lights going out and everybody chattering and snickering. Then someone turned over in his hammock, howled with fear, struggled desperately, and fell on the floor, as everybody laughed and yelled. Then it was someone poking Francis in the ribs at two o'clock in the morning, and saying, "Your turn for night watch, Martin," and Francis getting down from the hammock, putting on all his clothes again, winding on the leggings again in darkness, and wandering to and fro among the sleeping "sailors" for two hours with a club and flashlight. Then it was four o'clock, he was relieved from duty, he took off all his intricate leggings and jumpers again in darkness, struggled to climb into the hammock six feet off the floor, and swung there madly trying to sleep. Then it was morning, windswept and bitter and gray, and Francis jumping down again with all the others and winding on the leggings again and wrestling through his jumper, rolling up his hammock and airing out his blankets, and hurrying off as the Chief roared and clapped his hands. Then it was the long lineup before the messhall, the impatient crunching of shoes in the gravel, and some kid saying to Francis—"Geez, I wish they'd let us smoke before breakfast, stand still a minute while I stoop and sneak a butt!"

Then it was the marching and the cadenced singing "Hi-a-loop! Hi-a-loop!" as they swung and swaggered in formation over the frozen earth in the parade field, someone yelling hysterically at them between confused criss-crossing companies swaggering, and the whip of flags, and smoke, and dust in the wind.

On the third day, Francis realized in a sudden flash that he could not bear any more of this. He realized this with all the single concentrated force of a profound and incalculable aversion. So tremendous was his hatred of his new position in the world that he was literally blind, he bumped into people, sometimes he found himself staggering with rage, and once when he looked at himself in the mirror and saw the absurd haircut they had given him (there was no hair left, just the heavy furze of a really close clipping, with one tuft sticking up from the top of his head) he flew into a rage and kicked the board wall and almost broke his toe.

One night there was an air raid drill. Francis was ordered out to stand guard with rifle, bayonet and steel helmet, in front of a sandbag shelter, where he stood for an hour in total darkness as sirens howled and airplanes whined in the black skies. An officer came strolling by with a flashlight. Francis stared at him curiously.

"Confound it, you!" yelled the man suddenly. "Don't you realize that you're supposed to order me into shelter."

"Huh?"

"Don't you realize your duties, you idiot?"

"Well, now, I wasn't exactly certain—"

"You'd better address me *sir* or I'll report you right on the spot! How long have you been in camp? What's your name there, show your face!"

Francis was stunned, suddenly he was completely panic-stricken. With a feeling of unreality, he thought vividly of shouting: *It's none of your business who I am and I don't give a damn who you are!* He threw his rifle down in the dark, shivering with terror, and stalked away.

"Halt!" cried the officer in a sharp, clear, almost joyful tone of voice. At that moment a detachment of fire-fighters came running down the dark path with fire equipment on their way to a mythical "direct hit" in the course of the maneuvers, and in the resulting confusion the officer seemed to disappear on some more urgent matter. Francis, gloating and almost insane in the darkness, wandered around for a half an hour enjoying a strange freedom, chatting with guards who believed him to be a member of the fire-fighting units. Finally he made his way back to his station at the sandbags; at least he thought it was his station until he realized that some stranger from another company was standing there. Finally, after the drill, when the alley-lights came on again, he found his way back to his barracks.

The next day a form sheet was passed around to his company asking, among other questions, what they thought of the camp library. Francis took up his pen with a leer of joy, and wrote: "As an individual in this group, without the opportunity to exercise my own prerogatives, I should imagine that my opinion is of the least significance. Be that as it may, I feel most strongly that the selection of books represented in the camp library constitutes something that amounts to an intellectual fraud." He signed his name to this hopefully. He never heard anything from the officer-librarian.

When the realization came to him that he could not possibly bear another moment of military life—mild though it was at this stage—the overwhelming thought came to him that he was slowly being forced to the most important decision of his life.

"If I should revolt openly," he thought fearfully, "isn't it going to be awfully easy for them to destroy me? I'm caught between the stupidity and the danger of men. I ought to find some way to persuade myself that the stupidity of submitting to all this is at least not a threat to my life,—but I just can't submit to them. I think the submitting itself is more dangerous to me than the consequences of not submitting." And at this he smiled happily for the first time since coming to camp.

"There's only one thing to do," he brooded anxiously, "find some way of getting out somehow."

Two things happened that day that gave a tremendous impetus

to his plans to escape military life "somehow." Alexander Panos, with whom Francis had never exchanged more than a dozen words back home in Galloway, wrote him a letter from an Army camp in Virginia, on the impulse of some harried loneliness of his own in the swirl of military life.

> Dear Francis:
>
> To you, the brother of the greatest friend I have ever had, I write tonight from the guardhouse at Camp Lee here. If I sound a little drunk and maudlin, please forgive my very existence. These few things I have to say to you are important to me, they weigh so heavily on my heart. In spite of the beer I drank tonight, I write to you, unknown brother of my friend. Right now I am assigned to guardhouse duty and as you probably know I have two hours on duty and four hours off. The guardhouse is divided in two by a wire screening. The guards sleep on one side and the prisoners on the other. Just now the second lieutenant of the guard came along with the corporal and they were engaged in some silly conversation regarding how impossible it is for the prisoners to escape—when quite astonishingly one of the prisoners called out, quoting from Thoreau: "You are the prisoners, not I." How can I describe how I felt! And being a guard in this horrid little shack with the wire screening between us—not being allowed to talk to the victims who have broken some stupid little law— Aren't they our brothers? Francis, when I joined the Army I deliberately refused the chance for a commission (as you know, I was a major in the Galloway High School brigade) because I wanted to suffer with the masses and be among them, humble and patient. But I have found since, Francis, I've been cheated, I've been cheated! I wish with all my might there is a God!

The impassioned letter ended just like that. Francis felt that it was one of the most impressive documents he had ever read. He suddenly found himself regretting that he had not befriended the young Greek in past years.

"He's been cheated," he thought excitedly, "but I'm not going to give them a chance to cheat me, I'm not going to wait to find out if there's a God to punish the monsters of this world. . . ."

The second thing was this: while talking to two other sailors as the sun went down over the vast spread of barracks, one of them suddenly leaned over confidentially and said, in an awed tone: "One thing you don't want ever to do is complain about headaches. If you've got a headache just take a couple aspirins and forget it."

"Why?"

"There's a feller in my outfit who kept having headaches and going to the medics for aspirins and complaining. Next thing you know, poof!"

"What . . ."

"They packed him off home, right out of the Navy. They put him under observation for a week in the nut-wards and gave him his discharge. And that was all, brother."

With a convulsive feeling of the most ravenous glee, he hurried off the very next instant to the medical office, throbbing with excitement, foolishness and wild hope. "This is crazy!" he kept thinking. He complained of a headache, they gave him three aspirins to take intermittently, and noted down his name. He went back to his barracks and swallowed all three of them, hoping they might make him nervous and give him a real headache. The next day he went back twice for aspirins, and each time the Pharmacist's Mate made a note of it. Francis swallowed all the aspirins they gave him, ate almost not at all, kept himself awake at night to rack his nerves, and finally began to drink countless cups of black coffee. Finally, his heart pounding with the fear that none of this would work, he began to be actually nerve-racked and began to feel, or imagine, very real headaches indeed. Meanwhile he continued to drill and train with the other boys, all of whom seemed to Francis to be enjoying themselves idiotically. The whole experience was becoming so horrible to him that he actually began to derive a certain amount of morbid brooding pleasure in being there and doing what he was doing.

He went back the third day for aspirins, and at last the Pharmacist's Mate looked at him curiously.

"Say, you must have some pretty bad headaches. Don't the aspirins help any?"

"No. My head just keeps on pounding."

"Ever have 'em like that before, mate?"

"Oh," replied Francis casually, "yes, always."

He was summoned before an examining physician, a Lieutenant Commander, who gravely questioned him for fifteen minutes, made notes, and gave him an encephalography test with the complicated wire devices, which revealed at least that he had no skull injuries or defects of any kind. Whereupon the psychologist was called in. Francis was ready for him.

They sat in an office overlooking the gray stony day of the barracks, the psychiatrist behind his desk and Francis in a chair in front of him. Francis had purposely bought a pack of cigarettes for this interview: even before the psychiatrist was ready to begin questioning him, he had chain-smoked three cigarettes already. For some odd reason he expected that this performance, not only the harried chain-smoking, but the very fact that he would have the gall to smoke without asking permission from a commanding officer, would in some way arouse the doctor's suspicions. However the psychiatrist, who looked like he had had a bad night, seemed to pay no appreciable attention to anything that Francis did, including the violent convulsive trembling, and in time Francis dropped his pretense on the hunch that he was overdoing things. He even forgot to smoke when the conversation became interesting.

After the routine questions, about wetting beds and so on, the psychiatrist asked: "Now tell me, what is the funniest thing you ever saw?"

"Ah . . . let's see. Well, now. The funniest thing I ever saw was in—Boston. I was walking on Commonwealth Avenue and a pigeon got run over by a car. It was early in the morning."

"A pigeon got run over," repeated the psychiatrist without any curiosity or surprise. "And why was that funny?" Meanwhile he made notes.

"The sound of it," said Francis with a spellbound air, "the squishing, cracking sound it made, because the car was going very fast and that pigeon never had a chance, not even a chance to coo." He grinned widely, but the doctor was looking out the window with a kind of gloom. "The sound of it," pressed Francis. "It was very funny"—and he caught himself almost adding, "in a way," because he had actually experienced such a thing and it had struck him as horrible. "In its own way," he said severely now.

"All right," continued the doctor, "and now tell me, what is the strangest thing you ever saw?"

Francis pondered deeply. He was beside himself with excitement and even happiness, he had never been so deeply absorbed and pleased in all his life.

"You've never seen anything strange?" prodded the doctor.

"Hmm. Not particularly," essayed Francis, intently studying the man's face, and growing anxious when he saw no indication there of the success of his reply. Then he plunged. "Well now, I guess I could remember something." He waited.

"You could?"

"Well, I *can*—that is, I *do*, as a matter of fact." He grinned arrogantly into the man's face; never had he permitted himself such wonderful and absurd liberties with another human being. "I once saw a woman, she was shopping, and she bought a whole lot of groceries, that is, she picked them off the shelf, and put them all in a little wagon"—and here Francis leaned forward eagerly—"in a little wagon with wires on it, and she rolled it along like a baby carriage over the floor." Francis looked keenly at the doctor, and added: "Well, actually, it was in a big store in my home town, Galloway, on River Street"—and he grinned again, with a look of sly satisfaction.

The doctor was bored. "You say the little wagon had wires on it?"

"Yes," said Francis pensively. He suddenly thought of something. "And I didn't dare touch the wires because . . . well, electricity? Electricity in the wires, you see." He saw a flash of absorbed interest in the doctor's face as he leaned down to make a note, yet suddenly Francis felt confusedly disturbed by something, he had no idea what it was.

He was visibly disappointed when the doctor dismissed the interview at that point. He hated to leave the office. He was told to go back downstairs to the other office, where the Pharmacist's Mate was waiting, the Pharmacist's Mate who was quite definitely beginning to act like his keeper. Francis strolled along the hall grinning, however. And it was at that moment that he experienced the most mournful sensation of his life. He came to a halt, listening.

In one of the offices, through the flimsy barrack walls, he could hear an interview going on between a doctor and a patient. Regularly punctuating the sound of their voices was a series of heavy thuds that shook the walls.

He heard someone yell: "But that's not all. There's this one too, this one's the hardest!"

"I see," said another voice gravely.

And there was a great thud that shook the floor.

"Very good," said the grave voice.

"Oh, I can do a million others. You don't know the half of it, Doc, I'm full of terrific strength and speed, there's nothing like it. Sometimes I wake up in the morning and I feel so good I could blow up, blast, explode! You know, I like talking to a man who's really interested in acrobatics, it shows a sign of interest. Birds! birds! I used to have a lot of birds in my backyard, them little sparrows especially. But wait a minute, I just thought of another one—"

"It won't be necessary—"

But, after a short, almost electrified silence, there was a great shattering thud upon the floor, a cry of surprise, something, a glass, or a jar, fell on the floor and shattered, and someone giggled idiotically.

"Did you *hurt* yourself?" said the grave voice without any real consternation.

"Hell, no, Doc, I can usually do that one but I missed out that time! From the top of your desk I can do much better—"

"No, no! That's enough for now, that's fine."

"By geez, I like a man who shows interest!"

"Yes. And we'll do some more tomorrow. Now I think we better go back downstairs, it's just about time for lunch."

Francis, horrified, backed up against the wall and stared fearfully as the door opened. First there came a small, mournful, stooped, dejected fellow looking fearfully around him with rheumy eyes, his hands pressed to his sides, his head lowered and his eyes darting around with incredible furtiveness. Behind him was a tall bulky Lieutenant, carrying a briefcase and herding him along with one hand till they disappeared down the stairs. It was one of the most astounding sights Francis had ever seen.

"Was *he* the acrobat?" he thought with a wild fear. "And am *I* such an acrobat?" he asked himself wildly.

Yet Francis had made up his mind to pretend that he was insane. In a swirl of fear and confusion he prepared to spend his first hours in the "locked ward" of the hospital that night.

They had sent for his clothes and belongings back in his company's barracks. It seemed to Francis that there was something final in this decision, and he exulted. But while they were getting him a pair of pajamas and slippers and a bathrobe, and he was waiting in the ward office, he was suddenly conscious of someone watching him nearby. At one end of the office there was a window, or a partition, with a wire screening, opening into a long room with a row of beds. In this window now stood a dark, hairy, staring young man in a bathrobe, whose eyes were fixed on Francis, and whose hands, enormous hairy hands, were raised and gripped to the screen. Francis looked back into his eyes. They were like pools of illuminated water. Suddenly the hairy youngster opened his mouth and began to gibber and giggle with idiotic joy. Francis looked over this fellow's shoulder imperiously and noticed the others inside. They looked less fantastic, sitting around coolly playing cards and reading and talking. He turned to the attendant who was writing at the desk and said: "Look here, you're not putting me in *there* for the night, are you? It's like something in *The Inferno*."

The attendant looked up at him, kindly, with real sympathy, almost with the sort of affection undoubtedly developed after many experiences of this kind. Francis was suddenly aware that no matter what he could say, there would always be this wall of sympathy and affection separating him from these attendants to whom, now, he was just another deranged patient until proved otherwise by the powers of the place. He watched him coolly.

"Only for a few days. Your name is Francis, isn't it? Only for a few days, *Frankie*."

"But that fellow in the window is an absolute maniac, anyone can see that. Isn't there any danger?"

"That's Jeepo. Jeepo's okay, he wouldn't harm a fly, you'll be jake."

"Hello, Jeepo," said Francis, turning and gazing at the poor cretin who stood there grinning happily. He wanted to see what there was in him that could be depended upon.

Jeepo emitted a raving happy cry. Francis suddenly realized, with secret horror, that madness was the only key to uninterrupted, unobstructed happiness; he realized that in a flash.

"It's still not safe," said Francis, turning to the attendant. "How can you prevent him from going berserk or trying to kill somebody?"

"Don't worry, Francis, we've got that all taken care of—nothing's in there that could be used as a weapon and we watch everybody twenty-four hours day and night. Besides, Jeepo's leaving for Washington tomorrow. He's a scarey sonofabitch but he's harmless." The attendant smiled. "My name's Bill, Francis, just plain Bill."

"What's in Washington?" demanded Francis curiously.

"The last stop, Francis, the last stop." Bill grinned and returned his attention to the report he was filling out. "Look what I'm writing here, Francis: 'The patient shows excessive curiosity and alertness.' That's a good sign for you. You'll be all right. We'll take good care of you."

Francis decided to ask no more questions.

In the morning, after spending a surprisingly pleasant night in bed, enjoying his privacy of contemplation for the first time in weeks, and sleeping soundly, Francis woke up, ate a good breakfast, smoked a cigarette, and had his first look at the doctors of the place. He noticed certain things with his brooding, watchful, suspicious eyes.

In the first place, the head man, a dashing handsome Lieutenant Commander of about forty or so, had that look about him, as he strode hither and yon in the course of his duties, of a man who was much more of an organizer than a doctor of any kind: an executive, a man of efficiency. At the same time, there was that certain strut in his manner that reminded Francis of some of the smalltown "wheels" in Galloway, the aldermen, half-political businessmen who were always to be seen on Daley Square at high noon. He suddenly remembered his father's contempt for this kind of man. He studied the man carefully. Moreover, that same afternoon, he had an interview with this doctor and noticed his general blank disinterestedness. He also noticed, throughout the day, how the few women, the nurses and Red Cross workers and librarians who came around with books, seemed to adore this man and took every opportunity to follow him around and fawn over him.

Then he observed the other doctors, who seemed more competent, less Don Juan-ish, and somehow professionally humble. One of them particularly, a husky young Italian, obviously a New Yorker, who came around on the evening-call absentmindedly carrying a copy of the *New Republic* under his writing pad. Francis looked eagerly at this man, Dr. Gatti, who had a friendly and absentminded and almost amenable look about him. He noticed how Gatti jotted down all the important data, while the head doctor, Thompson, asked all the routine questions in a bored manner and moved on impatiently, glancing at his watch.

Francis also noticed that the head attendant, Bill, who had a sort of misty-eyed sentimental look and always spoke in a soft, gentle, and persuasive voice, could also be very cruel and sadistic at times. Francis had originally noticed this in his eyes, which were a little blank and unseeing, and in the shape of his jaw, the gross, heavy shape of it. Francis saw him beat up a stubborn patient that night when they were trying to calm down the poor creature off some tremendous yelling manic-depressive exultation. The other attendants held the boy's arms and legs, while Bill, beside himself with rage, pummelled him with his fists, occasionally hitting the other attendants who growled: "Watch what you're doing, for krissakes!" Finally they had the youngster calmed down for a moment as he nursed his bruises, and they forced a drink of paraldehyde down his throat, and put him away in one of the padded cells. Bill actually cried awhile, saying mournfully: "Geez, guys, I don't like to do things like that, nobody loves these kids more than I do, but what the hell can I do?" The other attendants consoled him.

Francis walked around noticing everything with great horror. There was one fellow who came up to him and said: "I know you, you don't have to act innocent, not with *me* you don't."

"Why?"

"You're an F.B.I. man, but you're not fooling me, not one bit; what's more I *don't care:* you've got nothing on me." And this young man smiled into Francis' face.

"You don't have anything to worry about," replied Francis gravely, "I'm not here to watch you, but someone else. You can relax now." He suddenly wondered why he should say a silly thing like that.

He made friends with only one patient in his ward, a tall, thin, sensitive-looking boy of twenty-four who continually smiled and behaved in the most genteel and refined manner. His name was Griggs. Griggs told Francis that he was a conscientious objector but that he hadn't had the nerve to announce it to the proper authorities. He was very nervous, yet dreamy, and spent most of his time reading a book, or staring over it for hours. Francis thought him very intelligent but noticed something indefinite and inconsecutive in his line of reasoning, brilliant and provocative though it was.

"The trouble with the world," said Griggs, absentmindedly running a long bony hand through his hair, "is not war or ignorance or anything like that, actually it's—well, you'll never guess what, it's the liver, the organism right down here," and he patted his side.

"The liver?"

"Yes. You see, people eat too much, they keep a continual sloppy stream of food going down all day and never give their liver a chance to kick out the bile. If they did, they'd never grow old and get gray hair, your Senators and Congressmen in Washington would not be a bunch of old petulant men, there wouldn't be wars. It all begins in the liver. The liver is the killer."

"That's an interesting play on words," sallied Francis.

"Oh, it's more important than that," said Griggs gravely, with a little reproach in his tone, "it's a question of the source of youth itself. Now I myself have experimented by starving myself on a controlled starvation diet, and you'll note that there's an unusual youthfulness in my eyes and in my movements."

This was almost true, except for the fact that he was a bag of bones with a gaunt, haggard mask of a face. "I hope to grow younger and younger as I go along, until finally, when I'm fifty, I'll be able to play football. . . ."

He overwhelmed Francis for days with his observations, but one day he grew silent, the day after that he just sat in his chair staring, and the day after that, steeped in profoundest silence, he refused even to look at the trays of food they brought him, and they took him away to a padded cell. Francis was terrified, especially since his single choice of a friend in the wards had turned out so disastrously.

Soon Francis had many panic-stricken moments when his only thought was: "I'm caught, I'm caught!"—and he racked his whole being wondering for how long, how long. . . . It was four weeks already.

One day he was lying on his bed with his slippers on, and one of the young attendants reminded him that this was against the rules. Francis did not budge: he suddenly had a feeling of the most intense pleasure.

"Take a rag in the corner, Francis, and wipe off the dirt from your bedspread. And don't do this again."

Still Francis did not budge, he simply stared away absentmindedly and hummed a little tune.

"Francis!"

Francis was swelling with a pleasurable indignation that brought a flush to his cheeks.

"Francis, you don't want me to lock you up in solitary, do you? Get up off that bed this minute and do as I say."

"All right," said Francis, getting up, "lead the way, lock me up if you want to."

The young attendant was startled, he began to blush, and all the other patients, who were watching, were amazed.

"Come on!" goaded Francis, waiting at the door. "Lock me up, Red!"

Red was confused for just a moment, he seemed to ponder the possibilities with no little hesitation, but the look of insufferable arrogance and pleasure on Francis' face irritated him and he made up his mind hotly. "All right, wise guy, I *will* lock you up!" Together they swaggered down the hall, Red found an empty padded cell, Francis walked in, Red locked the door, peeked in through the small screen (a little forlornly now), and Francis merely sat on the floor, on a mattress, with his legs crossed underneath him, and looked about him with intense pleasure. He suddenly realized that his privacy here would be inviolable and beautiful.

"What are you going to do, Francis?" said Red finally. "Are you going to do as I say, or stay in there?"

Francis grinned happily. He had been wandering around in a bathrobe so long that his usual severe taciturnity was all gone; and he said now: "Don't worry, my friend, I shall simply stay here and contemplate Vishnu."

Red went away, and a minute later the most mournful, grief-stricken, unhappy face in the world was looking in at Francis through the screen—Bill, the head attendant, who was actually crying, great real tears were swelling from his eyes and rolling down his cheeks. He just stared grievously through the screen for a whole half-minute, in ruefullest silence, he even sniffed and blew his nose slowly, wiped his eyes, and finally, in a low, tenderly pleading, almost inaudible voice, he said: "Francis baby, what did you go and do?"

Francis was astounded.

"Francis chappy, I don't know what to say, I'm so stunned, I never expected you to kick up like that, not you, not *you!*"

Francis only stared.

"A nice quiet kid like you, why, who would have ever thought it, now tell me, please tell me."

There was a long silence. New tears were welling up in Bill's eyes. Francis was conscious of an instinctive fear of the situation, of Bill's sentimentality which seemed somehow ominous. He promptly got up and agreed to go back and wipe the dirt off his bed. Bill affectionately put his arm around him and led him back to the ward like a mother consoled. And Francis was convinced that he had done the right thing at just the right moment, "or," he thought, "something would have exploded for sure."

That same afternoon something happened that Francis had long been awaiting: he had an interview with the youthful Doctor Gatti, and he was ready for him.

Gatti's curiosity in Francis had already been aroused by the reports he had read about him.

"They've got you down here as a dementia praecox case," he said affably after they had talked awhile in his office, "but I don't think so in the least, not after talking to you like this."

"I should hope not," said Francis urbanely. "By the way, I suppose that the diagnosis was made by Doctor Thompson?"

"Yes? How did you know?" smiled the doctor.

"I just imagine that he wouldn't waste much time with any of the newer, more complex diagnoses, assuming of course that he even understands the meaning of the old ones."

"Do you have any idea what is meant by dementia praecox?" smiled the young doctor.

"I read the definition somewhere in an ancient text. I do want to ask you one thing, though—I wonder if I'm being put through all this to convince somebody, including myself, that I must be insane because I can't submit to the absolutist discipline of military life."

Francis had conceived and memorized these phrases weeks before, on the very night he had first seen Gatti with his copy of the *New Republic*. He now recited them out with a strange and exalted nervousness. It was lucky that he was nervous, otherwise the phrases would have sounded mad and gravely memorized.

The young doctor was overwhelmed with curiosity. The fact that he was interviewing Francis in a capacity as psychiatrist, and that he was his commanding officer as well, seemed to be forgotten on both sides, and indeed, when it occurred to Gatti, he was disposed to overlook the matter.

"But that is a very bitter way of looking at it," he cried, lighting a cigarette and sitting on the edge of his desk.

"It's a bitter world, isn't it?" murmured Francis.

"Yes, but that's not our consideration at the moment. Right now we're concerned with your failure to adapt yourself to a given situation. We can talk philosophy later. . . . For one thing now, I'm ready to assume that the headaches you reported were entirely made up—"

Francis was deeply silent.

"Whether you had them or not is only interesting to me insofar as it shows your withdrawal from the realities at hand, whether psychologically or psychosomatically. In any case it's a withdrawal and it reveals a basic neurotic tendency. Do you understand that? I mean the terms? I assume you do."

"The terms, yes," replied Francis. He was busily considering the naïveté with which the young doctor had just mentioned "philosophy"—like some eager young student. "I did have headaches," continued Francis almost affably now, "as a result of having my teeth drilled and filled, twelve cavities in all, the second day here. But I was exaggerating things, I've always been a little—what's the word?" he demanded innocently.

"Hypochondriac?"

"Yes. By the way," he smiled, "another thing has occurred to me. Do you get impatient incidentally because I go on talking like this?—"

"Oh, no!" cried the doctor quickly. "Actually, the more you talk the better it is. I'm supposed to get an insight into your thought processes."

When he said that, they looked at each other curiously, with a sheer, foolish curiosity.

"Well then," continued Francis, "I've been wondering how you yourself, as a liberal, can reconcile your enlightened views with the system of military disciplines that are built up in the armed forces. You've got to admit that the absolute relationship between officers and enlisted men is a fascistic set-up. No one can deny *that* any more than you can deny that it's precisely such a system we're supposed to be wiping out." All this had been memorized.

"Ah-ha!" laughed Gatti jovially. "I think I expected that. I knew it was coming!" With a gesture of excited pleasure he went to the door of the office, which had been left ajar, and closed it.

When Francis saw this he could have hugged himself with delight, and the thought flashed across his mind: "Then it is *really* possible to be clever!"

He had many other interviews with Gatti during the following week and the upshot of it was that his fate in the Navy was decided once and for all, with no further hesitation and incompetent uncertainty. He was removed from the locked ward to the open wards, his diagnosis was changed from "dementia praecox" to "schizoid tendencies," and he was told that his discharge would be coming through soon, an honorable medical discharge. Doctor Gatti, who was nobody's fool, understood quite clearly that out of the millions of men involved in the Navy, good and bad, easygoing and wild, dutiful and undisciplined, Francis was numbered among those who could render no service at all to the organization because they were merely a jumble of incalculable reactions. He politely informed Francis of this opinion, and Francis was thoroughly pleased.

One rainy night an attendant came to Francis and notified him that he had a visitor waiting in the office.

"You've got only a half-hour, so step on it!"

Francis was astounded. As he hurried in the hall he passed a wet, shabby old man who, with a meek and humble air, was looking back down the hall in a gape of hesitation, clutching a dripping hat with both hands. It was a moment of awful presentiment before Francis, turning back to this woeful old man, realized it was his father George Martin. He had come a long way; he looked tired and haunted.

"Well, I didn't expect this!" said Francis, more pleased than he could have imagined.

"Francis," cried the old man anxiously, "there's a doctor here—Doctor Thompson? I wrote him a letter and asked him why they were keeping you here, and he told me you were a pretty sick boy."

"Oh, nonsense!" snapped Francis angrily. They shook hands firmly.

"You don't look sick to me, Francis. What's it all about? I was really worried—I took three days off from work to come and see you, that letter scared me so much. I'm going back tonight right away, I just wanted to see you myself, it's only for these few minutes they allowed. And, gosh, what a trip out here, a thousand miles, Francis, a thousand miles!" he said with amazement. "But your mother and I were so worried!—"

Francis was so exasperated he could hardly talk. Finally he explained everything to his father and assured him that it was going to be all right.

"Well then!" sighed the old man wonderingly. "Like you say, they'd have to prove you're nuts for not wanting to fight their silly wars. Well, that's one way of putting it. God knows, young Joe, and Petey too haven't given it much thought, they're right in the thick of it, and your little brother Charley's joining the Army next month."

The old man gazed at Francis. "But I understand you, kiddo, I understand you better than anybody else right now. You just made up your mind you wouldn't have any of it, so here you are, and it's all right with me, don't you worry, I won't wave a flag at you. If everybody was like you all over the world, they wouldn't be able to find anybody to fight their wars. God knows," said Martin, shaking his head, "I'm not the one to judge. You're a strange boy with your own quiet little mind. You're my son and you've got a conscience of your own, I hope! Everything is in chaos nowadays and none of us can explain it, none of us. You know something?" he suddenly grinned quickly.

"What?"

"Do you realize that this was the longest trip I ever took in all my life? That Chicago! You ought to see that town, a swell city! I had the time of my life this afternoon running around and eating in little restaurants." The old man chuckled gleefully. "If I had my way I'd travel clear on out west tonight! But the old lady and I have a budget to watch, dammit. It was a lulu of a trip, sonny. I enjoyed the beautiful Ohio farmlands, Indiana, that beautiful Indiana—"

"I'm glad you got *something* out of the stupid mess!" muttered Francis darkly. "Imagine that Thompson writing you a thing like that. The stupid fool!"

"I'll take your word he's a fool, Francis."

"*Ta-ake* my word!" breathed Francis madly.

The old man gripped Francis' hand and held it in his. "Don't let them get you down, sonny. Do as your old man says and take it easy, wait it out, be calm. Be humble, sonny, be *humble!* I'm going to have to be leaving, it's almost nine o'clock. Never mind what happens and what they say," he concluded with sorrowful gravity.

"Be humble," echoed Francis with a curl of his lips. "Be humble—among strutting fools?"

"Because it doesn't really matter," said the old man, frowning painfully over a thought of his own, "and a man is as strong as he's humble. There."

"That's ridiculous," sniffed Francis, grinning suddenly at his father. "A man's as strong as his strength and will, there's no two ways about *that*."

"No," replied the old man with awe and perfect seriousness, "a man's as strong as he's humble. He just doesn't have to prove his strength."

Francis glanced at his father with sudden curiosity. For some reason he thought of Alexander Panos and the letter. "That *may* be true, in a sad kind of way. But it's not for *me!* I haven't time to be humble."

The old man chuckled. "Well, you can bandy twenty-five cent words all you want, but— Say! we've never had a talk like this before, have we? Well, I'll be darned, I had to travel a thousand miles to have my first real chat with Francis! Ye Gods, what a family!" he cried. "Francis, Francis, Francis!" he chanted mournfully. "As long as you're *all right,* that's all I care!"

His father hugged Francis when it was time to leave, he grew sorrowful again, his eyes misting, his jaw almost trembling. Francis watched him go away across the courtyard and disappear, and he went back to his bed in a meditative state of mind. He realized in a flash of compassionate understanding, and with no little mortification, that his father had traveled a thousand miles to talk to him for thirty minutes, and that it was all over now. And he remembered his father's face and his voice and his big mournful presence, and it was strange to think of it, very strange and surprisingly sad.

[12]

GEORGE MARTIN stood on the steps of a great railroad station in Chicago and looked about him in the sea of night. He was a thousand miles from home, in the middle of America, alone, excited, feeling strange. He thought of himself poised on the great plains of the continent and in the great city of Chicago, and it was a spellbinding thing to think about. He looked around him. He listened to the murmurs, rumbles, and clangings of the big city, he smelled the corky coal-smoke from the railyards in the moist, drooping nighttime April air.

"If I had the time and money," he thought, "tonight I'd get on a train, tonight now, and I'd travel two thousand more miles to California. What is it like in California?"

He wandered slowly through the streets of Chicago and looked up gapingly at the State Street office-buildings deserted, dark and impressive at night. He crossed a canal bridge and walked among the grimy darknesses of South Halsted, and the Mills Hotel with its yellow light and dusty windowpanes and moving ruined shadows within. Then the old man roamed towards the throbbing halo of the Loop and found himself in the crowds and the lights, the music and the smell of chili beans. He walked—he walked beneath the elevated tracks, by saloons, across old deserted cobblestone streets, and finally on a railroad bridge, where he looked below.

There was an old wooden caboose abandoned at the side of the tracks, and inside an oil lamp burning, and six railroad men sitting around an old table drinking coffee, eating hamburgers, smoking cigars, and playing a heavy game of poker. And in the breathing murmur of the vast Chicago night, foremost before the hum and throb of the Loop, the distant soft thunder of trains, the Lake breeze like October, the far receded sighing—sharp and near beneath all that, he could hear the voices of the railroad men so harsh, gruff, good-humored and growling, he could hear the click of the poker chips, the scrape of chairs, the yawns, the sudden cries of laughter and surprise, and the muttering ruminations under the smoky lamp.

There leaned old George Martin on the rail above the tracks, brooding down and listening and watching with a grin, and thinking:

"Why, I remember seeing something like this years ago in New Hampshire. It was my uncle Bob, what did he call himself?—a railroad 'boomer'—and they used to have card games in a caboose just like this one, I remember the night now, it was that night the circus came to Lacoshua and Uncle Bob played poker with the circus men. I was watching from outside. Why, I must have been ten years old then—"

And suddenly he was wrung with a great confused desire to live forever.

"These fellows here—they've traveled with the railroad all over, up to Milwaukee, Minnesota, to Dakota—they must have been to Iowa and Nebraska and those places with the grain elevators—and even Wyoming, the West. And that Denver!—and all the railroad yards everywhere, all the way to long California . . . and down to Texas, the cattle pens, and over to Los Angeles, California, where they have palm trees by the railroad yards. Pshaw! Well! They've been there, been there a hundred times, they've had their whiskey and women, and they've had their wives and children too, and they've been everywhere and played a couple thousand poker games, and collected a thousand paychecks, and spent money, and eaten and slept and got drunk and walked around everywhere, and seen all that country. These fellows—"

He looked down and brooded. Why was it that he had not been with them all this time? What had he done, where had he gone, why was it that he could not live again, and live forever, and do all the things he had forgotten to do. And why were all the things that he himself had done so confused, so especial and definite and finished, so tattered and ugly, so incomplete, so unknown and half-forgotten now, yet so painful and twisted as he thought of them. Why were they so unlike the things other men had done? Why had he been born in New Hampshire instead of Illinois somehow? What would it be like to be on a train going West across the plains, on the old Union Pacific tracks, and to see a single small lamplight burning in a shack across the American darkness, the prairie darkness?

And he wondered what they would say if he went down the steps, crossed the tracks, mounted the boards in front of the caboose, knocked on the door, and asked them if he could join them for a few hands. No, he could not do that. It was too late for that now.

He stood on the steps of the railroad station at midnight in Chicago and watched the soldiers and sailors going to and fro with their packs and seabags. He thought of his children.

Joe was in England, across the sea of night in England, ancient unknown England. And Peter was coming and going on a ship in the Mediterranean sea, off North Africa, off the Carthaginian rocks. And Rosey, big genial yet woebegone Rosey, was in Seattle, a nurse in an Army hospital, and where was Seattle, how far across that wide darkness? Ruth was in Los Angeles, a WAC, and she was going to marry a soldier boy from Tennessee, she wrote and told her father. And Lizzy—poor fierce child of terror—was in San Francisco; in what chain of lights at night, in what sea-fog and night-fog was she? And Francis—across the pin-point lights of Chicago, near now, silent in the murmurings of the night, silent Francis. *Where* were all his children?

The old man stood on the steps of the station, and it began to rain, April rained again. He stood in the rain and smelled the rain, he remembered Galloway and the muddy sweet twinkling wash of rain at night in his part of the world.

In his part of the world!

"Lordy, Lordy, Lordy," he sighed.

He went on the train, found a seat, sat down, put on his old silver-rimmed spectacles, and opened the pages of the Chicago paper.

He was alone in the wide darkness of the world, but he was going home now, and his children were scattered like lights in the land. There was a war, he was on a train, he was old, he was George Martin.

[13]

PETER RETURNED from a voyage to North Africa in late September of that year. His ship, a cumbersome vast Liberty already old and rusty and battered in one year's incessant sailing, with one gaping patch in its bow from an old torpedoing, made its way round the Florida Keys and came up the mouths of the Mississippi, and into the ancient quays of New Orleans.

It was a glorious blue sky, and wild red flowers in Andrew Jackson park, the smell of molasses, loam and petals in the soft tropical air, the white shining marble balconies, the greeneries, the dark scrolled iron of balustrades, and even the ripple of women's laughter in a little open courtyard restaurant in the

French Quarter—everything that Peter would have wished New Orleans to be like.

But he was a deckhand, a seaman. He wandered and roamed the South Rampart Streets and Magazine Streets of his seaman's soul, he prowled and roamed, he was restless, feverish, drunken, seeking out the impossible ecstasies of the land as dreamed at sea, confused, brooding, crazy, lonely: he was a seaman.

He crowded at smoky bars with men in dirty shirtsleeves and greasy straw hats, he lurked in alleys with Big Slim and Red and drank raw whiskey from the bottle, he was blood-red drunk in whore-houses, sat in waterfront doorways waiting for something, anything, he even went aboard an antique Panamanian freighter one night to smoke hasheesh with the dark smiling Latins and he never forgot the weird drunken slant of that old ship's deck as he tried to cross it at dawn after a night in a jabbering crowded forecastle: it was as though the whole world had tilted over, like the moon, but it was only the old Panamanian freighter listing at the docks.

It was not until a week later, when he woke up one morning in a dirty room somewhere on Dauphine Street, that he decided to "pull himself together" somehow. He thought of going to see his sister Ruth in California. She had written and told him all about her marriage to the soldier from Tennessee eagerly, joyfully, and with her own rare simplicity of soul. "Oh, Petey, we had such a time getting Luke's leave so we could get married. I waited all morning at the marriage license bureau in Los Angeles but when he finally arrived all the boys were with him in a truck, including his Captain who turned out to be such a swell guy. They had wedding gifts and whiskey and just everything, and we got married and had such a grand time and I'll never forget it as long as I live. Now Luke is shipped out and I don't know where, and I haven't heard from him in a week. I guess he's going overseas now. Isn't it terrible and sad the way life is now? Are you taking good care of yourself away from home?"

After all the squalor of waterfront saloons, Peter longed to see someone sweet like his sister, to talk, and remember home, to do "something sensible" for a change, if only for a while.

"I could hitch-hike out to L.A.," he thought, and then he suddenly thought of his little brother Charley who was a kid soldier stationed in Maryland now. He could hitch-hike up there and meet him in Washington somewhere, and then go settle down a few weeks with poor wild Judie in New York.

He spent the entire afternoon sitting on a pierhead at the foot of Canal Street watching the Mississippi, the great uniting river of all rivers, and thought of everything and everyone in his life as the old late sun glowed upon the waters.

And that night, after writing a long harried letter to Ruth in California, and a postcard to young Charley telling him to meet him in Washington, and wearing his old black jacket and the same battered canvas bag he took everywhere, he thumbed the big trucks that started rolling at eleven o'clock across Louisiana on Route 90 . . . to Mobile . . . and Atlanta . . . and the big Southern night towards Washington.

He hitch-hiked all the way to Richmond blurry-eyed and dazed, boozing his way along till he was one shattered ecstatic nerve, slugging out of bottles with every soldier and sailor he met along the way, and suddenly growing weary and sick in Richmond, getting on a train and sleeping the rest of the way to Washington.

And in the morning he woke up, sober, and ate a big breakfast in the dining-car, and sat wondering what it all meant.

"Once," he thought, "once upon a time I was a crazy little kid rushing to football practice in Galloway and getting nowhere, and rushing back home to eat big meals—and I knew I was right. It was so simple and right in those days. I was a crazy little kid."

He was sitting by the window, watching the October earth roll by, the Virginia forest he had never seen.

"Five weeks ago I was in Casablanca, four months ago I was in Liverpool, a year ago I was at the North Pole! Arctic Greenland; who ever heard of Arctic Greenland! And before that? I was a crazy kid, rushing back from scrimmage to eat big meals in my mother's kitchen at home. What a simple good little guy I used to be. What happened? Is it the war? Where am I going, the way I do things, why is everything so strange and far away now?"

He saw his brother Charley that night in Washington. At first he didn't recognize him. They had arranged to meet on the steps of the Union terminal, and Peter stood there for thirty minutes staring at all the soldiers who passed and poured by him on the great pavement. He gazed at the Capitol dome looming in the

Indian Summer dusk, and wondered at the soft mysterious light in the sky overtopping this famous city that he had never seen before. He wondered at the ancient sadness of this city and the everlasting ghostly sorrowfulness of all the soldiers and sailors and Marines that came and passed.

He had expected somehow that Washington would be a scene of great international excitement with diplomats, ambassadors, foreign generals rushing by with eager entourages towards some indistinct place in the city blazing with light, all a-murmur with rumors, great preparations, mighty pronouncements. But it was just a lot of soldiers and sailors and Marines passing in the dusk, and sad girls strolling, and birds singing in the park, and trolleys clanging mournfully across the lowering darkness, and the lights coming on. Something was lost and forgotten, like sunsets vanished, and old names and dust, and the remembrance of history books, Civil War songs, and brown daguerreotype portraits of dead families.

One of many soldiers that had poured out of a bus in front of the station came hurrying towards Peter, smiling blurrily in the darkness. Peter looked and saw that it was Charley, his own kid brother, Charley Martin.

"It can't be!" he said with awe.

"Hi, Pete, don't you recognize me?"

"Sure I recognize you, but— Well, I'll be damned. I haven't seen you for so long—"

"I got taller, that's why you couldn't tell."

Peter shook Charley's hand and gazed at him. He had grown up, almost taller than Peter now, thin and wiry, graceful and sad, looking almost exactly like Joe Martin, except for the sadness, grace, and pensiveness of his face and whole slow-moving figure.

"You sure do look like a soldier!" smiled Peter. "Have you been home yet to show the folks?"

"Not yet. But I'm getting a furlough next month."

Peter had no idea what to say or what to do now that he was confronted by this sweet, sad brother, so much like a stranger and so quiet. "Well, hell! Look!—do you smoke? Have a cigarette!"

"I've got my own but I'll take one," said Charley, gravely wetting his lips and taking a cigarette with trembling fingers.

When Peter saw Charley's fingers trembling, he was suddenly

almost moved to tears. Once more he was struck with the haunted, guilty, mixed-up sorrow that weighed on him in the war from everything, all around, everywhere, all the time. The sight of Charley's trembling nervous fingers, his thin face lowered shyly, the gentle demeanor of him again, all this inexplicably filled him with the whole force of blurred-up time and sad change.

"Charley!" he cried, starting to say something, but suddenly not knowing what to say, and falling blushingly silent. They stood together on the steps, side by side watching the people and the servicemen going to and fro before the great railroad station. Then they started to walk aimlessly down the street, alongside a park, towards the lights and traffic.

"And do you drink too?" demanded Peter, assuming a gruffly tender air.

"Sure, I drink beer! Me and some joes got drunk the other night on beer, over at Hyattsville."

"Well, I'll be damned," said Peter. "And what else? What else, Charley?"

"Huh?"

"What else is there?"

"Well," grinned Charley, "I don't know."

They both looked away and grinned foolishly, and yet they realized that they liked each other somehow; their positions were changed, no longer big brother and little brother now, just two men walking down the street, yet they discovered this with a happy kind of awe.

"Well, what do you say," cried Peter. "How about a beer in that bar over there?"

"Let's go!"

So they stomped into the crowded bar together and leaned their feet on the brass rail and ordered two beers. But the bartender leaned over and peered at young Charley skeptically.

"Soldier, I've got a liquor license to worry about, so be a good boy and tell me how old you are."

"I'm twenty-one years old," said Charley gravely.

"Show me your papers, show me the papers!" said the bartender wearily looking away.

"It's all right, he's with me, I'm his brother!" cried Peter.

"That don't make no difference, he's got to be of age or I lose my license, so the papers, the papers."

"Okay," said Charley, "I ain't of age, forget it, give me a coke." He looked at Peter, and they burst out laughing. So Peter drank beer and Charley drank cokes.

"How old are you, Charley? Seventeen?"

"No, eighteen!"

"Well, I'll be damned!" They didn't have much to say, but they stayed together happily, quietly.

Then they wandered along the bright streets, looked at all the girls, bought popcorn and ate it as they strolled, stopped underneath all the marquees to look at the pictures, wandered on.

Finally, long after midnight, they sat down on a park bench when all the places had closed and all the girls and people had disappeared from the streets, and only the ghostly young soldiers and sailors passed and went away and came by again wandering aimlessly in the night, in the empty night. It was the same way Peter had seen it everywhere. And it was a balmy, soft, faded night, a southern night, with a vast warm dawn throbbing at the edges of the sky. Where they sat, not a leaf stirred in the trees.

There was silence in the world.

And sprawled everywhere in the grass and on benches, in a litter of newspapers and bottles—the ghostly young soldiers, the sailors, homeless and lonely and tired and trying to sleep, while a cop passed silently yawning, while a taxicab suddenly swept by and disappeared, while the empty streets clicked and glowed strangely as traffic lights continued to change red and green in the hollow desolation.

Just across the street from the park, in an impressive building behind great trees, a light glowed all night. There was silence, the only sound was the clicking of the traffic lights and a distant train along the Potomac—and the quiet light glowed in the building behind great lawn trees across the street.

"Well," said Peter, "I guess you'll be seeing some action all right, you'll be shipping out sometime. . . ."

"We had our maneuvers. We'll be shipping out pretty soon. . . ."

"That's the way it is. . . ."

"It'll be morning soon. The sun'll be coming up," said Charley. "Then I have to go back to camp. . . ."

"And I'll be taking off again. . . ."

Another soldier came by humming a song all by himself, and

disappeared across the park, his hands in his pockets, shuffling, looking around, prowling the empty night, kicking empty bottles, sighing.

"Nobody knows what to do with their leave. We were sitting just like this in a park here last month. No kidding, Petey, nobody knows what to do with their leave. There was some *twelve-year-old* kids, boys and girls, sittin' in the grass all night, gigglin' and singin' and everything—I don't know what they were doing out all night, but they were there till morning."

"It'll be morning any time now, look how gray it is over by those trees there."

"Yeah."

And behind the great trees across the street, the light glowed and burned in the windows. . . .

"What *is* that place across the street anyhow?"

"That's the Department of State or something like that. Yeah, the State Department I guess Tony said it was"—and Charley looked across the street gravely at the smudged façade of the old building.

4

THE MARTINS of Galloway, uprooted by war, had moved to New York City. The mother, so excited by this adventure, knew inscrutably as the movers unloaded her furniture from a truck in the streets of Brooklyn that she and her family were not destined to stay in the city.

"My goodness," she said to her husband, pointing to the high skyscrapers in downtown Brooklyn, "those buildings are so high they're going to fall someday. One good earthquake and it will all fall down!"

She knew a city like this could never last, but she wished somehow it could, because it was all so really delightful and splendid, and it pleased her to see it for the first time in her life. But she smiled secretly, and shrugged, and knew it could never really last.

It was October when they moved into Brooklyn, and the sun was shining russet-gold in the late afternoon. When the movers had left, George Martin, his wife, and young Mickey went out in the backyard of their new basement apartment and looked around.

An old wooden fence, or that is, two buttressed old fences, one wedged against the other and bent from behind by the pressure of built-up earth, leaned into their yard from the parking lot, and just above them flashed and glittered the bald tops of a thousand parked cars. Beyond this sea of auto-tops shining in the sun rose a great mournful structure of red brick, seemingly abandoned, with hundreds of dusty, dark windows, and curlicued eaves faded to a mouldy pale-green. One vast part of the red wall, windowless, displayed a huge advertisement, showing a man holding his head in despair. Some indistinct writing beside him, blurred and dirtied by weathers and soot, proclaimed the indispensability of some forgotten medicine. But most amazing of all was the crudeness of the drawing of the face itself and the huge hands, which showed only the faintest knowledge of line and design.

"Well, by golly, I won't be able to say that I can't see nothing outside my window on rainy days, will I, George?" laughed Marguerite, squeezing the old man's arm with delight. "That'll be my picture, I won't have to hang any on the wall."

All three of them gazed slack-jawed at this mighty portrait—this indistinct, faded, huge man holding his head in despair, as all around him, in the late afternoon of Brooklyn, there hummed and roared the multiple sounds of a great city.

"Gee!" cried Mickey, without knowing what strange excitement gripped him now.

"That big old red building looks like it was once a brewery, Marge, that's what it looks like. It's probably just a warehouse now."

"Yes, and notice the books in that window in that corner, they look like account books. There must be some old offices in that place."

They looked around at the yards of their neighbors, which were just like their yard, and the backs of their houses, which were just like the back of their own house, the wash-lines, the old fences, the black sooty drainpipes, and the dirty red-and-brown-brick look of it all which was somehow so clean and pleasant-looking in the ruddy late afternoon light of the sun. And all above this—the old brewery, the up-jutting office buildings a few blocks downtown, and the smoke curling from rooftops—soared the great golden clouds of October.

"By God!" cried the old man. "I will say this, it's certainly—it's really—big! There's a lot here a poor devil has never seen before."

"The truckdriver said the waterfront was a half a mile down the street!" said Mickey eagerly. "Let's go see the ships, huh, Pa?"

"The ships . . . You want to take a walk down there?" the old man cried.

"You two go down there now," said the mother, turning back to the house, "and I'll go in and unpack the dishes and get some kind of supper together, and when you come back we'll all have our first dinner in New York."

"By gosh, okay! Let's go, Mickey; we'll go take a gander at the waterfront and the ships!"

They went back inside the house, which was so mournfully disarrayed with piles of boxes and haphazard furniture just as the movers had left it, and stood for a while in the kitchen in silence as the mother began to unpack some boxes.

"Go ahead, go ahead," she cried, seeing them standing there, "I know where everything is and you'll only be in the way. Go down and see the boats and be sure and be back in a half an hour. And stop and buy some ice cream, why don't you, for dessert. And you can get yourself some beer, George."

"Well, okay, come on, Mick, let's go." Father and son went out and started down the street with awe.

The name of their street was State Street. As they walked along towards the waterfront, the redbrick and brownbrick houses became fewer in number until there was nothing but warehouses and old garages which had once stabled horses. When they turned into another street and turned again, they were lost momentarily, and suddenly found themselves on a height overlooking a lot of freight cars, rails, wharf sheds, and shining water by piers, and finally, the intricate topsides, stacks, and masts of great gray ships. Then they walked along a little further and came to a place where they looked up from the smoky waterfront scene, and—unbelievably—saw Manhattan itself towering across the river in the great red light of the world's afternoon.

It was too much to believe, and so huge, intricate, unfathomable and beautiful in its distant, smoking, window-flashing, canyon-shadowed realness there, and the pink light glowing on its highest crests as bottomless shadows hung draped in mighty abysms, and little things moving in millions as the eye strained to see, and the great myriads of smoke rising and puffing everywhere, everywhere, from down the shining raveled watersides on up the great flanks of city to the uppermost places—while, miraculously, way far away uptown, great October cloud-nations proceeded above the pinpoint of the Empire State Building.

Then, as by a natural impulse, and with great greed, their eyes followed the mighty swoop of Brooklyn Bridge and of Manhattan Bridge just beyond, the swoop across the river shimmering like pennies, over tiny smoking tugboats and the wakes and traceries of a hundred scows and boats and wind-ripples, to Brooklyn, to the teeming, ship-complicated, weaving, incomprehensibly ruffled water's-end and very ledge of Brooklyn.

"Aw! Well now!" cried the old man, adjusting his spectacles and staring proudly at this mighty scene, with his mouth twisted in a pathetic crooked smile—"it was almost worth it, almost worth it, to come and live out here without a cent to our name and not a friend in the world, just to see this!"

"Yeah," breathed Mickey, "gee, I guess this is the greatest city in the world."

"It's the greatest city in the world," said the old man, "but what it's like to live in it, I don't know. But when you see it like this"—and he waved his hand stiffly—"there isn't much you can say. Just think of all the people who've lived and died here . . . I guess maybe they might know. I myself certainly don't. No, I don't think I could say."

"Look!" cried the boy, pointing at Manhattan. "There's some lights starting to come on—see over there?"

And it was so: the sun was setting, leaving a huge swollen light like dark wine, and long sash-clouds the hues of velvet purple formed in apparitions above. Everything was changing, the river changing in a teeming of low colors to darkness, the abysses of the streets to darkness and a ghost-glow of lights, the pyramid structures from hard purplish stone with serried carvings of windows to a fabulous thousand-starred glitter in black steep cliffs.

"I guess we'd better go home," said the old man with a sigh.

"Let's stay and watch! It's all lighting up. Gee, what lights!"

"Yass, Mickey, lights! They've got lights in New York but they're not for people like you and me."

"Why not? Ma says we'll go to a show tomorrow night and see Broadway and all the places and eat in a restaurant."

"Yes, we can do that all right, with what little money we have we can do a few little things like that, but it'll never really be for us."

"Aw, Pa, you worry too much," laughed Mickey. He was fourteen years old now, gaunt and awkward and bashfully eager. "Ma says you worried too much about coming to New York. Look how nice it is! See?" he cried triumphantly, seeing his father's grin. "Even you know it. We can have fun here and lots to do. Boy!—the guys in Galloway wouldn't believe me when I told 'em we was moving to New York, now they know, all right!" And he thought about his chums in Galloway and what they were doing now at dusk under the trees.

"All right, Mickey, have it your way, maybe I'm just a scared old fool, maybe that's what it is."

So they walked back home along the dark bleak warehouses and by lonely arc-lights, realizing something else about New York City, and Brooklyn, the hollow streets at night, and came back to the mother in her basement apartment.

This woman had turned on the lights, swept the floor in the kitchen, rolled a bright linoleum on it, set the table with a clean white tablecloth, brewed some coffee, put out the plates, opened some cans and heated a supper. She put on a new flowery apron to celebrate, turned on the little radio, peered rapidly through her fortune-telling cards to see about the immediate future and now, as they came in lonely and dark and bewildered, she sat them down, kissed them with delighted understanding, brought the food steaming to them and bade them live, love, and abide in the earth, right there in Brooklyn.

Martin was a working man in his deepest soul. He had a new job, a nighttime job, so that on this first night of their arrival in Brooklyn, without sleep and really without more than a few coins in his pocket for coffee and sandwiches, he set out to work, to his printing job in Manhattan, with a deep and powerful joy that only working men know. Nothing in the world, no war, no city, no confusion, could alter the fact that he had a job and that he was going to it right off, into the vast complex of Manhattan streets and avenues, of which he had so little knowledge and just a vague hunch as to how to get to the printing plant that had hired him a week before. But they had hired him, he was supposed to start working that night, and he was going to work that night.

The printing plant was on Canal Street, eastward near the old abandoned city jail, in the dark, somber, ancient part of the city, near cobblestoned streets, near dark warehouses and old shoe factories, just above Chinatown and the Bowery. He had no real idea how to find his way, but he took the subway in Brooklyn. When he asked directions, men got up and peered at the subway maps, others came over to argue and shout and wave their hands as the train roared and plummeted in its black tunnel, others got disgusted with the argument and sauntered away, only to come back with a new way of putting it. They clustered around the bewildered old man, and they finally came to some sort of agreement and told him what to do.

He worked that night, and came back to Brooklyn in the dirty dawn, and saw all the scab of streets in the sickly light before sunup, the vast ruin of rooftops, the gray miles of beaten dust on sidewalks, the terrifying far-disappearing avenues reaching off towards more grayness, more alleys, more barrels and sidewalks, more bulking cities within the city, more debris and hugeness up-piled and sprawled in brick and girder, a shambles, a mournful cracked junkyard leaned non-ending in the gray world. If it were not for the fact that his wife and son were with him in this place he knew he would be like a dead man.

"Let me tell you," he told Marguerite and the boy after a few days, "not far from where I work there's the old city jail that's been abandoned, just an old broken down building, it must have been a fort or an armory once, but now it's just a big pile of stone and busted windows. But it had windows. . . . And you know what they've done, these New Yorkers? Right across the street they built a tremendous skyscraper for the police department and the district attorney's office and all that, but for the prisoners they built an underground jail, right under the street under this big beautiful new building, and it has no windows down there. They call it the Tombs."

"Why did they do that?"

And old Martin walked around on Sunday afternoons and looked at New York. On a raw November afternoon when the cold ruddy light of the sun was falling on dusty windows and streaming through El girders black with soot, he saw three old men, old Bowery bums, lying on the pavement against a wall trying to sleep, on newspapers. He stopped on the sidewalk to look at them. They looked dead, but then they stirred and groaned and turned over, just like men do in bed, and they were not dead, they were men. He thought of what must have happened to them that they slept on the pavements of November, and that their only belongings in the world were the filthy clothes that covered them. It also flashed through his mind that they were *old* men as well, rheumy-eyed, sorrowful, sixty or so, shaking with palsy, fixed against the weathers and miseries as though driven through with a spike, sprawled there for good. He had to walk away, he cried. . . .

On Hester Street he stopped with amazement as sixteen bearded Rabbis filed forth from a squalid tenement: he stopped, right in front of them, staring incredulously right into their faces: he stood there and breathed: "Good Lord-amighty!": and they filed past him deep in bearded thought, their hands clasped behind them, their heads cocked mournfully to one side, they stepped absentmindedly around smoking rubbish-fires on the sidewalk. There were sixteen of them, he counted them and could not believe it.

In front of an ornate old brownstone house on Fifth Avenue, in the late slopes of the sun, he saw a long sleek limousine pull up, and the chauffeur step out, wheeling briskly to open the door, as a butler ran out from the house wearing a derby hat. After vague incomprehensible fumblings within the funereal drapes of the back seat, he saw an old woman tottering on the edges of the runningboard, her tiny gray face lost in the folds and bulk of an enormous black chinchilla coat. He saw the two men reach out to support her, her gloved hand fluttering and failing. The two men led her into the house at an incredibly solicitous snail's-pace, as pedestrians rushed by unnoticing. He saw them labor the few steps together, someone opened the door from inside, they tottered over the threshold, and the door of the house was closed upon the red slopes of the sun.

In a cafeteria on uptown Broadway at dinnertime he entered pensively through the revolving doors. He had seen the cafeteria from outside, and people eating at tables, and he wanted to go in because it was cold outside and the street seemed suddenly deserted. Now he was shot around from behind and literally sent staggering into the place as a horde of poker-faced men and women streamed in from the street that had been empty and elbowed him as they passed. He just stood there gaping, as another fresh horde revolved in, streamed around him, jostled him, and rushed to the slot-windows and counters. Finally he ate a piece of pie sitting at a table with three other men. No one looked up or said a word, their eyes hidden beneath dark hat brims. When they had eaten they walked away, and new ones sat down silently as before.

Coming home on the subway train he sat on the hard, narrow, shelf-like seat and looked at the people with a modest, abashed, naked curiosity. They gazed through him idly, chewing gum, musing, waiting for something, for their station-stop or for someone to throw away a newspaper. He sat directly opposite a whole shelf-full of human beings and tried like them to gaze straight into space and through their faces and figures, but he could not do it.

He remembered a Negro youngster he had overheard talking in a men's room in Chicago, he suddenly thought of it now for the first time since it had happened. This boy, drunk, had been sitting on the floor in a smash of bottles, lolling and rolling his head and bleeding from some awful fight, saying: "I'm goin' to New Yawk! I been all over and I been beat aroun' and I been busted 'n' beat 'n' hauled-ass off to jail for nawthin', I been everywheah, I been all aroun'—but I ain't nevah been to New Yawk! And I'm goin' to New Yawk. Thass wheah I'm goin'—New Yawk! Yeah! NEW YAWK! *Thass* the place for me, *thass* wheah I'M goin'!"

He remembered how everyone had always talked about New York. "I hear there's plenty work down there, George, all kinds of jobs, no trouble at all!" "New York? Say now, there's one place where you can have a good time! My uncle Jerry was down there once on a weekend and you oughta hear about the hot numbers he hooked up with!" "I'd like to get out of this damn town and go someplace, New York maybe, do things in a big way. The Great White Way! Times Square! They say some of those Wall Street financiers down there started off as errand boys!" The movies about New York: Scene—Iowa City. Hero—"Darling, I know it's going to be hard for us being apart but I must go to New York and at least find out if I've got the stuff in me, just give me the chance to *find out!*" Heroine—"And if you fail, Jim, it won't make any difference to me, I'll wait for you here, always" (the waiting is always sad in Iowa). New York—the one place in all the roundaway world where everything is different from anywhere else, simply because it happens in New York.

One night, early in December, Martin stood huddled in his coat on Union Square and stared astoundedly as a man in a dirty tattered robe made a speech to a handful of shivering men. It was incredible. This poor demented man actually did look like a saint, he really wore the hairshirt of the wilderness. There he stood, a mournful ramshackle wreck of a being, bearded, rheumy-eyed, blue with cold, his mouth flapping and simpering with rubbery lips—the whole sickly ecstasy of him there on the Square beneath the sparkling towers of the city at night.

"Gentlemen," he was crying out, "your arguments do not touch me in the least, as my kingdom is not of this world, not-of-this-world!"

"What kind newspaper you got in your shoes?" cried a heckler.

"I do not read the newspapers. I know nothing of this world. I am *not* of this world. It is *not* my kingdom!"

"You can say that again!"

And they yaahed him in the cold winds.

"You there!" cried the saint, pointing at a youngster who carried books and listened in silence. "Pick up your pen, son, and write against the evil in this world. My little son and brother, if thou didst ever hold me in thine heart, absent thee from felicity awhile, and in this harsh world draw thy breath in pain, to tell my story!"

The youngster smiled thinly—he knew where those words came from—but he was moved, he stood there gazing confusedly away, almost blushing.

"And you, sir!" cried the saint, pointing straight at Martin, "pray for the deliverance of all our souls, in your heart of hearts, in the deep of your soul, pray! It is given you to pray in this world!"

The old man walked away, peeved, but he never forgot this rueful oddity of a madman with his beard and his rags and his melancholy stoop, and the mournful triumph of his great cry, right there in the streets of men—"My kingdom is not of this world."

Martin was more alone at this time of his life than he had ever been. He began to have the reveries of an irreparably lonely man. All his life he had taken it for granted that he could walk down a street and say hello and a few words to somebody he knew. Now he could only stare curiously at strangers. He began remembering, in his reveries, a particular boyhood friend from the old days in Lacoshua. He had no idea what on earth had happened to this fellow since then, but the memory of this lost friend—Shorty Houde—haunted him incessantly now whenever he walked alone down Canal Street in the black pot of night. He remembered how it used to be with Shorty—in the early morning streets of Lacoshua, Shorty would amble over, not smiling, not sullen either, just gravely puffing on his pipe, fall in step, and address him every day, almost without deviation:

"Where you headed for, Georgie me boy?"

"Oh, just going to work as usual."

"Goin' to earn your bed and vittles, hey, Georgie me boy?"

"I sure am."

"Well—I guess I'll join ye for a little perambulatin' down the streets of dear old Lacoshua-town, seein' as I'm headed for work myself." Shorty worked in the same sawmill with Martin, on the same shift, but he never mentioned that. And they would go down the empty street together without another word.

The memory of this strange, simple occurrence in his earlier life filled the old man now with a warm glow of recollection, and the thought that anybody would ever walk up to him in the gray sidewalks of New York or Brooklyn and say: "Where you headed for, Georgie me boy?" was utterly impossible, he thought of it with a grin, until the dark and serious sorrows of New York at night froze his heart and made it shrink miserably again. These were the dark last days of his life.

Yet one morning—the Saturday before Christmas—he woke up feeling fine and vigorous and looked out the window at the bright sun and the blue winter's sky and the snow. It was a splendid morning in Brooklyn. He got up and shaved, put on a clean white shirt and a new necktie, and went down to the corner store to buy a fresh cigar. And he suddenly realized that on every Saturday morning since his arrival a gray-haired old man took up his station in front of the bar and grille and began playing a cornet at ten o'clock sharp. Martin had never thought about it before, but now as the sun began to warm the streets, and people went to and fro shopping and hurrying off to the excitements of the big Brooklyn Saturday, the air rang with the sweet bugle-notes of some old song. The children flocked around the old musician and listened gravely as he blew just as gravely on the cornet, men came out of the bar and dropped dimes in his cup, and women paused with their groceries and listened with pleasure.

Back in his chair by the front window and the radio, Martin sat down, lit a deep-smelling cigar, opened the fresh pages of the *Daily Mirror*, tuned the radio to a barbershop quartet and there he stayed, comfortable, occasionally looking up at the feet of people passing on the sunny sidewalk with a new sense of order and joy. Then, as his wife moved about the kitchen preparing his breakfast, he began to smell the bacon and eggs and coffee of morning, and he thought—"Well, by God, it isn't so bad after all." And he grew hungry.

After breakfast he wandered out of the house and strolled to downtown Brooklyn, and there, around Borough Hall, he saw other men like him walking along the streets smoking cigars. He smelled the high sharp air of the harbor, he saw the great clear sunlight of winter falling on the busy streets, and he was suddenly almost glad that he lived in Brooklyn.

He strolled around, all the way to Williamsburg Bridge in the snowy streets, and found an elevated train that made the run to Manhattan.

"I never took this train, I'll try it," he said to himself absorbedly, and got on, full of the tingling joy a man has when he's off from work and just rambling around on a Saturday morning.

He thought this train would go underground at the river, but suddenly as it swooped higher near the Williamsburg Bridge, he realized that it was going to go over and soar in the morning sun. And there before his eyes again were all the waters, rooftops, streets and girders of a Brooklyn mysteriously whitened by snow.

He got off the train in Manhattan and walked around the slushy Delancey streets of winter, down mournful side-streets, over to East Broadway, down an Italianesque street, finally arriving at the broad cobblestoned way along the East River piers. And here the sudden loom of great ship's hulls stood high as though docked at the very curbstones.

He walked on, passing beneath the roaring high overpass of the Manhattan Bridge, he stared incredulously at the mountainous pylons that supported this bridge, that rose from dirty alleys as cathedrals rise from the earth, huge black stone supporting furious traffic above—and he saw the sun's winter light stream down from above in great smoky stabs.

He stood then on the corner of Charles Slip and Water Street as the sun finally disappeared behind clouds, and it began to snow again. He walked down a narrow street, filled with mute joy and sorrow because it was snowing, the air white with snow and dark with shapes and strangely silent. He came to an old building and stopped, and read the sign: "Haven Hotel, Established 1837."

He went in to an old taproom with a bare floor, spittoons, a potbelly stove burning wood, and a droning congregation of old-timers drinking beer at the bar. He ordered a beer. An old man with white hair was there singing a song, holding a beer in one hand, waving his other hand with a firm, grave, completely unselfconscious gesture of sincerity and pleased determination to sing. The others listened smiling. And Martin knew that some of these men had been drinking in this bar for almost half a century, he knew it for a certainty as he watched them. They lived somewhere in the shadow of the Bridges, they worked around here too, in old waterfront firms, and some of them had begun drinking in this bar in the 1890's of New York when the beer wagons were drawn thundering over cobbles by massive horses. They had begun drinking here after their fathers, and their fathers had been drinking in this taproom in the 1840's of New York when the waterfront streets were overspanned by jibbooms of ancient sailing ships. Martin was so certain of this.

He took off his hat and listened to the old man's song, and when it was over he bought the singer a beer and had it brought to him down the bar. They raised their glasses and drank to each other solemnly and respectfully across the room.

[2]

THERE ARE a lot of ways of traveling into New York, into the vital and dramatic heart of it—Manhattan—but only one way thoroughly reveals the magnitude, the beauty, and the wonder of the great city. This way is never taken by the spokesmen and representatives and leaders of the world, who come in airplanes and in trains. The best approach is by bus—the bus from Connecticut that comes down through the Bronx, along Grand Concourse, over to Eighth Avenue, and down Ninth Avenue to the Times Square carnival of light.

Busses coming from New Jersey or down the Hudson River drives do not penetrate by degrees into the city's heart, but suddenly emerge, either out of a tunnel or over a bridge, or out of forested parkways. But when the bus coming down from Connecticut begins to pass through places like Portchester and New Rochelle, the realization slowly occurs that these are not towns properly, but far-flung yet firmly connected doorsteps and suburbs of the great huge thing that is New York. And gradually these places are no longer vague towns, they are continuous and unending suburban sprawls. A tremendous feeling comes from this simple and terrifying fact: what vastness is this that feeds the heart in the throbbing center? How big can the city actually be? What in the world is it going to be like?

Peter Martin was traveling on this bus one rainy night in the spring of 1944, coming back from a nostalgic and sad visit to Galloway. Nothing had happened there. He had expected something intensely meaningful, dark, immense, and wonderful. Out of the sadness of his heart, he began to imagine that he had never been to New York and that he was coming into it for the first time in his life. He even selected an old woman who looked like a farmer's wife, who was riding in the same seat with him with a grin of awe and delight, as proof human and simple that coming into New York for the first time in one's life was an event of the most wonderful importance. He watched her greedily.

They came down through Mamaroneck and all the bright places, and in the soft rainy darknesses of April, they began to see apartment houses, huge ones, window-glowing in the night all around. Sometimes they saw these apartment houses where there was no town to connect them to anything. They just simply appeared, fifteen stories high with a thousand shining windows, innumerable cars parked in front, and dentists' offices and doctors' offices busy with lights. The bus would roll on and pass occasional dark parks, sometimes a field, sometimes even a farmhouse, and suddenly a roadside inn with pink neon, white gravel and parked cars, and then again the huge glowing apartment houses bulking up in the night, some of them built like forts on cliffs of rock.

Though there were more and more of these apartment houses and the distant spread of incomprehensible lights in the night rain—still they were "not anywhere near New York," according to the bus-riders who knew, they were "only in Larchmont" or "only in New Rochelle," and so on. Instead of the dazzling view of Manhattan towers in the night, there were just these same innumerable huge apartment houses standing high in the darkness with their thousands of windows, their thousands of parked cars, their unending drab shrubbery-vases in gravel courtyards.

Then bridges . . . incomprehensible bridges glistening in the rain, underpasses and overpasses, ups and downs along the crowded road, and still no dazzling Manhattan towers. Still the apartment houses—the Broadmoor, and the Cliffview, and the River Towers —but not the slightest sign of the tremendous Metropolis. The traveler in the bus grew more and more awed at the thought of the sheer numbers of people living in all the apartment houses that stretched back for miles, the uncountable nation of families that dwelled here "nowhere near New York," yet indisputably denizens and partisans of the huge unknown thing called New York.

Finally the apartment houses became so numerous and so vastly spread out in all directions that it became evident that something was coming up at last. What was this? "This is the Bronx." Peter watched greedily the grin of fascination on the old lady's face beside him. What was she thinking? Of the fabulous young Jew, Bronx-brooding and Bronx-fierce, who had written the play with that springtime yet Bronx-slain title, *Awake and Sing!?* Was she thinking about that? Why the grin of fascination and delight on her face? With her parcel of wrapped newspapers that passed for a traveling bag, with her big piano legs and her comfortable fat way of sitting back deep in the seat and possessing it whole, and her smile of delight because this was the Bronx and she was going through the Bronx at last. What was she seeing with her eyes and with her soul?

Now the bus crossed more bridges and suddenly the apartment houses loomed everywhere immediately above, and the streets were suddenly zooming by in explosions of light and traffic and thronging crowds. "We have just passed a shopping center." Some of the streets were darker than others, they merely glistened forlornly in the misty rain, cars were parked densely on each curb in the canyons between the apartment houses, a few people moved along the sidewalks, but the lights were not dazzling and many.

Then suddenly, between the apartment houses, strange tenements began to appear, darker, red-bricked, with lights in the windows that were somehow brown and dull instead of glittering bright. Then, in a flash, a great broad street exploded into view strung incredibly for a mile with lights and cars and trolleys and people, and this too disappeared, but only for a moment, as another thronging blazing street zoomed into view and passed flashing. "This is New York! O this is New York!" they thought gleefully, and Peter's old woman leaned back comfortably and began to grin a little more complacently, knowingly, with a shrewd old pleasure and joy.

But nothing changed: the tenements and the blazing crowded streets continued on and on, and this was certainly not New York. "We're still in the Bronx." So, all right, it was still the Bronx. The travelers leaned forward once more, the old lady leaned forward with a frown of perplexity, and they all searched outside through the beady panes for their New York that was not there. "Say, where the hell is it?" thought the old lady in secret.

The bus rolled on and finally began crossing great dark networks of bridges. They could see abutments and steel girders, black limbs of bridges swooping in the night, in the rain, backgrounded by a thousand scattered nonunderstandable lights, just so many swooping scaffolds and pinpoints of light everywhere. Where? What?

Then they were off the bridges and on solid ground again, and rolling fast. More dark tenements, a crowded blazing carnival scene at each corner, cars and trolleys and movie marquees, more and more of them except—well, by God—look! a million Negroes in the streets, all the Negroes in the world—fabulous and fantastic and thronging in the lights!—and what lights now! what lights! Every corner a blaze of lights and a blur of voices and klaxons and screeching trolley wheels. And one more thing!—now all the corners were absolutely square, the streets zoomed by in regular measured beats, everything was constructed in perfect squares, and such teeming tenemented carnival squares each one! It was Harlem, that's what it was! "Say—this is Harlem!" The old lady, no longer placid and grinning, leaned forward in her seat staring slack-jawed at everything that passed and blurred swiftly by her window. She even looked away for a moment to wipe her glasses, to stare appealingly at Peter, and then hunched her great bulk forward to feast her eyes on the dense blazing scenes that grew and grew in size as they plunged on.

But where were the shining towers of Manhattan?

The passengers waited as the bus lurched around a corner at a park, on a broad square lurid with marquee lights, and went roaring along the trees and by tenements on the other side. What was this? One could sense it for sure, something tremendous was coming up!

And in one brief fleeting blink of the eye, as the bus roared through the green light at 110th Street, they saw the magnificent space of Central Park West stretching almost three miles down to the glittering towers of Columbus Circle. In one instant they had seen it all! They had seen not only the tremendous "penthouses" of New York ranged along a great park boulevard, but they had seen the careful straight-distanced magnificence of Central Park and its stone walls and broad promenading pavement, they had seen a vision of one thousand yellow taxicabs speeding in the deep canyon-side by glittering penthouse fronts. This was it!

They had seen only the smoothness and swankness. Now they were going to see the unbelievable hugeness. For, as they sped down Ninth Avenue by store fronts and fruit markets and crowded tenements, as they saw the hordes of people moving about in the lights, they realized somehow that this street, as many others in New York, was as straight as an arrow, and broad and long enough to lose itself in vistas even on a clear day, and just as crowded as this on every inch of its miles.

And then they saw the cross-streets flashing by. When they saw how *these* streets, which numbered in the two hundreds, crossed seemingly endless avenues and were losing themselves over the curve of the island's rock to the east, they had a vision of hundreds of thousands, perhaps a million streetcorners in all of New York, perfectly square and measured, and each one, as well as the intervening space between corners, thronged and trafficked and peopled and furious. How could it be?

But the appalling hugeness had not revealed itself entirely. As they sped downtown past 59th Street, they began to see people in *multitudes*, they began to see a sea of heads weaving underneath lights unlike the lights they had already seen. These lights were a blazing daytime in themselves, a magical universe of lights sparkling and throbbing with the intensity of a flash explosion. They were white like the hard white light of a blowtorch, they were the Great White Way itself. And all the cross-streets were now canyons, each exploded high in the night with white light, and below were the multitudes of New York, the sea of heads, the whirlpools of traffic, the vast straggles and confusions and uproar, again and again at each block.

Was this the end of New York?

"Oh, no, this is Times Square, where we get off. But there's downtown, oh, about six miles more downtown, down to Wall Street and the financial district and the waterfront and the bridges —and then Brooklyn, you see."

And where were the sparkling towers of Manhattan now? How could they be seen when one was buried in them, how could one have possibly missed them from afar?

So Peter was back in New York that night, and it struck him with singular wondrous knowledge that this was one of the strangest and saddest moments of his life. The sight of New York now, the way it had unfolded itself in a horror of endless streets and uncomprehendable sprawl and distance, was as full of dark mystery and ghostly sorrow as the world itself—the world as it had become to him since the beginning of the war, or since some unnoticed time when he had begun to look around and say to himself: "It is not known, it is not known!"

Everything that he had ever done in his life, everything there was—was haunted now by a deep sense of loss, confusion, and strange neargrief. He had known a boy's life in Galloway, he had grown up there and played football and lived in the big house with his family, he had known all the gravities and the glees and the wonders of life. Now all that was lost, vanished, haunted and ghostly—because it was no more. And he had known youngsters like Tommy Campbell and Danny and Alexander Panos, he had known his own brothers Joe, Francis, and Charley, he had known a thousand young men like himself in Galloway who once roamed the same streets and places he roamed: but all that was lost, vanished, haunted and ghostly too—because it was no more. And there had been Liz and Ruth and Rosey, his sisters, and where were they?—what were their faces that he remembered in haunted dreams? And there had been his mother and father in the old house on Galloway Road: and now, more lost and vanished than anything could ever be, they were in Brooklyn, dark Brooklyn nearby, within a subway's distance from where he was, yet farther and more forlorn than ever.

He had gone to Galloway like a ghost and hovered there for twenty lonely hours, sitting in the Daley Square cafeteria, walking the old streets, revisiting the Monarch Theater, Galloway Road, Pine Brook and the Rooney Street saloons. He was a ghost there, and he had slept a few restless nightmare hours in the Y.M.C.A., among the angry soldiers from all over the country who had no other place to spend their leave. He had wandered among the strange men and women who had come there to work in the munition plants in the spectral night, and it was no longer Galloway, it was no longer the place of his boyhood, it too was haunted like all the world since the war—or since some time when he had begun to realize that it was not known, nothing was known.

He got off the bus at the station and sat down on a bench and watched all the others. He could think of nothing else to do, he tingled all over from sharp, pleasurable sadnesses and exciting suspenseful thoughts. He was back from a long five-month voyage to Guam and he had weeks and weeks ahead of him with nothing to do but abide and dwell on the land. He had nothing to do but go and involve himself in all the affairs and excitements and moods and glees and absorptions of his family, his friends, and his lovers in New York. It was all new . . . new seasons, a new circle of unutterable sweetness and confusion to be completed among things and people, he had known all this before and he knew that it was going to continue now with the greedy eager power of life.

He sat there in the bus station with his canvas bag between his feet—the canvas bag that had traveled with him all over the spectral prodigious world—a cigarette in his mouth, his hat pushed back on his head. He sat there thinking and looking around and expecting everything suddenly to happen: because it was joyful to realize that if there were no Galloway girls in this world now, somehow, there was Judie waiting for him that very moment as he sat in the bus station. And if there was no Alexander Panos in the world any more—(he was as lost as an autumn leaf)—if not Alex and Danny and the gang, then there were Kenneth Wood, and Leon Levinsky, and Will Dennison, his friends "waiting" in the city for him. And if there were not the father and the mother he had known as a boy in Galloway, then there were the father and mother he would know now in the city, and they were "waiting" too. Saddest of all was that when they did meet again, when they came face to face at the completion of some mysterious circle of life, what an unspeakable understanding they all had of one another!

Besides all these he knew he would meet some unknown woman; he knew in the pulse of his blood that he would meet such a woman, an inevitable woman who was "waiting" too—and he thought: "She'll just wait, she'll be there, and when I see her we'll both *know!*"

What was all the excitement and mystery and sadness in his soul? In all the world, the roaming, the going to and fro among family, friends, and lovers, he knew it was the *look* that was sad, the eyes of all human beings so enigmatical, so loathsome somehow, so wondrous and sweet. It never changed, it would always be like that. And what of himself, Peter Martin, his own nature: why was it so vast, false, complex, shifting, treacherous, saddened by the mere sight of life. Something complete, and wise, and brutal too, had dreamed this world into existence, this world in which he wandered haunted. Something silent, beautiful, inscrutable had made all this for sure, and he was in the middle of it, among the children of the earth. And he was glad.

He stood on the sidewalk, looked at the rain, and wondered: What is this rain falling on our houses and on our heads in this world, what is this rain?

[3]

HE WANDERED into Times Square. He stood on the sidewalk in the thin drizzle falling from dark skies. He looked about him at the people passing by—the same people he had seen so many times in other American cities on similar streets: soldiers, sailors, the panhandlers and drifters, the zoot-suiters, the hoodlums, the young men who washed dishes in cafeterias from coast to coast, the hitch-hikers, the hustlers, the drunks, the battered lonely young Negroes, the twinkling little Chinese, the dark Puerto Ricans, and the varieties of dungareed young Americans in leather jackets who were seamen and mechanics and garagemen everywhere.

It was the same as Scollay Square in Boston, or the Loop in Chicago, or Canal Street in New Orleans, or Curtis Street in Denver, or West Twelfth in Kansas City, or Market Street in San Francisco, or South Main Street in Los Angeles.

The same girls who walked in rhythmic pairs, the occasional whore in purple pumps and red raincoat whose passage down these sidewalks was always so sensational, the sudden garish sight of some incredible homosexual flouncing by with an effeminate shriek of general greeting to everyone, anyone: "I'm just *so* knocked out and you *all* know it, you *mad* things!"—and vanishing in a flaunt of hips.

And then the quiet men with lunchpails hurrying off to work across these blazing scenes, seeing nothing, stopping for nothing, hurrying for busses and trolleys, and vanishing. The occasional elderly gentleman wearing a look of fear and indignation at having to endure the proximity of such "riff-raff." The cops strolling by with nightsticks, stopping to chat with newsvenders and cab-drivers. The dishwashers who leaned in steamy kitchen doorways, all tattooed and muscular. The occasional crooks and thieves and murderous hoodlums who passed in silent, arrogant, gum-chewing groups.

This was the way Peter had seen it everywhere in these years of the war, but nowhere was it so dense and fabulous as on Times Square. All the cats and characters, all the spicks and spades, Harlem-drowned, street-drunk and slain, crowded together, streaming back and forth, looking for something, waiting for something, forever moving around.

Through all this passed occasional out-of-town visitors, in gaping happy families, the father and the mother grinning expectantly because "it's Times Square," and the young daughter clinging to her brother's or her fiancé's arm with gleeful excitement, and the young man himself glaring defiantly about because he burned at the thought of the word "hick" or the word "square" that must be on the minds of a thousand hoodlums.

Peter knew all these things. By this time he was on familiar terms with many of the young drifters who haunted Times Square day and night. Some of them he had met in other cities thousands of miles away but he was always certain of running into them again at Times Square in New York, the sum and crown of every marqueed square and honky-tonk street in America. It was the one part to which all the "characters" eventually migrated across the land at one time or another in their lone-wolf scattering lives. On Times Square he could meet a Norwegian seaman he had drunk with in the alleys of Picadilly, or a Filipino cook who had borrowed ten dollars from him in the Arctic Sea, or a young wrangler-poolshark he had gambled with in some San Francisco poolroom. On Times Square he would suddenly see a familiar face he had seen somewhere in the world for dead certain. It was always a wonder to see such a face and hauntingly expect to see it again years later in some other night's-market of the world.

To Peter the course of his life now seemed to cross and re-cross New York as though it were some great rail-yard of his soul. He knew that everything on earth was represented within the towering borders of New York. It thrilled his soul: but at the same time it had begun to mortify his heart.

He could stand on Times Square and watch a Park Avenue millionaire pass in a limousine at the same moment that some Hell's Kitchen urchin hurried out of its path. The gay group of young Social Register revelers piling into a cab, and some young bitter-fierce John Smith tempered by Public School No. 16 standing at a hotdog stand watching them, before going into an all-night movie to see them on the screen. The trio of influential businessmen, fresh from the convention dinner, strolling by absorbed in high conversation, and the tattered young Negro from 133rd Street dodging meekly out of their way. The meditative Communist committeeman brushing shoulders with the sullen secret Bundist from Yorkville. The Greenwich Village intellectual looking down his nose at the Brooklyn machinist reading the *Daily News.* The Broadway weisenheimer-gambler glancing at the old farmer with bundles wrapped in newspaper who gapes and bumps into everyone. The sartorial First Nighter frantically trying to hail a cab while the crowds swarm out of the second-run double-feature movie. The mellow gentleman in the De Pinna suit headed for the Ritz bar, and the mellow gentleman staggering by and sitting down in the gutter, to spit and groan and be hauled off by cops. The young Bohemian writer who couldn't pay his rent, always arguing about his art, and the sleek, smoothly-attired zooter twirling his key chain and eying the girls on the corner. The robust rosy-cheeked young priest from Fordham, with some of his jayvee basketballers on a night of "good clean fun," and the cadaverous morphine-addict stumbling by full of shuddering misery in search of a fix. The plug-ugly thuggish panhandler with the beery breath bumming a nickel from the embarrassed Methodist preacher waiting for his luggage in front of the Dixie Hotel. The hairy old Babylonian gliding lecherously towards an evening of pleasure in the Turkish Baths, and the trim little shopgirl hurrying home from work to take care of her aged father. The lissome blonde Hollywood "starlet" in dark glasses and mink in a Cadillac with her bald-headed "producer," and the two Vassar girls from Westchester with best-seller novels. Then the bleak young Negress who swept floors, in an old coat and cotton stockings, shambling along. The sad young soldier-boy, Private John Smith, U.S.A., wearing campaign ribbons, lonely and haunted, and the Lieutenant Commander, Third Naval District, Navy "E" for excellence in procurement, glancing at his watch impatiently, then waving at his blonde (he met her last month at the Waldorf bar) as she arrives in a cab, calling, "Here I am, darling!" Private Smith watched all this from the sidewalk in front of the White Rose bar and grille.

Peter watched too: he knew all these things and they were impressed in his heart, they horrified him. These were only some of the lives of the world, yet all the lives of the world came from the single human soul, and his soul was like their souls. He could never turn away in disgust and judgment. He could turn away angrily, but he would always come back and look again.

As Peter stood there, he recognized three young men strolling up the street. They were a strange trio: one was a hoodlum, one was a dope addict, and the third was a poet.

The hoodlum—Jack—was a sleek, handsome youngster from Tenth Avenue, who claimed that he was born "on a barge in the East River" eighteen years before. He was well-dressed, seemingly composed in his bearing and quiet, almost dignified, in his manner. It was only that he could never concentrate; he was always looking around as though anticipating something. His eyes were hard and blank, almost elderly in their stony meaningless calm. He talked in a swift, high-pitched, nervous voice, and kept looking away stonily, twirling his key chain.

The dope addict, whose only known name was Junkey, was a small, dark, Arabic-looking man with an oval face and huge blue eyes that were lidded wearily always, with the huge lids of a mask. He moved about with the noiseless glide of an Arab, his expression always weary, indifferent, yet somehow astonished too, aware of everything. He had the look of a man who is sincerely miserable in the world.

The poet—Leon Levinsky—had been a classmate of Peter's at college, and was now a merchant seaman of sorts, sailing coastwise on coalboats to Norfolk or New Orleans. He was wearing a strapped raincoat, a Paisley scarf, and dark-rimmed glasses with the air of an intellectual. He carried two slim volumes under his arm, the works of Rimbaud and W. H. Auden, and he smoked his cigarette stuck in a red holder.

They came along the sidewalk, Jack the hoodlum swaggering slowly, Junkey padding along like an Arab in the Casbah, and Leon Levinsky, lip-pursing, meditative, absorbed in thought, twinkling along beside them with his Charley Chaplin feet flapping out, puffing absently on the cigarette-holder. They strolled in the lights.

Peter walked up and greeted them.

"So you're back finally!" cried Levinsky, grinning eagerly. "I've been thinking of you lately for some reason or other—actually I guess it's because I've so much to tell you!"

"Why don't we go and sit down?" proposed Junkey wearily. "Let's sit in the cafeteria window there and we can talk and keep an eye on the street."

They went in the cafeteria, got coffee, and sat down by the windows, where Junkey could resume his pale vigil of Forty-Second Street—a vigil that went on a good eighteen hours a day, and sometimes, when he had no place to sleep, twenty-four hours around the clock. It was the same with Jack—the same anxious vigil of the street, from which the watchers of the Street could never turn their eyes without some piercing sense of loss, some rankling anguish that they had "missed out" on something. Junkey always sat facing the street, and when he talked, sometimes with intense earnestness, his eyes kept nevertheless going back and forth as he combed the street sweepingly under drooping eyelids. Even though Peter and Leon Levinsky sat with their backs to the window, they could not help turning now and then just to see.

Leon Levinsky was about nineteen years old. He was one of the strangest, most curiously exalted youngsters Peter had ever known. He was not unlike Alexander Panos, in a sense, and Peter had been drawn to him for this reason. Levinsky was an eager, intense, sharply intelligent boy of Russian-Jewish parentage who rushed around New York in a perpetual sweat of emotional activity, back and forth in the streets from friend to friend, room to room, apartment to apartment. He "knew everybody" and "knew everything," was always bearing tidings and messages from "the others," full of catastrophe. He brimmed and flooded over day and night with a thousand different thoughts and conversations and small horrors, delights, perplexities, deities, discoveries, ecstasies, fears. He stared gog-eyed at the world and was full of musings, lip-pursings, subway broodings—all of which rushed forth in torrents of complex conversation whenever he confronted someone. He knew almost everyone Peter knew, a few thousand others Peter did not know. Like young Panos, Leon Levinsky was also likely to show up suddenly morose and brooding, or simply disappear from the "scene" for months and Peter liked that too. He lived alone in some rooming house downtown. Before that he had lived with his family in the Lower East Side, where he had read a thousand books late at night and dreamed of becoming a great labor leader someday. That was all over with now, that was his "poor little Jew's past," as he put it.

"But just one thing, Pete," said Levinsky now, holding his chin judiciously and gazing at Peter with glittering eyes, "I wanted to talk to you about that Alexander friend of yours, the poet in the Army who sends you his social conscience bleatings about the brotherhood of man. I wanted to ask you not to class me with that—that sentimental fool, you might say. Don't be offended. As a matter of fact I understand and even appreciate your reverence for him—which is so *gone* for a person like you, really. On top of that I'm even honored that you should consider me an Alexander. But there are things so much more important now, at least more complex and interesting and illuminated you see, really, things going on right now, more penetrating and more intelligent somehow than your Alexander, your smalltown Rupert Brooke, your joy-and-beauty poet of the hinterlands—"

But Peter was about three years older than Levinsky and therefore he listened to all this with smiling indulgence. The young hoodlum Jack never had any idea what Levinsky was talking about, he just sat and looked around. Junkey, with his eyes sarcastically lidded, his mouth turned down at the corners in a mask-like expression of weary indifference and misery, listened to everything with earnest attentiveness and knowledge. He was wise in his own right.

Ever since Peter had known Levinsky, it was a matter of listening to his gentle torrential chastisements about his own ignorance and blindness to things. Levinsky was always urging him to "get psychoanalyzed" or to "come down" from his "character heights" and so on—a continual attempt to convert him to his, Levinsky's, point of view, for what reasons Peter could never understand.

"I do admit that there's a certain dignity to your soul," said Levinsky, jiggling his knee, "but it's not a sadness of understanding, it's really a neurotic failure to see yourself clearly. One more thing, Pete, I wanted to ask when I can meet your family, I'd like to meet your father again and some of your brothers . . . especially Francis.

"And now," he went on in the same breath, sticking a fresh cigarette in the holder, "I must tell you everything." He lit the cigarette avidly. "A lot of things have been happening since you've been gone. I see quite a bit of Judie—your Judie—and sometimes she is most charming to me, although for the most part she is not. I've had many long conversations with Kenneth Wood—yes, I know him now, I met him through Dennison: and of course

I've got so much to tell you about Dennison, but first we'll talk of Kenneth Wood. In the first place I wanted to ask you a few questions about him: you met him in the merchant marine, didn't you? I want to know what kind of family he has."

After months at sea Peter was only too pleased to supply the necessary fuel for Levinsky's talk. "I've been to Kenny's house only once and I met his father and great-grandmother. The old lady is close to a hundred years old and she still remembers old Abilene—"

"What is that?" demanded Levinsky, impatient and curious.

"That's where they made their fortune, way back. It's an old cow-town in Kansas . . . it was very wild in those days."

"Oh, never mind that nonsense. I want to know about *them*—I want something intelligent—"

"I'm telling you! His father is a handsome sort of man-about-town who's in some business on Wall Street. His mother's divorced and remarried to an Austrian count. How's that?"

"Hmm," mused Levinsky. "Then they still have money. Where do they live, what kind of a place is it?"

"It's an apartment towers on the East River, swanky as hell."

"What's his father like? What does he *think?*"

"How should I know!"

"The grandmother, the grandmother!" cried Levinsky—"what's *her* value, what's her vision, give me *information!*"

"Man, how annoying you do get!" spoke up Junkey suddenly with an earnest glance at Levinsky. "Give him a chance to get his bearings, the guy's been at sea, he's trying to relax and enjoy himself, ever since we've been sitting here you've been telling him what's wrong with him"—and with this Junkey returned his agonized gaze to the window.

"That's true," admitted Levinsky, deeply absorbed, "but it's somehow beside the point." And he suddenly giggled again, but in a moment fixed Peter with his beady glittering eyes. "I don't suppose you've ever heard of Waldo Meister?"

"A little . . . not much."

"Waldo Meister is a dilettante. It seems that he is a friend of Kenneth's family, a friend of his father's through some old business matters. They're *all rich,* don't you see!"

"Who?"

"Kenny and his family, Waldo Meister, and, of course, Dennison—all these evil figures of decayed families."

"What's evil about them?"

"I shall tell you, but first:—it seems that Waldo is a rare and curious person. He has only one arm. He's ugly, quite horrible, but impressive sort of. That is, impressive to everyone but Kenny Wood, who is eviler than Waldo somehow."

"What are you raving about!" cried Peter, frowning. "I shipped out with Kenny Wood, he's just a happy-go-lucky kid. What are you trying to say?"

"Don't give me that simple stuff. Nothing is simple, everything is complex and evil and audacious too . . . and that goes for your Kenny Wood. And let's not start arguing about simple normal happy-go-lucky Americans. Let me talk. Waldo is an execrable man straight out of some fin-de-siècle romance, a decaying Dorian Gray, a monster, and finally, a magician of darkness.—I'm using these symbols in a poem incidentally—an evil magician surrounded by the decline of the West on all sides . . . despised like Philoctetes, avoided, yet hypnotic and compelling . . . a doctor of horror, an organ-grinder of the angels surrounded by the vulgar pigeons of the West."

"What's all this?"

"I'm just amusing myself. To continue: out of the pure madness of his position in the world, this amazing Waldo Meister has turned right around to foist an even greater madness upon the world. There being only one person in the world who openly berates him for his physical disability, who openly despises him, mocks him, taunts him—your so-called simple-kid Kenny Wood—Waldo turns right around and refuses the company of anyone else but Kenny himself. A really sordid yet angelic situation. Strange angels."

"Kenny wouldn't mock a cripple. Who *is* this man?"

"I was coming to that. Before Waldo lost his arm in an automobile crackup, he was a close friend of Dennison's, they went to the same private school together, later to Princeton, they knew Kenny through his father, who was a gay blade and was everywhere, and when Kenny began drinking as a youngster he went out on binges with them. He was driving the car one night drunk, only about fourteen years old, and cracked it up somewhere in Long Island, and one of the girls in the party almost died from injuries."

"I never knew about that crackup. I knew Kenny was a wild

guy but I never knew about this Waldo guy," uttered Peter vaguely.

"Can't you see what an amazing situation it is?—Kenny is responsible for Waldo's physical defect, and he mocks him for it, and Waldo accepts his mockery with gratitude almost. It's the most evil and symbolic and decadent situation!—amazing! But I have a million other things to tell you, it all fits into the picture, a great canvas of disintegration and sheer horror. Right across the street from here there's an amusement center—see it there?" he pointed eagerly. "It's called the Nickel-O, see the big sign?—and there you have, at around four in the morning, the final scenes of disintegrative decay: old drunks, whores, queers, all kinds of characters, hoods, junkies, all the castoffs of bourgeois society milling in there, with nothing to do really but just stay there, sheltered from the darkness as it were.

"You see how bright the lights are?—they have those horrible bluish neons that illuminate every pore of your skin, your whole soul finally, and when you go in there among all the children of the sad American paradise, you can only stare at them, in a Benzedrine depression, don't you see, or with that sightless stare that comes from too much horror. All faces are blue and greenish and sickly livid. In the end, everyone looks like a Zombie, you realize that everyone is dead, locked up in the sad psychoses of themselves. It goes on all night, everyone milling around uncertainly among the ruins of bourgeois civilization, seeking each other, don't you see, but so stultified by their upbringings somehow, or by the disease of the age, that they can only stumble about and stare indignantly at one another."

"A mad description of the Nickel-O if I ever heard one," remarked Junkey with approval.

"But there's more to it than that!" cried Levinsky, almost jumping up and down. "Under the bluish lights you're able to see all the defects of the skin, they all look as though they're falling apart." He giggled here. "Really! You see monstrous blemishes or great hairs sticking out of moles or peeling scars—they take on a greenish tint under the lights and look really frightful. Everybody looks like a *geek!*"

"A geek?"

"The drunkards or addicts or whatnot who eat the heads off live chickens at carnivals . . . didn't you ever hear about geeks? Oh, the whole point's there!" he cried happily. "Everybody in the world has come to feel like a geek . . . can't you see it? Can't you sense what's going on around you? All the neurosis and the restrictive morality and the scatological repressions and the suppressed aggressiveness has finally gained the upper hand on humanity—everyone is becoming a geek! Everyone feels like a Zombie, and somewhere at the ends of the night, the great magician, the great Dracula-figure of modern disintegration and madness, the wise genius behind it all, the Devil if you will, is running the whole thing with his string of oaths and his hexes."

"I don't know," said Peter. "I don't believe I feel like a geek yet. I don't think I'll buy that."

"Oh, come, come! Then why do you have to mention it, why do you have to deny it?" grinned Levinsky slyly. "Really, now, I know you, I can tell that you have horrible guilt-feelings, it's written all over you, and you're confused by it, you don't know what it is. Admit it at least. As a matter of fact you told me once yourself."

"Admit what?"

"That you feel guilty of something, you feel unclean, almost diseased, you have nightmares, you have occasional visions of horror, feelings of spiritual geekishness— Don't you see, everybody feels like that now."

"I have a feeling like that," stammered Peter, almost blushing, "that is . . . of being guilty, but I don't know, it's the war and everything, I think, the guys I knew who got killed, things like that. And well, hell!—things aren't like they used to be before the war." For a moment he was almost afraid that there was some truth in Levinsky's insane idea, certainly he had never felt so useless and foolish and sorrowful before in his life.

"It's more than *that*," pursued Levinsky with a long, indulgent, sarcastic smile. "You yourself have just admitted it now. I've been making a little research of my own, I find that everybody has it. Some hate to admit it, but they finally reveal that they have it. He-he! And it's amazing who discovered this disease—"

"What disease?"

At this, Levinsky and Junkey exchanged secret smiles, and turned them upon the bewildered Peter. "It's the great molecular comedown. Of course that's only my own whimsical name for it at the moment. It's really an atomic disease, you see. But I'll have to explain it to you so you'll know, at least. It's death finally reclaiming life, the scurvy of the soul at last, a kind of universal cancer. It's got a real medieval ghastliness, like the plague, only this time it will ruin everything, don't you see?"

"No, I don't see."

"You will eventually. Everybody is going to fall apart, disintegrate, all character-structures based on tradition and uprightness and so-called morality will slowly rot away, people will get the hives right on their hearts, great crabs will cling to their brains . . . their lungs will crumble. But now we only have the early symptoms, the disease isn't really underway yet—virus X only."

"Are you serious?" laughed Peter.

"Perfectly serious. I'm positive about the disease, the real physical disease. We all have it!"

"Who's we?"

"Everybody—Junkey and me, and all the cats, more than that, everybody, you, Kenny, Waldo, Dennison. Listen! You know about molecules, they're made up according to a number of atoms arranged just so around a proton or something. Well, the 'just-so' is falling apart. The molecule will suddenly collapse, leaving just atoms, smashed atoms of people, nothing at all . . . as it all was in the beginning of the world. Don't you see, it's just the beginning of the end of the Geneseean world. It's certainly the beginning of the end of the world as we know it now, and then there'll be a non-Geneseean world without all that truck about sin and the sweat of your brow. He-he! It's great! Whatever it is, I'm all for it. It may be a carnival of horror at first—but something strange will come of it, I'm convinced. But these are my own ideas and I'm deviating from the conception we've all reached about the atomic disease." He mused with perfect seriousness.

"Listen, Leon, why don't you go back to becoming a radical labor leader," laughed Peter.

"Oh, it all ties in. But wait, I wasn't finished. The Nickel-O has become a great symbol among all of us, it's the place where the atomic disease was first noticed and from which it will spread, slowly and insidiously, that place there across the street!" he cried gleefully. "You'll see great tycoons of industry suddenly falling apart and going mad, you'll see preachers at the pulpit suddenly exploding—there'll be marijuana fumes seeping out of the Stock Exchange. College professors will suddenly go cross-eyed and start showing their behinds to one another. I'm not explaining it properly . . . but that doesn't matter, you'll begin to see it yourself, now that you're back. And now," he resumed gravely, "I wanted to tell you about Dennison. Incidentally he wants to see you, he heard your ship was back, go see him tomorrow. Dennison, I must tell you, has dropped his old habits of going to a psychoanalyst and idly biding his time learning jiu-jitsu and so on, and has begun an active participation in the phantasmagoria of modern life."

"What's he done?"

"He's got a morphine habit. He's moved to a new apartment now, down on Henry Street, right under the Manhattan bridge, a dirty old cold water flat with peeling disintegrating walls. His sister Mary's there with him taking care of the baby. Junkey sometimes lives there too"—and he bowed to Junkey graciously—"and the whole place is mad day and night, overrun with people who dash about getting morphine prescriptions from dishonest doctors. Mary takes Benzedrine, there's a mad character called Clint who comes around all the time with marijuana, and the whole place is a madhouse. You've got to see it—especially Dennison with his baby son in one hand and a hypo needle in the other, a marvelous sight."

"You don't really think it's marvelous. Incidentally, how's Dennison's wife coming along?"

"No—it's more than marvelous, really, and besides I've been talking to you almost maliciously all this time, insincerely in a way, of course. Oh, his wife's supposed to be dying now . . . she's still in that sanitarium in California or someplace. We've got to have a long serious talk, alone. That's another thing. Where are you going now, what are you going to do tonight?" Levinsky demanded eagerly.

"I'm going right up to Judie's."

"But we must talk. When? when?—and remember, I want to meet your family. Can't I go to dinner there sometime? There are so many things to settle, everything's happening, everything's changing—and also I want you to read some of my new poetry, and I want you to come in the Nickel-O with me some night so I can point everything out to you in its proper order."

"Well, all right," agreed the amenable Peter. He got up to go, but Levinsky jumped up solicitously.

"You're not leaving now, are you?" he cried.

"Yeah, I'm going to see my gal now. . . ."

"Ah! I knew something like that was coming, something about peace and normalcy and whatever else you may call it. . . ."

Peter looked gravely at him.

"Oh, never mind," snickered Levinsky. "So you're going to see Judie and forget all about the atomic disease in her arms. Actually, don't you see, I'm all in favor of it, I still believe in human love at the ends of the night. But may I ride on the subway with you?" he asked.

"It's okay with me," said Peter, who was growing more and more sullen at these sly manipulations. On the other hand, Levinsky had been like this ever since Peter had known him, and he understood somehow.

"You *do* feel like a geek, don't you?" Peter smiled. "But you know all the things you're talking about, people don't want them! They want peace and quiet . . . even if those things don't exist. Everybody's trying to be decent, that's all."

Levinsky was aroused with interest. "Let them *try!*" he brought out with an imitation of a snarl, and a malicious-looking smile—a smile he had learned from Dennison.

"There you go imitating Will Dennison again!" Peter taunted.

"Nonsense, my days of sitting at Dennison's feet are over—the position is almost reversed, in a sense. He listens to my ideas now with great respect, where it used to be just the other way around. Pete," said Levinsky eagerly, "wait for me just a minute while I make a phone call. I'll ride on the subway with you for a very specific reason—I want to prove to you that everyone is mad on the subway. Everybody's radioactive and don't know it." And with this he rushed off eagerly.

At that moment someone went by on the sidewalk. Junkey, starting with a jump, suddenly vanished from the cafeteria, almost before Peter noticed it.

The young hoodlum Jack leaned forward to Peter confidentially. "Junkey's connection just went by outside, the guy he buys the dope from. I don't go for that stuff, it costs too much, you get all hung up on it, then you're sick all the time when you can't get it." There was almost a note of conspiracy in these words, the first he had spoken all night. Now that they were alone at the table, the young hoodlum had grown quite voluble. "I tried it once, it gave me a good kick, but then I got sick and I puked. I like to drink myself, to get lushed . . . don't you?" he demanded anxiously, peering at Peter blankly. "Listen, you know? I got something on the fire that if it comes out right I'll never have to worry about money again, I'll be all set, man. A plan, you know?"

"Uh-huh," said Peter vaguely.

Jack gave him a significant look, paused awhile looking over his shoulder. Then he leaned forward, almost whispering. "I know a guy, see, and, well, last week I picked up on a sap from him, a blackjack unnerstand? So then I—well, you know what these guys are always talking about, that kid Levinsky, that's all right, you know?—sit around and talk and pass the time of day. But I believe in doin' something, you know? Action! They talk all the time, him and Junkey. But I met this guy in a bar, this is the plan I'm telling you, and this guy claims he's got all his money stashed in his room up in the Bronx, money and lots of suits and shoes and everything. The guy was drunk, and he's from out of town, lonesome, a shipyard worker, all that. Shipyard workers are always lonesome," he added vaguely. "I used to work in a shipyard myself, but I don't like to work, you know? . . . I don't dig guys tellin' me what to do all the time. I told him, this shipyard worker, I could fix him up with girls, see?" He paused significantly.

"Can you?" grinned Peter—who had never seen him with a girl. He was always standing around the street ruefully looking at girls swinging by under the lights.

"Well, sure, man—I know hundreds of 'em," Jack cried almost resentfully. "Girls! I know a guy who's got a way with 'em, you know?—a pimp the guy is. Well, on Saturday night I'm gonna go up there to this shipyard worker's house, with a girl I know, and beat him up and walk out with all his money and clothes. I won't even bring the blackjack, I'll just crack him a couple with my fists"—and he bared his fists from under the table and showed them to Peter. "That's all, man, that's the way I'll do it, I'll belt him a couple! wham! wham! I got it all figured out, one in the solar plexus, one on the point of the chin. Then I can kick him in the neck too . . . that knocks out a guy, you know?" he whispered earnestly. Then, confidentially: "Did you ever fight a guy? Did you ever knock out a guy? My brother's a great fighter, you know? How about comin' up there with me tomorrow night?" he concluded nervously, looking around the cafeteria over his shoulder.

Before Peter could muster up any sort of reply, Levinsky came rushing back. They left Jack sitting alone, worrying and brooding anxiously, and went out to take the subway.

"Everyone's mad around here," commented Peter sullenly, with a sense of foolish loneliness.

"But that's not the half of it! Just *wait* till you see my subway experiment which proves conclusively that the atomic disease has already made great headway!"

"You're not serious about all this, Leon! What the hell's happened to you?" cried Peter, exasperated.

For the first time that evening Levinsky grew serious, or seemed to, pursing his lips judiciously, glancing at Peter gravely and nodding his head. "Yes, I'm serious, but only in a way you see—"

"Only in a way—bull!"

"But no. Actually, you see, in a sense it's the invention of Dennison's sister Mary. There's no doubt about the fact that Mary Dennison is mad, but that's only because she wants to be mad. What she has to say about the world, about everybody falling apart, about everybody clawing aggressively at one another in one grand finale of our glorious culture, about the madness in high places and the insane disorganized stupidity of the people who let themselves be told what to do and what to think by charlatans —all that is true! All the advertising men who dream up unreal bugaboos for people to flee from, like B.O. or if you don't have such-and-such a color to your wash you're an outcast from society. Listen!—all the questionnaires you have to fill out in this bureaucratic system of ours asking all kinds of imaginary questions. Don't you see it, man? The world's going mad! Therefore it's quite possible there *must be* some sort of disease that's started. There's only one real conclusion to be drawn. In Mary's words, everybody's got the atomic disease, everybody's radioactive."

"It's a dumb conclusion," muttered Peter. "I wish you'd be serious."

"The amazing thing is this!" cried Levinsky gaily. "All the horror that Mary Dennison sees, and incidentally participates in—and there's more horror in that girl and in her view of the clawing world than Dennison himself ever dreamed in his greatest heroic moments—the amazing thing is that it all might be *awfully* true. Now I'm serious. Supposing it were! supposing it were! what then?"

"That's silly," muttered Peter again.

"But wait! There's a lot more to it!"

They were in the subway station. Levinsky picked out an old newspaper from a trash barrel and began folding it and tearing out sections, with a grave air, glancing slyly at Peter as he did all this.

"What does this remind you of?" he demanded.

"What?"

"This!—tearing and folding this old newspaper, haven't you ever seen mad people, how they behave?"

"Yes," laughed Peter, suddenly inexplicably amused by the performance, "that's pretty good."

When a train pulled in, they got on, and Levinsky stationed Peter at the door to keep a sharp eye on everyone in the car. "Remember," he instructed gleefully, "you watch closely anybody I pick on with my . . . my magical newspaper performance. With both you and I staring at the victim, he'll begin to feel vibrations of paranoid persecution. You'll see how everyone has become essentially mad—the whole insane world." He flung his arms around with a look of rapture. "Now watch."

Levinsky sat down, wild-eyed and fantastic in his military raincoat and flowery scarf, and the train got underway on the express run up to Seventy-Second Street. He sat opposite a distinguished-looking old man who had a little boy of four with him—a melancholy severe old man staring meditatively into space, full of stately thoughts, and a gleeful little child looking around at everyone with curiosity. They sat there holding hands as the train rocked along.

Levinsky opened up his newspaper and seemed to begin reading it, but suddenly Peter realized with horror that there was a hole torn in the middle of the page, through which the incredible Levinsky was intently studying the old man across the aisle. At first no one noticed anything. But gradually, of course, the old gentleman's eyes roved to Levinsky's newspaper. There, with an awful shock, instead of headlines he saw a great living picture, the beady glittering eyes of a madman burning triumphantly into his through a hole in the page.

Peter saw the old man flush. He himself had to turn away, blushing furiously with mortification. Yet at the same time he felt a wicked and delightful sense of pleasure. He had to watch, and he peeked around the door in a convulsion of horror and glee. What was most incredible and funny was that Levinsky himself continued to stare—through the hole—intently at the old man with perfect gravity and seriousness, as though he believed with his whole heart in the full significance of his experiment.

To cap everything, just as everyone across the aisle was beginning to notice Levinsky's stupendous act—and indeed, just as they began to fidget nervously, and look around furtively, sometimes glancing over to Peter as though they sensed his conspiracy in the matter (though he tried to look innocent and unconcerned), just as they were beginning to look to each other for confirmation of the fact that it was Levinsky who was mad, not *they*—the madman himself with delicate propriety, pleasure, and gentle absorption, began tearing strips out of the newspaper and dropping them to the floor one by one from gentle fingers. Meanwhile he smiled fondly at the page, never looking away, but eager, intense, pleased, and preoccupied with what he was doing, alone in the joys of pleasant perusal.

It was the maddest thing Peter had ever seen. Levinsky was perfect in his performance, solemn and serious. For just a moment he looked up from what he was doing to stick his forefinger in his ear and hold it there in deep thought, as if his brains might come spilling out if he didn't hold them in.

It was even more horrible to realize the small pitiable truth in his statement that everyone in the subway was somewhat insane. Some who noticed what Levinsky was doing looked away nervously and preferred to imagine that nothing at all was happening; they were perfectly stolid in their refusal of the situation, they sat like stones and brooded. Others were irritable and undertook every now and then to glance suspiciously at the performance; they seemed indignant and refused to look any more, they would not "be tricked" as Levinsky considered it. And there were those in the car who simply did not notice; they were coming home from work too tired to notice anything. Some were reading the paper, others were sleeping; some were chatting eagerly, others were just brooding without having looked, and others thought that he was some harmless nut and paid no attention.

There was one element Levinsky had not bargained for—the people in the car who had a profound curiosity and everlasting concern with things and a sense of funniness. All these elements, including the old gentleman's little companion, a Negro coming home from work, an eager young student, and a well-dressed man carrying a box of candy, stared with delight at Levinsky's antics. The old gentleman, who was the direct victim of the performance, was too painfully involved in the personal aspects of the matter to make up his mind whether it was funny, or absurd, or horrible:

he was fixed by a pair of mad burning eyes and could only look away with deep embarrassment.

Meanwhile he held on to the little boy's hand, almost frightened for his sake now, and certainly confused, while the little boy stared gape-jawed at Levinsky.

"What's he doing?" he cried, turning to the old man.

The old man shook his head warningly, tightening his grip on the little hand. The little boy was fidgety, and sat with his feet up on the seat gazing almost solemnly at Levinsky.

Suddenly the little boy unleashed a crazy screaming laugh and bounced off the seat across the aisle and stuck his face in the hole in the newspaper and began staring pop-eyed at Levinsky with huge delight, knowing it was a game, jumping up and down and clapping his hands and giggling with glee, and crying: "Do some more, mister. Hey, do some more!"

And at this, the eager young student, the Negro man, and the man with the box of candy all smiled and chuckled heartily, even Peter doubled up laughing helplessly—and then it was altogether too much. Levinsky himself became embarrassed, looked bashfully around the car at all the faces, blushed, stared sad-eyed at the mess he had made on the floor, snickered, and looked helplessly towards Peter. The whole experiment became disorganized. Others in the car who had been frightened or indignant a moment before began to laugh also. Everybody was grinning and craning and looking around and sensing something funny. Peter, like the rat deserting the sinking ship, hurried into the next car and hid himself in a corner and tried to keep from exploding. Once he peeked back to see Levinsky sitting there among all those people, absently musing.

He met the sad, subdued Leon Levinsky on the platform when they got to Seventy-Second Street.

"But don't you see, Pete, it all worked out the way I told you," he said, fingering his lips, "except for the little kid. Actually though," he reflected seriously, "it was in a way beautiful, because it showed that children cannot recognize madness. That is, they understand what is mad and what is not mad, they simply *understand*. And finally—they haven't had time to burden themselves with character structure and personality armors and systems of moral prejudice and God knows what. Therefore they're free to live and laugh, and free to love—like those few other men in the car."

Peter gazed at him with amazement.

Levinsky went back to the downtown side of the platform—while Peter had to go uptown to see Judie. When he last saw him, Levinsky was standing there among the subway crowds, gaping around and musing darkly about the puzzle of himself and everybody else, as he would always do.

[4]

JUDIE SMITH had an apartment on 101st Street, not far from Columbus Avenue, near the wild Spanish neighborhoods, yet within a short distance of the Irish tenements and saloons of Amsterdam, the blazing kosher-marts, hotels, and movie theaters of Upper Broadway, and the sleek towers of Central Park West. The park itself was nearby, big and doleful and gardened inside the walls of the city rising seven miles around it.

She lived six flights up in neatly furnished rooms, where she occasionally hid herself for days, knitting and thinking darkly with the terror of a child. Sometimes she worked as a model, or as a cigarette-girl in a night club, at one time as a girl longshoreman on the docks, but mostly she lived on her aunt's allowance checks from Philadelphia, and "waited" for something. She was furiously involved with Peter now, she was "waiting" for him.

It had begun raining hard, and Peter was dripping with rain when he got to her door. He smiled happily, took her in his arms and put his cheek against hers. He wanted to say everything he could think of saying, all in one instant, all about Galloway and what had happened there and all about the sadness of the bus and his thoughts, and Levinsky. But he only kissed her and turned away mournfully. "Honest, Judie, I had a lousy trip, I don't know why I went. You were right, I should have stayed here."

"Did you *just* get back?" Judie demanded, peeking around at him as he brooded, and finally putting her arms around him again and shivering against him.

"Just now, two hours ago. Why?" he grinned.

"Oh—just wondering. I thought maybe you went to Brooklyn to see your parents again." She brought that out with a curl of her lips, but suddenly bit her fingernails and looked flustered again. She loved Peter in a furious way.

"No, I didn't go and see the folks yet, are you satisfied? And *now* what's wrong? What are you so scared about tonight?"

"Scared?" she asked dumbly.

"What'd you do, buy another expensive fur rug with the dough I left?"

"Oh, no, nothing like that!" she cried joyfully, yet wincing a little at the sight of him. "Well, actually—no, wait, you take your shower first and I'll make you some coffee and give you a sandwich, and when you're all dry and clean and fed, I'll tell you."

Peter yawned and pretended that he didn't care, and went in and took his shower. When he came out she was sitting stiffly and primly on the edge of the couch with a look of new contented joy. She had a letter on her knees, and the sandwiches and coffee on a tray beside her.

"Petey, it's awful. While you were taking your shower, I've been trying to figure out what to say to you, one by one I tried to figure it all out—"

"Go ahead and tell me what it is, whatever you bought I don't care!" he laughed.

"No, no, no! Nothing like that!" she scoffed darkly. "I forgot all about *that*. This is something else. Petey, it's something else," she pleaded, "it's everything about us. I wanted to tell you everything! Do you realize that I knew that you were coming back this very night just because it was raining? You always come back when it's raining. . . . I knew you were coming, honest I did, so I sat down and wrote you a letter you could read when you walked in. Yes! And also I had it all figured out what I'd say to you—but, Petey, when you actually walked in, I didn't know what to do. I was cold and I trembled. Did you notice me tremble?" she cried anxiously.

Peter sat on a chair directly in front of her and gazed at her. "Yes," he grinned.

"But don't look at me like that, you make me bashful, Petey!"

"I'm not looking at you like *that!*" he cried, peeved.

"Petey!" she blurted, "I wanted to tell you I love you, but in a big nice way like in the books you made me read. In this letter I wanted to tell you how I feel deep down inside when I think of you, how it hurts! It hurts!"

Peter turned around in the chair and stared down at the floor. "The world isn't as sad as *that*," he spoke up finally. "Everybody's bats around here and I'm the battiest," he added mournfully, and he really felt that.

"Oh, I wish I could feel like we used to back home," she cried. "We used to go on wild rides in cars and go skating in the winter. All the boys wanted to do was neck, everything was so simple. That's the way you were, Petey—only you buried it, huh? The first time I met you that night, when you wore your bow tie and that sharp sport jacket, I fell in love with you. That bow tie!—You were so good-looking and sexy and collegiate. But nothing ever *happens!*" she cried contemptuously. "What a crazy place New York is. Nobody ever does anything, all they do is talk, nobody ever *plays* any more. We used to just drink and sit around, burping, back home at big beer parties. That's true, you know!" she cried sheepishly when Peter laughed. "There's something to that, it's not so silly as it sounds. You *know*, the high school crowd."

"I know, I know."

"I hate all these intellectuals around here. Why do you have to hang around with intellectuals?"

"Who's an intellectual?"

"Everybody's always talking about Rimbaud or something. Kenny Wood and Jeanne and Dennison and all *them*. I want fun, good things to eat, rushing around, beer! Don't you see all that, Petey? Didn't you ever do things like that?"

"Of *course* I did."

"What did you do with that bow tie? You never wore it since. All you wear now is dirty old sloppy clothes, khaki pants, and that old black jacket. But I like that jacket, it's you. But the bow tie, why don't you wear it again? Petey, let's dress up real sharp sometime and go out and eat lobster in a seafood place and go to a dance or something, or go riding with somebody, and laugh and sing with everybody and get plastered." She jumped gleefully on his lap. "You know what we used to do? We used to have a whole crowd and everybody who didn't belong to the crowd were frumps, that's what we called them. We used to yell out 'Hey, Frump!' or 'Hey, Cherry!' That was our yell. You never knew Bob Randall, he was so funny! He used to go up to old women and say 'Good afternoon, Mrs. Boonyak, how is Mr. Boonyak'—all kinds of things like that in Philly."

"Well, the kids around here aren't like that," said Peter absent-mindedly. "They've got more on their minds."

"Huf! Lot they know! All they can do is talk about books. They don't know how to have a good time. I hate everybody!" she concluded darkly, and pouted. She went to a dresser and took out a ball of wool from a knitting basket.

"What's that you're knitting?"

"Oh, never mind!—you don't deserve them."

"Socks?"

"Argyle socks. I'm going to give them to Bob Randall instead of you. Petey, what were you like in Galloway?" she suddenly asked, desperately.

"Just like Bob Randall."

"All right then, I'll give them to you."

They were silent for several minutes while Judie knitted in fierce pouting concentration and Peter stared gloomily into space. Meanwhile it began to rain hard outside, the rain slashed on the windowpane, and suddenly he got up and sat down at Judie's feet and leaned his head on her knee. She stopped knitting and started stroking his hair.

"That's not what I wanted, but that's all right," mumbled Peter. "What you were trying to tell me when I came in—you don't have to tell me, I can guess, I had the same things to tell you. We know each other by heart. We get all excited and nervous when we see each other after a long time, but that's the beauty of it," he pointed out almost slyly.

"Between us?"

"Yeah, but in the whole world too. *Everybody's* like that."

"The hell with the whole world. Why not just us?"

"Well, there's more to it than just us—"

"Oh, the hell with it!"

"That's women for you—"

"The hell with women. I'm not women, I'm me."

"You're you, you're you," grinned Peter. "Let's make believe I'm a mill worker," he said with a sudden happy grin of discovery, leaping up and grabbing her by the arm. "You're the boss's daughter and I'm calling on you on a Wednesday night and your father is sleeping in the next room, and we're sitting on the couch real coy and necking and whispering, waiting for your old man to start snoring. Then we start."

"You're crazy," she said, looking with meek seriousness into his eyes.

Peter was suddenly appalled. "Why?" he asked. He had a grin

on his face but it became foolish and flustered, he realized that he was not making sense. He was suddenly sad and mortified, with shame and a kind of misery, and the flashing sense that he was always lying now, always foolish somehow.

"Because . . . just because—well, you're not a mill worker and I'm not the boss's daughter."

"I know, we're us," he said with a sick feeling. He sat down on the chair again, but got up immediately and sat on the window-sill. "I'm going to make up my mind, right now, I'm going to make up my mind—if it's possible to make up my mind. And for the rest of my life I'll stick to it. I don't care what anybody says. Judie, I used to be just like that too, I mean the skating and the big times. Hell, I used to be just like any other kid. Something's *happened* to me!" he moaned. "My father knows it too!"

"Oh, *him!*" she almost snarled.

"He's a great guy, a great man, and I never really knew it till now. My mother too. They're real people, I ought to be a real son. Why does it always have to be *ought?* What the hell's wrong with all of us that it's always *ought?* And what happened?" He strode up and down the room nervously.

"Petey, don't . . . don't cry."

"What are you talking about!" he sneered.

"Well, you talk just like you were crying, Petey. Petey, let's play the mill worker and the daughter. I never really meant what I said."

"No!" he yelled furiously, opening the window and looking out at the rain.

"But it isn't nice to talk like this, and make fun of ourselves. That's what that damn book I was reading does all the time, everybody talks, talks."

"We won't talk," said Peter, getting up. He came up from behind her and put his arms around her shoulders and hugged her, leaning on her, with his head against hers. "We won't talk and we'll just lie still for hours and look at each other," he grinned triumphantly, and they swayed together, thinking.

They heard a strange sound an hour later. The apartment was on the top floor, and it sounded as though someone was wandering across the roof in the rain and leaning over the ledges to look down. Down on the street they heard shouts and the running footsteps. Then everything became quiet again.

Pete and Judie resumed their grave, cozy pleasures. The bed-lamp was on, shining warm and pink in the little room, the radio was playing, and there was a spread of avocado salad and ripe olives and asparagus tips in a big dish, from which they picked absentmindedly, with slow relish, as they went on with their reading and knitting.

Suddenly a window opened in the front room. They heard the loud splatter of rain, the window closed again, and there was a dead silence.

"Oh, Petey! what's that?" whispered Judie in a panic. "They were chasing somebody. Oh, it's a burglar!" she whispered almost gleefully now. "It's a burglar! Say something, say something!"

"Who's there!" growled Peter in a loud voice. He got up, put on his shoes, and glared into the darkness of the front room. "Of course it's not a burglar," he said, turning to Judie. "But there's somebody there, I can see the shadow. By geezus, I'm not scared" —he went on in a loud voice—"and I'm gonna brain somebody!"

Judie was staring greedily around the door jamb, utterly frightened.

Suddenly a little voice, like a four-year-old boy mimicking his little sister, was heard in the darkness: "It's me, it's me, it's only me."

Pete and Judie gaped at each other.

"Do you know that?" he demanded with amazement.

"No, but it's—"

"It's Kenneth Wood, Kenneth Wood," piped up the little voice. "Kenneth Wood climbing the fire escape and coming in from the roof. Tee-hee! tee-hee!"

"Is that you, Ken?" growled Peter.

"Well now, you can never tell," piped the little voice, "it might be an impostor playing Kenneth Wood and carrying a knife! Tee-hee! tee-hee!"

Peter lit a match, leaned into the room, looked at his friend, turned back to the bedroom, and lay down with his book again.

"You simply must finish that last paragraph!" said the little voice from the other room. "Tee-hee! the last paragraph is the false paragraph."

"Well, come in, come in!" cried Peter, grinning despite himself. "I won't read the last paragraph. What are you up to? What happened?" he demanded.

Judie went in the other room and turned on the light and

looked around. Kenneth Wood was standing in a corner by the window. He was all wet, his clothes were dripping, his hair was down in streaks in his face, and there was blood on his nose. One side of his suede jacket was black with ink, which was dripping on the floor.

"What happened to you?" Judie cried, startled. "There's blood on your face!"

Wood looked around him furtively, fearfully, in a mad imitation of fear, then suddenly made a long grave face, almost like the mask of a sad clown. He took off his suede coat, strode limping into the room, threw the coat on the floor, picked up a towel and began drying his head, and finally sat down on the floor lighting a cigarette with sudden profound gravity. He was a tall gangling youngster of about twenty, with a shock of black hair, great powerful nervous hands, and quick, peering eyes that looked up out of a screwed-up, sardonic, gravely astounded face. And he looked awful in his dirty inky rags.

They waited nervously for him to say something but he just stared at the floor moodily.

"Did you get in a fight?" inquired Peter finally.

"Yiss!" he piped up again in the small child's voice, but suddenly began speaking in his normal voice, rapidly. "Every time I go in a bar someone wants to buy me a drink and then fight. Jeanne was there, of course, flirting with a bunch on the other side, and this other bunch was buying me drinks and then they invited me outside for a fight."

"What did you say to them?"

"Nothing—that's the way it is, always. I boffed someone real hard and then they boffed me, about three of them, and I boffed someone else and started running like hell. I lost them downstairs, I went over the fence in the alley and came up the fire escape. Did you hear them bellowing down there?"

"Yeah . . ."

"That was the chorus and the end of the play . . . I should imagine."

At this Peter got up and began walking around the small bedroom nervously. Though he had little room to pace about because Kenneth was sitting on the floor and Judie was standing, he nevertheless brushed past them, walking around. "Dammit!" he kept muttering.

"What's the matter with you?" Judie laughed.

"Well, don't worry about it," said Kenny, jumping up and rummaging suddenly in the closet. "By the way, Martin, you look more woebegone than ever. What's the matter now? Don't you know what's so utterly sad about the past? It has no future. The things that came afterwards have all been discredited."

"Who's talking about that?" frowned Peter. He picked up his leather jacket and put it on and sat huddled on the bed, as though chilled. He gazed at Judie and Kenny as though he had never seen them before. "I'll tell you what I think," he said, "I think it's a lousy rotten world when three guys gang up on one guy like that—"

"Oh, let's have more of those splendid Galloway mill worker remarks!" grinned Kenny gleefully, coming from behind the closet door with an old pair of shoes and some shoe polish. He sat down on the floor and began polishing the shoes industriously. Judie sat down near him on the little hassock and watched what he was doing with happy pride.

"Ah!" she said. "Kenny always finds something to do, he's just like me."

"And I'm just a jerk, I know," said Peter. "But, hell, I *do* worry when things like that happen, I don't exactly worry so much as I get sore. I can't make out why guys are always starting fights, and with *you*, almost every time you go in a bar. Like that time we came back from Greenland—remember that fight in Boston?"

"Oh, that was a splendid fight," grinned Kenny, rubbing the shoes busily. "Polish soldiers, or I guess they were fliers, starting a fight with two Venezuelan seamen, and there's little Kenny and little Petey in the middle of it. And that Turkish seaman, remember that tremendous Turkish seaman who looked like he was all coal and oil from the top of his little red fez down to the bottom of his little curly toes?"

"Huh?"

"Remember how he broke it up and began making a speech about the compañeros and travalleros of the world, a Turkish Communist making a speech in Spanish. Oh, a splendid potpourri that was!"

"But it wasn't funny!" cried Peter, and gazed at Ken with amazement and curiosity, almost angrily.

Ken looked at him. "You *are* the most woebegone of all God's little pieces of shark feed!"

"Huh?"

"Shark feed! shark feed! Come on now, let's have the divine gossip, the little facts one by one about your woebegone state this evening. Let's get down to the bottom of it, quick!—or you shan't have your spinach!" Judie hugged herself with delight, devouring him with shining eyes, leaning gleefully towards him in the hassock. She was mad about Kenny.

"Both of you are bats," muttered Peter, not however displeased.

"Go down and buy a bottle, Martin, here's my share. You're in one of your Third Avenue moods, and Judie and I shall listen attentively to all you have to say." But as he said that, Kenneth, with the serious, slightly astounded look he always wore, glanced up at Peter sadly.

"Why don't you have Judie fix your face?" said Peter. "And I'll bring back a bottle."

"Yiss! yiss!"

Peter went down to the street in the dark misty rain to a liquor store, bought a fifth of whiskey, and wandered around the streets for a while, deep in thought. It wasn't raining any more, some stars were already appearing in one part of the sky over Fifth Avenue on the other side of Central Park.

He walked along the park. In Galloway there was no Central Park, no miles of traffic lights glistening on the pavement, no yellow cabs speeding by with the secrecy and dark luxurious mystery of New York at night. He began thinking with peculiar delight of a magazine he used to read as a little boy, the *Shadow Magazine*. In the *Shadow Magazine*, he remembered now, it was always raining mistily in New York, it was always night, and the Shadow, elegantly disguised as Lamont Cranston the man-about-town, millionaire esthete and amateur criminologist, was always speeding around Manhattan in a yellow cab and going somewhere swiftly, craftily, to cope with the "forces of crime." In the *Shadow Magazine* Lamont Cranston always stepped out of the cab as the Shadow himself, mysteriously leaving his fare money on top of the meter and vanishing in a mystery of cloaks. The cabby was always amazed and always rubbed his jaw in wonder. Peter used to read these stories and then go walking around the streets of Galloway, and curse his life because it was not New York and there were no yellow cabs and the rainy mysteries of penthouses at night. He was all of fourteen years old, still reading about the Shadow when even little Mickey began to peruse those pages.

He remembered the long earnest discussions they had had about the Shadow, he and Mickey, fourteen years old and seven years old, in the old house long ago.

What would he have thought, at fourteen, if he could have looked forward to this night? "I wouldn't have believed it!" he muttered out loud. "Wearing dirty khaki pants and an old leather jacket and walking around with a bottle of whiskey on Central Park West." He looked around him angrily. He remembered that Judie and Ken were waiting for him, he suddenly remembered *them*. Could he have foreseen them? Could there be an element of dark rainy adventure in living with a childlike gleeful girl or in having a friend who came in by the roof and called him "woe-begone"?

He wondered at that moment why he had really gone back to Galloway, and in the same instant he was riven with awful misty grief as he thought of his mother and father living in Brooklyn just across the dark of the sky—and Mickey there too, little Mickey.

Again he thought of Judie and Ken, and he thought of them with sudden tender feeling. It was true that he was Judie's lover, but she was like a child, a happy crazy child, and it seemed to him that she was his sister, after all—it was sad that she was his sister. And Ken was a boy he had met in the merchant marine, who stayed in New York now working for an advertising agency, his uncle's business, and was supposed to live with his family, his father and great-grandmother, in the East River apartment, but was hardly ever home, and got drunk every night and climbed fire-escapes and got in fights, and had been doing this ever since he was fifteen, and always ran around with blondes like Jeanne. It seemed that he was his brother after all, just like his brother, and that was sad too.

"And everything's like that," he thought, "I never did grow up since I was fourteen, none of us ever do. And all of us are crazy, I'm sure of that, not only me but all of us." He chuckled thinking of it. "Oh, everything'll be all right, I can feel it now. And one more thing!" he cried out, holding up his finger, alone on the sidewalk—"I'm going to make up my mind like I told Judie, although she doesn't know what I mean. I'm going to make a big decision and stick to it, some day soon." He hurried back to the apartment.

Jeanne, Kenny's girl, had come back from the bar where the

fight started. She was a beautiful blonde girl, lazy, sensual, always murmuring vaguely, always smiling dreamily—a hapless unconcerned kind of girl who yielded to Kenny's demonic wildness but more often drifted away, almost floating dreamily, to flirt with other boys. She was a professional model, her family lived in Long Island somewhere, she had been to Vassar.

Kenny had taken a shower and put on one of Peter's clean white shirts. He was lying on the couch, holding up a book at arm's length and reading to the girls. He threw the book down when he saw Peter, grabbed up the bottle, unscrewed it, and took one long preliminary drink. "Martin, I put on your clean shirt. I have responsibilities, responsibilities! I have to go to work in the morning!"

"It's all right with me."

"You can have my dirty shirt—it's very expensive. Well, well, well, you still look like the angel of sadness. Have a drink, quick, and tell us all about it!"

"All about what?" scoffed Peter.

"Very well then, I shall tell us all about it, I shall tell us a parable!" he said in the little boy's voice again.

"Do you know what Kenneth did tonight?" spoke up the languid Jeanne. "Just before the fight—you know, Kenny, they started the fight because you looked so awful."

"Oh, yiss, oh, yiss."

"Why did he look awful?" cried Judie.

"He took a bath in a puddle in pouring rain, right on the corner. He had a bottle of ink in his pocket and sat down in the puddle and began washing himself, all his clothes and everything with an old piece of Lifebuoy soap he found in the gutter. The bottle broke, all the ink spilled on him, and then he went in the bar like that." Jeanne recited all this with amusement, reclining on the couch with her dreamy smile.

"No wonder!" cried Peter, waving his hand at Kenny. "You're mad, man, you're mad—when you get drunk."

"But the parable!" cried Kenny, jumping up and pointing at all of them, and dancing around in a little jig. "See? first there's God, and God bemuses himself and says 'Well, now let's see, I must make a perfect world, that's what I must.' So he makes men and women and looks at them with that judicious air of a carpenter getting his boards and nails together. 'Hmm,' God says, and he walks away with his hands clasped in back of him, deep in thought, and all the little human beings jump up and down yelling 'When do we start? Yiss! Yiss! when do we start?' God strides down to the world and watches what happens."

Peter, sitting on the small table in the middle of the room, listening with a grin; Judie, hugging herself and jumping up and down on her chair; Jeanne, reclined, listening with a crazy smile—were all amazed, they were always amazed by Kenneth.

"God sits down on a fire hydrant and watches how everybody disports themselves in the world. That's when all the trouble starts, everything, all the things they cry about in books and newspapers, wars, crime, violence, adultery, deceit, and whatnot parlous. God says to himself, 'Now I will see just exactly how to make a perfect world. Hmm. There's a mistake here, it won't do! Poof! peef! He plucks up a little derring-do human being of a nobleman's son and throws him in the pot. Then he sees a little girl there and she's not doing right and poof! peef! to the pot with her!"

"What's the pot for?" yelled Judie excitedly.

"Wait! wait!" cried Ken, holding up his little finger. "This one won't do, poof-peef, in the pot! and this one won't do—same thing! In the pot!" He picked at the air with his little finger. "This one will do, this one is nice, a Pilgrim or something, John Bunyan, great man, and a Jude the Obscure sort of guy walking around down there in the field and deliberately not stepping on the worms. Nice! nice!—but, there's the *but* you see, there's always the but, because a perfect world is in the making and no one is perfect. God's trying anyway. This is not the finished copy. In the pot with John Bunyan, in the pot with the Jude the Obscure man, in the pot with the whole lot! Yiss! Now God is a cook."

"A cook?"

"A chef! In the pot he's making a stew, out of that stew he's going to make a broth, out of that broth he's going to make one drop of perfect essence, and that's what he's going to start his real heart's-desire world with, that drop from the broth of the stew in the pot. See?"

"But then what?" mumbled Peter sourly.

"Twang in the pot they go. Poof! peef!"—and Kenny plucked at the air daintily and finally ran around the room gathering things and throwing them on the couch—"God's real busy, sometimes he gets tired, his heart's overworked, he's pooped, his endodermis protrudes painfully. But he's got a goal, a goal! And look down there," he added with sudden gravity and absentmindedness, pointing at the floor, "the little human beings who haven't been plucked yet are looking around and wondering, and they're laughing and jumping up and down, no, they're crying, now they're scratching their heads, they don't know what to make of it all, now they have a look of positive gratitude on their faces, they're beholden to what they see down there and to what they think they see upstairs. Oh, nice! nice! they keep saying it's nice, they write poetry about the trees and bees. Suddenly," he jumped up, "poof! peef! they've been snatched up and thrown in the pot. And finally the time has come. The world is over, it's the end of the world and God rests. He goes over his notes. He boils up the contents of his pot and takes a million years extracting the juice and elixir that he wants just right, he smacks his lips, tasting it like a French chef, and says—'*Ah sacre-bleu! c'est ça!*' He's got just what he wants, now he knows how to beat the devil."

"The devil!" they cried.

"Didn't I mention the devil? But he was there all the time, he's God's arch competitor in fancy carpentry and cuisine. He's in business too, but he just doesn't know how to blow whoo! like God and make human beings, he has a pot but no little human beings to sample in it. So he watches and sneers, and he works his dirty fingers into all the human beings, he tries to make them perfectly wrong, but they're too disorganized even for that. God makes notes just the same, he learns something from every little life, bud-to-pot, bud-to-pot! And now he's got his drop of splendid juice and he goes over to the ocean and lifts the mish-mash pot and dumps the whole mess in the ocean."

"In the ocean!" laughed Peter, clapping himself on the head. "What for?"

"For the sharks, he's got to feed his sharks. And then he's going to start all over again a billion years from now." And Kenny threw himself on the couch beside Jeanne.

"So that's where the shark feed came from. . . ."

"Yiss! yiss!"

"Oh, Kenny, you're wonderful!" laughed Judie gleefully. "You're really an Indian."

Everybody burst out laughing.

"Oh, but yes!" cried Judie. "Don't you know anything about Indians? Don't you, Jeanne? Indians are the most wonderful people on earth, they walk without making a sound and they can see in the dark and they stand straight as trees, and everything they do is wonderful because they're Indians."

"There goes your pot," said Peter, grinning at Ken. "God doesn't throw little Indians in the pot."

"Petey's an Indian too," said Judie, pouting darkly. "I knew it the first time I saw him, by the way he walked and the way he looked at me and owned me." With this she suddenly went over to Peter and put her arms around his neck and leaned her head on his shoulder meekly. She was almost crying and Peter stared down at her gravely. Everyone was silent. They heard a sound out in the hall.

Suddenly Jeanne said, "Isn't that a rather skeptical philosophy?"

Kenny looked startled and jumped up from the couch. He picked up the liquor bottle deliberately, took a drink, and turned to Jeanne with a smile. "Do I have to put up with that, *ma petite?*"

"With what?" she cried confused.

"*One should go back to Vassar and try philosophy all over again,*" said a spectral voice from the hallway. Judie jumped with fearful surprise.

"I *do* believe in the devil and there he is!" shouted Ken suddenly, and began roaring with laughter. "Oh, Vassar, Vassar!" he howled, and slapped the wall with his hand.

"What the hell!" cried Peter. He ran to the door and looked in the hallway. There stood a well-dressed man of thirty-five, carrying a cane and a raincoat over one arm, with the sleeve of the other arm tucked neatly and almost modishly in a side-pocket, a suave, almost distinguished, kindly-looking figure of a man. Peter seemed to remember him from somewhere. The newcomer stood there, smiling.

"Oh, it's only *him,*" said Judie suddenly, looking over Peter's shoulder. She said this with utter contempt, but casually too. "That damn parasite, Waldo. I wish he would just stay home."

Peter was completely amazed. He looked at the man whom he recognized now as one-armed Waldo Meister whom Kenneth had once brought around to their ship. Ken now stood grinning in the middle of the room, and Jeanne remained stretched out on the couch.

"One shouldn't speak disrespectfully of their elders," spoke up Waldo mockingly. "Should one, Kenneth?"

"Oh, shut up, parasite!" Judie spat.

"Judie!" whispered Peter, mortified with horror, but she never looked up.

"What was that crack about my alma mater, Waldo?" Jeanne asked without stirring on the couch. "What was so apt about the Vassar remark, Kenny? I think you're both making fun of me."

"Of course not," said Waldo, "we wouldn't dream, would we, Kenneth?"

"I wouldn't know," said Ken, suddenly brooding, and disappearing into the next room.

"I like Dennison but this is the last time he's going to send you up here," spat Judie, "the damn last time."

"It wasn't Dennison sent me, it was Levinsky." The man appeared in the light and Peter saw the pitted, faintly perspiring, dark face with it rueful sneer.

"He's just a parasite too, so it doesn't make much difference—birds of a feather," cried Judie.

Peter was so mystified by all this that he could only stand in the room looking around wildly. Finally now, almost angrily, he walked up to Waldo and shook his hand.

"You don't know me," said Peter gruffly and with harassed confusion. "Please sit down, for krissakes. Here's the couch."

"But I *do* know you. You're Peter Martin!" said Waldo softly, and at that Peter recoiled and went across the room without a word.

"Ah, Waldo, you should thank the good Lord for the existence of well-mannered young Galloway mill workers who feel sorry for you," laughed Ken from the other room.

"Huh!" scoffed Judie, jumping up. "Petey, do you know what this awful man did? I didn't want to tell you because I'm afraid of you when you get mad. You remember the little cat that used to play around here?"

"Yes, what happened to the cat?" yelled Peter, turning around and glaring at Judie.

"*He* hanged it from the lamp!"

"Wait a minute, Judie, that's a lie and you know it!" said Waldo swiftly.

"Dennison told me. He was here, and he doesn't lie to me."

"Dennison is a first-rate fabricator of Gidean romances, my dear."

"I don't know what the hell you're talking about, but I know you hanged that cat and it's just like you, too! It could have died if Dennison hadn't taken it down. It was *your* necktie!"

"Lord, Lord!" yelled Ken from the other room and no one could tell whether he was laughing.

"It's a silly idle lie," said Waldo, leering pitifully around the room, "I don't want to hear any more about it. It's not true in the least. Dennison loves to make up things like that. The whole thing is just as absurd as that story he made up about my stealing a cripple's crutch in Paris in 1934 and hobbling around the streets. The whole thing is another one of Dennison's fancies—"

"We believe you," muttered Peter suddenly without turning from the window.

"Thank you, kind one," said Waldo, murmuring.

"Just the same, parasite, I wish you'd get out of here and never come back," Judie was shouting. "I can't stand your greasy sneaky ways."

Jeanne got up from the couch, stretching, saying, "Oh, this is perfectly marvelous. Poor dear Waldo. Nobody loves him."

"That should be perfectly obvious," came the voice from the other room, "and it should also be perfectly obvious to everyone that Waldo *did* hang the cat and that Waldo's going straight to hell someday and Waldo's not wanted and why doesn't Waldo leave."

"Good night, sweet ladies," said Waldo and left the house.

At nine o'clock in the morning Peter woke up and saw the sunlight streaming in the open window. His bedroom door was closed, but in the front room he could hear excited voices. For a moment he had difficulty remembering who they were and what he was doing there. Still forlorn with half-sleep, he recalled the dreams he had been having.

He was standing in his father's bedroom in the old Martin house in Galloway. Liz and his mother were reminding him that there was a "smell of flowers" in the air. "That means someone is dead," his mother said in the dream. Peter was terrified. "Who's dead?" he cried. Liz and his mother silently pointed into another room, the front room of the old house, and there, in a coffin surrounded by flowers, lay his father, George Martin, dead. And then, with the whole world rumbling with doom and dark, the scene shifted to a field, the weather turned gray and pallid, and Peter—little Peter, about five years old—was standing in the middle of the field filled with terror. On one side of the field was an old abandoned house—the "haunted house" of Galloway. Nearby was the house in which a "little boy" had died, a boy "like Julian, his brother." And there was an old shack in which "gypsies" lived, the "pockmarked gypsies who always kidnap little boys." And Francis was on that side of the field too, possibly living in the haunted house, or in the house where little Julian had died: that seemed most probable. In the field itself Peter stood terrified by a further danger—the "drunken men" who got drunk and fell on children and killed them, because "when men are drunk they weigh a thousand pounds." (This was a popular superstition among Peter's little chums of yore.) One of the drunks was lying senseless there in the weedy swamp. But on the other side of the field, in a vista of space, with the sun shining, there stood a bunch of tall raw-boned youngsters, including his brothers Joe and Charley, around a kind of tractor plow, talking and smoking. Nearby was his father's car, the old Plymouth, and his father himself sitting in it and smoking a cigar and looking at a roadmap (just as he used to do on Sundays long ago in New England)—and all of it in the great light of a plain, with mountains beyond.

These dreams overwhelmed Peter to such an extent that he continued them with his eyes closed, imagining himself walking away from the field and the haunted houses towards Joe and the raw-boned boys and his father in the car. He desperately had to do this, he even pretended to himself that he was fast asleep and dreaming so that he could make everything turn out the way he wanted. Yet he was only day-dreaming now.

Suddenly he jumped out of bed and thought: "I'll go see Ma and Pa in Brooklyn, we'll talk, we'll go to a movie, I'll talk to Mickey, I'll get news about the whole family. I won't be silly any more like these kids in the next room. Oh, yes, someday I'm going to begin to live," he cried to himself jubilantly. "Someday I'll show them all I know how to live!"

He chuckled and began dressing. When he opened the door to the front room, he was trembling with excitement.

They were all there, all the strange young people whose lives had become mingled with his in New York. Kenneth Wood was sitting on the windowsill looking at him sardonically, yet with that sadness that always happened when they looked at each other—as though there was something they knew that nobody else knew, a crazy sorrowful knowledge of themselves in the middle of the pitiable world. Judie was all dressed up to go somewhere. At the moment she was glaring angrily at Leon Levinsky, who had arrived with Waldo Meister. The latter was freshly attired and smiling. Jeanne was dressed in a bright new outfit, carrying a hatbox, apparently ready to go to work at the downtown model agency. They were all jabbering away.

Judie went to the door. "Everybody clear out!" she snapped irritably. "I'm going out and nobody's staying behind in my house. And that goes for you too, Levinsky: you bring Waldo here once again and I'll kick you in the teeth. I don't want you around, either of you."

"The lady is indiscreet," murmured Waldo, vaguely, getting up to go.

"I'll indiscreet you!" yelled Judie.

They all started down the stairs.

"Incidentally, Pete," Levinsky called back, "I saw Dennison last night and he said he'd like to see you today. Shall I tell him you're coming?"

"Don't go there!" snapped Judie, turning on Peter. "I don't like that Dennison character either, I don't want you to go see him. I want you to stay with me today."

"I thought you liked Dennison."

"Not any more! Oh, how I hate everybody around here! Someday I'm just going to leave and go out West and live on a ranch, Arizona or someplace!"

"What's the matter with you?" grinned Peter, taking her in his arms. "You're as mad as a wildcat this morning, and such a beautiful morning too."

"Petey!" she cried desperately, almost paling. "Let's go out in the woods today and sit in the grass and talk and eat oranges. I can't stand it here any more, everything's so horrible. I even hate Kenny because he keeps talking to that damn Waldo as though he mattered. I want to be alone with you, I want you to marry me. Petey, when are you going to marry me?" she demanded gravely.

He took Judie's hand and started downstairs to follow the others. "Judie, who do you think I am—Rockefeller?" he cried. "I haven't got any money, I don't know what I'm going to do, and I don't want to be tied down. You know all that."

"That's what you always say. All right!" she said angrily. "You'll be sorry someday, because there won't be another woman around who'll understand you the way I do. Remember that! You're awful dumb, Pete, so awful dumb. Any other woman would laugh at you, you'll find out that after I've gone away." She flushed and hurried down the stairs ahead of him.

Peter followed everybody gloomily. On the sidewalk they were all standing around talking, the sun was shining warmly and the street was thronged with coatless people strolling about on the "first real day of Spring."

Suddenly Kenneth yelled: "Hey! I've always wanted to explore that old abandoned house over there." He galloped across the street to a boarded-up brownstone house.

Without ceremony he ran up on the stoop and kicked in some boards. They had already been busted by children and collapsed immediately. Kenneth vanished inside greedily.

"Hey, wait for me!" yelled Jeanne, throwing her hatbox to Judie. She ran after him eagerly, and in a moment had vanished inside the dark wreckage of boards and masonry. Levinsky and Waldo strolled across the street after them with great curiosity. Judie stood with arms akimbo and glared at the whole crazy thing. People going by on the sunny street seemed to pay no attention whatever to what was going on. Peter leaned against a rail and watched everything with wonder.

"Jeanne, you fool!" Judie yelled. "You're going to dirty my new dress!"

They heard Jeanne's muffled cry, from inside: "Don't worry, I'll watch it!" There was a clatter of boards and much scuffling and banging-around as the crazy Kenneth roved about excitedly. With strange suddenness, he appeared in a third floor window looking down at them in solemn silence.

In a moment Jeanne showed up behind him, smiling foolishly.

"What idiots!" cried Judie, infuriated.

"What's in there, Kenneth?" Waldo demanded, in a low voice that carried all over the street with a strange articulate clearness.

Kenneth vanished inside without a word. Once more they could hear him kicking boards out of the way and scuffling over masonry and rubbish, and stamping down on the floor as though he wanted to see if it would collapse. They could hear Jeanne murmuring with laughter.

"Darkness, darkness!" yelled Kenneth suddenly. "Just your meat, Waldo . . ."

At this point Judie dropped the hatbox and walked away. She went down the street, not looking back, pretending not to know any of them, and finally, during a moment when Peter looked up to see Kenneth standing in the sun on the roof, Judie had just disappeared around the corner.

Peter remembered his dream about the old haunted house, and the house of death, and the gypsies, and all the darkness and helpless fear of it. It was strange to realize that he had obscurely and inexpressibly foreseen all this in that dream, and he was filled with a vague terror and premonition.

Before Peter hurried off to look for Judie, he handed the hatbox to Levinsky, who went inside the house with gleeful curiosity. When Peter looked back, he saw Waldo standing all alone looking up at the shattered windows and crumbling masonry above.

[5]

PETER WAS UNABLE to find Judie. He knew she would be around again in the evening when her sulking was exhausted. He decided to go and see Will Dennison before going to Brooklyn.

This strange man whose background included a wealthy family, Princeton, travel on the continent, and whose source of income was a trust fund established by his millionaire grandfather, lived in a cold-water flat which rented for twelve dollars a month. It was located in the lower East Side, down by the waterfront, near Henry Street in the shadow of the great Manhattan bridge.

It was a neighborhood where shapeless old men kept rubbish fires smoldering in the streets from dawn till nightfall for reasons as enigmatical as their own undiscoverable selves. Children from nearby Jewish and Italian tenements cavorted and yelled and played games all day in ancient streets. Old rabbis moved along the sidewalks musing and stepping around melancholy fires with their hands clasped behind them. Sometimes old women went by carrying bags of wood on their backs, or old men came down the middle of the street with pushcarts filled with rags. The grim tenements rose on each side of the street, some of them covered with weird inscriptions and signboards written in Hebraic letters, and others, nearer the bridge, alive all day with the brooding window-vigils of watching all-comprehending Italian mothers. Just a few blocks away, where the El roared and the trucks and busses rattled over the cobblestones of Chatham Square, was the Bowery with all its stews and saloons and grimy doorways and, just beyond, little Chinatown with its tiny streets. Soaring above, high and magnificent and as though sprung straight from the old soiled rooftop of these things, were the Wall Street towers distant and proud and looming.

Peter walked along these noisy crowded streets in the sunny noontime that day. He saw a fat mournful-eyed soprano, apparently an aspirant to the Metropolitan Opera, wild and mad, singing in her tenement—he gaped up with amazement at the sound of her piercing voice over the streets—and the little children raced and raced around him on the sidewalk. It was almost always a tremendous sadness when he walked the streets of New York. He had never expected the city to be that way at all, when he lived in Galloway.

He went up the dark musty stairs to Dennison's rooms, six floors up in the gloomy and decrepit tenement which was about to be condemned by the authorities. The door of the apartment itself was girded tight with a double lock, a padlock on the outside, not in lock at the moment, and a lock-and-chain inside, which slowly eased over as Peter began to knock. There was a moment of insane silence and suspicion, and then the door opened an inch or two. Dennison's long bony nose appeared in the crack: he seemed to be sniffing: and then Peter could see his pale eyes peering coldly.

"It's me, Will," explained Peter, grinning stupidly.

With this Dennison swung the door open a few more inches with a kind of gracious flourish. Peter entered, squeezing in with embarrassment.

"Nobody with you, is there?"

Peter looked foolishly behind him. "No, no, I'm alone."

"Fine." Dennison locked the door and slid the chain back in place. "I'm glad to see you, Pete," he said, shaking hands stiffly. "Make yourself at home, won't you? I'll be busy for a while now. We're all friends here," he added loudly, baring his lips and showing his teeth in a ratty grin. "I've got a few things to attend to. Just grab a chair."

The door through which Peter had come in opened right into a sort of kitchen which had an isolated bathtub sitting ridiculously high off the floor over antiquated plumbing. There was also a sink, a battered icebox that Dennison had bought in a second-hand store, and a greasy gas stove. The wash hung from the high ceiling on criss-crossing ropes. To the right was the back room of the four narrow "railroad" rooms that made up the apartment; in the moldy doorway hung a moth-eaten green drape that concealed whatever was behind it. To the left were the two front rooms—a kind of alcove with an ancient huge bureau, some chairs, and a card table and, beyond the alcove, the front room, also marked off by some old drapery, from which Peter could hear voices, radio music, and a baby crying. A girl with dark hair and horn-rimmed glasses peered at him from the drapery of the front room and vanished again without comment. This was Mary Dennison, who rarely spoke to Peter or anyone who chanced to drop in. She was a confidante of Junkey, whose voice Peter could hear in the front room, and she did the housework in the dolorous apartment.

Peter sat down in a chair in the alcove and watched Dennison and the other fellow, a tall, cadaverous, indistinct-looking man. At the moment they were busy boiling down morphine tablets in spoons. They bent absorbedly over their spoons and cottons and pills and hypodermic needles. They paid no attention whatever to Peter.

"This ain't bad stuff here," the tall skeleton was saying, as he picked delicately at an eye-dropper and inclined with the unction of a great chemist over his work. "This here Rogers is a pretty reliable guy, as doctors go, and he's never given me any cause for complaint."

"Well, the only thing is, as you say, he don't cotton up to me and Junkey so well," said Dennison out of the corner of his mouth.

"Well, he'll get used to you. He's jittery, you know, and he wants to make sure everything's all right with you guys. I've been getting prescriptions from him for four years now and he knows I've had the Chinaman on my back too long to jeopardize a good connection for stuff. The thing about Rogers is, get in his confidence and you can always score."

"Well, Al, put in a good word for me every time you see him," said Dennison, holding up a full hypodermic to the light. "I'll certainly appreciate it, in view of the fact that I ain't doing so well with these other characters. Last Sunday, Meyer up in the Bronx threw Junkey out of his office and told him not to come back. I think he got wise to the fact that Junkey's been lifting some of his prescription blanks from his desk."

"Well," said the cadaver, rolling up his sleeve judiciously, "I wouldn't fool around with forging prescriptions if I were you. You might get in trouble, you know."

"You know me, Al, always careful," smiled Dennison charmingly.

"And what about Doc Johnson out in Brooklyn?"

"Didn't you hear? The narcotics squad closed in on him last Wednesday. He's out on bail now but it looks pretty bad for him."

"Oh, that's too bad, Johnson wasn't a bad egg. Kind of nice guy, you know?"

"He certainly was," said Dennison, and both of them had rolled up their sleeves by now and were poising the needles on their arms. Al's arm was livid with one long scar along the vein. He seemed to be having difficulty adjusting the needle just the way he wanted it. Finally, after several unsuccessful attempts, he took the needle out and sighed.

"Well, I guess I'll have to try the leg again. This arm's just about raw this trip." And he put down his pants, ran his finger up and down a long livid scar on his thigh, and finally decided on a spot that seemed favorable. He sank the needle in and pushed the plunger down slowly. Meanwhile Dennison had concluded his own ministrations and was punctiliously cleaning out his needle and eye-dropper with water.

"Yes, Johnson wasn't a bad sort at all," he was saying.

"Yes," said Al, daubing his bleeding scar with a piece of cotton, "he came from a good family, you know, but found it hard going to live up to their square standards, you might say."

"Well, I suppose they'll take his license away from him, but he'll get another one somewhere else."

"Yes, I suppose he'll make out some way. We all have to take the bumps when they come and try to make the best of it."

They cleaned everything up, put away their pills and needles and cottons with great care, Dennison washing out glasses and spoons, Al rubbing the top of the table with a cloth, and everything was neat again. Al put on his coat and hat, and Dennison said he would accompany him downstairs.

"I've got to get a few quarts of milk at the grocery, Al, and some Benzedrine and codeine cough syrup at the drugstore, a few suppositories I want to try out, headache powders for pickup in the mornings, a few things like that, so I might as well walk with you downstairs."

Whereupon the tall cadaverous Al opened the door and said, "After you, Will."

But Dennison bowed slightly at the waist, smiling, "Please, Al, I am home here." They went out, ignoring Peter completely and he was left alone.

He had nothing to do now but go into the front room.

Junkey was there, sitting on a small barrel, painting lightbulbs blue in a kind of diligent absorption as he talked to Mary Dennison. She was bending over a broom as though in sudden thought. Jack the young hoodlum from Times Square was sitting there quietly. In a dim corner of the room, almost unnoticeable, sat another youngster whom Peter had never seen before, a small shriveled husk of a young-old man with beady gleaming eyes, a pale small face, and infinitely tiny hands that he kept folded primly on his lap as he sat staring at all the others.

"Well, man," greeted Junkey, with his somnolent gaze of dry reproach, "I was wondering when you'd come in and say hello." He had a crooked, pathetic way of grinning. "I've got no place to sleep," he went on. "I was up all last night in Beckwell's cafeteria on the Square waiting for a guy to show up with some shiazit. Don't you know, I'm beat and I need some sleep if I'm also going to score with the doctors for everybody around here." He continued with the bulbs in a dark ruminative chore. The purpose of the blue bulbs, he said, was to give the room a "weird, soothing effect" in the evenings. It was one of Junkey's many rudimentary decorations intended to ward off the stark street world he always had to live in. He hoped he could sleep in Dennison's that night.

Mary Dennison suddenly snickered secretly, and Jack the hoodlum and the staring madman in the corner said nothing. Peter wondered whether he ought to leave.

Suddenly the shriveled little man in the corner stood up and spoke. "Who wants a blast?"

"Everybody wants a blast, man," said Junkey reproachfully, but a little eagerly too. "I was wondering how long you'd hold out on us with that weed."

The shriveled young man methodically removed a long thin cigarette from an envelope and examined it carefully, with a dry, secret grin.

"I may as well tell you about Clint now that he has come out of his cocoon," said Junkey, addressing Peter gravely. "Clint is a guy who shows up once a week with the wildest tea in the world, which he has there in his hand. Then he disappears again for a week. I don't know where he gets that marijuana, but there's none like it in New York. And I don't know where he lives, or what he does for a living, or nothing and I don't ask him. He sits in his corner and says nothing at first, but eventually comes out, Pops, and comes *on* like you never heard."

As Junkey outlined these facts, Clint began painstakingly lighting the cigarette with the deliberation and suaveness of an after-dinner speaker who is about to say a few words, meanwhile looking around at the others with a gleam in his eyes.

"That's Clint," concluded Junkey, "and, man, they don't make 'em any weirder."

"That's right, Junkey!" piped up Clint proudly in a high-pitched voice. "Now try a drag on this here stick," and he handed the lighted cigarette to Junkey, who promptly inhaled prodigiously with a furious hissing intake of air that startled Peter, and then passed the cigarette along to Mary Dennison, who also "booted herself to it" (as Junkey put it). Then Peter tried it, and finally Jack the hoodlum "blasted" a while. Then it went back to Clint, who took it and gazed at it reflectively. He suddenly began talking.

"Tell you about cockroaches," said Clint with intense enthusiasm, leaning forward with a finger pointed. "Now! The place I live in has a lot of cockroaches, but I don't have trouble with them, understand, I'm on the best terms with them. Tell you how I do this. Some years ago I sat down and thought about the whole matter: I said to myself, cockroaches are human too, just as much as us human beings. Reason for that is this: I've watched them long enough to realize their sense of discretion, their feelings, their emotions, their thoughts, see. But you laugh. You think I'm talking through my hat. You doubt my word. Wait! wait!"

The others were giggling uncontrollably, even Jack the hoodlum in a sort of idiotic, insolent way.

"Now!" went on Clint, leaning over towards them even more, stretching out his arms with fantastic emphasis and holding their attention that insane way. "Time came when I got sick and tired of finding cockroaches in my bread and jam on the kitchen table. I like cockroaches, but it was too much, you dig? I got a little string"—and with this Clint dug into his pocket and pulled out a piece of string and held it up to display—"little string like this. Every time I found a cockroach in my bread and jam, I'd give it a little flip of the string, you see, a little whipping on the back. Not hard!" he warned breathlessly. "Not hard! Just . . . a . . . little . . . flick . . . of my wrist, like this!" He demonstrated gently, over and over again, while the others watched.

"Now," went on Clint, "time came when I not only had 'em trained so they wouldn't mess around my own bread and jam, but they were living in the pan under the table in peace and plenty, in a real orderly fashion, you dig? I used to lay down on the floor and talk to them and watch. Some of them lived in the pan, some of them were recluses and went and lived under the sink pipe. Others were just plain snooty, they had to live in the cracks way up on the wall. They had all kinds of domestic trouble, too. Sometimes a wife would desert her husband and run off with another character, sometimes two husbands would fight it out, sometimes one of them would run wild—a bandit, see?—and steal everything in sight, all the breadcrumbs and jam and carry it off, you dig? It was wild, I tell you, it was wild and weird. Well, here's what happened. Time came"—here Clint took another drag on the cigarette with a joyous fury—"time came when the cockroaches from next door began to drift into my place, and naturally, not being trained, there they were smelling around on top of my table. I thought I had a revolt on my hands and wasn't being firm enough, not realizing that these here untrained cockroaches were causing all the trouble and I was beating up my own trained ones for the sins of others. The way I found out is, my cockroaches were sulking and resentful, you understand? When I'd talk to them they wouldn't even look up. I could see their feelings was hurt. I said to myself, what gives here? Aren't they happy, ain't I treating them right? It dawned on me about the cockroaches from next door. Well, there I was, trying to figure out what to do, when my cockroaches sort of all got together in the pan and held a meeting. I could smell trouble was brewing, you understand? I just sat there watching. First thing you know they all take a beeline for the hole in the bottom of the wall leading to the next apartment and started fighting the cockroaches from next door. It was a real knock-out drag-down fight like something you never seen, a regular campaign with flanking attacks and charges and real crazy generals and everything. It was wild, man, it was wild! Next day, the cockroaches from next door stayed where they was put, my own cockroaches settled down to a peaceful disciplined life, and it's been that way ever since.

"They keep regular sentries posted at that hole," he went on.

"Nobody can come in. I cried for weeks realizing I was punishing my own cockroaches for the sins of others. I spent days laying on the floor trying to explain to them that I didn't know, that I couldn't have possibly dug what was really going on—and they forgave me. As a reward I used to blow a little hay smoke toward them, just a little bit at first, to give 'em some kicks, you understand, and they'd all perk up at first and lift up their noses and take a real deep sniff, like this." He sniffed deeply, to show them, and laughed scatteringly. "You dig? First thing you know, they was all high on marijuana. They're all teaheads now. I have to get more and more of the stuff all the time to satisfy them. It's a real killer, you oughta see it, I can almost see the expression of relief on their faces, dig, because they know they're really getting the good weed."

"Don't you know, Pops, it's the best weed in town," agreed Junkey impassively.

It was dark when Peter got off the subway in Brooklyn. The streets were thronged with people bound for movies, restaurants, bars, or just strolling pleasurably in the mild night and eating hot-dogs at the Fulton Street stands. With a feeling of orphan loss and mystery, and a kind of odd enigmatical consolation, Peter hurried towards home. Just because his parents lived in Brooklyn it seemed a more human place than Manhattan. It also struck him sorrowfully that while all his friends were engaged in their morbid demonisms, these people were working gravely and living earnestly and enjoying their evenings with quaint and homely gladness. He felt humble and strangely glad.

When he reached his new Brooklyn home, Peter stood in the dark street looking in at his family with inexpressible joyful confusion. His mother was ironing in the kitchen, his father was reading the papers, and Mickey was in the front room listening to the National Barn Dance with its cowbells and cheers and old-time music blaring on the radio.

For a moment Peter simply sat down on the iron railing fronting the sidewalk over their basement windows and looked about him, at the mournful-looking moon over the rooftops, at the corner where the boys stood whistling at the girls, at the lovers who passed arm-in-arm talking in low voices in the soft night. Nearby, with thrilling closeness and magic, among the murmurs of Brooklyn and the misty April night, was the deep sonorous quaver of a big ship in the harbor.

Peter was torn with a hundred confused desires. He wondered how he could have felt such empty bitter horror only a few hours ago in Manhattan.

"I was wondering when you'd get home!" his father cried happily. "So there was nothing in Galloway, huh, none of your friends? You didn't happen to bump into any of my old pals, did you? Pete Cartier, Old Berlot or someone like that? I'll bet that little old town hasn't changed a bit, I'd like to visit it myself sometime." He cackled hoarsely. "Say! you should have saved your money and stayed home with us and seen a couple good shows in New York. As a matter of fact, I was figuring on going to a movie later tonight. Say, Marge, give him some of that soup you made this afternoon and some of that nice crusty bread I bought. He looks half-starved!" The old man was so pleased to see his boy that he could not stop laughing and talking.

Peter sat at the kitchen table and had rich home-made soup and three porkchops grilled a deep brown, peas, mashed potatoes, fresh tomatoes, bread and butter, two glasses of milk, two pieces of chocolate cake, a small piece of home-made date pie, and hot coffee. His parents sat with him and drank coffee and talked, anxiously watching him eat, while Mickey shyly turned the pages of the newspaper and stayed beside them all.

"I suppose you saw your sweetie-pie?" the old man joked. "Your rootie-tootie Judie with the slacks? Boy, she certainly is a character if I ever saw one. You're not thinking of marrying her, are you?" he ribbed slyly.

"No, nothing like that."

"Just the same, Petey, you shouldn't be living with her like that," spoke up Mrs. Martin. "A girl doesn't really respect the man when she lets him live outright with her. Of course, I don't know about Judie herself, she seems a nice little girl, but I don't know."

"Oh, Ma, forget it! It's no great scandal, people do that nowadays. Times have changed—"

"Just like that!" grinned the old man, poking the woman in the ribs. "Did you hear that? People just do that nowadays. Here's your sophisticated man-about-town sitting right in front of you. I've spawned a Casanova! Times have changed, all right! Ha ha ha! Why, if I'd of pulled anything like that in Lacoshua the old man would have taken me out to the woodshed, but I guess this isn't Lacoshua and this isn't 1890. As far as I'm concerned, what did that English king once say? 'God won't punish us for taking a little fun along the way.' Ha ha ha! Say," he demanded eagerly, "how are all those whacky friends of yours making out?"

"They're all right, I guess," mumbled Peter.

"That Dennison guy? There's another character. What's he up to now?" demanded the old man curiously.

There was nothing Peter could think of saying.

"And that kid who was drunk that time, that Kenny fellow—he strikes me as being some sort of nut. When he dropped his beer glass on the floor that time in the bar, he just opened his fingers and let it drop. He told the waiter it was an accident, but he didn't fool me."

"Yeah, he does things like that."

"I don't know," said Mrs. Martin sadly. "I wish Petey could make friends with some nice normal young people. Everything I hear about those kids of yours sounds awful. They don't seem to have anything on their minds."

"They've got plenty on their minds!" laughed Peter sarcastically.

"Like your girl Judie. If she really likes you, why doesn't she save her money and make a nice clean little home for you for when you come back from sea? Instead of that, from what I hear, the place is always a mess. All she does is throw parties and hang around in bars and spend her aunt's money. You can say I'm just an old gossip, but I'd like to see you with a real girl that would look after you a little bit."

"But she does!" laughed Peter. "She cooks and everything, sometimes she works, gets jobs. . . . Why, right now she's knitting me socks, you know. It's only that she gets sick and tired sometimes and drops everything. All the girls in New York are like that now."

"Well, I don't know," his mother said, shaking her head sadly, "they don't sound wholesome and they don't sound right to me. I wish you could meet some nice young people like you knew in Galloway, like Tommy Campbell—the poor child—and Danny Mulverhill or little Helen you took to your prom in prep school—young people like that who take things to heart."

"That's New York, Marge!" the father cried, suddenly angry. "The place drives everybody crazy after a while. Any nuts that happen to pop up in the country come rolling into New York, they don't go anywhere else, they're all here." He brooded darkly. "We moved here, so we can't expect much more."

Peter looked at his father gravely. "Have you heard from Liz lately?"

The old man looked away. "We haven't had a word from Liz herself in more than a year, so there you are."

"That's true, Petey," said the mother mournfully.

"We haven't had a word from her and we never even know her address wherever she happens to be. I guess she doesn't give the slightest damn for her parents any more. She's been all over the country like a stray cat. Just went silly, like a lot of others nowadays, just as you say. Of course, that awful thing that happened to her in Detroit . . . that hurt. But it hurt us, too, more than she'll ever know, the little fool! I don't know, she doesn't give a hoot about our feelings. You might almost say you can't expect much more with the country turned upside down the way it is. Kids just don't have anything to lean on, any sort of faith, I guess. It gets the kids before it gets anyone else. Lord knows, the older generation is harassed enough." He spoke gloomily and looked away. "I could tell you a lot of the reasons why the whole shebang is getting to be what it is. I may be all wet, but it seems to me that everything is being turned upside down as completely as you might turn a cup over and spill everything out. Here you have a younger generation that doesn't believe in right and wrong. The cup's been overturned for sure. Isn't that so?"

Peter shrugged. "There's some truth in what you say."

"You know, Petey, I walk all around New York and Brooklyn here and watch people, and listen to their conversations in movies and subways and on the streets. And that's what I've come to realize. Understand—this generation *knows* right and wrong, they sense it all right and that's probably why they do so many crazy things, like those friends of yours. It makes them jumpy and neurotic. But they don't *believe* in right and wrong. There's a big difference there—and what I'd like to know is how this all came about, and I've been thinking about that too. With that other war we had, a lot of things changed, a lot of them to the better—like the standard of living and a decent job and so on and some good unions among the bad ones, better working conditions. But a lot of things changed to no good, like this business of ignoring the simple right and wrong of living. The other day I read about a girl who committed suicide in a New York hotel and she left a note explaining that she couldn't get along with her family, they 'repressed her life,' that's what she wrote. She was a student at one of those rich girls' schools—her family was rich, the father a Kansas businessman, and it seems that she had a lot of expensive clothes in her room when they found her, so that when all is said and done the family was doing all it could for her, the best schools, good clothes, and all that. How did they repress her? What I think of first is, what kind of guff did she learn in that school, what are they teaching nowadays that's doing so much, *so much* to separate the children of this generation from their parents?"

"That's a hot one," laughed Peter. "Just a minute ago you were criticizing *me* for the friends I have in New York."

"Yes, yes, I admit that, but *why* are the youngsters living the way they do? With no sense of right and wrong, no feeling of responsibility, no sincere hopes or things like that. You might say on account of the war. But think of the poor kids who haven't got time to feel one way or another about it right now, the kids on the fronts—will they all be like that *after* the war? It's like your sister Liz—she had one bad break and wham! She decides not to give a damn about anything any more. There's something missing somewhere. God knows your mother and I tried to make a good life for all you kids and we tried to teach you a decent sense of respect for certain things, but it didn't seem to work in Liz's case, or in Francis' either. He's become a sarcastic young punk. We didn't even know where he lived and one day I ran into him and a bunch of his friends, I guess it was on Lexington Avenue, and he talked to me for a minute or so on the street, didn't even introduce me to his friends as his father, said he was busy, looked ashamed, off he went!"

"Francis did that?" cried Peter, amazed. "When was that?"

"Sometime last winter, what does it matter?"

"He's got his own life to live now," said the mother, "but he should at least have enough love for his father to introduce him to his friends."

"Doesn't he ever come here?"

"Oh, no. He never even writes."

"Gone—just like that!" snapped the old man. "Good-bye to a son—who used to turn to me for help and to your mother for comfort. He's a prime shining example of what I'm talking about, your own brother. What's happening I don't know! Last month I got a book out of the library and I never read anything so ugly in all my life. The jacket said it was by a promising young author who should go far, all that kind of ballyhoo. So I read it. This story was about a young man who was the black sheep of his family, always complaining and whining around, and finally he comes to New York and whattaya know! He finds out he's a sissy. He likes boys better than girls. So the rest of the book is all about what he says to people in bars and how unhappy he is and finally he picks up with another sissy and whoopsidoo! they live together and have a big romance. It's all worked out with a lot of rigamarole and symbols and he even brings politics into it. It's a big world-shaking business—two big boys playing with each other like those morons who hang around men's rooms in the subway. He ends up talking about being grown up, *mature*, he used that word plenty in the last pages, and he seems to be criticizing everybody else for being *immature*, and blames all the troubles of the world on that. Gol-dang it, I remember Doc Kimball once telling me that thirteen-year-old boys are likely to fool around like that, but they always outgrow it at fifteen or so and start going for girls. So I figure that our *mature* genius was talking through his hat a little bit. Ha ha ha!"

"There's a lot of that in New York," said Peter meditatively.

"To have someone write a book about it and base the whole philosophy of the story on it is just the last straw as far as I can see it. I dunno. I often have a hunch that there are more nuts nowadays than ever, only now it's become a great *philosophy!*"

"That's what Leon Levinsky says," grinned Peter, "you remember Levinsky, that kid with the glasses—"

"Yes, I remember him, how could I forget him," sighed the old man. "I never did hear such a fast talker in all my life. I gotta hand it to you, Petey, you sure have a knack for picking out the screwballs. Your Alexander in Galloway was one. God knows, he was harmless enough and good-hearted—but these!"

He chuckled awhile, and then grew serious again. "I laugh, but it's damn serious. The country's going straight to hell if something doesn't happen. Some mighty funny things have been going on in the past ten years. Like I say, they've overturned the cup and they're trying to drain the country dry of whatever it used to have that made it strong. It's all these *foreign* ideas! I call it *gall* if nothing else, that they should come over here from Europe," he roared, "and get themselves jobs and then turn around and tell

American citizens who they should vote for and how they should spend their money, and on top of all that do their damnedest to change our form of government and economy after they themselves lived for centuries like beggars in the old countries. Why the hell do they think we fought all our wars—for the fun of fighting? Or just so *they* could come here and bring Europe back again? But don't you see," minced the old man savagely, "they're *cultured* and we're not, they *know* what should be done, they read Karl Marx or whatever his name is and they read this one and that one, while we're just a bunch of ignorant blockheads who just do nothing but work. Oh, boy, I hear plenty of that on Union Square, I go down there and listen every once in a while."

"You should meet Francis' great friend, Engels," laughed Peter, "he's one of those leftist intellectual characters—"

"I don't want to meet him or anyone like him!" shouted the old man warningly. "I might break their necks! I'm really afraid I *would!*"

And at this point Mickey laughed because his father was shouting so furiously and comically, and the mother got up and made another pot of coffee and brought out the date pie again, and they cleaned the pie-pan down to the crumbs. They sat around the kitchen table till after midnight. It seemed that something gleeful, rich and dark, something rare and wildly joyful, something ineffably glad, half-sad, hovered and lurked nearby, in corners somehow, in the dark hall, behind the curtains, in the very air of the midnight rooms leaning in, brooding around the lighted kitchen . . . something they could not say, which they all knew, and felt, mysteriously, eagerly, gratefully.

"I don't know," said Marguerite Martin with a wistful air, "but the best kind of life, as far as I'm concerned, was the life we used to live on my grandfather's farm in New Hampshire. That was before my father died, before I had to go to work in the shoeshops. You remember, George, when you first knew me and you used to call on me on weekends there. Gosh, how you ate that time! Petey, on a Saturday morning your Aunt Alice and I picked turnips and cabbage and carrots and potatoes and peas fresh out of the garden and made a big stew—oh, a delicious stew, with all the vegetables still juicy from the ground and tasting so rich and strong in the broth. Well now, at noon your father ate three heaping plates of that stew. I thought he was going to bust! Do you remember, George, I kept telling you you looked purple?"

"I'll say I remember!"

"Well now. My grandfather kept big barrels of apple cider in the cellar and all afternoon long you just drank cider until I thought you'd bust again—"

"I also went fishing with the old man at the creek, remember?"

"Yes. Then at night my grandfather went out in the yard and started his charcoal fire and broiled the dinner. And listen!—at night we made molasses candy. We stood on the porch pulling and pulling at it till it was nice and golden colored, singing songs, you know. And we ate that candy and sang at the piano and had a wonderful time. And you know, Petey, my grandfather would never let us go to bed without drinking a glass of hot wine—*vin ferré* he called it. He put a hot iron in the wine and it puffed up blue smoke, and when you drank that wine my grandfather always used to say you could go skating in your bloomers." She laughed delightedly.

"He was a funny old type—"

"In the morning, Petey, in the morning, my grandfather went out and milked his cows and brought back a pail full of thick cream you could cut with a knife. Then he cut some brisket and fried it in a pan, and then broke eight eggs in it, and fried them, and brought your father here all that for a breakfast, plus fresh bread your Aunt Alice made that very morning in her oven, and the cream to soak it in, plus some pure Vermont maple syrup."

"And, Petey," said the old man reverently, "if you've never eaten fresh bread with cream and syrup you missed the greatest food on earth—"

"Then remember, George, it was a Sunday, and my grandfather went out and shot some ducks and brought them back and plucked them, cut them in half, and broiled them over his fire."

"What a feast that was!"

"At night, Petey, we all went to church at Willamette's Corners for vespers. Your father here wanted to please me, so he came tagging along to church with us, but I knew he didn't go to church any other time." She winked gravely at her sons. "That was all so long ago, wasn't it, George? My uncles are still living like that in New Hampshire and others in Canada, and that's the best life there is. They work hard all right, but they get rewarded for their work, they live, and they're happy and healthy, and they're independent, no one can tell them what to do. You can have your

Communists and your neurotics and all that stuff, but give me a good old church-going farmer for a man, a real man—"

"That leaves me out, hey?" cried Martin, poking Peter in the ribs. "I guess that leaves the old man out in the cold, huh?"

"New York's all right," went on the mother, "it's all right for shows and stores and excitement and a lot of people, but when it comes to living the way people were *intended* to live, give me the country and the small town."

They talked on like that till two o'clock in the morning, till Mickey was dozing on the table beside them.

When they all went to bed, Peter stepped out in the back yard for a few minutes. He smoked a cigarette in the cool night air, and stared at the great portrait of the man holding his head in pain, on the wall of the warehouse, as the Brooklyn night rumbled and roared about him.

[6]

ONE NIGHT that week Peter joined Kenny Wood at a Second Avenue bar. They had to meet Judie and Jeanne and the others on Fifty-Second Street in a half hour, but lingered a while, drinking in this sad old place, before they went outside to hail a cab.

It was a strange bar, more like a saloon, where Kenny Wood went all the time, a bare, gloomy, drafty hall of a place in which the local Poles conducted great riotous polkas on Saturday nights that Kenny watched in grinning silence while tossing down his boilermakers. Sometimes he had to be assisted out of the place to a cab by these people who neither spoke English nor understood why he came there. On this night, as on most weekday nights, it was like a gloomy railway station with all the old men muttering over beers at the bar, in the one dim light surrounded by shadows, beside a small potbelly stove.

Kenneth was sitting forward with his head in his hands. "Someday I want to live in the Balkans among the Slavs. They're great mysterious people who just don't live like we live, nor love like we love, nor rave like we rave." He suddenly turned to Peter and said, "Why don't you go back to your splendid Galloway, Martin? What are you doing here?" He peered at him strangely. "Have you ever been haunted by a spook? Did you ever wake up in the middle of the night and find one leaning over your bed, leering? Did you ever feel that you were locked in a closet, smothering with such a spook?"

"What are you talking about?"

"I'm talking about Waldo. It's what he did at Judie's the night you came home. He came back after Judie threw him out. He was leering at me and he was leering at Jeanne, way in the middle of the night."

Peter was mystified and did not know what to say.

"Martin, do you know that some people are condemned, and some are not? Some gets *hanted* and some gets grace, so what are you doing here? You're the one that got grace. Why don't you go back to all those pretty little rivers and baseball fields of yours, that great home-vale of yours. Don't you appreciate the value of a vale? Where's that little Mickey-brother of yours you used to tell me about on the ship? Where's all those fine sisters that used to linger around so lovingly? Where's your Maw, your Paw? Where's your sense, boy?"

"Why, my whole family's living in New York now."

"Ah, Martin, you sadden me. Still, do you think you could possibly lend me a hundred dollars so I could run away to Mexico? You have money, don't you? You just got off a ship not so long ago." He was suddenly pale and earnest.

"I haven't got a *hundred dollars*. What do you want to run away to Mexico for?"

"To get away from the *spook!* The old man! Old leering one-arm Waldo! Old castrated mother-witch Meister with the meat hanging from her bones!"

"Why don't you just tell that guy to shove off?"

"Spook, spook . . ."

"Even spooks shove off," scowled Peter.

"Not faggot spooks like these. They tell tales of love and death. This here spook has followed me for years from one haunt to another, scaring little children and making old folks cry. Still, do you think you could round up a hundred dollars?"

"Not a *hundred*."

"A hundred or nothing at all!" said Kenny in a strange strangled voice, beating his knees with his fists. "Or I'll simply have to hitch-hike and try not to see spooks in trees at night." They paid their bill and went out for a cab.

When they arrived on Fifty-Second Street, Peter confusedly saw a large group of people standing on the sidewalk in front of a nightclub. Then he recognized Judie and Jeanne, Levinsky and Waldo, Junkey, and a tall shambling youngster who seemed strangely familiar. Kenneth ran up to them and suddenly seized Jeanne and began kissing her passionately in a long embrace. The others paid no particular attention to this, except Waldo, who raised his cane to his shoulder and watched with an intent smile.

"Yeah, there you are finally!" cried Julie, scowling at Peter. "I'd wait a heck of a long time if I waited at home for *you!*" But she took his arm and pulled him off.

Leon Levinsky stepped up in a curious little shuffle, hands clasped in front of him meekly, like a polite Oriental, bowing with a little nod. "Just now two fellows in the bar wanted to fight Waldo and Junkey and me because we had two *charming* young ladies with us. Apparently they felt some sort of unseemliness, and I rather admire their awful wisdom. Needless to say, we cut out." He giggled and stepped back.

"Well, let's not stand around here," emphasized Kenneth nervously, "let's walk or something, or go somewhere else." And he went over to Waldo Meister, who had been standing around listening with a vague smile, took a cigarette from his pack, and went back to Jeanne. Everybody began to move in straggling confused groups, Kenneth and Jeanne taking up the rear and stopping frequently to kiss passionately. It was a warm pleasant Spring night and the sidewalks of Fifty-Second Street were crowded.

"Well," said the tall shambling boy, putting a big hand on Peter's shoulder, "don't you remember me?"

It was Buddy Fredericks. Peter had to think twice before he realized it.

"We've been waiting for you since this afternoon!" cried Judie scornfully. "Buddy came to see you and had some beer and everything!"

"And where's Liz?" cried Peter.

"She's in town," smiled Buddy. "Look over there at that sign in front of the Opal Club, what do you see, man?"

Across the street in front of the nightclub there was a large sign, reading: "Billy Camarada and his sextet, featuring Ottawa Johnson, tenor; Curly Parker, bass; Mel Gage, drums; Lucky DeCarlo, guitar; and Buddy Fredericks, piano."

"Why, that's wonderful! I didn't know *you* were playing with

Billy Camarada. He's great! And where's Liz? How is she? How's the Lizzy?"

"She's singing in a nightclub down in the Village, the Village Haven."

"Singing!" yelled Peter astounded. "My own sister—singing in a nightclub? And I didn't even know about it! What do you know about that, Judie! Is she any good, Bud? Come on, man, give us a fair estimate!" He was suddenly overjoyed to be talking to Buddy, and to Judie too, after the strange tormented talk of Kenneth downtown.

"Liz is a pretty good singer," laughed Buddy, "a little on the Neets O'Day kick. She started in 'Frisco last summer—"

"And where are you two living?"

Buddy looked at Peter with sudden gravity.

"Say!" went on Peter enthusiastically, "did you happen to succeed a second time? Did you have a nephew for me maybe?"

"Well, no. Ever since what happened in Detroit Liz never wanted to have a baby again—"

"Aw, she'll get over that."

"Another thing—that is," stammered the big musician, "well, Liz and I are separated. I just got in from L.A. myself. Liz has been in New York for three months. We broke up, you see . . ."

Without so much surprise as disgust Peter looked away angrily. They had all come to a halt on the corner of Fifth Avenue and were milling around uncertainly. Waldo Meister, the leader of this aimless parade, looked north and south, east and west, and finally turned about face and said, "Well, there's no place to sit around here, we might as well go back this way"—and he started back in the direction they had come from.

"Say, why don't we find a park bench or something to sit down!" suggested weary Junkey to the general company. "I'd like to sit down and just relax. . . ."

"I understand there's a musician in the crowd," spoke up Waldo Meister with a smile. "What do you play?"

"Piano," said Buddy, looking down at him gravely. "They tell me you have a large collection of records."

"Yes. But I don't seem to enjoy it any more. . . ."

"Classical records, I imagine?"

"What else is there? Of course. Is there a connection?" Waldo demanded with sudden sarcasm.

"Oh, wonderful!" cried Levinsky, stepping in. "This is something that should be talked about! You haven't heard the new bebop jazz, Waldo, a complete departure from the old European forms. It's a kind of wild Dionysian American music, pure emotion and frenzy that sends great vibrations through everyone. It's just mad!"

"It seems cooler to me than that," smiled Buddy.

"Almost like an orgy, don't you see, in which everyone will explode and become as one. Actually!"

"Music does all that?" grinned Buddy with amazement.

"Yes. I've felt that. It creates a frantic, almost daisy-chain rapport similar to marijuana, you see! Oh, you should see the mad characters that go to jazz concerts now, right here in New York!"

"Well, *man*—but what about the music itself?"

"As far as I can understand it," snapped Waldo in a curious, piping, infuriated voice that sounded so forlorn and surprised everybody, "bebop or jazz or whatever you call it is just a lot of bleating noise. It certainly doesn't rate as music and whatever you may say about it, it's a lot of adolescent nonsense for adolescent American fools!"

"Hurrah!" cried Kenneth Wood from down the street.

Buddy was not visibly touched by these remarks which were flung at him in the general confusion and irritability of the moment. He only shrugged, smiled, and turned to look at Peter with cool amusement.

But at that moment Waldo had turned and said something, obviously pettish, to Kenneth, who suddenly flushed angrily and turned away. Jeanne was standing next to Waldo and listening to the general conversation with a dreamy smile, when Kenneth took Jeanne by the arm and said: "Come on, *ma petite,* let's go home now." Waldo clutched Kenneth's arm and hung on with a haggard look of abject supplication.

Kenneth looked at him. "Let go, old man, or I'll dispose of your carcass right now, I swear I will."

Waldo stepped closer, still hanging on. "Look here, Kenneth, let me come with you, please. Don't you think it's time to have a long talk? Don't you think it's time to understand?"

Everybody was watching with horror and confusion, though pretending not to notice.

"I said let go, you old fairy!" shouted Kenneth in a rage. He suddenly gave Waldo a tremendous push in the face with the flat of his hand that sent him sprawling flat on his back on the sidewalk. With a sickening thud his head popped back on the pavement and the cane he was carrying clattered tragically at his side. It was a gruesome helpless sight.

Waldo fumbled to sit up and Junkey leaned down to help him, as a small crowd gathered and the others stood around mortified. Kenneth went striding off up the street with his heels clacking loudly on the pavement. Peter suddenly ran after him and turned him around.

"Look here, for krissakes, Kenny, you don't have to knock down a poor cripple!"

Kenneth kept walking. "Since you're not acquainted with the facts, Martin, you might keep your conclusions to yourself."

"Ah, you're all crazy!" yelled Peter, suddenly feeling suffocated and sick with disgust.

"That may be so, naive one, but if someone wanted to kill *you* I don't doubt you'd knock him down too. Good night." Kenneth disappeared around the corner. Peter looked back at the others helping Waldo to his feet. Suddenly he wanted to go home and leave these sad nightmarish things behind. He hurried across the street towards the subway.

[7]

ONE MORNING the following week, after spending his days at home reading and studying, Peter got ready to go back to Manhattan. It was noon, his father was in the front room figuring out the horses in the *Racing Form* and smoking a cigar.

"Where are you going now?" he asked, looking up at Peter over his spectacles with a bland, affectionate, curious stare.

"Oh, I'm going back to New York."

"Still sold on them, hey?" The old man said that with a sly grin, chuckling heartily. Peter stood rooted to the spot, frowning, wondering why it always had to be so aggravating to talk to his father about his comings and goings—which, he realized ruefully, were always so useless. He had been thinking about it for days, just lying on his bed and thinking about it over his books. But a vast restless pendulum in him had swung back again, and now, inexplicably, he was burning with curiosity to go back and see what everybody was doing, what Kenneth was doing, and Judie, and Dennison, and Levinsky, even Waldo. And what else was there to do?

"What do you mean, I'm still sold on them?"

"Just what I said, you keep seeing them"—and old Martin, though not looking up at Peter, continued to pore over his figures with a secret pleased smile. He even began to hum a little bit.

"I'm not *sold* on them," scoffed Peter.

His father said not a word, but continued to hum a little tune, and suddenly he leaned forward with a swift busy movement and neatly flicked a little figure on the sheet.

Peter started to leave the room, but his father seemed to pay no attention to this, and suddenly, with a distinct feeling that he was being fooled, Peter sat down and quickly lit a cigarette. There was a long interval of silence.

Finally Peter blurted: "Is there any reason why I shouldn't see them?"

"I dunno. I think you ought to make better friends, that's all." And Martin wrote another figure on the sheet with a profound air. "Kids who'd take you seriously and be friendly and helpful and *real*, dammit."

"Well," smiled Peter almost sarcastically, "they aren't exactly like the boys who used to hang around the barbershop with you in Galloway, you know. This is New York."

"No, I guess they're not," said Martin with a certain amount of absentminded gloom as he turned over the page of the paper. "No, siree. 'Way back in Lacoshua we were just a bunch of country boys, just hicks, no fancy educations or anything like that. Just a bunch of simple boys, but we had a lot of fun and respected each other. Old Pete Cartier is one of those boys. Anything wrong with Pete Cartier?"

"Who said there was?" scowled Peter. "I only mean that these guys in New York have more on their minds—they're smarter in some ways—more interesting in some ways—you might say modern. You can't expect me to do the same things you did."

"Modern," smiled the old man dryly. "By the way, why don't you see some of those shipmates of yours, they seemed like a nice bunch of fellows."

"I don't need friends, I don't have to go around *looking* for friends. I can get along without them. When I'm ashore I like to do whatever I please. I'm just hanging around and taking it easy—"

"You're hanging around with a bunch of dope fiends and crooks, that's what you're doing."

"Who said that?" glared Peter.

"Oh, don't worry, I've got eyes and ears. As long as all that doesn't affect *you*. I'm *proud* of you to have dope fiends and crooks and crackpots for friends. It's just what I anticipated from you when you were a little kid, when you ran up to me that day crying and telling me that your little brother had died."

Peter was strangely reflective. "I want to know everything about New York, that's what it is." He realized that his father knew all about his friends. He felt that he was picking up the threads of an old conversation somehow. "I'm really het up on that, Pa. It seems I don't care what people do, as long as it's something different. I get curious."

"Well, yes," said George Martin, equally calm and judicious, "I used to be like that too, I used to get curious as hell about some things, wasn't satisfied till I knew all about it. Sometimes I'd make a fool of myself. I guess there was a streak of excessive curiosity in me. But some things disgusted me—I never liked crooks."

"*I'm* too curious for that," said Peter earnestly, wondering why this seemed so true. "I hate those punks on Times Square, the guys with blackjacks and sometimes guns, I can spot them. But I like to talk to some of the others. I don't know what you call them—they're just waiting around for something. I feel like an idiot sometimes, I really do."

"There was a little streak of that too, I guess—idiocy! I dunno . . . sometimes I feel like I've been an idiot at times, especially about my printing business. Yes, there's a streak, all right."

"I don't take any of that dope, you know. What interests me is *why* they start taking it, how they feel. Life is life."

"Look! You can say whatever you want, but I've no way of knowing whether you take it or not!" shouted Martin suddenly.

"You'd believe that of *me*?" cried Peter. "What do you think I am anyway?—a fool, a moron or something?"

"Your friends are, aren't they? There's an old saying that birds of a feather flock together.

"I don't swallow that stuff about curiosity, Peter," continued the old man, brooding away. "I don't know what's happened to you, frankly. It all went wrong long ago, you're another victim of the same things I was talking about the other night—"

"I do whatever I like! If I'm curious, I am! If I'm interested in certain people, I am! I'm not a victim of anything! I'm going to live in this world, I'm going to find out all about it, I'm not going to hide my eyes like a maiden in distress, or like an old Puritan either, or like a scared rabbit! I'm interested in life, any kind of life, all of it!"

"What could be your interest in that one-armed fellow?"

"Waldo Meister? I don't even know him."

"But he hangs around, doesn't he?"

"I don't want him around and neither does Judie. Kenny Wood knocked him down last week!" Peter was blurting away with child-like apologetic eagerness.

"I know, I know . . ." said George Martin.

"Well, now, how would *you* know!" Peter looked at his father, and marveled that he should know so much. Then he felt somewhat frightened by the sudden, unexpected, unknown twist of it.

"I didn't tell you, but your friend Levinsky came here the other night, I guess it was Monday night when you went to the movies with your mother and Mickey."

"Ah-*ha!*"

"And I talked to him," cried the old man angrily, "and I got a lot of information out of him, I got an earful. He likes to talk, he thinks he's making an impression. I bought him a few drinks down at the corner and he talked."

"You never told me he came."

"No, I didn't!"

"I don't care anyway."

They both sat staring away in irritated silence.

"If you want my opinion I think you're crazy to hang around with that bunch—head-crazy!" He tapped his head. "I can't think of any other explanation."

"If I'm crazy, so are you!" choked Peter.

"That's a fine thing to say."

"Ever since I can remember you've been telling me what *not* to do, what *not* to do. But you never did tell me *what* to do!"

"I'm not God, I can't tell you what to do, all I can tell you is what I *think* you should do—"

"Should this and should that—it's all I hear around here."

"That may be so. I'm your father and I'm older than you are and I've had more experience—"

"More experience, and yet you say there are some things you wouldn't look into—"

"I've lived longer and I should know what's best for you!" shouted the old man. "What about your future? The way you're going now, you're not headed for anything."

"The hell with the future."

"For all I know you'll end up a dope fiend yourself, a bum, a tramp, no better than the ones you hang around with. You threw away an education, you make a little money on ships and you spend it drinking and supporting a little slut—"

"She's not that at all," grinned Peter with a kind of mad satisfaction.

"Whatever she is! It isn't right and it isn't honest! You seem to have no sense of honor at all! Everything your mother and I taught you is gone, it's all twisted up in that damn silly head of yours till I can't make you out for the life of me. It hurts, you devil, it hurts!" he shouted. "I'm your father and I'm *worried* about you—"

"It's just another way of saying I'm a no-good bum, go ahead and admit it! So I drink, all right, I have my reasons! What's the great thing we're supposed to be living for now anyway? What's the great faith, hope and charity of the age that's been dumped on our heads—"

"On my head, too! On my head, too!"

"All right! But we don't have to blame the age, that's all they do, blame the age."

"It's simple enough," said Martin. "Your mother and I, your whole family, her people, dumb as they are, and *my* people have always been working people, we believed in working for a living and living *real* lives. That's what you can say about this country in general, or at least the way it used to be—"

"That has nothing to do with it!"

"This country doesn't mean a thing to you kids, it's just a big dumb place where you happen to be helling and spoofing around, that's all it is!"

Peter smiled.

"Sure, sure!" yelled the old man. "You kids know it all. But you'll get it in the neck all right and it won't—"

"You hope so."

"I hope so? Lordy, Lordy, you're getting it in the neck now," he said with an agonized expression, "but I guess there must be a kind of new courage among you. You can take so much and not give a damn and still go around with that smile. I give you credit for that, all of you. But you don't *care!* You don't care for your parents who love you. Something *evil* and awful has happened, there's nothing but unhappiness everywhere. And the *coldness* of everybody!"

"I don't know what you're talking about," said Peter.

"Life is living, working at it, planning, believing in it, things to do, living, living, simple living, and there's God in it, too!"

"Some people get bored." Peter was saying whatever would make his father mad.

"Oh, that's another tall tale made up for God knows what reason. It's all so insane. I would never dream that my own children would fall for it, *you*, and Liz, and Francis! I would never dream it! Why do you all want to be so unhappy, why do you want to punish yourselves? Lord only knows what'll happen to Charley and little Mickey in time, or you. In the end it just finally breaks a father's heart. Both ways!"

With a swift sweet insight, Peter suddenly heard himself blurt: "Why don't you come and visit Judie and me tonight and we'll go to a show. It's your night off, isn't it?"

"What for?" barked Martin, a little surprised. "I don't think she'd be glad to see us."

"She's got to, well, she's my girl, and she should meet you more. Why not?"

"Well, I'll talk to Marge about it. I guess you're pretty serious on the little girl, aren't you?" The old man looked away gently. "I didn't mean what I said about her, I don't even know her, that's the whole trouble—"

"I'm not *serious* about her, I guess I'm not serious about anything, or I guess I'm serious about everything and that just can't be done. I dunno," Peter was muttering sadly.

"Well—"

"Come on over tonight," he stammered. "We'll do *something.* I'll see you tonight? Huh? Don't forget." And Peter went out casually. When he closed the iron gate at the sidewalk, he saw his father sitting inside in an attitude of brooding loneliness.

"The most beautiful idea on the face of the earth," he thought unaccountably, "is the idea the child has that his father knows everything."

In the subway he brooded over the thought that *that* must be the idea men had always had of God. But he recalled sorrowfully that when the child grew up and sought advice he got only fumbling earnest human words, when the child sought a way of some sort he only found that his father's way was not enough, and the child was left cold with the realization that nobody, not even his father, really knew what to do. And yet, that children and fathers should have a notion in their souls that there must be a way, an authority, a great knowledge, a vision, a view of life, a proper manner, an order in all the disorder and sadness of the world—that alone must be God in men. No matter if men could live without inner stress and qualms, without scruples or morals or dark trepidations, without guilt or self-abasement or horror, without sighs and distressful spiritual worry that had no name—no matter, they continued to think that. The *should-be* in their souls powerfully prevailed, that was mightily so.

[8]

WHEN PETER barged into Judie's apartment, he found her in the front room entertaining a young man she had met in a bar that morning. They were drinking beer and talking. He was a young seaman just back from a voyage to Brazil, wearing dark glasses, cubana pegged trousers, and a weirdly colored silk scarf around his throat. At first he glared angrily at Peter, not understanding the situation, not knowing that he was a victim of Judie's incessant plot to make Peter jealous. Peter decided not to appear jealous and walked into his den and sat down and stared gloomily out the window at the gray rooftops of the day.

When the weird young seaman eventually left, Judie came in and sat on the arm of Peter's chair, with a wry, nervous air.

"Are you jealous?"

"No, I'm not jealous. When are you going to grow up, you damn fool."

"When are *you* going to grow up, Mister Martin! You disappear for days, and expect me to sit around and wait for you."

"I went home for a while, that's all."

"You went home," she mimicked sarcastically, "home to those damn parents of yours who don't do anything but criticize all day long. Well, you can have 'em, brother!"

"Listen," said Peter, getting up and gripping her by the arm and almost shaking her, "you want to get married, but you don't want anything that goes with it." Peter was yelling. "Sure, sure, you want to get married—and you won't even speak a civil word to my own folks. I don't even know what kind of mother you'd make—"

"Don't you love me?" she suddenly demanded, tearfully. He had frightened her. She moved to a corner of the room and stared at him appalled, and he felt a rush of sorrow for her.

"Look, Judie, dammit, I do! I *like* you! Maybe you and I could make a go of it, all our lives maybe, but there are some things you do that I don't like!" He was flustered and torn by these things he did not want to say.

"Well, you're not perfect yourself!" she cried.

"Okay, I'm not perfect—but what are we going to do?" he finally brought out wearily. He sat down. "Listen," he said finally, "my folks are coming over late this afternoon, I invited them. We're all going out to dinner and a show."

"I'm not going. I don't want to see them."

"Well, there you have it."

"I want to marry *you*, not them."

"Nobody's asking you to marry them. Where I come from young married couples get along with their folks—"

"I don't care where you come from, small towns and poor people and all their silly rules. I'm going to live the way I like and I don't care what anybody thinks. You're getting to be just like your old man, just a stuffy old goat always worried about something or other. You *love* to worry! Why don't you just try to enjoy life—like my father used to do before he died," she added contemplatively. "When I first met you, Petey, I thought you were just like him—your smile and the way you did things, a great athlete, and the way you liked to eat and make love and—*just be!* But now you're just like your father. Oh, I hate him!" she cried angrily.

Peter was sitting by the window where a mournful rain had begun to patter in the glass, and he was staring out. Judie saw him like that, and came over and sat in his lap, and leaned her face against his, softly. And just the feel of her temple against his cheek, her warm small skull pressed endearingly against him, and her little hand curling in his, made him forget all the trouble.

In the half darkness they stared at the shadowy sockets of each other's eyes, at the faint luminous eye of themselves, and brooded, and listened to the rain on the rooftops. They knew so much about each other, finally, that it must be impossible for them to fight ever again. The whole world was raining, but they were together in the warm sweet atmosphere of themselves, in the faint light their eyes made in the darkness, in the climate their bodies made embracing, in the season of their loving sadness. They were completely alone together in the sweetness of this, but it was then and then only somehow that they could remember the real enormous human love they must have for everyone else in the world. And the wisdom of the tender fact that they loved each other was so true and final. So much so that they did not say a word for hours together in the darkness, they were just quiet there.

When Peter's mother and father came at seven o'clock, Judie herself went to the door and greeted them with a bashful tenderness. Peter was happier at that moment than he could ever recall.

His father sat on the edge of the couch nervously, with the ponderous, modest, decent air of his kind of man, with the vast sad look of him more striking than ever, as he looked at little Judie and seemed to decide that she was a good girl after all. His eyes were luminous, moist, and shy as he looked up at her. Peter knew that his father was a forgiver before anything else, a forgiver within himself before he ever forgave in a formal sense. And his mother, with her shrewd peering eyes and her shy, jolly ways, she too was a person of whom he was proud—because of her great understanding which was always concealed under her gay rueful little manner. She would chuckle and "try to make the best of things" always, and Peter sensed the value of that strongly.

"Well," said the old man, "are we ready to hit a good feed and a show?"

"And I know just the place to go!" cried Judie, bubbling and blushing. "A restaurant I bet you never went to! *You!*"

"Me?" cried the old man pleased that she was addressing him. "All right there, my little one, name it and we'll see."

"Huh!" scoffed Judie. "I'm not telling you. We'll just go there and I bet you'll admit you never went there."

"It's a deal!" laughed the old man, taking out a cigar and lighting it. As Judie ran into her room to dress, the mother turned to old Martin and chuckled gleefully.

"She can be so cute! She's so nice, Petey! I'm so glad we came. You know, she has the same little mannerisms Lizzy used to have!" She dabbed at her eyes, inexplicably. "The little thing!"

When the doorbell rang, Peter hurried to it with the tremendous feeling that he had just learned how to live and love, and would never forget the secret. He opened the door with the air of someone accepting a challenge, like a little boy, vaguely conscious of the foolish joyousness of it all—yet with that mysterious fear of something overpoweringly unknown. He remembered this feeling later on, and recognized the prescience of it sadly. The man at the door showed a police badge and walked in nonchalantly.

"What's the matter?"

"You're Peter Martin? You'll have to drop downtown with us. We only want to ask a few questions to clear up something. There's been a suicide, fellow by the name of Waldo Meister. Jumped out the window of Kenneth Wood's apartment. But our investigations aren't complete yet. Just put on your coat."

The detective sat in the front room and began chatting with the others, telling them all about it affably. Peter lingered meditatively in his bedroom for a moment, full of sinking feelings. Waldo Meister was dead!

"Oh, is *that* all!" he heard Judie laugh scornfully. "It's just as well. And I hope Kenny did it himself!"

The detective pounced on this. "Look here, little girl! You may not know it, but that's a serious charge—"

"Uff!" she scoffed, and barged around the room in her old slapdash way. "That bastard tried to kill my cat and I'm glad he's dead, I was gonna kill him myself."

"Take it easy, Judie," said Peter angrily.

"Oh, shut up!"

"A fine thing!" roared the old man, pacing around the room. "Now my own son is mixed up in a murder case! Now it's finally coming out! I told you not to get mixed up with these people, I warned you a hundred times! Now you're in trouble! Well, good God!—Murder!"

The detective grinned as though enjoying the scene. "Well, we're not sure about *that!* I think personally it's a suicide, all right."

The old man glared at him. "Isn't that bad enough? That a man should go and throw himself out of a boy's window for some silly reason! That's what this damn world is coming to nowadays! You ought to know that yourself in your profession!" He was red in the neck and perfectly pale in the face.

Suddenly everyone noticed that Peter's mother was crying. Peter rushed to her and held her in his arm; she was trembling. "Take it easy, Ma, it's nothing, it'll be okay."

"All these terrible things!" she moaned. "Petey, what are they going to do to you?" She clung to him fearfully, shivering all over and pale.

Judie suddenly laughed almost hysterically. "Good God!" she cried, without elaborating any further, and Peter turned to her with a look of hatred.

"You watch what you're doing, you little—"

"Shaddap!" yelled Judie defiantly, and for a moment they glared at each other.

The old man was infuriated. "This is what I might have expected from brats! You're all alike, all of you! If you'd of stayed home and minded your business, or made decent friends, you wouldn't be getting in awful jams like this! Well, you didn't listen! Goddamit, you asked for it!"

"Ain't it nice to say I told you so!" cried Judie mockingly.

"Shut up!" cried Peter, out of his mind. He rushed to Judie and took her by the arm and, for some reason or other, in his agonized confusion, tried to sit her down in a chair. Judie shook him off with a loathing look. His knees were like water, he had to sit down. The detective by now was somewhat confused himself, but momentarily pulled himself out of that by assuming his official capacities and saying that it was time to go.

"You'll have to identify the body at the morgue."

"*Can* I come along too?" cried Martin, suddenly grabbing up his coat.

"It won't be necessary, Mr. Martin."

"But I want to come along. If my kid's in trouble I want to see if I can help. And I don't want him to get any kind of raw deal—"

"No, no, nothing like that, he's in no trouble—none that I know of. It's an open-and-shut case all right, but we're just checking. If I were you people I wouldn't go and get excited."

"But I can't help it!" sobbed Peter's mother. "It's just something that never happened to any of my children, they were never mixed up in anything like that. Can't my husband go along and help? Oh, Petey, you must tell them the truth, whatever you know, don't lie to them, Petey. George, why don't you go along with him. Oh, what am I going to do now?"

Peter was heartbroken as she said these things. He rushed back to her. He had a blind reeling feeling of stumbling about from one person to another in an awful nightmare. He had not seen his mother cry since he was a boy and it wrenched him to see her like that. He himself was crying, silently, great tears rolling down his face, which he brushed away wonderingly.

Judie was disgusted and suddenly threw on her coat and flounced out of the house.

"Where are you going?" yelled Peter, stumbling across the room after her.

"I'm sick and tired of all you damn serfs. I'll come back to my house after you're all gone. Do you know something?" she suddenly added, rushing back to the doorway. "It's just typical of poor people, always afraid of everything. Well, that's not for me! If you get in trouble and you need money to get out of jail, *I'm* the one who can get you out, not *them!*" she cried contemptuously. "So I'll see you later, fool."

"Listen, my young lady," roared old Martin after her, "you can always spray your nose with perfume, it will lessen your own odor! How do you like that!" He jammed his hat on his head and stalked around fuming, as Judie slammed the hall door and left. The detective standing beside Peter looked at everybody with amazement. "And that's that," sighed old Martin, taking off his hat and holding it and looking around mournfully, as though somehow paying respect to the awfulness of what had happened, not knowing what to do any more.

Peter went downtown with the detective in his car and his parents simply went home in the subway. The thought of how they would feel now in all their terror and innocence crushed him completely.

When they arrived at Kenny Wood's apartment at the Palmyran Towers, Kenny was pale and obviously scared out of his wits by the turn of events. He looked white-faced at Peter. His father was there making telephone calls to his influential friends all over town. He was a trim handsome man, graying at the temples, youngish in his energy and poise, a well-known broker on Wall Street and figure in New York society. Peter had never seen him before in all the years he had known Kenny. Now that the boy was in trouble, it was plain that the father was concerned only with the possibility of scandalous repercussions.

"You see," he was saying to another detective, "I have a reputation to maintain. I just wish that the investigation might have been conducted with more decorum. The tabloids are apt to make an awful splash about it."

"We can't do anything about the press, Mr. Wood."

"Yes, I suppose not." He smiled quickly. "Who is this?" he added, looking at Peter, but Peter hated him so much at that moment, with a kind of sullen pleasure, that the man got a dirty look for his curiosity. Eventually Mr. Wood left, explaining that he had to go for an important appointment, squeezing Kenny's arm, saying something in a low voice as the boy listened grinning, and bounding out energetically with a kind of embarrassed little gaiety.

Tired and confused, Peter wandered into the front room while waiting for whatever the detectives wanted. He realized as he crossed the threshold that Kenny's great-grandmother was in the room. He had almost forgotten her existence. Actually, he was a great favorite of hers from way back.

She was a withered old lady, but she still bore traces of some old rawboned strength. She sat with a plaid blanket over her lap, old gold-rimmed spectacles in her upturned hand, some flowers beside her in little clay pots that she tended, and a knotted cane resting against the chair. She frowned thoughtfully. "I was sitting here," she said, "and they came and told me about it. Do you know something? I don't think it's such a much. I've *seen* men commit suicide in my time. I saw a man jump off a bluff into the Missouri River a long time ago, I was a little girl."

"How long ago was that?"

"Well, Petey, I can't count any more, I guess it was in the Sixties, as I say I was a little girl. Did you hear *him* in there talking about his reputation? Do you know what he's talking about? The work and suffering of the men who came before him, my husband, my husband's son. When they heard there was gold, they went. They didn't find gold, none to speak of, that is, and you know they came *back* all the way. Some of 'em went West and a lot of 'em came back, but it was all the same then, they all craved work. My husband began cutting trees in Virginia and my son made paper and sold it. Then he went in the cattle business in Kansas. That's *his* reputation in there!"

The old lady was upset and some deep rancor against her grandson, Kenny's father, was coming out.

"He never was a father. He was never even a son. I've always wondered why a line of men starts strong and ends up like that. . . . Now little Kenny's got a lot of Wood in him, but he never got a chance. I was too old to make much difference anyhow. And the men who came before can't do much from the grave to spur their kin. There's no spurring in this house, never was—and the mother got herself married to an Austrian count, now *that's* something! We used to laugh at that, in the old house in Richmond. In those days in the Nineties we were as rich as you like, and Kenny's aunts were almost swept off their feet by two or three European counts that I can remember, but they ended up marrying some no-account Kentuckians and Missourians just the same. Ah, but I've seen this family change—from the big houses full of brothers and sisters down to this. This!" She waved a limp hand scornfully. "But I've got no say now—I just sit here and think about it."

She put on her glasses slowly and peered at Peter. "You come to see me again some time. Be a good son and you'll be a good father and that will keep going all the time." She frowned at him. "My gosh, a woman loves a good man—and you can keep that going all the time."

It was moving to hear these things after all that had happened that day, after everything that Peter had known in New York in the past years. This old lady sitting by a window in towering Manhattan, remembering Missouri in 1860 and the men and things of that time, remembering the first sawmills of Virginia, and cattle trail days, the early American time of great forests and wild plains. These places and raw simplicities had now gone into the night, far beyond the incomprehensible sprawl, the cancerous smoky suburbs, the street-demented scab and wreckage of New York City and its outflung Chicagos, Cincinnatis, Milwaukees, Detroits, and Clevelands—so easily forgotten in the turmoils of city-time and city-talk and city-life and city-sarcasm and city-weariness, in all the Brooklyns and Babylons, Baltimores and

Gomorrhas, Gazas and Philadelphias, and the pitted and blasted black Pittsburghs with all their Toledos and Bridgeports, ruined Newarks and Jersey Cities and the satellites thereof, the smoke-smothered Hobokens and Akrons and Garys of the land.

In her voice he heard the voices of all old people, voices without sarcasm and weariness and disgust, strong voices telling in a long way the chronicle of labor and belief and human joy. In her voice he heard his own mother's voice, the voices of his grandfathers and grandmothers, the voices he wanted to hear again, the voices that soothed in a harsh world, in a world of real struggle and true hope.

Peter kissed the old lady on the cheek and said good-bye. He never saw her again; she died a month later, just a few weeks short of one hundred years of age.

It began to rain in torrents. Peter and Kenny and the two detectives drove down to Bellevue Hospital to identify the body in the morgue.

They ran up the steps and ducked inside, almost boisterously, but at once they smelled the burnt odor of decay and death. An attendant behind a desk dozed over a magazine, an old clock ticked on the wall, the rain poured outside. Peter and Kenny looked at each other with terrified sadness. After checking some papers at the desk, one of the detectives beckoned the boys and started down a ramp of broad steps into the basement. As they descended the stairs, the sound of the rain lessened, the silence of death took over, and the boys' hearts pounded with horror and greedy curiosity.

In the cold damp cement atmosphere of the basement, in the catacombs of the city, there was the presence of something horrible and secret and guarded—the innumerable kept dead of the brutal streets above.

When Peter and Kenny saw what the morgue was actually like, they trembled in their bones. They expected to see rows of marble slabs and corpses covered by white sheets. They pitiably got this idea from movies and crime magazines. Instead—and with a feeling that it could not have been otherwise—they saw rows upon rows of big filing cases on all sides with numbers and handles on the doors. The detective glanced impatiently at the slip of paper in his hand, speculated with a finger pointing, selected a door, gripped the handle, called out jubilantly, "Here it is! Sixty-nine!"

—and yanked back. Slowly, on rollers, the corpse of Waldo Meister swung into view.

If it *was* Waldo Meister. The corpse that lay there on its back was a mangled thing, in no way human. Slumped, broken, with one elbow turned up the wrong way, one knee twisted around, brown clotty gobs where the face should have been, and hair like a mop used on the floor of an abattoir. A fly buzzed out as the filing cabinet opened, a lone fly that had remained inside the niche since afternoon, and now momentarily flew away.

Peter could feel his knees buckle. Kenny paled like a sheet. The silence all around was ghastly with the sudden presence of this apparition.

"That's him!" cried the detective, smiling at the youngsters and standing back to gaze with official impartiality at the thing on the roller-board. "Just identify him and we're all done for the night. My old lady's keeping my supper warm." As he spoke a huge attendant, a beefy red-haired man in an undershirt and white duck trousers, came shambling out of the shadows at the end of the aisle, munching on a sandwich and staring at them curiously. He was eating at a little table by the back door of the basement, where a truck backed up at that moment. Two men struggled in with a long box containing, presumably, still another corpse picked up in the streets above. They were swearing and shouting because the rain was dripping on them from a faulty drainpipe.

"Well, can you identify him?" demanded the detective.

"How the hell can we do that!" muttered Peter. "That doesn't look like anybody I ever saw. Why don't you just close it up and let's go!" He backed up instinctively, almost touching another row of filing cases. He jumped forward again in a stumble of nightmarish futility. He had the sudden urge to run like the wind right out of there.

"He won't hurt you, kiddo," growled the undershirted attendant with the sandwich, "not *now* he won't." And to the utter amazement of the two boys this man walked up to the corpse and plucked at the dry bloody hair with one hand, lolling the skull back and forth grotesquely, as he munched on the sandwich. "He had brown hair, didn't he? See the brown hair here underneath the blood? Come up *close* and look. You can't see nawthin' from there." He turned the head over, the pitiful head. . . .

"Come on, come on!" commanded the detective impatiently. "I can't stay here all night. Ain't you guys ever seen a weenie before?"

Kenny was trying to mumble something, stuttering and clutching his hands and looking desperately away. "I don't—know—who that is . . . honest to Christ I don't." His face was a contortion of grief and revulsion.

"Well, do you recognize the clothes? See the shoes there! How about the wallet!"

"Wallet?"

"Right under that broken arm, the wallet there. Did you ever see that wallet before?" shouted the detective.

The attendant reached over and plucked up the wallet and showed it to Kenneth, who glanced at it fearfully, and nodded, saying: "Yes, that's Waldo's wallet— I . . . I remember it all right."

"And the brown hair?" said the attendant, grinning with a leer at Kenny, and suddenly tearing up a fingerful of hair from the skull which cracked dryly, and holding the tuft underneath the boy's nose.

Kenneth dodged away with an agonized cry. "You crazy sonofabitch you!!"

"Hyah! hyah! hyah!" roared the attendant flinging the piece of hair away and twirling triumphantly on one foot. Without another word he walked back down the grisly aisle, munching on the sandwich.

"Please let's get the hell out of here," pleaded Peter. "What's the sense? Just push him back in and let's go." He turned and walked back to the stairs with the vision of the corpse burning as though it would never be erased from his mind. He saw it even when he closed his eyes, and he knew he would never forget it. It was not the corpse alone but the place where it was filed and registered, nameless and dead, in the dank underworld basement of the city.

As they waited in the office upstairs, a call came through from headquarters ordering Kenny Wood's release. The investigation was closed. The boys shambled out together in the rain and walked away from the morgue.

"Did I do that to the guy?" mourned Kenneth, looking at Peter in the downpour. His face was all wet from raindrops and tears, pale from terror, all twisted and stunned.

"You didn't do *that* to him, Ken."
"Oh, yes, I did—in my fashion. Just like Cynara and all that."
"There's life and death, man, and he's dead. Everybody dies—"
"You don't know what you're talking about!" scoffed Kenneth darkly.

They were walking along in the rain mechanically with no thought of sheltering themselves and no idea where they were and where they were going.

"Well, good-bye, Pete. . . ."

"Where are you going?" shouted Peter.

"How the hell should I know—where are *you* going?"

"Let's walk together anyway." Peter frowned and took him by the arm, and wondered what he could say. He could think of nothing. Perhaps they would go on walking all night in the rain. The neon lights of a bar were shining in the rain across the street.

"Let's go in there for a drink," said Kenneth. "I've still got some money Dennison gave me to go to Mexico."

"Okay. Don't worry, Ken, you'll be okay. . . ."

"You speak more nonsense—"

"Well, go to hell then."

"I've just been there. Let's have a drink and a toast to something, a toast to my grandmother maybe."

"Did you hear me talking to her tonight?" laughed Peter with a rattled little croak.

"I certainly did!" Kenny sighed, and suddenly, without any warning, he dug in his pockets, came up with a handful of bills, flung them away in the rain, and started running up the street. Peter stood stock still wondering what was going on. He started after Kenny, came back, searched feverishly for the bills soaking in the gutter, picked them up, and ran full speed after the boy, catching up with him at the corner.

"Where are you going? ! !" he shouted, gripping him by the arm and pulling him around impulsively.

Kenny turned and looked at him wonderingly, wearily, almost meekly, and sat down, without a word, on the curbstone—with his feet in a puddle—putting his head in his hands, drooping, shuddering suddenly with a spastic intwisted violence.

"It wasn't your fault, Ken. . . . For krissakes, forget it and pull yourself together. Let's go have that drink. Don't sit there in the gutter, you'll catch your death."

"I've always sat in gutters. I used to sit in gutters all the time. I once saw a dead guy in the street all mashed up by a car when I was on my way to see a girl I was loving-up at the time in Yonkers, and I thought, *Ever moreso gentle am I than death.*" He looked away up the street. "What the hell's a Kenny Wood to do in this world? Not on account of that, but on general watered-down principles. It's really fine to sit in gutters, by the by, it's a marvelous game that people always play at times like this. Don't you know anything, Martin? Maybe I should sleep in the river tonight."

Peter sat down beside him, but got up instantly because it was too cold and wet. He retreated to a doorway. "All I know's it's dumb to sit there in the gutter."

"Beautiful, beautiful."

"What's beautiful?"

"Everybody in the world's dumb and beautiful . . ." Kenny laughed sharply. "So the old man's disposed of at last. And ah! but he was beautifully chopped up. Mother Meister was always so thorough. . . ."

"Let's go to a bar," said Peter, shivering.

"Even as a weenie. Well, Pete, so long." Kenny came over and shook hands in the doorway, with drooped head.

Peter heard himself say "So long" faintly, but when Kenny walked away he followed him a few steps, and then, again, Kenny stuck out his hand, pitifully now. He had some change in his hand and when they shook hands the coins jingled and a few of them dropped on the sidewalk.

"I'll pick them up!" grinned Peter, nervously.

"Go ahead. So long, Pete."

"So long, Ken."

Kenny walked determinedly away in the rain, vanishing around a corner. Peter picked up the coins from the sidewalk and went back to stand in the doorway. He stood there staring in the rain, wondering where to go next. He looked up and down the deserted street and wondered who he was, and why it was raining so soft, and what it all was.

Suddenly he saw Kenny running towards him down the avenue. He ran out shouting, "What's the matter?"

Kenny stopped running and strolled casually in a little circle.

"My white gloves are beginning to chafe. I can't go home just now—you see, it's the white gloves."

"What white gloves?"

"They wear them, you know . . . the French dukes . . . when they face the firing squad. What'll I do with them? You want them?"

"What?"

"The white gloves! the white gloves!"

Peter looked around and down at the gutter, lugubriously. "That's easy, just drop them in the gutter, see."

And Kenneth plucked at the air over the gutter, magically, and opened his hand with stiff, dramatic fingers, and stared down.

"I'll walk you home," said Peter.

"All right. But on the other hand let's stay here awhile in this fine doorway. No, I think I'll go home. You go in that bar and have a drink on me, that toast to great-grandmama. So long, Pete."

"Okay," said Peter, turning away with sick confusion. "So long, man, so long."

Kenny walked away again, way up the avenue this time, in a straight line, disappearing in the rainy darkness as Peter leaned out of the doorway watching, watching. When he lost sight of the weaving form, he brooded in the downpour of rain, somewhere on Second Avenue, in the halo of a streetlamp, as the April rain slanted down and twinkled in the street, as the long dreariness lay spread, glistening and empty.

A solitary truck came rumbling down the avenue and vanished upstreet with a blink of tail-lights. The traffic lights blinked and clicked, blinked and clicked to the empty streets. Peter remembered Washington that dawn with his little brother Charley. And the tenement fronts were dark and asleep all around in the deathly rain of that night.

Around midnight he went home to Judie's apartment. It was empty. Just a few hours ago his father and his mother were there and Judie. Now they were all gone and he was alone with the haunted wreckage of their unhappiness, and his own, thinking of the irredeemable death and completion of Waldo Meister, the mad futility of Kenny Wood, and the foggy rain of the streets outside.

He wandered to his room and lay down in the dark, and lit a cigarette. In a moment he knew he would begin to imagine Waldo stalking blindly and bloodily into his room, arms outstretched, leering in death, with the great crab of suicide clutched over his mangled face. . . . He shuddered and sat up.

There was some mail on the desk beside the bed, two letters from Alexander Panos in Italy and another letter from his sister Ruth in Los Angeles. Peter reached for these letters like a man paralyzed. He put on the bedlamp, with the strange feeling that he was the only person left alive in New York, and began eagerly reading his sister's letter first. She was on leave in the California valleys with some friends, near Fresno, near the Fresno that Alexander loved so from reading William Saroyan's stories of Armenian children.

He began absentmindedly opening one of Alexander's letters, when he realized strangely that it was addressed in his own handwriting, addressed to A. S. Panagiatopoulos—alas! this was the boy's legal name—in Peter Martin's own thoughtless overbearing hand, looking so stupid there on the envelope. He looked meditatively at his own handwriting, with a blank sense of not comprehending something. Just below the address the words were stamped in red ink: "ADDRESSEE REPORTED DECEASED."

Peter snickered with a crazy little shudder of his lips. Quickly, with trembling fingers he opened the other letter and wonderingly read his comrade's last written words. He was sure someone had made a mistake. The little letter read:

> Dear Pete,
>
> Riding in a truck past fields scattered with the red leaves of last Fall, the bare little Italian trees and the dead, the English soldier boys who can't go home again now and are lying there among the red leaves together. I send you this leaf from a lonely Italian field.

All of Alexander's letters from overseas had been like this, brief, poetic, sorrowful. This scarcely differed from the others, yet somehow there was an air of weariness and finality in the words, something incurled, sad, complete. He mused over the red leaf Alexander had enclosed in the envelope, looking at it almost indifferently yet with a deep ungraspable stab of pain.

The letter was signed:

"I have kept faith, I have remembered—ALEXANDER."

It was as though something had broken inside him, all fallen and ruined. What had happened to his dear friend? Now his dark face was lost, Alex's face, in the strange unthinking world, all awful and raw and grieved.

5

IN THE FALL OF 1945 the great troopships began to arrive in New York Harbor crowded from stem to stern with returning veterans. On fabulous October days when the sun and wind made the harbor waters sparkle with all the allure of the sunny sea-world itself, when gulls swooped above ships' stacks and ships' masts, and circled the smoking tugs, and sat pecking on mouldy imperial dockpiles, and when flags cracked and whipped in the jubilant wind everywhere, and ships' whistles and horns brayed in the huge demented medley of war's end, and crowds waved on the docks—something furiously sad, angry, mute, and piteous was in the air, something pathetically happy too. Great ships lumbered slowly in the waters before the looming tumult and smoke-surrounded bulk of New York. And soldiers gazed with a sense of weary finality, some with a kind of sarcastic joy, others without a comment in their hearts, and others with sad-sack wonder and amazement that they were really back.

On one of these ships, leaning wearily on the rails, were Joe and Paul Hathaway, older, gruffer, darker, and more drunken than ever. Both of them were scarred and darkened and embittered by war, but calmer too, actually more at peace with themselves than they had ever been, sarcastic, weary, wise, vigorously sharp, ponderously amused. They looked at each other solemnly when the boys began to whistle at the girls a whole mile away on the piers. They shook their heads, turned away, stared glumly, sarcastically at big New York and its crested splendors, threw their cigarettes in the water below, leaned there on the rail in silence, and watched.

A few afternoons later they were striding through Times Square with bags over their backs, smoking cigars, looking around, hailing cabs with calm peremptory gestures and swearing up and down when the cabs swept by, tossing their bags on the sidewalk to sit and consult darkly. Then you saw them in a bar sitting at one end together, just drinking and not saying a word, ordering more drinks, staring straight ahead with bloodshot, weary, meditative eyes, lighting cigarettes with deliberation and afterthought, and just brooding there.

Both of them were sergeants. Paul had been a ground crew mechanic with a few flights to his credit, but his tremendous surly labors on the ground among littered wreckages of engines and tools and oil-rags and grease-guns had made him, and many other men of moody ravaged kind, indispensable in a war that had been won by work of all kinds. Joe had started off as a mechanic, and later had been assigned as flight engineer in a B-17 that survived forty-odd missions over Europe before it was shot up and had to make a crash landing on the English coast. In that crash Joe had gashed and broken his arm. It happened at a time when he was about to be transferred to the Pacific theater but by the time he came out of the hospital the European war was over. There were delays and confusions, finally the Japanese war was over, and he and Paul were shipped home on the same boat.

Something strange had happened to Joe in England, something like exasperation, disgust, terrific moody joylessness. He suddenly "didn't care any more." He went A.W.O.L. all over England and hardly remembered later on what he did over the fuzzy drunken days and nights. He spent some time in the guardhouse for this, but he didn't care about that either, it was all the same. Most significantly, he stopped writing to Patricia Franklin altogether. When he arrived in New York that October in 1945 he had not written to Patricia in eight months, he had no idea where she was now, and he didn't care. Sometimes it occurred to him how *thin* a line was drawn in himself between love or indifference, devotion or disgust, confidence or carelessness, and finally—between living joy or outlawish fury. He could laugh and have a good time, and then suddenly go off and break something with all the violence of a madman. He thought about it sometimes but most of the time he didn't give enough of a damn to think about it. He remembered feeling like this before, especially when he was twenty or thereabouts, full of wild recklessness and drunken, suicidal fury, and now it was back, but there was no more joy, somehow no more beauty in it, no more young man's awe and delight in it, and it seemed to him that something was over and done with.

He went home to Brooklyn with Paul Hathaway, to see the folks. He found his father in his sick chair. In the slanting afternoon light, by the basement window that faced the pavement, old

George Martin sat dying and brooding and thinking, with a blanket over his legs, an old bathrobe over his back, his antique silver-rimmed glasses magnified and skeletal in his lank face, his *Daily Racing Form* on a table beside the chair. The change that had come over him, in his face and physique, since Joe had last seen him three years back was enough to stun him back to an awful sense of boyish grief and terror.

There sat George Martin, gaunt and haggard with suffering, his once bulging chest shrunken down like the hollow bird's-breast of a consumptive, his hands pale and splotched with yellow cirrhosis spots (yet still inkstained at the fingernails), and his huge blue eyes gaping sorrowfully from out of the hollows of his bony face, full of fear, and dumb abashment, and an eager joyful awe that was more woefully intense than anything Joe had ever seen. The old man cried, and laughed and joked, and cried, and hugged his son, and talked and cried again. It seemed that all the tremendous eagerness and earnest sufferance in the old man's soul had grown in proportion to the waning of his body and had found a sad, wild, staring focus in his great blue eyes.

"Lord, lord, lord!" he cried. "I thought I'd never see you again, I thought they'd killed you, Joey! Oh, oh, oh!" he wept. "Now they've killed little Charley, I'm sure of that! Marge, you know that's true, you know it yourself."

"Charley?" cried Joe with amazement. "Isn't he in Okinawa? Did you get word from him?"

"No, oh, no," said the old man sadly, "he's finished. We haven't had a word from him in a long time. Little Charley's finished, just a little before *my* time, that's all, I'm sure of that."

"Well, maybe he just didn't write! Hell! The War Department would send word—"

"I know, I know. . . . I expect that any day now, Joey. God, you poor fellows! both of you! How are you, Hathaway? How are you feeling? A poor fellow your age . . ."

Sometimes the old man babbled like that and seemed to forget what he was saying a moment ago, or even that anybody was in the room with him. Then he paused and stared into the abyss of his approaching death and just stared wildly, coming out of it with a huge sigh and a cry and a mournful look around the room, and finally a heart-wrenched seizure of joy at the mere sight of anyone who happened to be there.

"Joey, you'll never know what your poor mother has been

through with me. I'm just a useless big hulk of flesh sitting here, I ought to be taken out and just thrown on the dump, for all the trouble I've caused that poor girl, all the trouble! Joey, she works and slaves, and I just sit here helpless, Joey! I can walk around all right, though . . . say, by the way!" he suddenly cried, gleefully, "you know something else? I sit here figuring the horses all day long, I can take care of myself a little. Ha, ha, ha! She comes home at night thinking maybe I'll be sitting here groaning and moaning, but, by God, here I am listening to the race results and figuring how I made out for the day—"

"That's true," said the mother, standing behind Joe's chair and stroking his hair, "he never complains, Joey. All he does is figure the horses"—and she shook her head, mutely looking at her husband.

"I could have gone to a hospital," grinned the old man slyly, "but they make you lay there doing nothing! At home I can play the radio and figure the horses. I thought I'd never see you again, Joey. I'm old and sick and dying and I'm full of thoughts of death. No, I thought I'd be meeting you wherever the hell they'd decide to send us!"

"Don't say that word!" whooped Joe, jumping up. "What do you want to do, influence the devil?"

"By gosh!" yelled the old man, laughing, "it feels so wonderful to have Joey back again. There ain't been a laugh in this house since I don't know when! And do I hate this hell-hole New York! Joey, do I *hate* it! If God would only let me die in peace back in beautiful New England, that's all I ask. Men don't live the way God intended them to live in this place! Whatever you do, Joe, don't stay here, please don't stay here! Marge, give Joe something to eat, something to drink, and, Paul, make yourself at home, and take off that damn soldier suit."

And then a moment later he brooded in the abyss of death, wrapped in thoughts and silent wonder, his great blue eyes staring, his hands limp, his lower lip pouting, his gaunt face lowered reverently over the mystery of his own life and the mysterious ruin of all life.

While the others were in the kitchen and he was alone in the front room, and as Mickey was just coming in the iron gate on the sidewalk outside, he looked up, startled, stunned from his reverie, and groaned in a low voice:

"God have pity on my soul."

When Joe had finished his second cup of coffee in the kitchen he took his wallet and threw an enormous amount of money on the table.

"Now listen to me, Ma, you're not going to work in that factory any more, you're going to stay right here at home with Pa and take care of him and take care of yourself. Do you hear me?"

"But, Joey, there's no more money coming in the house, and besides I don't mind the work, I like it, I've done it before—"

"Never mind that!" he cried angrily. "There's about twenty-two hundred bucks on the table there." He picked up the money and spread it out. "It's back-pay money, some of it, and most of it I won in crap games coming over. It's yours. Do you hear me? You're not going to work another minute, you're going to stay right here at home."

"But, Joey, I don't want to take your money—" she cried mournfully.

"Did you hear me? Never mind I said!"

"But what are you going to do?"

"I'll stay here when I'm discharged—and I'll get a job, I guess. But until I get discharged I've got a little money to horse around with. This is for you. I'll just have to get drunk on rotgut instead of Scotch for a change, that's all," and he turned and winked at Hathaway, and at Mickey, who stood gazing at him joyfully. "Why the hell didn't you write and tell me all this, I could have sent you a lot of money two months ago, I had thousands then!"

"Joey," said the mother, sighing, "I didn't want to worry you. But, gosh—this is an awful lot of money to just give away like that. You don't know what a relief it is," she finally admitted mournfully, and they saw, in her haggard worried eyes, how everything had become so grief-stricken, troublous, and hopeless for her in the past year in New York. She hugged Mickey broodingly. "I wanted him to stay in high school whatever happened."

"And what about everybody else!" shouted Joe furiously. "Is it true what he was saying about Francis and Petey and all them?"

"Petey's given us money, whenever he goes to sea. Francis—Well, we don't know what he's doing."

"What about Liz? What's *she* doing?"

"We don't even know where she is, Joey."

He waved his hand violently and snarled away, and stood at the window looking out, almost sadly, with a convulsive little gesture of sick disgust and sorrow. He was silent a long time, and said finally:

"What a hell of a family this turned out to be."

For a moment, as he looked out, his attention was diverted by the huge advertisement of the man holding his head in torment on the warehouse wall. He stared at it. "Hell knows, I was bad enough myself—but this! Who would have thought it, when we were all kids in Galloway, in the house—when *he* was big and fulla pep. If there was some way to make everything go back the way it was, or something like that, not let it go on like this till he dies. And he *is* going to die, anybody can see that, and it won't be long."

"No, Joey, it won't be long," said the mother, shaking her head slowly.

Liz was actually living in New York, in rooms on Fiftieth Street near Ninth Avenue, and had been living there a long time, at least a year and a half.

Peter went to see his sister one day. He was living alone now in a cheap room on the waterfront, in the Seaman's Church Institute, knowing that his father was dying, afraid to go home to watch him die, knowing that everything between Judie and himself was finished, hiding out in the great sprawl of the city with a sense of doom.

While he waited for Liz to come home he spent a pleasant hour chatting with a beautiful dark-eyed brunette girl who said her name was Pat. He never dreamed that she was Joe's fiancée, Patricia Franklin. He had never seen her before.

Patricia herself had looked up Liz a month or so after Joe's letters unaccountably stopped coming. It was with that astounding and inexplicable cleverness that women sometimes have that this girl decided to find her lover's sister, and having found her—which was something Buddy Fredericks himself could not always do—she made her way into her heart, into her confidence at least, and they became extremely close friends. Liz and Patricia were as different as night and day. Patricia was the same as she had always been, essentially a smalltown girl, somewhat old-fashioned even, fundamentally the same as Joe had found her—a sturdy, sensible, principled family girl.

Liz had changed a lot since the day she had lost her baby in a Detroit hospital. She had become one of the many girls in America who flit from city to city in search of something they hope to find and never even name, girls who "know all the ropes," know a thousand people in a hundred cities and places, girls who work at all kinds of jobs, impulsive, desperately gay, lonely, hardened girls. They run away from home at eighteen and never stop running, they can take care of themselves like men, have a woman's heart and a man's mind, are brusque, businesslike, ebullient, wild, passionate, forever in the course of relentless enterprises which are either successful or "laid low in the middle of nowhere." Searching for some kind of resting place in their lives, which they never really want, they travel in busses and trains and sometimes hitch-hike (in slacks). They are girls who "know everything" and know nothing at all, "hip-chicks" who are seen in Hollywood working in drive-ins or speeding along Hollywood Boulevard in some "producer's" convertible, or in Miami on a bookmaker's arm, or in Las Vegas with a gambler, or in a Chicago nightclub, or in New York going around with jazz musicians. They fall in and out of love a dozen times a year, go away in ragged clothes and return in a fur coat. They are girls who know their rights, know what they want, know how to go about it, and end up being insulted, baffled, and frustrated by every nighttime character in every night's-end of American life.

Liz had become one of these girls. She had grown somewhat hard-faced, due largely to the way she wore her hair and the way she dyed it blonde. The change was mostly in her mouth somehow, in the way it slackened sullenly in moments of reflection, with a grim set to it, almost surly and certainly bitter. Her shell-blue eyes which used to mist over in moments of sheepish joy were now constantly splintered and clear and hard. When Peter saw his sister after all the war years he was struck dumb and mortified.

Liz had a photo of him taken after he quit college in 1941, a melancholy sort of picture showing him gazing emptily into space and looking completely dogged—with the realization, almost, of what his life could very well become. She kept this picture and cherished it everywhere she went, hanging it in prominent parts of her room.

"Do you know why I like that picture?" she laughed. "It shows you just as you *are*, it's the picture of a young character who's been slapped in the face and doesn't know what to make of it."

"Haven't we all?"

"Man, I suppose all of us have—but some of us fight back, you know, some of us don't like to stay whipped. That's the picture of a whipped dog, a dog who's given up his right to snap back."

"You certainly have a fine opinion of your own brother," he muttered.

"Oh, come off it!" Liz cried, flaring up with her menacing way, stalking around the room like a caged lioness. "I like *real* things and that picture's real, besides, as I say, it *looks* like you. It should remind you of the fact anyway that you can't go around in this world with your shoulders drooped and expect to make a go of it."

Peter prodded her gleefully. "Now you're talking how to win friends and influence people, like the Chamber of Commerce, a great social rebel like you."

"Can anyone be anything but a rebel in a conventional world like this? But stay cool, I love you just the same, little one."

When she talked like that Peter remembered that summer night he had helped her elope with Buddy, when she was so fiercely yet so shyly proud, so sweet and mystified by the wonder and strangeness of her own heart. Now it was certain that nothing mystified her, that she had little faith in people, least of all in men, after all the things she had done and seen and all the distortions and venoms she had somehow acquired along the way.

She loved to prod at Peter's weaknesses. "Well, daddio, there you *go* pouting again. Isn't that stupid?"

"Pouting? Maybe I picked it up from Pa, he pouts all the time. I was reading in *Moby Dick* how the white whale pouts. . . ."

"What's this white whale routine? What kick are you on now?"

With Liz everything had become "kicks"—either you were "goofing off," on the goof-off kick, just being lazy and doing absolutely nothing in a deliberate, formal, almost desperate way, or you were listening to music which came under the heading of an emotional kick, or you were in love which was another kick, or you hated somebody and put his name in a little black book and *that* was a certain kind of kick—and so on, all of it divided into neat categories through which existence kicked along.

Liz and her husband Buddy were "just friends" now. There was a certain kick in their new relationship, a "cool kick"—Buddy was Liz's "mother." He came around every now and then to talk to her awhile, to swap news about happenings all the way from Los Angeles to Boston, from Miami to Seattle, news of other "cats" and "chicks" like themselves connected in some way with jazz music, nightclubs and show business, and after that he kissed her on the cheek and coolly slouched off back to his jazz music, that was all.

In New York Liz held down various types of jobs, singing in small clubs at times, at other times standing around showing her legs in second-rate floorshows, at other times wandering "beat" around the city in search of some other job or benefactor or "loot" or "gold." When you were loaded with loot and having your kicks, that was living; but when you were hung up without gold and left beyond the reach of kicks, that was a drag.

And it was all the more amazing to see Patricia living with Liz, to see the two girls conducting their separate lives in perfect understanding—Patricia working as a typist downtown with the same patient, musing, brooding silence as she had done in Denver to be near Joe long ago, Liz carrying on with her own slapdash fantastic affairs which always precipitated great and weird confusion in the apartment. At two o'clock any morning, there might be a procession of jazz musicians wearing berets and sporting California scarfs and dark glasses, or dancers and showgirls and models, and all kinds of strange characters from somewhere, or teaheads (Clint, the marijuana man who trained his cockroaches, was numbered among this host). While all this went on, there was Patricia Franklin, minding her wistful little affairs in the privacy of her room.

Joe knocked on Peter's door late one night. When Peter went to the door, it was like sensing the entire purpose of life to see him—to see why Patricia had come to live with Liz, and why, someway, she had inscrutably left it up to him to bring Joe back to her. Peter realized this in one clear, ecstatic moment of unearthly joy, when he saw his big brother standing there all wild and gaunt and racked with loneliness.

"Come on!" cried Joe. "Let's go out and have a drink and chew the rag. What the hell have you been doing? Why haven't you been home?"

Paul Hathaway was lurking in the hallway. It was about midnight.

"Did you see Pa?" demanded Peter with nervous curiosity.

"Yes, I saw him and he's got one foot in the grave, and you know it."

"Listen," said Peter, "I've got something to show you, I've got *somebody* to show you, that is. But wait a minute first—you don't have to get sore at me for not staying home. Do you think I love to watch the old man dribble away every day? I'd rather stay here alone, that's all, I'd rather do that any day—"

"Never mind what you like!" the older brother scowled darkly. "It's what you've *got* to do in this world that counts."

"Maybe you're right."

"You damn right I'm right."

The mood was ripe. Hathaway had a bottle and they all took a nip and started out into the warm October night to hit the bars. Suddenly, without warning, as they walked down a dark street, Joe took out a .32 automatic, looked around quickly, almost meekly, and pointed it into an ash barrel and shot. It made an astounding crashing noise in the murmuring stillness. Nothing happened, nobody was around. Peter was amazed, almost jubilant suddenly.

"You better look out with that thing, the cops'll get you on the Sullivan law—"

"The hell with Sullivan," muttered Joe darkly. "Sunday I just missed a sea-gull off a dock, you shoulda seen the look on a guy's face who was walking by. Hyah! hyah! hyah! Here, have a shot!"

He handed Peter the gun, not the bottle, but Peter waved it away with exasperation, though not without stifling a keen impulse to try it.

"I heard you got in trouble with the cops," said Joe. "You don't want to let those punks push you around, you're a merchant seaman, ain't you? Stand up for your rights, man! Here, take a pot-shot at that light. Let's see what kind of a shot you are!"

"You're crazy!" laughed Peter. "We'll hit somebody. But listen, I want to ask you, have you heard from Patricia?" He looked slyly at Joe. "Do you have any idea where she is?"

Joe twirled the gun on his finger, snapped it back and said nothing.

"Where is she?" pressed Peter.

"How the hell should I know? She's in Maine, I guess, and I guess she's all right in Maine."

"Everybody's all right in Maine," echoed Hathaway darkly.

"See? Everything's great in Maine," said Joe, and he let go another blast into an ash barrel, this time nonchalantly shooting from the hip without looking. A tenement window opened above and someone stuck his head out with suspicious curiosity. A man coming up the street suddenly vanished. The street was deserted and strange; they hurried away talking in loud voices.

Climbing the three flights of steps in the rickety Ninth Avenue rooming house where the girls lived, Joe wanted to know what it was all about. "What are you taking us here for, joker? What's all the mystery?"

But Peter was losing the sense of crafty joy he had felt at first in bringing Joe to Patricia. He suddenly felt dazed, and stopped in the middle of the stairs.

"Listen, Joe, this is where Liz . . . lives."

"Lizzy?" cried Joe gleefully.

"Yeah, Lizzy. And there's someone else here too. I may as well tell you, Pat's here too."

"Pat who?"

"Pat Franklin, for krissakes."

Joe gazed at him dumbly.

"So if you want to come up, come on—if not, don't say I didn't warn you."

"What do you mean, Pat Franklin!" Joe almost yelled, flushing angrily. "What are you talking about! What would she be doing *here!*"

"Go knock on that door and see for yourself."

They stood in the middle of the stairs in confused indecision, until finally Hathaway, who had not said a word for fifteen minutes suddenly pushed past them. He began pounding on the door with his fist, though softly. He looked back at them with a really sweet and radiant smile.

"I don't know about you guys, but if Pat's in here I'd like to see her myself."

Almost instantly the door opened and there stood Patricia Franklin.

For the next fifteen minutes Joe sat in a dark corner of the room with his elbows on his knees, just staring at the floor in complete perplexity, while Paul and Patricia and Peter carried on a meaningless nervous conversation about anything that came into their heads. Nobody knew what to do, or say—least of all Joe in his dark corner, and Patricia. The moment she must have been awaiting for so long had suddenly arrived, almost madly, and now all her thoughts of Joe were obscured pathetically in this one single tattered moment nameless with impurities. She and Joe went to extremes not to notice each other. Paul and Peter just bobbed around as though trying to conceal the lovers from each other. It was utterly insane, and suddenly, during a moment of silent perturbation all around, Joe got up and went out without a word.

"Where's Liz, by the way?" demanded Peter eagerly just as the door closed. "I thought for sure she'd be around."

"Oh," said Patricia, staring at Peter with burning eyes, "she's downstairs in that bar, that Kelly's place. . . ."

"I wonder where Joe went?" said Paul. He jumped up nervously, saying he was going downstairs to buy a pack of cigarettes, and left.

"I'm going down to see Liz," said Patricia firmly, and without even putting on lipstick or taking a coat, she opened the door, looked at Peter absentmindedly, and left. Peter, alone in the room, opened the window and looked out at the dark back-alley; sat smoking on the windowsill awhile. It was all over, his father was dying, it was dark and dirty outside, it was huge, walled-in, the great incomprehensible alley's end of the night. He hurried out and went downstairs in a swirl of meditations.

Joe was shuffling around the block with his hands in his pockets, painfully trying to recollect something, when Paul Hathaway caught up with him.

"Boy! I've never seen such a bunch of crazy goddam clowns!" snarled the oldtimer with infinite loathing. "What's the *matter* with you? There's nothing wrong with that girl, she's the finest girl I ever saw, I told you so a thousand times, I told you so years ago!"

Joe looked at him wearily. He was just simply weary—weary because it was all so mixed up and torn and at the same time because it was so unbearable and excruciating to a fierce new sense of pride that had just risen in him. He suddenly realized that he never wanted to do what he was *expected* to do. It made no sense at all. He could not even remember why he had stopped writing to Patricia—he had just stopped, that was all. A feeling of terror crept over him. He stared at Hathaway earnestly, fixedly.

"Honest to God, Paul, I don't know what's the matter with me tonight. I think I been drinking too much, don't you think? I feel sappy, I can't think."

"Do you or *don't* you like that girl, that's what I'd like to know," muttered Paul, lowering his surly face nervously.

"That's a fine question! It's like asking me . . . Ah!"

"It's like asking you what?"

"I don't *know* what! I just don't know nothing any more. I don't feel good, Paul, I feel sick, crazy, sick—everything. I tell you I don't know where I'm at no more. I'm not the same guy any more. Let's go back, I want to look at her, see what she looks like. I can't remember what she looks like!" he cried.

They hurried back to the rooming house. Paul put his hand on Joe's shoulder and began talking more earnestly and seriously than he had ever done, as though the deranged events of the evening had bitten into him deeply. "Do you know what it is, Joe? It's the feeling that everything is upside-down and turned inside-out and every which way and so to hell with it all, see? You want to be left out from everything on purpose! So you can go off and feel sorry for yourself and get royal drunk all the time!"

"Why should *you* care?" demanded Joe almost insolently, but with a hurt and subdued look at him.

"I'm just warning you, that's all, wise guy!" yelled Paul contemptuously. "Go ahead and do what you like, I don't care. Look, I'm going in this bar and you can find me here if you want." It was Kelly's bar. Standing in the entrance, like some disconsolate panhandler, was Peter, gazing at them gloomily.

"Do you guys want to know something?" he said, solemnly gesturing. "This is the end—all this." He solemnly pointed around the street and into the bar. "You see your sister and your girl in there? You don't see your sister, do you? That's because you don't recognize her. You never saw her the way she looks now."

"What are you talking about?"

Joe went to the window of the bar and looked in curiously. "Is that Liz sitting there with Pat? That crummy-looking blonde, Liz?" He stood there with a kind of dejected fascination. "The crazy little fool, I always knew she was going to be a nut from the start." And he kept staring at her unbelievingly, reluctantly, curiously.

"Let's go in and have a drink!" cried Paul emphatically.

They piled into the bar which was crowded at that hour with soldiers, sailors, regular neighborhood drinkers, and bevies of girls that seemed mysteriously to have come out of nowhere. Joe and the two others realized who and what all these girls were—girls just like Liz and Patricia for the most part, girls from other towns who had come to New York for one reason or another, part of a whole nomadic womanhood that had developed during the war. Because they knew Liz and Patricia so well and had seen them from all sides, human, sisterly, child-like, womanly, it was as though they knew all the girls in the place for what they lonesomely were, their real excruciating selves hidden beneath the lipstick, the hairdos, the studied poses. They saw all these girls as they truly were. They saw them with their hair in pins, ironing for mother in the kitchen; they saw them on the porch on warm nights gossiping eagerly with their girl friends; they saw them up in the attic furiously cleaning out the rubbish; they saw them streaking across the yard in dungarees to get to the swing before anyone else; they saw them hoisting great burdens down the cellar with wisps of hair over their brows and their tongues curled over their lips in ravenous exertion; they saw them sitting before the mirrors for hours with towels and cosmetics and lotions all about; and finally they saw them going down the soft dusty road at summernight hand in hand with the boy next door in the universe all blurred and transcendental with milky stars.

Finally a kind of merchant marine officer who was talking to Patricia—she pretended not to notice Joe—put his arm around her and began whispering in her ear amorously.

"See that, Joe?" grinned Peter. "I guess she's trying to show you a thing or two."

"Let her! And look at that silly Liz guzzling the booze like a Bowery hobo. Hey, I got an idea! Why don't we shoot up the joint, huh?"

Within the space of minutes, a great brawl developed. It started when Peter went over to talk to the girls and deliberately ignored the officer, who wanted to know who he thought he was, whereupon Peter told him and asked what *he* proposed to do about it, and the officer invited him outside. They marched out single file with pounding hearts—the hum of activity died down in the bar—

and outside, on the sidewalk, the officer absurdly struck up a John L. Sullivan pose with his fists. Peter, a little surprised by this unexpected twist, nevertheless started up a furious windmill of roundhouse punches that flattened the officer on his back from sheer numbers. But he bounced right up again. In another moment the officer's crony sailed into Peter with something that resembled a flying tackle at his neck but got the point of Peter's elbow flush in the face, and went sideswiping and sprawling on the sidewalk. But Peter's jig was up as they stalked him against the door, bloody-faced and snarling. For some reason or other Peter began to snicker.

"What!" he cried. "Two against one? What's the matter with you guys? Hey!" he cried with a crazy sheepish grin, but they pinned him against the wall without a word and hauled him down to the sidewalk as he twisted and spun in their grip. One officer, who had hold of Peter's hair, was trying to bat his head against the sidewalk. Peter, laughing foolishly, held his neck rigid and went right on chatting forlornly with them. Something grim, sad, and ugly had come into the fight now.

At that moment Joe came out of the bar and planted a kick on one of the officers with his G.I. boot and sent him sprawling. Paul, with an unexpected show of wild jubilance, took one great flying leap in the air and landed upon everybody, including Peter whose head was flattened in the act.

Sailors rushed out of the bar, and soldiers, and merchant seamen. By some invisible movement the Army lined up against the Navy, and the merchant seamen milled around. Peter joined the Army—and everybody stood around talking affably as the police cruiser came around the corner menacingly.

In the confusion Joe had herded Patricia and Liz both into a booth and was talking to them almost heatedly, while Paul and Peter stood at the bar loading up on shots of whiskey with great tact and sadness.

"I'll bet you loved that fight, both of you! That's the kind of thing you like, isn't it?" He was yelling at them above the hubbub and music, leaning madly across the table as he talked, while the two girls sat back watching him with amusement. "Get guys to fighting over you, that's the ticket, hey?"

"Will you *listen* to him?" scoffed Liz, laughing. "Big soldier comes back from the wars, tells his womenfolk what to do. Who do you think you are, hotshot? You may recall that neither Pat or myself started that fight. It was Pistol Pete over there in his eagerness to show what a—"

And Joe had suddenly gripped Patricia by the arms and turned her around to confront him. He was looking at her with his grave troubled eyes and she, taken aback by this strange beautiful circumstance, could do nothing but look back at him. Hathaway and Peter stood at the bar drinking silently.

Liz, alone momentarily, sat watching her brother out of the corner of her eye. She remembered now all the things that had happened long ago when Joe was her image of the fierce untamable youth who would be her husband forever. She remembered dark things, dark joys, and gorgeous hopes from the bottom of a girl's heart. She remembered the day Joe had appeared in a rickety old car to help her and Charley when they were struggling on the cold wintry plains of the city dump for reasons she could hardly remember now, but could never forget either. All the time her life must have been imbedded in something dark, something joyful and secret, something that her big brother was like, and something that young Buddy was like, something undiscoverably beautiful and now gone. Why had she run away from home to go to cities, honkytonks, and claptrap? When that dark secret gladness brooded back there in Galloway, and waited for her, and mourned like the wind at night in October, and something knocked against the house making summons and grieving, she was not there. A little girl in dungarees, she had lost her doll, climbed a tree in search of it, and seen, instead, great beacons turning and flashing on the night's horizon. Knowledge and awareness told Liz that sorrow was the fool's gold of the world, and she smiled, a smile that was her determined new key to things and understanding. But it was a poor key that did not fit, in any lock in the world, anywhere, ever.

She got up and took her things and walked to the end of the bar, touched Peter on the arm, said, "Good night, Pistol Pete," and went out alone.

Joe, sensing how many things he had to say to Patricia as he gazed at her, sensing the whole exfoliation of love and truth returning, held Patricia by the hand.

[2]

FOR FRANCIS, New York meant Greenwich Village freedom to live with a woman in a small apartment, to roam the little bookshops around Washington Square on misty nights, to haunt the bars where almost everybody had something to say about art, to attend parties where fantastic-looking people tossed off psychodynamic analysis, Jean-Paul Sartre, Orgone Theory, Jean Genet, and all the latest word in the easiest manner known to man, to writhe, finally, in the melodrama of "modern frustrative horror" in a chi-chi setting. It was the freedom to roam around deep in responsible thought from one foreign movie to another, from one art museum to another, from lectures at the Modern School of Cultural Research to the ballet, to the New Theater, to concerts, to political rallies, to performances by female impersonators, to poetry readings where some uncouth young poet yelled "Merde!" at everything submitted, to relief benefits, to demonstrations at cute little handicraft shops like the Taos (home of Kit Carson) Shoppe.

Francis had reached the point where people meant little more to him than single sentences:

"Oh, him? He's a disgruntled Chicagoan who loves Bach, spaghetti, Cris-craft cruises, tubercular women, and paints at Carmel in the summer." "Him, there? He just lives with his grandmother in Long Island City and writes novels. Very neurotic." "But *there's* a fascinating woman! Sold cocaine in the streets of Berlin in the twenties and married a Harvard boy to get away from the Nazis, and is now, I believe, having an affair with a famous ballet dancer's sister." "Her? . . . dull woman, a *type,* though. I think she once bound herself with chains to the Washington Square arch in broad daylight and finally got carted away to Bellevue. Knew Djuna Barnes." "Now *there's* someone you ought to meet! His translation of Isidore Ducasse is supposed to be the most beautifully sensitive. An intimate of Bauer the non-objective and Max Bodenheim and Eleanor Roosevelt. For some reason Joe Gould dislikes him." "*Who* is that mystifying creature standing by the bookshelf with such a sad look? She's looking at a book by Denton Welch. Well, isn't that triangular somehow! Do you know she looks just like the portrait of Madame de Castaigne, only more decomposed? Introduce me."

In all these scenes the grave Francis was like some young minister of the church who had been defrocked early in his career after a scandal of tremendous theological proportions. He was refined, dark, reflective, aloof, mysterious. There was something about him somehow; young ladies from Iowa and Georgia who had come to New York to be intellectual, and were merely drunk all the time, looked at him with ravenous fascination and said, "But *who* is that cloistral-looking person?" With Dora Zelnick on his arm at these gatherings—she with her olive-skin Scheherazade look and her trinkets and bracelets and Persian sashes that made her look like every other girl in the Village except those who were built like sticks and *had* to look like Madame de Castaigne—Francis seemed all the more mystifying and devilishly subtle. Everybody eventually learned that he came from Galloway, Massachusetts, had worked his way through college, had done a "hitch" in the Navy, was "working on a book," had a job in town, no money, and was just another joker like everybody else. Since Francis had not the gall to go around with a repertoire of mysterious ambiguous enigmas to perform—the technique of all intellectual stars—nobody trailed him to read the little scented meanings he might coyly drop.

After a year and a half in Greenwich Village, Francis began to drift to the East Side uptown. There was something there that the Village did not have: intellectuals who disclaimed all ties with Greenwich Village, of course, even if they were driven there by the housing shortage; intellectuals who leaned towards more sophistication, a kind of *Time* and *Life* worldliness, warier, fingering at the hem of wealth and society, less "politically wild-eyed" but, in another sense, in no real way different from the others.

The East Side "crowd" appealed to him more. He thought it was like the difference between Montmartre and Montparnasse, something like that. Through his friend Wilfred Engels he had managed to get a good job with the Office of World Information. He began to spend weekends at Connecticut estates where people casually dropped a remark that Secretary Morgenthau had made just the other day. Here at last, looming before him, was the opportunity not only to be superior in mind, but superior in advantage and position. He remembered the admiration he had for Balzac's young heroes when they struggled up from the poverty and obscurity of cheap boarding houses to great positions in the Ministry and favorable situations among the greatest women in the world, the Parisian women of wealth, diplomacy, and high corruption. Every well-married woman he met at cocktail parties held the promise of some great ruse that she would be able to develop for him, the brooding young de Rastignac so penniless and undiscovered and talented. He began to dress exceedingly well. Loneliness of this foolish woebegone existence sometimes made him laugh, and wonder, and groan in his pillow, and what was he to do next?

Wilfred Engels was head of one of the New York divisions at the Office of World Information. When he made trips to Washington on official business, Francis sometimes went along. He trotted after the bustling Engels like some young attaché trained in the very best diplomatic manner. Francis was thrilled, though he would never admit it, to meet the men who took direct orders from "top-level" Capitol figures.

There was a time when he dined at a palatial home in Chevy Chase with a French legation official on one side of him and the wife of an Army procurement officer on the other, and spent that pleasant hour speaking bad French with the legation man and casting sheep's eyes at the lady. To his utter and almost frightened astonishment he succeeded in finding himself alone with her at eleven o'clock that night in a little bar in Bethesda, and to her greater astonishment nothing happened.

One weekend Dora's brother Louis Zelnick, a Boston dentist, came down for a visit with his wife Anne, and all four of them got together on a program of theater and museums and French movies and that kind of thing. Dora and Francis met them at the train and they all had cocktails at a little Lexington Avenue bar.

All the excitement that New York meant to Francis was suddenly concentrated in that one moment. It was a rainy Saturday afternoon in January of 1946. On the way to the bar Louis Zelnick had purchased a fresh new glossy copy of the *New Yorker*, which he casually threw on the table when they sat down in the cocktail lounge by the street windows. Outside people were rushing, the air was gray and dark and some of the neon lights were already glowing at three o'clock in the afternoon. It was a somber, deeply exciting, and important scene to Francis. He realized that this was the first fine, pleasurable, perceptive feeling he had had for years.

He picked up the magazine with its fresh ink-smelling gloss, its new cover design for the week, the rustling, smooth, substantial feel of it in his hands, opened to a page casually and glanced at a few sentences. The sentences themselves were so fresh and glossy and new, "the latest," the very smartest somehow, the last thing in the whole huge scene that was New York and even Washington and Boston and Chicago, all connected together somehow by networks of rails and dining-cars on which people read the *New Yorker* and sipped martinis, a world connected by rumor, excitement, news, style, opinion, fashion, smart talk.

He looked up from the magazine and marveled at the chic look the two women had, Dora with her dark distinctive intensity, and Anne with her pale, fragile, intellectual look, her faint smile of reproach, vagueness, and withdrawn amusement. He loved their clothes and the way they wore them just as they wore the look on their faces. Francis sat there brooding happily and remembering the night long ago when he walked home from the Square in Galloway on New Year's Eve, young and exasperated and dark with resentment at the crude ugliness of the milltown, the ribaldry and coarseness of the people in it. All his old life swam before him in a kind of momentary nausea.

He sensed, though, that his present happy feelings were due perhaps to the fact that Anne was there, a married woman who had fascinated him so much in Cambridge. Every now and then they would exchange glances with a kind of faint amusement when the brother and sister argued heatedly about Yalta and such things.

"I can't seem to *feel* those things somehow," said Anne after a few martinis. "They're so far away and confused and unreal."

"My dear girl, those things should be of the greatest importance to you as a citizen of One World," her husband reminded her with an embarrassed little grin. "Those are the realities of the day. I can't think of anything *realer*."

"Oh, I suppose so. But I can think of realer things. Even this particular moment now," she looked around vaguely, "this particular moment is like something reflected on water and any minute the water's going to be rippled. That man at the bar seems as though he might ripple apart in an instant." She smiled forlornly.

"But that's within the realm of art," put in Dora Zelnick, darkly. "If it were ever carried into politics, we'd all be in a great Buchenwald concentration camp."

"But aren't we?" asked Anne, almost meekly.

Francis was amazed with her.

Two weeks later the Office of World Information began to cut down on personnel and Francis lost his job. He suddenly thought of Anne and what she had said in the bar about the world becoming rippled, unreal, vastly absurd. With a pang of something that felt idiotically like love, he began to see everything through Anne's eyes.

One misty night he was browsing in a bookstore. There was a book he particularly wanted but a young woman stood directly in front of the shelf, glancing through another book. He waited, hoping she would move away eventually, but she stood there rigidly with a kind of entrenched desperation. So he sauntered over, edging nearer along another shelf, looking at books. When he finally, meekly, reached out his hand for the desired book, he realized that he was too far away and could never make it. He moved to the other side of the young lady. He suddenly had an impulse to reach around in front of her and snatch the book. And as he just stood there deliberating uncertainly, the young lady snapped her book shut with irritation, glanced at him, and suddenly they recognized each other. It was Anne.

"But you know, you didn't have to pretend that you didn't exist at all when you tried to reach for the book," she laughed, as they sauntered down the street. "That was the thing that irritated me so much, that coy apology for simply *being* and taking up room."

"And you didn't have to bury your nose in your little sense of self as though the rest of the world wasn't there either!"

"Oh, nonsense, I wasn't pretending to be invisible. I at least had a sense of—of being in the way."

"Is that why you snapped the book?"

"That was wholly automatic."

"I'd prefer to think," said Francis, "that I tiptoed all around you from a sense of sorrow."

"How romantic!"

They talked a long while before it suddenly occurred to them to inquire about each other. Francis told her he was looking for a job. For a moment he almost told her that he had been thinking about her quite a bit lately, but he was rather afraid that she would say "Nonsense" again. She told him that things in Boston were dull and she had come to New York under the pretense of visiting her grandfather in Teaneck.

"And *does* he live in Teaneck?"

"Yes. But I always get a hotel room and go and visit him at the last minute so I can send the dentist a card postmarked properly."

"The dentist? Louis? It's strange that you should call him the dentist."

"He *is* one, you know. . . ."

With an almost lyrical feeling of freedom, Francis led Anne to his friend's apartment—he had the key—and began brewing a pot of coffee in the kitchenette.

"If you're going to try to seduce me, I wish you'd let me know in advance," called Anne from the front room. "Otherwise it would be terribly inconvenient to be caught unawares like a schoolgirl who's misjudged her beau."

Over black coffee, without any preliminaries, they began talking with a great deal of earnestness and with a sudden sense of pleasant rapport.

Anne looked around the room with a faint smile. "Do you know, it feels awfully strange to be here."

"Is the world rippling up?"

"Not at the moment. It's just a feeling of strangeness as though I'd been here before. . . ."

"Maybe it's because I'm going to inherit this apartment from my friend when he leaves New York next month," said Francis gravely.

In two months they were living together in that apartment in the East Fifties. Francis merely resumed an old argument with Dora Zelnick, built it up carefully over the space of a few days, and stalked out on her dramatically with his bag in the middle of a great flare-up. Again he had the feeling that he had experienced with a Navy psychiatrist, that it was really possible to be "clever" after all. Moreover, aside from some gnawing compunction at having broken up that deep sense of bitter kinship he and Dora had developed in their "Greenwich Village life" together, he felt he had a perfect individual right to break away completely from the past without lingering involvements.

Anne for her part simply dribbled away from her husband's home in Boston in small installments, without apologies, almost without a scene, leaving the earnest dogged dentist with the feeling that he had married some sort of ghost that eventually vanished from his life. There was no argument about the child; Anne simply went away and left the child in his care.

Francis felt the sheer delight and almost idiotic wickedness that truly indifferent men feel when they "steal" another man's wife without having given it much thought. Occasionally Francis held an astounded ecstatic grin on his face—but then he felt anxious too. He had managed to get a new job just about the time he inherited the apartment and he felt a certain sense of power from the whole unexpected situation.

Wilfred Engels again assisted him in getting a new job—this time it was an independent relief agency, for which Francis did a lot of paper work in a cramped little office on Madison Avenue. He was lucky to get another phoney soft job, inasmuch as Engels had just been cited by a Washington committee on un-American activities and had to take a vacation in Mexico to lay low for a while. There was talk of something that appeared to be a passport fraud. But Francis had no interest in these things; he became engrossed in an entirely new life with his haunting Anne. He had just started being psychoanalyzed.

Francis rushed home almost gleefully to tell Anne what happened every day. "Oh, God, if you only knew what happened to me today! What will my psychoanalyst *do* with it!"

"Begin at the beginning and I'll be the understanding wife," she smiled, and she handed him the Benzedrine. "Would you like an uppy first?"

"In a minute. It all started this morning when I had a benny depression from last night. Someone came in the office, one of the bosses, I guess, and he began talking most strangely, almost insanely. Gradually I understood that he wanted me to go to a certain hospital to pick up some supplies to be packaged—but, honestly, at first I couldn't understand what he was saying, *why* he was saying anything at all, with that utterly stupid look of urgency on his face—"

"I've had that feeling."

"So off I went! Down to the subway, where I had the most awful unreal feeling that my train would never arrive."

"How unpleasant!"

"It lasted ages! Finally I got on some train or other and went towards my destination. People were *staring* at me it seemed, I kept wondering why they were staring at me, I knew quite well I was having a fit of Benzedrine depression. When I got out on the street I saw the hospital and went straight for it, right up the steps and inside—with a feeling of buoyant, almost jubilant certainty, you see, but gradually I began to see signs of the fact that it must be a school instead of a hospital, and with a horrible feeling of limping futility I began hurrying towards the nearest exit. I didn't want to leave the way I came in, I just simply had to rush through my error and out another way!"

"You poor darling, I should have been there!" laughed Anne.

"Suddenly I encountered a *whole class* of children moving down the hall in formation. You know the way they all parade from one classroom to another? All of them were staring at me so curiously. Suddenly they all vanished, and on top of that I couldn't find another exit, there was absolutely no other way of getting out of there but by the way I had come in. It was rather amusing to find myself in the chalk and crayon atmospheres of a grammar school again, you know, but at the same time you can imagine my horror and defeat and everything. The whole experience just shattered me."

"Did you ever find the hospital?"

"Yes! But I got lost in it. It was a huge place, I was just simply lost, wandering along shiny corridors. I remember a nurse speaking to me solicitously, but she had to go away to do something else."

"Oh, you poor dear!"

"Do you know what crossed my mind then? I remembered what you'd said about Nietzsche's remark, 'Nothing is true, everything is allowed.' What was the way *you* had it? 'Nothing is true, everything is equally absurd?' Well, that's what I thought and I kept chanting it to myself. Finally I found the man I was seeking and he handed me the packages and said something and vanished. I left the hospital, only by the wrong door and found myself in some sort of empty lot—"

"Oh, God, just like Kafka!" screamed Anne with delight.

One day, on a Saturday afternoon, the doorbell rang and Francis went to the door. There, of all people, was his young brother, Mickey Martin. Mickey had grown a great deal, but Francis recognized him by his bashful eyes and the same soft fall of brown hair over his brow. Everything else about him had become gangly, crude, and powerful, to the older brother's incomprehensible amazement. The boy grinned at him with an astounded embarrassment and waved a big meaty hand in greeting.

"Hi, Francis!" he cried. "Is this where you live? What a nice place this is!" When he saw Anne, he almost tripped over the rug.

"Is there anything wrong?" wondered Francis out loud.

Mickey slowly fixed him with a serious look. "It's about Pa. He's sick as anything and Ma asked me to come and tell you about it. He's been sick a long time." He said this with that earnest mournful note in his voice, so Martin-like, that Francis had not heard for a long, long time.

"How long has he been sick? What is it?"

"For two months now he's been in the house and Ma's working in a shoeshop in Brooklyn and I work after school in a store there. The doctor says it's cancer."

"Cancer."

"Yeah. The doctor said he's had it for a long time and didn't know it. The doctor says he shoulda done something about it a long time ago. But Pa doesn't know he's got cancer, the doctor told him it's something else." And Mickey explained all these things with the same sorrowful, half-questioning, gravely troubled air that continued even at that moment to gnaw at Francis' memory. The last time anyone had spoken like that to him was when his father had visited him in the Naval hospital in Chicago on that strange melancholy rattled night two years back.

"So Ma wondered if you'd come over sometime," said Mickey slowly, "and see him and talk to him and just, you know, see him?"

"I see," said Francis absentmindedly. "Yes, well, of course I certainly must do that."

"I'll tell her," said the boy simply, and turned to go. Almost compulsively, Francis roused himself from his musing reverie and asked him to sit down and stay awhile. Whereupon Mickey sat awkwardly on the edge of a chair and seemed to blush continually. Anne got up and mixed him a coke with ice. Nobody could think of anything to say and there were long moments of embarrassing silence as Mickey sat there drinking the coke, looking up at Francis occasionally with a grave perplexed look.

After the boy had left Francis said, "Well, what do you think of my kid brother?"

"Really, after all, he *blushes* nice."

"God! Now I'll have to get down there sometime and pay my respects to my father. I'm sorry to hear that he's in such bad shape."

"I'm afraid you'll have to go," smiled Anne faintly. "There's nothing you can do about it. When they ask you like that . . ."

"Yes."

Outside, as it grew dark in the streets, young Mickey hurried home looking around him with the eager fascination of a boy raised in a small town who suddenly finds himself alone in the middle of fabulous and fashionable Manhattan. Everyone was so well-dressed, the men distinguished and handsome, some of them in Homburg hats, the women lovely, concealed, and secret in beautiful furs. They were all going to cocktails and restaurants and theaters as it got dark, and the lights glittered like diamonds. It was so different from Brooklyn, and of course, so different from darkest Galloway.

"What a nice apartment Francis lives in," he thought, "right in the middle of New York, and what a nice blonde he's got there, what a nice, quiet, pretty woman with him. Imagine having a girl like that right in the middle of New York, and a good job, and go out at night to big restaurants and then go to shows and everything. Yow! What a lucky guy!"

[3]

PETER WENT home to his family that Autumn.

A sharp knowledge had now come to him of the tragic aloneness of existence and the need of beating it off with love and devotion instead of surrendering to it with that perverse, cruel, unnecessary self-infliction that he saw everywhere around him, that he himself had nursed for so long.

His father was dying—and his own life was dying, it had come to a dead end in the city, he had nowhere else to go. Peter did not know what to do with his own life but somehow he knew what to do about his father, who was now not only his father, but his brother and his mysterious son too.

He spent the dying winter in Brooklyn and helped with the expenses of the house and doctors' bills by working in an all-night cafeteria. He came home from work every morning around seven, just as his mother was leaving for the shoeshop and his brother Mickey was getting ready to go to school, and brewed a pot of coffee and drank a cup with his father in the kitchen and argued and rhubarbed with him as much as ever. Now they both knew that the end was coming and their arguments were fewer and fewer, they were no longer arguments. They laughed together more than they had ever done. The father was very happy that his closest, saddest, more serious son had come back to him at last.

"Ah, Petey, life isn't long enough, there's so many things I could have done!" cried Martin in the morning. "If I had done the right thing, invested my money carefully in something good, in a home or a farm or something like that, just think how different it would be now, maybe I wouldn't be sick and your mother there wouldn't have to be working in a shoeshop in my dying day. Ah, now I know how much I underestimated that kid in my time!"

"Kid?"

"Your mother, Petey, your mother. Don't you know how men are? They play down their women, they call them knuckleheads all their life, until finally it dawns on them who's the knucklehead in the end? Hah? And, sure enough, if I had done the right thing, maybe I wouldn't be dying from all the disappointment I've had since I lost my shop back home, since I came to New York. Somehow, somewhere, we'd be living a better life and we'd be happy enough to make it click. By gosh, I wish I could start all over again!" he cried, slapping the arm of the chair with his intense, tearful, emphatic look of mournful determination.

"Feel good this morning, huh?"

"*Sure*, I feel good! I'm not dead by a long shot, you know! By God, sometimes I feel so good I can almost feel this damn junk in my body falling apart and healing itself someway. It could happen, you know," he added shrewdly, "it could happen just as sure as I'm sitting here. Sometimes I don't wonder but it will! And I'd bounce right up again and do something although I'd be pretty weak, I'm weak, all right, I'm weak, Petey, and I'm a lot older, I don't know if I'd be worth much any more—" He trailed off painfully.

"The way you've got the horses beat maybe you could go to Florida and make a profession of it!"

"Why, *sure!* Did I show you last week's figures, how I came out?" Eagerly, with the wild absorption of a little boy at play, the old man produced his complicated jumble of figures and explained them at length with many gestures and ejaculations and wishes that he could be in Florida at that very moment. Then they had more coffee and talked for hours.

Peter worked at his job, a lonely miserable dishrag of a nighttime job that ticked away in the dreary midnights of city-time and city-blackness, and came home in the gray dawns along streets covered with butts and newspapers and chewing-gum wrappers, along sidewalks with gratings that breathed the stale air of subways. When the sky itself was a dishrag and the earth was covered with the rat-gray paving that city people lived on—he came home from his job, smoking and silent and trudging, his mind blank, his soul deadened, his heart breaking: he came home to see his father wasting away throughout the Winter and into the Spring in the midst of dreadful wreckage. Something like Spring came into the air, something that suggested birds swinging on branches in sweet alluring singsong, and sweet air, and Homeric dawn—but it was a suggestion for only a short while, soon forgotten in the roar of Brooklyn morning.

Old Martin swung with amazing courage from joyous, almost robust days when he loved to talk and drink coffee and listen to the radio and read books, and days when he just sat slumped and ravaged of all his strength, almost dead, buried in the huge ennui of sickness and dizzy sorrow.

There were strange nights, too, when he woke up in the middle of the night and sat in the kitchen alone and talked to himself while the others slept. He talked to his own mother and father long dead, he addressed them his appeals as a son, he mourned them so long buried, he asked them their dark advice, he remembered the pale flowers of their faces strangely. And he talked to God, sometimes with heated familiarity and argumentative fury, he asked why things had been made so hard for men, why, and if there was no why, then *what* it was that was so strange, beautiful, sad, brief, raggedly real, so hurt and inconsolable. He asked God why he had been made by Him, for what purpose, for what reason the flower of his own face and the fading of it from the earth forever; why life was so short, so hard, so furious with men, so impossibly mortal, so cruel, restless, sweet, so deadly. And he talked to the lone self that would die with him for always. "George," he said, "George, all the misery in the world and what can you do about it in the end? George, there's too much misery in you, too much headache, you can't last. All your life went through your fingers and you laughed it off because you thought you had all the time in the world. You had all the time in the world, all right, all the time it gives you and no more. And I was always sore when something went wrong, and all the time it was just *me* that was wrong. George! why the hell didn't you do what you were always just about to do! When you woke up in the middle of the night sometimes, you knew, you *knew*, George! That big thing we were always waiting for and no one ever did . . . We? Yass, *all* of us, *all* of us— Oh, we're all dying! All the others and all the misery in store. But what's misery, George?—your own ignorant foolishness in the middle of life. In the middle of life. Oh, God, I want to be in the middle of life! It's sad, it's sad to die, it's misery dying like this, knowing. I don't want to die!" He bit his lip thinking of it. "But I'm ready to die, God, I guess because it's all I've got left. I'm ready—but, God, whoever I am and whatever reason you made me live, I know one thing, God, I wish I was certain about one thing—about my wife and children. I know *them*, God!" He laughed, scratching his chin. "Ah, but I know them well, everything about them. Ha ha ha! I've *seen* them and heard them and felt them all right. Just see that they'll be all right after I'm gone." He raised his face mournfully to the poor cracked ceiling of midnight, he looked at heaven through the plaster-cracks of Brooklyn. "See that I can look back from the grave and find out how they're coming along, some way or the other, there must be a trick like that to make up for this. See that they're happy, God!"

He puttered around the kitchen at four in the morning talking like that. At times he stared out the window at the black Brooklyn night and cursed it up and down for what it seemed to have done to him.

And when Peter came back in the mornings, the old man asked him what had happened all night in the cafeteria. Nothing had happened, people just came in to eat doughnuts and drink coffee in the dead of night, and left, all in the middle of life. And then father and son looked at each other, and talked about the past, all the things in the million-shadowed blazing past, and about what they would like to do, what they might have done, what they should do now. Father and son were also two men in the world, sitting idle for a moment together, recognizing in sad-voiced commentary that the destiny of men is to come up to rivers, and cross them one way or another, this man's way and that man's way and any other possible way, and get over them or turn back in defeat and sarcasm. At these times they experienced moments of contentment talking to each other. This was the last life they would ever know each other in, and yet they wished they could live a hundred lives and do a thousand things and know each other forever in a million new ways, they wished this in the midst of their last life.

These things began to work their change on young Peter who

saw, as in an ancient vision spaded up from his being, what life must be about, at last. He saw that it was love and work and true hope. He saw that all the love in the world, which was sweet and fine, was not love at all without its work, and that work could not exist without the kindness of hope. He gazed into the face of these things at last just as he gazed at his father's impending death, into eyes that would soon be blind and dead. He understood these things when he helped the feeble old man out of bed in the mornings and supported him on wandering feet that used to stride and clack along on Saturday nights in Galloway, he saw these things when his father roused himself from fevered reveries to eat, wash himself, and settle his things around his chair to resume another day.

He saw that all the struggles of life were incessant, laborious, painful, that nothing was done quickly, without labor, that it had to undergo a thousand fondlings, revisings, moldings, addings, removings, graftings, tearings, correctings, smoothings, rebuildings, reconsiderings, nailings, tackings, chippings, hammerings, hoistings, connectings—all the poor fumbling uncertain incompletions of human endeavor. They went on forever and were forever incomplete, far from perfect, refined, or smooth, full of terrible memories of failure and fears of failure, yet, in the way of things, somehow noble, complete, and shining in the end. This he could sense even from the old house they lived in, with its solidly built walls and floors that held together like rock: some man, possibly an angry pessimistic man, had built the house long ago, but the house stood, and his anger and pessimism and irritable laborious sweats were forgotten; the house stood, and other men lived in it and were sheltered well in it.

Peter and his father, by just looking painfully at one another, seemed to understand that to question the uncertainties and pains of life and work was to question life itself. They did that every day, yet they did not hate life, they loved it. They saw that life was like a kind of work, a poor miserable disconnected fragment of something better, far greater, just a fragmentary isolated frightened sweating over a moment in the dripping faucet-time of the world, a tattered impurity leading from moment to moment towards the great pure forge-fires of workaday life and loving human comprehension.

And old George, when the blindness of pain and disintegration dimmed his brain, rolled his eyes mad in their sockets. When he was like that, having his gloomy dying days of demented terror, Peter was stabbed in his own heart with the loneliness and brutality of it, and tried to cheer him up, and sat with him, and worried himself white.

"Oh, I've been sick so long, and so damn tired. . . . Petey! Petey! life is too long, it takes too long to get it over with. . . ."

This was unbearable to Peter, locked in his own vision of death, trying to come out of it like a man crawling out of a Black Canyon as the vultures darkened the sun. What if he should succeed in clawing and clutching out of this abyss only to meet his father dead, without hope? What if he should suddenly see the whole terrible bleak enigma as no man had ever seen it, and die of it himself?

But gravity, glee, and wonder would return to his father by the miracle of everyday heartbeat, and he would look up out of a dream of death to see the mother and Mickey and Peter moving around the house, he would see the slow, somehow stupid motions of the world around him, the dear pathetic things of it, and some vast pity would sink through him like a drug, some vision would inflame his inflammable brain with its pictures of joy and regret and trembling sad affection, and he would come talking and laughing back to them, back to the noonday staple of his life's blood. All that, and his slow unfolding amazement, his knowledge of poor mortality, of the awe of little children, of the workaday purposes and passions and loves of men in their prime, of the silence and sorrow of old men, all these things would flame in his mind like explosions of light, like the powerful flutterings of candlelight near the end.

But the candle, which is light, is extinguishable just because it is light. And one morning in May he died.

A strange thing had happened the day before he died. For some reason or other the old furies of contention had risen between him and Peter, and they had argued again. It had started when Peter mentioned something that he was reading.

"Listen to this, Pa, just to show you what an amazing sort of guy Tschaikowsky was—*you* know, the composer. It says here that he came to a hotel and was taken upstairs, ordered his dinner, saw to all the towels and whatnot, tipped the waiter, and when everything was all settled and he was alone in his room, he just threw himself on the bed and started crying . . . for no reason at all."

"Why did he do that?"

"That's the kind of guy he was, *you* know, a melancholy Russian composer. I'm amazed that he did that."

"Sure, sure!" cried the old man bitterly. "You're amazed, all right. You're amazed because he's a Russian and because he's a composer and because they all write about him, he's not an ordinary joker like *me!*"

"I didn't say that!"

"Ah!" cried Martin, waving his hand violently. "Chekooski and Plakooski, just as long as it's some fancy Russian name it means a hell of a lot more when *they* cry!"

"Why are you saying all this!" demanded Peter, who was deeply hurt.

"Why? Because I find out what you damn kids nowadays are thinking about all the time, that's why! Why does it have to be Chekooski that you admire! Why! Just because he cries?" he yelled furiously, pounding the chair. "Goddam it, I cry, I cry too! But it doesn't mean a goddam thing when *I* cry, I'm not Chekooski, I'm not a Russian composer, I'm just a poor ordinary American slob, that's all, when *I* cry it's because I'm a slob not because I'm amazing!"

Peter stamped out of the room angrily and went barging around the kitchen in a blind reel of fury and embarrassment.

"I cry too! I cry too!" his father was shouting in the other room. "Remember that, my fine-feathered young son with all your fancy books!"

They hardly spoke a word the rest of the day. Peter was off from work that night, a time he would have ordinarily spent chatting with his father in the kitchen over a carton of beer while the mother and Mickey slept. Instead of staying home, he went walking all over Brooklyn in the profoundest daze he had ever known in all his life. Never had he felt so low that he had to shuffle his feet, compulsively, as he moved along the sidewalks that night. He tried to walk in a normal way but ended up shuffling and dragging along feebly, helplessly, wondering vaguely why. He covered miles and miles of streets that way, with his head lowered, his hands dangling at his side, his shoes scuffling slowly on the pavement, not looking particularly at anything along the way.

When he came back home at three in the morning, his father was in bed sleeping. From the kitchen where he sat with his head down on the table in deep and helpless thought, Peter suddenly began to try breathing in rhythm with his father's snores, just on a whim, almost in a lighthearted way, and realized wearily that he could not keep up with those rapid desperate wheezings without becoming dizzy and sick. It never occurred to him that anything was wrong, although, by the fact that he was so utterly and physically depressed, he realized later that his very furthermost nature must have known that his father was slowly nearing death during those very hours. The doctor had come the evening before to tap some more water out of the old man's ravaged belly, as he had been doing for almost a year's time, and weakness and shock were conspiring at last to bring the end, something which the doctor had expected many months ago.

At dawn Peter raised his head from the table when his mother shuffled into the kitchen to get ready to go to work. The old man called them from the other room and said that it made him dizzy to lie in bed, so they helped him to his chair. He stared blindly at them and said:

"If I'm going to die, dammit, I want to die in my chair."

Peter settled him back comfortably in his chair and arranged the blankets around his legs. His father said, strangely:

"That's right, my poor little boy."

His wife asked him if he wanted a little breakfast and he said he wasn't hungry, just a glass of grapefruit juice would do. She brought him that and held the glass to his lips while he gulped blindly. She gazed at him with tender pain, gravity, and sorrow, and then she had to go to work and told Peter to make him a little breakfast later. She went off to work silently, sadly, and Mickey went off to school. Alone with his father in the gray morning, Peter brewed a pot of coffee. He could hear him snoring in the other room beneath the music of the little kitchen radio.

After twenty minutes spent gloomily over a cup of coffee, Peter went in to ask him if he wanted some coffee or breakfast, and saw him there with head lowered, perfectly still in the chair, his lower lip pouting, the ragged hair askew on his head. He called his father in the empty stillness of the house. The old man did not look up with his air of stunned wonder. Peter's blood crawled with awful understanding. His father was not breathing, his stomach was not rising and falling in tortured wheezes as before, and there was sudden stillness all around him.

George Martin had died as though in his sleep, so quietly that no one had even guessed. And what Peter had imagined to be his snores had really been the lonesome death rattle.

But Peter, understanding that he was dead, refused nevertheless to believe it was so. He went over and picked up a limp wrist and tried to feel the pulse. The old hand slumped back. He placed his hand on his father's brow with fearful anticipation of cold fleshly marble, but the brow was warm, almost hot. He knelt down in front of his father and cried out: "Pa! Are you dead, for God's sake? Pa!"—and there was no reply.

"You poor old man, you poor old man!" he cried, kneeling in front of his father. "My father!" he cried in a loud voice that rang with lonely madness in the empty house. He still refused to believe it, with a sense of terrible wonder he reached out and stroked his father's cheek, like a child, and the notion that now he could stroke his father's face at will because he was dead and did not know it was awful, it strangled in Peter's throat. That he could cry out and talk like that, mad and foolish, even though his father was sitting there, too flooded his brain with uncomprehending horror. Without thinking he wiped the mouth of spittle, brushed back the poor ragged hair a little, held his hand on his father's head unbelievingly, and kissed him on the forehead with a feeling of gentle crumbling grief, and madness, and fear.

"Ruthey!" yelled Peter, looking around the room, his thoughts suddenly fixed feverish on the image of his sister Ruth, that trim sweet daughter of the old man who was so far away as he sat dead. "Hurry up, Ruthey, for Christ's sake!" Peter was out of his mind as though she would hear him and come rushing immediately. "Oh, somebody hurry up! All of you! Pa's dead, Pa's dead!"

He stumbled around the room, stopped to gape at the wall, mused almost absentmindedly, suddenly lashed out with a terrific smash of his fist against the plaster, stared at his bruised aching hand with crazy satisfaction. Almost as suddenly he calmed down, sat down in a chair across the room, gazed at the dead old man, and began to decide what he must do now, what he must do now.

"What will I do?" he asked his father with growing dullness.

He stared at his face, his lowered, pallid mask of a face, the poor face so soon to gape dumbly in darkness, so soon to weep the juices of the grave, to look upon black exfoliating loam and silence and decomposed night. He stared at the lowered eyelids in their last acquiescent prayerful vow, their gloomy sleep, their devout sorrow, their inward-turned religious knowledge, their human tenderness and secret final understanding. He could not believe it. What had killed his father, in God's name? He had not done it himself, it was not true that he had done it himself! A thousand times it seemed he had done it himself, but it was not so! Who could say that he had done it himself! How would he ever learn that he had not done it himself!

Why was he alone with his dead father like this, what had happened? Where was sweet Ruth, and striding Joe, and poor sarcastic Liz, and dark Francis, and big Rosey, and little Mickey, and lost Charley? Where was his sad and silent mother? Where was the house back home in Galloway? And what was it that had killed his father? Why did he sit there in his chair with his dead lips pouting as from some suffering awful knowledge and experience of hopelessness?

Why did he lie drowned now in the strange ocean of Brooklyn far from the verdant home of his youth? What had happened to him in the fifty-seven years of his life among the scramble and scatter of losses and the impossible griefs and weepings of the poor exasperated world? Amid haunted disappointment, and worrying love, and dear wild wants and mysteries, among wars where the children of the earth go mad—no use, no use . . .

He had died from the things Peter knew he would die of. . . . There was his father, the rare flower's image of him in the world, who had come to live, and care, and work, and die, and go away—leaving nothing now, no seal and mark of his caring anywhere, no monument to his meek figure, no plaque to commemorate his deeds of foolish and woebegone devotion. There was his father, slumped and done in the raw catastrophic world, dead among dust and fury, dead even in his own way, his own suffering true way, his sweet real excellent way, his great way. His embarrassed sheepish shy eyes, modest ways, strong heart, strong hands, true inkstained hands, his strong legs and corded neck and bony jaw, and the love of other men and of children, and the ravenous strange love of attentive delicious women—his admirable life all finished, his soul complete. . . .

Peter went outside to a candy store and telephoned his mother at the shoe factory, and Mickey at the high school, and then came back in the house and sat looking at his father for the last time.

"In a minute now, in a minute now," he kept saying anxiously, "everything'll be all right in a minute now."

[4]

SEVERAL DAYS or so after the death of George Martin in Brooklyn, around the curve of the earth, in Okinawa, two men were running a bulldozer against a pile of rubble at the edges of an air field when they noticed a soldier's dark, twisted, dusty body turning over in the rock and sand. They shut off the motor, one man wiped his brow, jumped off, walked to the pile of rubble, and the other man jumped down and leaned against the big machine and lit a cigarette nervously.

"What's the matter with you?" asked the first man in a loud, abrupt voice. He kicked away a few rocks from the pile and leaned his elbow on one knee to examine the body.

"What's it say on his dawg-tag?" demanded the other man nervously. "Has he got a dawg-tag, Thompson?"

Thompson said nothing, but just leaned there meditatively at the side of the rubble pile, as though thinking about something else.

"Ain't he got a dawg-tag, Thompson?"

"Aw, he's turned over, I don't want to move him."

"Well, why don't you see if he's got a wallet there in his back pocket."

Thompson pulled out a wallet from the limp-hanging trousers and began looking through it slowly.

"What's in it?"

Thompson was silent in contemplation of something he had in his hand, and the other man was watching anxiously. The afternoon darkness was deepening, something almost cold had come into the dusty air, a dog barked far away.

"What's it say, boy?"

Thompson groped slowly through the wallet with a grave. searching, sullen curiosity.

"Did you find his name?"

Thompson wiped his brow and deliberately said nothing.

"Did you find his *name?*"

Thompson lost his temper, turned, held the card up before the other man's face, and yelled, in a loud irascible voice: "Charles Martin! Charles G. Martin! Galloway, Massachusetts! Born June 16, 1926! *Now* are you satisfied? ! !"

"Is that his name? Charley Martin." The soldier sitting down thought foolishly about the name for a moment. "I reckon I didn't know *him*."

"Did you think you'd know him, jerk? Do you think you're the only guy out here, you and your cousins from Louisiana?"

"Well, I *could* have known him, couldn't I? What are you making bad jokes about with a fella daid right in front of you?"

"I'm not making bad jokes. All *you* can do is sit there and ask foolish questions."

"Lord, I cain't stand looking at daid fellas, that's all."

"You shoulda been around here three months ago, that's all."

Silence, grave and sullen silence . . .

"What's thet you're a-looking at now?"

"A letter, a letter. And if you think I'm gonna read a guy's letter, you're crazy. It's *his* letter, ain't it? Why do you ask so many stupid questions?"

"I didn't axe you to *read* the letter, I just want to know what it says on it," moaned the other man.

"It says Private Charles G. Martin, APO San Francisco, that's all it says, and it comes from a guy called George Martin, that's all. George Martin of 255 State Street, Brooklyn, U.S.A."

"Didn't you say he come from Massachusetts?"

"Yeah, he came from Massachusetts but he's got a letter here from Brooklyn, some guy he knows, maybe his brother or his father or a cousin or somebody"—Thompson was speaking with gentle defeated weariness now—"somebody with the same name, living in Brooklyn, you see?"

"Well then, thet's all I wanted to know, boy."

Thompson came over and sat down and lit a cigarette, and stared at the tip of it in moody silence. They just sat there looking around and wondering about the dead boy called Charley Martin, the dusty figure they had just dug up.

[5]

THEY BURIED George Martin in New Hampshire, on a long grassy slope off the foot of a hill, in the middle of the farming country around Lacoshua. It was a small cemetery over one hundred years old, with old stones leaning woefully among the waving grass, others fallen and half-buried in the loam, the husks of ancient wreaths mingling with pine cones, wild flowers, and a stonewall that had become a vine in the wild undergrowths of the earth. A great grove of old pines surrounded this burial ground, bending over it shaggily on three sides. From the dirt road at the bottom of the slope wound up an old wagon path over which had marched the funeral of little Julian Martin two decades ago and, before that, the funeral of Jack Martin, George Martin's own father, almost fifty unclaimable years before.

On this hill, in the distance, one saw the misty lands and farmfields and pine woods of the old New Hampshire earth from which the Martins of two centuries had risen secretly, hidden and unknown, enveloped and furious, to live and work and die in the brooding presence of themselves and the earth, in the dark atmospheres of their own moody dream of things. Many of them were buried there, grandfathers, grandmothers, unknown lost progenitors of them, forgotten infants, dark aunts, uncles, cousins, ancient brothers and sisters and sourceless kin, and the kin of other families.

The old man had requested that he be buried in this place and his wife agreed as though she had known all along that he had such a longing in his mind.

When Peter heard this he was amazed. Yet he knew that his father never would have consented to be buried in New York among the unnumbered strange dead of the world's city. He was amazed because his father had never mentioned it to him and because, between his parents, this secret unspeaking pact had long existed, older and deeper than his own mere sonhood. And when Joe heard about it, and Mickey, and the sisters, Ruth and Rosey, they were awe-struck with the realization of some inevitable rule in the huge dark circle of things. But Liz wondered what difference it could make where you were buried. And Francis, receiving a telegram that notified him of his father's death and of the funeral in Lacoshua, remarked to Anne: "He evidently wanted to be buried among his relatives. It seems rather pathetic, doesn't it?"

The Martin mother made arrangements in Brooklyn to have her husband's body shipped to a funeral home in Lacoshua operated by a man who had known Martin in his youth and who knew the old cemetery seven miles out of town. The mother realized now why her husband had been so intent on having his little boy Julian, Francis' twin, buried there among generations of Martins long ago, as if he had sensed that he himself, these many years later, would have to be buried there before anyone else in the family. She was glad he would be laid to rest close by the dark little angel of the family, the waif of eternity in their souls, "to guard over him." The Brooklyn undertakers carried the body direct to Lacoshua in a hearse on the second night of his death, after he had lain in state one night in a lonely funeral parlor on a dark neon-winking street in Brooklyn, with no one to see him but his wife and children and a few strangers who wandered in by mistake. When his family left after midnight the lone commercial light was left shining beside his bier and the alley night outside murmured and muttered till dawn. On Saturday afternoon the hearse rolled out of Brooklyn and carried him north to New England. That night the mother, Joe, Patricia Franklin Martin, now Joe's wife, and Mickey and Peter journeyed up overnight in a car that Joe had bought just a few weeks before.

Then the mournful odysseys for the funeral began. Ruthey and her husband Luke Marlowe, back from the war, drove up from Tennessee and arrived Sunday morning only a few hours after the mother's party. Rose flew in with her husband and child from the far West, from Seattle, and arrived at the same time. Liz came up with Buddy Fredericks on a train, arriving Sunday afternoon. Francis, the last of the Martins to show up, arrived late Sunday afternoon, alone.

In Lacoshua, the body was laid in state in a great white frame house of noble proportions, now converted into a funeral home, a neat, expansive structure with green shutters, set at the top of a great lawn, under aged trees, far back from a quiet street. The dead man's wife and some of his children were pleased that he would lie there, if only for a night, in the kind of a house that he had often thought of living in when he was younger and still thinking of following his desires.

How many times they had heard him, on his Sunday drives

through the New England countryside in the old days: "Golly! will you look at that beautiful old house there in back of the trees. Just imagine how peaceful and dignified it would be to pass the rest of your days there! Sometimes I wonder why I break my head working and spending money when I could buy a house like that in a few years and live so sweet and peaceful. . . ."

The mother and the youngsters had arrived at ten o'clock. It was a beautiful May day, a Sunday morning in the small town, fresh with odorous new greenery, thronging faintly with the sound of churchbells in the distant air of the New Hampshire countryside. The mother shook her head sadly as she stood on the lawn of the great house. "Oh, Joey, your father waited and waited for a day like this all Spring, he lost so much blood and he was so cold in the house. . . . I only wish he could see this now."

"Well," said Joe gravely, "he's here anyway. . . . This is where he wanted us to bury him."

"New Hampshire, New Hampshire," sighed Marguerite Martin, looking around at the beautiful morning and the trees and the distant fields. "He wanted to come back here the worst way. He hated it so much in New York! Joey, this is where your father and I were born and raised, this is where we were married. When we came into town there at Millis Street that was the little church where we were married. And he wanted to come back so bad, to finish his days here. Joey, you'll never know how unhappy he was down there. . . ."

"I know, I know."

The old man was laid out in his coffin among baskets of flowers. He looked like a sweet, saintly young man, pure and inwardly devout in contemplative sleep, silent, virtuous with death, richly content on his satin pillow. Joe and Peter agreed that it did not look like him at all. There was no mournfulness and no eager harassed intensity in that padded and powdered face, but the mother, sentimental in her grief, was moved, even astonished at the transformation the embalmer had wrought in his Brooklyn moratorium. She whispered sorrowfully at the rim of his bier:

"Well now, he looks exactly the way he was when I married him! See how young and handsome they fixed him, isn't it marvelous? *Just* the way he looked. There, you see him now, that's what he looked like when he was a young man. Poor George, poor George!" she whispered entreatingly. Peter and Joe and Mickey were mortified with crushing sadness, and clustered around their mother. She preferred to stay there gazing at his youngish face, shaking her head with slow amazement and recollection, and they retired and left her there alone.

The boys were exhilarated when Ruth arrived with her husband whom they had never seen. A few minutes later Rosey arrived with her baby in her arm and her short, squatly powerful, gravely scowling husband from Seattle. It was sweetly consolatory to see these two men, these strangers who had married their sisters, bearing regrets for an old man they had never really known. Ruth's husband, Luke, had seen George Martin once, but both had had tumultuous letters from him. To see them, grave and uncomfortable and tenderly discreet, craning rawburnt necks, moving with the stiff and awkward solicitude of strong men at solemn gatherings, arriving over the long raw night of travel with the grim air of determination and sympathy, was consoling. The Martin brothers clasped their hands gratefully and smoked with them out on the porch.

Luke Marlowe was a strapping slow-spoken Tennessean who looked like the hunter and woodsman that he was. He said very little, smiled a lot, was extremely polite, considerate, vast with deep instinctive knowledge, and kindly as a bird. Yet they marveled at the huge bulge of his shoulders and something raw and powerful in the weighty hang of his hands beneath his clean white shirtcuffs.

Big Rosey's husband, whose name was Tony Hall, at first glance seemed to be the very opposite of Marlowe. He walked on twinkling bandylegs, whirled about with quick attentiveness whenever someone spoke to him, turned his head convulsively aside in swift decisive consideration, answered with a kind of curtness—and yet they saw that he too spoke very little, that he was depthless with earnest attention and regard, keen, sensitive, nervous with polite apprehension and, like Marlowe, raw with strength, in his case a kind of packed, furious strength that seemed to strain and throb in the thrust of his neck and in the quick action of work-gnarled hands. He and Rosey and the baby were going to go live in Alaska within a year. Young Hall had ideas and vigorous muscles that were suitable for that raw unknown country.

Sweet Ruthey looked smaller than ever now that she was faintly pregnant. The big powerful Rosey had already begun to look like the young mother of uncountable children, with her flushed cheeks, dark blazing eyes, big forearms and authoritative speech. "Did any of you eat?" she demanded almost angrily. Nobody had—and she went off straightaway to look for food to make a lunch for everybody.

"And, Petey!" cried Ruth, embracing her brother joyfully. "I haven't seen you for so long! What did I tell you about Luke! . . ."

"Boy, am I glad for you!" cried Peter with unexpected feeling, looking away mournfully. "That's the kind of guy you *should* marry."

"And I did!" she cried gleefully. "We're buying a house in Tennessee next month and settling down. What about Liz? Do you think she'll be coming? Do you think maybe she won't come?"

"I don't know, I don't know. . . ."

They all stood before the bier of the dead father, before the mother who was kneeling and whispering softly over her rosary beads. All these young people, flushed and excited with life, bursting with a thousand things to tell each other, saw, in that silence and brooding candlelight, how all their endeavors and glees and absorptions would end. Yet the stillness that crawled into their hearts was not convincing. Yes, death had happened, but somehow it would not happen to them. It was their own father, and their own bending, repining, rosaried mother, but somehow they themselves would be fathers and mothers who would never end, who would never die, who would never bend and pray over the sad sweet consummation among flowers that they saw there. But when they thought: "This is my father, this is the man they called George Martin, this is the George my mother called in the house, this is him so sad and excitable and full of fun and arguments, so near now, still alive, I can still see him, I can hear him, where is he? Where is he? THIS IS PA!" When they realized that, they looked at each other and knew that they would all die too.

Ruthey was almost angry because her father had been so prettily made up by the embalmer. "For God's sake, that doesn't look like him! I wanted to see *him*, I thought I was going to see my father's face again, I thought about it all night long. I said to myself, 'Well, Pa is dead, but, by God, I'm going to have my last look at him.' And now look what they went and done to him! Did you ever see anything so silly!"

At that very moment, the Martin mother was telling her two new sons-in-law how wonderfully her husband looked—exactly the way he looked when they were married long ago. They listened with haggard sympathy and sudden affection for her.

In the afternoon the relatives began to arrive. The mother had telephoned the Galloway newspaper the day before from New York and a small notice was printed in the Sunday obituaries there. But in Lacoshua everybody knew that George Martin was dead, almost everybody knew who he was, and many of them had known him personally in the past. And now, to the amazement of the Martin youngsters, and as the Martin mother watched with her shrewd and ancient understanding, whole hosts of undiscoverable kinsmen began to arrive at the funeral home. The children knew Uncle Harry Martin and the aunts Martha and Louisa—they had been jiggled on their knees many times—and they knew a few cousins, but they did not know the strangers who came trooping into the old house smiling sadly at them.

"Don't you know your own cousin?" cried the mother gleefully. "This is a son of your grandfather Jack's brother William, and these are his children. You don't remember, you don't know them all—but I know them. Oh, it's so grand to see you again, Arthur!" She embraced the man and kissed his children, young and old, and the Martin youngsters were amazed. Unknown relatives arrived in old cars spotted with country mud, with their troops of children, their young mothers, their wise and melancholy old folks, their dark young men all dressed in their Sunday best, and paraded before the coffin of George Martin with grave and respectful demeanor. They came from all over New Hampshire, they all knew that George Martin had died.

"Will I ever forget that argument I had with George almost forty years ago, do you remember, Marge?" cried a very old man, taking the mother's hand and gazing at her fondly. "Do you remember that night? We were all drinking beer in my backyard, I believe it was the Fourth of July, it was summertime anyway, and we were talking about politics, that's to say we *started* talking about politics but when we were finished we was *yelling* politics and we had the whole town listening on the back fence. . . ."

"I remember that night. I was a little girl. George was eighteen and he was always arguing with older men to show he was the cock of the walk, and we used to listen to him and laugh, all my little cousins and me!" She chuckled eagerly. "Oh, but he was a big showoff in those days!—"

"I'll say! He was always arguing with his old Uncle Ray!" Almost letting out a whoop in the solemn house, old Ray hugged the Martin mother and whirled her around. "Margie, do you know you haven't changed much? Why, I could recognize you. Who's this? Which sprout is this? Mickey? Is he your youngest? Look here, Mickey boy, I knew your sweet little mother here when she was so high and I want you to know that she's the grandest little girl that ever lived! Look at him! What's the matter with him? Cat's got his tongue! Who's that tall boy over there, is that the Joe Martin I heard about? Come here, Joe, don't you remember your Uncle Ray?!!"

Joe had seen him once, he had been jiggled on his knee at the age of two on a forgotten night in a farmhouse kitchen when a great circle of laughing faces had surrounded his infant's awe.

"Well, he grew up, didn't he? He grew up all right. He shore grew up!"

Faint flashes of remembrance and recognition haunted the minds of the young Martins as the relatives trooped about, faces remembered from some childhood comprehension, faces changed and grown older yet still hauntingly familiar, faces that reminded them of the brooding pine forest and night of New Hampshire long ago when young George Martin and his young wife so proudly visited the innumerable relatives to present their children.

"Who's the college football player? What was his name? Charley?"

"No, Pete. That's him on the porch there."

"So *that's* him, so that's the guy I read about in the papers. *Say!* He looks just like my nephew Barney Martin—you know Barney, did you ever see young Barney? He's not here today, he's up in Maine now, he grows potatoes up there with his young wife Althea. Do you know Althea Smalley?"

"Well, now," considered the Martin mother, "if I'm not wrong, I think I do. She was the daughter of Emma Martin, wasn't she, who married a second time after her husband died, married a Jim Smalley—from Welford, wasn't it?"

"That's *right!* that's *right!* Say, Margie, you *do* know them all, don't you! Hyah! hyah! hyah! That's who it was, the daughter of Emma Martin—"

"No relation to your people," added the woman with satisfaction.

"That's right! No relation! Boy, I'll say you know them all!"

And then, to add to the innumerable Martins and kin of the Martins by marriage, came the mother's own people, the Courbets. They were numerous too. No one there that afternoon could keep track of all the families and all the lines represented, all the in-laws and spreading generations and inweavings of that something that wove and wove and begat mysteries in the earth, no one but the Martin mother in all her immortal knowledge of these things.

And then came the friends of George Martin, trooping from Galloway, Massachusetts, thirty miles to the south; and they came from around Lacoshua, men who had known him as a boy and had gone swimming with him, men who had worked with him in the sawmills, men who had known his father well, men who had hung around the Lacoshua barberships with him, who had vied with him for the affection of the town belles in the long ago summer nights. The mother remembered most of them, the children had never seen them and yet it seemed they knew them well. It was all so deeply moving, so deeply mysterious, so deeply joyful to see their father honored and remembered by the intensity of modest sorrowful men.

"There he is," said one man softly, holding his hat against his breast.

"Yep. That's Georgie, old Georgie," whispered another man, and these two old partners turned slowly, spoke awhile with the widow, smiled at the children, stood about awkwardly, gravely in the candle-flickering parlor for a few minutes, and then left, walking back to the sunny town together.

The great crowd of friends from Galloway was a joy and a solace that tore at their hearts. Old Joe Cartier arrived with his entire family, a gay raucous troop that had enlivened many a party in the old Martin house on holidays. To see them lunging in, one after another with earnest troubled looks of pain and regret, to see their true sadness, their perturbation, their loss, was a sight to warm the soul. Old Cartier had not changed a bit, he was still the big sturdy man who had been Martin's lifelong crony, still the redfaced, stolid, white-haired oldtimer with the powerful bulging stare of unbendable determination, still loyal, still unbending in his feelings.

He stood before the bier gazing at Martin. He held the Martin mother by the hand, shook his head, and said only: "George, George, you poor kid!" And he turned away with a griefstricken sense of some impossible mistake.

Martin was dead and they came and stood and passed before his coffin, remembering him as he was "only yesterday it seems," recollecting the huge eagerness of his soul from the powdered husk of flesh that lay there. For him death had seemed so impossible, especially to these old friends who had not seen him in the last dark years away from Galloway.

There was young Edmund, who had worked in Martin's printing plant so long, and old Berlot the barber, who came looking like death himself in his discouraged old age, and young Bill Mulligan and his wife, who had never seen Martin without a drink and a cigar in his hand. And there were many other friends who had once formed an informal association of rotating house parties in Galloway, people who had known Martin at his wildest and most wonderfully affable. And finally there was Jimmy Bannon the spastic editor, who swayed grotesquely before the coffin, craning his tortured neck, straining with awful effort to hold his gaze upon this man he had known and worked with. He had always thought so well of "Joth, big Joth!" as he struggled to explain it to Mrs. Martin in the antechamber.

The day wore on towards late afternoon, the Martins were exhausted and hungry, many visitors had come and gone, many heavy condolences had been borne, much pounding grief had returned again every time they saw their father's face on the satin pillow. And they all knew how barbarous it was to keep their dead father on display so long. He was dead, he was gone, they hated the waxen sheen of his forsaken flesh, they wished he could be buried and remembered as he actually was.

"When Pa died in Brooklyn," said Peter to Joe as they sat smoking on the porch railing, "I should have gone out and dug a hole for him, something like that. That's the way I feel. But, God, did you ever see so *many* people in all your life?"

"Hell of a lot of good it does him now."

"He'd be glad if he knew. He'd *laugh* if he knew!"

"He sure would."

Finally Aunt Martha took the harassed mother by the arm and led her out on the porch, and said: "Now listen to me, Margie. You can't say no. I've got a big dinner waiting for all of you at the farmhouse. That's what I've been doing all afternoon and I've got the finest turkey you'll ever eat. Louisa and John are waiting for you, and Uncle Ray, Arthur, and all the others. We're all going to eat and enjoy ourselves for a few hours, so get your things and don't say no."

"Oh," sighed the widow, looking up at her husband's sister with an air of weariness and humorous defeat, "I should say I won't say no. I can't tell whether I'm coming or going any more. But,

Martha . . . did you ever see so many people in all your life?" she added fervidly. "I didn't think it would be *anything* like this. . . . They *all* came!"

"Certainly. My brother was always popular. Everybody liked him. I see he had a lot of friends in Galloway, too!"

"But, Martha . . . he was so *lonesome* in New York, he didn't know a soul down there, he used to sit for hours and just talk about the old days up here and wish that he could be back. I tell you, he was *so* unhappy."

"Well," said the stern and judicious aunt, "he should have stayed home."

Everybody got in the cars and drove off to the old Martin farm seven miles across the fields and woods of late afternoon, Luke Marlowe, Tony Hall and Joe driving the three crowded cars over the dirt roads.

Just after they left, as a few raven-garmented old ladies who always visited funeral homes hovered around the coffin of George Martin, Francis Martin arrived.

The three old ladies peered with gimlet eyes at him. "Why," they said, "that must be one of his *sons*, yes, that's one of his *sons* right there!" And they whispered and cronied up like eager excited buzzards. "Yes," they said, "and he *is* a nice young man, isn't he? Oh, he dresses *very* well, he looks *very* nice. It's a pity, such a *pity*, tsk tsk tsk!"

Francis went out and walked around the block, and when he returned, wondering what in heaven's name he was doing in a small New Hampshire town on a Sunday afternoon in May, he was almost pleased to see that Liz and Buddy Fredericks had arrived. Actually they had been in town for several hours looking for a room for the night.

"Well, hasn't it been ages since I've seen *you!*" cried Liz with astonishment. "Francis! I'd almost forgotten all about you, man! Where have you been all these years! Where's everybody?" She embraced Francis with the amazing recollection of never having done this before.

"I don't know where everybody is and I have a vague idea that all of this is some kind of crazy dream. . . ."

"Solid! Let's get out of here and go to the hotel and goof off awhile, I can't stand it here. I don't mean disrespect to Pa, but this is the *end!*"

Francis and Liz had to wait awhile on the porch while big Buddy Fredericks, who had always liked old Martin, went in and paid his silent respects to the man who had been like his father long ago, before something, perhaps little Liz, had gone out of the world. She was going back to the Coast to sing; he was going to New York and his bebop night.

The old Martin farm had been run by great-grandfather Joseph Martin and his sons, and Jack Martin had been one of the last to leave and go to the little town and become a carpenter. The farm was now owned by the last of George Martin's sisters, Louisa and Martha, and it was run by Martha's husband, a gnarled, stubby, silent oak of a man called Will Goldtwaithe who seemed to live in a world of his own while his wife and sister-in-law conducted their vast family interests and absorptions.

The farm was laid deep in the woods. A marsh in back divided the house and barns from a railroad track. On one side were ten acres of cornfield, and on the other two sides a solid wall of pine forests as dark and as dense as a fabled wood in old fairy tales. These woods and the farmhouse were well remembered by the Martin kids who had spent summers there in the mystifying past of childhood glee.

Even the old collie dog Laddy was still alive, shambling about slowly, grown dim and drooling with age. The kids remembered him when he ran flashing across the marsh after stray rabbits, when he barked on moonlit nights at old cars rattling over the dirt road by the railroad tracks, when he roamed his stamping grounds like an adventurous prince of dogs. Now he sat at old Goldtwaithe's feet growing blind.

A great many people were there. It was a vast tribal out-spreading of the life that had been born and begun on that farm generations before, from the oldest gaffer who sported a handlebar mustache and still remembered great-grandfather Joseph Martin to the little one squawling in his mother's arms. The Martin mother seemed to know them all, to trace them, sourceless, to the furthest reach of folding earth and darkness.

Young men in clean white shirts, cousins, stood about the yard smoking in clusters, talking about their cars and their work. Inside, the older women got dinner ready in the big kitchen and the younger women gathered in the livingroom with the babies. The old men sat in the parlor smoking, discussing matters solemnly, sometimes erupting in loud guffaws of laughter. And the little ones who were old enough ran loose throughout the house and around the yard and into the woods.

The sun sloped and reddened, the grass cooled, smoke whipped from the farmhouse chimney. It seemed to Peter, in the yard with the young men, that something, some inexplicable fertility, had risen from the earth to honor his father's death. He looked around and thought, "I should have known!" There was a pretty girl, a young cousin of his, he was given to understand, who kept looking at him blushingly and had eyes for him. This too was something he had never realized before, something sudden, inexplicable, and fertile. He was amazed and delighted and saddened all at once. It seemed as though he had been gone a long time, almost longer than he could remember, from these things, from this place, from these people who were his people.

When the fragrant turkeys were taken out of the oven, everybody sat down and ate. Then, just as the sun was beginning to set, Joe and Peter sneaked out to do a little fishing at the creek before nightfall. They borrowed Luke Marlowe's rod and reel and flies and took off in the car.

They had heard that Francis and Liz and Buddy Fredericks were in town so they drove through the little streets of Lacoshua until they saw Francis buying a pack of cigarettes in a corner store.

Joe tooted the horn and yelled: "Come on, boy, we're goin' fishing!"

Francis jumped in the car a little surprised, and they drove off to the creek in the woods. When they got there Joe took out the rod and reel and stationed himself on the bank and started casting about with a lonesome concentrated air, while Peter stretched out on the ground and Francis sat on the runningboard of the car a little ruefully. The soft red sky, mellifluous with low colors, melted warmly in the pool of the creek, pine-shapes darkened all around, the summerbugs flip-flopped in silent air, a dog barked far away, voices murmured across the hush of the fields from farms and from Lacoshua. All over the woods among thickets and leaves and tree-tops, and on the secret enveloped floor of the forest murmurous with crickets, was something dark and splendid and soft . . . nightfall in the land in May.

"I guess the old man would be here with us if he could," suggested Joe, looking at his brothers and grinning, "so I guess he won't begrudge us a little fishin'."

"He'd be the last one to stay in that coffin," said Peter, gazing dreamily up through the trees. "This is great—or at least," he turned to Francis, "at least it's a hell of a lot better than sitting in Central Park. . . ."

"Oh, yes . . . it's the *real* thing," murmured Francis, smiling.

"Tell you what," said Joe, casting off again, and wetting his lips in a brief and businesslike way, "I've made arrangements to buy old man Bartlett's farm outside Galloway. You know the one, just near the Shrewsboro line. He's an old hellcat, you know, and he's so sick and tired of sitting there all alone he's willing to sell out cheap, equipment and everything. I'm going to make a home for Ma and Mickey and for my own kids. There's forty acres there, I could plant corn, potatoes, feed, everything."

"You need money and help to start a farm, don't you?" observed Francis.

"I'll get a G.I. loan and handle the work myself. What the hell, I've got two hands, haven't I?"

"You've never done any farming before."

"I learned a little on the farm here when we were kids, and besides I can learn, can't I? Mickey'll go to high school, but he can help."

"If you can stand it out in the country. . . ."

"*Shore* I can stand it!" laughed Joe good-naturedly. "Give my kids a lot of room to play in! Let 'em roam! I want to live a good life and have good times! Boy, after that damn Brooklyn I'd rather live out in the middle of nowhere, Wyoming even, and if you've ever seen Wyoming you know what I mean. Hyah! hyah! hyah!"

"I haven't had that pleasure," laughed Francis.

"What are you going to do now, Francis?" asked Peter suddenly.

"Oh," smiled Francis, "didn't you hear? I'm going to Paris."

"Really?"

"Oh, yes. I've already received my letter of acceptance at the Sorbonne."

"And what are you going to do there?" demanded Peter curiously.

"Nothing, I suppose. Perhaps I might get a perspective of some kind."

"Perspective? What do you mean?"

"On this country, I guess. Everyone who's going there is saying the same thing, I'm only repeating what I hear." And Francis smiled ever so faintly. "*You* know, from a different vantage point—a different culture and so on. It ought to be nice in itself in any case. And so," said Francis, smiling, and holding out the palm of his hand, "what are *you* going to do now?"

"Me?" cried Peter, almost dumbfounded by this kind, unexpected query. "Why, I don't know." He stared at Francis foolishly. "Not an idea in the world, I haven't thought of it at all."

Francis simply nodded, as it were decisively, and fell silent, and seemed amused but at the same time delicately satisfied with this answer. And Joe wandered up along the creek with his pole.

A moment later they heard him whoop as he reeled in a catch, a glistening, wriggling black bass that fought for its life in a lonesome furious splashing in the silence of dusk. He brought it back and hung it over the bank in the water, by a chain, to keep fresh, with a hook torn through its dumb mouth.

Peter sat on the bank, deeply silent, watching the fish swimming back and forth on the tugging chain.

"Okay, Willie, take it easy," laughed Joe, looking over Peter's shoulder, "you might as well relax, I'll see if I can catch your brother to keep you company"—and he cast off again, nudging Peter exuberantly.

Peter could not take his eyes off the struggling enchained fish. He had done some fishing as a boy but now after all these years, and perhaps after the strain of his father's death also, there was something he could not understand, something hurt, something inexplicably troubled in his feeling about the fish and the fact that a hook was torn through its mournful mouth. He watched its gaping eyes almost with terror. Unaccountably he remembered something he had read a few days before, in the New Testament, something about Jesus and his fishermen casting their nets in the sea.

"This is what happens to all of us, this is what happens to all of us!" Peter kept thinking over and over again. "What are we going to do, where are we going to go, when do we all die like this?" For a moment he thought he was going to cry, as though he had no control any more. He looked at Francis meekly. Francis noticed; and Peter had no idea what made him look at Francis that way, he felt abashed and childish.

"Come here and look at this," Peter finally said.

Francis came over and looked with a smile, nodding as though with appreciation.

"Back and forth, back and forth, with a hook in his mouth."

"Yes," said Francis.

"A minute ago everything was all right . . . and now! Like people, don't you think?"

"You mean the fish!" yelled Joe from down the bank. "He don't feel nothing or know nothing, he's just a fish."

"From which arises the term 'poor fish,' I guess," said Francis.

"Did you ever hear that expression they use in New York, Francis? I mean the Village writers especially. They say 'salvation through sensibility.' What little sensibility this fish has is not saving him at the moment, it's only telling him that he's doomed for certain suffering."

"You get so wrought up. Why trouble yourself?"

"Where did you learn not to trouble yourself, *you* of all people. Don't you remember that time we talked up in the attic, all the things you said?"

Francis laughed.

"Why do you laugh?" demanded Peter, looking hard at him, almost paling, suddenly, with a terrified sense of anger, resentment, dumb loneliness.

"Well, heavens, why shouldn't I laugh!"

Peter was flushing with embarrassment, he realized he was acting like an idiot, nervously, foolishly, yet there was "no other way," he kept thinking, there was no other possible way for him to be in the world, as though he himself had a hook torn through his mouth and was chained to the mystery of his own dumb incomprehension.

He watched Joe fishing and wondered what Joe thought, silent and absorbed as he was. He watched Francis and the inscrutable halo of indifference that always seemed to surround his pale, narrow face.

"And therefore," sighed Peter, "we catch a fish, we lock him up in the compartment where there's no water and he suffocates and dies, alone, while we drive along in the fresh New Hampshire air. He had the water of this brook and the sunshine in the afternoon . . . and now we're going to throw him in the back of the car and let him die. There it is."

"What the hell you want me to do," called Joe, "throw it back?"

Joe was irritated and impatient with the whole thing, foolish as it was on a little fishing excursion that he wanted to enjoy. But Peter, riven with the idea, idiotic before his brothers, persisted, with strange disaffected nervousness, gaining sheepish gloating satisfaction by the moment, and yet infuriated because that was not what he wanted at all.

"It's all right, he's only meddling in God's system," joked Francis almost kindly.

"I'm not God, I'm not supposed to meddle," cried Peter, staring at him worriedly, "and even if I could, say if I had the power of miracle, I couldn't alleviate the suffering without breaking up God's purpose in the whole thing."

"There, perhaps, is the cream of the jest."

"Ah! that's so easy to say! What are we supposed to do in a suffering world . . . suffer? That's not enough to satisfy the big feeling we might have of wanting everything and wanting to like everything. How can we be fair in an unfair situation like that?"

"Why do you insist so much?" joked Francis again, to a degree grimly now.

"Why is it that we can bear our own troubles and pain because we believe in . . . in fortitude—"

"Soap opera talk, my dear boy. You should say 'quiet desperation.'"

"—and we have to believe in fortitude," ignored Peter, "of course we have to, but we don't grant that fortitude to fellow creatures like the fish here." He pointed at it, hesitantly.

"How strange!" breathed Francis with sudden curiosity. It suddenly occurred to him that his brother Peter must be mad.

Peter seemed to sense this. He pointed his finger, almost accusingly, but with a grin, rattling along: "Jesus warned against the sin of accusing any man of madness, Francis, he even said that no man was mad!"

"Well?"

"Oh, for God's sake, don't sit there with that *look* on your face!" cried Peter, jumping up jubilantly. "Stop thinking that I'm insane. Did you know, for instance, that Jesus always got angry when they brought a lunatic before him? He knew who was responsible, always, he knew what madness meant better than anyone has known since. He said to one woman who brought her mad daughter, 'It is not meet to take the children's bread and throw it to the dogs.' How do you figure that one? That's all he said. Then another time when his disciples complained they couldn't heal a certain lunatic, he said, 'Oh, faithless and perverse generation—it is because of your unbelief.' It was unbelief that created and aggravated the madness of the madman. The faith that moves mountains didn't recognize madness anywhere, it only recognized people, people who are responsible, like the annoyed parents you see sometimes on the streets slapping their kids around . . . don't you see those things?"

"Why do you keep asking don't you see, don't you see?" Francis was peering at Peter with curiosity and amused interest, yet with genuine, almost troubled concern now.

"And why do you keep asking that?" cried Peter, flushing.

"Why, I haven't the faintest idea," laughed Francis, looking up. "But your parent, by the way, slapping the child, it would be rather weary, wouldn't it, to trace that responsibility back to the original slap in the face that everyone got? Wouldn't it now?" Francis was smiling with urbane amusement now and blushing too, furiously.

"Is that why *you* give up?" Peter looked up with sudden soft curiosity.

"Oh, no. Not at all. You see," Francis reddened, "it's just . . . really . . . that the original slap in the face has completely . . . vanished. It cannot be known who did it. It's all wearying—no one knows . . . no one can be blamed. . . . Where is your original annoyed . . . parent . . . or unbelief . . . or whatnot? *Therefore,* you see . . ." Francis leaned forward with the palm of the hand held out.

Peter stared at him. Francis was still leaning forward with his gesture.

And Joe, who had been listening in silence, came over and sat down and lit a cigarette, and said, "I didn't know you read the Bible, Petey." He looked at Peter gravely, with an awe-struck seriousness that was full of kindness, even to Francis who noticed.

They drifted off into other things, talking warmly, enjoying each other's company with a kind of understanding they had never had among one another before. It was as though Peter had revealed their common situation, and their differences in it, their individual sorrows, and the sorrows of Francis, by exposing himself like a child and agitating the drama of their secret and especial concerns, making them see one another with serious eyes. This was, after all, so much like the action of the man who had been their father.

In the morning the burial took place. The mother's people, the Courbets, were there, as well as the Martin relatives. The Martin children noticed for the first time with peculiar impact the tremendous difference between their father's and their mother's people. The Courbets, Uncle Joe and all the others, were white-haired, calm, almost beautiful people of silence, aloofness, and dignity. Like their mother, nothing fazed them, and they were strong and determined. But the Martins, all of them so abundantly similar to the dead man, were mournful, tempestuous, argumentative, sensitive, nervous, furious.

At nine o'clock the coffin was closed, and four solemn strong young men, Luke Marlowe, Tony Hall, and two of the Martin cousins hoisted the box off the bier and carried it to the hearse in the bright morning sunshine. The Martin boys, even Francis strangely, watched with a proud and inexplicable sense of gratitude, since as sons of the deceased they were not supposed to carry the coffin and the sight of these grave young strangers supporting the weight of their father was like penitence, humility, labor, and honesty, like all those things as unquestioning as the very honor of mankind itself. They felt no grief any more for their father—the modern funeral had done its sleek gloved work—but this ritual, this last ritual, was good, and somehow true.

The procession got underway. Luke Marlowe drove the first car with Joe and Patricia sitting in front, and the mother, Ruthey, Mickey and Peter in the back. The others followed in their cars. They proceeded through the streets of little Lacoshua following the beflowered hearse, and the townspeople, who all knew the name of the dead man, paused in their Monday morning affairs to watch, the men removing their hats—briefly—before walking on. Somewhere a churchbell was ringing, and everywhere Lacoshuans knew that George Martin had died.

"Oh, Ruthey," said the mother, gripping her daughter's hand, "now I *know* I did the right thing bringing him back home. I'm *so* glad! And look over there . . . our little church, where we were married, thirty years ago."

She began to cry, at last, in the privacy of the car with her children, as they passed the old church. Her whole life with the man gripped at her heart and memory, she gazed at the hearse in front and thought of him lying there underneath flowers, and there was a groan in her breast. She had been an orphan, lonely in the world, and then George Martin had found her and married her, and they had lived a lifetime together, and now she was a widow, the mother of grave young people silent at her side. They passed the church beneath the trees, and later the dark house where she was born, and then the places where she had played as a little girl, the place where the circus had come to town with Sitting Bull and Buffalo Bill long ago, the park where she had first seen Martin, the fields where they had strolled under forlorn moons, and then the countryside, the old cemetery under brooding shaggy pines, in the hills, where he was to be buried forever.

[6]

ON A HIGHWAY one rainy night in the summer of that year, by glistering waters of a river in a place not far from the lights of a town, among hills and river-bluffs that were like shadows, a big red truck stopped at the one-light junction. Peter Martin, in his black leather jacket, carrying the old canvas bag in which all his poor needments for a long journey were packed, got down from the truck.

"Don't worry about me," he cried, waving. "It's not raining hard at all. See? Just a drizzle, just a little drizzle. I'll be all right."

The driver of the truck, enshrouded in his high cab, sadly called out: "Well, I guess you'll be okay then. Remember what I told you now. Walk a quarter mile down the road, just follow the river, till you get to the railroad overpass. If it starts raining hard you can wait there. Then you come to the red lights at the big junction, and there you'll see the gas stations and the diners, and there's the main highway that'll take you right in. It goes over the bridge. Got that straight? Good luck to you, man!" He shifted into gear and lumbered off the highway.

And Peter was alone in the rainy night.

He was on the road again, traveling the continent westward, going off to further and further years, alone by the waters of life, alone, looking towards the lights of the river's cape, towards tapers burning warmly in the towns, looking down along the shore in remembrance of the dearness of his father and of all life.

The heat-lightning glowed softly in the dark, and crowded tree-top shores and wandering waters showed through shrouds of rain. When the railroad trains moaned, and river-winds blew, bringing echoes through the vale, it was as if a wild hum of voices, the dear voices of everybody he had known, were crying: "Peter, Peter! Where are you going, Peter?" And a big soft gust of rain came down.

He put up the collar of his jacket, and bowed his head, and hurried along.

Also available in paperbound edition from
HARCOURT BRACE JOVANOVICH, INC.

WILLIAM GADDIS: THE RECOGNITIONS (HB 169)

The theme of Gaddis' monumental novel is forgery —emotional, spiritual, actual—in the chaos of contemporary life. Wyatt, the central figure, forges Old Masters; Basil Valentine is really a double agent; Mr. Sinisterra counterfeits money, passports, and mummies; and each of the many other characters is busy pursuing his own deception. The book has been widely praised for its brilliant language, erudition, and black comedy.

". . . as great a work of art as has been produced by an American writer in this century. . . . Gaddis must be reckoned not only with Hemingway and Faulkner but with Joyce and Proust and Mann."
—*The Village Voice*